WHAT READERS HAVE SAID ABOUT ANNE PAOLUCCI'S
ESCAPE AND RETURN. THE SEARCH FOR IDENTITY: A CULTURAL JOURNEY

We are a nation of immigrants. All of us will be captivated and held by the memories, story, and history of renowned author Anne Paolucci as she brings us into her family and her new book, *Escape and Return, The Search for Identity. A Cultural Journey*. From the very beginning, as she tells us about her parents' birthplace, Acuto (Frosinone), a town walking distance from the famous spa-resort of Fiuggi, we are captured by her family album style of juxtaposing photos and stories.

We learn how she grew up in New York, where she began her academic and professional career; how she became the genuine literary artist and scholar she is today. Her self-effacing method of spelling out her own and her husband Henry's works and extraordinary accomplishments, literary and otherwise, only enhances them. This book is another chapter in the preservation of their tremendous intellectual legacy. I especially like the charming accolades and asides when she speaks of Henry as her husband and mentor, describing his words as "an intellectual feast" and a "banquet of the mind." It was truly a "partnership that was to last a lifetime."

Her chapters on Columbus, "Columbus: Countdown 1992," and her dedicated service to the Humanities as Chairwoman of the Board of Trustees of The City University of New York, shed new important light on the vital issues they record. I believe readers of the chapter on Columbus will agree that "those who came after the First Immigrant," Columbus scholars and admirers and all Americans, owe her a great debt of gratitude for her courage, tenacity, and scholarship — "her faith truly was boundless." Especially relating to CUNY, there is no question that she is to be credited with unheralded Herculean accomplishments that even today are still bearing fruit.

All these vignettes, stories, photos, and clippings have been brought together in a unique totality that lets us know not only what Anne Paolucci has accomplished, but truly who she is.

From first to last page — a joy to read and savor.

SENATOR SERPHIN R. MALTESE
Chairman, NYS Senate Committee on Arts and Culture

This long-awaited and richly illustrated book is about an extraordinary life, a compelling, humorous narrative with sharp insights into the unexpected turns of fortune. The chapter about her two-year tenure as Chairwoman of the Board pf CUNY, gives us a new side of the story. Equally riveting is her account of the "flak" during the Columbus Quincentenary. The book is not only excellent good reading; it is also an archival storehouse of materials, especially news stories and documents relating to her controversial public activities.

FRANK D. GRANDE, D PHIL. (OXON)
President, Griffon House Publications

Writing about the impact of European nations on their African colonies, the noted scholar Albert S. Gérard of the University of Liège observes in that "hordes of people in the late twentieth century regard themselves, as bilingual because they find it easy to communicate naked facts and their own rudimentary thoughts in the world's vehicular language, Bad English. . . . But the Conrads, the Nabokavs and the Samuel Becketts form a very meager phalanx indeed . . . only exceptionally gifted bilingual individuals can describe and voice the response of their community to the traumatic experience of colonization and cross-cultural contact."

I was reminded of those words in reading Anne Paolucci's *Escape and Return*, especially where she speaks of her deliberate effort to master English beyond mere competence. She has given us a brilliant description of the "traumatic experience" of adjusting to a new community, a new language, and "cross-cultural contact," an experience that hones her many talents to perfection. . . . What struck me most was her ability to create "distance" while drawing us close, in an idiom that is never casual, yet beautifully colloquial.

DR. CLARA SARROCCO
Vice-President, C.S. Lewis Society

Having spent a lifetime in the world of American academia, Anne Paolucci provides fascinating insights into its politics, and into the struggles of a young foreign-born newcomer in coping with assimilation. Her experiences and considerable success in achieving high recognition from her peers in education and literature offer the reader an exhilarating and entertaining narrative. Her life is a fine example of the contribution to be made by melting-pot Americans to a constantly evolving American culture.

EDMUND A. BATOR
Foreign Service Officer (Ret.)

If you have ever sat, furiously taking notes, as an important author or professor lectured, you might wish Anne Paolucci was the speaker. The next best thing is to read *Escape and Return*. The book follows the author's career, her many and varied intellectual interests and her impact on a variety of academic and professional fields, including Shakespearean studies, translation, Theater of the Absurd, Dante, Machiavelli, Pirandello, and her pioneer work in multi-comparative literary studies. We are treated with remarkable ease to insightful reporting on higher education, brief excursions into Hegelian dramatic theory, tips on teaching, how to care for elderly parents, and much else. Not surprisingly, this book reads like a novel.

A. DOROTHY ARTHUR
CEO, Imprimatur, Inc.
Public Affairs Dept., Dupont Co. (Ret.)

■□■

(ABOUT *FROM TENSION TO TONIC: THE PLAYS OF EDWARD ALBEE*)
One of the terrors facing a creative writer early in his career is the awareness that sooner or later critics and scholars are going to start interpreting and dissecting his work, beginning the long and wearying misunderstandings and misinterpretations that will plague any writer who is brave or foolhardy enough to go on writing in the face of it. . . . It is a lucky writer, indeed, who finds an Anne Paolucci at him early on, writing with intelligence, insight and perception. Her book, *From Tension to Tonic*, made this writer a happy man, and while Dr. Paolucci's accomplishments are many and varied, and her championing of Pirandello essential to our understanding of 20th century drama, her lucid and encouraging essays on my first handful of plays still burns bright for me.

EDWARD ALBEE, *Playwright*

I am proud to call Dr. Anne Paolucci my friend. She is perhaps one of the outstanding intellectuals of our time. She has traversed the literary world as well as the educational and governmental with ease and a profound sense of what is real and enduring. And yet, with all this talent, she has remained a compassionate and humble woman.

CLAIRE SHULMAN
Former President of the Borough of Queens, New York

(ABOUT *SEPIA TONES. SEVEN SHORT STORIES*) If more Italian-American writers do not speak up soon, much of their experiences in the 20th century will go unrecorded. Anne Attura Paolucci's slim volume helps dispel the silence. . . .

NANCY FORBES
New York Times Book Review

(ABOUT "BURIED TREASURE" IN *SEPIA TONES. SEVEN SHORT STORIES* (REPRINTED IN *THE VOICES WE CARRY*) The jewel in [the final] section — indeed the masterpiece of the entire anthology — is Anne Paolucci's "Buried Treasure," a brilliant, haunting memoir of an unforgettable Italian American man narrated by his daughter-in-law.

WOMEN'S REVIEW OF BOOKS (Wellesley)

(ABOUT *SEPIA TONES. SEVEN SHORT STORIES*) These seven short stories, beautifully written and utterly absorbing, are the work of a genuinely literary artist. The author's insight into her various characters is of such clairvoyance as to make them universal. [She] combines qualities seldom found in the same writer: a sure sense of narrative, a marked talent for writing effective dialogue, and a distinctive style that constantly engages the reader with its warmth. . . . I cannot imagine any discriminating reader experiencing the pleasure of these stories without wanting to read more of the author's writings.

JERRE MANGIONE
Award-winning novelist

■□■

(ABOUT *SEPIA TONES. SEVEN SHORT STORIES*) This elegant volume
has high literary merit. The characters are vivid; the style, impeccable.

MARIO FRATTI, *Playwright*

(ABOUT *IN WOLF'S CLOTHING (A MYSTERY NOVEL*) She got me. That
means I hated having to put it down and couldn't wait to get back to it.

VICTORIA SCHNEPS, *Columnist and CEO, Schneps Enterprises*

(ABOUT *PIRANDELLO'S THEATER: THE RECOVERY OF THE MODERN
STAGE FOR DRAMATIC ART*) . . . impressive both in its . . . research and
its limpid presentation.

VICTOR CARRABINO
Review in *Books Abroad*

(ABOUT *SELECTED POEMS OF GIACOMO LEOPARDI* [Winner of the
2004 Special Recognition Award from the Italian Ministry of
Foreign Affairs]) I keep reading the Leopardi poems. The translations
are exquisite. The commentaries, too, are truly excellent.

TALAT HALMAN
Former Cultural Ambassador-at-Large for Turkey

(ABOUT *SELECTED POEMS OF GIACOMO LEOPARDI*) Leaving aside
the enormous difficulties of translating into English the expressive,
musical, and poetic language of Leopardi, but not ignoring them, we
must say indubitably that she has surpassed the limits of semantic
possibilities in her arduous task.

ORAZIO TANELLI
Review in *Il Ponte*

(ABOUT *THE WOMEN IN DANTE'S DIVINE COMEDY AND SPENSER'S
FAERIE QUEENE*) Nothing of cultural value is lost as an end in itself
but is decanted, as it were, interpreted along unpredictable and
sometimes unusual lines. . . . [She] does not limit herself to finding and
tracing similarities, but throws new light on a great many of the themes
that have continued to attract the best critical minds: the allegory, for
example, as well as or perhaps above all, Dante's ethical-political
message (Spenser's as well). [Translated from the Italian.]

FRANCO BORRELLI
Senior Editor and Feature Writer, Oggi

(ABOUT *QUEENSBORO BRIDGE [AND OTHER POEMS]*) *Queensboro
Bridge* is mature, "educated," meditative poetry beyond the need to be
hip and modish. . . . These are "comfortable" poems, poems written with
large vistas and backed up by all sorts of comfortably worn erudition . .
. [whose author] doesn't feel a need to keep sweatily up to date with the
latest evolution of swinging lingoes. . . .

HUGH FOX
Critic, Small Press Review

■□

(ABOUT *QUEENSBORO BRIDGE [AND OTHER POEMS]*) [the images] are so apt and true! It is a wonderful book. . .

MARIA MAZZIOTTI GILLAN
Director, The Poetry Center, NJ

(ABOUT *QUEENSBORO BRIDGE [AND OTHER POEMS]*) I am slowly savoring it with a mixture of pleasure, admiration, and — yes — envy. I recall particularly poems like the superb "Sailing Out": "We can hardly begin to find definition / For what we think we know best."

JOHN BROWN, *Poet, Critic, Translator*

(ABOUT *QUEENSBORO BRIDGE [AND OTHER POEMS]*) . . . beautiful . . . a work of art inside and out.

DIANA DER HOVANESSIAN
President, New England Poetry Club

(ABOUT HER PIONEER WORK IN MULTI-COMPARATIVE LITERARY STUDIES) Readers more familiar with the story will find it difficult to separate their admiration of the dynamic personality of Anne Paolucci from their appreciation of what she has accomplished for comparative and interdisciplinary studies through the series *Review of National Literatures* (1970-2001) and *CNL/World Report* (1985-2001) — not to speak of countless panels and symposia on a rich variety of topics in literature and art held at numerous venues because of her organizational efforts. One of her remarkable strengths has been the capacity to inspire a wide range of leading scholars and artists to join collaborative projects, to take the lead as experts in shaping valuable teams, and to produce a rich harvest of studies that no simple taxonomy can describe with justice.

GERALD GILLESPIE
*Professor Emeritus of Literature, Culture,
and Languages Stanford University;
Former President, International
Comparative Literature Association*

WHAT CRITICS HAVE SAID ABOUT
REVIEW OF NATIONAL LITERATURES

- "One of the most important journals in the U. S." (*YEDITEPE 13* [TURKEY])

- "An essential title for libraries . . . ." (*CHOICE*)

- "A valuable addition to literature collections."(*LIBRARY JOURNAL*)

- " . . . Excellent . . . New and fresh . . . ." (HENRI PEYRE)

- "Splendid periodical . . . ." (PETER NAGY)

- "An admirable publication . . . ." (SIR MALCOLM KNOX)

- [*Columbus, America and the World*] "Provocative and contemporary . . . a true bouquet of cross-cultural perspectives, scholarly criticism, history and literature . . . beautifully diverse." (Arnold B. Levine, *NYSFLT Bulletin*)

- "The main event in critical writings on Indian literature was the special *India* issue of *RNL*." (*ENGLISH STUDIES*)

- [*Armenia*] ". . . rich, diverse, informative, . . . highly recommended." (*CHOICE*)

- "All issues of *RNL* have been most enjoyable. I am quoting extensively from the one on Russian literature in my book *Beast or Angel* . . . ." (RENE DUBOIS)

- [*Machiavelli '500*] "An excellent discussion!" (ISAIAH BERLIN)

- [*The Multinational Literature of Yugoslavia*] "Gli autori si riallaciano alle intenzioni della rivista di esplicare . . . l'infinita e necessaria varità dello spirito umano." (OLGA TRITNIK ROSSETTINI, *CULTURA E VITA SCOLASTICA*)

- [*Norway*] "Ably edited by Anne Paolucci . . . contains a first-rate selection of essays. . . . An excellent introduction to modern Norwegian literature . . . as well as up-to-date discussions of recent trends." (*THE SCANDINAVIAN-AMERICAN BULLETIN*)

- "*German Expressionism* . . . has superb articles . . . . It is one of the best [*RNL* volumes] yet put together." (TALAT S. HALMAN)

- "During the past few years several reviews have published special issues devoted to Africa. To my knowledge, however, none equals the importance in size and scope of the *RNL* volume on *Black Africa* . . . ." (F. Michelman, *JOURNAL OF GENERAL EDUCATION*)

- "*RNL* is covering areas with which the academic world is far too little informed, and has therefore its special kind of contribution to make." (EDNA STEEVES, *CELJ*)

- (*HUNGARIAN LITERATURE*) "A first major overview in English of Hungarian literature after the political changes of the late eighties . . . ." (GEORGE TOTH, *INSIGHTS*, LIBRARY OF CONGRESS)

- (*HUNGARIAN LITERATURE*) ". . . contributes significantly to the eradication of the Chinese wall that has surrounded our literature for centuries." (J. TELEK, *VICTORIA*)

ESCAPE AND RETURN

THE SEARCH FOR IDENTITY:
A Cultural Journey

ANNE PAOLUCCI

Copyright © 2008 by Anne Paolucci
ISBN: 978-1-932107-17-3

Publisher's Cataloging-in-Publication Data

Paolucci, Anne.
    Escape and return: the search for identity: a cultural
journey / Anne Paolucci. 1st ed. — Middle Village,
NY : Griffon House Publications, c2008.

        p. ; cm.
        ISBN: 978-1-932107-17-3
        1. Italian American women—Biography. 2. Italian
Americans—Biography. 3. Women educators—United
States—Biography. 4. Women authors—United States—
Biography. I. Title.

E184.18 P36 2008
973/.04510082   0810

GRIFFON HOUSE PUBLICATIONS

(THE BAGEHOT COUNCIL)

P.O. Box 790095
Middle Village, New York 11379
griffonhouse_bagehot@ctkrhs.org

CONTENTS

I'm nobody! Who are you?
Are you nobody, too?
Then there's a pair of us — don't tell!
They'd advertise, you know!

How dreary to be somebody!
How public like a frog
To tell one's name the livelong day
To an admiring bog!

EMILY DICKINSON

1981

AUTHOR'S PREFACE

People have often asked why I don't write a book about my life. My answer has always been the same: I'm not a celebrity of any kind; I haven't won a Nobel Prize; and surely enough has been written about ethnicity and the "hyphenated-American." Who in the world would want to read about me, or want to hear more stories about family gatherings, reminiscences about the "old country," adjustment to the "new" one?

When a friend asked that familiar question recently, I was ready to shrug it off again with my usual response; but then he added something that made me pause. "You've got a lot to say," he went on, "not just about your personal life, how you came to be here — although that's a rather unusual story — but about your influence on so many different academic fields and your public impact, especially on higher education reform. You've been in the public eye and you've left your mark. A success story, sure, but what's really worth sharing is your rigorous commitment to certain principles, the stands you took in trying to improve things at The City University of New York, your courage in the face of tremendous opposition, not only at CUNY but during the Columbus quincentennial. Certainly, that's worth telling!"

My friend may have a point, I thought, especially since there had been a great deal of misapprehension and misunderstanding surrounding certain positions I'd taken, certain tasks I'd assumed. He was right also in saying that my early history had some unusual twists and might be of some interest — but it could be told quickly. I began to reconsider my objections.

I thought a book of this kind might be useful, after all: besides the interweaving of old and new, the dialectic of ethnicity, the paradox of escape and return, my observations might also have some bearing on the urgent issues of our time. My own experience, I realized, was relevant in this context insofar as it dramatized the enormous pressures our nation faces as new waves of nationals come into the country, legally or illegally, from all over the world. The tremendous ethnic diversity in New York City alone has created and will continue to create major problems — critical ones, in education. I became painfully aware of those problems during my tenure as Chairwoman of the Board of Trustees of The City University of New York.

Other thoughts ran through my mind as I debated whether or not to write this book. It might indeed have a certain historical value. The idea of "escape and return" emerged as part of a larger ongoing dialogue that is more than personal. But other compelling arguments forced my attention.

In my various roles as an educator, I have relentlessly pursued historical accuracy, both in the classroom and in my writing, presenting as best I could the wide spectrum of opinions, facts, and theories that are available to scholars. Today, alas, contemporaneity rules. More often than not,

1

current fads determine values; history is viewed through the distorted mirror of prejudice and factional interests — even by many who should know better. As a teacher, I entertained all kinds of questions and doubts from students; I tried to answer opposing views without trimming facts to suit my argument. As a historian, I tried to present events within the context of the time. As an administrator, I approached change with an organic yet flexible plan, resisting the practical appeal of the "band-aid" approach to problems. As a "hyphenated-American" I've insisted on the ongoing dialectic between the familiar and the unknown, the spiraling toward a new identity in which the past is thoroughly explored and preserved, the future made secure through that solid base.

These and similar thoughts brought me around to accepting the idea of writing this book.

Having made the decision, I chose to follow my educational growth and professional life chronologically, reviewing my early years quickly, in Part One. The "Highlights" of Part Two bring into focus some of the more interesting moments of my life — in particular, the difficulties encountered in certain public offices I assumed and my response to situations and events that made daily headlines (chapters 7 and 8). Part Three is a brief concluding chapter, in which I relate more recent events, especially my efforts to consolidate my husband's accomplishments as well as my own past activities and insuring their preservation. Throughout the book, but also at the end of each chapter, under "From the Files," I've added news stories, letters, and photographs from my personal files, archival materials that are worth preserving and give a wider historical perspective to my account of things, especially on the controversies surrounding Columbus and "discovery" (Chapter 7) and the crisis at The City University of New York (Chapter 8).

I am always grateful for reactions to my work — but, in this case, especially thankful for the encouragement received from friends and colleagues to write this book.

Among them, I must once again single out for special mention my indefatigable researcher, Azar Attura, who never failed to find the answers I needed and in record time. I am indebted also to my long-time friend Edmund Bator, who read the manuscript carefully and not only offered useful suggestions but also sent me information I lacked, including documents he tracked down related to the founding of the American Legion in Rome and my father's role in that endeavor.

To those who followed the making of this book with the kind of interest that often verged on enthusiasm: I treasure their loyal support. I hope I have not disappointed them.

July, 2007

PART ONE

SHAPING THE PAST

THE CREST AND HISTORY OF THE GUIDONIS AND ATTURAS
(RESEARCHED BY MY BROTHER GEORGE).

GUIDONI

Antica e nobile famiglia oripinaria dalla terra di finale (Prov. Modena). La sua oripine monta al secoli XI. Nel 1200 un ramo si trapiantò in Orvieto ate ha dato un Ranieri, capitano del popolo nel 1257. Cesare vesti l'abito di Cavaliere di Santo Stefano il 2 Giugno 1596 e fu poi Capitano di una palea. Marco di lui fratello militò nelle palee pontifiche.... Si trapiantarono negli Abbruzzi circa il 1600. Giovanni Castellano di Sassuolo e fattore ducale nel 1697. È nobile di Velletri. Alla Chiesa ha dato Prelati e Canonici.....

ATTURA

famiglia oripinaria della città di foppia. La sua oripine rimonta al 1600. Giacomo Antonio Attura era Governatore di Capitanata nel 1511. Un ramo fiorì nelle Marche circa il 1700....
    Ambrogio e Pietro furono Senatori di Perugia. Altro ramo attualmente finisce nel Lazio....
Antonio Vescovo nel 1600.....
Nazzareno Cavaliere nel 1950. Roma Giorgio Inventore, dal ramo che si trapiantò in America, nel 1928.
    Dato a Roma......1920
    Copiato negli Stati Uniti di America......1955

LUCIA (LUCY) GUIDONI ATTURA

GIUSEPPE (JOSEPH) ATTURA

1. BLACK HOLES IN MY GALAXY

"mi ritrovai in una selva oscura. . . ."

Like so many others who sought a better life in this country, my father, Joseph (Giuseppe) Attura, had a large dream. I never got to know exactly what it was; but apparently he was a practical man as well as a visionary, for his dream had already taken root when in 1913, not yet sixteen — the oldest of six children (another yet to come) — he left his father's small farm in the mountain village of Acuto (province of Frosinone, a forty-minute train ride from Rome, a ten-minute walk to Fiuggi, famous even then for its spa and mineral waters, boasting today over 300 hotels and a five-star splendid resort spa at the top of the mountain) to sail, together with an older cousin, for America. He worked briefly in the Pittsburgh area, as a gofer for construction gangs — an easy target for the older men, who stole his meager pay and played tricks on him. But by early 1914, he seems to have come to some important decision about his future, for we suddenly find him in Texas, where he had gone to join John J. Pershing's border patrol and probably saw action in Mexico the following year. We do know that when America entered World War I, he volunteered to remain with Major General Pershing, as part of the newly-formed 1st Infantry Division of the American Expeditionary Force and was among the first American soldiers to land in France. Sometime in the late Spring or Summer of 1919, he was brought down by mustard gases. At first given up for dead, he was hospitalized for several months. By early 1920 he was well enough to be released: he returned home, where he married in February of that year.

IN MY FATHER'S HAND, IN PENCIL, ON BACK OF PHOTO: "C.G. OF 1ST DIV. WITH HIS CAR ON HEAD OF TROOPS AFTER BRIDGE FINISHED 5.6.19." (FRANCE, WORLD WAR I.)

What was he thinking when he walked down the *vialozzo*, the rough narrow path that led to the fields he'd help tend as a child? He seemed to pick up where he'd left off but obviously did not intend to settle down to a poor farmer's life. Newly-married, he managed to win the sought-after government concession for the sale of tobacco and stamps. This interval lasted about four years. By 1925, the first two children had arrived — my sister Sylvia (1921) and my brother George (1923) — and the young family was settled in Rome, where my father had found a much better government job and where I arrived the following year. He soon managed to get similar jobs for two of his three younger brothers, hoping to better their lot as well. A fourth brother, born the same year as my sister, separated from his siblings by a whole generation, followed easily in their footsteps, when he was old enough to do so. Even their two sisters were brought to Rome before long, where they married and remained to raise families. My father had led the way.

JOSEPH ATTURA WITH HIS FAITHFUL GERMAN SHEPHERD (FRANCE, 1919)

I don't know if settling in Rome was meant to be a temporary strategic move, part of his original dream, or simply an unexpected opportunity which he was quick to grasp. Did he intend to make Rome his permanent home? His job insured him not only financial security, but plenty of perks — for himself and his siblings. Nino, the next-oldest brother, was the first to benefit. Shrewd and enterprising, he managed, soon after settling into the job my father had found for him, to get government subsidies for building a co-op on the outskirts of the city. There were no paved roads at the time, no shops, no other structures nearby; but it gave Nino and the other family members who soon joined him there a handsome state-of-the arts apartment complex, which Nino controlled. Today, the area is a thriving part of the city. It could well have been my father's project, and we might have moved in there ourselves; but by then, we were out of the picture.

VIEW OF ACUTO (2007)

ARCH LEADING INTO THE CENTRAL SQUARE

LAND OWNED BY THE ATTURAS

My father must have realized, soon after moving to Rome, that with a few more bold moves, he could completely transform his life and that of his family. His war service had opened important doors; he'd glimpsed a whole new world of possibilities. America was still a vivid reality for him.

In 1925, he joined the small coterie of American war veterans to help set up the Rome chapter of the American Legion. A photograph of the time shows him in a large group of men, standing up front, next to a gentleman in a straw summer hat, who was obviously their leader.

Whatever his immediate plans when he settled the family in Rome, by 1927, my father's sights were clearly focused elsewhere. By the time I was eighteen months old, he had made up his mind. He left what anyone else would have considered excellent prospects in Rome and brought us all to America. I never knew if my mother really went along with this decision. I suspect not.

MEMBERS OF THE AMERICAN LEGION, ROME, 1927. JOSEPH ATTURA, FIRST ROW CENTER, BETWEEN MAN IN WHITE SUIT AND MAN WITH STRAW HAT.

FAMILY PASSPORT PHOTO, 1928.
L/R: LUCIA (LUCY) GUIDONI ATTURA,
A.P., GEORGE, SYLVIA, GIUSEPPE
(JOSEPH) ATTURA

NEW YORK, MAY, 1928

Cutting all ties to come back to this country with a wife and three small children was a bold move; but he knew his advantage. He wasn't the usual immigrant; he wasn't an immigrant at all. He was an American war veteran, an

American citizen. Through him, his children too could claim American citizenship. He must have been convinced that there was little to lose and everything to gain by relocating permanently in the United States. When other Italians were struggling to escape poverty and a bleak future, my father chose to abandon his secure new life in Rome for an undefined future in New York. No doubt he worried about the changes that lay ahead— he was no longer alone in the great adventure — but in the end, his determination prevailed, sparked, no doubt, by a visit he seems to have made to the States as one of the founding members of the Rome Chapter of The American Legion between 1925 and 1927 (see below). While there, he seems to have met a number of public officials; he may have been promised a job. I doubt it would have made a difference. He was determined. And with his energetic optimism, his fluency in English, his commitment to forge a great future for himself and his family, his creative skills — not to mention his appealing manner and presence (he resembled Gregory Peck, my mother would later recall) — he was sure to succeed.

(This inscription was typed on the back of the photograph reproduced below. Nothing more could be found about the "Tilson Law" — which seems to have secured American citizenship for Italians who fought on the American side in World War I — or my father's sailing to the States on American Legion business.)

"SAILING ON THE S.S. DUILO.

L/R: JOSEPH ATTURA, SERVICE OFFICER AND ADJUTANT OF THE ITALIAN AMERICAN LEGION DEPARTMENT; JAMES G. RODGERS, ADJUTANT OF ROME POST AND EDITOR OF THE *AMERICAN LEGION MONTHLY* OF ITALY; ENRICO SARTORIO, MEMBER OF THE EXECUTIVE COMMITTEE OF THE ITALIAN-AMERICAN LEGION DEPARTMENT; FRANK B. GIGLIOTTI, ROME ADJUTANT OF THE ITALIAN-AMERICAN LEGION DEPARTMENT (NOT SAILING). GIGLIOTTI WAS RESPONSIBLE FOR THE PASSING OF THE TILSON LAW, WHICH ADDRESSED THE PROBLEM OF THE 10,000 SOLDIERS, WHO WERE BARRED FROM RETURNING HOME."

He had made other, personal, friends in the States. Among them was a young priest, Michael Paris, who was also a distant relative. Through Father Michael Paris, my father had met the Di Marcos, who were destined to become our new "family" (before long, Assunta was *zia* and her husband Aurelio, *zio*). Father Paris, had, in fact, recruited the Di Marcos to help furnish the small apartment on Crotona Avenue, in the Bronx, where we would spend the next three and a half years.

My memories of that time, like those of my interrupted infancy in Rome, consist of few vivid scenes and images. I remember walking along what seemed like an endless corridor, balancing a small cup of *espresso* for my father but somehow managing to steal a tiny sip before delivering it to him, where he was resting on the bed. I remember his killing roaches (I had never seen one before) as they came out of the hollow handle of a dust pan. I remember bouncing on his shoulders as he paraded me through the small apartment, when he still had his strength — for it had soon become clear that whatever work my father was ready to take on could be nothing more than wishful thinking: he was taken ill soon after we settled in. The symptoms were the same as those he'd experienced in France as a result of the mustard gases. He was in and out of hospitals. His last stop was Bellevue Hospital.

REV. MICHAEL PARIS

The doctors there were baffled; they couldn't figure out what was wrong with him. In the end, they simply gave him more and more morphine to ease his pain. The mustard gases (and the morphine) won out. He was thirty-three years old when he died on February 12, 1931. I was four and a half.

I remember two visits to Bellevue. On one occasion I shouted up to him from the street, after we'd left, to where I thought I saw him peering at us through a closed window: "Papà, quando torni a casa?" ("Papà, when are you coming home?") The second time, we were leaving and my mother lifted me so I could reach over and kiss him. He held my head between his hands and whispered "Sì buona!" ("Be good!). I remember being held up to kiss him goodbye, in his coffin. I remember someone pulling me away, crying.

Today, psychiatrists might frown at allowing a four-year-old to see her dead father lying in a coffin, not to mention kissing him goodbye before the lid was closed. If I experienced some kind of trauma, it seems to have had no negative impact. Not that I didn't grieve; I still think of my father often and still mourn his early death. My time with him is preserved with the clarity of inevitability. The memories of his last days and of his funeral are among my most vivid. Of course I cried. I cried for happiness lost, but happiness it was. I treasure those memories.

FUNERAL PROCESSION OF JOSEPH ATTURA, FEBRUARY 16, 1931

1931

WITH BROTHER GEORGE

The rest of the family suffered the shock of my father's death in different ways. I suspect it was then that we began to go our separate ways, emotionally. My older sister and brother became restless, hard to manage. My mother, of course, had a terrible responsibility: three children to raise on a scanty pension. Whatever light had brightened her eyes before my father died had gone out. She was an attractive young woman, but in black she looked drab and suddenly old. She had never been very demonstrative, but now she grew even more withdrawn and made no effort to reach across her grief to comfort us. All that too, I seemed to have taken in stride. In any case, there was no time to brood; we all recognized the need for survival. The land of opportunity had suddenly turned into a desert, where we'd been left to wither and die.

In July of 1932, a year and a half after my father's death, showing unexpected resolve and no doubt longing for familiar surroundings, my mother sold everything, packed our belongings and took us back to Italy. Maybe she thought her American pension would do better there. Maybe in order to heal she needed familiar faces, familiar surroundings, a familiar language in which to communicate easily. Whatever triggered her decision, by Fall, 1932, we were soon settled in a beautiful high-ceilinged apartment on the square behind the basilica of Santa Maria Maggiore (St. Mary Major), where I was later confirmed.

SAILING BACK TO ITALY ON THE "ROMA" (JULY 29, 1932)

This third phase in my young life lasted 18 months. Here too, my memories are few and scattered. I have absolutely no recollection of attending school, but I must have, since I own a large framed certificate with an imposing gold seal and ribbon and a bronze medal — my first award — for excellence in first grade at the Alfredo Boccarini school.

I suspect my mother put most of what she and my father had saved into buying the apartment on the square behind the basilica, an investment that strongly suggests she meant to stay put. It was not to be. Events of the time and new financial pressures forced her into drastic action. Not long after we'd settled in, President Roosevelt — preparing for the inevitable — had cut veterans' pensions abroad roughly by half, no doubt to draw American families back home before war broke out. With no other means of support except that meager pension (she had no intention of ever marrying again and never did), knowing that her parents were too poor to help her and that other relatives were unwilling to take on a second family, my mother made what she must have known was an irrevocable decision: she sold the apartment and its furnishings at a tremendous loss, and after many delays managed to get the visas we needed before a crucial deadline expired. A few days later, on February 23, 1934, we sailed back to the States.

CERTIFICATE AND BRONZE MEDAL FOR EXCELLENCE IN FIRST GRADE (ROME)

CLASS PHOTO, FIRST GRADE, ALFREDO BOCCARINI GRADE SCHOOL, SIGNORA GINA MOLA (INSTRUCTOR), ROME, SEPTEMBER 1932. A.P. IN BACK ROW, FOURTH FROM THH LEFT.

All of us were uneasy, anxious, fearful; but for my mother this second parting from parents, relatives and friends must have been especially painful. Although I can't begin to imagine the depth of her despair at this second wrenching, it must have seemed like another death.

And so, at the age of eight, I was crossing the Atlantic for the third time. My life was beginning again from scratch. Our brief interlude in Rome was reduced to a few vivid scenes, shards of memory. I can still see myself yelling from the courtyard of our building to a playmate, who was looking down at me from the open window of her apartment, "Veng' acoppa?" ("Should I come up?"). I don't remember if I went up or not, and I still don't what other dialect phrases I'd picked up.

SAILING BACK TO AMERICA ON THE "REX" (FEBRUARY 23, 1934)

Another isolated memory of those years in Rome was my being confirmed, in 1933, in the imposing basilica across from our building, with my great-aunt as my godmother. Her name was Cornelia Macciò, and she had been a school principal when she met and married Antonio Longo, my mother's uncle, my maternal grandmother's brother. Antonio had forged a career in education and had risen to become chief superintendent of schools for the district of Rome and the immediate areas beyond the city. When Cornelia, an imposing-looking woman, every inch the rigorous educator, asked what I wanted as a confirmation gift, I didn't hesitate. I knew exactly what I wanted: not a gold watch, not a fancy doll, nothing like that. Ever since I'd laid eyes on her, I'd longed for a pair of lorgnettes, like hers. And that's just what I got (and no doubt saved her some money). The only difference was that the glass in mine was not prescription lenses, and it was tinted blue.

My grandmother had a second brother, Augusto Longo, who had remained in the village and, like his brother Antonio, had done very well for himself as the overseer for a large ducal estate. He lived with his family in a palatial home, across from my grandmother's small modest house, on the main thoroughfare that led into the village square. "Signor Augusto" was by far the most influential, certainly the wealthiest man for miles around. Concetta, the one sister, had not fared so well. She had married a carpenter, Antonio Guidoni, and was anything but wealthy. A soft-spoken woman, resigned to what fate had allotted her, my "nonna" never complained about the injustice of not being given some portion of what their parents had left their three children. Augusto very likely had been the executor and had taken matters in hand, but that hand did not reach out to his sister or to Antonio. Perhaps for the sake of appearances or simple decency, he would send his sister occasional gifts of fresh fruit, eggs, game meat, or other foodstuffs, but he never visited her, although she lived just across from him.

My grandmother had resigned herself to the role of poor relative, but my great-uncle Antonio — certainly not a poor relative — never stopped ranting against his brother. Time and again, as I was growing up, I heard my mother refer to the continuing feud between the two brothers. On my return to Italy as an adult, I witnessed the extent of that feud for myself.

My mother had never lost contact with her uncle Antonio and his wife; and I myself would write to them occasionally about my activities and my school work. It was usually Cornelia who replied, encouraging me in my studies. When my husband and I settled in Rome for a year as Fulbright scholars from Columbia University (1951-52), we paid them a visit. They were both retired by then. In no time, Antonio zoomed in on Augusto Longo. I can still see him as he paced the small study where we sat, ranting against his brother, whom he accused of all sorts of villainy. A short, stocky man, at least a foot shorter than his tall, patrician wife, he made a ludicrous picture, walking back and forth in that small room, his brown robe open over a white shirt and dark trousers, the belt of the robe trailing behind him as he walked restlessly, gesticulating, raising his voice to make a point, pausing at moments in a dramatic pose to punctuate what he was saying. He seemed laughable but vulnerable too, in the intensity of his tirade. Before we left, he gave us a copy of the book he had just published, in which the family quarrel is eloquently recorded.

Perhaps, because this aunt and uncle had no children of their own, my mother may have entertained the notion that they would take a practical, ongoing interest in *hers.* They certainly had the means to do so; but in this, my mother was mistaken. Besides offering her an *espresso,* and treating us to milk and cookies when we were kids, nothing more ever materialized. Clearly, we had to fend for ourselves.

In the wake of leaving Rome again, at the age of eight, the normal continuity from infancy to childhood was denied me: circumstances had made me rootless. The first time, I'd been too young to understand the enormity of what my father had done by moving his entire family to America. This time, leaving Rome seemed an exciting adventure; for me, there was nothing traumatic about it; but settling again in what was for all of us an alien land proved, in fact, an ordeal. My mother had fallen into a deep gloom. She had not only lost her husband but whatever little money they had managed to put aside had been spent to return to the States, after selling, at a tremendous loss, the lovely apartment overlooking the square behind the basilica of St. Mary Major, an investment which at the time spoke clearly about her intentions to stay close to family and friends. Separated from the people she loved and the places she knew, stranded on a distant shore with only a small veteran's pension to provide for four people, having to learn a new language as quickly as possible, she must have seen what lay ahead as a bleak prospect, indeed.

1934-1936

At this point in our lives, Father Paris looms large. For as long as we knew him, he was a parish priest, assigned to "St. Patrick's Old Cathedral," on Mott Street. The church catered to Italian immigrants and was by no stretch of the imagination an imposing cathedral, but it did house a number of prominent priests of the New York archdiocese, several of whom were destined for high places in the Church. Occasionally, Father Paris would bring one or more with him to our apartment in the Bronx, to sample Mom's excellent cooking. I think one later became a bishop or cardinal on the West coast (MacIntyre? McGuire?).

Without Father Paris, our lives would have taken a very different turn. It was "PP" (the short form of address we kids devised for "Padre Paris") who had found and furnished for us the new apartment on Garden Street — again, with the help of the Di Marcos, with whom we were to establish an even closer friendship that would continue for decades. Our new place was at right angles to Crotona Avenue and the building where we had lived the first time around, until my father died and mom took us back to Italy. It was "PP" who had helped my mother over those difficult days of my father's illness and death, who had done the paperwork and saw to it that my father was buried in the National Cemetery in Cypress Hills, in Brooklyn. He now picked up where he'd left off, ministering to us in every possible way, as he'd promised my father he would.

His presence gave us strength. He became our guardian angel. I grew to appreciate him more and more as I got older. He watched us grow up, spoiled us with ready cash whenever he could spare it (over my mother's loud protestations). For Mom, he was like an older brother to whom she could always turn for advice.

The "rest of my life" began with the certainty that we were here to stay. Circumstances had uprooted me three times, but now I started to take in the new world around me, like a child absorbs its environment: quickly and effortlessly, including the sounds and words of the new language that was to become my medium as a writer. I seemed to have picked it up naturally, the way infants learn to imitate sounds, then words, then begin to form sentences. My mother took longer to learn English, but even when she'd grown fluent in it, we continued to speak Italian at home — something that served me well, in later years.

Still, it was a time of unease, of trial and error. I don't remember having friends, although I often played with other children in front of the building or in the tiny park across the street. Instinct, honed to a shrewd awareness by loss and uncertainty, guided me in all things and made me cautious. What were for other children quite ordinary experiences for me were wary steps into unknown, often hostile territory. Not surprisingly, I matured quickly. I came to realize early in life that I had to fend for myself in this new world full of unknowns; I had to build stone by stone, brick by brick, the road on which I was destined to move ahead. I could take nothing for granted.

Our new apartment was a far cry from the high-ceilinged, spacious rooms in the stately building on the square behind the basilica of St. Mary Major, but the novelty of things enabled me to adjust fairly quickly to our cramped new living quarters. The rooms overlooked the street and a small triangle of green, with trees and benches. On the other side of the tiny park, facing our building, was P.S. 32, in which I soon was enrolled.

The Di Marcos had not moved; they still lived several blocks from us on Prospect Avenue, near the Bronx Zoo. They were excellent cooks from near Pescara, in *Abruzzo,* on the Adriatic coast, and loved to prepare meals for their relatives and friends. They prided themselves on such gourmet dishes as calf's brain and *trippa.*

On cue, after a hearty meal, while the women washed the dishes, Aurelio would clear the dining table, which practically filled their tiny living room, and the grown-ups would sit down again to play cards, often into the early morning hours; while we kids, with the Di Marcos' older children, Nicoletta and "Anna Piccola" (to distinguish her from me, the other, older-by-a-year, Anna) sought out mischief around the crowded apartment, until sleep would overcome us. Aurelio, who was a barber in one of the big downtown hotels, sometimes took us aside before dinner and cut our hair. That wasn't too bad; but sometimes he tried out new products on us, especially perms. I hated them; but mom was delighted to get them for free. She couldn't have afforded them otherwise. So, who was I to complain?

"PP" came often to the Di Marcos for supper and usually stayed on to play cards with the rest of the gang, which included "Zia Elvira" (an older cousin and *comare* of Assunta's) and her husband Nicola, and Angelina Nobilio and her husband Joe. They all remembered my father and often recalled stories about him.

(Right after the war, Angelina's daughter, Irma, married my brother. My mother did what she could to postpone the wedding; she needed him at home. When he ignored her and went ahead with his plans, she refused to attend the wedding. Nor did my sister and I. It was the first of many disconcerting episodes in our family life in America.)

Although we attended the modern church of St. Martin of Tours, which was up the block, just around the corner (where I was later married in a simple ceremony held in the rectory) and not the much larger church of Our Lady of Mount Carmel, on 187th Street, the church most Italians frequented at the time, my mother went marketing along that wide street in front of the big rococo church, often walking a bit further, to Arthur Avenue, especially when she wanted to buy a chicken. I can still see the long blood-spattered white coat of the attendant, the wet sawdust on the floor of the chicken market. A rabbi was always on call. The place reeked; the door always stood wide open. Inside, my mother would choose the chicken she wanted from the crowded cages and the white-coated attendant would pull it out, twist its neck, and wrap it up for us. When I visited the old neighborhood several years ago, the chicken market was still doing business (although I didn't see a rabbi). Across the street, the delicatessen (*salumeria*) was still there too, but I'm sure it has changed hands several times.

At home, my mother would prepare the chicken: she would pluck the feathers, clean out the entrails, scrape the stomach and put it aside with the liver, heart, and neck — a special treat for "PP."

I don't remember going marketing with my mother in Rome; I guess I was too young then to be of any use. Here, old enough to be called on to accompany her on errands, I felt unjustly burdened. I realize, looking back to those days, that my mother had no choice. Someone had to help her carry back the groceries and fresh vegetables, and I was the only one available to serve as family gofer and general *factotum*. My sister (the first-born, six years older than I) had grown into a moody teenager and was going through a critical time. No doubt my mother wanted to spare her. My brother couldn't be relied on: he had made some rough friends and had grown hard to handle. When his behavior became a serious concern, it was "PP" who, through contacts, managed to get him into the Salesian High School in New Rochelle as a special non-paying student. The priests were rigorous disciplinarians and kept him under control. When my mother and I visited him on Sundays — a trip of over two hours by bus and train — lugging large valises full of clean clothes and whatever delicacies my mother had managed to prepare for him, within her limited budget, he offered no thanks. He resented being where he was; he wanted his "freedom," missed his rowdy friends back home. For my part, I resented having to travel for hours, dragging a heavy suitcase, to visit a brother who scarcely spoke to me at home and who had nothing but complaints when we visited. My mother suffered her son's rebuffs in silence. He, in turn, continued to blame her years afterwards, for "putting him away."

By now, I was doing well in school. To this day, I can't be sure how or where I picked up the language — but I'm sure the Di Marco girls had a lot to do with it, since I saw them practically every day. I certainly didn't learn it at home; there we all spoke Italian. My mother trailed us in picking up the new language, but she soon did. Years later, she took a night course in a nearby public school to make sure she had it right. She was still reading newspapers both in English and Italian when she died at ninety-four.

In my case, what I can say for sure about my magic transition into the English-speaking world is that I started out in P.S. 32 getting "A"s in Art, Math, and Music and failing History, Civics, and English; being left back three times as a result (ESL courses were unheard of in those days); and then making up the lost time by skipping three times. To me it seemed perfectly natural to be left back, just as it seemed perfectly reasonable that I should be rewarded, once I caught up. I graduated on target and went on to junior high school (P.S. 57), a few blocks away.

The two years in junior high stretched out to three, when I came down with rheumatic fever. I remember lying in bed for more than a year, some fellow students and a teacher visiting, once or twice.

By the time I entered Evander Childs High School, we had moved from Garden Street to Allerton Avenue, two blocks from White Plains Road and Pelham Parkway North, with easy access to the Lexington Avenue train. It may have been "PP" who suggested the strategic move, since the high school was within walking distance and at the time had a good reputation. I'm sure he had chosen the apartment across from P.S. 32, earlier, with the same idea in mind.

At fourteen I got a work permit and began to earn some money after school, on Saturdays, and during the summers. I continued working part-time right through college. I had no choice. My mother could not afford an "allowance" for any of us.

Two of my part-time jobs stick in my mind because of incidents I provoked. In one, I was hired by the advertising firm of Young and Rubicam to ring doorbells and get answers to a consumer survey. It didn't last long. Trying to spare my tired feet and yet fill my quota, I began to sign a number of questionnaires with fictitious names and addresses. I still remember the embarrassment at being found out; facing the personnel manager; not saying a word (what excuse could I possibly give?). I knew I deserved to be fired. The incident taught me a lesson I never forgot.

The other part-time job, still vivid in my mind, was with Fortune Pope. This taught me a lesson of a different kind. I was hired to write advertising copy in Italian for olive oil Mr. Pope imported from Italy. I saw it as a real challenge, since the space I had for promoting the product was only 2 inches square. I quickly warmed to my subject and was rather pleased with myself until one day, Mr. Pope stopped by my desk, holding a copy of *Il Progresso*, the Italian newspaper in which the most recent ad had just appeared. I was proud of the fact that I'd managed to squeeze into that small space all the excellent qualities of the oil Mr. Pope imported — the printed version, in four-point type, now being held in front of my eyes. He didn't have to explain the obvious; I had to lean forward to peer at the almost illegible type. If I wasn't fired it was probably because it was hard to find someone who could write ad copy in Italian for a meager hourly rate.

In the summers, I would take on full-time work in places like Lord and Taylor and B. Altman's. I lacked basic office skills and usually ended up running the big manual elevators, opening and closing the heavy doors of the steel gate on every floor. (I still have the muscles to prove it!)

Two things stand out from my otherwise blurred and confused high school years. One was the senior prom, which I went to with a blind date, in a gown my mother had made for me. The dress was a dusty pink satin with a wide mesh skirt in plum. My mother made all my clothes in those days, to save money. She was pretty good at it, but it was an embarrassment to me. I used to look longingly at the store-bought dresses, skirts, and blouses other girls wore. That night was no exception. I was self-conscious about my appearance; I didn't think my dress stood scrutiny. I also remember six of us driving in someone's car to the Glen Island Casino and dancing to the music of what was already known as the legendary Glen Miller band. I drank my first cocktail that night: a Manhattan.

The other thing I remember from those days was the school's senior advisor suggesting I go to Barnard College rather than Mount St. Vincent or New Rochelle (my mother's two choices; "PP" opted for Barnard). My advisor knew I had access to some scholarship money because of my father's war service; my brother had claimed his, three years earlier, to study electrical engineering at Manhattan College. The $350 check from the government was, at the time, enough to cover roughly half the annual tuition at Barnard.

With "PP" on my side, I chose Barnard. It was a long and tiring train ride every morning and evening, walking with my load of books from the 110th Street Lexington Avenue station in Harlem, across Morningside Park (empty and desolate in the early morning hours and darkly silent in the late afternoon and evening). It never occurred to me, no one ever told me, and I never suspected and therefore never asked if there were a better way to get to the west side. Nor did it ever occur to me that the Park might be dangerous. I would get off in the heart of Harlem and return home the same way, every day. This went on for over a year, until I discovered that there was a West Side Seventh Avenue subway that stopped right at the entrance to the Columbia campus, across the street from Barnard, at 116th Street and Broadway.

Commuting still wasn't easy, but I had no choice. I certainly couldn't raise enough money to pay for room and board in the dormitories. I was happy enough to have found a shorter route that saved me close to an hour and (I later realized) was infinitely safer than the ride to Harlem and the steep climb through the park.

A new world was opening up for me. I didn't know what to expect, what college life would be like. I had one friend, Marie Mancuso, who lived near us (by that time we had moved again to better quarters on Pelham Parkway North). Marie and I did all kinds of things together, including finding seats in the first row of the Paramount Theater to hear Frank Sinatra when he gave one of his great early recitals there. But college separated us.

Later, I was destined to cross to the other side of the street, walk through the massive gates that led into the campus of Columbia University. I didn't know it at the time, but my life was about to change dramatically. I was about to enter a Dantesque journey that would correct my weaknesses, rid me of many errors, and strengthen my faith in my own potential.

🗁 *FROM THE FILES* 🗁

JUNE 4, 1928

1929-1936

WITH "NICKY" DI MARCO

WITH SYLVIA AND GEORGE

IN FRONT OF CROTONA AVENUE
HOUSE WHERE WE LIVED
BEFORE MY FATHER DIED

WITH SYLVIA AND GEORGE

1929-1936

1937-1943

1937-1943

WITH MARIE MANCUSO

WITH IRMA NOBILIO, "NICKY" AND ANNE DI MARCO

WITH IRMA, GEORGE AND SYLVIA

2. REACHING FOR THE UNKNOWN

"la dritta via era smarrita. . . ."

COLUMBIA UNIVERSITY'S LOW MEMORIAL LIBRARY, CA. 1950

Choosing Barnard was a crucial decision. Not that I got much out of those four years: for me, they were a waste of time. No one understood my special needs; I could hardly articulate them myself. With no one to guide me, I drifted along, shifting my "major" several times. Nothing appealed to me, except writing. I had been filling notebooks with poems and short stories long before Barnard. Finally forced into making a decision, in my junior year, I opted for "creative writing" as my major field of study for the next two years — a risky choice for any student; the worst possible choice for someone still culturally illiterate, without any kind of literary foundation in either Italian or English, ignorant of even the most common children's stories.

In other ways too Barnard was a difficult time for me. The strange mixture of ignorance, innocence, and a kind of defensive arrogance set me apart. I soon became a target for the well-established, well-bred, well-prepared wealthy young ladies, for whom going to Barnard (where, many of their mothers and grandmothers had gone before them) was practically a birthright. Coming from socially prominent families, they were the insiders; I was the intruder, the uncouth foreigner. They kept me from joining their clubs and activities, made no effort to be socially or in any other way "correct" — that sorry myth was for a later time. For these young women, born into wealth and ease, who were assured a predictable future, who married into equally rich and prominent families, who were raised to assert in their every gesture their inbred sense of superiority, I was the unpolished immigrant. It hurt, but I also understood it — even when they played cruel tricks on me — and took it in stride. My only friends during those years were two other Italian girls, not quite as new to this environment as I was, since their families had been here much longer than mine.

All this was unpleasant, but I was not one to brood. I knew my life was different from that of the well-bred, well-dressed, well-prepared aristocratic young ladies with whom I shared classes. I had learned to survive much greater setbacks. I ignored the snubs and went about my business. I became Art Editor of the college magazine and got myself elected as head of Press Board (I've forgotten what we did there). Somewhere along the line, I won the college competition for a poster design advertising the musical that was then the rage on Broadway, *Oklahoma!* — for which accomplishment I was presented with two free tickets to that play. (My poster depicted a surrey with a fringe on top, seen from behind, as it moved down a country road, a man and woman sitting in it, their backs to us, leaning into one another, their heads close together, touching.) I loved art almost as much as writing and had for the previous two years been Art Editor of *Barnard Quarterly*, the college magazine and designed several covers and other drawings for it.

PRESS BOARD (THIRD FROM LEFT), 1946

At times, I wondered if I'd made a mistake going to Barnard. I probably had, in a way. The privileged young ladies who avoided me no doubt thought so, as did some of the people in the administration. My doubts were answered in an unexpected way at the end of my Freshman year, when I was called in for a routine interview with the Dean, who reviewed my work. The woman seemed genuinely surprised that I had done so well and told me bluntly — though not unkindly — that "they" almost hadn't accepted me when I applied for admission but decided at the last minute to give me a chance. She never explained the reason for their wavering; she didn't have to. She went on to tell me that I had done exceptionally well in my final exams for the year. It did me good to hear those words: I was sure I'd done badly in the English exam especially, where I had barely glanced at the directions and had answered all five essay questions instead of choosing two out of five, as instructed on the top of the exam sheet.

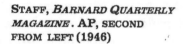

STAFF, *BARNARD QUARTERLY MAGAZINE*. AP, SECOND FROM LEFT (1946)

I moved through those years unfocused, uncertain. I took advanced math and radio communication courses and discovered Freud, before ending up in "creative writing" — a subject which, I soon realized, cannot be taught and which no student in his right mind should ever waste time trying to master in that way. To presume to write without the great authors of past and present echoing in your ears, to express feelings and emotions without having gone through a certain amount of experience to sensitize reactions to people and events, is a useless effort at best. Not that writing should not be encouraged as early as possible; but it should always be accompanied with a good healthy and varied diet of good books to sharpen one's awareness of language at its best, its function as a tool of logic; to nurture respect for the tried and tested skills needed to realize one's individual talent.

I had become painfully aware of my mistake, during my senior year. I felt a terrible lack inside me, the years in college a sorry experience. Still, I was bent on going to graduate school, had applied and been accepted. I didn't pause to congratulate myself: I knew perfectly well that Barnard's close connection with Columbia made the transition almost automatic. The sheer fact of my having gone to Barnard was a big "plus." For that, I was grateful.

All through my years at Barnard, I continued writing on my own. Several poems even found their way into print before I graduated. It was only when I began to seriously consider going on to Columbia and graduate studies that I suddenly realized how much I'd missed. It struck me, then, how large a vacuum waited to be filled; how much I needed to learn, how hungry I was for real intellectual challenge, how superficial my life still was. When I was accepted for graduate work, I asked my history professor at Barnard — whose class I had enjoyed immensely — to recommend some graduate courses I might take, telling him that I needed "more substantial" fare. He replied, without a moment's hesitation: "Ah, you want Dino Bigongiari!" There was a kind of awe in his voice. I must have asked more questions, he must have given me more answers. All I remember is that when I left, Professor Bigongiari was top on my list of people to see before I registered for courses. I didn't know it then, but my life was about to change forever. Confident in a yet unchartered future, I was about to enter on a long search for cultural identity. I was twenty-one.

Around this time, we had moved again, a few blocks away, to Pelham Parkway North, with the Bronx Botanical Gardens close by. My sister, with her Iranian husband and their two young daughters, had moved in with us while my brother-in-law (who had come to Columbia as an exchange student) waited for a job to materialize in Washington. My brother, having joined the Navy Reserve while studying for a degree in electrical engineering at Manhattan College, had been called to active duty in the Pacific soon after graduation and had gotten married and moved out as soon as he returned home. Our beloved "PP" had died just before my graduation from Barnard, in May, 1947.

It was no time to relax. Mom and I had to find a way to carry on, with even less resources than before and the new, unexpected responsibilities of an extended family.

WITH BROTHER GEORGE

GEORGE WITH WIFE IRMA NOBILIO

Barnard was a thing of the past, a necessary but not too pleasant experience that had served to bring me closer to the new world I was just discovering. But now, there were new pressures — the most immediate being the need to earn the money needed to pay for my courses and other expenses for graduate school and to help as best I could at home. Surely there was some decent full-time job for me out there?

Several, in fact, were open to me. One was with Metromedia TV, which was just taking off and no doubt would have catapulted me into a glamorous future as a talk show hostess or some such thing. (My courses in radio production and communication, and my writing — such as it was — carried a certain weight). I chose instead a rather humdrum job as Administrative Assistant to the head of Teachers College, just a few blocks from the main campus, and therefore walking distance to Butler Library and Philosophy Hall (where most graduate classes in the Humanities were held). As a career, the job was a dead-end; it had none of the bright prospects of the Metromedia offer. I didn't care. All I wanted at that point was a fairly decent salary to see me over the new hurdles. The biggest attraction for me was free tuition: as a full time member of the University staff, I could take as many courses as I wished, for as long as I continued in the job, without having to pay a single penny. For me, this last was manna from heaven.

It was not the first time I had followed my instincts and found myself safe and sound on the other side of difficulties that ignorance or a naive self-confidence had blithely ignored. Fate seemed to be on my side. It rewarded me, in fact, with unexpected gifts.

I don't remember just when I first met with the legendary Dino Bigongiari, but it was not long after I had settled into my new job, right after my graduation. I was eager to meet him before enrolling in Fall courses. In the interim, I had discovered that not only was he the head of the Graduate Italian Department at Columbia but he was also the University's most prominent scholar and teacher.

DINO BIGONGIARI

I was more than a little nervous on meeting him, toward the end of that Summer. He must have sized me up quickly: a nice Italian girl, inexperienced but wary, not clear about the future but eager for something still undefined, seemingly interested in learning, proud of her heritage but not too familiar with it. As for me, I took to him at once. His quiet concentrated manner, his kindness, his obvious willingness to help me, in every way he could, at once put me at ease. I must have told him a great deal about my family and circumstances. Somewhere into our conversation, he mentioned a scholarship available in the Department of Italian. There was still time to apply, he told me, although classes were soon to begin. I never stopped to consider alternatives. I was in the presence of the Master. I would be taking his courses. What more could I ask?

To this day, I'm not sure that the deadline for the Garibaldi Scholarship was as flexible as I had been given to believe. Much later, I came to the conclusion that Bigongiari could do pretty much what he wanted and had decided on a long shot.

I held the Scholarship for two years, while I earned credits for the Master's degree, which I received in 1950. It provided me with some ready cash (my tuition was paid for); it also gave me credentials that would make a big difference later on.

Bigongiari had assigned to me, as my mentor, an extraordinary man who had come to Columbia at Bigongiari's invitation (backed, of course, by his good friend, President Nicholas Murray Butler), the brilliant European journalist and man of letters, Giuseppe Prezzolini. "Prezzi," as everyone called him, also happened to be the world's leading scholar on Machiavelli, and before long I was deep in the *Commentaries on Livy*, as well as *The Prince* and other works of the master of *realpolitik*. It was my first in-depth encounter with one of the great authors of the Renaissance. I read everything I could get my hands on, including that last profound commentary on man's depravity, *Mandragola*. Some years later, my husband and I translated the play into English — my first major academic publication. (It has gone through several publishers and almost 40 printings.)

I wrote my Master's thesis, however, not on Machiavelli (as one might expect, with someone like "Prezzi" around), but on the critical language of Giosuè Carducci, the major Italian poet (and critic) of Italy in the latter part of the nineteenth-century and the second Italian Nobel Laureate in Literature. I don't recall whose idea it was originally, but I'm not sorry I settled for it. In addition to sharpening my insights about the nature of literary criticism, it gave me a chance to hone my skills in the language, since all the research and the thesis itself had to be in Italian. It also made me conscious of poetry in a different way, in a different "key," one might say. I heard beautiful cadences in a different language, words and phrases fashioned in a new way. A short English version of the Master's thesis was later published in *Italica* (June,

1956) with the title, *Moments of the Creative Process in the Literary Criticism of Giosuè Carducci.*

"Prezzi" taught me to read texts carefully. He was a wiry man, not very tall, full of enthusiasm for his subject, caustic at times, sharply critical as a rule, but always ready to explain, to help. He remained at Columbia until his retirement — when he returned to Italy, picked up his journalistic career, continued to write and lecture on Machiavelli, and died, still lucid, at 102.

Somewhere along the line, I quit my job at Teachers College and came closer to the heart of the action, manning the check-out desk of the Business Library, in Butler Hall, Columbia's main library. It was a strange job for a college graduate, but I recognized it as a temporary move. For the moment, it suited perfectly, especially since it was the place where discarded library books were brought in and sold for fifteen cents each. During the several months I worked there (and even after I'd transferred to another part of the building and another job), I managed to collect an impressive number of excellent books — some valuable and irreplaceable — which the library had to get rid of to make room for recent acquisitions. One of the treasures I found was an unabridged Century Dictionary, which I still own. Bound in heavy corduroy, it weighed a ton. I remember lugging it six or seven blocks, to where I then lived, resting on every car fender along Broadway, to catch my breath. I paid a bit more for this one: all of three dollars.

I was in the Business Library for just a few months. Dr. Richard Logsdon, the Director of the Columbia Libraries, had met me and offered me a job that had opened up in his office, as his administrative assistant. This was more in keeping with my credentials, but for me it was just another temporary measure. I still did not have big or clear plans for the future, but I think I had come to realize that I should not rush things, that I was still adjusting to my new world. Like my other jobs, this one too enabled me to walk to work and continue my research and writing easily. During this time I continued to read new authors and write articles and poems. The biggest boon was to be able to audit Bigongiari's Dante course as often as I wished, since I had already taken it for credit during my first year in graduate school.

The first two years of graduate work were immensely satisfying and instructive. The University was like a magnet; I couldn't pull away. I knew I would go on for the Ph.D., but there were no pressing decisions to be made. I felt I could stay on forever.

Bigongiari had repeatedly been re-elected Chairman of the Italian Department, but one year — perhaps anticipating his retirement — he allowed someone else to take on the job, someone who had been teaching mostly language courses but whom Bigongiari felt was capable of taking the administrative burdens off his shoulders. In preparing faculty schedules, the new Chairman arrogantly assigned the Dante course to himself, forcing Bigongiari to "retire." It was a bad move. The faculty community was shocked.

Marjorie Nicolson, then Chairperson of the Department of English and Comparative Literature, acted quickly and decisively, inviting Bigongiari to teach the Dante course in her Department. In what seemed a perfectly natural and appropriate move, I too shifted departments. I had given little thought to my future, but I knew for certain that I did not want to limit myself to the teaching of Italian. My Master's degree was a first step toward realizing a larger goal, not yet fully understood. When Bigongiari moved into the Department of English and Comparative Literature, I simply followed him there for my Ph.D.

By then, my personal circumstances had undergone another dramatic change. In the first year of graduate work, I had met, in Bigongiari's Dante class, Henry Paolucci, who had returned to the States between 1945 and 1946, after serving as a navigator in the U.S. Air Force in Europe He had signed up for the Air Force even before graduating from City College in 1942 and was called to duty soon after. His first assignments had been flying from a Florida base to Dakar, in North Africa. Later, and for most of the war, he was based abroad, his main targets Italian and German cities. After the war, he had stayed on another year, to supervise the "processing" of ten thousand German prisoners of war waiting to be sent back to Germany. He took the occasion to become fluent in German and to learn to drive a jeep built for him by the men in his charge, who respected him because, although rigorous, he was fair,

When I met Henry in 1947, he had been at Columbia for over a year on the "G.I. Bill." He'd earned his Master's degree by then, had taken Bigongiari's course and, when I entered the picture, was auditing the class.

From the outset, I couldn't help noticing that there was a special kind of relationship between Bigongiari and this unusual young man who asked questions — I soon discovered — not because he didn't know the answers but as a way of encouraging discussion and input from the rest of us. It was as if the two men had reached a tacit understanding to liven things up. It worked, of course; and I realized as I got to know him better, that Henry had already read many of the authors Bigongiari brought into the class discussion. He was very much like Bigongiari himself, often indulging in long comments that made all of us sit up and take notice. Bigongiari was always pleased by his participation and never interrupted him. Like Bigongiari, Henry was a natural teacher and anything but shy about speaking his mind or taking on the hard topics that often came up in reading Dante's poem.

A story I heard later helped explain not only Henry's character but also the role he played in the Dante course.

Bigongiari (so the story goes) had been explaining the implicit contradiction in accepting free will and the omnipotence of God. I suppose that from the beginning of religious awareness men have argued that if God is omnipotent there is no room for free will: if we are truly free, then God becomes a mere bookkeeper, keeping inventory of our good deeds with a check mark, putting a cross next to our transgressions, and, at the end, adding up the two columns to determine our fate. Bigongiari cited St. Augustine, who admittedly had no simple answer to that dilemma and had cautioned "silence." One must accept both on faith, Augustine had written; it's a dilemma and can't be explained logically. To Bigongiari's reference to St. Augustine, Henry had countered, bluntly: "That answer may satisfy you, but it doesn't satisfy me." No one expected him to return to class after having in effect insulted both the Professor and St. Augustine, but he had continued to show up — only, he no longer participated. One evening, Bigongiari addressed him as others were leaving at the end of the 2-hour class and asked: "Why don't you raise questions any more?" Henry replied: "Because I know everything you know —" then added quickly "— but you've turned it right side up for me."

It was typical of Henry. No one else I've ever known could transform what appeared to be an insult into the highest compliment possible. He never undermined his own worth but was ready to admit his shortcomings just as honestly. His answer to Bigongiari was true and direct. An apology would have been out of place. He had read most of St. Augustine's works and knew them well. His comment had reflected not a personal view or an arrogant skepticism but, rather, a large question that even the great Augustine could not answer in rational terms.

Henry had read a great deal, in fact, long before he even went to college. An older brother, Louis. a self-made writer/poet/critic/music lover, had introduced him, when Henry was still a youngster, to a number of great authors, old and new, to great composers; had taught him all about music — an education that went beyond what is available in any classroom. He taught Henry to play the piano as well. There were books everywhere in the family's crowded apartment in the Bronx and, later, in their house in Yonkers. Louis took time to share with his younger sibling everything he knew, from the time

LOUIS PAOLUCCI WITH MOTHER "NANCY" (ANNUNZIATA). ON THE WALL: DONATO PAOLUCCI'S OIL PAINTING OF COLUMBIA'S LOW MEMORIAL HALL.)

Henry was a child (the last of five children; Louis, the second, eight years older). Louis was, for a time, curator of the Paterno Library of Columbia, an Italian-style stone structure reminiscent of the Sforza palace, but he chose never to attend college or get a degree. He loved to talk at length about the things that mattered to him, something that must have impressed Henry even as a child, not only because of the mastery of subjects Louis displayed but also because of the manner of his delivery. Both his enthusiasm and his sharp critical observations taught Henry what argument and debate were all about; he learned to be intellectually articulate when most of his peers were still struggling with grammar.

Henry had returned to academe with a rich legacy that he never minimized. Louis was his unofficial mentor as he was growing up, but they both owed a good deal to their father, Donato, a resolute and clever man, who had learned many skills on his own.

DONATO PAOLUCCI

HENRY WITH HIS MOTHER "NANCY"

Donato Paolucci had come to this country with his father, as a boy, an early immigrant, and quickly found work. A perfectionist, he was never satisfied with less than the best. He was one of the few workers kept on by the Krakaour Piano Company, during the depression, for he had learned how to build a piano from beginning to end. Some years earlier, he had bought with his savings, the small apartment building where they lived, on 149th Street in the Bronx; and now he tore down walls to create bigger units where married children with young families could move back with their parents to economize, during those hard times. Later, with the same clear-headed efficiency, he restored the smaller apartments into the larger units they had been before the depression. Still later, he sold the building and bought a house in Yonkers, where the family lived for many years.

When he retired at sixty-five and sold their house in Yonkers, he took up painting. He gutted a small closet in the apartment they had rented in Rego Park, put a light bulb in it, and used the tiny enclosure as a painting studio. He turned out more than two dozen paintings, landscapes from a far-off past or copied from photos and pictures: the Bay Bridge in San Francisco, surreal village scenes and people as he saw and remembered them, or as his imagination gave them shape. They all have a Neapolitan feeling to them, those paintings — the lush colors of the south. Even his Assisi, with its sloping hills and the cluster of familiar buildings, beautifully rendered, shows a landscape of miniature trees and giant grasses hard to find anywhere, least of all in Umbria. His experience as a draftsman is evident in the precision of the lines of buildings and in the shadows exquisitely traced on them. At any one moment, he made the best possible use of everything he knew, everything he had learned. Nothing escaped him. He was an intelligent, self-educated man, well-read in Italian literature, Machiavelli especially. He passed on to his children his love of music as well. He was also, for most of his life, a confirmed atheist and an intellectual anarchist.

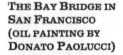

THE BAY BRIDGE IN SAN FRANCISCO (OIL PAINTING BY DONATO PAOLUCCI)

It would be misleading to say that Henry, coming from such a home, went to Columbia to learn from his professors. He wanted a degree, of course; but, even more, he wanted others against which to test his knowledge.

On campus, he quickly earned a reputation as a reputable scholar. William Westermann, for many years the head of the Graduate History Department at Columbia, would say to anyone interested in Aristotle and Greek philosophy: "Talk to Henry Paolucci." Always fair, always careful in his assessment of people, always ready to admit excellence in others, Henry greatly admired Westermann's honesty as a scholar, Gilbert Highet's elegant and witty manner, Jacques Barzun's easy way of carrying his well-earned renown — but he could also be openly critical of the witty Renaissance scholar, Maurice Valency (who, later, was assigned as a reader for Henry's dissertation — with almost disastrous results). Bigongiari, of course, was the Master and later his close friend as well. I basked in the light they shed. A great deal of what they knew and of their classroom manner rubbed off on me, even before Henry became an integral part of my life.

Often, in the early evening, after Bigongiari's Dante class, Henry and I would stroll down Broadway and stop for coffee at places like "Tom's Restaurant" (in recent years, a familiar venue on the "Seinfeld" series). He too, I discovered, was working toward a Ph.D. and, like me, was in no great hurry. We'd spend hours talking, or rather Henry spent hours educating me in subjects and authors I had never heard of or reviewing things Bigongiari had said and I had not wholly taken in. Just as I knew, as I began graduate work, that I had found the direction and purpose I had been unconsciously searching for all through my college years, I was equally certain now about Henry's influence and place in my life. I was never more exhilarated than when I was with him, never more eager to hear him explain things, recite long passages of poetry and prose. His store of authors seemed endless. I learned that he was an Augustinian pessimist without St. Augustine's unshakeable faith and that his favorite poets, after Dante, were James Thomson, author of *The City of Dreadful Night* (what one critic called "the most pessimistic poem in any language") and Giacomo Leopardi, the second great poet of Italy, he too a profound pessimist. I also learned that, in spite of his professed atheism, Henry had a profound respect for the Catholic Church and for Church history and had collected and read such impressive works as Adolf von Harnack's *History of Dogma*. He had also developed a keen interest in astronomical theory, especially the massive work of Pierre Duhem, *Le Système du Monde,* an authoritative, documented history of astronomical theory, with original texts, from the time of the Greeks down to the present. (We acquired the several huge tomes of that invaluable work several years later, from the Columbia book discards, for 15 cents each!)

When I met him, Henry was already a thoroughgoing Hegelian. I was soon introduced to the *Philosophy of Fine Art*, a subject I was not altogether ready to take on, in spite of my interest in Shakespeare and the Hegelian Shakespearean critic, A. C. Bradley. Wisely, Henry did not push me; but he was persistent and relentless in talking about Hegel's theory of the arts and of tragedy especially. He made sense, and he always left me wanting to hear more; but it wasn't easy at first. My questions were endless, but he was always there with the answers. It was the beginning of a major and still ongoing intellectual experience for me, one that continues to illuminate what I know about ancient and modern drama, and Shakespeare.

That first year of graduate school at Columbia, I discovered not only the world of Prezzolini and Machiavelli, of Bigongiari and Dante, but also the world of Henry and Hegel. Listening to my new friend was an intellectual feast, another *Symposium*, a banquet of the mind the likes of which I had not remotely imagined, much less expected to find. On his side, Henry had found a passionate acolyte. I had come far enough to understand that he had everything I yearned for: ease in the intellectual life (not so common among academics, I was to find out), confidence and assurance. What he knew, he knew perfectly. He was also kind and generous (often to a fault, I would soon discover) in sharing his knowledge with others.

At the end of that first year of my *vita nuova*, Professor Bigongiari sponsored Henry for the Eleanora Duse Fellowship, which carried a generous stipend. He would spend the entire academic year 1948-1949 in Florence, perfecting his Italian, meeting prominent writers and (although he was not obliged to do so) attending university lectures of renowned scholars. During that time, I continued my studies at Columbia; but even before he left, we had both come to a tacit understanding that our separate ways had become one and that our futures were about to merge.

☞ *FROM THE FILES* ☞

MY FIRST PUBLISHED POEM APPEARED WHEN I WAS NINETEEN, IN A THIN "NATIONAL" ANTHOLOGY OF COLLEGE POETRY. ITS ONLY MERIT PERHAPS IS A CERTAIN RESPECT FOR METER AND RHYME, AN HONEST EFFORT TO DESCRIBE THE VAGUE BUT POWERFUL FEELINGS THAT PLAGUE MOST TEENAGERS.

LOVE RUSTLED IN THE WIND
Love rustled in the wind, sighing forlorn.
And the little golden drops of withered song
Echoed in the breeze.

I called to the bloodless rose, a wretched plea
To still eternity. And as I stood upon the shore
   of sighs,
Receding in the cool darkness of the night
I wept bitterly. Love rustling in the wind forlorn,
Sighed for me.

(In *America Sings*. National Poetry Association, Los Angeles, 1945, p. 84.)

THE YEAR I GRADUATED FROM COLLEGE, THREE OF MY POEMS APPEARED IN A HUGE HARD-COVER VOLUME — MORE OF THE SAME KIND OF TENTATIVE EFFORT. ONE OF THEM IS REPRODUCED BELOW.

A DREAM
I saw it flee, a shining rolling sea heaving away from me.
I watched it roaring past — too swift, too fast the die was cast!
And still I stood and watched the flood
The foamy blue turning to blood.

Yes, I cried. I shed the shadow at my side
Flung it in Heaven's golden tide
For the sunbeams eager to convey their minstrelsy
Of dancing glee, dissolved their passion in the murky sea.

(In *Poetry on the Air. An Anthology of Contemporary Verse*, edited by
Michael Everett. Poetry House, New York, 1947, p. 42.)

THE FOLLOWING POEM IS FROM LOUIS PAOLUCCI'S POEMS BY PAUL.

ISOLATION

Men are like trees,
I walk around them
And wonder why they grow,
And women are like winds
That stir the trees to frenzy,
To carry off their seeds.
And I am like a shadow,
Lost among the trees
And hidden from the winds.

COLUMBIA UNIVERSITY'S "ALMA MATER" (ON THE STEPS OF LOW MEMORIAL LIBRARY)

**WITH MOM
AND SYLVIA
(1944)**

HENRY (R) WITH HIS
NEPHEW MATTHEW (L)
AND BROTHER ADAM

WITH MOM

THE FOLLOWING EXCERPT FROM MY SHORT STORY, "BURIED TREASURE" FOCUSES ON MY FATHER-IN-LAW. (IN *SEPIA TONES* [RIMU PRESS, NEW ZEALAND; GRIFFON HOUSE PUBLICATIONS, NEW YORK], ORIGINALLY REVIEWED IN THE *NEW YORK TIMES*.) REPRINTED IN *THE VOICES WE CARRY*, AN ANTHOLOGY OF WRITINGS BY ITALIAN-AMERICAN WOMEN, "BURIED TREASURE" WAS SINGLED OUT AS "THE MASTERPIECE OF THE ENTIRE ANTHOLOGY" (*WOMEN'S REVIEW OF BOOKS*, WELLESLEY).

. . . There was a tacit understanding between us [about music]. I knew that he wanted to hear me play; and I never disappointed him. It was a ritual of sorts. (Later, painting took its place.) I simply wanted to please him. And, although my own piano was a 1929 Steinway and had an impeccable tone, I know that he heard the same perfect sounds in his imagination, when I played on his old permanently out-of-tune reject from Krakaour Piano Company, where he worked. To me, those sounds were better than the ones I got from my Steinway. Not that I played any differently on his piano, but something about his interest and his commitment to the music Henry had taught me to love, gave me a little extra something, a bit more energy and daring at the keyboard. Even my mistakes were somehow glossed over in the intensity of our mutual dedication.

The piano, especially, figures in all this. The old man was 67 when he decided finally to sell the house in Yonkers and move with his wife into an apartment in Rego Park, Queens. It took a lot of doing; he was a house man, had been for many years. And they always lived close to Lucy, the oldest of the five children, who had the upstairs quarters in the house; so Lucy had to make a decision about whether to move to Rego Park, close to them. Well, everything was settled, finally, when it became clear that he could not go on doing all the heavy chores he had insisted on doing right up to that moment. The rest of the family had worried for months and months about that. Because he would not listen to anyone; he always did what he thought was right and did not consult anyone else about the need of the household or his tasks in keeping things going. He had insisted on refurbishing the roof in its entirety, and almost fell because of a dizzy spell at one point. He continued to trim the trees that got battered in the winter storms. He replaced doors, cut the hedges, built a patio with a grapevine, tended his vegetable garden in the summer. He had a mind of his own and didn't want to be pushed around. So for the last two years he continued to do everything he had always done (which was the work of several strong men), but eventually he must have realized he couldn't carry on at that pace and came around. I guess he knew in his heart it couldn't last forever. The arbor and the hedges had to be pruned, the lawn had to be mowed, the ivy on the north side of the house (which housed hundreds of birds) had to be cut down when the starlings began to threaten the structure. He had some help, of course. His son-in-law and grandson lived in the upstairs apartment, and they had their chores too. But the heavy jobs were the old man's, he simply wouldn't give them to the younger people. He was never satisfied with any one else's work. In the years they lived in Yonkers, he never called in a workman from the outside or ever asked his sons or son-in-law or grandson to help him with the tasks he himself took on. He was justifiably proud of his skills.

When they finally decided to move (when my father-in-law finally consented), the piano became a real problem. There was no room in the apartment for it; no one was interested in buying an old gutted player-piano; he couldn't even give it away and refused to call in someone to dump it. I suspect he had a sentimental attachment to it and could not bear to see it carted away.

He brooded about it and found a solution he could live with.

First, he took the piano apart, chopped the wooden frame into pieces and threw those out. That was simple enough. But the trouble was the innards. The metal strings could not be taken apart, It was a big piano, you have to understand. One day, after watching him struggle with it, my sister-in-law (the witch) took her mother aside and whispered to her. "Keep him out of the house tomorrow. Find something for him to do in the City. Willie and Donald will get rid of the piano. He's going to rupture himself if he goes on like this." The old lady managed to get him out of the house on some pretext or other. Willie and his son worked most of the day, but they could not get rid of what remained of the piano. It couldn't simply be left outside. There was too much of it still. They took it out into the yard and looked for some solution there. When the old man finally returned, late in the afternoon, he surveyed the scene but said nothing. The next morning, before anyone else was up, he got back to work. He had sized up the situation and had reached a decision. He dug a deep hole and buried the innards and everything else that could not be chopped up into small pieces. He buried it between the garage and the strawberry patch. Just like that.

Bozo is buried there somewhere too. It's only natural. What does one do with a 17-year-old dog who has been part off the family all that time? Someday, someone is going to get a big surprise!

And the rock. That's not treasure exactly, but it's a good story. The house had a two-car garage, but the driveway was narrow. It was an old house and only one car could drive up the narrow space, straight into the first garage. That was my father-in-law's space — not for a car (he didn't drive) but for his tools lawn mower and much else. Willie's space was the second garage. To get his car inside it, he had to maneuver around the sharp corner of the house and into the second space, attached to the first — avoiding, as he did so, a huge rock that lay between the two.

Willie had taken on the challenge, since he liked to brag. He managed, of course (he was a good driver, I'll say that for him), but, upstairs, with Lucy, he'd curse the day and everybody and the rock. In front of the old man he never said a word. There was a silent running battle between them because my father-in-law was so damn good at just about everything and so critical of a shabby product that Willie, who was not as competent as he liked to think, but who insisted on competing, had trouble holding his own. Willie did not want to *scompari*. He did not want to lose face. So he suffered the garage and the rock in silence in the old man's presence, complaining only to his wife and son, knowing that he was in a way getting back at the old man through them. Lucy would report everything to her mother and alert her to what was going on, Willie's moods, the predictable binges that would sooner or later take place. Willie had to be handled with care. He was on the wagon for a while because of my sister-in-law the witch, who managed to put some kind of fear in him; but eventually he cut loose and, well, that's another story. At that time, he hadn't yet reached the boiling point, his problems did not filter down into the apartment below. Lucy made sure of that. Her mother knew everything, but nothing was ever reported to the old man. I'm sure, myself, that he knew anyway. But they respected a certain protocol. And the bottom line was that nothing should actually be said to the old man about Willy or anything that Willie said out of earshot.

Personally, I think my father-in-law knew everything about everybody. But the convention called for a mask of ignorance on his part for *quieto vivere* (what a marvelous phrase!) — for, well, keeping the lid on. I'm sure of this because the old man kept out of Willie's way as much as possible. He didn't like arguments or confrontations; on the other hand, it was his house and he knew that no one else could care for it as efficiently as he — even at the age of 68. But when emergencies arose, when things *really* had to get done, he pulled no punches. Willie or no Willie, he would simply get to work and do what he thought was necessary. At those moments, everybody was in the way, Willie especially, because he was given to grumbling and bragging while watching the old man at work. . . .

One day Willie said to his wife: "Lou, tell your mother to keep your father off my back tomorrow. I don't care how you do it, and believe me you'd better do it, because I don't want him around. I'm going to get rid of that damn rock in the back." This triggered long whispered and agitated exchanges between the women. My mother-in-law, poor soul, was frantic. There was bound to be a confrontation if the two men were together, Willie trying to get rid of the rock, my father-in-law watching, chafing at the bit and trying not to butt in. It was an old story. Willie was certain to blow his top if the old man said anything to him while he worked. The rock had finally made him desperate. He had to get rid of it because he was tired of maneuvering to get around it. And even if my father-in-law were simply to watch from the window, Willie would resent it, anticipating the old man's suggestions and interpreting them as criticism. There would certainly be sparks.

It was hard, but the women succeeded in getting my father-in-law out of the house on some errand into Manhattan. Once the old man had left for the subway, Willie went into the tool shed and got to work. He dug carefully around the huge rock and then tied a heavy rope to it. His car was already in position for pulling the rock out of the ground. He spent all that morning and part of the afternoon trying to get the rock to budge. No luck. Finally, my sister-in-law, who had been watching from her kitchen window upstairs, called down to him.

"Come on up, Willie. Eat something. You've been at it all day." Willie went inside. He was still upstairs when the old man returned. He took everything in and made his decision.

"Keep him upstairs," he told my mother-in-law. "Tell Lucy to keep him busy. I don't want him down here until I'm finished." My poor mother-in-law tried to stop him, but it was useless. So she ran upstairs, drew Lucy aside and told her what was happening.

Lucy did the best she could. She kept Willie upstairs for as long as she could. She didn't dare tell him that the old man had taken over his job. They couldn't hear anything, which made the women all the more apprehensive. How in heaven's name was the old man going to get rid of that huge rock that even Willie couldn't budge with the car and all? Willie was strong and he'd been at it all day. The old man was, well, old and might rupture himself trying to do something beyond his powers.

When Willie finally went back downstairs, the women scurrying after him, my father-in-law was standing there, a devilish gleam in his eyes, his hands in his pockets, a familiar pose. The rock was gone. The ground was covered over as though nothing had happened. Willie just stood there staring. For the first time in his life he was at a loss for words. Finally he asked" "Where is it?"

"I buried it," said my father-in-law, relishing the moment of triumph.

"Buried it?" Willie took this in slowly, obviously in a mild state of shock. It was the only time he did not respond in character. He was actually too surprised to be annoyed. "How the hell did you manage *that*???"

"I just dug around and down a bit more and slipped it into the ground," said the old man, smiling with tremendous satisfaction. Everybody else was tense and nervous. The women hovered nearby, waiting for all hell to break loose. Willie was hard to deal with on any occasion, but this was enough to send him into a week-long spree. He always felt the old man was trying to show him up, and when he thought he was in fact being criticized openly, especially in front of the women, he became sullen and morose and sometimes disappeared for days on one of his binges. But this was the exception.

"My God!" he burst out, "why didn't I think of it?"

My father-in-law, obviously pleased at this kind of recognition, said:

"You tried to pry it out of the ground. I just pushed it back in." Years later, Willie still told the story and always with a touch of awe. "God," he would always end, "why didn't I think of that?". . . .

1943

HIGH SCHOOL YEARBOOK

HIGH SCHOOL PROM

HENRY WITH
MY MOM, LUCY

1945

**Sketch by
street artist
(New York**

3. FATE CALLS THE MOVES

"ed io li tenni retro. . . ."

Henry returned from Florence in May, 1949 and we were married in September of that year. At Columbia he took up where he'd left off, expanding his master's thesis on James Thomson's *The City of Dreadful Night* into a doctoral dissertation: a close critical reading of the poem from an Augustinian viewpoint. I was finishing my Master's thesis, still working as Dr. Logsdon's Administrative Assistant. Together, we continued auditing Bigongiari's Dante course. We felt no pressure to find permanent jobs.

ANNE ATTURA PAOLUCCI
AND HENRY PAOLUCCI,
SEPTEMBER 5, 1949

In 1951, our studies were pleasantly interrupted when the Chairman of the Department of English and Comparative Literature recommended us, separately, for Fulbright Scholarships to Italy. (I suspect that Bigongiari had something to do with that, too.) And so, in the Fall of that year, I found myself once more in the city of my birth, this time with Henry. We had a marvelous time. In addition to attending lectures and events at the University of Rome, we took trips to other cities, including Munich, Vienna, and Barcelona, and spent many pleasant hours with my extended Attura family, most of whom were now settled in Rome. I enjoyed visiting with them and developed a close and lasting affection for those aunts and uncles and cousins.

We also took time to visit Henry's maternal uncles and cousins who had moved to Benevento from Circello, a tiny village in the mountains of the region, where his mother had been born. They had all done well; many had gone into politics (some in the Christian Democratic Party, others in the Socialist Party). We then went on to Circello, as well as to Colle Sannito, a short distance away, where his father still had relatives. Both places were impossible to reach without a car; even then, it was a bumpy ride, with sharp turns as the narrow road twisted around the rocky slopes.

As we drove up the mountain, Henry told me about his first visit to his relatives, soon after the end of the war in Italy — driving up those steep slopes, on rough mountain roads, in the jeep that had been built for him by the German prisoners entrusted to his care. He had reached Circello and had parked the jeep so that he could ask where he could find his Uncle Louie, his mother's brother, the oldest living family member. As he started walking into the village, a tiny old woman, holding two children by the hand, approached from the other direction. Henry smiled a greeting. The old woman stopped. She and the wide-eyed children stared after him. Henry — who was five feet seven inches tall — must have given a strangely misleading impression all bundled up in his air force pea jacket, scarf and hat, with heavy boots on his feet, for as he glanced back he heard the old woman exclaim, "*che gigante!*" ("what a giant of a man!"). Henry always enjoyed telling that story.

Uncle Louie, about whom I'd heard a great deal from my mother-in-law,

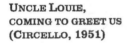

**UNCLE LOUIE,
COMING TO GREET US
(CIRCELLO, 1951)**

remains fixed in my memory in a special way: a gentle man with smiling eyes and, like his sister "Nancy,", a great storyteller, with a quiet sense of humor. He was always ready to share with us family anecdotes and details of the family history. We took a day also to visit Henry's father's only sister, who lived in the nearby village of Colle Sannito, walking distance from Circello, where a huge meal awaited us. Unfortunately, the pleasure of our visit was marred somewhat by the legion of flies that zoomed in to share the feast with us.

When we first arrived, the Fulbright people were waiting for us in Naples to take us directly to Perugia, where we joined the other students for a month's orientation. At first Henry and I were "billeted" in a modern house on the outskirts of the historic city. It was quite comfortable but some distance away from the Center and from the activities scheduled for us. We had arrived later than the other Fulbrights, and those were the only quarters still available. Nonetheless, we asked the Fulbright people to please try placing us closer to the Center; we felt isolated where we were. They finally came up with a large room in a house right in the main square. It was the home of the Coen family, the leading Jewish family of the area. There were quite a number of Coens living together under the same roof, including two unmarried older sisters of the head of the family. I remember those two ladies clearly; they wore blue sweaters and were always helping out in the kitchen. The Coens had not advertised for boarders, but when asked they agreed to take us in. Henry and I enjoyed our big room with its large stove, its high bed with its thick down comforter, the colorful cupids painted on the high ceiling. But what left a lasting impression on us was the number of Jews who came there during the high holy days that September, to attend services at the only synagogue in the entire region: the room adjacent to ours, which we had to cross every day as we left and returned to our own quarters. When services were to be held, we were gently reminded to plan our day so that we would not intrude.

While in Perugia, I was prodded by Henry to enter an essay contest in Italian, on some aspect of the city. My entry, "Sulla cima della montagna, dove tutto è più puro" ("On the Top of the Mountain, Where Everything is Purer") found its way into print, as a winner. By now, writing in Italian came easily.

Sulla cima della montagna dove tutto è più puro

La pianura ondulata che si estende dal piede del Subasio verso Perugia, è forse più di ogni altra regione d'Italia, pienamente adatta alla vita umana. Non sfolgorante come il paesaggio molle di Napoli, nè quasi pauroso come quei vasti panorami delle città alpine, la natura umbra sembra in tutto misurata ai bisogni materiali e spirituali dell'uomo. Chi passa per quella pianura verso Perugia, si trova circondata da una bellezza naturale, da una verde fertilità, che fa amare la vita terrestre, ma che nello stesso tempo fa rivolgere gli occhi verso il cielo in gratitudine. Quasi non c'è da meravigliarsi, dunque, che Assisi, risplendente nel sole sulla costa del Subasio, e dov'ella franse più sua rattezza, abbia dato al mondo il gran Santo che per primo, dopo lunghi secoli oscuri, vide e ispirò altri uomini a vedere la natura, non come cosa vile, corrotta dal peccato, ma bella, illuminata dappertutto dall'amore divino.

Ma se si passa da Assisi a Perugia, si nota subito come l'atmosfera cambia. Pochi chilometri separano le due città, eppure rappresentano civiltà diverse. Perugia non s'estende al sole su una costa di montagna, come s'estendono Assisi e le altre città di aspetto veramente umbrico. Perugia è di un aspetto etrusco: il suo centro è sulla cima della montagna, e tutte le abitazioni s'aggruppano intorno all'altura come se volessero ritirarsi il più possibile dal mondo della pianura. Attaccate lì in un punto che sembra inaccessibile, le case sono spesso battute dal vento, e molte rimangono nell'ombra, della costa settentrionale tutto l'anno. Chi entra per la prima volta nelle stradette tortuose che portano alla cima, può sentirsi per un momento soffocato, come se in quel mucchio di case non ci fosse abbastanza spazio per respirare. Ma quel primo momento passa subito. Una stra-

da si volge, ed ecco ad un tratto apparire una piazzetta o un largo. E quando finalmente si arriva alla cima, si trova che tutto è aperto, tutto è arioso.

Ma il centro di Perugia, che comprende il Corso e la Piazza del Duomo, non è un vuoto qualunque, piazzato lì nel mezzo di una massa di case per ragioni di simmetria geometrica o per motivi igienici. Non è vuoto, ma un vero spazio spirituale, ancor oggi come sempre centro vitale di vita di Perugia. Nel disegno di quel centro, nella sua situazione architettonica, si può studiare un'attuale soluzione del problema sul quale ancora oggi i più grandi architetti del mondo si scervellano. Ciò che è stato concepito astrattamente dagli architetti moderni che cercavano un modo da poter trasformare una massa di abitazioni in una comunità veramente organica, si vede realizzato storicamente e perfettamente lì nel centro di Perugia. Eppure uno scettico potrebbe domandare: — ma questa soluzione, era veramente necessaria realizzarla sulla cima di una montagna? Non si poteva ritrarre la presenza delle antiche generazioni che fa di Perugia una grande città. Gli abitanti viventi son pochi in numero. Spostato dalla cima antica della montagna, ristabilito in qualche pianura lontana dalla presenza delle passate generazioni, sarebbe un aggruppamento di trenta o quarantamila persone? Sarebbe nient'altro che un paesetto provinciale, come quei paesetti dell'Australia e dell'America, che contano non più di venti o cinquanta anni di vita. Abbandonando l'altura i cittadini perugini si troverebbero isolati spiritualmente, senz'altro sostegno culturale fuorché quel poco che una sola generazione può darci.

Ma tutto questo forse s'inten-

de meglio dal punto di vista di uno straniero. Sono loro, più che gl'italiani, che si meravigliano di vedere paesi collocati sulle cime delle montagne. E di stranieri che si meravigliano, in Perugia ce ne sono molti. Vengono lì da tutte le parti del mondo, certi per perfezionarsi nell'insegnamento dell'italiano, altri per facilitarsi la strada nella vita commerciale con un po' di lingua straniera, altri ancora per soddisfare una curiosità, o perchè il vivere è meno caro in Perugia che nel loro paese. Quasi tutti questi stranieri frequentano l'Università per stranieri. In un gruppo con interessi così vari è naturale che manchi una vera materia accademica. Però fanno male quegli studenti d'altre università italiane, che per questa ragione ne parlano quasi con leggerezza. Chi si fa conto del poco interesse, che la cultura italiana desta oggi in altri paesi, deve ammettere che l'Università per stranieri di Perugia rende un gran servizio all'Italia. Ogni straniero che viene a Perugia per studiare, e che poi porta via almeno una conoscenza elementare della lingua italiana, può eventualmente servire in qualche modo per spandere la cultura italiana all'estero.

Ma forse la più grande cosa che l'Italia può dare al mondo, è simboleggiata da quelle città che, come Perugia, resistono alla tentazione della pianura e si mantengono sempre sull'antiche altezze delle loro origini. Come Perugia emerge dalla pianura umbra, così l'Italia stessa emerge dalla pianura della civiltà occidentale. In tutta l'Italia, come in Perugia, sembra che manchi spazio per respirare. Battuti da tempeste politiche ed economiche, in gran parte nascosti nell'ombra perenne della povertà, molti italiani di oggi, certi anche non ignari delle somme altezze della cultura tradizionale d'Italia, spesso rivolgo-

no gli occhi in basso, verso la vita della pianura moderna, e sognano di rifare la loro vita in qualche punto meno vertiginoso, più accogliente. Una volta era il capitalismo protestante che li tentava: ancor prima era stato il repubblicanesimo francese; ora è il materialismo grossolano che li tenta.

Molti non resistono affatto alla tentazione: e scendono dall'altura, abbandonandosi alla vita della bassa pianura. Ma c'è da sperare, credo, che ci saranno sempre in Italia degli uomini che sapranno resistere e ogni tentazione, tenendosi fedelmente alla cima, pronti a difendere ad ogni costo i valori più alti del cristianesimo romano contro i barbari che minacciano dalla pianura.

ANNA MARIA PAOLUCCI

Ecco un'altra concorrente dal nome italiano ed italiana di origine anche se è nata New York. La giovane studentessa ha sospeso i suoi studi alla Columbia University per venire alla nostra Università ed apprendere la storia e la lingua dei suoi genitori.

Ogni lettore può esprimere il suo giudizio sugli articoli concorrenti a mezzo del tagliando pubblicato in questa stessa pagina.

Questo della signorina Paolucci è il decimo articolo pubblicato.

Christmas in Rome meant making the rounds of relatives. We tried to cover as much ground as possible. (By now, all my father's siblings had moved from Acuto and had pretty good jobs in Rome; their small houses in the village had become summer homes.) A visit to one uncle, one aunt, and not to others would have been construed as preferential and therefore an insult. Even more distressing was that those on whom we did call were waiting for us to arrive in order to serve the holiday meal: heaping dishes of pasta, followed by a roast and vegetable, after which came cheese and fruit, all eased down with plenty of wine. Trying to explain to Uncle Neno that we weren't used to such large meals, and telling my Aunt Caterina, whom we visited later that same evening, that we had already eaten much more than we were accustomed to was like trying to communicate with the Inuits. Somehow we got over that hurdle. For the rest of the year, we made sure we were not available to relatives for holidays. We did visit them often, however (avoiding dinners) and always with great pleasure.

That Fulbright year went by all too quickly. Soon we were back in New York and several months later had moved out of the apartment we'd been sharing with Mom on Pelham Parkway North and moved into a place of our own on West 110th Street, between Amsterdam Avenue and Broadway, a few blocks from Columbia. It was an incredibly small apartment. You entered directly into the main "living" space. Kitchen appliances were hidden behind louvre doors on the left; and a few feet further was a tiny bedroom and bathroom. Henry's nephew Donald built us two bookcases to separate the entranceway from the "living room." We placed a small couch just past the bookcases and two small vinyl tub chairs against the wall, opposite the couch. The two-foot aisle between the bookcases and the louvre doors was our "dining" area; our "dining table," a metal typewriter stand. Once we had a "dinner party" of six sitting around that green metal stand, its "wings" open, all of us sitting on borrowed hard plastic-mold chairs.

IN OUR "LIVING ROOM" ON 110TH ST. (KITCHEN APPLIANCES BEHIND LOUVRE DOORS IN BACK)

Two years later, we found a larger place in a stately building on the corner of 111th Street and Broadway: two large airy rooms, right off a tiny vestibule, a separate narrow kitchen and a bedroom and bath. We had waited for this apartment, for over a year. It was on the west side of the building and overlooked the Hudson. Although there were buildings below us on Riverside Drive, they did not obstruct the much sought-after view of the river — all but one room overlooked the water. Soon we were tracing the movement of barges, small boats, and the water itself with a pair of binoculars bought for the purpose. In the evening, I would look for a neon sign in the window of a small tavern across from us, on the New Jersey side, trying to imagine the people who went there, the stories it held. Several times a month, we would also watch containers the size of freight cars taken off huge barges that had carried them across long distances to that point. Cranes would quickly swing them to the ground, where they were hitched to waiting truck cabins and driven away.

VIEW OF THE HUDSON RIVER IN WINTER FROM OUR APARTMENT ON 111TT ST., BROADWAY (1953-1969)

VIEW OF THE THROGS NECK BRIDGE FROM CRYDER HOUSE APARTMENT, QUEENS (1969 –)

That view of the Hudson spoiled us forever. When some years later we moved into Queens, we made sure the apartment we chose was on the water — a high-rise on the northern tip of Whitestone, where the Long Island Sound turns sharply into what becomes the East River. A picture-postcard view of The Throgs Neck Bridge outside our windows was an added attraction. On a clear day, we could see Connecticut on the northern horizon.

By the time we'd settled in the Broadway/111th Street apartment, both of us had found teaching jobs: Henry in the English Department at Iona College at the same time that I was hired at Rye Country Day School, a private all girls' school in Rye, New York, where I taught grammar to seventh- and eighth-graders. The school was about an hour's drive north of the City. Both of us commuted by trains and buses.

For me, it was an especially long trip each way. When my Department Chairwoman, who lived with her teen-age son in New Rochelle, offered to rent me a room in her big house, Henry and I agreed it was an excellent solution for me. The woman was also kind enough to drive me with her to the school and back every day, from Monday afternoons to Friday mornings. After my last class on Fridays, I took the train back into Manhattan. This lasted two years. Some thought it unusual, bizarre even — Henry taking the train from Manhattan to New Rochelle while I lived in New Rochelle and drove with my colleague to Rye — but we ourselves had no problem with the arrangement. We knew it wouldn't last long.

I am sorry to say that it was during my two years at Rye Country Day School (1955-1957) that I took up smoking. It was something to do while chatting with colleagues in the faculty room between classes or during lunch break. At first it was only a few cigarettes a week; later, more. Eventually the habit set in, and I found myself smoking even before breakfast. At one point, I was chain smoking three packs a day — shallow breaths at the typewriter, like Hoagy Carmichael smoking at the piano. I had told myself that the smoke was not really going into my lungs: I didn't inhale in long drags, the way most people did. I was deluding myself, of course; but it wasn't until twenty-five years later that I began to realize just how much damage my smoking was causing. Not only had the smell and taste of tobacco begun to annoy me; my nose was often bloody and my cheeks were puffed up. I couldn't postpone the obvious decision. In fact, there were no real options, only the stark reality that smoking would force me into the hospital . . . at my great inconvenience. On the morning of November 18, 1981, sitting at the typewriter, about to light a fresh cigarette from the one-inch stub still between my lips, I paused, put down the fresh cigarette, put out the stub, got up from the typewriter where I'd been working and threw out all my cigarettes. I never smoked again.

I remember thinking how appropriate Aristotle's definition of virtue was. It had seemed simplistic at first but I'd come to realize how profound a truth it carried. Virtue (he'd written) is a good habit and vice is a bad one. I also understood St. Augustine's prudent warning that wanting to experience and know all things in life is not a virtue; on the contrary, it is both misleading and dangerous. One need not rape in order to know what rape is about and to grasp its devastating effects; one need not kill in order to know all about murder. . . .

On the positive side: teaching at Rye Country Day School forced me to learn quickly on the job (not without stumbling, once in a while). Grammar wasn't exactly my strong point yet. There were quite a few embarrassing moments. I was much better at it two years later, when I came back into Manhattan to teach at the Brearley School on the upper East Side. This too was an all-girls school, but seriously academic, possibly the best private school of its kind in the country, catering to daughters of prominent families.

TEACHING STAFF, RYE COUNTRY DAY SCHOOL. AP IN FIRST ROW, FOURTH FROM RIGHT (1956).

"FATHER-DAUGHTER NIGHT" DINNER, RYE COUNTRY DAY SCHOOL (1958) A.P., SEATED, CENTER, SECOND FROM RIGHT.

The Summer of 1958, I took Mom on a "grand tour" of Europe — London, Lucerne, Paris, Versailles, Florence, Milan, Venice, and spent some weeks in Rome and Acuto, visiting relatives (on both sides).

ON THE "GRAND TOUR": LUCERNE (SUMMER, 1958)

PIAZZA SAN MARCO
VENICE (SUMMER, 1958)

LONDON (SUMMER, 1958)

WITH COUSINS, FONTANA DI TREVI,
ROME (SUMMER, 1958)

We stayed for two weeks in Acuto, with my mother's unmarried sister
(my Aunt Maria Guidoni) and Uncle Lello and his daughters. We spent a day
with my Uncle Luigi, one of my father's brothers, who had settled with his

family in a nearby village. I can still recall our walking down the wide main street and seeing a man coming toward us who looked so much like my father that I knew without asking that it was my uncle coming to escort us to his house. I'd never set eyes on him before; but like everyone else in the Attura family, he shared certain physical traits I knew well and recognized as my own.. Even his movements were familiar. He had my father's easy manner, what now drew me in a special way to my Attura uncles, aunts, and cousins.

WITH FAMILY FRIEND (ACUTO, 1958)

PERFECT REFLECTION ON THE ARNO, AT DAWN (SUMMER, 1958)

I always wanted to be part of my father's clan, have those cousins aunts and uncles close to me, enjoy their company. My mother's relatives were sullen and withdrawn, by comparison (except for my Uncle Lello, who had a great sense of humor . . . but also a tendency to ramble). I found little warmth in them and could not bring myself to relate to them easily, in the same way that I'd always found it difficult to reach out to my mother.

We returned from our tour late in August, and I resumed my teaching job at the Brearley School in early September. The transition from Rye Country Day School had been made especially easy by the woman who headed the English Department. She had studied at Oxford and was surprisingly flexible in allowing her teachers a free hand in choosing their texts and preparing their course syllabi. I remember spending most of one semester discussing *Macbeth* and *Oedipus Rex* with my seventh graders (my notes later became an important comparative analysis of the two plays). In my second year, I treated the ninth graders to an entire semester of William Hazlitt, the English essayist — a name, I suspect, unfamiliar even to many graduate students today!

Following Henry's example, I had for the first time asked students to keep journals. At the beginning, there were moans and groans. I reassured them that a journal was not a personal diary; I didn't want to hear about their personal problems, their quarrels, or their love life. A journal, was an intellectual exercise, I explained. They could enlarge on comments made in class, describe people they knew, review books they had read, plays they had seen, share fiction and poetry they'd written — whatever had tickled their imagination. They soon caught on. I found myself on Fridays carrying home a stack of notebooks, literally hundreds of pages of writing. I had unleashed a *tsunami* that threatened to drown me in paper work. They couldn't write enough about things they had never before dreamed of talking about, much less put down on paper. I had my work cut out for me. I would return the notebooks on Monday mornings, with marginal comments and suggestions, as well as grammatical corrections (I was getting better and better at that!) — all of which they took in with utmost seriousness, deriving pleasure and satisfaction in the knowledge that we were (in a way) carrying on an interesting conversation. I made sure I always found something to praise even when criticisms were in order. I gave a great deal of time to this project, but it was worth it. My own critical faculties were sharpened in the process, even as my students learned to probe their own minds and practice their writing skills. In all my subsequent teaching, keeping a journal would remain a central requirement in all my courses.

The students at Brearley had a definite advantage, of course, and made teaching a pleasure. They came from privileged families, had read a good deal on their own, most of them routinely visited museums, galleries, concerts, plays. They were familiar with art works and music. Many of them had been to Europe more than once. They were still young enough, however, not to flaunt their advantage, as my fellow-students at Barnard had. For me, it was a time of expanding literary interests; satisfying, also, in the response to my teaching.

Several occasions and people stand out. One of my ninth graders was Sylvia (Kalitinsky?), whose mother had started reading Shakespeare out loud to her when she was three. Sylvia would sit doodling in class, but I never scolded her because I knew she didn't miss a word and that she would speak up when she had something to say. Sylvia could turn a simple book report into an incisive critique. One particular assignment became a comparative essay on the relative merits of the Dickens novel we were reading and Thomas Hardy (whose novels had not been mentioned in class). Sylvia would have been perfectly at home in a graduate class in English.

Nina Hirschfeld (daughter of the cartoonist, Al Hirschfeld) also comes to mind. She was one of my seventh graders, a small girl with flowing red hair. We had been discussing Shakespeare's *Julius Caesar* when she came up to me with a few friends one day, after class, and asked excitedly if we could stage the play. I had to think fast: I didn't want to discourage her, but I knew it was an impossible request. They already had a full schedule (as I had); preparing for such an event would require hours that were not available to any of us. My first response was to remind her and the others who had approached me that the school already was rehearsing a play (a Greek tragedy in which even faculty took part: I myself had been assigned a walk-on role). I told Nina that a second production, no matter how modest and informal, was impossible. Even a one-night performance required rehearsals and supervision for which we could not make time. As I said all this, I racked my brain to come up with an outlet for their enthusiastic response to Shakespeare's play. I hit on a compromise: "Why don't you choose a scene and prepare a dramatic reading?" I suggested. "When you're ready, we'll bring seventh, eighth and ninth graders together during home room period, to watch you perform." They seemed satisfied with the arrangement in those terms. I stepped back at that point and left them to it.

And so, it came to pass that at 7 AM one dreary winter morning, before classes got under way, five little girls, all in the dull blue outfit that was the "working" uniform at Brearley (a shorts/blouse combination that served for athletics, and a button-down skirt worn over it for the rest of the school day) came to the front of the large room in which a still sleepy audience of students and teachers had assembled, to watch Nina Hirschfeld, as Caesar, fall under the blows of Brutus, Cassius and the rest of the assassins — her skirt (read: cloak) thrown over her head in an effort to ward off the blows. Incredibly, the little group had memorized their lines, which were delivered with great energy, booming voices, much gesturing, and tremendous enthusiasm. By the end of the performance, everyone in the audience was wide awake. My own reaction was a combination of joy and amazement.

Teaching at Brearley was an immensely instructive experience. I learned, among other things, that one can't be taught how to teach; the art of communication can only be mastered by facing the hard, sometimes embarrassing questions students ask — especially those in their early teens, who never hesitate to speak their minds and are completely unself-conscious about it. I also learned to aim higher than what students expect, forcing them to stretch their faculties just a little bit further.

I loved my Brearley students. I nurtured their childlike wonder, watched them grow in their perception of the world, guided them in developing their critical awareness of things. I could have stayed on forever.

One afternoon I received a call from the head of the English Department of The City College (now part of the City University of New York [CUNY]). One of their instructors was ill. Someone at Columbia had recommended me to take over her class on Spenser that afternoon. Was I available? It was another of the unexpected turns Fate had decreed for me. I knew I had only a few hours to bone up on *The Faerie Queene*, but I accepted without hesitation. A second and third call followed in the next few days. These too I accepted. Before the end of the academic year, I was offered a full time, tenure-track appointment with the rank of Lecturer for the next year. It was an important move; I couldn't turn it down. But it was a sad one, too. It meant leaving the school that had given me a chance to try my growing skills as a teacher. It meant leaving the best, most receptive students I would ever have.

All this time I had been writing steadily. The year I left Rye County Day School for Brealey saw the publication of a translation Henry and I had done of Machiavelli's dramatic masterpiece, *Mandragola* — the first new version in English in over thirty years. The work quickly found its way into the political science departments of many universities because of Henry's Introduction, where he explains the play, in the context of Machiavelli's other writings, as his last and most bitter political commentary, as well as his most dismal statement on the depravity of human nature left to its own devices in a state without strong leadership.

COVER OF MACHIAVELLI'S
MANDRAGOLA
(15TH PRINTING, 1980)

The play's obscenity, especially the corrupt characters, all of whom (including the monk) are ready to do anything to satisfy what they want — seduction, abortion, murder even — is brilliantly depicted as an exercise in diplomacy. It is an ironic commentary on the use of whatever "means" are available to justify personal and private ends — the very opposite of what Machiavelli meant by "the end justifies the means." For him, only one end justifies whatever must be done to achieve it: the safety of the State. Applied indiscriminately, especially in an epicurean environment without firm moral values, "the end justifies the means" not only encourages every kind of personal gratification but also leads to anarchy.

We met Eric Bentley as a result of that translation: he wanted to use it in one of his anthologies. We told him we couldn't consider his offer; we had already signed a contract with Oskar Peist, founder and President of The Liberal Arts Press. That meeting and the others that followed were the beginning of a long friendship, coming to focus eventually on our common interest in Luigi Pirandello, the Italian Nobel Laureate in Literature (1934), "father of the contemporary theater" (Robert Brustein). My translation of Pirandello's insightful essay on the history of the Italian theater appears as the Introduction to Bentley's anthology, *The Genius of the Italian Theater;* but I confess I never would have tackled it if Bentley had not asked me to.

Teaching at City College was invigorating in a new and different way. The students were older and therefore more cautious, not as forthright or naively questioning as those at Brearley. Most of them were also less prepared, limited in their interests — many of them holding jobs in their "off" hours. Still, in the classroom, they were serious enough about wanting to learn. In this new environment, I found myself preparing my lessons even more conscientiously, so as to lure these underprivileged students into an intellectual world that was not always related to their immediate needs or their practical outlook on life. Most of them came from low to middle-income homes: — mostly Italian, Jewish, Irish, some Blacks, not the wide ethnic spectrum that prevails today. In those days, one could expect even the most ignorant students to be fluent enough in English to understand their teachers and to follow classroom discussion. The language was there, even if the understanding of how it worked and the accessibility to its many possibilities were limited.

Again, following Henry's example, I started to get up earlier in the mornings to type out outlines of what I intended to say in this or that course on that particular day. I never used those notes; but writing out a rough draft of what might have been a lecture, with passages I wanted to cite and authors I wanted to quote helped clarify my thinking and gave structure to my seemingly impromptu presentation. I soon discovered that students always remembered passages that were read to them out loud, especially if accompanied by a bit of dramatic flourish. Those outlines proved valuable, later, in providing me with materials for articles and books.

At City I was initiated into the politics of academe. Those wishing to run for the office of Department Chairman had to win the backing of their Personnel and Budget Committee, the support of the tenured, permanent staff, and the approval of the administration. Many hours were spent recruiting such "backing," and working out "deals" behind the scenes, but many thought it worth the effort. A Chairman enjoyed special "perks," not the least of which were course reductions and the potential for higher-ranking positions, there or elsewhere. In the English Department, the Chairman in place at the time I left, Edmond Volpe, soon after became President of Staten Island College (CUNY); another professor moved out of the state to take on the job of Provost in a major university in Pennsylvania; Alice Chandler became President of one of the upstate colleges of the State University of New York (SUNY) system; still others found second careers after early retirement, as high-level administrators elsewhere.

During my years at City, there wasn't the least hint of discrimination against women or against me, as an Italian-American woman. That came later, after my time, when minorities began to assert themselves as factional groups with distinct interests and often conflicting priorities. There were already three "high-power" women in the English Department when I joined it: Alice Chandler, Rose Zimbardo, who later moved to SUNY at Stonybrook, and Marcia Allentuck, for whom I had substituted when I'd first started out at City. They all had excellent credentials, were fine teachers and productive scholars. We were all treated with respect; none of us was ever held back for promotion because we were women.

Everyone in the Department had to teach at least one course in grammar and basic skills. By now, thanks to Henry, I had learned to respect every aspect of language; I actually enjoyed parsing sentences. More important, I had grown confident in my use of English: I saw grammar as the means to clear thinking and effective expression.

I will never tire of saying that I owe my command of English to Henry — among the first of his many gifts to me. He had quickly become my taskmaster, urging me on, giving me all the help I needed to improve my skills in writing. I knew he was right in wanting to help me, but I wasn't always happy about it. I was restless: taking time to do what he was asking when there was so much to be discovered in the world of literature and the arts was frustrating. These mixed feeling persisted for a long time: I often complained, but I knew he was right. Sometimes I resented that too; but in the end, I would follow his advice. In this case, I had learned that one can be fluent in a language and yet not a master of it.

Henry had been persistent, incredibly patient in the task he had taken on to perfect my skills. It paid off. I learned to love and respect grammar. In an Honors freshman course in basic skills I taught at City, one year, I took to reading, for our parsing exercises, from all kinds of interesting books, including classical texts in translation. One day, I read a short passage from *Plutarch's Lives,* from which I chose some sentences for our parsing exercise. I had chosen carefully; it was an excellent translation, the English impeccable. After the exercise was over, a hand went up, and one of the students asked, somewhat tentatively: "Dr. Paolucci, could you read something less interesting next time?" I didn't, of course. I wanted them to hear good writing even as they perfected their basic skills. They were understandably distracted — I would have been disappointed if they had not been — but it was easy enough to get back on track. The point was, they heard me read passages from works and authors they would never have heard otherwise — certainly would never have found in a grammar book — excerpts which, howsoever brief, whet their interest and nudged their imagination. Grammar, I had come to learn, was not simply a matter of knowing the names of the parts of a sentence and using them effectively; it was the primary tool for rational communication, a function of logic. Using examples that clearly reflected its ultimate purpose was the best way to impress students with its importance.

Somewhere along the way, I even proposed an elective course in grammar. I was amazed at the response. On one occasion, I recited to the class the opening sentence from an essay by the renowned Jacques Barzun, one of Columbia's "stars," as well as an internationally acclaimed author of literary and critical essays and books. I didn't tell them where it came from until later; I asked them instead to develop a short paragraph with that sentence as their opening. After a few minutes, I went around the room, asking each student to read what he or she had written. We discussed continuity, the directional signals implicit in any opening statement and in that particular case what must follow once the idea had been introduced, how even the placement of words served to provide emphasis and mood. I then read the full paragraph to them, noting transitions, the movement from the introductory sentence into the general argument, and the implications of that opening statement. The class — made up of resolute juniors and seniors — quickly learned how deliberate scrutiny of a good piece of writing could improve their own basic skills. A number of students asked where they could find the essay, so they could read it in its entirety.

Even in those classes where perfecting grammatical skills was not the primary focus, I used part of every hour for writing or for oral drills of one kind or another. I was never a great believer in long essays prepared at home; even less, in term papers. There was homework, always; but I would tell my students that their writing in class, howsoever brief, had to accord with the writing prepared at home. The usual objections would be voiced; I would always counter them by saying that I could tell, even in brief exercises in class, written under some pressure, whether the same person had written the home assignments that were handed in at the beginning of every class hour. I never accused anyone of plagiarism; I didn't have to. When there was clear evidence that the writing at home was of an altogether different quality, I simply marked the assignment "NG" ("No Grade"). Without giving a student an outright "F" (*Failed*), I made my point. Even if he or she rewrote the piece for our next class meeting, the original "NG" remained and was worked into the final grade for the course.

The plan worked. In all my experience, on every level of teaching, I've found that the truly good students are always consistent and predictable in the quality of their written work. Even as they answer questions or comment in class, that quality surfaces in the way they present and give shape to ideas, in the clarity of their statements and their choice of words, as they speak.

In every class, students were given short writing exercises. I would collect them and read each one out loud, without identifying the writer. No one was ever singled out for criticism. Instead, I had my students keep a list of "common errors." They soon realized by the sheer force of repetition where their weaknesses lay. There was nothing personal or offensive in this approach.

My years at City were productive and satisfying in other ways, too. I saw a number of articles and books published. The most important thing for me, however, was the collaboration that had built up between my husband and me. It was a partnership that was to last a lifetime. Over the years, we never gave out a manuscript without consulting one another. At first, Henry played the larger role; but after a while, I caught up.

It was Henry who re-introduced me to Aristotle *via* Hegel. I had read Aristotle's *Poetics*, but Henry made a point of having me read the *Rhetoric* — an even more important and timely work. The *Rhetoric*, written by Aristotle himself (unlike the *Poetics*, which was compiled from notes taken by his students) is rigorously structured and contains wonderful examples. What I found especially intriguing was his discussion of the *enthymeme*, the rhetorical syllogism, which is the basis of the art of persuasion or what we today often refer to as "propaganda." Aristotle explains that the *enthymeme* is a rhetorical tool like any other, and that it can be put to good or bad use, like any tool. He warns that one should become proficient in it, since (especially in politics) the "other guy" will surely find a way to use it against you, if he possibly can. The work could have been written today: it describes effective propaganda in any age.

The *enthymeme* is not structured like the syllogism in logic. Its aim is not to convince the mind (as in the case of the syllogism) but to move to action. It often rests on assumptions, but these must be credible for the *enthymeme* to be effective. When Shakespeare, in *Julius Caesar*, has Antony remind the crowd that has gathered around the body of Caesar that the dead man was responsible for the Roman victory against the Nervii, he knew his listeners understood the implications of that contracted statement: the victory over the Nervii was not just another victory but a *decisive* victory, the one that saved the Roman world at the time. The rhetorical question then could be asked, without fear of contradiction: "Was that ambition?" The rhetorical question, in fact, contains the compressed argument of the *enthymeme*. Brutus has called Caesar ambitious, but the man who led the Romans to victory in the crucial battle against the Nervii, putting his life at risk many times, was obviously not thinking of his own welfare but bent on saving Rome from its greatest enemy. He never wavered in that purpose. Were those the actions of an ambition man? Well, some might interpret them that way, and probably with some success; but the facts themselves are unanswerable and therefore the conclusion (in the form of a rhetorical question — still one of the best examples of the many uses of the *enthymeme*) is implicit and self-evident. Bad uses of the *enthymeme* would include introducing partial for full information (to avoid or hide something), making assumptions not altogether clear or reliable, basing arguments on prejudicial, accepted premises or loose popular cliches, etc. etc. But, as Aristotle said centuries ago: you better learn your way around in this arena or your opponent will knock you down. It's not a question of who is really "good" or "bad"; it's a question of knowing how to use the tools of rhetoric to get what you want. We hope the goal is a good one, Aristotle tells us; but those tools will serve, either way .

I used the oration of Antony in many of my classes, besides those I taught on Shakespeare, as an excellent example of the art of persuasion and, naturally, of Shakespeare's incredibly versatile genius.

Perhaps Henry's greatest gift was introducing me to the world of the German philosopher, G. W. F. Hegel, who has left his stamp on so many areas of thought (not just Marxism). I had already been impressed by the work of the famous Shakespearean/Hegelian critic, A. C. Bradley, one of a group of Hegelians at Oxford University, which included A. C.'s brother, F. H. Bradley (whose work was the subject of T. S. Eliot's dissertation, abandoned for many years and finished at Oxford, late in life), and Bernard Bosanquet, whose translation of the first hundred pages or so of Hegel's Introduction to *The Philosophy of Fine Art* is a model of what translation should aim for: accurate and written in impeccable English — a work I still recommend as an introduction to anyone interested in the influential German philosopher.

Henry knew that my interest in A. C. Bradley and Shakespeare would make the transition natural if not altogether easy. Predictably, I resisted at first; I was a humanist, not a philosopher, I would argue; I wasn't at home in the rigorous language and abstractions of philosophy. Henry, relentless but also perceptive, found the right approach. He would catch the right moment to read passages to me that he knew I would understand and appreciate: the long discussion on the use of the metaphor, image, and simile in dramatic poetry (where all Hegel's examples are drawn from Shakespeare); the detailed account of the accusations against Socrates, the actual trial, and its aftermath, where Socrates is described as "the tragic hero in history" (by then I knew and had accepted the fact that the word "tragedy" for Hegel was never to be taken casually; it had a very particular significance with respect to drama); the excellent definition of the genres, which T. S. Eliot made good use of in his well-known essay, "The Three Voices of Poetry," acknowledging the source of his distinctions to be Gottfried Benn, the German expressionist poet and critic who, in turn, openly credits Hegel as his source.

I was soon hooked. What I didn't understand, Henry was there to explain. He never grew weary of my ignorance; he ignored my impatience and answered questions indirectly, approaching the answer in large concentric circles that allowed me to grasp the important base on which the answer rested. I recognized Bigongiari's classroom approach in his way of presenting material. It came naturally to him, also. He knew how to rivet the attention of an audience, large or small, Even at social gatherings, Henry inevitably drew people if he started to talk. He never initiated those conversations; some even thought him shy. The truth was, he was ready with answers if questions were asked, and always drew an interested group of listeners, once he got started. I also came to realize that for Henry the intellectual life was a reality, just as daily routines are a reality for most of us. Unlike many academics I have known, he was perfectly at home in the world of thought. I was still struggling to get a foot in the door.

THE HEGEL MEDALLION, PRESENTED TO HEGEL BY HIS FORMER STUDENTS ON HIS 60TH BIRTHDAY (1830) THE YEAR BEFORE HIS DEATH.

"FROM HIS STUDENTS"

THE SEATED FIGURE ON THE LEFT: HEGEL AS THE MODERN ARISTOTLE. ABOVE HIM, THE OWL OF MINERVA, SYMBOL OF THE GREEK SPIRIT OF WISDOM. ON THE RIGHT, THE CROSS, SYMBOL OF CHRISTIANITY.

His persistence got me over the threshold. By the time our anthology, *Hegel on Tragedy,* was published by Doubleday (Torchbook) early in the seventies (later by Harper & Row, Greenwood Press, and Griffon House Publications), I was perfectly at home in Hegel's exposition of the arts. I am still uncomfortable with modern philosophers spouting a language that distances them from the rest of us, but Hegel (in particular, the Osmaston translation) has not been difficult reading. With Henry's help, Hegel has become a steady diet for me. His influence has had a life-long impact on my sensibilities as well as my thinking. I have actually grown fond of the Ostmaston translation, which I've learned to respect in spite of its often "dated" language.

No attempt has ever been made to produce anything remotely resembling *Hegel on Tragedy*. It is a seamless collection of passages on tragedy, comedy, and dramatic theory, drawn from the entire Hegelian opus. Henry, perfectly at home in the Hegelian texts, chose the passages to be included; my role was to refine and edit the result, making suggestions along the way and helping with the Index (a painstaking job, but well worth the effort). In bringing the book to the attention of students and colleagues, I still recommend what Henry encouraged me to do: find in the Index those names and subjects you know well or that are of particular interest to you and read them first (and more than once). There's plenty of time, later, to tackle the book from beginning to end.

One of my favorite passages in the anthology is the brilliant account about Socrates, who never wrote a word of his own (two of his "students," Plato and Xenophon, took notes, most of which have come down to us in the form of dialogues). In it, Hegel presents Socrates not simply as the "teacher of morality" but as the "inventor" of it. Hegel's account of that moment in history is the most thorough and most profound I have ever come across. The name of Socrates comes up many times in Hegel, but this long excerpt, primarily from *The Philosophy of History,* on the accusations made against him by the Athenians, of "corrupting" their young men, who ignored their family obligations and flocked to hear him speak; the actual trial that followed; and the aftermath of that trial, which according to Hegel was the beginning of the end for those remarkable freedom-loving Greek city-states, is a passage everyone should read. I've gone back to it many times and have read it to many audiences. It is one of the most touching descriptions of events which ultimately lead to the death of Socrates. The account is compelling, without being polemical, and factually accurate (since Hegel knew and read Greek easily and could easily relay the events to his readers. Even in translation, the account produces a powerful effect.

Hegel on Tragedy was well-reviewed in a number of journals, here and abroad, but apparently American Shakespeareans (and to some extent the British, as well) were not ready for Hegel — still aren't. Not only have they continued to ignore Hegel's provocative pages on modern or Shakespearean drama, but in many cases have had the temerity to criticize him without having read any of his works. Even Shakespearean colleagues who respect my interest in Hegel and have sought me out more than once for lectures and articles on Hegel's views on drama, have not read him. One well-known Shakespearean critic actually wrote, some years back, that Hegel not only preferred Greek to modern or Shalespearean drama, but that he hated Shakespeare because he depicted (among other things) characters who experienced powerful emotions! Aside from that idiotic generalization, he might have been embarrassed to discover that the very opposite is true. Hegel considered Shakespeare's plays far more powerful and with far greater universal impact than those of the Greeks. His final estimate is clear enough and can be found not only in any number of passages in the *Philosophy of Fine Art* but also in many of his other works as well. For Hegel, Shakespeare is the playwright *par excellence* because of (among other things) the emotional depth of his characterizations. He is the greatest of all dramatists "soaring above all the rest at an almost unapproachable height."

One wonders what it will take to nudge the new generation of Shakespeareans into reading Hegel. For Shakespeare studies in America, his insightful discussion on modern drama is still virgin territory.

Such failings, even in the most renowned scholars, strengthened in me a perverse desire to "go it alone," to educate not just my students but my colleagues too (if possible), whatever it took! I had found my calling. I had become an acolyte. My faith was boundless.

HEGEL ON TRAGEDY

DOUBLEDAY (ANCHOR BOOK EDITION)

HARPER & ROW (TORCHBOOK EDITION)

Academics, I had long discovered, indeed are not perfect. I had been initiated into the self-serving priorities of the academic profession in the sixties, watching colleagues at City College vie for the Chairman's job in the English Department, like politicians campaigning for high public office. I wasn't shocked, exactly — how could a Machiavellian be shocked by any kind of human behavior? — and surely academic politicking was the least grievous of academic sins! It was a minor infraction (in my book), predictable, even acceptable compared with the brazen attitude, for example, of Shakespeareans toward Hegel. Still. academics are supposed to be above such petty battles, right? They are the guardians and purveyors of truth, right?

WITH JAMES MCMANAWAY (ED. *SHAKESPEARE QUARTERLY*) AT HIS HOME IN CHEVY CHASE, MD (OCTOBER, 1977)

WITH MARVIN SPEVACK AT THE SHAKESPEARE INSTITUTE CONFERENCE, STRATFORD-ON-AVON, ENGLAND (1974)

Not quite . . . but I'd come to terms with all that. What I couldn't accept was the kind of disillusionment I experienced at Columbia as I was nearing the end of my work for the doctoral degree. The incident confirmed me in the sad reality that academics are not beyond question or above reproof. They're often prejudiced, irresolute, insensitive to students, and, yes, self-serving, too. What happened in this case strengthened my resiliency in the face of difficulties.

Long before Henry and I had even begun to think about *Hegel on Tragedy*, I had decided to write my dissertation on A. C. Bradley and Hegel on Shakespeare and had prepared an outline for the Shakespeare "expert" in the Graduate School, who was to be my mentor. He approved it, without any major suggestions or changes. In the hot summer months that followed, I sat at the typewriter and wrote over a hundred pages of what was to be a major section of the book. In the Fall, I returned to him with what I had written. He quickly scanned the sheaf of papers I'd handed him, then said, without raising his eyes: "I hope you intend to criticize Hegel. . . ." I was stunned at first; then angry. Making every effort to control myself, I told him that I would criticize Hegel, if I found reason to do so; but that I hadn't chosen to spend long months on a subject that was disagreeable to me or simply to put a certain writer down!

I don't remember what else was said, but I realized quickly that I had a problem. I had wasted four months, working relentlessly, only to be told by my "mentor" in effect that my project didn't appeal to him. Why had he approved the outline in the first place? He could have said four months earlier what he had just said. I felt I had been misdirected, betrayed. I left as soon as I could and rushed across the hall to Maurice Valency's office, to report what had happened. His reaction distressed me even more. "If he's to be your mentor, you can only expect more of the same," he said bluntly. "You'll find obstacles all the way down the road." My dejection, my helplessness must have been evident, because he added, almost without a pause: "Why don't you write on Dante and Spenser instead? Most people would give their right arm to have your training in Dante!" I recognized the soundness of his words. He knew I had studied with Bigongiari, and although he included Dante in his Renaissance seminar in the Department of English and Comparative Literature, he never asserted himself as a competitor. Like the rest of us, he had the utmost respect for Bigongiari. I accepted his suggestion on the spot. With Valency as my advisor and — as of that moment — my new mentor, I completed my dissertation on the role of the women in Dante's *Divine Comedy* and Spenser's *Faerie Queene* (the great epic of Protestant England) in four months. To my surprise and pleasure, the work won the first Woodbridge Honorary Fellowship in the Department. (An interesting postscript: The Shakespeare "expert" was fired soon after for incompetence.) Looking back on that incident, which routed me into a completely different area, I suspect that our "expert" hadn't read a word of Hegel and didn't want to tackle him.

It was an unconscionable thing to do to a student; but as it turned out, it was a blessing in disguise. The experience also taught me that if one followed one's instincts honestly and with conviction, a pattern would eventually emerge. What might at first appear to be arbitrary and casual points of intellectual curiosity were likely to emerge eventually as part of a larger interrelated structure. This wasn't clear to me at the time, but I was already deep in several areas of research and writing that suggested some kind of implicit pattern tending heavily toward drama and dramatic criticism — Shakespeare, A. C. Bradley, Hegel, ancient and modern tragedy and dramatic theory. Eventually, those interests expanded to include "Theater of the Absurd," Pirandello, Edward Albee and the new French dramatists, in addition to Spenser, Dante, and Italian literature generally. Colleagues warned me that I was "spreading myself thin." They were right, in a way: there is always the danger of treating superficially too many subjects taken up casually. I didn't need to be warned, however. My interests were clearly interconnected, and I approached them with enthusiasm and a willingness to spend time exploring them in depth. Still: I have never called myself a Dante scholar, although I've written enough and with enough dedication to qualify as one; I don't consider myself a "Shakespearean," although I certainly have written as much as (and perhaps more than) many of my colleagues in that area; I have translated major works from Italian and French, without labeling myself a "translator." I've never called myself a writer, even, although I've written more and on a greater variety of subjects than most of my colleagues — poetry, short fiction, mystery novels, and plays, in addition to more than two hundred scholarly articles and books. Each step of the way, I moved from one area of interest to the one that suggested itself next. The transition was always organic and systematic, although I gave it little thought as it happened. And I may well have pursued those interests even if I had not been an academic.

The incident with the Shakespeare "expert" at Columbia strengthened my resolve to follow my irresistible impulses to widen my horizons. It also taught me that nothing meaningful is ever lost: the pages I had prepared on Shakespeare and Hegel became a major article in *Comparative Literature*, and years later I found it listed, together with A. C. Bradley's essay on Hegel (*Oxford Lectures on Poetry*), in the brief bibliography under "Hegel," in an important British reference guide on European literature.

Another incident comes to mind — this one less traumatic perhaps, but embarrassingly revealing with respect to the preparation of even well-known and otherwise proficient scholars in high places.

In most universities, after course work is completed for the doctoral degree in some area of the humanities, the student has to pass a three-hour oral examination that tests his or her knowledge of the entire field of major interest. Mine was the Italian and English Renaissance, with the focus on Dante. I was already working on my dissertation on Dante and Spenser and was still auditing (with Henry) Bigongiari's Dante course. As a member of Maurice Valency's Renaissance seminar, I had also continued to audit that class (as was the custom), even after I had completed the needed credits for the Ph.D. I'd come to admire Valency's elegant and witty style; and he had also won my respect as a fair and honest scholar. He was a caustic critic, but always ready with praise and gave credit where credit was due. In Bigongiari, the most renowned Renaissance scholar anywhere, certainly the most important Dante scholar of his day, Valency (the Renaissance and Dante expert in the English Department) saw not a competitor but a treasured colleague. I never heard him say anything that undermined Bigongiari's authority; he knew his own worth and limitations and was comfortable with what he was. He too was generous with his time and encouraged students in every way. The informal environment of his Renaissance seminar was conducive to bringing out one's best potential — quite a different story from my unfortunate encounters with the Shakespeare "expert" or the dramatic confrontation which took place during my oral exam for the doctorate.

I was relieved that Valency, as my mentor, would open and continue to direct my oral exam.

For several days before the exam, after I came home from teaching, Henry had grilled me with questions he concocted, covering works and authors that were likely to come up. I had to answer (as I would at the exam) without consulting notes or books: that came later, after we'd gone over my performance. Then, he would pull out this or that volume, read passages to me from this or that critic, tell me where I went off course, suggest ways of answering a question indirectly etc. etc. Never in my life had I experienced such an intensive drill (nor would I, ever again!). I complained, of course; but I could see that Henry had put aside his own work and had spent precious hours collecting what he thought were relevant texts, to cover as much ground as possible with me. He was a natural teacher, a dedicated mentor. To the end of his life, he never turned away anyone who needed his help. He would give his entire attention to whatever problem was brought to him and would spend hours talking to the person or making notes for him. Needless to say, I admired this selfless dedication but grew uneasy, too, when, again and again, he put aside his own work to do the work of others, sometimes rewriting entire book manuscripts. In later years, I sometimes complained that he was wasting his time patching up the mediocre product of others, but his answer was that one could learn even from a bad manuscript. He was kind enough never to remind me that I had been one of the first to benefit from that kind of dedication! The night before my "orals," I was so keyed up that I slept less than three hours. I was sure I would drift off during the exam and that, when awake, my brain would draw a blank.

The next morning, a sunny bright day, I walked the short distance to Philosophy Hall in a blur. I felt like a zombie. Somehow, I made it to my destination, where panic set in and the adrenaline began to flow. Professor Valency, as expected, opened the proceedings. I heard words come out of my mouth, but I was in a haze from lack of sleep, not sure if my answers were what they wanted, if I was talking too much, if I was straying from the subject. I blurted out whatever I had stored away and hoped for the best.

In answer to a question by another member of the Committee, about the nature of Dante's poem, I replied boldly what Bigongiari had drummed into us: that the *Commedia* was first and foremost a political poem. The professor who had asked the question (the Department expert in English Renaissance prose) took strong objection to my answer; but before I could go on, Valency raised an objection to the objection and, as the rest of us watched, our heads turning from one to the other, the two experts carried on a vigorous word match for several minutes. That exchange is etched in my memory. Valency put down his colleague in no uncertain terms before the exam continued. By then, I was running on sheer nerves. When the exam came to an end, I was still awake but utterly exhausted. I was escorted outside to sit on a bench in the corridor and wait for the decision of the committee. I seemed to have sat there for an eternity, but it was only a few minutes later that Professor Valency escorted me back into the room to tell me the result of the exam. I had passed "With Distinction." Everyone applauded. I gasped.

Soon, the dissertation too was behind me. At City College I was rewarded with tenure and the rank of Instructor. The next year, I was made an Assistant Professor.

Everything had started coming together when I accepted that first desperate call from the English Department Chairman at City College, but I wasn't altogether sure where my future lay. When it finally became clear, it was not a conscious decision, made after deliberating and weighing other possibilities, but a realization, rather, of actions already under way — much like a child crawls naturally, then tries to get up, stumbles, and suddenly begins to walk. I had never given serious thought to anything else, but now I came to realize, with utter certainty, that teaching was my future — not a career so much as a natural inclination, a way of life that would give me time to develop my growing interests and allow me to expand them, together with my writing.

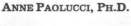

ANNE PAOLUCCI, PH.D.

WITH HENRY

WITH MOM

SYANDING ON THE STEPS OF LOW MEMORIAL LIBRARY, IN FRONT OF COLUMBIA'S "ALMA MATER"

I began to realize, then, just how much I owed to Dino Bigongiari, how much trust he had placed in me. His kindness and generosity had enabled me to find my stride at Columbia, bolstering my ego and helping me gain confidence with prizes and awards that were not overlooked by those who later had occasion to ask for and review my credentials. His recommendations had earned me two scholarships for graduate work in the Italian Graduate Department and a Fulbright Scholarship to the University of Rome. Because of the excellent preparation I had received in his class, I had won "Distinction" in my oral examination for the Ph.D., where my major author was Dante and my major area the Italian Renaissance. His influence and training surely had something to do, also, with my being singled out for the first Woodbridge Honorary Fellowship for my dissertation on "The Women in Dante's *Divine Comedy* and Spenser's *Faerie Queene*." His earlier recommendations surely worked for me, when I applied for and received a Fulbright grant as Lecturer in Modern Drama at the University of Naples for 1965-1966. He was quite ill by then and about to return to his native town of Seravezza, near Lucca, where he died on September 5, 1965, on my sixteenth wedding anniversary.

My writing continued without pause, not because of the "publish or perish" mandate that often forced academics to produce an article or a monograph or a book in order to get tenure or promotion, but because I loved to write. During the years that followed, I not only wrote for academic journals – *Shakespeare Quarterly, College English, Comparative Literature*, etc. – but also produced books of short stories, poetry, plays and translations. At City College, I suggested and was given approval to prepare and edit a volume of commemorative essays for the 400th anniversary of Shakespeare's birth. Professors and students submitted papers. The volume launched a series, *The City College Papers*. I called that first volume *Shakespeare Encomium*.

The energy that had fueled my trials and errors at Barnard had finally found its proper outlet. For me it was a time of exciting new activities, growing teaching skills, and bold extra-curricular ventures. It was during these years at City that I began to explore the work of the 1934 Nobel Laureate in Literature, the Italian playwright, Luigi Pirandello. I had met, in the mid-sixties, Gino Rizzo, a colleague in the Italian Department at City, then head of The Pirandello Society, founded in 1958 by George Freeley and Marta Abba, Pirandello's beloved leading lady, for whom he wrote several of his later plays. Abba had come to America after the playwright's death in 1936 and eventually married (and later divorced) an American businessman. The Society met at the Lamb's Club in Manhattan and, for a while, flourished. When I met Professor Rizzo, it had dwindled down to just a few members and was meeting sporadically in Rizzo's apartment. He soon resigned. I decided to revive the Society, if possible.

The first thing I did was bring in some new blood. With the help of friends and colleagues in theater, I started a newsletter and planned a few dramatic readings and lectures. A crucial move was to bring the Society under the aegis of the Modern Language Association of America (MLA) — the largest professional organization of professors, graduate students and academic groups in the country. We applied for and received status as an "Affiliated Association," entitled as such to hold two sessions at the annual MLA convention as well as at regional MLA meetings. Our presence at the MLA conventions gained us visibility and enough papers to insure a larger annual publication, launched in 1985, under the title *PSA*, which I edited until I withdrew from the Society in 2001.

LUIGI PIRANDELLO

MAETA ABBA

Rather than have colleagues present papers at our MLA meetings, I encouraged dramatic readings with mini-commentaries and, when possible, in a comparative spectrum. Such programs found ready audiences in community groups, as well. One such "production" drew an overflow audience of over 80, in a local church basement in Queens. We decided to repeat the program in the auditorium of a nearby school, where over 300 people showed up. The playwright from Agrigento, until then virtually unknown in these parts, even to many Italian-Americans (even Sicilians!), was a huge success. Had there been money, the program could have been repeated, offered to schools as well.

THE PIRANDELLO SOCIETY OF AMERICA

The Pirandello Society of America was founded in New York City in 1958 by Marta Abba and George Freeley. By the mid-sixties, the original Board was no longer active and the Society eventually began to attract academics. Even then, its activity was limited, partly because Pirandello was still not well-known outside of Italian studies, partly because his stage work suffered from major publishing restrictions, and partly because he was not yet recognized as an important international playwright. The President of the Society during this time was Professor Gino Rizzo (Italian Department, The City College).

The Society picked up momentum in the early 70s, under the leadership of Comm. Anne Paolucci of St. John's University and, later, that of Professor Maristella Lorch (then Executive Director of the Casa Italiana of Columbia University). After some years, during which the Casa Italiana hosted a number of dramatic programs, lectures, and conferences on Pirandello, the Society once again called on Comm. Paolucci to serve as its President. She remained in that position for the next 17 years, encouraging dramatic readings at the annual meetings of the Modern Language Association of America (MLA), planning special events and — in 1986 — launched an annual publication, *PSA*, to replace the Society's *Newsletter*, first introduced some years earlier and edited by Professors Nishan Parlakian and Philip Fulvi.

In 1997, the Society's status as an "Affiliated Association" of MLA was reviewed and renewed for the next seven years — mainly because of the uninterrupted publication and high academic quality of *PSA*.

In the late eighties, the Society hosted the first Pirandello Awards Dinner. In the years that followed, we honored a number of Pirandello scholars or theater people who were connected with Pirandello's works. One was Edward Albee, whom I had described in several articles, as well as in my book, *From Tension to Tonic: the Plays of Edward Albee,* as "America's Pirandello." I continued as President of the organization and editor of *PSA* until other urgent commitments forced me to resign, in 2001. Even so, my interest in Pirandello, the playwright Robert Brustein has called "the father of the contemporary theater," has never diminished.

THE PIRANDELLO SOCIETY OF AMERICA HONORS EDWARD ALBEE.
"PLAYERS," NEW YORK, 2000. A.P. (FAR LEFT); ALBEE (FAR RIGHT).

ALBEE (FOURTH FROM RIGHT), NEXT TO ACTRESS ROSEMARY HARRIS. A.P., FRONT RIGHT.

During my active teaching years, I made sure to include Pirandello in all my drama classes, graduate and undergraduate, both at City College and, later, at St. John's University. I "promoted" him every chance I got, included him into any lecture on drama I was invited to give at other colleges and universities. If the choice of topic was left to me, I invariably chose dramatic readings from Pirandello and other playwrights, placing the Sicilian dramatist in the mainstream with Shakespeare, Camus, Sartre, Beckett, Ionesco, Genet, Giroudoux, Pinter, Edward Albee and others. I would, if asked, provide the "script" for "comparative" readings around a critical theme (*e.g.* "The Language of Non-Communication in 'Theater of the Absurd'," "Open-Ended Action in the Plays of Pirandello and Edward Albee") with brief commentaries in between readings from the plays.

ONE OF THE REVIEWS OF *FROM TENSION TO TONIC: THE PLAYS OF EDWARD ALBEE*

476   THE TWENTIETH CENTURY (AMERICAN)

Brian Lee and David Murry. Vol. 53 (1972), published 1974.

Anne Paolucci's *From Tension to Tonic: the Plays of Edward Albee*[86] is an enthusiastic study of Albee's work (excluding the adaptations of other plays or of fiction), which sees Albee as the only modern American playwright to attempt 'serious articulation of the existential questions of our time, recognizing the incongruity of insisting on pragmatic values in an age of relativity'. She sees Albee's real master as Pirandello rather than O'Neill, and his technique, described as 'an oscillation between the prosaic and the absurd, obvious and mysterious, commonplace and revelation', is designed to incorporate the advances of the French absurdists and to avoid the narrowly *social* commitment so often demanded by critics. Paolucci therefore sees the critical stress on social themes in *Bessie Smith* or *American Dream* as misleading, in that to view Albee as a writer of social protest leaves us ill-equipped to cope with *Tiny Alice* for instance. The most interesting part of the book is in fact the long chapter on *Tiny Alice*, perhaps because it best fits Paolucci's claim that Albee has done more than most to revive in modern terms 'the glorious tradition of polysemous writing' exemplified by Dante.

[86] *From Tension to Tonic: The Plays of Edward Albee*, by Anne Paolucci. Carbondale and Edwardsville: Southern Illinois U.P. pp. xvi+143. $5.95.

I did this in cities as far away as Los Angeles and San Diego and at places like the University of the South. Although I read the occasional "paper," I was more interested in drawing audiences, anyone willing to listen, to Pirandello by more direct means. In some places (including the ones just mentioned) the students recruited for the readings, and most of the audience as well, had never heard of Pirandello before.

Albee and Pirandello are still the two most underrated playwrights in America. There are many reasons for this, and I have discussed them at length elsewhere. Here I wish simply to point out that Albee's plays, like most of Pirandello's, have a veneer of "realism" that gives them a stage life that tends to mislead audiences, addicted to traditional action, "message" plays (political, social, religious, psychological themes, etc.). Drama critic John Gassner's harsh judgment, in the forties, that the American theater was still "provincial," still in a state of "protracted adolescence" unfortunately still holds: we are still bound to the realism of Ibsen and Strindberg, introduced on the American stage by Eugene O'Neill and turned into what seems a permanent acquisition in the deep-rooted "message plays" and American social commentary of Arthur Miller. It is not surprising that Miller has fared so much better among us than Albee. We have not gone much beyond that kind of theater, as the French and British have. In Pirandello's case, we must also remember that, except for occasional college productions of the universal favorite, *Six Characters in Search of an Author,* he is rarely staged in commercial theaters — partly because of the bad translations and adaptations, partly because the stage language of the "Absurd" is still a mystery for most American critics and audiences. Unlike the French playwrights — Beckett, Ionesco, Genet and others — who have enjoyed receptive audiences for decades, Pirandello and Albee are still out of bounds in America. I hate to say it, but Albee's well-deserved Tony awards and Pulitzer prizes I suspect were given for all the wrong reasons.

THE PIRANDELLO SOCIETY OF AMERICA HONORS (L) MAURICE EDWARDS (PRODUCER, DIRECTOR, WRITER); (C) ANNE PAOLUCCI (PRESIDENT OF THE SOCIETY FOR ALMOST TWO DECADES); AND ® ROBERT DOMBROSKI (PIRANDELLO SCHOLAR). SECOND FROM LEFT: NISHAN PARLAKIAN, PRESIDENT OF THE SOCIETY.

UCLA. STUDENT READING OF PIRANDELLO'S *THE LICENSE (LA PATENTE)*

Hegelian insights had helped me grasp the new theater of Pirandello, especially the so-called "theater plays" (*Six Characters in Search of an Author, Each in His Own Way, Tonight We Improvise*, and I would also include here *The Emperor Henry IV*), as well as "Theater of the Absurd" and Albee's new kind of stage. I came to recognize in the extraordinary similarities that brought these playwrights, and others like them, to the edge of non-theater the truth in Hegel's provocative statement that in an age when "spirit" has exhausted itself there is a possibility of "art transcending itself," when existing rules seem to give way to new compelling structures that elude definition. Certainly this is evident in painting (*e.g.* Picasso), in twentieth-century fiction (*e.g* James Joyce), in music as well as architecture (*e.g* Wright and others), but it has yet to be acknowledged in drama. Albee is the only American playwright who has successfully mastered the delicate shift from an exterior world to an interior landscape, changing forever our view of what is depicted on stage.

For starters: both Albee and Pirandello elude established critical criteria. It is nearly impossible to discuss a Pirandello or an Albee play intelligently in the usual way, according to the familiar categories of action (events structured toward a predictable ending), character (insight into motives and behavior that bring out a certain potential in the personality depicted), theme (read: "message" of some kind), and language (in its familiar forms). Pirandello's stage action is a point seen through a powerful telescope, a revolving around a core, leading not to traditional closure but to a question of some kind. He turns familiar reality upside down, right side up, creates a new universe, as it were. Character is no longer idiosyncratic in a recognizable context but a mosaic of states of mind, no longer a well-defined personality moving toward insight and enlightenment but a state of being. The dialogue is often built on paradoxes and *non sequitors*.

In Albee's case, I was helped enormously in my efforts to probe the "eccentricities" in his plays by Alan Schneider's extraordinary staging, especially his *Who's Afraid of Virginia Woolf?* and *Tiny Alice*. With *Virginia Woolf*, audiences had responded well (on a realistic level, at least). They were drawn to the critique of upper middle-class life in suburbia, to alcoholic-induced arguments, to family quarrels — themes they could easily relate to. The imaginary son remained a problem, but for the most part it was ignored. On the level of realism, the play had merit and worked. The movie version strengthened this view and gave Albee's reputation a large push in the wrong direction. Critics still were unable to see behind the thin scrim of realism, to what lay behind it.

In its realism, the Schneider production was a huge success. Returning to the text after seeing the play performed — perhaps still the Albee favorite with audiences — I found some measure of reassurance for my conviction that this was an altogether new kind of theater. . . . all very exciting, but perplexing, still. Perversely, I focused on what most audiences and critics minimized: the imaginary son. I didn't try to get at "meaning" but simply searched the text for clues that would clarify the strange "character" who was central but never appeared on stage. Here, Dante and all that I knew about Catholic rituals came to the rescue. Careful reading of the text convinced me that the play was essentially a Mass for everything dead that demanded burial, for the imaginary son who had to be killed off in order for the living to survive. Illusions that held no hope, denial of the harsh realities of our daily lives, unwillingness to face the dilemmas that threaten the delicate balance of our daily routines — all these (Albee was telling us, I was convinced) and much else had to be destroyed for our true selves to emerge. I felt the text stood up against critical scrutiny along such lines, and, thus encouraged, went on to try my ideas on some of the other plays. *Tiny Alice* was the eye-opener.

I resorted to Dante again. In probing the layered structure of *Tiny Alice*, I recognized the transparent kind of allegory found in the *Divine Comedy*. I anticipated that some critics would find the comparison far-fetched (they did), but I went ahead anyway. These efforts led me back to Pirandello as well. In *Tiny Alice* I discovered not only Dantesque and Augustinian echoes but also the open-ended closure Pirandello had forged, particularly in his "theater plays." In the unresolved dilemma of Albee's play, the spiraling to an ever-increasing awareness of faith (or non-faith) is depicted as an unanswerable and unanswered mystery, much like the central mystery of all religions that accept an omnipotent God. The Chinese-box arrangement of the great house, receding into a silent eternity, tells us we are in a dimension not easily defined, a provocative scenario that is almost lyrical in quality. The familiar critical categories of Aristotle seem no longer adequate to explain a play that is transformed into an internal "landscape" and calls for subjective rather than objective correlatives: in Hegelian terms, traditional theater seems to have been "transcended." Audiences were faced with a totally new and unfamiliar kind of stage (and language).

Dante and Pirandello became my unexpected guides in assessing "Theater of the "Absurd." I found that like Pirandello, Albee often created "voices" and "moods" rather than traditional full-bodied dramatic characters; that his language was made up of paradoxes, contradictions, questions. rather than statement and "message." I also saw in his transparent symbolism, in his unmistakable religious implications, familiar Dantesque effects. I agreed with Robert Brustein, that "Theater of the Absurd" was one of many results of Pirandello's innovations, a new kind of stage that answered the needs of a disillusioned generation living in an existential world. In that context, Albee was the genial American heir to the new drama created by the Italian playwright — a drama quickly mastered by the French but totally ignored by other American playwrights.

By the time I was invited to the University of Naples as a Fulbright Lecturer in American Drama, for the year 1965-66 (the appointment was later renewed for a second year), I had pretty well sorted things out. It was no accident that I chose to focus my lectures on Eugene O'Neill, Arthur Miller, and Edward Albee. I had already started to organize a book on Albee, for which I had contracted with Southern Illinois University Press, through Harry T. Moore, the leading scholar on D. H. Lawrence and, at the time, General Editor of the prestigious Crosscurrents/Modern Critiques series. I planned to finish at least a good first draft of the book while in Italy. But an unexpected opportunity to start working on the Albee book came my way in the Spring, several months before I was scheduled to sail, when I was invited to spend time at Yaddo, the artists/writers colony located on a lovely estate in Saratoga Springs, New York. I spent the two summer months there, and in that time I prepared a tentative outline, jotted down ideas, and wrote bits and pieces. It was a productive prelude to what was to be my major personal project while in Naples. I did some other writing, as well, in that relaxed atmosphere.

The New York Times

Arts & Leisure

Section 2

Sunday, March 13, 1994

EDWARD ALBEE

'New Language Of the Stage'

To the Editor:

It was a pleasure to read Vincent Canby's essay on Edward Albee's "Three Tall Women" ["A Season of Albee, Obsessions Safely Intact," Feb. 20]. It is a work that I consider, with "The Man Who Had Three Arms," among the playwright's best accomplishments in recent years.

As a longtime scholar of Mr. Albee's plays, I have seen changes in his approach to familiar themes (marriage, death, noncommunication in relationships, etc.), which I would characterize as his obsessive effort to trim and reduce the realistic flab of most of our modern plays to an almost abstract musical design. Mr. Albee's approach is already beyond Theater of the Absurd, a form of legitimate theater never properly understood in this country.

In France and Germany the new playwrights have moved beyond the Absurd, which has proved to be — as Mr. Albee once noted — not nearly as "absurd" as some Broadway offerings of the last decade or so. And in moving beyond the Absurd, the Europeans have carried national audiences with them.

Ripeness is all.... What I have been urging for years is now perhaps possible: a menu of Albee plays on a regular basis, as well as a national outlet in New York and elsewhere. If we don't see new plays of quality on a steady basis, even the best drama critics will not be able to absorb the new language of the stage as it evolves.
                                    ANNE PAOLUCCI
                                    Beechhurst, N. Y.

The writer is author of "From Tension to Tonic: The Plays of Edward Albee."

I made good progress on my Albee study while in Naples, but the book wasn't actually published until 1972. Two other printings quickly followed; and in 1974, Southern Illinois University Press also brought out *Pirandello's Theater: the Recovery of the Modern Stage for Dramatic Art*, which I wrote when I was back in the States. (Both volumes have since been reprinted by Griffon House Publications.)

ARTISTS AND WRITERS AT YADDO, SARATOGA SPRINGS, N.Y.
A.P., STANDING, FAR RIGHT (JULY-AUGUST, 1965)

The Albee book has become a classic in its field. Albee himself was pleased with it and praised it publicly a number of times. On one occasion — an entire week's "celebration" of his work, hosted by Albright College in Pennsylvania — Albee asked that I be invited to give the keynote address. It was my first meeting with him. I was stunned when he called to me from the audience and had me join him on stage, as he spoke to students who had prepared a reading of one of his short plays. He pulled up a chair and waited for me to sit down, then turned to the audience and said: "Every writer should be fortunate enough to have a critic like Anne Paolucci!" I felt as though I'd won the Nobel Prize!

Not long after that, I was again invited at Albee's request to take part in a three-day conference at Northern Ohio State, where I had the good fortune to see productions by talented local theater groups of two plays I had never seen before and have not seen since: *Listening* and — what I consider to be one of Albee's absolute masterpieces — *The Man Who Had Three Arms* (forced to close in New York, after a few performances, because of bad reviews by critics, who felt the play was aimed at them). I found the work intriguing, especially in the breakdown of the barrier between the stage and the audience (very similar, in this respect, to Pirandello's *Tonight We Improvise*) and in the almost manic energy of the "lecturer" who, in addressing the audience of the script is also addressing the real audience in the theater. This is an extraordinary drama, a tour-de-force reminiscent also of Pirandello's Enrico *IV*, an excellent vehicle for a truly first-rate actor. I remember thinking that Richard Burton, with his stage stamina, his exuberance, and his many-faceted talent would have been a natural choice for the leading role. I hope the play will be staged again in the not-too-distant future. Perhaps critics will be ready for it, the next time around. But all this was yet to come. . . .

In late August, I left for Naples with Mom (Henry would join me later), who had not seen her siblings since circumstances had forced her to leave her people and return to New York, over thirty years earlier, a widow with three children. Her mother Concetta Guidoni had died during the war; her father Antonio not long after; but her brother Lello and her sister Maria were still alive. When I invited her to accompany me and stay on for as long as she wished, she agreed. It would give her a chance to visit with her relatives (one last time, as it turned out).

WITH MOM, SAILING TO NAPLES (AUGUST 1965)

On our arrival, my cousin Giuliano (Uncle Neno's son) was there to welcome us. He had taken time off from his job to see us through customs and settle us in Hotel Paradiso, where he had reserved rooms for us and remained with us until we found an apartment. The Hotel was built on the face of a hill, on the *Vomero* (the high section of Naples) with a marvelous view on all sides. Unfortunately, it later had to be closed down permanently because the sloping land on which it was built began to crumble. We were probably among the last to enjoy the place.

Giuliano remained with us until Mom and I were settled in an apartment we found on Corso Europa.

WITH COUSIN GIULIANO ATTURA

ON THE TERRACE OF HOTEL PARADISO
(NAPLES, SEPTEMBER, 1965)

September was coming to an end, but I still had plenty of free time: even before our arrival, the general unrest that was plaguing so many cities around the world had found its way to Naples. Student demonstrations kept the University from opening on schedule. The unexpected hiatus — I didn't actually begin lecturing until early January — not only allowed us to visit family in Rome and Acuto but also enabled me to finish a first draft of my book on Albee. Uncle Lello died soon after we returned to Naples; but we were comforted by the memory of his pleasure at our visit.

By the time January rolled around, we were — thanks to my cousin Giuliano — enjoying our large, airy apartment on the Vomero. From our terrace, we had a magnificent view of the Bay and Vesuvius. The one drawback was the so-called "central heating" the realtor had boasted of, when my cousin inquired. I had made the mistake of insisting on a place that had the kind of heating we were accustomed to in the States. When the cold weather finally set in, we discovered that "central heating" was nothing more than a thin metal filament, about half an inch in diameter, set against the wall behind a large (strictly for show) radiator unit. I quickly recognized my mistake and did what I should have done in the first place: rented a "bomba," the standard movable gas appliance Italians everywhere used for heating.

At the University, I found my students receptive but overly deferential, in keeping with a more rigorous, more formal protocol than ours. Although I was a woman (at the time, a rare bird in a top level university teaching job in Italy), my rank as a Fulbright Lecturer gave me a certain status and (I soon realized) the right to walk alongside Professor Chinol (the top man in English and American literature). His *assistenti* (something like our Assistant and

Associate Professors) were much older than I but never presumed to walk alongside us. I also discovered that students could come and go to classes as they pleased. Attendance was not important. What counted — at least in the liberal arts — and the only real requirement was an oral exam at the end of a course.

VIEW AT DAWN FROM THE TERRACE OF CORSO EUROPE 9, ON THE VOMERO, NAPLES.

One incident stands out in particular in this context. Edmund Bator, an American Consul and Director of the United States Information Service in Naples, who had set up a mini-tour of lectures for me in major Italian cities, escorted me one evening to the recently renovated museum of Benevento, where I was to speak on Arthur Miller. We were somewhat late. The great lecture hall was packed. We walked inside, but no one was there to greet us. Finally, Bator approached a small group still standing on the steps outside and nodded in my direction. They quickly approached and apologized profusely. Ed told me later, they had expected someone much older.

It was Ed Bator who took the initiative in getting my first play, *The Short Season*, produced under the auspices of both The American Studies Center in Naples, U.S.I.S., and the American Playwrights' Showcase. He had been around longer than I and knew where to go and who to tap for what was needed. He approached a group of NATO people who had started a little theater group and recruited the actors for my play — who were more than happy to cooperate. The two leading roles were played by Jack Ryan and Peter Migliaccio. Jack became a life-long friend of ours; Pete, unfortunately, died not long after, still a young man.

The Short Season was not the first play I had written, but it was the first to be produced. It was an exciting event, but I didn't need that to hook me. I was already well into theater as well as dramatic theory and critical studies about the stage and playwrights. Seeing my play produced simply reinforced that interest and gave me fresh incentive to continue not only writing about plays but also writing plays of my own.

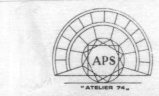

AMERICAN PLAYWRIGHTS' SHOWCASE

presents

THE SHORT SEASON
(LA BREVE STAGIONE)

A Three-Act Play
by
ANNE PAOLUCCI

June 17, 18, 19 - 1967

Sponsored by the American Studies Center and USIS -

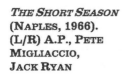

THE SHORT SEASON (NAPLES, 1966). (L/R) A.P., PETE MIGLIACCIO, JACK RYAN

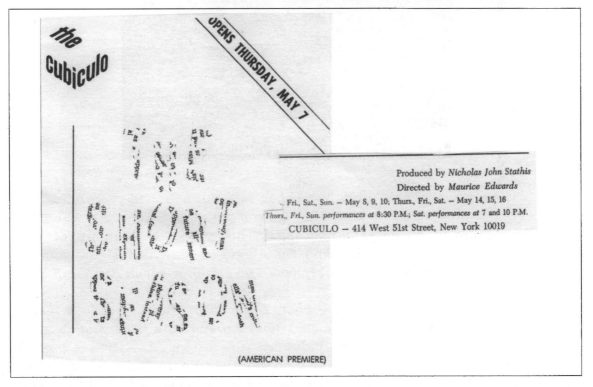

Produced by *Nicholas John Stathis*
Directed by *Maurice Edwards*
Fri., Sat., Sun. — May 8, 9, 10; Thurs., Fri., Sat. — May 14, 15, 16
Thurs., Fri., Sun. performances at 8:30 P.M.; *Sat. performances at* 7 *and* 10 P.M.
CUBICULO — 414 West 51st Street, New York 10019

(AMERICAN PREMIERE)

The Short Season had an excellent staging on my return to the States, where it was produced Off off-Broadway in 1968 at the Cubiculo, by Nicholas John Stathis, under the direction of Maurice Edwards. It was my first contact with these two talented men, the beginning of a long friendship and many shared projects at the Cubiculo and, later, at The Classic Theater, where Edwards and Stathis put on many forgotten classics, Greek and Elizabethan masterpieces, modern plays, and unusual new plays. An excellent actor, singer, author, translator of German, Italian, French and Russian texts, Edwards was always ready to entertain my suggestions and, over the years, put on a number of Pirandello plays, including the American premiere of *La vita che ti diedi* (*The Life I Gave You*) — always with the help of Nick Stathis, a successful lawyer who loved theater and chamber music and gave generously to both.

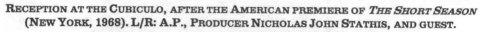

RECEPTION AT THE CUBICULO, AFTER THE AMERICAN PREMIERE OF *THE SHORT SEASON* (NEW YORK, 1968). L/R: A.P., PRODUCER NICHOLAS JOHN STATHIS, AND GUEST.

The renewal of my Fulbright grant in 1966, for a second year in Naples, had made the production of *The Short Season* possible. Soon after, when Ed Bator asked me to do another play, again under the sponsorship of The American Studies Center, U.S.I.S., and The American Playwrights' Showcase, I decided to direct Albee's early masterpiece, *The Zoo Story*. Jack Ryan and Pete Migliacci were cast in the two roles.

The timing could not have been better. The film version of *Who's Afraid of Virginia Woolf?* had reached Italy around that time and dazzled Italian viewers. It had been expertly dubbed (the Italians had already proved themselves masters in that field). The voices of the principals speaking Italian sounded exactly like Elizabeth Taylor and Richard Burton; and what they said was couched in idiomatic, fluent Italian, as though they actually knew the language and had been speaking it all their lives.

Given these circumstances, it was no surprise that our production of *The Zoo Story* — modest as it was — should attract more than local interest. It received a great deal of coverage in the press. I was pleased, of course; we all were. The audiences enjoyed the play. The actors had done a good job. At the same time, I'd discovered that I wasn't cut out to be a director. It was, in fact, the one and only time I assumed that role. I still cringe recalling the daily "crises" I had to deal with, my constant frustration in the effort to produce the perfect blend of voices, the perfect timing, a fast-moving pace in what was a deceptively static action. It was the ideal production in my head that I wanted to see on stage. . . .

AMERICAN PLAYWRIGHTS' SHOWCASE

presents

THE ZOO STORY

A One-Act Play
by
EDWARD ALBEE

Produced and Directed by
ANNE PAOLUCCI

Sponsored by the American Studies Center and U.S.I.S. - Naples
Cover: From Vetruvius' drawing of the Greek theater.

ROMA — Venerdì 10 marzo

DOMANI AL TEATRINO « ATELIER 74 »

"The Zoo Story,, in inglese

Domani sera alle ore 21 (con repliche nei giorni 12 e 13) al teatrino « Atelier 74 » in via Filangieri 36, verrà presentato —in lingua originale — « The Zoo Story », un atto unico del drammaturgo americano Edward Albee, autore di « Chi ha paura di Virginia Wolf? ».

Il lavoro — messo in scena sotto gli auspici del Centro studi americani e dell'USIS di Napoli — è stato realizzato da Anne Paolucci della City University di New York nel quadro dell'American Playwrights' Showcase, una nuova iniziativa sorta a Napoli allo scopo di promuovere l'allestimento di alcune delle migliori commedie americane.

Per i biglietti d'invito rivolgersi all'USIS, via Filangieri 36 oppure al Centro studi americani, via Andrea d'Isernia 36.

● NELLA FOTO: *Peter J. Migliaccio e Jack Ryan in una scena di « The Zoo Story ».*

In the years that followed, watching Maurice Edwards and other friends work their magic, transform a script into a living and compelling stage experience, I came to appreciate how the best directors use to advantage the raw material they are given to work with. They know how to transform the text of a play into a reality that has consistency and immediacy.

During my two years in Naples, I found new friends like Martha and Ed Bator, wrote most of what was to become the major critical work on Edward Albee (*From Tension to Tonic: the Plays of Edward Albee*), gave lectures on American drama and theater not only at the University of Naples but also at other academic and cultural centers in Italy and Austria. I had a chance to travel and see parts of Italy I had not seen before and would not see again, refined my critical views of our major American playwrights, spent the summers of 1966 and 1967 at Urbino, teaching courses in American drama (for which I prepared three "dispense" — official course "notes" by professors — in Italian, for their students), and enjoyed those long summer days below, on the beach in Pesaro, with cousins who had come to spend time with Henry and me.

I was able to accomplish a good deal, while in Naples; but my most important acquisition during those two Fulbright years was discovering a certain skill for writing plays. I have honed that skill in short historical and literary plays. All of them have been produced, some more than once; but for me, the high point was always the conception and actual writing of a play, I have also come to recognize the play as an educational vehicle, through which history and literature can be filtered through a heightened critical awareness by creating voices and words that bring to life such figures as Christopher Columbus and Machiavelli, Thomas Cromwell and Thomas More. I never wrote anything with social or political or religious "reform" or "message" in mind: I wrote, always, to satisfy an irresistible and irrepressible urge.

☞ *FROM THE FILES* ☞

SPEAKING AT
WAGNER COLLEGE,
STATEN ISLAND
(EARLY 1950s).

PART OF THE LIVING ROOM OF
OUR FIRST APARTMENT (110TH ST.
BETWEEN BROADWAY AND
AMSTERDAM AVE. (MID 50S).

ON A CRUISE WITH
(L.) HELEN MCGIRR,
AND (R) "RORY,"
SINGER JULIUS
LA ROSA'S WIFE

Tuesday, November 10, 1964

A REVIEW

'Shakespeare Encomium'

By Bob Weisberg

Harvard has the Harvard University Press, Oxford has the Oxford University Press, and now City College may have a press of its own.

The College's English Department decided to participate in the quadricentennial celebration of Shakespeare's birth by publishing a

(continued)

Shakespeare Encomium. And this collection of essays, poems, and articles on the Bard of Avon has been designated by the College's Cohen Library as Volume I of *The City College Papers,* a proposed series of publications that will be sold to the public and exchanged with the libraries of other institutions. Unfortunately, no one seems to have plans for Volume II. But the library has certainly encouraged further publishing under the auspices of the College, and hopefully, other departments and individuals will add to the *Papers*.

The encomium is a joint literary effort of students and faculty, and a joint financial effort of the administration, Student Council, Professor Edward Mack (English), and a benevolent printer who happens to be an alumnus.

Edited by Mrs. Anne Paolucci (English), it speaks well for our academic community. In particular, the critical essays combine liveliness and perspicacity, and almost warrant the price at which the book is being sold. Generally, the essays avoid obscure subjects, but deal with the personalities of some major Shakespearian characters and with an order that underlies the huge geometric plots of the plays.

In the first category we find Mrs. Paoluccoi's "Macbeth and Oedipus Rex: A Study in Paradox." The author draws some fascinating parallels between two seemingly opposite characters, especially in regard to their relationship with supernatural forces, prophecy, and fate, and in the dramatic irony of the respective tragedies. Henry Warnken offers an interesting interpretation of Othello in which he recognizes Iago, the completely evil man, as an actual projection of Othello. Mr. Warnken sees in Iago the embodiment of Othello's potential for evil, and he shows how the two personalities blend with one another as the play progresses. . . .

Another essay worth note is Leslie Freeman's on the influence of Machiavelli on Shakespeare. The Bard may have known *The Prince* through secondary sources only, but Miss Freeman clearly establishes the influence and points to one Shakespearian king, Richard III, who loses his hereditary crown because he fails to exercise Machiavellian techniques, and to two others, Henry IV and Henry V, who rely on these techniques to maintain their reigns. It is a convincing bit of scholarship.

As for the second category, Naomi Conn studies the major comedies in light of her thesis that a universal order in nature underlies the comedies, and that the plays progress from disorder to resolution.

Shakespeare's survival on the European continent concerns three articles in the encomium. Philip Roddman, who in 1946 was the director of a Parisian radio program, presents the text of that program's interview with Andre Gide. Gide had just completed a widely acclaimed translation of *Hamlet* and discusses the problems involved in French translations. And one of the two contributions to the encomium dealing with production is David Gild's article on Andre Antoine's staging of *King Lear* in Paris in 1887, which, says Mr. Gild, ended the French tradition of ornate and "emasculating" Shakespearian productions.

The College has made a worthy contribution to the quadricentennial.

SAILING FOR NAPLES WITH MOM.
(AUGUST, 1965).

NEW YEAR'S EVE IN MONTE CARLO WITH COUSIN GIULIANO ATTURA AND HIS WIFE (1966)

WITH COUSIN ITALO
GUIDONI (1967)

WITH GODCHILD/NIECE,
BARBARA ATTURA
(EARLY 60S)

WITH BROTHER-IN-LAW,
JAVAD HAIDARI (CA 1950)

VISITING PUGLIE
(BARI LECTURES, 1967)

WITH STUDENTS FROM
UNIVERSITY OF URBINO
(SUMMER, 1966)

PORTOFINO
(APRIL, 1967)

WITH UNCLE NENO AND HENRY
FONTANA DI TREVI (ROME, 1967)

WITH COUSIN LEA
(ROME, 1967)

SCUOLA DEI BARNABITI (APRIL, 1966)

WITH COUSINS LEA AND RENZO (PESARO, SUMMER 1966)

WITH MY ALFA-ROMEO "GIULIETTA" (NAPLES, 1966-57)

MOM (SARATOGA SPRINGS, EARLY 60S)

CAMPAIGNING WITH HENRY IN UPSTATE NEW YORK, 1964 (L.) KIERAN O'DOHERTY, VICE CHAIRMAN, CONSERVATIVE PARTY OF NEW YORK STATE)

YADDO (JULY, 1965

Jack Ryan and Pete Migliaccio in Edward Albee's *The Zoo Story* (Naples, 1967)

IL MATTINO — Domenica 12 Marzo 1967

TEATRI E CONCERTI

Al Teatrino «Atelier 74»

«Racconto allo zoo» di Edward Albee

Racconto allo zoo, l'atto unico col quale Edward Albee (il drammaturgo di «Chi ha paura di Virginia Wolf») entrò di prepotenza a far parte del ristretto numero dei commediografi della nuova generazione nordamericana, già si vide un paio di anni fa a Napoli, proposto dall'Ente Teatro Cronaca. Non si tratta di un capolavoro, si tratta di una prima e già seria prova di impegno, una proposta in chiave più assurda che crudele della solitudine umana di oggi. Il colloquio a due voci fra Peter e Jerry su una panchina del Central Park di New York con la morte di Jerry assassinato da Peter, quasi senza motivo se non quello tutto esistenziale e moderno di cercare una maglia rotta nella rete convenzionale che tutti ci stringe è già del buon teatro, magari qua e là venato da influssi surrealistici, beckettiani, espressionistici. Ma Albee mostrò a sufficienza di saper tenere una scena, di farvi muovere, agire, morire dei personaggi di carne e non delle astratte maschere.

Questo testo è stato rappresentato ieri sera in inglese da Peter Migliaccio e da Jack Ryan, due attori americani di buona fama per le loro interpretazioni sotto la regìa della signora Paulucci, esperta e critica di teatro, in uno scantinato di via Filangieri adibito per l'occasione a teatrino. «Atelier 74» si chiama questa «cave» dove altre volte si sono svolti incontri, anche polemici, di cultura promossi dal Centro di Studi Americani e dall'USIS nonché dallo Youth Leader Club. Per quanto ci è dato di poter giudicare l'edizione presentata di «The zoo story» ci è sembrata fedele al punto giusto al significato poetico del testo, ben meritando quindi i nutriti applausi di un pubblico che conoscendo la lingua inglese ha potuto meglio apprezzare finezze ed eleganze della recitazione. Si replica.

ma. st.

* * *

A causa delle numerose richieste pervenute, le repliche di «The Zoo Story» di Albee, all'«Atelier 74», avranno luogo, oltre questa sera e domani, anche martedì 14, sempre alle ore 21. Per i biglietti d'invito rivolgersi all'USIS oppure al Centro Studi Americani.

ROMA

GLI SPETTACOLI

« THE ZOO STORY » DI E. ALBEE | Domenica 12 marzo 1967

Incomunicabilità stile americano

Inaugurato il nuovo teatrino « Atelier 74 » sotto gli auspici dell' U.S.I.S.

Si è inaugurato con successo il nuovo teatrino «Atelier 74 » (settantaquattro sono i posti a sedere) in uno scantinato, rimesso a nuovo con gusto, in via Filangieri 36: spettacolo d'apertura *The Zoo Story*, atto unico dell'ormai famoso drammaturgo americano Edward Albee, noto soprattutto come autore di *Chi ha paura di Virginia Wolf*.

Lo spettacolo è stato ben realizzato sotto gli auspici del Centro Studi Americani e dell'USIS di Napoli, nel quadro delle attività dell'*American Playwright's Showcase*, gruppo statunitense che intende mettere in scena, non solo a Napoli ma anche in altre città italiane ed europee, una serie di produzioni — in lingua originale — di capolavori teatrali americani.

The Zoo Story (Storia dello Zoo) è un moderno dramma dell'incomunicabilità a due personaggi: un breve ma intenso saggio espresso in forma anticonformista, quasi sul piano del teatro dell'assurdo. L'azione si svolge al Central Park di New York, un pomeriggio domenicale d'estate. Il dialogo avviene tra due sconosciuti, uno dei quali attende le morte (e l'altro non lo sa). Una sorta di quasi-monologo più narrativo che letterario — in trasparenza all'ombra di Kafka, un Kafka contemporaneo all'americana — esplode lentamente in un'attanagliante quanto suggestiva azione teatrale. Lo sbandato Jerry incontra il signor Peter — che tranquillamente seduto su di una panchina sta leggendo un libro — e gli chiede se è a conoscenza di quanto è accaduto al vicino Zoo. E' chiaro che Peter non desidera essere disturbato; senonchè sarà costretto suo malgrado ad accettare la conversazione con l'inquieto Jerry il quale, in cerca di «comunicabilità», narra alcuni esempi dei tentativi effettuati invano per cercare, appunto, di comunicare con gli stessi esseri ed anche con gli animali, in special modo con un cane. Gli è proprio impossibile, insomma, essere compreso dagli altri, vivere con gli altri: adesso, appunto sulla stessa panchina occupata da Peter, che si mostra borghese conformista. Al contrario Jerry è un ribelle «arrabbiato». E vorrebbe far sua la panchina sulla quale da molto tempo, ogni domenica, siede Peter. Nasce così fra i due — a causa di quelli che i cronisti chiamano «futili motivi» — un concitato litigio che si concluderà, in maniera imprevista, tragicamente. Evidenti sono i reconditi significati sociali, di umana problematica, racchiusi in questo allucinante atto unico.

The Zoo Story (di cui rammentiamo una buona edizione in italiano realizzata nel maggio 1964 dal «Teatro Cronaca» al Politeama, protagonista Glauco Mauri, regia di Mico Galdieri) è stato ottimamente interpretato dall'incisivo Jack Ryan (nella parte di Jerry) e dall'altrettanto valido Peter J. Migliaccio (nel ruolo di Peter). Entrambi recitano con dizione chiarissima. Assai apprezzabile la regia della colta e provveduta Anne Paolucci, della City University di New York, che si è valsa della collaborazione di Jack Pearson (bozzettista), di Amos Force (direttore di scena) e di Ed Wiley (datore di luci).

I due protagonisti e la regista sono stati più volte calorosamente applauditi dallo scelto pubblico.

se. lo.

* * *

In seguito alle numerose richieste pervenute, le repliche di «The Zoo Story» avranno luogo, oltre questa sera e domani, anche martedì 14, sempre alle 21. Per i biglietti d'invito rivolgersi all'USIS, oppure al Centro Studi Americani.

Naples gets 'arrogant' theater treat

Sunday-Monday, March 19-20, 1967

NAPLES—It has become quite a truism to say that there is so much theater going on in the streets of Naples that there hardly seems any need to bring artificial drama or comedy into its playhouses. Two of the city's theaters are anyway dedicated for a good part of the year to presenting plays which are slices of the Neapolitan human comedy—the Bracco and the San Ferdinando, the latter being the traditional home of the great Eduardo De Filippo who, unfortunately, now rarely plays there himself.

For more refined theatrical fare (and in Italian rather than Neapolitan dialect) local audiences get the pick of the season's offerings during the current months at the Politeama. Between now and May there are promised shows that range from a Milan company's production of a contemporary French farce to Franco Zeffirelli's forthcoming production of Albee's "A Delicate Balance" (which Rome and Milan won't see until next season).

If Neapolitan audiences have to wait until May to see Edward Albee's most recent play, this last week they have had a chance to see, or re-see, the American dramatist's first play, "The Zoo Story," and in its original language.

Experimental

Now Naples too, has its English-language theater group dedicated to experimental productions of contemporary American theater. Added to the Rome experiments of Ben Ardery Jr., and his New American Theater, the interesting recent English Players presentation of "Telemachus Clay" and the current Italian tour of the New York Living Theater, this means that American theater really does seem to be catching up with us.

The Naples group calls itself the American Playwrights' Showcase which gives a clear idea of their program. The animator of the group is Anne Paolucci who is currently a Fulbright Lecturer in American Drama at the University of Naples. Mrs Paolucci chose Albee as the first playwright for the "Showcase" because she considers the author of "The Zoo Story" and "Who's Afraid of Virginia Woolf" the most eloquent voice of the new "poetic or dramatic arrogance" in American playwright.

Anne Paolucci staged "The Zoo Story" in the Atelier 74, a pocket-sized theater (seating 74 people) which is housed in the basement of the USIS building on Via Filangeri. It was a straightforward interpretation of the play, acted with a fine sense of emotional awareness by Peter J. Migliaccio as Peter and Jack Ryan as Jerry.

The Naples group aims to take this production and subsequent presentations on tour to American cultural centers in other Italian cities and eventually to other parts of Europe, beginning with Austria and Yugoslavia. It would be a good idea if this group and its sponsors could get together with some of the other English-language groups now functioning in Italy and arrange to coordinate their activities.

I was intrigued, incidentally, by Mrs Paolucci's reference to the "arrogance" of American playwrighting and to her conviction that the American theater todays offers a 20th Century equivalent to the Elizabethian theatrical renaissance that gave England its Marlowes and its Shakespeare.

Teatri e concerti

Un dramma di Albee al teatrino «Atelier 74»

IL MATTINO

Giovedì 9 Marzo 1967

Nei giorni 11, 12 e 13 marzo, alle ore 21, al Teatrino «Atelier 74» in via Filangieri 36, verrà presentato — in lingua originale — «The Zoo Story», un atto unico del drammaturgo americano Edward Albee, autore di «Chi ha paura di Virginia Wolf?».

Il lavoro — messo in scena sotto gli auspici del Centro Studi Americani e dell'USIS di Napoli — è stato realizzato da Anne Paolucci della «City University» di New York nel quadro dell'«American Playwrights' Showcase», una nuova iniziativa sorta a Napoli allo scopo di promuovere l'allestimento di alcune delle migliori commedie americane.

Per i biglietti d'invito rivolgersi all'USIS, via Filangieri 36 oppure al Centro Studi Americani, via Andrea d'Isernia 36.

NAPOLI NOTTE

«The Zoo Story» all'Atelier 74

Giovedì 9 - Venerdì 10 Marzo 1967

Nei giorni 11, 12 e 13 marzo, alle ore 21, al Teatrino «Atelier 74» in Via Filangieri 36, verrà presentato — in lingua originale — «The Zoo Story», un atto unico del drammaturgo americano Edward Albee, autore di «Chi ha paura di Virgina Wolf?».

Il lavoro — messo in scena sotto gli auspici del Centro Studi Americani e dell'USIS di Napoli — è stato realizzato da Anne Paolucci della City University di New York nel quadro dell'American Playwrights' Showcase, una nuova iniziativa sorta di Napoli allo scopo di promuovere l'allestimento di alcune delle migliori commedie americane.

Per i biglietti d'invito rivolgersi all'USIS, Via Filangieri 36 oppure al Centro Studi Americani, Via Andrea d'Isernia 36.

● *Nella foto:* Peter J. Migliaccio e Jack Ryan in una scena di «The Zoo Story».

CORRIERE DI NAPOLI

Lunedì 13 - Martedì 14 Marzo 1967

LE PRIME TEATRALI

«Zoo Story» all'«Atelier 74»

Ad Anne Paulucci — una esperta di teatro che insegna alla City University di New York, e che si trova attualmente a Napoli per ragioni di studio — si deve la felice iniziativa di questa serie di rappresentazioni in lingua inglese.

La sede è stata messa a disposizione dall'USIS e si chiama «Atelier 74»: un locale sotterraneo non molto ampio ma confortevolmente attrezzato, che il pubblico ha gremito con entusiasmo e che certamente potrà ospitare, in avvenire, molte altre manifestazioni interessanti e stimolanti.

«Zoo Story», di Eduard Albee, fu da noi recensita un paio di anni fa, allorchè — interprete Glauco Mauri — ne presentò una edizione in lingua italiana la compagnia del «Teatro Cronaca» diretta da Mico Galdieri. Rispetto a quella, la rappresentazione data sabato ha avuto il vantaggio, per gli spettatori che intendono l'inglese di fare gustare in lingua originale un testo di apprezzabile valore che — pur embrionalmente e in forma alquanto schematica — introduce al mondo di uno dei più famosi scrittori americani di teatro e anticipa quei motivi di solitudine, di delusione, di disperata «incomunicabilità» che lo stesso Albee svilupperà poi in «Chi ha paura di Virginia Woolf» e nelle altre sue opere.

La regia della Paulucci e la interpretazione di Jack Ryan e Peter Migliaccio si sono proposte, soprattutto, obiettivi di linearità e di accuratezza: il testo è stato presentato in maniera nitida, distaccata, precisa, con forza di penetrazione affidata alle parole di Albee, con l'ausilio di un misurato gestire e di una incisiva dizione.

Lo spettacolo — per il quale hanno collaborato con Anne Paulucci lo scenografo Jack Pearson, il direttore di scena Amos Force e il datore di luci Ed Wiley — ha riscosso calorosi applausi. Dopo la affollata replica di ieri, verrà ancora ripetuto stasera e domani, sempre alle ore 21. Biglietti all'USIS, in via Filangieri 36.

e. f.

LE CONFERENZE

Anne Paolucci
al Centro studi americani

« L'eroe tragico in Arthur Miller » è stato il tema di una conferenza tenuta ieri sera al Centro studi americani dalla prof. Anne Paolucci della City University of New York, attualmente a Napoli con un lettorato presso l'Università.

Attraverso una rapida analisi dei drammi più famosi del discusso commediografo americano da « Erano tutti miei figli » al recente « Incident at Vichy » rappresentato qualche settimana fa a Milano, la Paolucci ha illustrato l'evoluzione del complesso carattere del protagonista milleriano.

Il protagonista dei primi drammi — ha osservato l'oratrice — eroe in senso classico, con una morale ben precisa, colpevole e consapevole di esserlo fino alla decisione di distruggersi come Willy di « Morte di un commesso viaggiatore » si è man mano trasformato in un eroe quasi innocente e certo inconsapevole delle sue colpe.

La svolta nel pensiero drammatico di Miller avviene — secondo la Paolucci — proprio con « Dopo la caduta », il discusso dramma autobiografico che può considerarsi il « turning point » della poetica milleriana.

ROMA   Giovedì 16 giugno 1966

**
Ieri, nel corso di una conferenza al centro studi americani, la prof.ssa Anna Paolucci, della City University of New York, ha tracciato un quadro dell'evoluzione del teatro americano contemporaneo.

* * *

ROMA   Mercoledì 15 giugno 1966

La prof.ssa Anna Paolucci, della City University of New York, terrà oggi, alle ore 18,30, al centro studi americani in via Andrea d'Isernia, una conversazione in inglese sul tema: « Il dramma americano contemporaneo ».

* * *

IL MATTINO   Giovedì 16 Giugno 1966

MOSCONI

IL SANTO DEL GIORNO

Oggi 16 giugno, S. Quirino e S. Aurelio.

Auguri al comm. Aurelio Pasquini, ad Aurelio Annunziata e a tutti quelli che festeggiano oggi il loro onomastico.

Domani, 17 giugno, S. Ranieri.

Gazzettino

Brillante ieri il cocktail che ha riunito al Centro Studi Americani il qualificato uditorio della conferenza «Contemporary American Drama» della prof. Anne Paolucci.

IL MATTINO

Paolucci al Centro di studi americani

Oggi, alle ore 18,30, al Centro studi americani in via Andrea d'Isernia, la professoressa Anne Paolucci della City University of New York terrà una conversazione in inglese sul tema «Il dramma americano contemporaneo»

Mercoledì 15 Giugno 1966

L'«eroe» del teatro di Miller in conflitto coi valori assoluti

La prof. Anna Paolucci dell'Università di New York ha illustrato tutta l'opera del drammaturgo americano

Ieri sera, in un'aula dello istituto universitario di Magistero, la prof. Anna Paolucci, docente di letteratura comparata all'università di New York, ha tenuto una dotta conferenza sugli eroi tragici nel teatro di Arthur Miller.

L'oratrice, che è stata presentata dal prof. Lindsay Hopie, incaricato di lingua e letteratura inglese nella nostra Università, ha parlato con competenza di studiosa e di critica di tutta l'opera del drammaturgo americano, molto noto anche in Italia, particolarmente per la rappresentazione sulle scene di «Morte di un commesso viaggiatore», «Uno sguardo dal ponte» (queste due ultime realizzate anche in film) e «Dopo la caduta», che rivela alcuni spunti autobiografici in rapporto alla sua sfortunata esperienza coniugale con l'attrice Marilyn Monroe, suicidatasi due anni or sono.

La prof. Paolucci ha puntualizzato il particolare aspetto degli «eroi» di Miller, i quali non hanno, in effetti, nulla di quell'eroismo che è presente nei personaggi tragici della tradizione classica. Essi, infatti, sono uomini comuni, gente semplice, con difetti e vizi comuni, privi di responsabilità pubbliche e spesso afflitti da una sorta di monotonia che tende a distruggerli.

La maggior parte di essi sono eroi quasi innocenti incapaci di vedere gli errori che commettono e, quindi, bisognosi di essere aiutati e protetti dalle forze esterne che creano in loro conflitti insanabili.

L'oratrice ha affermato la concezione ideologica che affiorava nei primi drammi del Miller («Erano tutti miei figli», «Il crogiuolo», eccetera) ora è andata scemando nella sua ultima produzione, dove lo scavo psicologico e il conflitto interiore prevalgono e si identificano con un significato simbolico altamente umano, al di fuori di un vero impegno di natura sociale. In questi ultimi lavori («Dopo la caduta» e «Avvenimento a Vichy», non ancora tradotto in Italia) l'evoluzione tragica dell'autore rimette a posto i valori assoluti che prima erano stati trascurati: il senso di colpa, le responsabilità, che scaturiscono come da un incubo, spingono costantemente i protagonisti a tentare una giustificazione, a volte sottile, a volte violenta. Gli estremi del bene e del male sono valutati sia nell'«eroe» innocente sia in quello perverso e pericoloso che ha la convinzione assoluta della propria presunta innocenza. Anche se il Miller non raggiunge, qui, l'unità artistica e poetica dei primi drammi, è auspicabile che il suo lavoro di drammaturgo continui ad approfondire verità e situazioni umane al di fuori di una propaganda d'ordine politico.

L'oratrice, che è stata molto applaudita dal folto uditorio, ha esemplificato la sua efficace esposizione con letture di interessanti brani della opera di Miller.

LA CONFERENZA ALL'ISTITUTO DI MAGISTERO

SCIA Sabato, 19 marzo 1966

ROMA

Nuova iniziativa teatrale a Napoli

Successi americani in lingua originale

Una nuova iniziativa, l'American Playwrights' Showcase (Vetrina di successi americani) che ha lo scopo di favorire l'allestimento — in inglese — di copioni americani di successo e di avanguardia, è sorto a Napoli. Animatrice dell'interessante iniziativa è Anne Paolucci della City University di New York, attualmente a Napoli con una borsa di studio Fulbright per tenere un corso sul teatro americano presso la nostra università.

Il primo lavoro che andrà in scena è un atto unico di Edward Albee, «The Zoo Story», realizzato sotto gli auspici del Centro Studi Americani dell'USIS. Esso verrà presentato nei giorni 11, 12 e 13 marzo, alle ore 21, nel Teatrino «Atelier 74», in via Filangieri 36. Sarà regista dello spettacolo la stessa Mrs. Paolucci.

Protagonisti di «The Zoo Story» saranno due attori americani: Peter J. Migliaccio e Jack Ryan, già applauditi interpreti di drammi di Sofocle, Shakespeare. Pirandello, Lorca, Inge.

I biglietti d'invito per le tre serate possono essere ritirati all'USIS, via Filangieri 36, oppure al Centro Studi Americani, via Andrea d'Isernia 36, tutti i giorni, tranne il sabato e la domenica.

Lunedì 6 marzo 1967

il Resto del Carlino

Letteratura inglese

Oggi 9 maggio, alle ore 16, presso l'Istituto di lingua e letteratura inglese della Facoltà di Magistero, (via Zamboni 32) la professoressa Anne Paolucci, commediografa e insegnante universitaria americana, terrà la sua prima conferenza sul «Teatro di Edward Albee». La seconda avrà luogo mercoledì alla stessa ora. Le conferenze sono in lingua italiana.

Martedì 9 Maggio 1967

CORRIERE DI NAPOLI

conferenze

Al Centro Studi Americani, Anne Paolucci ha tenuto ieri una conversazione interessantissima su: L'eroe tragico di Arthur Miller.

Venerdì 6 Maggio 1966

LA SICILIA

Il teatro di Arthur Miller

La prof. Anna Paolucci dell'Università di New York, voce autorevole nel campo degli studi sul teatro americano contemporaneo, terrà una conferenza sul tema «L'eroe tragico nel teatro di Arthur Miller» all'istituto universitario di Magistero (via Ofelia), alle ore 17.30 di oggi, venerdì. Il pubblico può intervenire

Venerdì, 18 marzo 1966

CORRIERE DI SICILIA

Conferenza al «Magistero»

La professoressa Anna Paolucci dell'Università di New York, voce autorevole nel campo degli studi sul teatro americano contemporaneo, terrà una conferenza sul tema «L'Eroe tragico nel teatro di Arthur Miller» all'Istituto universitario di Magistero di Catania (via Ofelia), oggi alle ore 17,30.

Catania, 18 marzo 1966

LA GAZZETTA DEL MEZZOGIORNO

Conferenze Paolucci su Miller ed Albee

Oggi, 21, e il 28 aprile, alle ore 17, la prof. Anne Paolucci, dell'Università di New York e autrice di teatro ella stessa, attualmente «fulbright lecturer» presso l'Università di Napoli, terrà due conferenze, in italiano, nell'aula prima del Corso di lingue dell'Università (Largo Fraccacreta) la prima su Arthur Miller, la seconda su Edward Albee. Le conferenze sono aperte al pubblico.

Venerdì 21 aprile 1967

NEWS WRITEUPS OF HENRY'S LECTURES, SPONSORED BY USIS (1967)

MESSAGGIO d'oggi

SETTIMANALE POLITICO CULTURALE INDIPENDENTE

20 Aprile 1967

AL CIRCOLO CULTURALE BENEVENTANO

Le tre fasi della storia U.S.A. in una conferenza di H. Paolucci

E' seguito un interessante dibattito

Benevento, Aprile

Mister Henry Paolucci, professore emerito della St. Johns University di New York nella facoltà di Scienze Politiche, è stato in questi giorni ospite della nostra città per iniziativa del Circolo Culturale Beneventano, presso il quale ha tenuto una interessantissima conferenza sul tema: « Le tre grandi fasi della storia degli Stati Uniti ».

Non è la prima volta che il Circolo Culturale ospita studiosi di altre nazioni (e non sarà certamente l'ultima se si tien conto che il programma del presidente prof. Antonio Margherini è di portare il Circolo ad un'importanza molto più che provinciale: per quest'anno si prevede addirittura l'intervento di un giovane scienzato italiano che ha condotto numerose ricerche negli Stati Uniti e da poco è rientrato in Italia per continuare qui i suoi studi e riprendere lo insegnamento universitario), ma la presenza del prof. Paolucci ha destato un più vivo interesse soprattutto negli ambienti politici, essendo egli un uomo politico di primaria importanza nel suo Paese, anche se la sconfitta del suo partito, quello Conservatore, ha impedito la sua elezione a Senatore del Governo degli Stati Uniti, a tutto vantaggio del suo illustre competitore Robert Kennedy.

Mister Paolucci, nella conferenza tenuta al Circolo Culturale Beneventano, ha anzitutto affermato che, per un principio generale della storia, ogni popolo nuovo deve attraversare tre fasi fondamentali di formazione e sviluppo, per acquistare dignità di nazione e forza di stato. Esso anzitutto deve rivolgere tutti i suoi sforzi al conseguimento dell'autosufficienza; in un secondo momento deve provvedere a determinare e chiarire il suo « essere » ad affermare cioè le sue peculiari caratteristiche, e a raggiungere un altro livello di benessere; in terzo luogo deve affermare la sua egemonia nel mondo.

Alla luce di siffatto principio, l'oratore ha esaminato con profondo acume e dottrina, le tre fasi della storia degli Stati Uniti, soffermandosi a lungo sulla considerazione della attuale politica americana.

IL MATTINO

SABATO 10 GIUGNO 1967

Dibattito all'USIS sui diritti civili

Nel quadro della serie di iniziative dedicate alla rassegna storica della Guerra Civile Americana 1861-1865, rassegna che comprende — com'è noto — una mostra di fotografie e cimeli ed un ciclo di manifestazioni sugli aspetti storici, giuridici e sociali della guerra fra l'Unione e la Confederazione, lunedì 12, alle ore 18, all'USIS, avrà luogo un dibattito sul tema: «La Guerra Civile Americana ed i diritti civili». Vi partecipano il prof. Paolo Tesauro,

ordinario di diritto pubblico americano all'Università di Napoli ed il prof. Henry Paolucci, ordinario di scienze politiche all'Università di St. John, New York.

Il programma delle manifestazioni proseguirà martedì 13, alle 18 ed alle 19, con la proiezione del film «Il ruolo della Marina nella Guerra Civile Americana» e si concluderà venerdì 16 con una tavola rotonda su «Il ruolo della stampa negli ultimi 100 anni: l'influenza dei corrispondenti di guerra». La mostra invece, che può essere visitata tutti i giorni tranne la domenica dalle ore 9 alle 20, rimarrà aperta fino al 20 giugno.

CORRIERE DI NAPOLI

Sabato 10 - Domenica 11 Giugno 1967

Dibattito all'USIS sui diritti civili

Nel quadro della serie di iniziative dedicate alla rassegna storica del periodo della Guerra Civile Americana 1861-1865, che comprende — come è noto — una piccola mostra di fotografie e cimeli ed un ciclo di manifestazioni sugli aspetti storici, giuridici e sociali della guerra fra l'Unione e la Confederazione, lunedì 12 giugno, alle ore 16, all'USIS, avrà luogo un dibattito sul tema «La guerra civile americana ed i diritti civili». Vi partecipano il prof. Paolo Tesauro, Ordinario di Diritto Pubblico americano all'Università di Napoli ed il prof. Henry Paolucci, Ordinario di Scienze Po-

litiche all'Università di St. John, New York.

Il programma delle manifestazioni proseguirà martedì 13, alle 18 ed alle 19, con la proiezione del film «Il ruolo della Marina nella guerra civile americana» e si concluderà venerdì 16 con una tavola rotonda su «Il ruolo della Stampa negli ultimi 100 anni: l'influenza dei corrispondenti di guerra». La mostra invece, che può essere visitata tutti i giorni eccetto la domenica dalle ore 9 alle 20, rimarrà aperta fino al 20 giugno.

4. AN OFFER YOU CAN'T REFUSE

"l'ubidir, se già fosse, m' è tardi. . . . ."

While I was in Naples, Henry visited several times. Mom had left at the end of 1965, and Henry had arrived before Christmas to spend the one-month "break" with me. When we learned that my Fulbright grant would be renewed for a second year, he did not visit for the Summer in 1966 but surprised me by coming for what I thought was the Christmas break. As it turned out, he'd resigned from the English Department of Iona College, and part-time teaching assignments in Roman history at City College and Brooklyn College, in order to accept a full-time position in the Political Science Department of St. John's University, in Queens. The new job would start in the Fall of 1967; until then he was a free agent. He flew to Naples and remained for the next nine months, until my assignment was over. I was happy to have him with me and more than pleased to find that Ed Bator found in him a kindred soul. Ed soon arranged for Henry to give a number of public lectures on current American affairs.

HENRY (RIGHT) WITH ED BATOR

We all had a great time. In August, we sailed home, in time for me to resume my teaching at City College and for Henry to start his new job at St. John's, where he was welcomed warmly. No one objected when he proposed that they rename the Department "Government and Politics." His reasoning was that both their Department and the St. John's Law School (where a good number of the Department graduates went on to get their Law degree) had and still produced a large number of high-ranking city and state officials. The new name would focus interest on the Department in a special way.

RETURNING HOME ON THE "INDEPENDENCE" (AUGUST, 1967)

In the course of his long teaching career in that Department (he retired in 1991), Henry designed elective and graduate courses on Hegel's philosophy of history, on Greek and Roman political structures, and — his favorite subject — American foreign policy. In the sixties, he launched a non-profit independent organization, The Walter Bagehot Research Council on National Sovereignty, named after the famous English economist and man of letters, Walter Bagehot, editor of the *Economist* and author of *Lombard Street*, who lived in the latter part of the nineteenth century. For almost four decades, Henry planned meetings sponsored by the Bagehot Council at the annual convention of The American Political Science Association (APSA), where colleagues took part in panels and programs covering all aspects of American politics, especially foreign policy. He was an unrelenting critic of Henry Kissinger, whom he believed had deceived the President he worked for and the American people by posing superficially and ambiguously as a hawk when he was really a dove, bent on stretching out the war in Vietnam at a needless loss of life, until he had achieved détente with Russia. Henry wrote books and articles to make his point, quoting chapter and verse to show that Kissinger, contrary to what he said publicly, had other priorities, not the least of which was to educate Americans to the need for giving up our sovereignty and "live in impotence" as a nation, in order to insure world peace.

My husband also had an active political life and was briefly in the national spotlight. In the late fifties and early sixties, we spent our summers in Saratoga Springs, where we helped friends produce musicals (one a week) at the Spa Summer Theater.

THE HOUSE, AT THE END OF TOWN, IN WHICH WE RENTED AN APARTMENT FOR SEVERAL SUMMERS.
RIGHT NEXT TO US WAS THE ENTRANCE TO SKIDMORE COLLEGE.
(SARATOGA SPRINGS, LATE 50S, EARLY 60S.)

OUR FIRST CAR, A USED BLACK BUICK CONVERTIBLE FOR WHICH WE PAID $150
IN SARATOGA SPRINGS (EARLY 60S).

One day, before leaving for Manhattan for a dental appointment, I suggested to Henry that he get tickets for us to attend the New York State Conservative Party convention. We had joined the new Party at Bill Buckley's invitation, two years earlier, when it was first launched. In 1964, the nominating convention was conveniently being held in Saratoga Springs. When I returned from Manhattan, later that day, I found reporters impatiently waiting to interview me. In my absence, Bill Buckley had nominated Henry for the U.S. Senate!

Scholarly Candidate

Henry Paolucci

THERE may have been at some time a politician with odder qualifications and ideas about campaigning than the Conservative party's candidate for the United States Senate for New York. But diligent research fails to find one who can compare to Henry Paolucci, B.S., M.A., Ph. D., Associate Professor of History and Political Science at Iona College, New Rochelle. Item: He has no illusions about being elected. Item: He intends to kiss no babies, shake no hands, make no stump speeches. Item: His chief interest, aside from politics and teaching, is chamber music.

Item: While running for public office for the first time, and probably continuing his classes at Iona (although he's not sure about that), he may also find time to continue work on a novel and on a play about Galileo that he is writing. He has written the music for a Pirandello play "Liola" that is to be produced by the Spa Music Theater at Saratoga Springs where, during the summer, he is the co-producer.

If all this makes the 43-year-old, second-generation Italian-American sound like an intelligent, likable, scholarly college professor who is enjoyed by his students, then that, old friends say, is exactly what he is.

James D. Brophy, a fellow faculty member at Iona, said he would rate Dr. Paolucci among the more popular professors at the suburban Roman Catholic men's college, among both the students and the faculty.

"I just sent him a telegram saying: 'Congratulations from the first Democrat for Paolucci,'" Mr. Brophy said.

Associated Press Wirephoto

No kisses for babies
(Mr. Paolucci at Convention)

Wife Also a Teacher

Mr. Brophy collaborated with Dr. Paolucci on a book about Galileo two years ago, one of several that Dr. Paolucci has written or translated from Italian either himself or in collaboration with his wife, Anne, a teacher at City College of New York.

Dr. Paolucci was born in New York City on Feb. 4, 1921, and still lives in Manhattan, at 600 West 111th Street. His father was an immigrant cabinet maker.

He was educated in the public schools and at City College, where he took his B.B.S. degree in 1942. On graduation, he joined the Air Force and went to Italy as a bomber navigator. He had completed four combat missions when the war ended.

Dr. Paolucci stayed in Italy as an intelligence officer with an air base guard unit for several months, then returned to New York to enter Columbia under the G. I. education bill.

After taking his master's degree and a doctorate in

English at Columbia, Dr. Paolucci spent two one-year periods of study abroad, first on a Columbia University traveling fellowship and then as a Fulbright scholar. He taught at City College and at Brooklyn College before joining the history and political science faculties at Iona eight years ago. Up until three years ago, he also taught night classes in Greek and Roman history at C.C.N.Y.

Friends say he has a cyclopedic mind and a pleasing style of address. He intends to do most of his campaigning through radio and television, or at large rallies.

Described as Sincere

"He's an excellent speaker," Mr. Brophy said. "I'm looking forward to hearing him expound his philosophies."

Mr. Brophy said Dr. Paolucci was not obtrusive with his political views, nor particularly argumentative.

"There's no question he is sincere about them, though," Mr. Brophy said.

Dr. Paolucci said yesterday at Saratoga Springs at the party convention, that he joined the party three years ago through the urging of a student at City College, Regina Kelly, who works in the conservative party headquarters in New York.

Before accepting the senatorial nomination yesterday, Dr. Paolucci had intended to run for a seat in the House of Representatives from his home 20th District, where the Democratic incumbent is Representative William Fitts Ryan.

What had happened was that Clare Boothe Luce, the playwright and wife of Henry Luce, of *Time Magazine*, etc., had made herself available for the slot, but it turned out that, for some reason, she could not run on the Conservative Party line. Henry, who had written for *National Review* and had had many occasions to share his views with Bill Buckley, was chosen to replace her (while I was at the dentist's, in Manhattan). The nomination of an unknown professor of political science received front-page coverage in all the major newspapers. The *New York Times* featured him as "The Scholarly Candidate" and even carried a review of the play that was still running at the Spa Music Theater, the last offering of the season, an early work of Luigi Pirandello's, called *Liolà,* for which Henry had written the musical score. The production was a "first," an unusual offering, especially for that part of the world; but Ray Rizzo, the theater's producer and a good friend, appreciated

Pirandello as much as we did and was more than pleased to put on Eric Bentley's translation of the play, with Henry's music. In one of his interviews, on the day he was nominated, Henry made clear that he would not start campaigning until the Spa Summer Theater production of *Liolà* ended. The *New York Times* carried that as a separate story, with a review of the play, and the phrase Henry quoted from Aristotle — "music tunes the heart" — as the "quotation of the day."

NEW YORK TIMES, SEPTEMBER 9, 1964

HENRY AT THE PIANO. ON THE WALL: DONATO PAOLUCCI'S OIL PAINTING OF LOW LIBRARY (COLUMBIA UNIVERSITY)

PLAY WITH MUSIC BY PAOLUCCI OPENS

Conservative Candidate for Senator Puts Off Politics

By THEODORE STRONGIN
Special to The New York Times

SARATOGA SPRINGS, N. Y., Sept. 8 —Henry Paolucci, Conservative candidate for the United States Senate from New York, threw his hat into another ring tonight. "Liolà," a play by Pirandello, was given its first American performance at the Spa Music Theater here with incidental music written by Mr. Paolucci.

"Liolà" may be headed soon for an off Broadway production, says Raymond Rizzo, producer of the Spa Theater.

Mr. Paolucci undertook his musical commitment in June at Mr. Rizzo's request. The political commitment came this month. But when he accepted the bid to run against Senator Kenneth B. Keating and Robert F. Kennedy, Mr. Paolucci insisted that his heavy campaigning not begin until after the nightly run of "Liola" ends on Saturday.

To Mr. Paolucci, music and politics belong together. He teaches political science at Iona College in New Rochelle (where Mr. Rizzo teaches speech) and one of his favorite books is Aristotle's "Politics."

Quotation of the Day

"I agree with Aristotle that music is the foundation of a well-ordered life. Music tunes the heart."—Henry Paolucci, Conservative party candidate for the United States Senate from New York. [40:4.]

Agrees With Aristotle

"The whole last part is devoted to music," he said today in an interview. "I agree with Aristotle that music is the foundation of a well-ordered life. Music tunes the heart.'

It can put the heart out of tune, too. Mr. Paolucci believes. He went on: "I see in the civil disorders of our great cities a kind of fulfillment of the incitement of the immoral songs marketed by high-pressure methods to our teen-agers.

"What the kindly teacher says to children in the sheltered schoolroom is nothing when compared with the power of suggested words and rhythm constantly pounded into the ear of children through screeching transistor radios, record players and TV sets."

Mr. Paolucci would like to end what he called "the monopoly of monsters who aim everything at teen-agers."

While he is not entirely opposed to Government support of the arts, he views President Johnson's activities in the field with suspicion. "Johnson is not a sophisticated patron of the arts," he said. He added however, that culture as a cause "is far above the buying of popular votes."

He has supplied "Liola" with sentimental and serviceable background music that is simple with a tang of Sicilian folk music. It was played on a piano tonight, but if it reaches New York, it will be heard on mandolin, guitar, concertina and a zampagna, an Italian form of bagpipe.

Mr. Paolucci's father played the mandolin and violin, and his wife plays the cello. He started writing music at the age of 17—"strictly imitations of Chopin."

Since then he has set words to music in both classical and popular style. Jimmy Durante is interested in a "Christmas Song" Mr. Paolucci wrote, and will sing it if it is published, the candidate said.

But win or lose in November, Mr. Paolucci will go on with his music. "Music is to me," he said, "what touch football is to the candidate from Massachusetts. It is an exercise and a relief."

During the campaign for the U.S. Senate seat, Henry drew the attention of the media in a special way. He was witty and articulate, well-informed on all issues, especially sharp on foreign policy. He was a guest on all the major talk shows and made quite an impression. One afternoon, as we were entering our building at 111th Street, just off Broadway, another tenant was leaving. He went through the revolving doors then came back inside to stop us and ask my husband: "Are you Henry Paolucci?" When my husband replied that he was, the gentleman — who introduced himself as a producer for one of the major TV networks — replied: "I don't agree with you, but I wish we had more like you on our side!"

There were no illusions about winning the senate seat; Robert Kennedy was obviously a formidable opponent. But Henry's handling of the campaign brought the Party into prominence in New York State. In the next major election. James Buckley, Bill's brother, ran for the U.S. Senate exclusively on the Conservative Party line and won. Henry prepared the way for that.

He continued as Vice-Chairman of the Party, until his death on January 1, 1999, avoiding a more public role but always available to those who sought him out. He was instrumental in getting John Marchi to step into the limelight and run for the New York State Senate and helped New York State Senators Serphin R. Maltese and Frank Padavan to get started (currently the three senior members of the New York State Senate). He worked closely with Mike Long, who became the Party's State Chairman (and still serves as such). An astute and honest critic of the political scene, he earned the respect of all who knew him and was often referred to as the "conscience of the Party."

He never sought attention or recognition, not even when it came to getting his articles and books published. Others initiated exchanges that resulted in book contracts. Editors approached him for articles. He himself never touted his credentials or his special gifts to promote himself. The idea for his first major political study, *War, Peace, and the Presidency*, was suggested to

---

THE NEW YORK TIMES, MONDAY, OCTOBER

Two Conservatives Bitterly Attack G.O.P. Rival

Paolucci Calls for Boycott of Keating as 'Turncoat'

O'Doherty Includes Lindsa in 'Band of Renegades'

Associated Press

Henry Paolucci

Two Conservative candidates made bitter attacks yesterday on their Republican rivals, Senator Kenneth B. Keating and Representative John V. Lindsay.

Henry Paolucci, an associate professor of history and political science at Iona College, New Rochelle, who is running as a Conservative for the Senate, denounced Mr. Keating as a "trojan horse" and a "turncoat." He argued that voters should boycott the Senate contest rather than vote for the Republican candidate.

Kieran O'Doherty, Conservative opponent of Representative Lindsay in the 17th Congressional District, accused the Congressman of being a member of a "small band of renegades" who continually cross party lines to support the Johnson Administration's legislative program.

Dr. Paolucci was interviewed on WABC-TV's "Page One" program and on WINS radio. Mr. Keating was not present. Mr. O'Doherty made his attack on answering questions on WNBC-TV's "Direct Line" program, in the presence of Mr. Lindsay and his Democratic opponent in Manhattan's so-called Silk Stocking District, Mrs. Eleanor Clark French.

Representative Lindsay re-plied that Mr. O'Doherty was out to destroy the Republican party. Declaring that he acted "independently" when the good of the country or his district demanded it, Mr. Lindsay said he had voted according to principle and had never put party regularity above principle.

Mrs. French supported Mr. O'Doherty's view. Senator Barry Goldwater, the Republican party's Presidential nominee, is the issue, she declared, adding that if Mr. Lindsay could not support

Senator Goldwater he ought get out of the Republic party.

Dr. Paolucci denied that h nomination was a "Stop Keating" move. "Oh, not a bit," h said.

"It's a move," he said, " get for the Goldwater-Mill national ticket as many vot as possible in this state." F said he hoped to attract to t Goldwater-Miller ticket "at lea 100,000 votes that would n otherwise be drawn to that tic et and could well make the di ference for Goldwater-Miller carrying the state or losing it

Dr. Paolucci said the Conse vative aim was to get in Ne York "a conservative Repub can party."

"We work at it two way Goldwater on the national lev calling for unity, and we in th local level reminding this par which has submitted to liber domination that it ought not do that," he declared.

The college teacher said th in recent issues the overwhelr ing majority of the Republica in the Senate voted with Sen tor Goldwater but Senato Keating, Jacob K. Javits a three others voted against ther He did not name the other

"I think it's clear that the people are the ones who a preventing us from having distinct choice nationally," asserted. "That's my objective

someone at McGraw Hill Book Company by a friend and Columbia neighbor, Robert A. Rosenbaum. The book is still considered one of the most penetrating analyses on the subject, still dramatically relevant today; and still used as a textbook in a number of colleges. Even his position at St. John's was the result of a young colleague's efforts. He never vied for special privileges, never sought to head the Department (although urged to do so several times). He was there for anyone who needed him and ready to help in whatever way he could, but always quietly, behind the scenes.

Keating Camp Sees Union Rift Over RFK

DAILY NEWS, MONDAY, SEPTEMBER 7, 1964 • C8

(NEWS foto by Tom Baffer)
Conservative candidate for Senate Henry Paolucci goes over notes with wife, Anne, before television interview.

Even the Bagehot Council programs at APSA were initiated by others. I, for one, had realized early on that this peculiar attitude of his would work against him, if colleagues (myself included) did not help out. I never resented the time or effort that went into getting him the visibility he richly deserved. He had always supported my activities; I was more than happy to do something for him, if I could. In time, I automatically took on most of the preliminary arrangements for APSA meetings, suggested or backed new ideas as he came up with them, encouraged him when, in 1969, he launched *State of the Nation*, a political newsletter, and helped prepare copy for the printer every month. I didn't mind giving him the kind of nudge he needed; besides, I had learned a great deal from him about sharing, never turning anyone away who asked for advice or help. I also had learned that interrupting one's own work to give someone else a helping hand could be a distinct advantage; in my case, I absorbed a great deal about the strategies of political debating as well as the substance of many important arguments. I eased his chores so he could do what he did best as an orator, debater, and especially as a writer. At this time, he was writing for *National Review*, *Il Borghese* (in Italy), and other journals and periodicals, and contributing Op Ed articles to *New York Times*.

OP ED ARTICLES IN THE *NEW YORK TIMES*

Acheson Remembered

By HENRY PAOLUCCI

The New York Times

NEW YORK, THURSDAY, OCTOBER 12, 1972

Tragic nemesis is apparently catching up with Richard M. Nixon. He is being forced, as President, to pursue the same temptations of naive statesmanship that once led Alger Hiss, on a much lower level, to collaborate secretly with Communist officials and to lie about it when caught.

In 1950, Dean Acheson had to decide with great public embarrassment how to treat a friend charged with espionage and convicted of perjury. Now it is the turn of some of Mr. Nixon's supporters to be similarly embarrassed. The editors of National Review, for instance, have already followed Acheson's example to the point of refusing to turn their backs on their friend in the White House, even though he is charged in their own pages with having compromised the nation's safety.

Apart from his crimes, Alger Hiss was, after all, essentially an Ivy-League New Dealer who professed to believe in the late forties what Mr. Nixon (belatedly tutored by Harvard's Henry Kissinger) professes to believe in the early seventies. The Hiss view back then—which is now the Nixon Doctrine—was that America shouldn't try to be an armed custodian of the world's freedom, that it should instead pursue peace as an end in itself, and that collaboration with Communist regimes, rather than anti-Communist militancy, is the only risk-free way for Americans to pursue peace in the atomic era.

That was, of course, the pre-Truman legacy of World War II. Winston Churchill had rejected it with his Iron Curtain speech of 1946. President Truman's rejection followed in 1947. The occasion had been the crises of Greece and Turkey, where the British acknowledged that they could no longer afford to guarantee the independence of small nations threatened by the expansive might of world Communism. Guided by Dean Acheson, Mr. Truman took up the challenge.

When first announced, the Acheson policy aroused a storm of protests from the left. Walter Lippmann led the attack. The policy would oblige us, he complained, to play policeman and, worse, involve us in the "repression of legitimate nationalistic or revolutionary movements."

But there were attacks also from the right, and, before long, Mr. Nixon was leading them. As General Eisenhower's running mate in 1952, he ranted fiercely against what he called "Dean Acheson's College of Cowardly Communist Containment." Mere containment was not enough for that old Nixon. He talked of freeing captive nations and, occasionally, of rooting out Communist imperialism in its Peking and Moscow capitals as well.

Now, twenty years later, the tables are turned. The leftist critics of the Acheson-Truman doctrine are having their way, and Mr. Nixon, having suffered a sea-change, has been the means. Is there not a sense of tragic nemesis in this turn-about? As Walter Lippmann said when Henry Kissinger's secret mission to Peking was first disclosed, "only Nixon, among the available public men, could have made such a reversal . . . because he had been such a violent and unscrupulous anti-Communist."

For Dean Acheson, the new Nixon Doctrine was the same old pre-Truman doctrine he had rejected as Secretary of State. It was wrong then; it was doubly wrong now.

Henry Paolucci is professor of political science at St. John's University and vice chairman of the New York State Conservative party.

The New York Times

THE NEW YORK TIMES, SUNDAY, SEPTEMBER 30, 1973

The Shabbiness of It All

By Henry Paolucci

Mr. Nixon cannot serve as a valid test of ultimate Presidential prerogatives. In his heart, as in his peace and disarmament deals, he has long since abandoned the source of his prerogatives, which is the principle that the nation's safety is its highest law. He survives now only as a crippled captive of his old enemies.

On the back wall of the Lincoln Memorial in Washington, we read these words inscribed in stone: "In this temple, as in the hearts of the people for whom he saved the Union, the memory of Abraham Lincoln is enshrined forever."

Lincoln's temple is the crown of a mighty cross in our nation's capital—a cross that has Capitol Hill at its base and the White House and Jefferson Memorial at the ends of its cross beam. Washington's Monument, rising near the point where the long and short beams intersect, is like a spear in the side of an invisible savior of our body politic, for whose ultimate agony Lincoln Memorial, with all its solemn words, will one day serve as a fitting crown of glory.

Washington, Jefferson, Lincoln — each of them confirmed in word and deed that profoundest truth of our Western political tradition, which is that coercive government is at best a necessary evil, and that when free men deny either its evil or its necessity they must soon cease to be free.

The Watergate affair recalls our attention to that painful truth, but unfortunately with misplaced emphasis and miscast spokesmen. Surly John Mitchell, to the delight of the Ervins and Weickers, has put the brand of "White House horrors" on what officious John Ehrlichman has professed to defend as Presidential prerogatives in national security affairs.

Hoping to save himself with his old boss, Mr. Ehrlichman has made a cynically ruthless appeal to the old principle of *raison d'état*: a principle of statecraft that Winston Churchill summed up accurately when, to justify the Anglo-Soviet alliance against Hitler, he snarled: "Madam, I would make a friend of the devil himself if it would save England."

But the principle of *raison d'état* is ill applied in Mr. Nixon's case. Guided by Henry Kissinger, our President has committed his Administration to pursue peace as an end in itself, thereby invalidating the traditional grounds on which Presidential prerogatives ultimately rest.

What about the Nixon Administration's prosecution of Daniel Ellsberg? Was it a "national security" prosecution in the traditional sense? Senator Sam Ervin, a stanch defender of our nation's sovereignty against the supranational pretensions of the so-called Genocide Convention, correctly rejects the Ehrlichman-Haldeman-Nixon claim that it was. Ellsberg was charged, he notes, not with giving treacherous aid and comfort to Communist powers but merely with "stealing some papers that belonged to the Government."

On this same point, Presidential spokesman John T. Lofton has tried to set the record straight, arguing in the August issue of First Monday that Mr. Nixon had little motive for political vindictiveness against Ellsberg, "since the Kennedy and Johnson Administrations were hurt by the disclosures." Revealing that President Kennedy, hardly less than Lyndon Johnson, had been tempted to try to win a military victory in Vietnam, the stolen papers validated, in effect, President Nixon's claim that he, rather than Kennedy, deserves to be honored by the liberal establishment's conscience élite as the first American President of the Atomic Age to be thoroughly committed to peace.

But why then did so many presumably anti-Nixon liberal academicians and journalists collaborate to get the pro-Nixon Pentagon Papers published? Mr. Lofton's explanation reads: "It is evident that the liberal media had, by 1971, written off the Kennedy-Johnson Vietnam policy as a disaster. If, in order to save high-priority liberal fantasies about Vietnam, they had to destroy some liberal myths about Kennedy and Johnson, the liberal media were ready." And that statement helps to explain also why the cases against The Times and Ellsberg were so ineptly argued. The Nixon Administration was not about to go to court to injure itself!

Where does Mr. Nixon really stand on the question of ultimate Presidential prerogatives? Is he prepared to defend even so shabby a version of *raison d'état* as Mr. Ehrlichman has advanced? Hardly. With Watergate, as with Kissinger's peace strategy and Moynihan's welfare reforms, the President apparently intends to pursue a Disraelian course, hoping to "dish" his opposition by claiming its positions as his own.

Emerson must have had a prescient vision of the post-Watergate, crippled Nixon Presidency in mind when he wrote in "Compensation": "The President has paid dear for his White House. . . . To preserve for a short time so conspicuous an appearance before the world, he is content to eat dust before the real powers behind the throne."

Henry Paolucci is professor of government and politics at St. John's University and vice chairman of the New York State Conservative party.

The New York Times

FRIDAY, JUNE 30, 1972

The Thin Line: Settlement or Surrender

By HENRY PAOLUCCI

How far to the left has President Nixon moved in his quest for "peace" in Vietnam? He has himself said that if he took a single step further to the left, he would be in the camp of the enemy whose combat-fire has already killed over 45,000 American soldiers.

President Nixon is deluded if he thinks history will not charge him with having lost a war and humiliating this nation in the eyes of the world. His latest peace plan closely parallels the peace plan offered to the Allied powers by Italy's little King in 1943, after he broke with Mussolini. The Italian King offered to give the Allies all they wanted compatible with "Italian honor." But the Allies insisted on unconditional surrender; they insisted that, in addition to giving up, the King would have to declare war on his German allies. To her disgrace, petty-monarchic Italy did just that.

How close to being America's little leftist monarch has Nixon become? Characterizing his latest "peace" offer, the President has said: "The only thing this plan does not do is join the enemy to overthrow our ally, which the United States of America will never do. If the enemy wants peace, it will have to recognize the important difference between settlement and surrender."

The fine professional hand of Henry Kissinger is discernible in that distinction between settlement and surrender. Surrender, here, obviously means "unconditional surrender," while settlement is used as a euphemism for "conditional surrender."

In his first "on the record" news conference, Secret Agent Henry Kissinger explained why the Nixon Administration refused to submit to the nine-point North Vietnamese peace plan of June 26, 1971. "One of the nine points," he said, "is a demand for

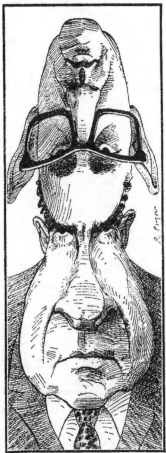

Robert Pryor

reparations. We told them that while we would not include reparations as part of a settlement, we would give a voluntary massive reconstruction pro-

gram for all of Indochina in which North Vietnam could share to the extent of several billion dollars." In other words, the Nixon Administration is prepared to pay reparations, like a defeated country, provided they are not called reparations and included as such in the "settlement."

Kissinger defined the limits of America's willingness to surrender (just short of unconditionally) in the following terms: "They are asking us to align ourselves with them, to overthrow the people that have been counting on us in South Vietnam. They are asking us to accomplish [their ends] for them. If we will not do it for them, then the longer the war continues the worse that situation gets which they are trying to avoid, and they may settle for a political process which gives them less than 100 per cent guarantee but a fair crack at the political issue."

In other words, short of unconditional American surrender, the North Vietnamese Communists cannot hope to get more for themselves than the Nixon peace plan offers. We repeat: a single step to the left of where Nixon stands today would take him, like the little King of Italy in 1943, into the camp of the enemy as a cobelligerent.

How low have the mighty fallen! Nixon has had a Metternichian adviser constantly at his ear. He has therefore been reduced to thinking and acting like the head of a third-rate power—like a 19th-century Austrian "emperor" —trying to eke out an existence in the crevices of *realpolitik*. Or, as the tough-minded French critic André Malraux recently summed it up: "President Nixon maneuvers as if he were the President of Luxembourg."

Henry Paolucci is professor of political science at St. John's University and vice chairman of the New York Conservative party.

Much of his political activity, especially his 1964 campaign and his long and active role as Vice Chairman of the Party, is being recalled in a book I'm preparing. In addition, I have reissued many of his political and literary writings and have edited and seen through publication several of his manuscripts. An arrangement with Griffon House Publications (a small mail-order academic press started by Ted Dabrowski in the late 60s, initially as the outlet for Henry's political newsletter *State of the Nation*) has enabled me to carry out a long-term plan to make Henry's written legacy available for years to come. Since Henry's death, about two dozen books authored or edited by him, out of print or hard to come by, have been issued and distributed to a list of selected libraries, here and abroad, free of charge. The first such book is a collection of important essays published originally in a number of journals and magazines. Recently, I also prepared a selection of articles written over the years by him or me (or jointly) for *Review of National Literatures*, a journal I launched in 1970, when I joined St. John's, and continued to edit through 2001, with Henry as its chief researcher and feature writer. This "Bonus Gift Book" project has been expanded to include books by other scholars and colleagues, new titles and reprints which Henry would have wanted to see published. (All this happened after I'd left St. John's and will be described later.)

In the Spring of 1969, two years after Henry joined the faculty of St. John's, I received a call from the President of the University, Father Joseph

Cahill. Could I find time to visit the campus some day, before the end of the semester? He wanted to meet me. I suspected what might be coming: he had approached Henry to ask if I might be interested in a change of venue.

When I drove to the University one morning, President Cahill asked me bluntly if I would accept an offer he was prepared to make. I was to answer directly to him, as part of his Presidential staff. There would be no direct department affiliation. My title (created expressly for me) would be "University Research Professor" — the first such position on campus. I was not expected to teach or to serve on university committees. Besides a substantial raise in salary, I would also be given tenure on appointment.

It was an offer I couldn't refuse, the kind of offer every academic dreams about but rarely receives. There might be better candidates somewhere, I admitted briefly to my stunned conscience — in fact I was sure there were — but who was I to question fate for having dropped this good fortune in my lap instead of somebody else's? I accepted on the spot.

Of course, I knew that what had singled me out and brought me a measure of academic recognition (as well as a tailor-made new job), were the kind of credentials the University needed to chalk up for itself, especially in the light of upcoming accreditation visits by New York State agencies. I would have been surprised if that had not been a factor in President Cahill's decision.

My colleagues at City thought I had gone a little bit crazy when I announced, in April, that I would be leaving the Department where my name had already been submitted for promotion to the rank of Associate Professor, with a hefty increase in salary. Besides, I suspect that most of my colleagues, including the Chairman, couldn't bring themselves to believe that everything I reported to them about Cahill's offer was true. On the other hand, we all knew that the president of a college or university could do just about anything he or she wanted, so long as the decision did not require approval from below. Cahill had skillfully skirted around the difficulties by making me a member of his staff, with no department affiliation. I could ignore the complaints (and, I was soon to discover, the resentments) of many faculty members.

Ed Volpe, my Chairman at City College, was especially vocal in warning me against rash decisions. In the end, however, he had to admit that it was an unusual opportunity. (He himself left, not long after, to assume the Presidency of Staten Island College, one of the larger and older units of the growing complex of 2- and 4-year colleges within the City University of New York [CUNY].)

At St. John's I had my own private office, a secretary, and an assistant, all made accessible to me so that I could implement my personal projects, especially my writing. I was grateful for these "perks" (who wouldn't be?); but even as I prepared to implement my own agenda, I felt a strong need for doing something special for St. John's. After discussing with Henry what I might initiate to give the University a truly dramatic academic push into the limelight, we decided on a journal, one that was different from all other academic journals around at the time. Following the mandate on campuses and in private industry for greater global awareness, we decided on a publication that would feature literatures outside the traditional canon of Western literatures. We named the new journal *Review of National Literatures*. It was a bold idea; even the use of the plural, "literatures," was new at the time and brought some criticism.

Henry's common sense quickly asserted itself. He suggested I start with volumes that we could control, subjects we knew pretty well, so that together we could plan and see those volumes through on our own, if necessary, tap experts we knew and could count on for the articles needed. Our plan would give us time to find special editors for future volumes. It was a good idea. More important: it worked. We had decided that the series should also include European authors and literatures, but always from a fresh and unusual point of view. With that in mind, I proposed that we focus in the first volume on Machiavelli, the father of *realpolitik*, who although a perennial offering in most history departments is more often than not undermined and misunderstood. And so, using the occasion of the 500th anniversary of his birth, I planned and hosted, in the Fall of 1969, as my first major project at St. John's, a conference commemorating that anniversary. I invited several well-known Machiavellian scholars to present papers that would later be printed as the first volume of the new series, under the title of *Machiavelli '500*. These included Leo Strauss ("Machiavelli and Classical Literature"), Joseph Mazzeo of Columbia ("The Poetry of Power: Machiavelli's Literary Vision"), John C. H. Wu ("Machiavelli and the Legalists of Ancient China"), Gian Roberto Sarolli ("The Unpublished Machiavelli"), and Giuseppe Prezzolini, perhaps the most eminent Machiavelli scholar of the century ("The Christian Roots of Machiavelli's Moral Pessimism"). These conference speakers had been carefully chosen to provide the kind of spectrum we wanted, a solid assessment of the great Renaissance writer quite different from the popular controversial image that prevailed.

The conference was not only a success; it also served as a model for subsequent *RNL* issues. *Machiavelli '500* confirmed me in the need for carefully planned volumes, not an aggregate of papers, as is the case with most academic journals. Because each issue reflected a "special" approach (even those dealing with European literatures and traditional themes), *RNL* could have no backlog. Every volume was in effect a book, each one with its special priorities. I soon discovered that my major task as general editor of the series was to maintain that focus. The journal was in every way *sui generis*.

From the outset, I supervised every phase of the operation; I even designed the cover for the first issue, using a typewriter to get the effect I wanted. By the time I got around to the second issue, I had taken the advice of a friend and commissioned a professional designer to work out my idea into a more sophisticated format. It cost $500 (a lot of money in those days), but I quickly admitted that it was money well spent. I used the same cover design for all subsequent *RNL* volumes, changing only the combination of colors each time. The very next issue carried the new cover, in which the artist had picked up my idea of displaying the names of as many countries as possible and had arranged them in an attractive pattern that not only became our permanent *RNL* cover but, in 1976, also was introduced as the logo for Council of National

Literatures, the independent non-profit organization I set up to carry *RNL* and other publications and activities, when the operation became independent.

Hegel in Comparative Literature — the second volume issued in 1970 — was a subject in which I felt confident and for which, in a pinch, I could help recruit contributors. The Special Editor was a young disciple of my husband's, a committed Hegelian named Frederick G. Weiss. Henry is represented in that volume with a major article, "The Poetics of Aristotle and Hegel," the first of his many contributions to *RNL.* By the end of my first year at St. John's, I felt I'd accomplished one of my major goals: I'd given the University an unusual publication, one that was already drawing attention, here and abroad.

FIRST *RNL* COVER

PROFESSIONAL COVER DESIGN

The latest issue of the *Review of National Literatures* is devoted to Norway. Under the direction of special editor (and longtime *WLT* reviewer) Sverre Lyngstad, the issue's contributors examine such topics as "Norwegian Literature in the Scandinavian Spectrum," "The New Norse Literary Tradition," "The Female Voice in Norwegian Literature," "Norwegian Literature between the Wars" and "New Directions in Norwegian Literature," all tied together by Lyngstad's own lengthy introductory overview. *NRL* editor Anne Paolucci is represented with the essay "Norway's Literary Languages: English Contrasts and Greek Parallels." Subscription and purchase only via membership in the Council on National Literatures; dues $35 per year in the U.S. $45 elsewhere. CNL / P.O. Box 81 / Whitestone, NY 11357.

Of course, the real test was yet to come. How would I fare with the literatures of emergent and neglected literatures, those outside the traditional canon or academic mainstream of comparative literary studies? Would I be able to find top scholars who wrote well in English to produce the eight to ten articles needed, and locate — for each issue — a Special Editor who could help design and implement such an issue, preferably someone who knew the language or languages involved, even though I had made a firm decision that articles should be written only in English? (I had no intention of adding to the many already existing difficulties those inherent in any effort at translation.)

The Hegel issue was followed by the first volume on a literature not in the traditional mainstream: *Iran.* Here too, however, I had made sure that I had within reach someone who knew the literature and the land: in this case, Javad Haidari, who had come from Iran over two decades earlier to study at Columbia and had eventually settled in Washington D.C., working for The Voice of America.

These first three issues insured the continuity needed to establish a new journal and gave me the time I needed to plan later volumes. The search for experts became my most important and pressing concern. Reviewing those years, I am sometimes surprised at the good fortune I encountered in locating well-known scholars as special editors and contributors, and never having to pay for the articles we commissioned.

The volumes that followed the first three already mentioned were:
Black Africa (Albert Gérard, University of Liège, Sp. Editor);
Turkey: From Empire to Nation (Talat S. Halman of Princeton, Sp. Ed.);
The Multinational Literature of Yugoslavia (Albert B. Lord of Harvard, Sp. Ed.);
Greece: the Modern Voice (Peter A. Mackridge, Sp. Ed.);
China's Literary Image (Paul K. T. Sih, Sp. Ed.);
Canada (Richard J. Schoeck, Sp. Ed.);
Holland (Frank J. Warnke, Sp. Ed.);
India (Ronald Warwick, Sp. Ed.);
Australia (L. A. C. Dobrez, Sp. Ed.);
Norway (Sverre Lyngstad, Sp. Ed.);
Armenia (Vahe Oshagan, Sp. Ed.);
Hungarian Literature (Enikö Molnár Basa, Sp. Ed.);
Japan: A Literary Overview (John K. Gillespie, Sp. Ed.).

Surprisingly, the volumes on the familiar European literatures and authors proved just as interesting — especially the ones on the age of discovery and early America, which have preserved important materials for the archives. These include:
Russia: The Spirit of Nationalism (Charles A. Moser, Sp. Ed.);
Shakespeare and England (James G. McManaway, Sp. Ed.);
The France of Claudel (Henry Peyre, Sp. Ed.);
German Expressionism (Victor Lange, Sp. Ed.);

Comparative Literary Theory: New Perspectives (Anne Paolucci, Sp. Ed.);
Pirandello (Anne Paolucci, Sp. Ed.);
Columbus, America, and the World (Anne Paolucci/Henry Paolucci, Sp. Eds.);
Native American Antiquities and Linguistics (Anne Paolucci/Henry Paolucci, Sp. Eds.);
Cultures of the Aztecs, Mayas, and Incas (Anne Paolucci/Henry Paolucci, Sp. Eds.);
Spanish, French, and English Relations with Native Americans (Anne Paolucci/Henry Paolucci, Sp. Eds.);
Italy: Fiction, Theater, Poetry, Film Since 1950 (Robert S, Dombroski, Sp. Ed.);
*Romanticism in its Modern Aspects and Early Discussions on Expanding Comparative Literary Studies (Virgil Nemoiani, Sp. Ed.) and;
*Literature as a Unifying Cultural Force and Comparative Studies and Non-Western Literatures: a Retrospective (Anne Paolucci, Sp. Ed.).

RNL was a semi-annual until 1975, when St. John's, like so many other universities, was forced to economize. One of the things that had to be sacrificed was *RNL*. I knew the forces at work were beyond our control, but at the same time I didn't want to abandon the series — too much hard work had gone into·it . . . but could I carry it by myself? Membership fees established at the outset, to encourage subscribers (mostly libraries), were modest. Without major changes, *RNL* could not survive.

After brooding a while, I told my secretary to hold the renewal checks that were coming in. I needed time to weigh very carefully what had to be done to continue the series as an independent operation. Until all the details were clear in my mind, I wouldn't take action.

It took me almost a month to work out the new arrangements — discontinuing *RNL* had been a fleeting thought only, discarded almost immediately. I finally worked things out so that the series could continue, but with some inevitable and vital changes.

I dictated a form letter that was sent out to all member libraries, here and abroad, announcing "exciting news." I informed our subscribers that a non-profit organization, Council on National Literatures (CNL), had been formed as the independent parent group for *RNL* and its new companion publication *CNL/World Report*. This last, begun as an occasional newsletter, had become a small quarterly pamphlet, *CNL Quarterly Report*, then a semi-annual, *CNL Report*, and in 1985 emerged as the annual *CNL/World Report*. It provided what I still believe to be a much-needed forum for the ongoing dialogue among comparatists about the future of the profession.

As I had done with the Pirandello Society of America, I quickly asked for and soon received from the Modern Language Association "Affiliated Association" status for the new organization. This enabled CNL (like PSA) to claim two sessions at every MLA convention — annual meetings that drew thousands of college and university professors, as well as graduate students and provided us with a potential audience (even if small) for our meetings.

I planned our panels (as I had our PSA/MLA panels) as potential sources for material that could eventually be published. The strategy worked: speakers soon learned that they were expected to provide longer versions of their presentations for possible inclusion in *CNL/WR.*

CNL/WR was published, without interruption, from 1985 to 2001 (the last two issues were combined with the last two *RNLs* (marked with an asterisk [*] in the list of titles given earlier). The first two issues — *Problems in National Literary Identity and the Writer as Social Critic* and *New Literary Continents* — were the result of joint meetings with Columbia University's School of International Affairs. Other issues were:

What Price Glory — in Translation?
Comparative Literature and International Studies.
Selected Papers on Columbus and His Time.
The Doctor of Arts Degree: Re-assessing Teaching and Research Priorities.
Modern Views on Columbus and His Time.
Multicultural Perspectives: New Approaches.
Toward the 21st Century: New Directions.
Latin America and its Literature.

In issuing the new announcement about the future of *RNL*, back in 1975, I minimized the fact that new membership-subscriber fees had to be dramatically raised (a crucial decision that might have brought on financial disaster) and that instead of two volumes a year (which we had managed to put out from 1970 up to 1974), there would now be only one. On the plus side: the notices and reviews we had been getting throughout the world made what one colleague had called "a pioneer effort" worth continuing. It was a risk, of course; taking on a major independent publishing venture; on the other hand, our new subscription fees were not too far off from what other academic journals were charging. In any case, I thought *RNL* deserved the chance.

Once the decision had been made to carry on independently, there was no time to worry or look back. The series had to continue without an obvious break in continuity, if at all possible. I focused on refining the preparation for the volumes, especially those on emergent and neglected literatures. By now, I knew what had to be asked as a new volume was taken on. I had made a list of questions to be shared with every special editor working with me. The early years of *RNL* had convinced me that a major "history" of a literature not well known or not in the traditional canon was essential and basic. We tried for one, whenever possible. Questions were designed to bring out the characteristics of a particular literature, *e.g.:* What historical forces shaped the literature? What literary genre has prevailed? Who is considered the most characteristic writer? What author or work has gained international attention? What critical reference works exist in English or should be translated into English as a guide for comparatists?

The questions were pretty much the same in each case, but the answers were always different, often surprising and even intriguing at times. Titles often carried the vital message found in our statement of purpose (which appeared on the first page of every *RNL* issue), *viz.:* that literatures develop from a cultural and linguistic base that reflects the many-faceted life and history of a people, their national identity (e.g.: *Russia: The Spirit of Nationalism* [long before international Marxist rule collapsed in that country]; *Shakespeare and England*, etc.). Younger readers may find it hard to believe that until recently, in the light of long-standing internationalist priorities — in and out of the academy — such a view as ours was considered outrageous if not blasphemous. In today's climate of strong ethnicity and national pride, on the other hand, the search for roots and national identity is pretty much a commonplace. Political challenges to national values still exist, but they emerge more as a dilemma than an uncontested priority. In any case: back in the seventies, the response to the series was positive and enlightening, in spite of the internationalist atmosphere that prevailed.

Each volume produced surprises. In planning the Greek issue, the big question was: Where does one start? The Greeks are the direct heirs of a heritage that shaped the Western world. Could one avoid talking about it? We decided we had to, or the past would overwhelm the present. The volume, appropriately, was called *Greece: The Modern Voice*.

A similar problem arose in preparing the issue on Turkey. Should we include the Ottoman Empire out of which modern Turkey emerged? The answer again had to be "No." Whatever was relevant historically could be included in one or more of the articles projected, but the parameters of the volume were clearly defined in the title we gave it: *Turkey: From Empire to*

Nation. We focused on the years following the impact of the "Young Turks," starting around 1950.

Am altogether different problem emerged in preparing the issue on Norway. Sverre Lyngstad — the special editor for that volume — had written to me in Australia, where I happened to be at the time, a 6-page single-space letter in which he described the major forces at work historically (what became a splendid introductory essay) and raised an important question: should we really include Ibsen? He would clearly overwhelm the rest of the volume. I came to the conclusion that, in spite of his world-wide reputation (which could indeed obscure the rest of the volume), or perhaps because of it, Ibsen could not legitimately be ignored and wrote back suggesting an article on the influence of Ibsen on other Norwegian dramatists. This skirted around the difficulty and gave the author of the article a chance to discuss playwrights well known in Norway (and perhaps more characteristic and representative of Norwegian culture) but not familiar to audiences and readers abroad.

In the case of the Yugoslav volume: the first of two invitations by the Ministry of Culture to tour the country in 1974 and talk with their writers and publishers brought a major difficulty to light. Noting what their top authors and academics had to say, as I visited the various regions and national groups, I was soon convinced that although Tito's efficient rule had managed to bring together in a delicate balance those various regions and nationalities into a single south slav nation-state, they were still autonomous and separate in many ways. I had to agree with my hosts that there was no such thing as "Yugoslav literature." I explained, however, that I couldn't possibly consider several *RNL* volumes to make that point. The result was *The Multinational Literature of Yugoslavia.* (Sadly, the point was made in a violent way twenty years later, when those diverse "nationalities" or "literatures" seceded from the slavic union Tito had built.)

The following is the statement of purpose which appeared on the first page of every *RNL* issue:

REVIEW OF NATIONAL LITERATURES *is a forum for scholars and critics concerned with literature as the expression of national character and as the repository of national culture in the most vital and most readily communicable form. The editors recognize the validity of the critical perspective of recent decades when, as a corrective against the excesses of an exclusively national orientation, it has seemed important to emphasize internationalist and even anti-nationalist tendencies in the study of literature. But they also recognize the validity of Professor René Wellek's strictures against deliberate cultivation of an internationalist point of view which has the effect, as he says, of encouraging "an indiscriminate smattering, a vague, sentimental cosmopolitanism" that often mistakes the poverty of national literatures for their wealth.*

Professor Wellek has remarked correctly that in the comparative study of what is sometimes called world literature, it is "the problem of 'nationality' and of the distinct literary process which should be realized as central."

On the assumption so ably expressed by a distinguished statesman of the 20th century that "it should be reactionary to abolish those distinctions of language, literature, and art, which give to the human mind its infinite variety," REVIEW OF NATIONAL LITERATURES *undertakes to encourage a continuing reassessment of the wealth of national literatures — from the earliest to the most recent — as a prerequisite to the understanding and diffusion of "world literature" in its profoundest sense.*

Each issue will focus on a national culture, or, on a representative theme, author, literary movement, or critical tendency, in an effort to provide substantial and concentrated materials for comparative study. To insure competent presentation of highly specialized or novel topics — such as contemporary literary developments in a new or emerging nation — the series editor will, when necessary, enlist the collaboration of "special editors."

The quotation from Abba Eban (a genial addition, which I owe to Henry) bolstered René Wellek's argument — and mine. At a time when efforts to restructure comparative studies were at best arbitrary, at worst confused and misleading, *RNL*'s commitment was clearly spelled out, its goal defined. That commitment and goal remained firm, even when *RNL* became independent and I was forced to trim the operation.

SAMPLE *RNL* REVIEWS

■ THE TIMES OF INDIA, SUNDAY, FEBRUARY 21, 1982

Sunday Review

The Literary Page

Like Dante's eloquent plea for Italian, Mahatma Gandhi's plea for Hindustani should be considered in its historical context.

Do We Need A National Language?

by Vasant A. Shahane

REVIEW of National Literatures is an annual publication of the Council on National Literatures in New York. The Council has already published special numbers on the national literatures of Iran, Black Africa, Turkey, Canada, Yugoslavia, China, Greece and Australia. The 1979 publication is devoted to an elaboration and assessment of the national literatures of India.

Anne Paolucci's introduction to the India volume, "India's Banyan : As Many Trees as Branches", focusses attention on the epiphylic image of the Banyan tree, and the Latin motto *Quot rami tot arbores* of the Royal Asiatic Society of Great Britain (derived from the Asiatic Society founded by Sir William Jones

in 1784) which symbolises the true spirit of Indian literature. While modern culture-vultures call it 'Unity in Diversity', the emphasis in the India volume is on the diversity in unity, which is meaningfully symbolised by the mighty fig-tree.

By far the best and the longest essay in this volume is on "Dante and the 'Quest for Eloquence' in India's vernacular languages" by Anne and Henry Paolucci. They raise a basic question : Does modern India have a national author whose work has given it a national literary expression? Does India have a national language? The case of Sanskrit has been ably examined as an instrument of national renaissance. Like Dante's eloquent plea for Italian, Mahatma Gandhi's plea for Hindustani should be considered in its historical context. The explora-

tion of the Dantean approach to Italian sheds new light on our quest for vernacular languages and, in fact, the 'ground-rules' for the competition for primacy among modern Indian literatures could be derived from Dante's *De Vulgari Eloquentia*. In my view, Anne and Henry Paolucci offer a very original approach to India's vernacular languages and literatures.

William Walsh's perceptive comments on R. K. Narayan and Alistair Niven's "Introduction to Indian Fiction in English" express both sensitivity and judgment, though they seem like old wine in new bottles! K. K. Chatterjee's essay on modernity in Tagore explores a much-debated field with refreshing ideas! The articles on recent Indian literatures, contemporary women's poetry (P. Lal) and Europe's impact on India (P.

S. Guptara) are both informative and analytical. Ronald Warwick and Richard Clark offer extremely valuable comments on the major genres and also a much-needed bibliographical spectrum.

To attempt to sum up the vast treasures of Indian literatures in a single volume of 235 pages is almost like trying to paint the Himalayas on a small postage stamp. However, the effort is admirable specially because it projects a new Dantean perspective on this vast panorama of a rich literary treasure.

REVIEW OF NATIONAL LITERATURES—INDIA: Edited by Anne Paolucci and Ronald Warwick (Griffon House Publications, Whitestone, New York, $14)

The
Modern Language
Review

Review of National Literatures. Volume x: *India*. Edited by ANNE PAOLUCCI and
RONALD WARWICK. New York: Griffin House Publications for the Council on
National Literatures. 1981. 235 pp. $23. (USA), $25. (outside USA).

India is the fourth in the new annual series of the Council on National Literatures'
Reviews. Through this series the Council acts as an inter-cultural agency exploring
the literatures of various countries and languages. In this particular volume the aim
seems to be, on the one hand, to collate information from specialists in comparative
literary studies and, on the other, to introduce general readers to a wealth of Indian
literatures in the regional languages and English. The subjects in this symposium
range from early European influence on Indian literary activities to the present-day
impact of Western ideologies and critical fashions on contemporary Indian writing
in a complex of different languages.

Anne Paolucci, in an extended essay on the development and role especially of
Bengali and Hindi as instruments for the expression of national identity and
sensibility, pays tribute to the notable contribution of Western and Indian scholars
and creative writers. She gives due prominence to Mahatma Gandhi's unsuccessful
championing of Hindustani as the official language because of its widespread nature
and potential for synthesizing Hindi and Urdu. Professor Paolucci draws striking
parallels with the history of the Italian language and the contribution of Dante in
giving it the national stamp through his advocacy of the vernacular and the genius of
his own poetic achievement.

Other Western and Indian scholars deal with fiction and poetry in English,
pointing out various themes and trends in the Indian literatures generally which
have been stimulated by the events associated with partition and independence as
well as the penetration of critical ideas from the West into a literary tradition
dominated by classical Sanskrit poetics and Hindu conservatism. Two writers
selected for individual treatment are R. K. Narayan and Rabindranath Tagore, the
latter reinstated as a national poet in a well-balanced reassessment. A rather brief
review of the work of some Indian women poets writing in English suggests the
dubious advantage of a cultural emancipation no less dubious than statements in
other reviews about the 'progress' towards modernism evident in the treatment of sex
in Indian writing today. There is inevitably some overlapping, especially between
observations on works in English, but this is not to the detriment of the scheme of the
book since it provides some comparisons between the views of different critics.

The crucial point in discussing the composite culture of such a vast country as
India, reflected in its complex of literatures in a variety of languages, is the matter of
language itself. In spite of the illuminating essay by Professor Paolucci, this matter of
the language medium is dealt with only from a Western point of view. How can a
discussion conducted entirely in English give adequate attention to the theme of unity
in diversity? The fifteen major languages of India have all a closer affinity to Sanskrit
than English has. How then can literature in English have a truly Indian character
until it has assimilated something of the classical and folk mythology of the sub-
continent? Indian writing in English generally lacks the metaphoric quality which
derives naturally from vocabulary, if nothing else, in the fifteen regional languages.
The exceptions in English are some of the works of writers like Tagore, Narayan, Raja
Rao, and Desani because these authors, steeped in the philosophy and mythology of
the Sanskrit classics and the folklore of their country, succeed to a greater or lesser
degree in bringing across something of the colour and resonance of the imagery or
merely verbal associations of non-English traditions. This is naturally so with the oral
artists and with a writer like Premchand, who has a ready rapport with his readers not
least because of the linguistic and stylistic qualities of the language he employs, be it
Hindi or Urdu or the combination of both in the Hindustani that Gandhi wished to see
adopted as the national language of India.

Translation or 'transcreation', to borrow a term from the Calcutta Writers
Workshop, should have been given a prominent place in a volume that is ostensibly
transcultural in its aim. There will be no very useful dialogue until a more vigorous
attempt is made to overcome the difficulties of translating from or into the regional
languages as well as to appreciate Indian literatures from both an Indian and a
Western standpoint.

J. A. RAMSARAN

IGHTHAM, KENT

RNL continued to be my personal top priority for the next twenty-five years, just as it had been when under the aegis of St. John's. Looking back, I would say that *RNL* was one of my most significant contributions to the University — and the profession — but I did much else during those years. I was often asked to represent the President at fund-raising events and speak for him. I also prepared special projects and events, such as the three-day production of Goldoni's *La Locandiera* (*Mistress of the Inn*), which was followed by a reception hosted by the Institute of Italian Culture on Park Avenue. Since parking is always a problem in the City and especially in that part of it, I hired buses to bring guests into the City and, later, back to the campus. No one had to drive in on his own. The turnout was impressive, the play (which most of those who attended had never seen or even heard of) was an educational as well as a dramatic success.

A.P., WITH JOSEP[H VALLETTUTI, ACCEPTING A $10,000 DONATION FROM THE FEDERAZIONE ITALO-AMERICANA DI BROOKLYN AND QUEENS, FOR A 3-DAY WEEKEND PRODUCTION OF CARLO GOLDONI'S *LA LOCANDIERA* (*MISTRESS OF THE INN*) AT ST. JOHN'S. (L/R) JOSEPH VALLETTUTI, A.P., RAY RIZZO, WHO DIRECTED THE PRODUCTION. RAY ALSO PRODUCED AND OFTEN DIRECTED MUSICALS AT THE SPA MUSIC THEATER (SARATOGA SPRINGS).

Another production which St. John's helped sponsor some months later was Eric Bentley's translation of Pirandello's *Six Characters in Search of an Author*. The play was shown at Brooklyn College with a reception at the Italian Cultural Institute in New York. By now, Henry and I had come to know Bentley rather well, especially for his interest and continuing work in Italian literature. I was particularly pleased when he asked me to translate for his anthology, *The Genius of the Italian Theater*, Pirandello's insightful essay on the history of the Italian theater. I would never have thought of undertaking the task, except for his request.

RECEPTION AT THE INSTITUTE OF ITALIAN CULTURE, FOLLOWING THE PRODUCTION OF ERIC BENTLEY'S TRANSLATION OF *SIX CHARACTERS IN SEARCH OF AN AUTHOR* (1970) (ERIC BENTLEY, SECOND FROM LEFT; A.P., THIRD FROM LEFT.)

I was often invited to speak at community group meetings as well as other universities. One year, I was invited to give a special graduate course in the Italian Department of Queens College (a short distance away). I could choose my topic. After checking with the President, to make sure there was no conflict of interest, I accepted the one-semester offer as "Distinguished Adjunct Professor" and gave a series of lectures on Dante's *Inferno*, James Thomson's *The City of Dreadful Night*, and T. S. Eliot's *Wasteland*. I enjoyed that course at least as much as the students seemed to enjoy it: I was able to bring together three of my favorite authors and three major works. Most important, it gave me an opportunity to talk about Dante in a contemporary spectrum, making the poem accessible to readers in an immediate and comparative context.

For two Summers I was a guest lecturer at the Oregon Shakespeare Festival. The invitations for the two-week visits came from Homer ("Murph") Swander of the University of California at Santa Barbara, who at the time also headed the Renaissance Institute in Ashland, Oregon. Both times, there was a second guest lecturer — someone who taught theater (I've forgotten the names). Classes were very informal, although students could get credit, if they wished. On both occasions, I suggested to my colleague that we work together. In the morning, I would discuss the plays: the modern or contemporary play being featured in the late afternoon, in one of the lovely indoor theaters, and the Shakespeare production being offered on the outdoor stage in the evening. My colleague would cover the same ground, but from an actor's viewpoint. He'd get the students on their feet, moving about, reciting the lines, so that they heard the words out loud and got to know the text in a more intimate way.

Guests of the Institute were asked at some point during their stay to give a public lecture in the giant auditorium of one of the buildings adjacent to the theater complex. On the day of my lecture, the first summer I was there, I entered the large hall, already filled to capacity, and noticed that workmen painting the back area had brought on stage (to get it temporarily out of their way) a worn wooden storage chest, about three feet high and six feet long. Someone had thought to cover its worn and scratched surface with a dark green cloth. A lectern and microphone had been placed on top of it.

"Murph" introduced me. He seemed intent on leaving nothing out. I squirmed in my seat as he went on and on. When he was finally through and started up the long aisle to find his seat in the back, I walked on to the stage, put down my notes on the makeshift podium, and racked my brain as to how to begin. Suddenly there was no more time to think about it. I raised my eyes from what — it suddenly occurred to me — resembled an altar and heard myself say: "I guess, the only thing left for me to do is to become Pope!" Without interrupting his stride up the aisle, my friend and host turned, shook his finger at me, and yelled (above the laughter my comment had evoked): "*And you will!*"

I don't remember what I said in my lecture, but that drawn-out embarrassing introduction still echoes in my head. . . .

One day, Win Kirby, director of TV activities at St. John's, came to see me about a TV series he thought I might do. I liked the idea and we settled for a number of weekly interviews with editors of academic and other journals. We named the series "Magazines in Focus." It was taped in the University's state-of-the-arts television studio and (through Kirby's contacts) was aired on prime time (8 PM, Sunday evenings) on Channel 31, for an entire year. The first series was later repeated, even as a second series was aired.

WITH RICHARD SCHOECK, ED.
SHAKESPEARE QUARTERLY

WITH ANTHONY PELLEGRINI,
ED. *DANTE STUDIES*

Before each taping, I wrote out questions I intended to ask my guest but also made sure the cameraman knew that he was not to focus on me when I consulted my notes. The result was an illusion of spontaneity and continuity, of easy but provocative conversation that never dragged. There were in fact no cue cards or rolling teleprompters. The program was singled out for several months in a row, in the *New York Times* TV listings, with a black dot (●) that signified "Notable Rating." With that, calls began coming in from all over the country, from editors asking Mr. Kirby to include them in the program. Among those interviewed were the editors of *The Yale Review, Columbia Forum, The Massachusetts Review, Intellectual Digest, Antioch Review, American Scholar, Glass, Dante Studies, Shakespeare Quarterly, Commentary*, and others.

During that time I also appeared as a guest lecturer for a segment in a CBS/TV series called "The Evolution of the Cities."

SJU MORNING SERIES ON CBS-TV

St. John's University began teaching a million early risers about the development of modern cities when WCBS-TV, Channel 2, began telecasting "The Evolution of the Cities" on May 22.

The fifty-four part, half-hour color series is seen at 6:30 A.M. every Monday, Wednesday, and Friday on approximately one hundred twenty-five CBS network stations throughout the nation.

A non-credit course essentially designed to give the viewer a comprehensive, contemporary look at the evolution of urban life, the series is divided into seven key sections: Pre-Village; Village and Town; Early Cities; Pre-Industrial Cities; Industrialization; Industrialization in America, and Tomorrow.

Major stress is being placed upon "Industrialization in America," and that section includes lecturers on such topics as migration, immigration, xenophobia, slums, crime, pollution, media, recreation, morality and ethnicity.

"The Evolution of the Cities" is the first early morning educational series to offer viewers a totally interdisciplinary approach to this topic. St. John's professors from diverse academic fields—history, fine arts, sociology, comparative literature, communications, psychology, etc.—are cooperating in its teaching. Several guest lecturers from other universities in the New York metropolitan area are also lending their special perspectives.

Visual aids such as photographs, slides, charts and maps are being used to illustrate each lecture, and a topical outline and select bibliography is available to viewers upon request.

Explaining the rationale of the program, Winston L. Kirby, Director of St. John's Instructional Television, commented: *"People today are more conscious of urban life than ever before. Problems in the cities are the consistent focus of national attention, and city dwellers are seriously questioning their environment. When 'The Evolution of the Cities' takes a close, hard look at the cities of the past, the public will be able to see that, in any point of time, urban life was both pleasant and unpleasant. And the comparisons which can be drawn will help city people to better perceive their relationship with city life."*

While "The Evolution of the Cities" becomes the first national TV network program for St. John's, the University has produced two television series. "University Roundtable," a general interest program, has been seen weekly on WNYC-TV since 1970. "Magazines in Focus," a series designed to explore prestigious intellectual and academic journals, debuted in May on WNYC-TV.

"Magazines in Focus" probes the editorial aims and policies, contents, and influence of such well-known magazines as *The Yale Review, Columbia Forum, The Massachusetts Review, Intellectual Digest, Antioch Re-*view, *Worldview*, and St. John's own *Review of National Literatures*.

Dr. Anne Paolucci, St. John's University Research Professor, hosts the new series. A prolific author, playwright, lecturer, and editor of *Review of National Literatures*, Dr. Paolucci is a former Fulbright scholar and lecturer and one of the foremost comparative literature scholars in the United States.

"Magazines in Focus" is seen on Sunday evenings at 8:00 P.M. Each Sunday program is repeated on the following Thursday evening at 5:00 P.M. □

DR. PAOLUCCI

Another series I hosted, "Successful Women: Before, During, and After *Women's Lib*," was shown live on Channel 7 for the week of June 25 to 29, 1973. It featured Margaret L. Rumbarger, Associate Secretary of the American Association of University Women (AAUP); Kathleen Carroll, film critic for the *Daily News*; Ponchitta Pierce, co-host of NBC's "Sunday" Show, contributing editor for McCall's, and special correspondent for CBS News; Margaret Stephenson, Administrative Vice President, NBC Radio Division (the first woman in the history of that organization to reach a "top level" position); and Margaret Kelly, Executive Vice President of St. John's.

"SUCCESSFUL WOMEN: BEFORE, DURING, AND AFTER WOMEN'S LIB"

Monday-Friday
June 25-29, 1973

Channel 7 (ABC-TV)
6:30 AM

- - - - - -

HOST: DR. ANNE PAOLUCCI

Monday, June 25. MARGARET L. RUMBARGER. Associate Secretary, American Association of University Professors (AAUP), concentrating on the area of academic freedom and tenure. Member, Committee on the Status of Women in the Profession. Administrator and writer.

Tuesday, June 26. KATHLEEN CARROLL. Film Critic, New York Daily News; Adjunct Professor (St. John's University); "Film Critic of 1972" (Yeshiva University). Lecturer and writer.

Wednesday, June 27. PONCHITTA PIERCE. Co-Host, "Sunday" show (NBC-TV); Contributing Editor, McCall's; special correspondent, CBS News (1968-1971); New York Editorial Bureau Chief, Johnson Publishing Company (1967-1968); Director: African Student Aid Fund; Director: American Freedom from Hunger Foundation. "Headliner Award" (1970); "Women Behind the News Award" (1969). TV personality, lecturer, writer.

Thursday, June 28. MARGARET KELLY. Executive Vice President and Vice President for Academic Planning (St. John's University); Associate in Higher Education (Office of Higher Education, New York State Education Department); Member, Middle States Accrediating Association. Highest ranking woman administrator on the university level in the U.S.A.

Friday, June 29. MARGARET STEPHENSON. Administrative Vice President, NBC Radio Division and its parent company, RCA. First woman in the history of that organization to reach "top" level. Member of the International Radio and Television Society, Broadcast Pioneers, and American Women in Radio and Television. Member also of the State Department's Inter-American Advisory Council.

> ANNE PAOLUCCI. University Research Professor at St. John's University and editor of REVIEW OF NATIONAL LITERATURES, a semi-annual in comparative literature. She has written extensively on Shakespeare, Dante, Machiavelli, and Pirandello. Her books include FROM TENSION TO TONIC: THE PLAYS OF EDWARD ALBEE (1972) and LUIGI PIRANDELLO: THE RECOVERY OF THE MODERN STAGE FOR DRAMATIC ART (1974). She has appeared on TV in SUMMER SEMESTER (1972), in FOR WOMEN ONLY and GIRL TALK. Author, playwright, critic, editor, and lecturer.

We had no trouble recruiting these women for the week-long panel, partly because of the success of "Magazines in Focus," but also because of Win Kirby's contacts. He was totally at ease in the television world, knew any number of producers, and had their ear. I enjoyed working with him, exchanging and developing ideas. He was a good listener, always cooperative, always ready to take on a new project. Looking back to those days, I almost wish I had opted for more television exposure, educational programs where I could lecture to a wider audience. The response that came in after each of my appearances convinced me that it was a medium I could handle easily and effectively.

I appeared on other TV talk shows during my years at St. John's and prepared several "in-house" lectures and programs for students and the

University community, but there was no time for indulging the prospect of more shows of my own, no matter how interesting and rewarding they might turn out to be. The commitments I had already taken on kept me busy enough. *RNL* and *CNL/WR*, as well as CNL business generally, took a great deal of my time; attending conference and giving lectures outside the University was a continuing priority, as was my own writing (and this included much else besides my academic articles and presentations). In addition, in 1981, my mother joined our household as a permanent guest. She remained with us for ten years, until 1991, when she died of an infection in her leg, which quickly spread and could not be contained or cleared. She was 94. Until the end she was lucid, still read and spoke two languages, and was easy to care for. I found there was always time to give her a shower, cut her toe nails, keep her as happy as was possible. During those years, I was the mother, she was the child entrusted to me.

There were difficult moments. Mom took every opportunity to indulge, whenever possible, her litany of past miseries — especially as I helped her dress or prepared her for bed or waited for her to take her medications. I was a captive audience, forced to listen to her self-righteous complaints, hating myself for feeling that way but unable to hold back the complex and deep-rooted reactions she unleashed in me. At those moments, I was the forgotten youngest member of the family, unable to escape from the oppression of her memories, the real and imagined suffering others had inflicted on her. In this too, Henry was a tremendous help, reminding me that in order for things to function smoothly, I had to keep a certain distance. I had to remind myself that I was now Mom's caretaker.

I tried to keep that in mind when I discovered that she didn't always swallow her pills in the morning. She would hold them in her mouth until I left the room then spit them out and hide them. I would find them in the night table drawer, carefully wrapped in tissues, or under the mattress, or, on one occasion, at the bottom of a discarded panty hose in the trash.

Aside from such moments, she was easy enough to please. She especially enjoyed watching the Merchant Marine Academy training ship, directly across from us, on the Bronx side, as it was getting ready to lift anchor and take the cadets into northern waters for their six-week summer training period. I would get her up early on those mornings, postponing her breakfast, so that she could sit in our alcove, with the binoculars we had given her, and watch the ship move slowly away from its mooring, cross under the Throgs Neck Bridge and head for the Sound and the ocean, beyond. She would follow it until it disappeared on the horizon. I often wondered if the cadets in full dress uniform lined up on the deck ever suspected they drew such interest from at least one of the apartments in Cryder House, directly across from them, in Queens.

Henry was especially supportive with regard to Mom. I always tell people who are contemplating caring for an elderly parent or relative at home: make sure the rest of the family is in full accord or it won't work. Don't even suggest it if there is the slightest hesitation or doubt on the part of husband, or wife, or children. In our case, Henry was devoted to Mom as though she had been a blood relative. She often got on his nerves, but he was never abrupt with her, never criticized her. He explained to me once that what I was doing was not, should not be done out of love but as a commitment, a job taken on and to be seen through no matter what. I didn't quite understand his reasoning; it seemed impersonal, cruel even. But I came to grasp it soon enough. I had, in fact, taken on the obligation, when my sister and brother could not or would not do so. I knew that Mom would have preferred to stay with my brother, who had a large family Mom had helped raise and to which she was devoted. But it didn't turn out that way. I had no illusions about the situation. There were periods when we had not communicated for months at a time. She was manipulative and critical of even her best friends. I did not welcome her comments, her criticism. But I knew she needed me, and I took her in as another job that had to be done. And I realized in due course that Henry was right. The boundary lines had to be drawn to make things work; there was love, of course, but — more important — a conscious commitment. Arguments were minimized (Henry saw to that), and the days passed without the confrontations that could easily have been sparked by Mom's self-righteous comments and my aversion to them.

MOM WITH HENRY (CA. 1964)

MOM (ON TERRACE OF CORSO EUROPA 9, 1966)

Still we were both disconcerted when she began to get up in the middle of the night, put on slippers and her long housecoat over her nightgown and wander out of her bedroom in the dark, into the large living room and down the long corridor leading to our bedroom, calling "Anna! Anna!" When we jumped out of bed, still groggy with sleep, to see what was happening, she was clearly relieved. "Oh, there you are!" she would said with an embarrassed little smile. "Credevo d'esser sola!" ("I thought I was alone!") This became a regular occurrence and her words a familiar refrain. I realized how deep her fears were, how even the ticking of a small clock in her bedroom announced imminent danger to her. I learned to interpret what were on the surface misreadings or frustrating exaggerations of perfectly normal occurrences as what they really were: an old, vulnerable woman's fears of the unknown, of what she didn't recognize or understand. One's attitude inevitably changes in the light of such knowledge.

On many occasions, when Mom came searching for me at two or three in the morning, Henry would tell me to stay put, that he would take Mom back to her room and help her into bed. His quiet efficient way of handling her was typical and in character. I was committed, and out of deference to me, out of love for me, he willingly shared that commitment and all the obligations it carried. He never once complained. When I lectured outside of New York, I knew I could leave Henry in charge. If I was to be gone for one or more days, I would prepare and freeze meals for both him and Mom, I would try to minimize his chores, but he did them all. He never discouraged me from accepting professional invitations, even when they meant rather long absences from home. I could not have asked for a more supportive companion, on all levels of our relationship.

I did in fact have occasion to travel a good deal during these years, most of the time alone. I visited Stratford-on-Avon twice, at the invitation of T. J. B. Spencer, head of the Shakespeare Institute — a scholar as well as a kind and gentle man (also a contributor to our *RNL* issue on *Shakespeare and England*). I lectured twice at the Institute, and on both occasions found time to visit the theater. I was fortunate to be there for a production of *Antony and Cleopatra*, an experience I shall never forget. At first, I was somewhat surprised at the choice, since the play has a number of problems when it comes to staging, not the least of which is the incredible number of shifts from one part of the world to another, some scenes only a few lines long. Critics, unable to explain what they consider an aberration, have put forth all kinds of arguments to account for the play's seemingly scattered action, the most popular being that Shakespeare probably wrote it in a hurry and therefore somewhat carelessly!

I've never been able to accept such excuses for what critics won't admit is a failing in their judgment rather than a failure in Shakespeare's creative faculty. Seeing the play in Stratford, with the remarkable Janet Suzman as Cleopatra and Robert Johnson (I'm almost sure it was he) as Antony, I was made acutely aware of the play's fractured structure and came to realize how vital and organic it was to the action. Rather than an aberration, the fast-changing scenes are an essential part of the play, deliberately introduced for a certain effect. As I watched, I saw how those quick changes in location dramatized the two places at opposite ends of the world, the two opposing forces coming closer and closer together, toward a destructive confrontation. A revolving stage, often with no props at all, made the changes easy and quick, creating, in the nervous shifting from one place to the other, an ever-increasing intensity of expectation. The whole production was a far cry from the extravagant movie versions that had come out of Hollywood — especially the Elizabeth Taylor "megaspectacular." Perhaps the most striking thing about the Stratford production was Suzman herself. She was a small woman, made to look rather ordinary. There was nothing extravagantly seductive about her; but her delivery, her movements, her gestures, her manner generally, her entire presence on stage had the audience riveted. For most of the play, she wore a simple green gown, without any trimming or jewelry. At some point, I suppose she wore a crown; if she did, I don't remember. I still have a vivid impression of her moving on that unadorned stage; I can still hear the rush of words, feel their raw emotion, all of which explained her mysterious fascination, her incredible attraction. It was an experience I'll never forget.

Shakespeare (with Hegel in the wings) had obviously become a major part of my life. For a time I was a member of The Shakespeare Association of America and even served briefly on its executive board. When possible, I attended their meetings and took part in their programs, panels, and other activities. In turn, my Shakespearean colleagues had come to know my work with CNL and the Pirandello Society and, when invited, would agree to participate in programs and panels planned for those two groups at the annual Modern Language Association convention.

I was surprised, nonetheless, when early in 1981, Maurice Charney (with whom I had shared a number of Shakespeare programs and for whom I had written an article on "Hegel on Comedy" for a book he was editing on the evolution and history of comedy) asked me to join him and other Shakespeare scholars in planning an ambitious multi-faceted project featuring the life, times, and work of the great playwright. The project was to be funded by grants from EXXON and other corporations, the Folger Library, the National Endowment for the Humanities, the National Endowment for the Arts, and with the cooperation of a number of universities, libraries, theater groups and other private and public agencies. I was to be Associate Director of the four-month event, which came to be known as "Shakespeare Summerfest," (the title I suggested and the one chosen by the Committee). The event was to be hosted by and housed at the American Museum of Natural History on Manhattan's West side; but additional activities, exhibits, and stage productions sponsored by participating groups outside the area would be available to the public at a number of other locations.

The project included lecturers, exhibits, an audio tape that visitors would have access to at the entrance, to explain what they were about to see along the way in their tour of the various exhibits. There were musical programs, recitations, a mini-production of *Othello* as an opener, and related activities in other parts of the City, even as far away as Stratford, Connecticut and Washington D.C. As visitors entered the area where the Shakespeare project was housed, an actor or actress in costume (in most cases, students recruited for the occasion), standing on a tiny eight-inch platform, greeted them with a few lines from one of the plays or from the sonnets.

HENRY UNDER THE LARGE BANNER ADVERTISING "SHAKESPEARE SUMMERFEST" OUTSIDE THE MUSEUM OF NATURAL HISTORY, NEW YORK, JUNE, 1981.

My experience with CNL, Charney had explained, would give the project a multinational dimension and reflect Shakespeare's world-wide influence. I decided on dramatic mini/readings by theater groups or actors brought together for the purpose, each program representing a national culture. For a while I thought I'd bargained for more than I could deliver; but with the help of friends in theater and colleagues who knew of my work with CNL, I managed to plan twelve separate one-hour programs. These were held every Saturday, for the duration of the project, in one of the little theaters in the Museum. They drew full houses every week. The purpose was to give the audience some idea of what Shakespeare sounded like in other languages: what came out of my planning was a remarkable variety of approaches and presentations. Several of the groups came with their own costumes but there were no props and no stage sets.

DRAMATIC PROGRAMS PREPARED BY CNL FOR THE "SHAKESPEARE AND THE WORLD" WEEKLY SATURDAY THEATER SERIES, PART OF "SHAKESPARE SUMMERFEST," JUNE-SEPTEMBER, 1981).

Shakespeare — *Summerfest*

"SHAKESPEARE AND THE WORLD"

PROJECT DIRECTOR: Shakespeare Summerfest
Bernard Beckerman, Chairman,
Theatre Arts, Columbia University

DIRECTOR: "Shakespeare and the World"
Anne Paolucci, President,
Council on National Literatures

June 17: Opening Address by TOM STOPPARD.

June 20: "Shakespeare and the Afro-American Community" (opening lecture by Professor Errol Hill). Scene from *Othello*, directed by Darryl Croxton, Artistic Director and Producer (Daragon Productions) with Mercie J. Hinton, Jr., Robert Jackson, Darryl Croxton, Albert Neal, Elizabeth Page, Sundra Jean Williams. Brief informal talk by Earle Hyman: "An Actor's Experience with Shakespeare."

July 11: "Shakespeare in the Hispanic World," the impact of Shakespeare on Hispanic theatre and letters. Introduction: Dr. Andre Franco (Coordinator/Director), with Raul Davila, DavidCrommett, Francesco Prado, Elia Enid Cadilla, Soledad Romero.

July 18: "The Greeks Meet the Elizabethan." Introduction: Yannis Simonides (Coordinator/Director), with Anna Makrakis and Isadore Sideris.

July 25: "Shakespeare in Germany": Scenes, Songs, and History. Maurice Edwards (Coordinator/Director), with Annette Becker, Warren Kliewer, Will Taylor, Robert Corman (pianist).

August 1: "Shakespeare in Japan." Introduction and showing of 1957 production of *Throne of Blood*.

August 8: "Shakespeare and the Armenian Theatre." Dr. Nishan Parlakian (Coordinator/Director), with Herand Markarian, Elizabeth Khodabash, Hovhannes Bezdikian, Shoghere Markarian.

August 15: "Shakespeare, Our Contemporary." Lecture by Dr. Anne Paolucci, Director of "Shakespeare and the World" and Associate Director of *Shakespeare Summerfest*.

August 22: "The Hamlet-Myth in Nineteenth-Century France." Dr. Rosette Lamont (Coordinator/Director), with Joanna Adler, Noble Shropshire, David Warrilow.

September 5: "The Many Faces of Love: Shakespeare's Italy." Dr. Ben Termine (Coordinator/Director). Music.

September 12: "Shakespeare in Russia": excerpts from poetry, fiction, and music. Maurice Edwards (Coordinator/Director), with Andrej Kodjak, and others.

September 13: "Shakespeare in the Yiddish Theatre." Wolf Younin (Coordinator/Director), with Mel Gordon, Michael Gorrin and Rita Karin.

September 18: "Shakespeare on the Turkish Stage": an informal talk on "Shakespeare in Ataturk's Turkey," by Tunc Yalman, and selections and reminiscences by Cigdem Selisik-Onat and Shirin Devrim-Trainer.

A local Spanish troupe took on "Shakespeare in Spain" and did readings from *Romeo and Juliet,* partly in Spanish, partly in English. The Armenian segment began with critical remarks by the director of the group, which led easily into bilingual readings from *King Lear* (an Armenian favorite, which I understand is beautifully translated into Armenian). The Italian and German programs, prepared by Ben Termine and actor/director/singer Maurice Edwards (already mentioned as the inventive director/producer of the Cubiculo and The Classic Theater, but also, for twenty-five years, Artistic and Executive Director of The Brooklyn Philharmonic), focused on songs and operas inspired by Shakespeare.

"SHAKESPEARE IN THE HISPANIC WORLD" (DIRECTED BY ANDRÈ FRANCO)

SHOGHERE MARKARIAN: "SHAKESPEARE AND THE ARMENIAN THEATRE"

"THE MANY FACES OF LOVE: SHAKESPEARE'S ITALY"

The French offering, prepared by Rosette Lamont (official biographer of French playwright Eugene Ionesco) consisted of "spoofs" of *Hamlet*. Talat Halman, who later became U.S. Cultural Ambassador-at-Large for Turkey, brought in for his presentation two well-known Turkish actresses who recited scenes from *Hamlet*. (They habitually played both male and female roles in Turkey, and were quite famous for them.)

ISADORE SIDERIS,
ANNA MAKRAKIS,
YANNIS SIMONIDES:
"THE GREEKS MEET
THE ELIZABETHAN"

JOANNA ADLER, DAVID WARRILOW:
"THE HAMLET-MYTH IN
NINETEENTH-CENTURY FRANCE"

ROSETTE LAMONT, JOANNA ADLER
AND NOBLE SHROPSHIRE:
"THE HAMLET-MYTH IB
NINETEENTH-CENTURY FRANCE"

The Turkish segment had a life of its own. Professor Halman, a true cultural ambassador, saw further possibilities for the Turkish segment he had prepared — "Shakespeare on the Turkish Stage," an informal talk on "Shakespeare in Ataturk's Turkey" by Tunc Yalman, and selections and reminiscences by Cigdem Selisik-Onat and Shirin Devrim-Trainer (the two actresses he had flown in from Turkey) — and decided to take the program, with his two distinguished performers, to Washington D.C. and other places, after the New York closing.

"SHAKESPEARE SUMMERFEST" POSTER, A COPY OF WHICH I WAS FORTUNATE TO GET BEFORE THEY RAN OUT.

Early in September, while "Shakespeare Summerfest" was still going on, I flew to Yugoslavia to represent the United States at the "Struga Poetry Evenings," an international poetry festival held annually since 1966. I was immensely flattered but curious too as to why I had been chosen. Although by then I had published poems in a number of journals and had three collections to my credit, I knew I didn't command the attention certain other poets enjoyed, who had worked their way into major reviews and had made a greater impact than I had. I knew realistically that my work drew only a limited audience and hardly any critical attention. Some of my poetry had been translated, however — into Turkish (by Talat Halman), into Spanish and Greek, by others who liked my work and took it upon themselves to help promote it. Perhaps my being invited to a week-long Canadian conference on Isabella Crawford, some time earlier, and having shared poetry readings and interviews with May Sarton may have had something to do with it. Or some members of the planning committee may have remembered me from my two earlier invitations to Yugoslavia, as the editor of *RNL*. At that time, I had spent a few days in Macedonia and had met several of their writers.

It was an elaborate affair, which lasted almost a week. Very few of the participants spoke English or any language other than their own, but the committee had made provision for simultaneous translations. The meeting, attended by poets from all over the world, was an interesting break in my schedule and, as it turned out, my last trip abroad. I had been invited to attend the annual International Pirandello Conference in Agrigento, scheduled right after the end of the poetry conference in Yugoslavia (an invitation I had accepted on several occasions in the past), but this time I declined. I didn't want to miss the final programs of "Shakespeare and the World" or have to cancel my public lecture.

I returned in time for both. When I got back to New York, "Shakespeare Summerfest" had three more weeks to go. I gave my lecture, as planned (it was later videotaped at St. John's; still later, it was picked up by Everett & Everett Co, in Florida, on audio-cassette). I already had resumed my teaching.

WITH DR. ENZO LAURETTA, HEAD OF THE PIRANDELLO INSTITUTE IN AGRIGENTO, SICILY, THE PLAYWRIGHT'S BIRTHPLACE.

"STRUGA POETRY EVENINGS," STRUGA, YUGOSLAVIA (EARLY SEPTEMBER, 1981)

WITH HOST, METO

WITH POET FROM SENEGAL

WITH MEMBER OF THE "STRUGA POETRY EVENINGS" PLANNING COMMITTEE AND HIS WIFE

"STRUGA POETRY EVENINGS," STRUGA, YUGOSLAVIA (SEPTEMBER, 1981)

At St. John's, I had in fact agreed to head the Department of English and to help promote the Doctor of Arts Degree Program in English, as its Director — two jobs I held for the next eleven years. My main goals were to minimize "turf wars" within the department and encourage colleagues to prepare new syllabi to enhance the D.A. program. I succeeded in part in the first but failed in the second. I went ahead anyway and streamlined D.A. offerings to give the program a much-needed comparative component, including a seminar on "Multicomparative Literary Perspectives"— a course which I ended up teaching myself, since no one else was prepared to do so.

The Doctor of Arts students were not the usual Ph.D. students. The D.A. Degree was designed for and attracted teachers already in place, mature and experienced in the classroom. The majority taught in private and public high schools, a few on the college level; but the one thing they all had in common and were eager for was a desire for subject-oriented courses that offered, not methodology (as in the Ed.D. and Ph.D. degree programs in education) but substantive material designed to help them enlarge their knowledge of what they actually taught and therefore improve their classroom presentation.

Instead of taking the usual graduate offerings in Shakespeare, for example, the D.A. student in our program at St. John's could choose the specially-designed course on "Shakespeare and the Media," in which Shakespeare's plays were studied on a variety of different levels, starting with the usual critical assessments of a given text and moving quickly into the "translations" of that text for stage and television, the different forms it assumed in order to be appreciated by different audiences, especially students in the classroom.

In a course I named "Playwriting as Basic Communication," students were asked to develop, in slow stages, a short play, This was not an exercise fashioned to encourage or produce playwrights; it was meant to measure the awareness on the part of the teacher of the many kinds and levels of communication needed in the classroom, the various approaches or "masks" one had to assume to get something across to others. I was gratified to hear students say, at the end of the course, how much they had learned about how to present a subject to students — even though most of them had not succeeded in the experiment to "get out of themselves" and assume different voices, as in a play. I was especially pleased that they recognized their shortcomings, knew that they had much to learn still about getting the attention of a mixed group of listeners; but I reassured them that knowing where they went wrong was half the battle won.

Another new course was "Political Writers of the Renaissance" in which students were introduced to Dante's *Inferno,* Spenser's *Faerie Queene,* Shakespere's *Richard II-Henry V* sequence; Machiavelli's *Prince,* More's *Utopia,* and excerpts from the French writer, Jean Bodin. Though my students were all mature and well-read, and all were practicing teachers, most of them had not read the *Divine Comedy.* Even Machiavelli was for most of them nothing more than a name. By bringing such important texts together under a common theme, my students were introduced to major authors of the Renaissance in an intellectually stimulating context, one that was meaningful in itself and gave their readings much greater impact than if they had been approached separately.

The most important and certainly the unique addition to the program was the seminar I added on "Multicomparative Literary Perspectives," where authors and works from other parts of the world were read and the difficulties of expanding comparative studies were explored.

These were challenging years for me, given the captious nature of my colleagues. Most of them were old-timers, unwilling to take on anything new. They resisted change, produced very little in the way of publications, basking in their tenured status, as though nothing more should be asked of them. My greatest frustration was the opposition of those still wedded to the Ph.D. kind of "research." They rejected the more practical approach of the D.A., which gave teachers a better grasp of subject matter and helped them find ways to present material more effectively. Instead of the laser-sharp research of the Ph.D., usually in a limited (and often esoteric) area, or the methodological and psychological focus of an Ed.D. or Ph.D. in Education, the D.A. provided teachers with subject-oriented courses that gave them fresh perspectives and suggested new ways of handling material in the classroom.

My colleagues had never adjusted to this new degree and continued to teach as though they were preparing Ph.D. students. Even though the course requirements for the D.A. were a hefty 54 credits beyond the Master's degree (instead of the additional 30 required for the Ph.D.), most of the faculty members in the English Department simply refused to change their offerings or streamline their syllabi to accord with the demands of the D.A., nor would they relinquish the impossible hope of some day getting the Ph.D. degree in English (lost some years earlier) reinstated.

In my opinion, the D.A. degree has great potential. Unfortunately, it has not taken root in our country, although it still flourishes on many campuses. One of the difficulties that prevents its wide acceptance is the variety of ways in which it has been structured; another is that the offerings chosen to suit a particular kind of degree (*e.g.* "creative writing") are not necessarily vital to another program, elsewhere. Even the number of required credits differs from one campus to another. D.A. programs in any one area (*e.g.* English or History) are often so different from one another that it is hard, in fact impossible to come up with a much-needed evaluation mechanism that will serve all of them.

My new assignments at St. John's did not change things in any drastic way. I continued to write and to attend academic meetings; I continued to publish *RNL* and the *CNL/World Report*; I continued to accept invitations to speak on other campuses; I even took leave without pay to spend time in Australia. And since teaching had become a natural and integral part of my life, which I thoroughly enjoyed, I admit I welcomed the chance to do so, whenever there was time for it.

I could not always count on my Department to support my initiatives, but the deans and other administrators took every opportunity to recognize my work. In addition to annual "merit bonuses," they presented me, in 1985, with St. John's "Faculty Outstanding Achievement" medal. Community groups I had helped with cultural programs, lectures, and special events also found occasion to single me out from time to time. In May, 1982, I was chosen for the City-wide "Teacher of the Year" Award." Some years earlier I had been chosen by Lucille De George and her committee for an "Amita Award" (to women of distinction) and for several years after that I served on their awards committee.

CITY-WIDE "TEACHER OF THE YEAR" AWARD" (MAY, 1982)

ACCEPTING THE AWARD

WITH FORMER CONGRESSWOMAN
GERALDINE FERRARO
AND JOSEPH SCIAME

THE AMITA AWARD DINNER (1969)

The New York State Grand Lodge of Order Sons of Italy in America (OSIA), one of the largest Italian-American groups in the country, with lodges in every state, had singled me out in 1980 for the Elena Cornaro Award (named after the first woman in the world to receive a Ph.D. [ca. 1648, from the University of Padua), and in 1993 presented me, at their annual convention at the "Breakers" in West Palm Beach, with the first (and for some reason the only) national Cornaro award "for academic and professional achievement." A few years later, they presented me with the "Golden Lion" award at their annual dinner (this time, at the New York Hilton).

"GOLDEN LION" AWARD (L/R) JOSEPH SCIAME, A.P. JOSEPH VALLETTUTI (1980)

RECEIVING THE ANNUAL AWARD OF AMERICANS OF ITALIAN LEGACY (PLAZA HOTEL, 1997)

A real surprise was learning that, as part of the commemorative celebration of the centenary of the Statue of Liberty, the Italian newspaper *Il Progresso* had conducted a poll of its readers to find who they thought should be honored as the ten leading Italian-Americans in the country. I knew nothing of this initiative and was truly stunned when I was invited to Washington D.C. to meet with the Italian Ambassador, Rinaldo Petrignani, early in October, 1986, to receive, with the nine other Italian-Americans who had been chosen as the "winners," a gold medal made for the occasion.

The idea (I subsequently learned) came about in March, 1986. On the 13th day of that month, the national Commission chosen to select twelve representatives of ethnic groups to be honored on the Fourth of July with the "Freedom Medal," commemorating the centenary of the Statue of Liberty, had published the names they had selected. The absence of even one Italian-American drew loud protests. Given the many contributions Italian immigrants had made to their communities and to the nation as a whole, the absence of even one Italian name was both offensive and unacceptable. The result was an initiative launched by *Il Progresso* to come up with distinguished names to put forward for the occasion. The initiative was supported by both the Ambassador and the President of Italy, Francesco Cossiga, who hailed the event and sent congratulations from Italy to the ten who had been chosen by their own to represent the Italian-American community in the national celebrations.

It was a memorable occasion. The Ambassador hosted a reception and dinner for us and presented each of us with a specially-designed gold medal. My fellow honorees were Nobel prize winner in economics Franco Modigliani, Judge Marie Lambert, industrialist Marco Cangialosi, composer and lyricist

Giancarlo Menotti (founder of the Festival of Two Worlds), Soprano Licia Albanese (President of the Puccini Foundation), Latinist, poet and writer Joseph Tusiani, Father Joseph Cogo (National President of ACIM), producer/director Frank Capra, and Nobel prize winner for his work in physics, Emilio Segrè.

IL PROGRESSO

★ Venerdì 10 ottobre 1986 - Friday October 10, 1986 ★

Oggi, a Washington, saranno consegnate le medaglie ai 10 italoamericani scelti dai lettori che hanno partecipato al "referendum" indetto da "Il Progresso": eppure, la commissione dei festeggiamenti del 4 luglio per "Lady Liberty" li aveva dimenticati...

Ecco, sono i nostri giganti

Una lezione per tutti Anche per noi

di ANDREA MANTINEO

"Li premieremo noi", avevamo titolato in prima pagina lo scorso 16 maggio, nell'annunciare il referendum tra i nostri lettori per la scelta di dieci italoamericani distintisi nella loro patria di adozione. Lo faremo oggi. O meglio, lo farà l'ambasciatore Rinaldo Petrignani ospitandoci nella sua residenza di Washington.

Il ricevimento, al quale oltre ai premiati interverranno numerose personalità del mondo della politica e della cultura della capitale, sarà la degna conclusione di un'iniziativa del nostro giornale particolarmente felice che ha suscitato entusiastici consensi.

Il referendum è nato infatti da una protesta corale del nostro gruppo etnico per l'esclusione di un americano nato in Italia dall'elenco dei 12 insigniti con la Medaglia della Libertà. Gli italiani erano stati i "grandi dimenticati" dalle celebrazioni del lungo weekend del 4 luglio.

I dieci italoamericani scelti dai lettori che hanno partecipato al referendum indetto da Il Progresso saranno premiati oggi nel corso di una cerimonia alla Firenze House, residenza dell'ambasciatore italiano a Washington Rinaldo Petrignani.

A ricevere le artistiche medaglie ricordo, coniate dalla Zecca italiana, saranno:

Franco Modigliani, premio Nobel per l'economia;

Giancarlo Menotti, fondatore del "Festival dei Due Mondi";

Emilio Segrè, premio Nobel per la fisica;

Joseph Tusiani, latinista e poeta;

padre Joseph Cogo, segretario nazionale dell'Acim;

Marie M. Lambert, prima ed unica donna premiata con il "Law Day";

Licia Albanese, soprano, presidente della Puccini Foundation di N.Y.;

Marco Cangialosi, industriale, cavaliere al merito della Repubblica;

Frank Capra, regista cinematografico;

Anne Paolucci, docente presso la St. John's University, fondatrice del "Columbus Countdown 1992".

Come i lettori ricorderanno, la vicenda che ci ha portato ad indire il referendum ha avuto inizio il 13 marzo scorso quando la commissione preposta alla selezione di dodici illustri americani nati all'estero, da premiare durante i festeggiamenti del weekend del 4 luglio per il centenario della Statua della Libertà, ha reso noti i nominativi. Tra di essi non vi era nessun italiano.

Subito abbiamo protestato facendoci portavoce dei sentimenti della nostra comunità. Massiccia è stata anche la protesta dei nostri lettori. Tra le moltissime lettere giunteci in redazione ina un particolare inviataci da padre Graziano Battistella del Centro Studi sulle Migrazioni di Staten Island, proponeva che il giornale promuovesse un referendum tra i lettori.

Abbiamo subito accettato l'idea. Il referendum, lanciato il 16 maggio e conclusosi a fine giugno, è stato un successo: la redazione è stata inondata da migliaia di tagliandi, giunti da ogni parte degli Stati Uniti. I nostri lettori, con i loro voti, hanno scelto democraticamente i dieci italiani ai quali verrà oggi conferito il meritato riconoscimento per l'opera svolta negli Usa.

La scelta della "Commissione dei 24" era stata particolarmente offensiva per gli americani di origine italiana, considerato il contributo di opere e di idee dato nell'ultimo secolo al progresso di questa grande nazione.

Poco importava se dall'elenco dei premiati erano stati esclusi, oltre a quello italiano, anche un altri gruppi, quali quelli irlandese e polacco, fortemente rappresentati nel mosaico etnico americano.

Il nostro referendum è servito quindi a colmare una lacuna, a rimediare a un'incredibile "dimenticanza".

I dieci premiati di oggi, scelti democraticamente dai nostri lettori, hanno di che essere orgogliosi: le dieci medaglie che l'ambasciatore Petrignani consegnerà loro, costituiscono anche un simbolico riconoscimento dei sacrifici di milioni di nostri connazionali che, negli anni della grande migrazione, giunsero su questa sponda dell'Atlantico lasciando alle spalle un passato di privazioni per un futuro incerto, in un Paese del quale non conoscevano la lingua e i costumi.

Il ricordo dell'epopea dell'immigrazione italiana in America, con le sue tragedie e i suoi successi, non deve però riempirci soltanto di orgoglio. Deve anche essere una perenne lezione di umiltà. Deve insegnarci a non discriminare verso altri gruppi etnici. Ricordando le nostre sofferenze passate possiamo comprendere chi soffre oggi.

Il Progresso naturally carried the event in a big way. The editor had written the front-page story himself. There was also a centerpiece of photographs and accounts of the event. In was in those pages that I learned what had triggered such a dramatic reaction on the part of the Italian-American community.

A.P. ACCEPTING THE GOLD MEDAL FROM AMBASSADOR RINALDO PETRIGNANI

After supporting Henry for his U.S. Senate bid, in 1964, I ventured into political campaigning a few more times. In support of the much-decorated former NYPD officer who was running for the New York mayoralty, I set up "Women for Biaggi." Henry had been asked to manage the campaign and had brought together the county leaders of the Conservative Party in support of our candidate. Mario Biaggi did not win the election; but I think Henry was as pleased as I was to have helped promote his candidacy. He would have made a great mayor; and in spite of the setbacks he experienced later, both Henry and I remained his loyal friends. We felt that the sentence served on him was harsh — especially in the light of what others in high office were getting away with. The rumor was that someone with influence wanted to put him down. . . .

I gave time also to the Reagan-Bush campaign, recruiting members for a political action group called "*conservative* Women for Reagun-Bush" (and later "*conservative* Women for Bush-Quayle"), emphasizing "*conservative*" in its generic application. I felt that in many issues — *e.g.* improving education, discouraging factional interests, etc. — most people were more or less conservative, regardless of party affiliation. Our main activity was writing and distributing press releases on subjects that were of public interest, reminding readers of certain priorities. There was no money to speak of and no time to raise any; but we managed to get out a number of press releases to as many potential voters as our limited means allowed.

WITH MARIO BIAGGI: "WOMEN FOR BIAGGI"

Human Events

THE NATIONAL CONSERVATIVE WEEKLY

OCTOBER 27, 1984

●

Conservative Women for Reagan-Bush '84 is a new organization involved in taking the President's message to female voters. Dr. **Anne Paolucci**, who chairs CWRB's New York State Campaign Committee, said the group "will be working for a Reagan-Bush victory in November, but is also the beginning of a national movement to bring conservative-thinking American women together on fundamental issues and values between elections."

New York CWRB's plans for the current election include supporting voter registration drives aimed at conservative women, preparing campaign literature for mailings, and recruiting and briefing Reagan-Bush volunteers for "telephone clubs" to get out the vote. The group is also supporting veteran conservative activist **Serph Maltese's** bid for the 9th Congressional District seat being vacated by Geraldine Ferraro.

"Symbolically and substantially,"

CWRB leader Paolucci declared, "This is the most important local race in the entire state." Maltese "has proved his effectiveness as executive director of the Conservative Party of New York State. I have watched Serph Maltese at work over the years," she added, "and I can say with confidence that he speaks true, he is always there when needed, and, most important, he always delivers. I wish we had more like him in all political parties."

For more information on CWRB, a project of Conservative Women of America, contact Dr. Anne Paolucci, Director, 166-25 Powells Cove Blvd., Beechhurst, N.Y. 11357; (718) 767-8380.

During my years at St. John's. I wrote constantly on academic subjects but also indulged my irresistible impulse to write fiction, poetry, and plays. After *The Short Season* in Naples, I turned to short dramatic pieces.

The first was *Minions of the Race*, written in 1972 for a competition the Medieval Institute of Western Michigan University was sponsoring for a short play on some medieval or renaissance subject. The winning play would have a dramatic reading at the Conference, scheduled for later that year.

My submission was in five sequences; the most important of which was the trial scene, where I dramatized the dilemma of authority, what the two great ministers of the unpredictable and self-serving Henry VIII of England were up against. It portrays the difficulties Sir Thomas More and Thomas Cromwell (disciple and friend of Cardinal Thomas Wolsey) had to sort out: More's unyielding faith and Cromwell's Machiavellian strategies to divorce England from Rome. *Minions* was one of the two winning entries.

In it, I tried to bring out the paradox implicit in that truly historic confrontation. More, the great statesman and astute lawyer, the staunch Catholic, could not bring himself to sacrifice his faith on the altar of opportunity or secular necessity. He was ready to acknowledge Henry's divorce from the Queen (and indeed did so) but could not bring himself to accept what Henry had promised he would never ask of him, but (true to his erratic nature) ultimately insisted on: that he recognize the King as head of the Church of England and thereby renounce Rome and the Pope.

THE MEDIEVAL INSTITUTE

of

WESTERN MICHIGAN UNIVERSITY

presents

THE WINNING PLAY OF THE

1972 CONFERENCE DRAMA PROJECT

MINIONS OF THE RACE
by ANNE PAOLUCCI, St. John's University

Cast of Characters

Cardinal Wolsey	M. Robémarque
Thomas More	P. Greenquist
Thomas Cromwell	C. Muldoon
Archbishop Cramner	J. Stevens
Richard Rich	M. Malloy
Audley, the Lord Chancellor	J. Glenn

Directed by: William V. Roberts

"You would God's work! But do you really know what that is? Surely not the work of ROME! God's kingdom is NOT of this world . . . Where there is REAL RESPONSIBILITY there is never a real choice."

"The simple truth is . . . first one Thomas, then another . . . and . . . of necessity . . . a third."

—Anne Paolucci

Although in many quarters Cromwell is regarded as the villain of history, I saw him as a worthy opponent to More, a man dedicated to his king and country, ready to sacrifice all lesser needs in order to promote and preserve the integrity of England. He is denounced by many for having destroyed the monasteries and having brought down the holiest of churchmen in order to insure the cooperation of weaker prelates. He did in fact do those things, wiping the slate clear, as it were, paving the way for England's new destiny, one that would make her independent and bring her into prominence in the family of world nations. With the defeat of the Spanish Armada, a new England began to assert itself. Cromwell's Machiavellian maneuvering brought on the golden age of Elizabeth and Shakespeare. Ironically (and history is full of ironies, as Hegel tells us), Cromwell too became a victim of Henry's arbitrary rule. Not long after More's death, he too was executed.

MINIONS OF THE RACE AT THE CHURCHYARD THEATER

The play was done Off off-Broadway in New York a number of times — at the "Little Theater" of Columbia University, at St. John's, at the Churchyard Theater in Manhattan, and at other places. Often, people in the audience would approach me afterwards to urge me to turn *Minions* into a full-length play (they wanted "more of it"), but I knew that the laser-sharp focus would dissipate and disappear with that kind of change. I had realized by then that I had a certain skill with short plays (and short stories). I liked the fast pace of the form and responded best to the need for a strong central point around which the rest of the play gathered. I was not prepared to stretch out the story, as in the genial *Man For All Seasons*. Much as I admire that excellent play, I knew, even then, that its structure, the evolving story, its biographical emphasis would not work for me. My play was meant to depict a mini-tragedy in true Greek (and Hegelian) terms: two great men at odds — both right, both wrong in their absolute claims. I recognized in the More-Cromwell confrontation the essential formula of Greek tragedy, where both sides are justified. I dramatized the *dilemma* which ensues when both parties insist on justifying inflexible positions. In the confrontations which inevitably occur, both sides (as Hegel points out) end up losers. The short play was the perfect medium for this.

WITH CAST OF QUEENS PUBLIC TV PRODUCTION OF *MINIONS OF THE RACE*.. A.P. (STANDING, FRONT LEFT); DIRECTOR EMELISE ALEANDRI (STANDING FRONT RIGHT).

Over the years slight revisions were made. The final version appeared in my *Three Short Plays: Minions of the Race, Incident at the Great Wall, The Artist in Search of His Mask*, published in 1994, with an Introduction by Mario Fratti, co-author of the play that won the Yale Drama prize and went on to become the hit musical *Nine*. It was that final text that was turned into a television script and used for a production funded by a grant from Queens Public TV (New York). It is still shown from time to time on Queens cable network channels.

Another short play, *Incident at the Great Wall*, was a kind of literary "spoof." It centered on the resemblance noted by many scholars between Sophocles' Orestes and Shakespeare's Hamlet. I'm not sure where the idea came from, but Greek tragedy was (still is) one of my favorite subjects and one that I return to often when dealing with drama. It's a funny play but also a literary lesson. It was staged twice Off off-Broadway and also at St. John's. One production was staged as a kind of *commedia dell'arte* showcase: the play lends itself to this kind of interpretation because the characters have agendas of their own and seem to be improvising, adapting themselves to the action around them. The second production, staged at The Churchyard Theater, was given a more conventional staging.

FROM PROGRAM NOTES FOR *INCIDENT AT THE GREAT WALL*

INCIDENT AT THE GREAT WALL *is not only a comedy but also a lesson in literary-critical archeology which dramatizes the popular question of the Hamlet-Orestes-Oedipus relationship and the larger historical question of the development from ancient to modern tragedy and drama. For those who recognize these familiar notions, the play has a special value. But it is, first and foremost, a funny piece, which works well for all kinds of audiences, including the very young.*

The Sophocles-Orestes-Oedipus combination is balanced with the Confucius-Monk combination, creating the Absurd comic mood which characterizes Ms. Paolucci's dramatic works. The fifth member of the cast, the Harvard student doing research in Chinese lyrics, in the middle of nowhere (or in some dark corner of the library), reminds us that all that we see is in effect part of our daily life, the juxtaposition of real and unreal, the play of the mind as it tries to find release from the routine activities of our existence in flashes of insights that are at once frustrating and exalting.

The casting for the *commedia dell'arte*-type was an interesting mix. Confucius was played by a woman, and the actor chosen for Hamlet was a rather stocky young man, whose costume was a tunic that reached just beneath his bare knees. The director focused on the humor implicit in the movements of this rather obese Hamlet and on the other self-assertive characters with their petty quarrels — but never undermining the historical and literary elements of the play. In The Churchyard Theater production, a young woman dancer was cast as the "Student." She very cleverly seized the opportunity to display her dancing and choreographical skills to advantage. Her doing so (and, of course, we didn't stop her) gave the play an extra dimension that I had not envisioned or anticipated but which worked very well.

CONFUCIUS AND SERVANT IN THE CHURCHYARD THEATER PRODUCTION OF *INCIDENT AT THE GREAT WALL*

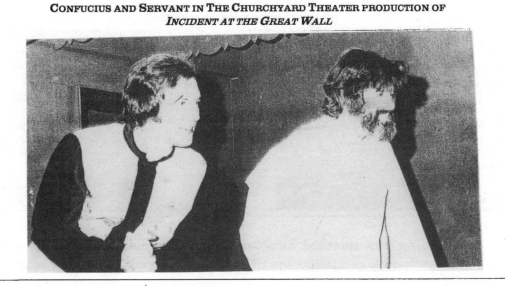

Like Beckett's *Waiting for Godot*, my play has no traditional closure; it circles on itself in an ever-widening awareness of unfinished business. Audiences had no trouble with that or with the array of characters moving against a timeless scenario. Even excerpts from a sequence of poems I'd written years earlier while taking a summer seminar in Chinese history at Columbia with William De Bary — "Fragments from the Chinese Lyrics" — and put into the script for the "Student" to sing while strumming his guitar, blended in nicely. An informal production of the play was also done at St. John's during a one-day conference sponsored by the Asian Institute.

STUDENT AND CONFUCIUS IN THE *COMMEDIA DELL'ARTE*-TYPE
PRODUCTION OF OF *INCIDENT AT THE GREAT WALL*

SCENES FROM THE CHURCHYARD THEATER PRODUCTION
OF *INCIDENT AT THE GREAT WALL*.

Watching how talented directors "read" the play and what they chose to stress in each case reminded me of how vital staging is. Drama is meant to be seen and heard as an immediate experience. Alan Schneider comes to mind again, as the epitome of the genial director who managed to give an extraordinary life on stage to several Albee plays.

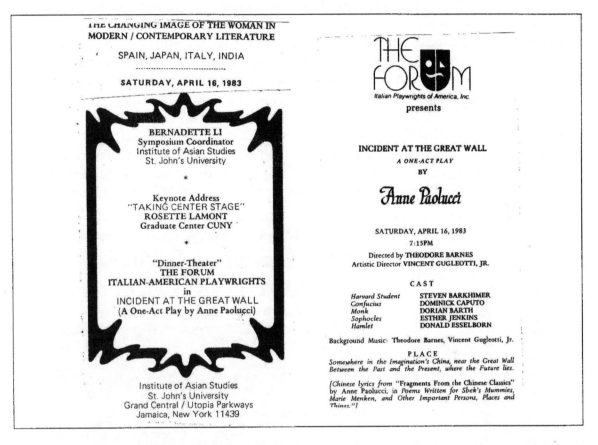

Cipango!, a 90-minute videoplay, was written for the quincentenary of the landing of Columbus in the "new world," also won an award, this time as an "Official Project of the Christopher Columbus Jubilee Quincentennial Commission," the federal organization set up by President Reagan to help celebrate that historic anniversary but which quickly was forced into the background because of the heavy flak created by certain factions and special interest groups, out to undermine any and all "celebrations" of the event. There was enough interest in the play, however, for it to be done several times, as readings and full productions, both in New York and in Albany, where certain members of the New York State Senate, especially Senator Serphin R. Maltese, stood firmly behind the historic anniversary and supported wholeheartedly projects like mine. I visited Albany several times during the "countdown" to 1992 with a variety of programs — panels, lectures, dramatic readings and even original music and publications — under the aegis of "Columbus: Coundown 1992," a non-profit foundation I set up in 1986 anticipating the quincentenary. In spite of much frustration, I was gratified to find my 90-minute videoplay about the ironies of the Columbus story not only singled out by the Jubilee Commission but also listed in commercial catalogs and sold by Educational Video and other distributors. (More about Columbus in a later chapter.)

Still another short literary-historical play, *The Actor in Search of His Mask,* was done as a reading several times here in New York; but through the efforts of Etta Cascini, an Italian producer and writer whom I met when she came to New York on business, it found its way to Genoa, where she translated it, had it staged and also read on radio. In this, there are only two characters (except for a brief appearance by the wife, at the very beginning): Machiavelli and "The Actor." We see the exiled statesman reading and writing to fill the leisure forced on him by the government of Florence, which will not call him back from exile to serve his country again. The play centers on the creation of his play, *Mandragola,* more particularly, the character of the Monk. It received notices in the Italian press, not only in Genoa but also in Milan and Naples.

At the request of friends in Italy, I undertook, in 1975, the translation of *L'Apocalisse di Gian Giacomo* (*The Apocalypse According to J. J. [Rousseau]*), an interesting play by Mario Apollonio, an Italian professor of drama at the Catholic University of Milan. The play recalls events in Rousseau's life, as they are called forth by the writer's own arrogant demand for immediate judgment of his life. Instead of the kudos he is confident he will elicit, Rousseau is put down by all who have known him: a chorus of school boys berate him, prostitutes belittle him, a whole universe bears down on him.

The play is humorous and cleverly avant-garde. My translation (the first and only one in English to-date) was produced and directed by Maurice Edwards at The Classic Theater in New York. The modest production was remarkably effective and received an excellent review in *Show Business*. One of the interesting features of the staging was the use of wooden benches at different heights to create a tiered effect that facilitated the quick changes in time and place, which the script called for.

I was surprised to learn that this treasure had been buried in a desk drawer with several other plays left behind when the author died. I have not seen any of the others, but I found this work not only intriguing as a literary commentary but also interesting as a stage experiment. No doubt, the author dwelt, in his teaching, on Beckett, Ionesco and others, certainly on Pirandello, and was no doubt inspired (as I was) to try his hand at their new kind of plays.

REVIEW OF THE *APOCALYPSE* IN *SHOW BUSINESS*

Thursday, April 15, 1975.

SHOW BUSINESS

THEATRE REVIEWS

THE APOCALYPSE ACCORDING TO J.J.

at the Classic Theatre

* and ½ *

Review by JON BERKELEY

Opened 3/30/76
Seen 4/8/76

The Classic Theater's production of Mario Apollonio's THE APOCALYPSE ACCORDING TO J.J. (Rousseau) is described by its director, Maurice Edwards, as "a symphony more than a play" which seems to be an accurate description.

The play tells the story of Jean Jacques Rousseau on the threshhold of invading his past to write his "Confessions." Friends, lovers, and characters from his works weave in and out of a narrative that is noted for originality of concept, and moments of poetic lyricism, but as theater is very, very dull.

The author of this scholarly work has presented a series of highly intellectual conflicts that never reach a human level. As such, the play might well make fascinating reading, but is a trial to endure on the stage. Occasionally, a scene will show possibilities, as when Rousseau's real life mistress confronts the perfect heroine of one of his works, but each scene is rendered ponderous by weak dramatic construction and verbosity.

The author, a professor of drama at Catholic University of Milan, has an obvious affection for these historical characters, but is unable to convey this to his audience.

Director Edwards has been entirely faithful to the author and made no attempt to make the "symphony" theatrical. As a result, the play is presented clearly, but uninterestingly.

Anne Paolucci's translation is excellently poetic and many passages are memorable for their lyric beauty, an added reason for thinking the play would make rewarding reading.

The Classic Theater, however, does boast some fine actors. John Michalski, who plays Rousseau, is a striking presence with a powerful voice that would do justice to the best of Shakespeare, while Wendy Nute is alluring and commanding as Zulieta. Also memorable were Annette Hunt and Jillian Lindig. Many of the supporting cast, however, especially Joseph Frisari, lacked the requisite vocal, physical and thespian training needed for classic theater.

Tony Giovanetti provided a workable set of many levels and playing areas, which the director made little use of.

The Classic Theater, produced by Nicholas John Stathis, has presented a list of plays that is awesome in its scope and difficulty. After this world premiere, they will present Kafka's REPORT TO THE ACADEMY. It is hoped that they will continue to present unusual works of this nature.

CREDITS

The Apocalypse According to J.J. by Mario Apollonio. (World Premiere). Original translation by Anne Paolucci. Produced by Nicholas John Stathis. Directed by Maurice Edwards. Sets and lights by: Tony Giovanetti. Costumes: John Ahrens. Cast: John Michalski, Joseph Frisari, Annette Hunt, Tom Jarns, Ellen Kelly, Jillian Lindig, Robert Hilton, Wendy Nute, Emile Van der Noot, Craig Wyckoff, The Loyola Boys' Choir. At the Central Presbyterian Church, Park Ave. at 64th.

I had never heard of Apollonio before this manuscript came into my hands. It has yet to be "discovered"— ideally, in my opinion, as a musical.

SCENE FROM APOLLONIO'S *APOCALYSE*

Music has always been a vital part of my life, but Henry turned it into a passion. After our marriage, I took up the piano again. I had learned to play it as a teenager but had not touched it for years. It was Henry who introduced me to the composers he had learned to love. Soon I was playing rather well: at first on the old Krakauer player-piano, a discard from the factory where my father-in-law had worked, during the depression, and later on our own pianos.

We bought our first (used) grand piano in the early fifties, when we moved to 600 West 111 Street and had room for it. Later we replaced it with a Steinway grand, which came with us to Cryder House in Queens. (I sold it back to Steinway after Henry's death.) For many years, I spent about six hours every day going through the "repertoire" I had built up from the large collection of music books Henry had brought with him from home: German songs by Brahms and Schubert, piano/violin sonatas by Mozart and Beethoven, passages (arranged for piano and voices) from the "St. Matthew Passion," and a few piano sonatas of Mozart, Haydn, and Beethoven.

Henry was not as agile on the keys as I was, but he played with great feeling. He also composed. Some of his songs and lyrics (as I had occasion to mention earlier) were used in a musical version of Pirandello's *Liolà*. I myself chose some of his tunes as background music for my play *Cipango!*

In the spare time that remained — first in Manhattan, later in Queens — I also took up oil painting. Music "tuned my heart"; painting gave me first-hand knowledge of how an idea or emotion can be expressed visually by means of lines, shadows, and color. Both refined my sensibilities and my writing.

Officially, I retired from St. John's in June 1996; but at a time when most people are planning to slow down, to indulge in things they could not do while actively employed earning a living, I was about to be drawn into a new and totally unforeseen adventure: a no-pay assignment that put me on the front page of the *New York Times* more often than I would have liked. At the age of seventy, I was thrust, if only briefly, into the limelight and a new career. But before continuing, I must go back to certain events that took place while I was still at St. John's — events that had nothing to do with the University but which were an important part of my life.

🖅 *FROM THE FILES* 🖅

REVIEWS AND STORIES CONNECTED WITH CNL PUBLICATIONS AND EVENTS

"A rich, informative, and diverse collection by 11 specialists on Armenian and comparative literatures. The articles provide a comprehensive perspective of ancient, medieval, modern, and Soviet Armenian literature and also focus on several key literary figures .... highly recommended ....   MAY 1985

Review of National Literatures Releases "Armenia" Issue

By **Shoghere Markarian**

NEW YORK, NY - It was an unprecedented event that took place at the New York Public Library at Fifth Avenue on Friday evening, November 9. Dr Vartan Gregorian, President of the Public Library, accepted from Dr. Anne Paolucci, President of the Council on National Literatures, the first copy of the **Armenia** issue of Review of National Literatures, CNL's prestigious annual volume.

Armenia was edited by Dr. Paolucci and Dr. Vahe Oshagan. Its contributors, too numerous to mention here, embrace Armenia's literary heritage - Shakespeare, medieval poetry, classical drama, 19th century realism and more. To quote our literary champion, Dr. Paolucci, "I consider this volume in the RNL series one of the most important since it focused on a literature that is in every way a national cultural expression by a people who cultivated and cherished their cultural heritage with ardor."

Anne Paolucci, Chairperson of the English Department at St. John's University, Distinguished Visiting Professor in Italian at Queen's College, is the driving energy behind the Council of National Literatures which she founded in 1974. In over 40 countries, it is the first and perhaps only organization in comparative literary studies dedicated exclusively to integrating neglected and emergent literatures into the traditional European spectrum of the major national literatures.

Dr. Paolucci has fostered Armenian literature for many years. With close friend, Dr. Nishan Parlakian, was conducted the memorable Shakespeare and the Armenian Theatre at the American Museum of Natural History. The idea for the Armenian volume came from Leo Hamalian, **Ararat** editor (we regretted his absence). When Dr. Paolucci went to Italy, Professor Hamalian suggested she write something on the San Lazzaro Monastery in Venice. She did - for Ararat.

The cocktail reception was hosted in the office of the President, a room reflecting its literary memorabilia. Leaning over a huge oval table, the dynamic and indefatigable Vartan Gregorian gave a brief history of the library, pointing out valuable vintage portraits of Benjamin Franklin and John Jacob Astor, Percy Bysse Shelley and his wife Mary painted by Romney, Shelley's mother-in-law, Mary Wollencraft, commissioned by Aaron Burr. He noted with pride on his desk a stone head of a young Barbara Tuchman, given by her. Dr. Gregorian expressed his gratitude to Anne Paolucci and Vahe Oshagan. He reminded the select group of writers and scholars that culture was too important to be left to the bureaucrats, that in diversity was the strength and we celebrate not just Armenian culture but all cultures.

Among the list of distinguished invited guests were: Alice Antreassian, Fred Assadourian, Nona Balakian, Paul and Madeleine Bleecker, Susan Carlin - Public Affairs Director of the Armenian Assembly in Washington, Mario Fratti, Professor Nina Garsoian, Frank D. Grande - President of Griffon House, Michael Kermian, Rosette Lamont, Dr. Richard J. Logsdon - former Director of the library at Columbia University and Chancellor of CUNY Library, Sverre Lyngstad - Special Editor of the Norway volume, Maryann Morgan - assistant to Dr. Gregorian, Mrs. Nikit Ordjanian, Dr. and Mrs. Nishan Parlakian, Dr. Henry Paolucci - Professor of Government and Politics at St. John's University (and an invaluable aid in his wife's efforts), and Peter Sourian.

This writer proudly walked away with an autographed copy of **Armenia**

THE ARMENIAN REPORTER

NOVEMBER 29, 1984

ARMENIA

REVIEW OF NATIONAL LITERATURES

THE WHITE HOUSE

WASHINGTON

June 20, 1989

Dear Anne:

Thank you for sharing with me the Council's recent publication. I appreciate your gesture -- and I am particularly grateful for your friendship and support over the years.

With my best wishes to you and the members of the Council,

Sincerely,

George Bush

Dr. Anne Paolucci
President
Council on National Literatures
Post Office Box 81
Whitestone, New York 11357

JANUARY 10, 1985   THE ARMENIAN REPORTER   PAGE 11

N.Y. Public Library President Vartan Gregorian Honored by Council on National Literatures

REVIEW

WORLD LITERATURE TODAY

FORMERLY BOOKS ABROAD

A LITERARY QUARTERLY
OF THE UNIVERSITY
OF OKLAHOMA
NORMAN, OKLAHOMA
73019 U.S.A.

FROM THE
AUTUMN 1984 ISSUE

New Literary Continents is not a journal in the strict sense, though published by the Council on National Literatures in a paperback format quite similar to the *Review of National Literatures*, the Council's annual magazine (see below). The *NLC* instead offers "Selected Papers of the Fifth NDEA Seminar on Foreign Area Studies" (Columbia University, 1981), including an introductory essay by *RNL* editor Anne Paolucci and individual area contributions by Caroline Eckhardt (the Americas), Norman Simms (South Pacific), Rosette Lamont (USSR) and Edmund Keeley (Greece), plus a sixth on "the multinational curriculum" by Marilyn Gaddis Rose.

LIBRARY JOURNAL/FEBRUARY 15, 1994

MAGAZINES
BY BILL KATZ & ERIC BRYANT

CNL—World Report & Review of National Literatures

1974. a. $35. Ed: Anne Paolucci. Council on National Literatures, PO Box 81, Whitestone, NY 11357. Illus. adv. Aud: Ac (Subject: Literature. Issue examined: "World Report" No. 6, 1993)

These two annuals are supported by a nonprofit educational foundation though they are not directly affiliated with a university. Both aim to highlight lesser-known literatures from around the world and offer a "forum for the ongoing dialog as to how to expand comparative studies," in the words of the editor, a professor at St. John's University. In the 1993 *World Report,* there are seven articles, based loosely on the theme of "Multicultural Perspectives: New Approaches," ranging from Haitian writers to Armenian theater. Each *Review of National Literatures* solicits essays from leading scholars worldwide on a specific tradition, such as Hungarian literature or "Japan: A Literary Overview." Both journal subscriptions, along with occasional supplements, are included with membership in the council.— *BK*

ENGLISH STUDIES

VOL. 63 NO. 4

The main event in critical writings on Indian literature was the special India issue of the *Review of National Literatures*, Vol. 10, guest edited by Ronald Warwick and published by the Council on National Literatures. New York. This enterprising publication, whose general editor is Anne Paolucci, contains ten essays, some on specific writers (Tagore, Narayan), some on more general themes ('The Impact of Europe on the Development of Indian Literature'. 'Contemporary Indian Women Poets in English'). P. 343

books abroad

Winter 1975

AN INTERNATIONAL
LITERARY QUARTERLY

foreign criticism

Anne Paolucci. *Pirandello's Theater: The Recovery of the Modern Stage for Dramatic Art.* Carbondale, Il. Southern Illinois University Press. 1974. xvi + 159 pages. $6.95.

One thing in common between Sartre, Livingstone, Pitoëff, and Brustein is the fact that they categorically acknowledge Pirandello to be "the playwrights' playwright par excellence of the contemporary theater." Paolucci's ambitious study affirms this statement wholeheartedly. This is indeed the only published study on Pirandello's theater from *Liolà* to *The Magic Giants* which traces both the Pirandellian leitmotif of the "destruction of personality through self-deception," and the world as will and faith. Paolucci's accent on the dialectics of consciousness and self-consciousness brings into the study of Pirandello's dramatic art Hegel's phenomenological dichotomy of Master/Slave—the mirrored self-consciousness, leading to both the wholeness and the fragmentation of the self.

Proceeding from the Sicilian naturalism, of which *Liolà* is the most exemplary play, Paolucci classifies Pirandello's plays in three parts. The first deals with the "theater" plays, which "dramatize Pirandello's commitment

to the *maschere nude*"—how Pirandello handles the modern stage, the shaping of personality on the stage, and the experience of catharsis. Life invades art and the dichotomy reality/illusion is shattered. In the second section, she discusses the "character" plays—phenomenological externalization of the character's emotions—which anticipate the existential drama and the theaters of the absurd, revolt and of protest, dramatizing what later becomes Ionesco's concern: the difficult, painful and vain effort of human communication. The dramatis personae live in a Dantesque limbo of reality/illusion. The separate chapter on *Henry IV* leads to the Pirandellian universe where "the Dantesque journey into the depth of personality finds its darkest and most sublime expression." Henry IV is appropriately compared to Hamlet, for both indulge in an endless game of "roles." The third and final part examines the "myth" plays—synthesis of Pirandello's dramatic art—which concentrate on the efficaciousness of art transcending itself. Paolucci brilliantly ties Pirandello's conception of art to the Sicilian Saracen olive tree which in Pirandello's view has survived the vicissitudes of life and the agonies of time itself.

Paolucci's volume reads very well. It is impressive both in its laborious research and its limpid presentation.

Victor Carrabi
Florida State University

SELECTED PAPERS OF THE FOURTH ANNUAL NDEA
SEMINAR ON FOREIGN AREA STUDIES
COLUMBIA UNIVERSITY, FEBRUARY 28-29, 1980

FROM . . . **C R N L E** [Australia]

Anne Paolucci (ed.), **Problems in National Literary Identity and the Writer as Social Critic,** New York: C.N.L./Griffon House Publications, 1980, pp. 72, US$5.95, paperback.

This is an important publication of the Council on National Literatures. Its Executive Director, Anne Paolucci, edits the papers delivered at the Fourth Annual NDEA Seminar on Foreign Area Studies, held at Columbia University in February 1980. The papers range from Africa (Bernth Lindfors on "negritude") to India (Robin Jared Lewis) and Soviet Russia (Elena Klepikova), and are all socially and culturally oriented. The relevance of the Council's endeavours — mainly to promote comparative literary study in a wider interdisciplinary context and to spotlight the quality and relevance of relatively neglected literatures outside the "western" world — to the study of the New Literatures in English is obvious. The Council's *Quarterly World Report* summarises the Council's work and gives useful information and book reviews. New members are always welcomed.

No. 2, December 1981   H.M.W.

REVIEWS OF *THE ACTOR IN SEARCH OF HIS MASK* (GENOVA PRODUCTION, 1967)

IL SECOLO XIX Mercoledì
21 gennaio 1987

Sala Garibaldi

Teatro di parola: domani sera un doppio spettacolo dell'Atelier

GENOVA — Nono spettacolo della rassegna Teatro di parola domani sera alle 21 alla Sala Garibaldi. L'ultimo se si esclude quello fuori concorso che andrà in scena giovedì 29 gennaio.

Lo presenta la compagnia teatrale «L'Atelier» ed è composto da due atti unici: «L'attore e la maschera» (che Etta Cascini, alla quale lo consegnò a New York l'italo-americana Anne Paolucci ci propone in una versione tradotta e adattata per l'occasione) e «Storia di un biologo», opera prima del ventenne Andrea Ovcinnicoff.

Nel primo si assiste alla creazione della Mandragola da parte di un Macchiavelli immaginato tra le pareti della sua casa, dove vive confinato dal nuovo governo di Firenze in seguito alla caduta dei Medici.

Vi si narra con la genesi di una commedia vista come uno scontro tra l'autore attento soprattutto ad esprimere le proprie idee, e l'attore che vuole ottenere gli applausi del pubblico.

Nel secondo atto unico alla Sala Garibaldi ascolteremo due amici scambiarsi un dialogo assurdo nel quale le frasi dette dal primo vengono recepite prive del loro significato logico dall'altro.

Secondo Sergio Maifredi e Fabio Alessandrini, rispettivamente regista e aiuto regista di questi due lavori, i due testi apparentemente dissimili hanno qualcosa in comune: rappresentano entrambi la lunga introduzione ad una storia che non verrà raccontata.

Infatti «L'attore e la maschera» termina là dove dovrebbe iniziare la Mandragola, e «Storia di un biologo» non dà al suo protagonista la possibilità di raccontarla.

Gli interpreti di queste due commedie sono Paolo Portesine, Fabio Alessandrini, Maurizia Grossi, Giuliano Pastorino, Sergio Maifredi e Francesco Berlinghieri.

G. Gibb.

GARIBALDI HALL

A DOUBLE PROGRAM BY "WORD THEATER" TOMORROW AT ATELIER

GENOA: —Tomorrow night at 9 PM Word Theater will present its ninth production of the season at Garibaldi Hall. This will be the last regular production of the season (not counting the special show scheduled for January 29th.

The production is by the Atelier Theater Conpany and consists of two one-act plays: "The Actor in Search of His Mask" (in the translation and adaptation of Etta Cascini, who was given that charge in New York by Italian-American playwright Anne Paolucci), and "Story of a Biologist" 20-year-old Andrea Ovcinnicoff's first play.

In the first play we are witness to the creation of Mandragola on the part of a Machiavelli who has been restricted to his home by the new government of Florence after the fall of the Medici.

All this in the context of how a play comes into being and by means of a dramatic confrontation between the author trying to shape his ideas and the actor intent on getting the audience's applause.

In the second one-act play we hear two friends talking in an absurd exchange in which the words of one are picked up irrationally by the other.

According to Sergio Maifredi and Fabio Alessandrini (the Director and Assistant Director of both works), the two texts though seemingly unrelated have in fact something in common: both dramatize the long prelude to a plot that never materializes.

"The Actor in Search of His Mask" ends, in fact, precisely where Mandragola should begin, and "Story of a Biologist" denies the protagonist any possibility of telling his story.

The cast of the two plays included Paolo Portesine, Fabio Alessandrini, Maurizio Grossi, Giuliano Pastorino, Sergio Maifredi, and Francesco Berlinghieri.

G. GIBB

Anno VIII
1987, 1-2
gennaio-giugno

SEGNI

Conte · G.B. Vico Editrice
Napoli

RIVISTA DI CULTURA ITALO-AMERICANA

ANNE PAOLUCCI - The Actor in Search of his Mask (A one act play - Griffon House Publications - New York 1987, p. 37)

È un atto unico brillante e vivace, ma anche penetrante, vero. Il personaggio principale e Machiavelli al momento in cui, accantonato dai Medici, sta pensando alla sua *Mandragola*. C'è anche una scena affettuosa con la moglie, ma ciò che costituisce la parte vera dell'atto, comica e drammatica allo stesso tempo, è il dialogo tra lo scrittore e un attore entrato non si sa come nel suo studio a sera tarda, un personaggio irreale, che sa già della commedia che l'autore del *Principe* vuol fare. L'argomento principale della discussione tra l'autore e l'attore è la figura di Fra Timoteo, come deve essere, se la figura di un perfetto manigoldo, una presentazione satirica di un uomo di chiesa, assolutamente cinico che si presta a favorire l'inganno che Callimaco ha pensato per possedere Lucrezia, la moglie del notaio Nicia, o sarà un semplice personaggio comico, l'orditore di una burla, senza nessuna intenzione satirica. Come si sa, si tratta di far credere a Nicia che se vuole avere un figlio deve dare a Lucrezia una pozione di mandragola, ma non deve giacere con sua moglie subito dopo che essa ha preso la pozione perché egli morirebbe. Ad andare a letto con Lucrezia dovrebbe essere Callimaco che conseguentemente dovrebbe morire. Nel dialogo, molto animato, tra Machiavelli e il fittizio attore viene contemplata l'idea di una farsa, con allusioni sessuali e quella di una presentazione satirica, pessimistica, conforme alla visione pessimistica dell'autore del *Principe*. L'autrice evita sia l'una che l'altra direzione. È un poco una situazione pirandelliana rovesciata: un autore in cerca del personaggio, dibattuta tra una inclinazione realistica e il giuoco della fantasia.

ANNE PAOLUCCI. *The Actor in Search of His Mask* (A One-Act Play: Griffon House Publications, New York 1987, pp. 37)

This is a brilliant, lively one-act play, but profound, as well, and true to life. The chief protagonist is Machiavelli at the time when, dismissed by the Medici, he turns to writing the *Mandragola*. There is even an affectionate scene with his wife, but the true core of the play—comic and dramatic at the same time—is the exchange between the writer and the actor who suddenly appears in his study late at night, an imaginary character who seems to know all about the play which the author of *The Prince* is bent on writing. The main argument between playwright and actor is how Fra Timoteo should be drawn—whether to depict him as an out-and-out ruffian, a satirical portrayal of a man of the Church, a complete cynic who lends himself to the deception Callimaco has conceived to seduce Lucrezia, notary Nicia's wife, or show him as a simple comic character who succeeds in playing a joke on others, without any satirical intention. Machiavelli's play, as everyone knows, calls for persuading Nicia that if he really wants a son he has to force Lucrezia to drink a potion made from the mandrake root, but he must not lie with her after she drinks the concoction because it will prove fatal. It is Callimaco who must somehow be brought to Lucrezia's bed and who will die as a result. In the fast-moving dialogue between Machiavelli and the imaginary actor the play is first considered as a farce built on sexual allusions then as a satirical pessimistic vehicle in keeping with the pessimistic vision of the author of *The Prince*. Paolucci steers clear of both these scenarios. The result is something of a Pirandellian situation in reverse—an author in search of a character—traced as an argument between realistic motivation and a purely genial exercise of the imagination.

[January/June, 1987: VIII, 1-2, p. 53: Naples, G.B.Vico Publisher]

A.P. ACCEPTING THE PIRANDELLO BUST BY SCULPTOR JOSEPH FINELLI (MID 70S)

THE PIRANDELLO SOCIETY OF AMERICA

The Pirandello Society of America was founded in New York City in 1958 by Marta Abba and George Freeley. By the mid-sixties, the original Board was no longer active, and the Society eventually began to attract academics. Even then, its activity was limited, partly because Pirandello was still not well known outside of Italian studies, partly because his stage work suffered from major publishing restrictions, and partly because he was not yet recognized as an important international playwright. The President of the Society during this difficult transition period was Professor Gino Rizzo.

It was only in the early 70s that the Society picked up momentum under the leadership of Comm. Anne Paolucci, later that of Professor Maristella Lorch (then Director of the Casa Italiana at Columbia University). After a number of years during which the Casa Italiana hosted a number of dramatic programs, lectures, and conference on Pirandello, the Society once again called on Comm. Anne Paolucci to serve as President. She remained in that position for 17 years, encouraging dramatic readings at the annual meetings of the Modern Language Association of America, special events, and — in 1985 — the launching of an annual publication, *PSA*, to replace the Society's Newsletter, first introduced some years earlier and edited by Professor Parlakian and Professor Philip Fulvi, two of the most hardworking members of the Society.

In 1997, the Society's "Allied Organization" status in MLA was reviewed by that Association and — mainly because of the continued production and high academic quality of *PSA*, the Society's annual volume — "Allied Organization" status was renewed for the next seven years.

SAMPLE PROGRAM AT MLA MEETINGS OF THE PIRANDELLO SOCIETY OF AMERICA

PIRANDELLO society ———— PIRANDELLO society

1988 MODERN LANGUAGE ASSOCIATION

NEW ORLEANS

7:15 - 10:15 PM*
Thursday, December 29

"JACKSON"
MARRIOTT HOTEL

PIRANDELLO'S *HENRY IV*
[Program arranged by the Pirandello Society of America.]

Presiding: Franco Zangrilli (Baruch College CUNY)
Opening Remarks: Anne Paolucci (President PSA; St. John's University)

PART I (PANEL PRESENTATIONS)

Alberto De Vito *(Long Island University):* "Time in *Henry IV*"; Angelo Spina *(Dickinson College):* "'The Masks from *The Late Mattia Pascal* to *Henry IV*"; Maria Rosaria Vitti-Alexander *(Michigan University):* "Madness as a Mask: Variations on the Pirandellian Central Theme in *Henry IV*"; Nishan Parlakian *(Award-winning playwright; John Jay College CUNY):* "A Director's Assessment of *Henry IV*"

PART II (DISCUSSION)

Philip A. Fulvi *(Pace University):* Respondent. OPEN DISCUSSION WILL FOLLOW.
*PLEASE NOTE: PART I AND PART II ARE LISTED AS SEPARATE
BACK-TO-BACK MEETINGS IN THE MLA PROGRAM, WITH A BREAK IN-BETWEEN.

Papers read at this meeting will be eligible for consideration in PSA, the official annual publication of The Pirandello Society of America.

June 12, 1991 • THE CHRONICLE OF HIGHER EDUCATION • A5

RESEARCH NOTES

■ **Computer scientists make robot perform checker-playing tasks**

■ **Molecular analysis links coelacanth to first terrestrial vertebrate**

■ **Themes of Pirandello's plays are seen in earlier works of fiction**

■ **Effects of divorce on children said to occur before parents split**

Notes on Research: Plays of Pirandello

Themes explored in the plays of Luigi Pirandello were introduced by the author in earlier works of fiction, says a literature scholar at St. John's University in New York.

Pirandello, the Italian playwright and novelist who died in 1936, is best known for his 1921 experimental drama, *Six Characters in Search of an Author*. The play takes place on a stage on which actors are gathering for rehearsal. Six people arrive at the theater, claiming that they are unfinished creations of the author's imagination and demanding to be allowed to play out their personal dramas on the stage. Their stories then unfold, as the lines between actors and "real" characters become increasingly blurred.

In the current (March) issue of *Modern Drama*, Anne Paolucci, head of the English department at St. John's, notes that, until he wrote *Six Characters*, Pirandello's reputation had rested largely on a body of fiction that depicted in realistic terms the harshness of Sicilian life. But with the play, and others that followed, he began to explore a new kind of theme—the interior search for identity and how that search can liberate a person from the constraints of the environment.

Ms. Paolucci argues that the themes of Pirandello's plays, written later in his career, were actually announced in some of the earlier fiction. His 1904 novel, *The Late Mattia Pascal*, for example, is the story of a man who, returning from a solitary holiday, reads a mistaken announcement of his own suicide. He takes the error as an opportunity to escape his old life and begin a new existence. He finds his new life even more constraining, however, and fakes a second suicide in order to return to his earlier existence, albeit on different terms.

The novel, Ms. Paolucci argues, was Pirandello's first direct expression of a pessimistic view of humans trapped by hostile forces but overcoming that condition through their gradually evolving sense of identity and consciousness of freedom.

—ELLEN K. COUGHLIN

WITH MARISTELLA LORCH, EXECUTIVE DIRECTOR, CASA ITALIANA, COLUMBIA UNIVERSITY , AND TWO-TERM PRESIDENT OF THE PIRANDELLO SOCIETY OF AMERICA

READING OF PIRANDELLO'S *THE LIFE I GAVE YOU*, "PLAYERS," MID-70S

THE CITY OF NEW YORK
OFFICE OF THE MAYOR

CERTIFICATE OF RECOGNITION

presented to

DR. ANNE PAOLUCCI

*Upon being named one of the Top 10 Women in Queens Business by Queens Business Today.
This is a tremendous honor that recognizes your significant contributions to your field and your community.
You have paved the way for future generations of women leaders and all New Yorkers
join with me in wishing you continued success in your endeavors.*

Michael R. Bloomberg
Michael R. Bloomberg, Mayor

"A.C. BRADLEY AND HEGEL ON SHAKESPEARE" CITED IN
THE EUROPEAN *PENGUIN COMPANION TO LITERATURE*

THE PENGUIN COMPANION TO LITERATURE

EUROPE

EDITED BY

ANTHONY THORLBY

ALLEN LANE THE PENGUIN PRESS

Hegel, Georg Wilhelm Friedrich (Stuttgart 1770–Berlin 1831). German philosopher. He published only four full-scale works: the *Phänomenologie des Geistes* (1807), the *Wissenschaft der Logik* (1812–16), the *Encyklopädie der Philosophischen Wissenschaften* (1817; revised 1827 and 1830) and the *Philosophie des Rechts* (1821); the rest of his major output consists of posthumous reconstructions of his lectures. In terms of cultural influence, Hegel is probably the most important of modern philosophers, not only in virtue of his relation to Marx, and of the support European theories of nationalism and 'social democracy' seemed to find in the *Philosophie des Rechts*, but also because of his impact upon nearly the whole range of the humanities. Thus the accelerated growth of intellectual history during the 19th and early 20th centuries continued to receive powerful stimulus from Hegel's phenomenology of culture long after his metaphysics had fallen into disrepute; Hegel's interpretation of Christian doctrine as a symbolic expression of 'philosophical truth' inaugurated modern philosophical theology; and many aestheticians, critics and poets have been irresistibly drawn to his dialectical categories. Central in this latter connexion are, firstly, Hegel's remarkable synthesis of organicist aesthetics and historicism in his *Vorlesungen über die Aesthetik* (1835–8); and, secondly, the fact that what is broadly true of Hegel's philosophy as a whole is also true of modern poetics: both attempt to give coherence to principles of disparity and conciliation, dissonance within harmony, transcendence and yet immanence, tension, paradox, irony. Significantly enough, recent scholarship shows that Hegel developed his characteristic modes of thought and utterance while he was absorbed in the aesthetic works of Diderot, Rousseau and Schiller. [MM]

W. Kaufmann, *Hegel: Reinterpretation, Texts and Commentary* (N.Y., 1965) (bibliography); A. C. Bradley, 'Hegel's Theory of Tragedy', in *Oxford Lectures on Poetry* (1909); A. Paolucci 'Bradley and Hegel on Shakespeare', in *Comparative Literature*, XVI, 3 (Summer, 1964); G. Lukács, *Beiträge zur Geschichte der Aesthetik* (Berlin, 1954); B. Teyssèdre, *L'esthétique de Hegel* (Paris, 1958); G. Morpurgo-Tagliabue 'Attualità dell'estetica hegeliana', in *Il Pensiero*, 1–2 (1962); Wellek, HMC.   pp. 355–6

GUEST OF HONOR, WITH THE CONSUL GENERAL OF ITALY, AT AWARD CEREMONY
OF THE AMERICAN ITALIAN CULTURAL ROUNDTABLE, JUNE 5, 1997

New York Post

FOUNDED 1801. THE OLDEST CONTINUOUSLY PUBLISHED DAILY IN THE UNITED STATES.

| Vol. 171 No. 112 | NEW YORK, TUESDAY, MARCH 28, 1972 © 1972 New York Post Corporation | 15 Cents |

NEW YORK POST, TUESDAY, MARCH 28, 1972   60

Random Notes

RICHARD WATTS

Anne Paolucci, a Research Professor at St. John's University, is a warm admirer of Edward Albee, and she writes thoughtfully of his plays in "From Tension to Tonic" . . . Dealing with all his works that aren't adaptations, she offers many subtle and illuminating insights into them, although I must admit that at the end of her detailed analysis of "Tiny Alice" I found its enigma more puzzling than ever . . . While not always agreeing with her, I think she is correct in her high regard for his stature as a playwright . . . More than

Incidentally, I was gratified by her approving mention of my description of Albee as "an angel of darkness."

* * *

Comfortable

Queensboro Bridge (and Other Poems).
By Anne Paolucci
60pp; Potpourri Publications Co., PO Box 8278, Prairie Village, KS 66208. $8.00.

Hugh Fox

Queensboro Bridge is mature, "educated," meditative poetry beyond the need to be hip and modish. Here's the beginning of a poem not about the Queensboro but the Throgs Neck Bridge: "The bridge straddles obscenities/As I watch dawn's early light/Pounding against my daily rocks. I water plants and look for mites/Squint for a sight of nesting/Peregrines under the span..." (p.60).

These are "comfortable" poems, poems written with large vistas and backed up by all sorts of comfortably worn erudition. There are travel poems, poems about the author herself as a professor, poems about her Italian mother facing the New World, poems about literary award banquets, readings in Soho. It's refreshing to come across someone beyond kineticism and hip stances, someone who unapologetically taught Hegel, Spencer and Dante at City College in New York and doesn't feel a need to keep sweatily up to date with the latest evolution of swinging lingoes, but accepts a kind of aristocratic autumnal ending of things with dignity and resignation: "Now, in my atlas age,/I visit orchards heavy with apples,/Wrapped in a brown parka. I drive to country inns in Maine/For Sunday brunch. Sometimes I bring a friend." (p.40).

FROM *QUEENSBORO BRIDGE (AND OTHER POEMS)*, 1995

QUEENSBORO BRIDGE

My favorite too, of all crossings
Into the City. Fitzgerald was right,
Canyons, gorges, suddenly rising
Before you, are part of a mystery
Never unraveled, a wild promise.
I understand the words,

But when I try to see what *he* saw,
In his leap across the span
Of his own startled vision
I'm not sure I can.

And yet, as I turn off,
The bridge behind me,
Driving faster than he ever could
Or did, down the avenue,
I know I'm in Gatsby country.

PREPUBLICATION COMMENTS ABOUT *QUEENSBORO BRIDGE (AND OTHER POEMS)*, 1995

"The rhetorical turning upon one's old self, so dear to many other Italian-Americans, pointless and predictible in its form and expression, is light years removed from Paolucci .... Viewed from the Queensboro Bridge, said F. Scott Fitzgerald (author of Gatsby), New York is always new, as though seen for the first time, as if suspended in the blue sky, always rich in promise and mystery and beauty. And Paolucci's *Queenboro Bridge* is just that, a bridge between two islands of being, a turning in surprise toward the skyscapers of Manhattan and of the spirit, a silent vigil . . . ."
REVIEW BY FRANCO BORRELLI ("MAGAZINE," *AMERICA OGGI*, SEPTEMBER 17, 1995 [TRANS. FROM ITALIAN]

" . . . terse and infinitely suggestive language . . . a kaleidoscopic imagination that never strains for effect but always succeeds in evoking surprising yet seemingly natural responses . . . an education in literary and historical sensibilities . . . ."
REVIEW (*THE ITALIAN VOICE*, AUGUST 24, 1995)

" . . . beautiful . . . a work of art inside and out."
DIANA DER HOVANESSIAN (POET, TRANSLATOR, PRES.IDENT NEW ENGLAND POETRY CLUB)

"I am slowly savouring [QB] with a mixture of pleasure, admiration and — yes — envy. I recall particularly poems like the superb "Sailing Out,' 'We can hardly begin to find definition/For what we think we know best.'"
JOHN L. BROWN (POET, TRANSLATOR, AUTHOR)

" . . . bellissima raccolta . . . sto pensando alle poesie di Sylvia Plath, che contengono più pessimismo e più amarezza della vita. Le tue poesie tra il reale e l'onorico: mi piace molto 'Looking Back' in cui accenni alla scomparsa di tuo padre sulla collina."
ORAZIO TANELLI (POET, PUBLISHER, TRANSLATOR)

" . ∴ intensely palpable verbal fleshiness (and, not least, truthfulness!!)"
VIRGIL NEMOIANU (CATHOLIC UNIVERSITY OF AMERICA; EXECUTIVE COMMITTEE ICLA)

" . . . bellissime poesie . . . ."
MARISTELLA LORCH (DIRECTOR, THE ITALIAN ACADEMY [COLUMBIA UNIVERSITY])

"[the] images are so apt and true! It is a wonderful book . . . ."
MARIA MAZZIOTTI GILLAN (DIRECTOR, THE POETRY CENTER [PASSAIC CC])

"[These] poems remind me of the first time you catch a lightning bug and put it in a glass jar and watch it. You know it's going to light up but you don't know when. I'll be reading and every so often a word just jumps out at you. Every line or two really. There is a freshness about that word in that place that givec you joy."   M. MILLS

"*Discovery, surprise, wonder, hypnotic impact.* In her latest volume, Anne Paolucci still draws from her favorite literary and historical sources to startle the reader into a fresh image: a phrase from a medieval hymn, a suggestive line from Goethe, a classical reminiscence, an echo from the Brahms sound of a Heine song . . . . Perhaps her literary schoes account for the sense of awe the reader experiences in her poetry, a feeling of shared greatness modulated by modesty, as though she writes to exalt those great poets who have helped to mold her talent . . . . Perhaps what Chandler Beall wrote about her poetry best sums up Anne Paolucci's special talent: "Her unique style is a combination of thoughtful, observant, yet muted commentary on moods and things, the lively and attractive personality that shines through, the self-knowledge and the wisdom, the feeling of the feel of things and of feelings, the language lean and apt and rich in culture . . . .'"
(FROM THE "INTRODUCTION" BY NISHAN PARLAKIAN [PLAYWRIGHT, TRANSLATOR])

"I have read the poems, some of them more than once, with great pleasure. Besides making xerox copies of the ones I liked best I am sending the book to the keepers of my archive at the University of Rochester."
JERRE MANGIONE (AUTHOR, EDUCATOR)

FICTION

SEPIA TONES: Seven Short Stories. By Anne Attura Paolucci. (Rimu Publishing/Griffon House, Box 81, Whitestone, N.Y. 11357. Paper, $10.) If more Italian-American writers do not speak up soon, much of their experience in the 20th century will go unrecorded. Anne Attura Paolucci's slim volume helps dispel the silence. The scenes alternate between the farmland north of Naples and the outer boroughs of New York. Cast in an implicitly documentary mode (owing, partly, to the photographs that herald each story), the tales have the sentimental "sepia tone" the title suggests, with several of the same characters figuring throughout. The author, who teaches English at St. John's University, is often in danger of turning characterization into tribute; one feels the taboo against exposing, and thereby dishonoring, the family and community. The exceptions are two New York stories. In "Rarà," a priest in Little Italy helps a 9-year-old girl drag her sick, drunken father to bed, then learns he is terminally ill when he visits his old friend, an atheistic doctor. He then goes on to help a young woman with college applications. The "and then" quality creates a sense of the daily jumble of events. "The Oracle Is Dumb or Cheat" begins and ends with the neighborhood women. The rambling narrative is written as if learned secondhand, the narrator's voice yet another gossip. In this way we hear of Louise Quattrocchi and Frank Guardino, two young lovers torn between their new American freedom to choose as individuals and their old imperatives to live as the family and community dictate. By the end of the book, the author has invoked the world of an ingrown community where family pride cautions, "Keep your eyes shut and say nothing. . . . Dust always settles."

—*Nancy Forbes*

The New York Times Book Review — February 16, 1986

RIMU PRESS, P. O. Box 13049, Hamilton, New Zealai

"These seven short stories, beautifully written and utterly absorbing, are the work of a genuinely literary artist. The author's insight into her various Italian characters is of such clairvoyance as to make them universal. Anne Paolucci combines qualities seldom found in the same writer: a sure sense of narrative, a marked talent for writing effective dialogue, and a distinctive style that constantly engages the reader with its warmth. SEPIA TONES should bring its author the recognition she merits as an important American writer. I cannot imagine any discriminating reader experiencing the pleasure of reading these stories without wanting to read more of the author's writings."
JERRE MANGIONE, *Award-winning novelist*

"A superb chronicle of shifting ethnic values in the American setting . . . ."
NISHAN PARLAKIAN, *Playwright*

" . . . versatile . . . sensitive . . . they portray accurately; they interpret life among Italian Americans [with] the mind-probing of Pirandello, here and there Verga, and maybe O'Henry in "Rarà." But no, it's straight Anne Paolucci."
PETER SAMMARTINO, *Educator*

34 The Women's Review of Books / Vol. XI, Nos. 10-11 / July 1994

After immigration

by Rita Signorelli-Pappas

The Voices We Carry: Recent Italian/American Women's Fiction, edited by Mary Jo Bona. na. Montreal and New York: Guernica Editions, 1994, 376 pp., $18.00 hardcover.

I RECOGNIZED FEW NAMES as I read down this book's table of contents, but that is not surprising: Italian American women authors were until recently an almost invisible presence in our literature. Why has it taken so long for their words to reach the printed page? According to Mary Jo Bona's introduction to this anthology, their prolonged silence was in part a result of the conflict that the daughters and granddaughters of immigrants experienced when they were given educations but told not to leave the traditions of the family behind. Above all, they were warned against breaking the traditional code of *omertà* (silence), an unspoken but deeply ingrained taboo against revealing family secrets.

The conflicts of Italian American women who turned to fiction writing have been intensified by the negative stereotyping of their ethnic culture by the media. Films and television still portray Italian women as overweight, oversexed and obsessed with a need to cook pasta, and Italian men as oafs in pompadours and undershirts or as murderous gangsters. What I particularly admire about the selections in *The Voices We Carry* is the absence of these stereotypes, which suggests just how distorted they are.

Indeed, although the book presents itself as having a special focus on "ethnicity in American culture," the selections often downplay ethnic considerations to explore subjects that are more universal: childhood, the difficulty of relationships with spouses or lovers, life within loving but troubled family circles, the poignancy of growing old.

The final section is a tribute to the pioneering first generation of Italian immigrant grandparents. Although it too is somewhat misleadingly titled, it contains some of the best writing in the book. The jewel in this section—indeed the masterpiece of the entire anthology—is Anne Paolucci's "Buried Treasure," a brilliant, haunting memoir of an unforgettable Italian American man narrated by his daughter-in-law. The admiring portrait of an impassioned painter who lacked formal training but possessed the sensibility and discipline of a real artist has clear, eloquent power:

Perhaps it was simply his lack of training; but I like to think it was his vision, quirky and poetic, strangely haunting in its stiff configurations, its lines never quite straight, never quite even, that had such an ambiguous effect on me. I saw the effects all too clearly, always; but at the same time I saw his soul trying to tell me something, everything. (p.344)

"MAGAZINES IN FOCUS" ENTERS SECOND YEAR

St. John's University is producing a second season of its half-hour television program "Magazines in Focus" which last year received consistent "Notable" ratings in the New York TIMES.

The program, a lively exchange between guest editor and host, is designed to explore the editorial policies, purposes, contents and goals of academic and other journals. Hosted by St. John's Research Professor Dr. Anne Paolucci, "Magazines in Focus" is taped in St. John's own Campus Television Center and is seen on Saturday evenings at 6:30 P.M. on Channel 31 in New York.

LIBRI DALL'ESTERO

IL VELTRO EDITRICE

5-6 ANNO XXX – SETTEMBRE – DICEMBRE 1986

A. Attura Paolucci, Sepia Tones

Rimu Publishing Co., Hamilton, Nuova Zelanda, 1985, distribuito in USA dalla Griffon House di Whitestone, N.Y., pp. 128, $ 10.

Una strana tensione accomuna tutti i personaggi di questi racconti, quella che non si ferma all'apparenza, quella che scava nel proprio animo alla ricerca di nuove ragioni per vivere, quella che non si accontenta di restarsene ferma ma sogna nuovi cieli nuovi paesi nuove certezze economiche, quella che rende simili in fondo tutti gli emigranti, e ne sottolinea l'ansia, i dubbi e le abitudini ataviche, i vizi dell'antico vicinato trasposti nel nuovo. Queste della Attura Paolucci non sono tuttavia storie d'emigrazione soltanto, ma quadri di umanità che soffre e che spera, che esige i propri diritti e che per orgoglio finisce spesso per non accettare le proprie colpe, sia che si viva nell'assolato Sud del Lazio, o nei paesi/vicoli del Beneventano o di Napoli, o nei «neighborhoods» della Big Apple.

Il paradiso spesso è nel paese vicino, o al di là dell'Atlantico (per chi vive nel Meridione della penisola) o in California (per chi vive invece sull'East Coast). Una strana tensione, dicevamo, non solo a non quietarsi ma anche al dubbio, all'incertezza esistenziale (la verità, infatti, sarebbe pace, quindi stasi). La realtà sfugge e non rientra nei disegni di queste creature pirandelliane indecise o incapaci a decidere o «costrette» in certo qual modo da necessità incomprensibili e tiranne. Eppure si può uscire al di là di quel cerchio che le circostanze e gli altri costantemente ci impongono. Oppure no?

Queste figure, reali e fantastiche ad un tempo, non subiscono gli eventi, il fatto per loro è sempre qualcosa cui si può reagire, per affermare la propria libertà, e per essere più tranquilli con la propria coscienza. Ma non sempre questo ha successo, e di tanto in tanto si accetta supinamente anche quanto ci viene «consigliato» dagli altri, dal vecchio padre o dagli amici: ma ciò solo se non si scorgono altre alternative.

Sono storie di «compari» e di «comari», di matrimoni mancati o di «sistemazioni» dettate dalla convenienza; sono storie però di sole e di colore, che riescono a trasportare anche al di qua dell'oceano quel folklore e quella «paesanità» che si rimpiangono solo quando non si hanno più. C'è sempre un paradiso perduto o dimenticato nel fondo dell'animo di ognuno di noi che, per strana ironia, non coincide mai con quanto viviamo quotidianamente.

I personaggi di *Sepia Tones* non sono poi tanto vincolati dal ricordo o da ciò che è irrimediabilmente «passato». In loro c'è un'accettazione del presente coraggiosa e forte. Non c'è mai debolezza, anzi. Un'aderenza quasi filosofica a ciò che si è e a ciò che si ha; certo, si potrebbe avere di più e si potrebbe essere diversamente, tutti i personaggi lo sanno, ma non bisogna farne un dramma; la realtà prima va accettata e poi cambiata, se ci si riesce, altrimenti non è peccato o colpa l'adeguarvicisi.

Una lezione eroica di vita, e anche un'occasione per sentire tutta l'aderenza ad una doppia cultura, la coscienza chiara di appartenere contemporaneamente a due mondi che, all'apparenza così lontani, finiscono invece con il ritrovarsi vicini e quasi coincidere.

Storie di emigranti, dicevamo, storie comuni di gente comune, personaggi che continuano a vivere nei centri piccoli e poveri del Meridione d'Italia, che ci passano accanto nel «neighborhood», il passo svelto, un saluto appena accennato.

FRANCO BORRELLI
«Il Progresso», New York, 5-1-1986

WITH MARTHA AND ED BATOR

IL PROGRESSO - DUE MONDI   DOMENICA 14 DICEMBRE 1986

Machiavelli pirandelliano

"**The Actor in Search of his Mask**", di Anne Paolucci, pp. 37, Griffon House Publications, New York, 1986, $ 10.00

Questo è il terzo "atto unico" della Paolucci, dopo il colombiano *"Cipango!"* e *"Minions of the Race"*. Il dramma è d'ispirazione pirandelliana e si impernia sul ruolo diabolico dell'attore con un intreccio interessante di finzione e storia. Machiavelli (nella riproduzione qui sopra) qui rappresenta un commediografo qualunque alla ricerca della forma ideale per la sua creazione. La Paolucci decide di riandare alla genesi della *"Mandragola"*, opera spesso incompresa o interpretata tradendo lo spirito dell'autore. Cardine della sua ricerca è la figura di fra' Timoteo, la figura più complessa in questo dramma di seduzione e di magistrale esercizio diplomatico.

Attraverso quest'atto unico conosciamo i due livelli in cui opera la fantasia dell'autore: da un lato vediamo un uomo che vorrebbe occuparsi di cose ben più serie, dall'altro egli si trasforma in un Machiavelli idealizzato, in un commediografo simbolico che cerca di far coincidere i suoi personaggi con gli attori sulla scena. Fra' Timoteo, ad esempio, viene continuamente "rifatto", fintanto che il dio creatore non resti soddisfatto della sua creazione.

L'attore è chiamato ad esistere dalla pressione derivata dall'atto della creazione e dall'ossessione dell'intuizione dell'autore. L'attore diventa così flessibile una volta che ne ha compreso in pieno tutto il potenziale. Ne vien fuori così una commedia di buon livello, equilibrata e in diverse parti anche umoristica.

Qual'è il fine dell'autrice? Semplicemente quello di dimostrare che la storia non è mai solo "passsato" ma "contemporaneità".

E ogni lettore finirá per essere trascinato dall'incastro di fantasia e realtà. Un'opera quindi che oltre ad istruire si fa anche d'intrattenimento, soprattutto per i giochi della personalità (di chiara matrice pirandelliana) che la rendono viva e piacevole.

2/B | ATTUALITA' | IL PROGRESSO - DUE MONDI | DOMENICA 30 SETTEMBRE 1984

"Gli Italoamericani leggono e scrivono come chiunque altro..."

...e i nostri scrittori sono vivi e vegeti

Mancano però editori e conferenzieri che mettano in giusto risalto il nostro retaggio culturale - Occorrono idee chiare e precise per il futuro

di ANNE PAOLUCCI

Sono rimasta colpita dall'articolo *Intellettuali e popolo: un rapporto difficile*, di Anthony Pedatella, pubblicato nel supplemento *Due Mondi* dell'8 luglio scorso.

Nell'articolo in questione, l'autore ci fa sapere che gli Italiani che vivono negli Usa non "scrivono" semplicemente perchè "non leggono". Come le streghe nel *Macbeth* shakespiriano che, parodiando l'oracolo di Delfi, predicevano solo metà della verità per indurre in errore e distruggere, l'autore sfonda una porta aperta affermando delle verità che, in fondo, non sono poi che "mezze verità". Sono certa che, come me, molti altri lettori abbiano avvertito sentimenti di frustrazione e di noia, oltre che di imbarazzo e di rabbia, per le suggestioni che un simile articolo comporta.

Si sa che gli Italoamericani non leggono come un tempo usavano fare, ma non certo perchè essi siano perseguitati ancora da pregiudizi derivati dallo storico binomio Chiesa-Stato, che molti dei nostri emigranti si sono portati dietro al di qua dell'Atlantico e che hanno prodotto una strana forma di anticlericalismo che, in molti casi, non ha cancellato tuttavia del tutto la fede cattolica dei singoli.

Lo strapotere dei mass-media

Gli Italoamericani, come qualunque gruppo etnico, soffrono di quella malattia generale che sacrifica il leggere e lo scrivere all'ansia di riuscire in fretta nella vita e goderne presto i privilegi. Scrivere bene è infatti così raro oggi, anche da parte dei migliori studenti universitari; tanto che leggere è diventata quasi una causa persa in partenza a causa dello strapotere della televisione e degli altri mass-media, con i "news" ventiquattro ore al giorno, con il creare eroi in un batter d'occhio, col fare dell'attività politica un "dramma" da seguire, con il "suspense" relegato nei cosiddetti dibattiti spesso ridotti a degli assoluti semplicistici: cosa che un grande filosofo ha definito "diritto astratto" cercato da coloro che non hanno reali responsabilità.

Tutti abbiamo sofferto per la riduzione e la dispersione dell'apporto culturale, ma, ciò che è peggio, molti di noi non riescono nemmeno a riconoscere cosa in effetti sia o debba essere questo apporto culturale. Ma è senza dubbio errato e senza senso attribuire tale fenomeno a qualcosa di inerente la stessa natura degli Italoamericani.

E' un fenomeno comune: questa è l'amara novità dei nostri tempi.

Quelli che vissero dopo l'invasione degli Unni e prima del "revival" umanistico, durante il regno degli imperatori di casa Hohenstaufen (che diedero inizio alla letteratura italiana con la *scuola siciliana* e rimpiazzarono la poesia dei Provenzali), non sospettavano certo di vivere nei "secoli bui".

Un'occasione storica

E' difficile oggi, suppongo, riconoscere che anche noi abbiamo perso una grande occasione storica, permettendo che i nostri legami col passato si allentassero così tanto. Ma, come ho già detto prima, non risponde a verità e, peggio, conduce in ulteriori errori, pensare che tale fenomeno sia solo da addebitare agli Italoamericani.

Gli Italoamericani, proprio come gli altri gruppi etnici, leggono. Essi, allo stesso modo degli Ebrei, sentono le pressioni sociologiche del nostro tempo, e non di meno sostengono, come chiunque altro, - al con-

trario di quanto affermato da Anthony Pedatella - quella letteratura e quei film (come *Il Padrino* di Mario Puzo, a lungo in testa alla classifica dei best-sellers mondiali) che trattano di gangsters.

Certamente, è doveroso trattare, capire e far conoscere quella realtà, piuttosto che far finta di niente, come se si stesse nascondendo la polvere sotto il tappeto. E ogni qualvolta da un libro si trae un soggetto per un film o per una rappresentazione teatrale di successo, lo stesso autore e l'editore finiscono col trarne dei guadagni finanziari in quanto gli spettatori richiedono quell'opera facendone un successo editoriale. Così, se l'*Enrico IV* con Mar-

Mario Fratti

cello Mastroianni venisse negli Stati Uniti, sarebbero in molti a scoprire ed apprezzare l'opera di Luigi Pirandello.

Il dramma "artificiale"

La spiegazione di ciò è sempre da ricercare nello strapotere dei mass-media e della Tv in particolare, che allontana dal leggere e crea il dramma artificialmente (avvenimenti di cronaca e di politica) anche là dove il dramma non c'è affatto.

Bisogna anche respingere un'altra delle affermazioni del Pedatella, laddove egli afferma che gli Italoamericani non vogliono che i loro figli siano istruiti nel reale senso del termine. Forse non ho inteso bene il significato voluto dall'autore, o forse egli intendeva parlare solo di *una certa educazione*.

Non c'è alcun dubbio infatti che gli Italoamericani preferiscano per i loro figli un lavoro sicuro e ben retribuito, piuttosto che saperli "artisti" (poeti, musicisti, etc.) senza alcuna sicurezza economica: quante volte abbiamo infatti sentito dire da amici e parenti che loro non erano daccordo con il figlio o il nipote che sognavano di diventare uno scrittore o un artista in genere? Ma, in questo, gli Italoamericani sono forse diversi dagli Ebrei o dalle altre minoranze razziali e culturali?

Gli Ebrei, si sa, hanno gran rispetto per la posizione che uno occupa, per il denaro che si guadagna, e per il prestigio che da ciò deriva - e chi non lo sarebbe infatti? -; essi prima cercano una solida posizione, e

La statua di Dante Alighieri nei pressi del Lincoln Center di Manhattan e, in alto, un'incisione raffigurante Francesco Petrarca.

SI/B   ATTUALITA'   IL PROGRESSO - DUE MONDI   DOMENICA 30 SETTEMBRE 1984

Niccolò Machiavelli

poi pensano a dedicarsi alle arti o alle altre attività culturali. In questo particolare campo, forse si sono sinora mostrati più responsabili degli industriali ed uomini d'affari italoamericani.

Priorità culturali

L'errore che sta alla base del fatto che i nostri connazionali non leggono abbastanza e non scrivono sarebbe, seguendo le argomentazioni del professor Pedatella, il risultato di una scelta di priorità culturali. Saremmo finiti nella massa amorfa perché i nostri leaders culturali non hanno saputo indicare, come dovevano, le varie priorità e, di conseguenza, è stato impossibile vedere le cose nel modo migliore possibile. Ripetiamo però ancora una volta che tale fenomeno non può per nessuna ragione al mondo essere addebitato esclusivamente al nostro gruppo etnico.

Certamente, in un particolare forse siamo tutti colpevoli: migliaia di dollari sono stati, ad esempio, investiti nell'insegnamento dell'italiano e, molto spesso, ciò è anche diventata materia di un vero e proprio dibattito politico, ma ciò che ancora manca, in fondo, è la definizione della meta da raggiungere: il fine è quello di poter ordinare un pranzo al ristorante quando si va in viaggio in Italia o è altrove e diverso?

L'amara verità

L'amara verità è che molti che hanno eccellenti capacità e titoli accademici debbono scegliere l'insegnamento della lingua come loro lavoro fondamentale. Alcuni di loro scrivono durante il tempo libero e molti sono anche bravi in questo, ma, per la maggior parte del tempo, la loro attività primaria è quella dell'insegnamento linguistico nelle varie classi. Le classi non sono poi molto numerose (così pure quelle nei dipartimenti di inglese sono minori che non in passato).

Molti bravi studenti preferiscono infatti dedicare le proprie attenzioni verso quelle aree (legge, farmacia, commercio, comunicazioni di massa, medicina, etc.) dove il futuro sembra meglio garantito. Questi studenti non hanno tempo per lo studio di una lingua straniera (e l'italiano non fa certo eccezione). Perciò a che serve porre al di sopra di tutto la necessità di insegnare la lingua? L'insegnamento della lingua non porta infatti automaticamente all'apprezzamento dello studio di Dante o di Leopardi.

E ciò non per deficienze congenite agli italoamericani, ma semplicemente perché nessuno ha mai seriamente considerato la necessità di riportare alla ribalta tutto il curriculum di studi umanistici in cui autori come Dante, Petrarca e Boccaccio siano presentati in buone traduzioni inglesi, insieme a Goethe, Shakespeare ed altri.

L'insegnamento di una lingua straniera, così come è congegnato adesso, non sem-

bra, purtroppo, avere alcun futuro. Ciò verso cui invece dovrebbero essere rivolti tutti i nostri sforzi è nell'incontro pieno tra cultura e lingua.

La comunità degli scrittori

La comunità degli scrittori italoamericani è molto vivace in questa direzione. Mario Fratti, ad esempio, nel preparare una convenzione di scrittori italoamericani da tenersi a Perugia, ha trovato circa sessanta autori; gli è stato invece difficile trovare le opere di detti autori. Nel mio caso personale, questa difficoltà è stata superata in quanto avevo a disposizione miei libri da dargli, ma per gli autori che non sono più in vita o che hanno pubblicato le loro opere molto tempo fa come si fa?

Ciò di cui abbiamo fortemente bisogno è una casa editrice che pubblichi regolarmente le opere dei nostri autori, come Jerre Mangione (una cui opera è l'unico libro di italoamericani attualmente in circolazione), Helen Barolini (della quale si è recentemente ricordato il suo *Umbertina*), Di Donato, lo stesso Fratti ed altri.

Avremmo bisogno di maggiori premi letterari (come, ad esempio, il Poggioli, dato alla migliore traduzione dall'italiano). Avremmo bisogno di industriali e di uomini d'affari italoamericani che promuovano attività culturali (in questo gli Ebrei hanno mostrato sinora una migliore organizzazione e diversa volontà).

Il mondo però è quello che è. Gli ultimi avvenimenti hanno portato alla ribalta personaggi come Mario Cuomo e Geraldine Ferraro che possono certamente contribuire al rilancio culturale desiderato, soprattutto se riusciremo a far tesoro delle lezioni del passato e se avremo idee chiare e precise per il nostro futuro. E' giunto il tempo di appoggiare con coraggio e decisione i progetti italoamericani, e tra questi anche quelli di natura squisitamente culturale.

Le diverse radici

Dobbiamo distinguere, nei far ciò, le radici italiane da quelle italoamericane. Dante fa parte di ogni letteratura, come Shakespeare. Lo stesso Machiavelli è conosciuto ovunque nel mondo per le sue idee politiche. E, ironia della sorte, molto spesso sono state altre comunità a promuovere e far conoscere tali autori che, in parte, vengono trascurati dai nostri.

E' assurdo affermare che gli italoamericani non leggono a causa del pregiudizio del binomio Chiesa-Stato di cui si è detto prima. Non riesco infatti a ricordare nessun italoamericano che voglia nessuna educazione per i suoi figli: tutti vogliono che i propri figli ricevano l'istruzione adatta, almeno quella che li aiuti a farsi una posizione decente nella società.

Nel mio caso personale, ad esempio, ho imparato l'inglese quando avevo nove anni, dopo essere nata a Roma e aver conservato la lingua nativa; a quattordici anni ho dovuto poi iniziare a lavorare per procu-

Luigi Pirandello

Helen Barolini

rarmi i mezzi per poter andare all'università. Mio suocero ha sempre ripetuto ai figli che per essere rispettati qui in Usa è necessario conservare il più possibile il proprio retaggio culturale: è l'unica via per aver successo. E così è stato fatto. Egli stesso, del resto, era un lettore accanito.

Non aveva alcuna educazione scolastica che andasse oltre la seconda-terza media (settimo-ottavo grado della junior high-school), ma conosceva Machiavelli e Dante e riusciva a capire fino in fondo il loro pensiero, e avrebbe certamente fatto arrossire molti dei miei colleghi universitari per le sue conoscenze letterarie e culturali. Non ha mai spinto i suoi figli a diventare professori universitari ma, quando uno lo è diventato, ne è stato oltremodo felice.

Sociologia e politica

Questa questione dovrebbe comunque essere affrontata anche sotto l'aspetto sociologico e politico.

Gli italoamericani sono stati tra i primi gruppi etnici (insieme agli irlandesi ed agli scandinavi) ad integrarsi nella nuova realtà sociale. Hanno spesso dimenticato il loro linguaggio naturale (il dialetto), hanno sposato appartenenti ad altri gruppi etnici e sono diventati dei leali cittadini americani.

Ma, ad un certo punto, sono stati costretti per ragioni pratiche a ritornare al rango di minoranza per raccogliere alcuni dei benefici che sono emersi di recente per le varie minoranze. Le pressioni politiche, a torto o a ragione, hanno fatto sì che anche i figli o i nipoti italiani solo per un quarto (che non conoscevano né la lingua né la cultura dei loro antenati) fossero inseriti nel gruppo degli italoamericani per esercitare quella pressione messa in pratica dalle altre minoranze, alcune delle quali stanno ancora lottando per asserire la loro identità e per loro posto nel panorama degli Stati Uniti.

Perché non usare il teatro?

Alla richiesta di come fare, ho recentemente risposto: "Perché non provare con il teatro?" E' sempre efficace infatti rappre-

sentare una commedia o parte di essa e reclamare l'attenzione dovuta da parte degli spettatori. Pirandello, ad esempio, è uno degli autori che meglio si prestano ad un'opera di divulgazione culturale simile.

Ci fu un momento di panico: qualcuno tra coloro che mi avevano fatto tale richiesta non conosceva affatto l'opera del nostro premio Nobel. "Chi è Pirandello?", mi è stato infatti chiesto. Era una maestra i cui genitori erano siciliani e siciliani erano molti dei suoi colleghi, eppure Pirandello, come ha detto Robert Brustein, è il più rappresentativo drammaturgo dei nostri tempi, il creatore del teatro contemporaneo. La lezione fu imparata molto rapidamente e ogni dubbio scomparve. Ma quante volte bisogna trovarsi in una situazione imbarazzante come questa per iniziare a fare qualche cosa in proposito?

Arte e letteratura

Gli italoamericani leggono e scrivono sotto l'influenza dei mass-media, come chiunque altro intorno a loro, e non è certamente una loro caratteristica esclusiva. Tutto può essere cambiato. Abbiamo bisogno di editori, abbiamo bisogno di corsi che ci istruiscano sul nostro retaggio culturale, abbiamo bisogno di abili conferenzieri che ci entusiasmino verso il nostro passato, abbiamo bisogno di teatri ove mettere in scena le opere di Goldoni e di Pirandello, abbiamo bisogno di programmi scolastici umanistici che inseriscano lo studio della nostra cultura nel suo reale contesto, e, ovviamente, abbiamo bisogno di conoscere e di parlare bene la nostra lingua.

Ma prima di fare ciò, occorre costruire una chiesa (il cui dio sia l'arte e la letteratura, ed in cui noi possiamo intimamente sentirci parte vivente del nostro passato culturale, e avere con ciò conferma della nostra identità di italiani e di italoamericani ad un tempo.

La dr. Anne Paolucci è Chairperson & Director of Arts Program in English presso la St. John's University di Jamaica (N.Y.).

SHORT STORIES, ESSAYS, TRAVEL AND VERSE

Potpourri

A Magazine of the Literary Arts

December 1993

Vol. 5, No. 12   Not-for-profit national publication dedicated to readers and writers

Two poems by Anne A. Paolucci

CANBERRA (1979)

I was christened in small doses
Vulnerable in slow erosion.

To touch without accident
As you break bread
Is the greatest gift.

My own timing grew parched
Like trying on French on thin lips
Or stretching the Nile
Beyond discarded Africa.
Blue beetles ride the red dust of my
Translated winter,
Upside down on the edge of the world
Who wouldn't twist and bend
Out of shape
Listening for the moon to fall, eh?
The southern stars rewind to their beginning
Thread me back.

CARIBO
(FOR HARRY T. MOORE)

"... L'altre tre se fero avanti,
danzando al loro angelico caribo."
Purgatorio XXXI (131-132)

Every curve of your Tiber flows epic.
You sweep us beyond the gift of tongues.
Somewhere in that familiar landscape
Of Tuscan hills tawny litanies
The best of whispering trees
We join catechumen in vigil
Crowned and mitred for a glimpse
Of your face.

Poet's is emerald burning
Snow a breath of fire
The air between is dancing light.
Mosaics teach us how to stare.
And when, still fleeing in terror,
Our body rooted in forest fears,
Rush of waters at our back.
High noon a haloed visitation
Too far across the curve of vision
As it bends to sound,
When in quiddity we stop,

Check the road map,
Others, some few, touch once, gently,
Forever, like you, with perfect skill,
White on white angelico caribo.

MOM WITH GRANDSON JOSEPH ATTURA

Dr. Anne Paolucci, Director
CONSERVATIVE WOMEN FOR
REAGAN-BUSH '84
166-25 Powells Cove Blvd,
Beechhurst New York 11357

New York Tribune

TUESDAY, SEPT. 11, 1984 / **3B**

ALLEN ROTH

N.Y. Women believe Reagan has earned bid for re-election

" I'm fed-up with those who say we don't have to spend more money to modernize our Armed Forces," Patricia McCrann says. "My husband served in Vietnam and the enemy frequently had more sophisticated weapons than he did. I think it is very important that we go ahead and modernize our Armed Forces."

McCrann is not a right-wing fanatic who longs for war. She is a concerned citizen who served in prominent administrative positions in the League of Women Voters and the Girl Scouts of America. She is now co-Chairman of New York Women for Reagan-Bush.

Dismissing the conventional political wisdom that New York and women will not vote for Reagan, Pat McCrann is confident the president will triumph. While she readily admits that she disagrees with Reagan on some issues ("You can't agree with someone all the time"), she believes the president is doing a splendid job with those issues of greatest importance.

Educating the public

She gives Reagan high grades for making Americans deservedly proud of their country and for improving Carter's rapidly deteriorating economy. On these and other issues McCrann is upset that the truth about Reagan's accomplishments is not public knowledge. She believes that if the Reagan record became known he would sweep the votes of women and men in New York and across the nation.

To educate the public, Pat is actively reaching out to any organization that will give Reagan-Bush an opportunity to set the record straight. Despite the lack of cooperation from a host of supposedly non-partisan women's groups which are really biased in favor of the Democrats, Pat feels she will succeed. She is especially optimis-

Allen Roth is a free-lance writer and columnist living in New York.

tic because she has the Reagan record of achievements on her side.

She notes that more women than ever before have started businesses because of the opportunities provided by the economic recovery, and feels that the appointment of Sandra Day O'Connor is a prime example of how this president is anxious to give talented women the opportunity to serve their country. She is also proud of the important roles Elizabeth Dole, Margaret Heckler,

> *The reality is that, except for some activists, men and women are concerned about the same issues.*

Jeanne Kirkpatrick and more than 1,500 other women are playing in this administration.

Pat's enthusiasm for Reagan is echoed by Dr. Anne Paolucci. Asked why Paolucci has taken time out of her busy schedule as Chairperson of St. John's University English Department to organize Conservative Women for Reagan-Bush, Paolucci answers that Ronald Reagan has earned reelection because of his diplomatic successes, his strengthening of our defense capabilities and his improving our economy.

Giving Reagan credit

Paolucci also thinks Reagan deserves credit for making Americans proud of being Americans. She feels the Carter Administration paid too much attention to those who make a profession out of denouncing America, and not enough to defending our national

interests. She also contends the Democrats promise what they cannot deliver and are advocating a policy of turning Latin America and South America over to the Soviets. Paolucci believes it is imperative that Reagan's realistic, hard-nosed policy toward the Russians and Cubans continues.

These and other New York women have raised questions about the validity of the Gender Gap theory which maintains American women have entirely different concerns than their male counterparts. The reality is that, except for some fringe political activists, men and women are primarily concerned about the same issues.

Anyone who thinks President Reagan's opposition to the Equal Rights Amendment and abortion will cause an overwhelming majority of women to vote for Mondale is in for a rude awakening. Women and men support the president because they are benefiting from the booming economy, tax reforms and tax reductions, which allow many more people an opportunity to enjoy the fruits of their labor.

Women in particular are benefiting from the gradual elimination of the estate tax which imposed unfair burdens on widows. Because of President Reagan's support, women can now invest more in IRA accounts, and families can take advantage of increased tax credits for child-care programs. The list of Reagan's record on women's issues could continue, but the main reason Reagan should gain a majority of votes of both men and women is that most voters think of themselves as Americans, not members of interest groups. If the president successfully delivers his pro-American, pro-family values message, he stands a good chance of carrying Geraldine Ferraro's home state of New York.

Anyone interested in information about Conservative Women for Reagan-Bush should write to Dr. Anne Paolucci, 166-25 Powells Cove Blvd., Beechhurst, New York, 11357.

CW **CONSERVATIVE WOMEN FOR REAGAN-BUSH '84**   **NEWS**

FOR IMMEDIATE RELEASE: November 3, 1984

CONTACT: Dr. Anne Paolucci - Judy Stupp (718) 767-8380

"BACK TO BASICS: GRAMMAR IN THE GRAMMAR SCHOOLS":
EDUCATIONAL REFORM UNDER PRESIDENT REAGAN

The report of President Reagan's Commission on Education makes dramatically clear that the next four years are crucial in the assessment and restructuring of all levels of education in the United States, said Dr. Anne Paolucci in a recent interview.

"Return to basics is essential both in the lower schools and in higher education. Grammar should be taught in the grammar schools, and ideally through one or more foreign languages. It is appalling to find that the greater percentage of incoming college freshmen have little real command of language and that they consider courses in humanities a waste of time. No doubt television, with its instant gratifications, is responsible for a measure of erosion in the humanities, but that reality can be countered quickly by reorganizing priorities in the lower and higher schools as well as in the colleges."

Dr. Paolucci, who spoke as Director of Conservative Women for Reagan-Bush '84, and Interim Director of Conservative Women of America (in formation), is Chairperson of the English Department of St. John's University, and Director of its Doctor of Arts Degree Program in English. "We shall soon be talking to ourselves," she commented when asked about the morale and role of the humanities instructors in colleges and universities. "We have to start much earlier, reinstating humanities courses, so that students know the names and works of Homer, Aeschylus, Dante, Machiavelli, Spenser, Shakespeare, as well as those of Andric, Mofulo, Borges, Ibsen, Ionesco, Pirandello, Hemingway, Senghor and other great writers of our modern world. We should not have to apologize for teaching humanities. By the time a student reaches college, he should expect and want to continue a basic program—ideally a four-year program, as in the old days—which is humanitistic and not predominantly career-oriented.

"We have given too much attention to preparing students for jobs," Dr. Paolucci emphasized. "The result is that students are now impatient with any courses that are not specifically focused on their field of career specialization. This situation has already resulted in a certain measure of cultural illiteracy. Students should understand that a humanities curriculum is a lifelong acquisition and that the only formal access they will ever have to subjects that enlarge the human spirit and establish a love for knowledge in its own right is during the school and college years."

Asked about President Reagan's plans for education in the next four years, Dr. Paolucci said: "I don't know the details of President Reagan's plans for education, although the recommendations of the National Commission on Excellence in Education appointed by the President reflect unmistakable concern and a firm commitment to stricter standards and basic requirements. I am certain that President Reagan will follow the priorities he has already established and which have guided us in the formation of Conservative Women of America: national excellence in all fields and areas; national strength in the world; and organic and viable programs that will serve all our people domestically. In terms of education I feel that a complete overhaul of the system is in order at this time. Special or experimental programs should be re-examined and tightened or changed; and the basic programs in the schools should be firmly rooted in a strong and expanding humanities curriculum, with the classics reinstated, at least two foreign languages required as in past times, and grammatical skills, including fluency in writing and speaking, again made the center of all teaching programs from early grades through high school."

Dr. Paolucci, whose academic specialties include Shakespeare, Dante, Machiavelli, Spenser, dramatic theory, ancient and modern drama, is founder and President of the Council on National Literatures, which has members in over 40 foreign countries. The aim of the Council, according to Dr. Paolucci, is "to do for our colleagues in comparative studies what I have proposed for our students: reconsider priorities and work out new definitions and approaches that will enable us to reorganize comparative literary studies systematically within a multinational spectrum in which all literary cultures will have 'separate and equal status' among the nations of the earth.

"Our Doctor of Arts Program in English at St. John's," Dr. Paolucci noted, "is structured as comparative, interdisciplinary, and professional—and it includes multinational approaches to literatures. In its special structure the Program is perhaps unique."

Dr. Paolucci commended the Reagan administration for its insistence on high quality education and concluded: "It's easy enough, of course, to say we want high quality education for our children; what is hard is to implement that commitment along realistic and humanistic lines. It means taking a long look at the primary and secondary schools, at the colleges and post-graduate programs, and work out a total organic structure of excellence that will give scope to all students, and make provision for those who need special help along the way.

"I congratulate President Reagan and his Commission for having had the courage to look at the situation in a non-partisan way and for having called attention to the serious problems that face us in the years ahead. The Commission's report, 'Nation at Risk,' is unambiguous in stating the seriousness of the situation; but it has also shown the way to solid improvement."

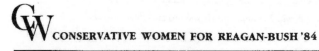

CONSERVATIVE WOMEN FOR REAGAN-BUSH '84   **NEWS**

FOR IMMEDIATE RELEASE: October 15, 1984

CONTACT: Dr. Anne Paolucci - Judy Stupp (718) 767-8380

"THE MISCHIEF OF FACTIONS": WOMEN AND POLITICS IN A DEMOCRACY

Now that the candidacies of our highest elective offices are within their grasp, it is important to remind ourselves that women in America *do not* constitute the sort of majority faction that James Madison warned us against in *Federalist* Paper 10.

That the "women's rights" movement of recent decades should have tended toward the excesses of majoritarian factionalism—at least in its most publicized manifestations—was perhaps inevitable. Its self-appointed and most radicalized spokespersons have usually indulged themselves in the rhetoric of abused minority rights: but in fact women greatly outnumber men in this country; and the political reality has been that, if they could ever be brought together to vote as a factional bloc, they would obviously have the numbers to sweep the field. Still, women haven't so voted, and it seems unlikely that they ever will.

To avail themselves of the rhetoric of abused minorities, advocates of "women's rights" have had very deliberately to narrow their constituencies. They have had to limit their advocacy more or less specifically to the claims of sexist discrimination in public or private sector employment, life-style preferences, the rights of pregnant women to abort unwanted children, or of un-wed mothers to un-qualified public support of their children. Any attempt to identify such distinctly minority claims as majority interests of American women as a whole have consistently failed. And we are reminded, on that account, of the important distinction James Madison drew between factions that consist of less than a majority and those that in fact include a majority.

For the "mischief" of factions that consist of less than a majority, "relief is supplied," as Madison put it, "by the republican principle, which enables the majority to defeat its sinister views by regular vote." Unwed mothers, or victims of discrimination in the work force, certainly have a right to be heard as minorities expressing discontents in the process of petitioning the majority government for justice, for redress of wrongs. As minorities, they can hardly hope to get very far by threatening to outvote the majority. When, on the other hand, "a majority is included in a faction"—as would be the case if women voted together simply as women—the form of popular government itself, as Madison explains, enables it "to sacrifice to its ruling passion or interest both the public good and the rights of other citizens."

What if American women as a whole were ever to abandon themselves to a ruling passion or interest? Madison at no point singles out women in his discussion of the evil or mischief of majority factionalism, but his pessimism about the prospect certainly applies. If we were dealing with a small community, say a democratic city-state of the size of San Francisco, or Manhattan, the danger would be very real, for, in a relatively small democratic society, a common passion or interest can very easily spread to infect a majority of the whole. In Madison's words: "A communication and concert result from the form of government itself; and there is nothing to check the inducements"—in the ranks of a passionately aroused majority—"to sacrifice the weaker party." Fortunately, from Madison's vantage-point, our country is much larger than Manhattan or San Francisco. According to Madison, when a democracy or republic has a large citizenry spread out over a vast territory, the excesses of majority factions are less to be dreaded; for a majority made up of large numbers is not likely to **act as** one, not likely to have "a common motive to invade the rights of other citizens; or if such a common motive exists, it will be more difficult for all who feel it to discover their own strength and to act in unison with each other."

The division of the American sovereign national Union into sovereign States is defended by Madison as a primary check upon the mischief of majority factions. "The influence of factious leaders may kindle a flame within their particular States," he says, "but will be unable to spread a general conflagration through the other States." Again, Madison does not refer to women as potentially constituting a majority faction in the electorate; and that was prudent of him, since more than a century and a quarter was to pass before the Federal Constitution was amended to accord them their right to vote. But he speaks of religious sects that might degenerate into political factions (something much in the news these days), noting, however, that while a politicized sect might conceivably gain majority adherence for its political ends in one section of the country, the "variety of sects dispersed over the entire face of it must secure the national councils against any danger from that source."

Madison speaks also of factions animated by the "rage for paper money," or "for an abolition of debts," or "for an equal division of property." Such factional passions, pressing for these or "for any other improper or wicked projects," he concludes, "will be less apt to pervade the whole body of the Union than a particular member of it, in the same proportion as such a malady is more likely to taint a particular county or district than an entire State."

The examples cited by Madison may not be as compelling for us today as they were for his fellow-citizens of those early days; but the principle he expounds remains viable and vital. Within the majority group of American women there are many different interests and concerns. There are Geraldine Ferraros and Jeane Kirkpatricks, there are liberal and conservative women, as well as pro- and anti-abortionist women. Despite superficial representations in the newsmedia, the *conservative* women of

America probably constitute a majority of women, at least potentially. But, even if they do not, they certainly constitute a sufficiently large, and sufficiently active minority to prevent the radicalized factional advocates of minority female concerns from ever rallying a true majority. to their cause.

The *conservative* Women of America are determined, as women, to perfect our national Union as a whole; they are determined to preserve our diversity in unity as a community of individuals born free and equal, or raised by democratic means to equality in freedom; and, most importantly, in the spirit of our founding fathers, their concern is to secure the blessings of such freedom, to themselves, of course, but also to the whole of their posterity, male and female.

CONSERVATIVE WOMEN FOR REAGAN-BUSH '84   NEWS

FOR IMMEDIATE RELEASE: October 23, 1984

CONTACT: Dr. Anne Paolucci - Judy Stupp (718) 767-8380

RATIONALE FOR THE ORGANIZATION OF A NEW YORK STATE CAMPAIGN
COMMITTEE OF CONSERVATIVE WOMEN FOR REAGAN-BUSH 1984

The Reagan-Bush Administration has plainly earned its right to "four more years" in Washington. Since the chief challengers to the re-election of Reagan-Bush have given their national campaign a New York focus, with an Italian-American woman from Queens nominated as the Democratic Party's Vice-Presidential candidate and the Italian-American Governor of New York State chosen to give the key-note address at that nominating convention, Reagan-Bush supporters must do their best to counter the attempts of the Democratic challengers—particularly their argument that the Democratic ticket will be especially appealing because of the presence on it of a liberal Democratic woman from New York State. This "cosmetic" argument must be shown for what it is: there are issues at stake in this campaign that must and should be faced squarely. There are indeed many relevant and distinctive matters that bear directly on the issue of women voters and these matters should be brought into focus.

Conservative Women for Reagan-Bush 1984 mean to confront these matters directly by emphasizing why, from a woman's point of view, it is imperative to re-elect Ronald Reagan and George Bush for "four more years." Some of these matters have to do with the state of the *economy, ethical-family values, and national preparedness internationally.* As against the counter-claims of the liberal standard-bearers of the Democratic Party, it can be clearly demonstrated that

1) The *economy* is much better off now, nationally, and in New York State, than it was four years ago. The Governor of New York makes the same claim for our state but, as Republican-Conservative Edward V. Regan, Controller of the State of New York, correctly says, it is on the strength of Reagan's national economic programs that New York State is holding up economically, despite the Governor's sustained liberalism in economic matters.

2) The appeal to *ethical-family values* made by New York State liberal Democrats now in the national limelight owes much more to the Reagan appeal on those same values than it does to the liberalism of those same New York State Democrats, for which they have been severely criticized, at least implicitly, not only by outstanding religious leaders but also by Democratic leaders in other parts of the country.

3) The Reagan-Bush *defense policy* has restored confidence in an overwhelming majority of Americans. Conservative Women for Reagan-Bush in New York can be proud of the fact that two of the finest spokespersons of that policy, on the highest levels of international diplomacy, are indeed women: Jeane Kirkpatrick. U.S. Ambassador to the United Nations. and Jean Girard, U.S. Ambassador to UNESCO. Both these women were appointed to office by President Reagan.

The Reagan-Bush administration has worked positively and responsibly in both domestic and foreign policy, keeping the interests of all Americans in clear focus at all times and working sincerely and honestly to promote international understanding and communication.

That Administration deserves our enthusiastic support.

COMMON SENSE
By Allen Roth

BROOKLYN SPECTATOR—September 5, 1984

About a year ago the news media reported that American men and women have very different opinions about the major issues facing our society. Public opinion surveys supposedly showed that females and males were going to cast their votes on Election Day for different candidates because they disagreed on so many fundamental policies.

After learning of these statistics Democrats and feminists jumped to the conclusion that women are ready to vote as a block against Ronald Reagan. This in large part is the reason why Walter Mondale chose a woman for the vice presidential slot. If the so-called gender gap theory is correct, women, both because they are opposed to Reagan's political agenda and because one of their own is on the Democratic ticket, would vote to replace Reagan and the Republicans with candidates who represent their special-interest points of view.

I never believed the theory that America has become two different and competing societies—one male, the other female. And recent political polls suggest that a majority of women have joined a majority of men in support of President Reagan's reelection. It seems that rather than having their own selfish political agenda, women are primarily concerned about the issues that effect our entire society and not just "women's issues."

One woman who belies the gender gap theory is Dr. Anne Paolucci. Given her impressive professional achievements one might think that she would be in the forefront of the National Organization For Women's crusade to retire Ronald Reagan. Instead, this accomplished poet, author, and educator is the driving force behind Conservative Women For Reagan-Bush.

Why is the chairwoman of St. John's University's English Dept. and an expert on Dante, Shakespeare and Comparative Literature, so committed to winning the election for Reagan? For one, she believes that the Democrats promise the moon even though they cannot deliver it. And she feels President Reagan has done a splendid job "settling the economy" at a time when all national economies are to a large degree affected by international forces beyond any president's control.

Dr. Paolucci is also critical of the Democratic Party's foreign policy. She agrees with Ambassador Jeanne Kirkpatrick's analysis that the Democrats are like ostriches who bury their heads in the sand in hopes that the Soviet threat in Central America and elsewhere will disappear. Like Kirkpatrick, Dr. Paolucci applauds President Reagan's initiatives that have strengthened our nation's defense capabilities and have improved our standing in the international community.

Furthermore, Dr. Paolucci admires President Reagan's "love" for the United States of America. Unlike Jimmy Carter and the Democrats, she feels Reagan is most concerned about the interests of the United States, not the world as a whole. "And we are selecting a president of the U.S., not the world," she declared.

After listening to Dr. Paolucci's enlightened analysis of the Reagan presidency we began talking about the state of education in our nation. She is concerned by the large numbers of high school graduates who cannot read and she is supportive of President Reagan's campaign to make excellence a part of our educational system. And she feels, excellence cannot become reality until our children master the basic disciplines.

As our delightful conversation came to an end, Dr. Paolucci informed me that Conservative Women For Reagan-Bush '84 is open to Democrats, Republicans, Conservatives, and Independents who feel it is important to carry on the work of the Reagan Administration. Anyone interested in more information should write to Dr. Anne Paolucci, 166-25 Powells Cove Blvd., Beechhurst, N.Y.

ADVERTISING SPA MUSIC THEATER PRODUCTIONS, WITH RAY RIZZO (1964)

OIL PAINTINGS ON CARDBOARD AND BOARD (1968-1975)

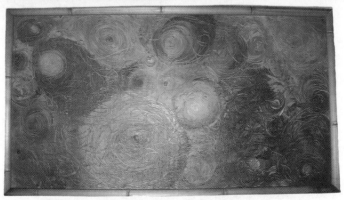

PART TWO

MOVING INTO THE PRESENT:
HIGHLIGHTS

FIRST VIEW
OF AUSTRALIA
FROM PLANE

"THE GAP:"
LOOKING OUT
TOWARD THE
OCEAN

5. THE OTHER SIDE OF THE WORLD
THE HUMANITIES RESEARCH CENTRE OF
THE AUSTRALIAN NATIONAL UNIVERSITY, CANBERRA

My book on Luigi Pirandello, the Sicilian playwright and Italian Nobel Laureate in Literature, published in 1973 (this too with a Preface by Harry T, Moore) and my reviving the Pirandello Society of America and encouraging dramatic readings, panel discussions, and lectures at Columbia, St. John's, Pace and other colleges and universities, as well as The Classic Theater and the Roundabout Theater, had had a certain impact, the result of which was several invitations to Agrigento (Sicily) — the playwright's birthplace — to take part in the annual Pirandello International Conferences held there. Other academic and professional activities, while at St. John's, took me to many parts of the United States and Canada, to England, Italy, Austria, Yugoslavia and Germany.

During this time, I also read a paper at the very first International Shakespeare Conference, held in Vancouver, Canada. It was a memorable event, primarily because of the impact made by Japanese colleagues, who, in the plenary session at the close of the conference, reminded us of the many Japanese scholars who, not only had been writing about Shakespeare's works for many years, but had also produced some of the best translations of the major plays, thereby making them accessible to Japanese readers. Their appeal for greater and more effective networking around the world was the beginning of a new attitude among Shakespeareans. The impact by those Japanese academics would last into the present. Their presentations gave a new dimension to Shakespeare studies and encouraged new translations.

I gave scores of lectures here and abroad, during my 27 years at St. John's; prepared academic articles and, when the spirit moved me, relaxed writing fiction, poetry, and plays. I also continued to edit the publications of Council on National Literatures. But by far my most interesting professional trip during that time was a prolonged stay in Australia.

The invitation came from the Humanities Research Centre of the Australian National University in Canberra and was for the entire year of 1979. I was pleased but also puzzled. Not only had I not applied for anything like that; I had not even heard about the Centre, or about Canberra, before receiving the invitation. I found out later that one had to be nominated by a person who knew the candidate's professional work well, someone obviously of some standing and reputation, whose opinion would be considered seriously. Still later, I learned that my sponsor (although he had said nothing to me and never referred to it) had been the distinguished scholar Victor Lange, Professor of German and Comparative Literature at Princeton University.

I had met Professor Lange in the mid-seventies, at a conference held by the International Comparative Literature Association (in Tallahassee, I think). I had been asked to read a paper, and — as always on such occasions — I stayed on to hear other presentations, especially the keynote speakers. They turned out to be Henry Peyre, then Sterling Professor of French and Comparative Literature at Yale University (later, Distinguished Professor at the Graduate School of The City University of New York [CUNY]), and Victor Lange of Princeton, two of the most prominent comparatists and literary scholars in America, both also with strong European connections. At the reception that followed their presentations, I had a chance to speak with them. I found Professor Peyre witty, and (in spite of his many awards and ten honorary degrees), very much down-to-earth. Professor Lange, who had studied at Oxford, Heidelberg and the Sorbonne, was just as pleasant and easy to talk to.

They knew and had seen issues of *RNL* (their university libraries subscribed), and we soon got around to the possibility of their editing an issue for the series. But what I treasured for years to come was the easy and pleasant professional friendship that evolved. They were always eager to help, always took time to explain, always courteous, more than generous with their time.

When I first started to plan *The France of Claudel*, I contacted Professor Peyre, who graciously invited me to lunch. The meeting is etched in my memory. We chatted amiably as we ate. He shared with me a number of funny stories. Then I told him I was planning to do a French issue of *RNL* on Paul Claudel, the French Catholic playwright and Nobel Laureate, who wrote a number of plays on religious themes, as well as one about Christopher Columbus, plays that resembled our early American spectaculars and that often required a stadium to be performed. Peyre told me bluntly that he wasn't a fan of Claudel's. I quickly countered with my own admission that I much preferred Theater of the Absurd and the plays of Edward Albee. Why then did I want to do a volume on Claudel?

I told him exactly what had happened. A colleague of Henry's and good friend of ours, Boris De Balla, a Hungarian *émigré*, was visiting us with his wife one evening, when the subject of *RNL* came up. I told him I was thinking of a volume on France, but that I hadn't yet decided on a suitable theme or subject. He mentioned Claudel. I told him I wasn't that interested in his work. His answer set me thinking. "He represents an entire era that is fast disappearing," he said. "It should be preserved." I wasn't convinced, but I was ready to consider the possibility.

Professor Peyre nodded, but obviously he too was not convinced. Still, he kindly volunteered to help me in whatever way he could, if I decided on Claudel. In the weeks and months that followed, true to his word, he found time in his busy schedule to reach colleagues here and abroad for contributions to the volume and, in addition to writing a piece of his own, also translated two articles he had obtained from French colleagues. I allowed the translations in this case, knowing that the translator could not be faulted.

After a number of weeks, I proposed that he take on the title of Special

Editor for the issue. He refused in a nice way. I couldn't help myself and burst out: "But you've already done most of the work of an editor. You should take credit for it!" After a pause, he accepted. To my surprise, in the weeks that followed he worked even harder than before. It was something I had rarely met with; most colleagues I knew, with much less to their credit and much less to occupy their time, were most often than not "too busy" to help others. Here was a world-renowned scholar putting his own important work on "hold" in order to share his vast storehouse of knowledge — and contacts — with me on a subject he wasn't even too keen about.

Victor Lange was of the same breed. He was always ready to listen, give advice, make suggestions, provide names for our panels — I couldn't have found a better supporter, not only for my own writing but also and especially for the work of CNL and especially the *RNL* series. He readily accepted the task of Special Editor for the issue on *German Expressionism*, not only planning the issue with me and providing excellent contributors, but also writing a brilliant article himself. I treasured the support of these two extraordinary men, particularly their encouragement and cooperation in the preparation of *RNL* volumes. I was gratified by their attention (who wouldn't be?) and under their influence tried to better myself in every way. They actually read whatever new articles or publications I got out and would write me little notes thanking me and telling me what they found of special interest in what I'd written. It was exhilarating for me to be in contact with them.

I'm sure it was my work with CNL and my interest in Hegelian dramatic theory that made Professor Lange submit my name to the Humanities Research Centre. There were no duties attached to the invitation, except for one lecture to be given at an international conference the Centre hosted every year, on a subject that reflected the interests of the guest scholar in residence. The rest of the year, I could do whatever I pleased.

I was still, as I had always been, a wife and, if not exactly a parent, a "den mother" of sorts to nieces and a nephew, who took turns staying with Henry and me in Queens during the years they attended St. John's University. At this time, my nephew Joe was staying with us. Henry, as always, was supportive and wouldn't hear of my turning down the offer. On the other hand, I was concerned about the daily chores (among other things) that I would have to entrust to my husband and nephew. When I decided to accept, I spent days cooking and freezing meals, writing out instructions, showing Henry where the bank book was and how to make out the monthly checks, and silently prayed that, with my nephew Joe's help, my husband would be able to cope. I trusted my nephew more than my husband for taking care of the day-to-day business (including marketing), since he had been well-disciplined by his parents. Besides, I had decided to accept the invitation for six months only.

My trip to Canberra took 24 hours. I first flew out to the west coast, where I waited several hours for the connecting flight that would take me across the Pacific. In Sydney I had another wait, for the train to Canberra. I arrived at my ultimate destination on an absolutely brilliant afternoon. I learned later (and discovered for myself) that most days were like that, all year round. I was told that it rains for a whole week in June and that's it. The sun is out for the rest of the time.

Professor Ian Donaldson, the Director of the Humanities Research Centre, was waiting for me at the station. He first escorted me to the apartment they had reserved for me, one of the few on campus, a short distance from the Centre, helped carry my luggage inside, then turned to me pleasantly, with: "Shall we join the others for tea?"

I was ready to collapse from the long journey and lack of sleep; I could hardly keep my eyes open. Didn't the man realize I was in no condition to socialize and sip tea? I quickly decided it was best to go along rather than postpone my "introduction" to the Centre staff, who had come to meet me.

We walked across a bright expanse of green to the Centre. Donaldson kept fanning away big flies with a magazine he had brought along. I had to use my hands. The flies, he explained, were on account of the Merino sheep, which were more numerous than the human population in Australia. He went on to explain that Australia, although about as large as the United States, is — except for its populated eastern strip and the city of Perth on the west coast — a huge desert, most of it uninhabitable. The sky is brilliant and the unobstructed sun dangerously hot most of the year.

When we got to our destination, I went through the motions, had my tea, chatted, and stayed longer than I intended. What caught my eye and kept me staring from the moment I entered the lounge were three giant spheres, four feet in diameter, resting inside wooden stands. One was of the earth, the other two were celestial spheres. I felt as though I'd fallen asleep and walked into a surrealistic dream. I'd never seen anything quite like those huge globes.

TWO OF THE THREE GIANT GLOBES I FOUND AT THE CENTRE, THE DAY OF MY ARRIVAL

They had been brought there from somewhere else, I was told, and would be delivered elsewhere the next morning. I don't remember what was said or who else was at that afternoon tea, but those three enormous globes are still vivid in my memory. I was glad I'd gone to the Centre that day, instead of postponing my visit for the next afternoon.

In the days and weeks that followed, I discovered that Canberra was a very small "city," built expressly to serve as the capital, to avoid difficulties between the major contenders: Sydney on the eastern coast (a much smaller and less hectic version of New York City) and Melbourne in the southeast (reminiscent of London). Either of these two established centers was a more likely venue for the national capital, but Canberra was built instead, thus preventing disruptive and lingering resentment had one or the other of the two major cities been selected.

Perhaps deliberately, Canberra was built in the middle of nowhere. There is nothing close to it. Its major attraction is an artificially-created lake (a wonder, where water is scarce) surrounded by thriving trees, carefully tended gifts of foreign countries. The sight is unexpected in a place where vegetation is scarce and where trees, where they grow naturally, are a far cry from the large centuries-old majestic redwoods of our West, the tall firs of Vermont and Maine, and the many other varieties of trees we are accustomed to. I remember watching the landscape go by, on first arriving and later as I approached Sydney; taking in the sorry spectacle of what appeared to be dying trees shedding their bark, with tiny tufts of pale thin leaves reaching upward here and there, in a valiant effort to survive. I later learned that the trees were not dying but had adjusted to the dry climate in that peculiar way.

I soon found a buddy, a retired nurse (or "Sister," as they are called there). Her name was Pat Sorby. She was a tiny, energetic woman, with a small

WITH "SISTER" PAT SORBY

car, who took me under her wing and drove me everywhere. One of her sons was a barrister and had set up an elegant office in one of the buildings on the central square. I met him once only, when Sister took me to see his new quarters. But offices like his, government buildings and all the shops, I soon discovered, shut down promptly at noon on Saturdays and didn't open again until Monday morning. For two days, Canberra resembled an abandoned MGM or Universal set. I wondered what people did on the weekends, with everything closed down. Sister soon made me wise. She took me, as her guest, to several of the "private" clubs in the area. You couldn't really see these places from the street. You had to know where they were and then gained access only if you were a member. Inside was a hidden other world: playgrounds for the children, soccer fields, "casino" game rooms, cinemas, and restaurants, of course.

VISITNG A "CLUB" WITH PAT SORBY AND FRIEND

Sister took me also on long drives and, on several occasions, we spent the day in Sydney. One of the things that most impressed me about Sydney was the sleek ferries that serviced dozens of points, moving swiftly across the water — a far cry from the lumbering old New York ferries that make the crossing from lower Manhattan to Staten Island. Inside, the famous opera house was smaller than I had imagined, but truly a striking structure. I returned to Sydney on my own, near the end of my stay, to give a lecture at the University. I had decided by then, to visit some of the college centers before returning to the States. Having made myself available, I was surprised at the number of invitations I received — La Trobe, Deakin, Adelaide, Flanders, Monash, Melbourne, Queensland, in addition to Sydney and the Australian National University itself.

My visit to Brisbane, Queensland, on the northeastern coast, where I gave a series of lectures, lasted a whole week and gave me time to see that part of the continent. My stay was made especially pleasant by the Provost of Queensland University, Sam Rayner, who took me to places of historical interest; showed me the local "sights"; drove me to see the endless stretch of white-bleached sand along the flat, uninterrupted smooth northern coastline, where I expressed surprise at finding the place deserted. I was reminded that, tempting as those lovely sands might be, exposure to a sun that beat down on them mercilessly was dangerous and should be avoided.

DINNER WITH SAM RAYNER, PROVOST, QUEENSLAND UNIVERSITY

ON THE BEACH — BRIEFLY) — (BRISBANE)

The record showed that there was a high incidence of skin cancer among people who had ventured to lie under those powerful rays, even briefly. I recognized the foolhardiness but couldn't resist. I love the ocean. I talked my host into spending part of a morning on a stretch of beach, the sand sparkling in the white hot sun. There was no one else around all the time we were there.

I enjoyed my tour of the universities, but I was also somewhat disconcerted to discover that, everywhere I went, my Australian colleagues rejected both the phrase and the idea of "comparative literary studies." They felt strongly that comparisons tended to dilute the subjects approached in that way. A student should have in-depth preparation in one area, they insisted, before presuming to move into another. It was no accident that my lectures were always hosted by the separate language and literature departments of the universities I happened to be visiting: French, Italian, German, and English (depending on my topic). I trust that by now, things have changed.

I also discovered — and this too came as a surprise — that Australian academics distanced themselves from their British heritage. Shakespeare, Thomas Hardy, T.S. Eliot were dismissed impatiently in favor of Australian authors who wrote about their own evolution, who described Australian life and the people who lived it: the difficulties encountered by settlers in a land that was essentially a vast desert; the routines of people who had to adapt to an inhospitable, even hostile, environment; the long separations when men had to leave families behind, moving from farm to farm at sheep shearing time to earn money; the loyal bonds that evolved among "mates" forced to live in close proximity during such times; bush fires that destroyed homes and acres of land; people struggling to eke out some kind of living from an arid land. The preferred authors were Alexander Harris, Marcus Clarke, Henry Lawson, Edward Dyson, Ethel Florence Robertson, Patrick White, and the contributors to the renowned *Bulletin*, the journal that launched many Australian writers.

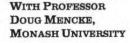
With Professor Doug Mencke, Monash University

The University of Adelaide

Australian literature focused on preserving and consolidating accounts of the life their grandparents and great-grandparents had had to overcome, the ineradicable and harsh reminders of a society originally settled by convicts expelled from England and sentenced to spend the rest of their lives in that desolate colony on the other side of the world. Contemporary Australian writers seemed to have "escaped" their British roots. I couldn't help noting the difference between their experience and that of the liberated colonies, following World War II.

When the Dutch, French, British, and Italians gave up their colonies in Africa, those emergent nations were not a *tabula rasa*. In their efforts to establish a national identity, they could not discount or ignore the experience they had gone through. The occupation by European countries had left behind habits, new skills and traditions that were deliberately or unconsciously absorbed by the former colonies in the shaping of their new future. In spite of their many struggles, battles, and sufferings, they had a wealth of experience to build on as they shaped their new independence. India, for example, in spite of many confrontations with its British rulers, emerged, after the War, with the imprint of the British clearly stamped on it, the language especially, which, adopted as the official form of communication for the entire country, helped to give its parts the unity needed to facilitate networking among the diverse regions and nationalities. The French colonies in Africa benefited even before the War was over — many of its men leaving to find work in France and, in most cases, settling there. Although the circumstances that produced Australia are not quite the same, it has — unlike many European colonies after World War II — consciously rejected the past, what shaped it, the dialectic of escape and return, by means of which the past is acknowledge and absorbed. At the time I was there, Australians seemed bent instead on completely distancing themselves from England.

What I liked most about Australia was that it didn't have the frenetic pace of most other places. At times, I felt I had been caught in a time warp, that I had come down in a land that was at least twenty-five years behind the rest of the world. The air was uncontaminated (in spite of the megaflies). Nothing here of the nervous intensity of New York. Life was predictably pleasant, reasonably simple, things got done without stress. Only occasionally were there surprises. One story is worth telling.

On this particular afternoon, I'd walked across the green meadow to University House, where I had moved into a large room and bath. The space was much smaller than the apartment across from the campus, but I preferred the single room for several reasons. I was isolated in the apartment; it was the only one in the area, directly across from the University administration buildings and student dorms, to which I had no access (nor did I have any reason to want access). My new quarters at University House were much more suitable; I became part of the group of colleagues and HRC guests who happened to be in residence. I could join others at dinner, or, after dinner, sit in the common lounge to chat with colleagues over a glass of wine or a cup of coffee. It was an ideal arrangement.

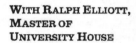

WITH RALPH ELLIOTT, MASTER OF UNIVERSITY HOUSE

With the sun blazing down, as usual, I took the familiar path across the grass to the residence. No one was around, and I was in no hurry. As I drew close and approached the archway leading into the building's large grassy quadrangle, I saw a small cluster of people standing about expectantly. I was surprised and curious: The place was pretty deserted at that time of day — it was about four-thirty — and I wondered what might be going on. I didn't have to wait long to find out.

I paused as three sleek back cars came into view. They came to a stop a short distance across from where I stood, just underneath the archway leading into the building's open quadrangle. Several men emerged from the second and third cars and casually approached the first car. They stood there as a young man stepped out of the lead vehicle and started to walk toward me, or, rather, toward the archway. The others slowly followed. No one hurried. The informal procession had to pass by me in order to reach the grassy courtyard and turn onto the walkway that led to the building. The young man walked alone, leisurely; the others behind him keeping a discreet distance. In spite of their unhurried, casual appearance. I (and I'm sure the others who were watching) knew this was not an ordinary occurrence. We all recognized the visitor though I am pretty certain no one there had ever met him before.

To my amazement, I watched Prince Charles nod and smile at me, as he strolled by. I could have reached out to touch him, trip him, shoot him! Then, suddenly, someone was rushing forward to greet him and escort him inside. Official protocol had taken over.

Thinking back to that day, I'm still amazed at the casual way in which the next King of England strolled by. It could have been a tourist stopping at a roadside inn for tea. I learned the next day that he was on an official visit to Australia; for some reason, University House was on the itinerary.

PRINCE CHARLES, COMING TO VISIT UNIVERSITY HOUSE

A month after my arrival in Canberra, I chaired and delivered the main address at the conference that had been set up on "International Tragedy." The subject of my talk was "Hegel on Tragedy: A Review of Bradley Criticism," a topic of which I never tired and to which I kept returning, expanding and refining my arguments each time. The most recent version, "Shakespeare Revisited: Hegel. A.C. Bradley, and T.S. Eliot," was written not too long ago, for a *Festschrift* in honor of Talat Halman (Special Editor of the *RNL* volume on *Turkey*, for a number of years Professor of Turkish literature at the Middle East Institute of New York University, then "Cultural Ambassador at Large," and after a distinguished career in the United States, a professor again, in Turkey). The article also appeared in *Hegelian Literary Perspectives,* a collection of essays by my husband and me, issued by Griffon House Publications in 2002.

Between the conference and the lectures which I delivered at a number of universities toward the end of my stay, I had plenty of free time to write, read, or just relax. What I actually did was write short stories and poems; correspond with Sverre Lyngstad, my special editor for the *Norway* issue of *Review of National Literatures*, who had expressed some concerns with regard to Ibsen's role in that issue; and answer Henry's long and informative letters with equally long ones of my own. I kept my socializing at a minimum: "Sister" was always available for brief excursions by car, into neighboring areas; I could join colleagues in the lounge for an hour or two in the evening; but I liked also strolling by myself into the center of Canberra to visit the shops. The one thing I carefully avoided was walking "tours" or nature hikes into the countryside.

Once only did I succumb. At the prodding of a visiting scholar from England, and his wife, I agreed to join them in an early morning excursion into the "wild," to see the sun rise from behind nearby hills. I regretted my decision almost before we were out of sight of human habitation.

On the way, we looked into a large deserted cabin. There was no glass in the windows, no door on hinges, nothing in the way of "accommodations" or the usual facilities. A huge old coal stove was the only thing in the place. It stood right in the center of the large room, which was otherwise empty and open to the elements.

WATCHING THE SUNRISE OUT IN THE "WILD" WITH HRC COLLEAGUES

The sun was just coming up. My companions stood perfectly still, watching in awe as the light grew around us — their concentration that of neophytes at a religious ritual. All I could think of was what I had heard about huge wild boars in the area. What if one suddenly charged through the underbrush? Where could we run? Even if we made it to that abandoned cabin, there were no door or windows we could shut. Had my companions given any thought to that? I didn't dare ask.

Their attention was riveted on the rising sun. Wasn't it awesome? Wasn't it worth getting up before dawn, walking through the rough terrain, missing breakfast, to witness the birth of another day, with the hills picking up light slowly and opening up the world again for us? I tried to appreciate the poetic moment but found I had nothing to contribute. Their glances told me they wondered at my silence. Perhaps they sensed my nervousness. Surely they must have seen my relief when we started back. . . .

My writing and outings with Pat Sorby and others kept me busy. The days blended peacefully into one another until it was suddenly time to fly home. It was sad leaving my new friends; sadder still, knowing I probably would never return. Moreover, I'd learned to appreciate the Australian way of life. I had also met some interesting people: the historian Manning Clark (who became a contributor to the Australian volume of *RNL*); Val Vallis (the only true and respectful Heglian I'd ever encountered, besides Henry); poet Rodney Hall; and the legendary writer, A. D. Hope.

WITH PROFESSOR VAL VALLIS

WITH POET RODNEY HALL

The HRC staff hosted a going-away party for me at the Centre. I was touched to see how many new friends and colleagues had come to say good-bye. It made me sad to think I probably would never see them again. On the eve of my departure, the Institute staff treated me to dinner at a Thai restaurant, one of the many in and around Canberra. Ian Donaldson ordered dozens of different dishes, all delicious, delicately prepared, reminiscent of the best in French cooking, but with a character of their own. I remember trying and enjoying every one of them. There were also little parting gifts and a lovely book on Australia, with many photographs.

One of my sharpest memory of HRC is of Mary Theo, the Centre secretary, proudly showing me a poster hanging in her tiny office: a photograph of Vermont in the Fall. It was the kind of promotional advertising poster tourist agencies put on display. Mary had gone to a lot of trouble to get it. The brilliant colors of the autumn leaves was something she had never seen but yearned for. To her, that poster was a work of art. It was off limits; no one could get near it.

AT MY GOING-AWAY PARTY: (L/R) MANNING CLARK, A. D. HOPE, A.P., DR. JEN, PROFESSOR LIVIO DOBREZ (LATER, PRESIDENT OF BOND UNIVERSITY)

DINNER WITH HRC STAFF AND FRIENDS, IN THAI RESTAURANT, THE EVENING BEFORE MY DEPARTURE.

I didn't fly directly to the States. I stopped for a few days in Hong Kong, where the American Embassy had arranged for me to give two lectures at the Chinese University of Hong Kong: "The Future of Comparative Literary Studies" and "Eugene O'Neill's *The Iceman Cometh*."

After the lectures, my hosts and some of the Embassy people took me to lunch at a restaurant on the border of or just inside the Chinese mainland. It was not the usual restaurant, as I recall, more like a private dining room in a big house. The meal apparently had been ordered ahead of time so that I could sample many wonderful dishes. There were no windows but open arches that looked out toward a brooding landscape of low hills surrounded by water. I can still bring up the details of that view, still feel the strange effect it had on me. I also still have, as a reminder of that wonderful day, a glazed brown earthen jar from which our wine had been poured. It was urged on me as we left. I gladly accepted it. I still have it. . . .

As in a quick "zoom to" in a film script, I was suddenly back in Queens. After an affectionate reunion, Henry thrust the checkbook at me. "It's all yours again, thank God!" he said, with obvious relief. I wasn't surprised. I'd known from the time we were married that he wasn't cut out for certain tasks. I'd made up my mind that it was simply easier for me to take on the daily routines, including paying bills and sorting documents for IRS returns than to make a fuss about "sharing" household responsibilities. I knew I couldn't change him in that respect; and I knew that ultimately it was more practical for me to handle them. I thought it best to let him apply his talents elsewhere.

I had plenty to keep me busy on my return from Australia. I resumed my duties at St. John's, picked up my writing again, continued to plan and edit the two CNL volumes, as well as the annual volume of The Pirandello Society of America. I gave lectures at a number of universities across the country; wrote *Sepia Tones* — a collection of short fiction drawing upon the Italian-American experience; published poems and wrote plays. I settled down into our familiar life, never suspecting what surprises still lay ahead.

☞ *FROM THE FILES* ☞

FROM THE SEQUENCE "TROPIC OF THE GODS" (*RIDING THE MAST WHERE IT SWINGS,* 1980). THE POEM WAS INSPIRED BY THE SIGHT OF THREE HUGE GLOBES IN THE HRC LOUNGE.

BOOK TWO. POETS IN THEIR SPACE
3. HAPPENINGS

Huge globes all in a row
For a bowling tournament of giants.
Constellations walk round and round.
I sit sipping tea, resisting temptation
To follow my own footsteps where they grow
Up there in the snow.
The Southern stars had followed me instead
Across the sea.
I never thought they'd reach in here
To crowd us in this reading room
Where tired scholars shape huge myths,
Dive for pearls, rape locks,
Map such dreams as invite
New sails new prows.
"The spheres above the moon"
(Said Galileo to the Grand Acoond)

"And those below as well
Have all been plotted, Your Exalted Grace!
All that's left to do
Is roll ourselves into position
And kick the ball.
You'll see how Aristotle lied! . . . ."
I felt my head begin to spin
Grow dizzy as rectilinear intentions
Took shapes hyperbolic. A voice
Boomed somewhere not too far:
"I don't need telescopes
To tell me ships still need
A Ptolemaic sky to sail! I'll nominate
You for the Nobel Prize,
My friend, but don't come back
Until you have some better proof!
Even Copernicus knew that! . . . ."

Other poems about my Australian sojourn (Riding the Mast Where it Swings, 1980).

THE OPERA HOUSE
(FOR NEAL, IN SYDNEY)

Rain charged with pellets of cold
Hammered us to the water's edge
For cover. All other sap
Drained into the smell of sea.
We fingered oranges pears
Bought macadamia nuts.
Against the wind white-peeled
Ready to drop anchor
I wondered at the bridge so long in faith
Tried the wetness where it lapped
The music in me still untapped.

GARRAN HALL (FOR PAT SORBY)

Lovely parrot lady quick and small
Full of talk
Large in your wing
When you felt ripe and tall,
The drive into weekend places
Was vintage. I learned to read
Your hands on the wheel,
Drumming the chair too large
For tired evenings
You took flight. The Indian sculpture
Had a friendly look.
You hosed down treasure,
Willed flowers out of the ground.

THE COLOR OF BLACK (FOR RODNEY HALL)

In you it wears well, what others
Avoid for pale spring colors,
For the sesame street
Of small rounded joys —

You paint our wonder in white and
Mostly black, giving us back
For roses a wide sweep of fragrant shadings.
Sleep is gentle in your words
Death, a friendly voice.

THE DIRECTOR OF THE HUMANITIES RESEARCH CENTRE RECENTLY INVITED GUEST SCHOLARS WHO HAD SPENT TIME AT THE INSTITUTE TO CONTRIBUTE TO A COMMEMORATIVE VOLUME. I SENT IN THIS:

I reached Canberra on a sun-filled day in January, about 24 hours after leaving a typical dreary, icy cold winter day in New York. I was groggy, sweaty, utterly exhausted. Ian Donaldson had been waiting for me at the train station, the last lap of the long trip. He took me to the tiny apartment that had been reserved for me, a short distance from the Centre, helped me settle my luggage, then . . . "Shall we join the others for tea?"

Half asleep on my feet, looking out my window at that blinding sun, I resisted the temptation to turn down the invitation. I didn't want to disappoint colleagues and staff who were waiting to meet me. Later, I realized that had I not gone to the Centre that afternoon. I would have missed seeing three giant globes in the lounge, waiting to be taken elsewhere the following day.

I recorded some of these impressions (including the effect those awesome globes had on my tired eyes and travel-weary spirit) in "Tropic of the Gods," which appeared in my second book of poems: *Riding the Mast Where It Swings* (1980). I also have a still-vivid memory of a poster advertising the state of Vermont, which the secretary of the Centre had managed to get (very likely from a travel agency or from the state department of tourism) and had on prominent display on her office wall, showing trees in a blaze of Fall colors. . . . For her, that ordinary blown-up photograph, depicting such a variety of extravagant foliage and the rich colors of a northeastern autumn, was the equivalent of a work of art. For those of us who took such seasonal changes for granted, her treasuring that poster was a humbling experience.

My best wishes and congratulations to all of you at the Centre, and a very special greeting to Professor Donaldson, whom I shall always remember as the Centre's genial and gracious host!

THE FOLLOWING TWO EXCERPTS ARE FROM A LONG POEM, "CRADLING MY YUGOSLAV FANCIES," PUBLISHED IN *RIDING THE MAST WHERE IT SWINGS*, 1980.

V.

God in his mercy gave us this mountain top
That road, settled us in this spot.
Socrates is a voice among many
And our own shouting seems best.
While sipping wine
We trace intentions on paper napkins
Coffee stains remind us of a joke.
After a while we learn to sketch
Rough maps of buried treasures.
I think of Njegos in black granite
Watching the sky we share. . . .

VII.

I bought napkins and stole
A poster on the road.
I was shy and bold and slept through
One whole afternoon.
I swam and talked with editors
Under a large umbrella at lunch.
The ambassador invited us to cocktails
And in the new hotel I had a sauna.
I don't remember what was said,
But sitting here I see the faces
Across the way, and the chair
Tilts under me, on the sloping ground,
In the open, with the mountains
Looking over our shoulders.

PRINCE CHARLES BEING
GREETED AT UNIVERSITY HOUSE

THE RACES AT EAGLE FARM (BRISBANE)

WITH WENDY
AND SAM RAYNOR
(BRISBANE)

VIISITING THE UNIVERSITY OF QUEEBSLAND (BRISBANE)

MY TEMPORARY OFFICE AT THE UNIVERSITY OF QUEENSLAND

TREK TO MT. FRANKLIN

**WITH PAT SORBY
AND FRIENDS**

**WITH MARY THEO
AND FRIEND,
SYDNEY AIRPORT**

**THE "SUNSHINE
COAST"
QUEENSLAND**

VISITING WITH
KANGAROO

ELIZABETH BAY HOUSE, SYDNEY

My office
at HRC

With HRC
friends

Hong Kong
seen from
the air

6. A CALL FROM THE WHITE HOUSE
THE NATIONAL COUNCIL ON THE HUMANITIES
(BOARD OF TRUSTEES, NATIONAL ENDOWMENT FOR THE HUMANITIES)

In the early 1980s, friends in Washington and New York, including a well-known U. S. Senator (still in office, still very active and articulate), offered my name as a candidate for the top post at the National Endowment for the Humanities. It was an awesome job. Was I ready for it?

Well (I reasoned), I knew plenty about the humanities, and the years spent running both the English Department and the Doctor of Arts Degree Program at St. John's could certainly be cited to claim a fair amount of academic administrative experience. I could even put forward the years spent running three non-profit organizations: CNL (1975 –), The Pirandello Society of America (1968 – 1986) and Columbus: Countdown 1992 (1984-1993), set up to encourage new literary and art works to commemorate the upcoming quincentennial of the landing of Columbus in a part of the world Europe did not dream existed.

Of course, the NEH job was in an altogether different league. The importance of running a top-level federal agency with an annual budget in the millions precluded over-confidence. Still, I felt I had a chance, especially with the support of the influential people who were backing me. The competition was fierce, but I was not prepared for what happened.

For weeks I filed official forms, went to preliminary interviews, signed affidavits that I had indeed complied with the government regulations that had to be met, and submitted IRS returns. I got clearance from the FBI and waited to be contacted for final meetings at the White House. Rumors reached me that I had made the "short list" and, soon after, that I was the top contender. In due course, I was called to Washington for a final and decisive interview.

I realized almost immediately that I had been invited simply as a formality, for the record to show that I had been properly "processed," my application "considered," an interview set up — but just for the record, as it turned out. I was effectively already dismissed. The decision had already been made, long before I boarded the shuttle for my Washington interview.

The first clue I had that the interview was not all it should be was that only one person, a young woman, was conducting it, not an official committee. She seemed in a hurry and was anything but friendly. It soon became evident that she had a bone to pick. She told me at once, without wasting words or time, that she didn't approve of the Modern Language Association. I was astonished. What had my membership in MLA have to do with my interview? Her harsh words about the organization jolted me into awareness. Everyone knew that the people who ran it often expressed liberal views and often were critical of the White House. But it was also obvious that the huge membership they boasted could not all be liberal. Was my being a member of MLA (I'd joined when I'd started to teach at City College) the one argument she could pounce on, to dismiss me as a candidate? I told her I rarely agreed with the statements the Executive Director and her people put out, that I ignored them as a rule, that the membership represented the entire spectrum of political thinking, that MLA was not a political action group but the only organization where an academic in literary studies could keep up with news of the profession and take part in its annual and regional meetings, where they could learn about ongoing research, hear lectures and take part in panel discussions on subjects they taught or wrote about, where they could meet with colleagues from all over the country.

I realized we had reached a dead-end even before starting. There had to be more to it, I concluded. This young lady could not possibly be the only person authorized to make a decision in such an important matter. I could not help thinking that she was merely carrying out instructions and had hit on the MLA as a convenient though flimsy excuse to get rid of me. The political wheels seemed to have been put into motion long before my interview. The meeting was soon over. I had effectively been dismissed in just a few minutes.

Brooding about what had happened, as I flew back to New York later that afternoon, my suspicions grew. The young woman's vitriolic attack of MLA seemed excessive and, yes, irrelevant. The only explanation I could come up with was that she had been chosen to meet and dismiss me on whatever pretext she could find. My membership in MLA (God save us!) was all she could dredge up for the purpose. I was made to feel I should never have had the temerity even to consider myself a candidate!

The experience was disheartening but not traumatic. I was still able to do all the things I loved to do. Neither my writing nor my other activities on or off campus suffered because of this setback. I merely had taken the opportunity offered, as I had so often done in the past, and given it my best shot. Rejection wouldn't break me. It never had. At the same time, I was particularly grateful for the support of so many good people, whom I respected and admired. They had gone out of their way for me; I had no intention of dragging them into a fight or insisting on a public outcry against a young woman's prejudicial remarks about me. She was probably simply following orders, expediting an unpleasant task as "low-man" on the totem pole. I was pretty sure by now that she had not acted on her own. "Insiders" close to the White House were soon saying that the person who was to become the new Chairperson of NEH had many powerful people backing her. In spite of excellent academic credentials and an impressive track record in the humanities, what chance did a little known Italian-American professor have?

I soon learned that, although the job at NEH was a dead issue for me, my sponsors in Washington were still pushing on my behalf. One day I received a call from one of them. Apparently he and others were intent on getting me some kind of recognition. Before long, I was asked to serve on a brand-new panel, the National Graduate Fellows Program (later renamed for Jacob Javits, former United States Senator from New York State). The handpicked panel was to select and provide generous cash awards to Ph.D. candidates working on their dissertations. The panel members were sworn in by William Bennett, who came in somewhat late for the morning ceremony, somewhat distracted. I remember noticing that his shirt collar needed pressing. He left as soon as the formalities were over.

My appointment was for four years, but one year into my tenure, I received another call. President Reagan had nominated me for a six-year term on the National Council on the Humanities. (Actually, I continued until 1995, under Presidents Bush and Clinton, as well.)

PRESIDENT REAGAN RECEIVES NEW MEMBERS OF THE NATIONAL COUNCIL ON THE HUMANITIES IN THE OVAL OFFICE. A.P., THIRD FROM LEFT (1986)

When I started my term on the National Council on the Humanities, Lynn Cheney had settled into her new job as Chairperson of NEH. We met three times a year to review grant applications and recommend the disbursement of the millions of dollars that Congress allocated to NEH every year. We were assigned to committees that corresponded to the working committees within the agency. Stacks of folders were sent to us prior to every meeting. When we all came together in Washington for a day-and-a-half of working sessions, we wasted no time. The NCH committees met with the staff committees on a Thursday morning, for as long as necessary. The plenary sessions, open to the public, were always on a Friday morning. At those meetings, NCH committee chairpersons presented the proposals their people had reviewed and relayed the committee recommendations to the Chairperson, who, of course, made the final decisions that would allow the disbursement of moneys.

I enjoyed my years on NCH. I was assigned to two committees: historic preservation and state grants. The first reviewed requests for the restoration and/or upkeep of important landmark buildings, historic materials, and anything else that deserved to be saved from the inevitable erosion of time. The second committee — state grants — decided what state projects should be funded beyond the minimum sum mandated annually by Congress ($25,000 during my tenure). The territories and some states often lagged behind, primarily because of their lack of experience in preparing grant applications. In those cases, the NEH staff dutifully traveled around the country, as well as to places abroad, to help give direction where needed, and to advise in the planning of projects as well as the writing of proposals. In other instances, state grants were accepted almost routinely.

To Anne Paolucci
With best wishes,

Ronald Reagan

It was during my tenure that Ken Burns first came to our attention, with his television project about a series on the Civil War. NEH Chairwoman Chaney, a strong supporter of historical projects, set up an informal meeting with the Council members, at which time Mr. Burns explained his idea and answered our questions. We all know the rest: NEH was instrumental in providing him with national exposure of the best kind. The Civil War television series won instant acclaim when it premiered on PBS.

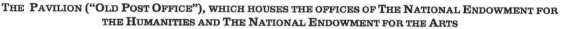

THE PAVILION ("OLD POST OFFICE"), WHICH HOUSES THE OFFICES OF THE NATIONAL ENDOWMENT FOR THE HUMANITIES AND THE NATIONAL ENDOWMENT FOR THE ARTS

Besides our own committee projects, there were other excellent proposals we learned about and voted on in plenary sessions. One that has stuck with me was a proposal for the teaching of Japanese from Kindergarten to grade 12, from a mid-west school district. It was a stunning reminder of one of the side effects of the shifting economic "plates" that realign the centers of world trade.

One of the questions that kept bothering me and which I finally raised had to do with NEH's funding of "intermediary" groups. These submitted proposals and then distributed the funds at their discretion, either to individuals or to other groups. Most of these groups had a good track record: the moneys they received were usually well spent. Nonetheless, I felt that tighter monitoring was needed in scrutinizing both the proposals and the reports that were sent in to close the books, at the end of the grant period. My concerns had grown in connection with "Columbus" projects NEH was receiving, especially one submitted by a state agency.

ENTRANCE TO THE PAVILION ("OLD POST OFFICE")

There were already strong indications that special interest groups and factions were planning to undermine both Columbus and the quincentenary celebration. In the light of those rumblings, I thought the description of the proposal in question should be more explicit. I expressed my concern to our Committee, but the consensus was to accept the proposal as submitted and wait to examine the results. I went along.

When the reports came in, I took time to examine what had been submitted and came away with the distinct impression that Columbus and his bold venture had not been treated fairly. By then it had become clear to everyone that Columbus had been a target: his name had been denigrated, the historic "first" had been trashed, the events of those years turned into a dark age of conquest and violence. Native Americans, especially, raged, prodded by other factional interests into accusing Columbus of all kinds of criminal actions, including genocide. The facts of history were interpreted by self-interested groups, for reasons of their own, to fit a prejudicial pattern. It was too late, obviously, to do anything about federal and state NEH money having been allocated in good faith to expand our knowledge of Columbus and his time. History had been approached with a vengeance and turned into propaganda.

THE INTERNAL GRAND STAIRCASE FACING THE OPEN PUBLIC AREA
AT THE BOTTOM OF THE "WELL."

THE PUBLIC AREA OPPOSITE THE GRAND STAIRCASE OF THE "OLD POST OFFICE."

I knew first hand how mercilessly Columbus had been bashed, how the great age of Renaissance expansion had been turned into a holocaust. Even the federal commission that had been set up by President Reagan in 1986 had kept a low profile as 1992 drew near. The damage had been done. I expressed my disappointment to the rest of the committee, but we all knew it was too late to probe any reports. Both the staff and NCH committees had done their best to be fair. The state agency in question represented a major state and no one had ever thought of questioning their allocations. They were given the benefit of the doubt.

At a committee meeting held in 1992, one of the NEH staffers who had been present when I expressed my concerns about how NEH money had been used, approached me and urged that I stay on into the Saturday morning and stop in at the Smithsonian Institution, where a conference on "The Violence of Conquest" was going on. The main theme was, of course, the consequences of Spanish rule in this part of the world and the horrors inflicted on the native inhabitants by Columbus and those who followed him. I decided to stay into the next day, at my own expense, to see and hear what was going on. I already knew that the Smithsonian was not honoring the 500th anniversary of Columbus's landing but subverting it. They had brazenly said so when I had inquired, months earlier, about their plans.

The conference was heavily attended by Native Americans. It was mid-morning when I arrived to be met by a great deal of shouting. People were standing up, yelling at one another. I finally was able to make out that the subject was burial rights and the responsibility of the government to provide funds to reclaim bodies and bury them properly, according to the established rites and rituals of individual tribes or "nations," each of which had its own particular protocol in such matters. I remember thinking in one case, where tradition called for the dead to be placed in trees, how the government would proceed to set that right. By then I had heard enough and left.

I had paid for an extra night at the hotel, since NEH took care of our expenses only through Friday morning. They would reserve at discounted prices a certain number of rooms in the area hotels, usually the major hotels on Pennsylvania Avenue, walking distance from the NEH building. On several occasions, when the rooms at the large hotels had run out, I was sent to a much smaller place, more like a cozy inn, but at some distance from the NEH offices. It was a charming little hotel which, I'd been informed, served English tea every afternoon in the tiny lounge to the right of the entrance, across from the reception desk. It also had a small but rather good restaurant, where I had eaten dinner several times. The lobby was the smallest I've ever seen, quite attractive with its Spanish tiles and gleaming mahogany desk. Just beyond the lounge, a passageway that led into the restaurant had been fitted out as a narrow bar with room for a few stools. Every inch of space had been attractively utilized.

One Thursday afternoon, our committee meeting had ended earlier than usual, and I had returned to my hotel (this very one) with time to kill before dinner. I thought I might take a short walk; with that in mind, I stopped at the reception desk to ask the clerk for information and possibly a map. No one was there at the moment, so I walked casually into the lounge. It was deserted, which allowed me to admire the furnishings unself-consciously. Suddenly, I heard someone call out, "Hello! Can I help you?" I turned to see a friendly face smiling at me from behind the narrow bar. I walked over to the pleasant gentleman getting things ready for the cocktail- and dinner-hour customers and told him what I was looking for. He answered my questions, and we continued chatting for a while. As I was getting ready to leave, he offered me a drink "on the house." I asked for a small Glenlivet. "Have you ever tried Macallan?" he asked. I had not. "Well, let me offer you that. It's the best." I'm not an expert, so I couldn't vouch for its being the best, but it certainly was smooth, without any trace of the slight medicinal taste most scotches have. I told him that. He seemed pleased. I never saw the man again, never had a chance to tell him that Macallan had become my scotch of choice (on the rare occasions when I drank at all).

Several months later, booked in the same hotel, I came back late from our Thursday meeting to find the place literally overflowing with people. They were spilling out from the bar and lounge into the reception area. I was making my way toward the elevator, but curiosity got the better of me and I allowed myself to be jostled into the entranceway to the lounge. The first thing I noticed was that someone else was behind the bar. Around me, everyone seemed to be having a great time. Nice party, I thought, nudging my way toward the elevator. I never got there. Someone well into the "happy hour" thrust a glass of champagne into my hand. "It's free," the man's voice rang out, with an equally large smile. I was about to comment that all drinks are free at parties, but before I could get the words out, the person at my elbow went on to sing the praises of the bartender who had been on duty the day I wandered into the place and had tasted Macallan's for the first time. The words I heard suggested that the man being described was the guest of honor. I craned my neck to see if I could spot him in the crowd, when I suddenly realized that my companion was talking about someone who was dead. Apparently, the bartender had collapsed while on duty, one day. He'd left precise instructions in his will that, in place of the usual wake, he wanted a party for his clients and friends, right there, in the hotel he had served for so many years. I had to admit, it was a genial idea. That "party" is still vivid in my memory.

When my term on NCH expired, I was asked to stay on until a replacement could be found and "cleared." George Bush was then President, but by the time my replacement was ready, Bill Clinton was in the White House. By then, Lynn Cheney also was gone. Following an established precedent, she had resigned when the Democrats won the election and took over the White House.

What came as a surprise and embarrassed many of us were her outgoing comments to the Press, in which she suggested that Congress discontinue funding NEH. Disbelief was the immediate reaction of many of us on the National Council. To some, it seemed a betrayal. All of us had worked hard over the years to counter the charges leveled against NEH from time to time by people in Congress and other high places. Private groups had bitterly contested the granting of federal funds to projects that were thought to be highly controversial, pornographic, or anti-religious. The Press had made the most of such accusations. But even more shocking was to read what the Chairperson had to say, when she left office. I never fully understood what prompted her to speak out in that way, so late in the game.

The Old Post Office or "Pavilion" is still there, of course, and the NEH and NEA offices still take up several of its upper floors. Inside, the building resembles an early Hyatt, the central area open from the bottom up to the highest floor. Offices are situated on the inside perimeter. On the street level are shops and stalls, where one can buy hand-made Indian jewelry, local art, cards and other mementos, sports goods, clothing, just about anything and everything except furniture and heavy equipment. At one end of the lower level, reached from the street entrances by a large central stairway, there is a low platform, where musicians, actors and other groups perform during the lunch hours. Opposite that, behind the stairway and just below the street level — the only area not gutted to the top — is a food mall, where people can buy all kinds of ethnic specialties as well as the usual fast-foods and then sit and eat at the small tables that take up the rest of the food mall area, while enjoying the music of a band or listening to singers perform at the other end, or watch a dramatic skit or a poet reading from his or her work.

I regret not having found time to take at least one leisurely stroll around the public area on my visits to the building. On one or two occasions, I purchased some small mementos from stalls conveniently placed just inside the main entrance, a few feet from the elevators and from the large room where our plenary sessions were held on Friday mornings.

The meetings at NEH were important to me, and I found I could handle them without disturbing equally important established and ongoing routines, especially the thankless task I'd taken on in 1984 (even before joining the National Council on the Humanities) to support and promote Columbus activities against an increasingly hostile response to preparations for the quincentennial celebrations. Against the rising tide of criticism, I perversely insisted on doing everything I could to encourage fair discussion and new literature, art, music, and lectures about Columbus and his time. Toward that end, I had organized a non-profit organization, "Columbus: Countdown 1992" and set about gathering Columbus scholars and others interested in reviewing and adding to the history of the events surrounding the discovery by the old world of a continent no European had ever heard of before. It was perhaps the biggest challenge I had yet faced.

📂 *FROM THE FILES* 📂

THE PASSAGE BELOW IS TAKEN FROM "LOWEST OF THE ARTS," THE THIRD CHAPTER OF MY NOVELLA, *TERMINAL DEGREES*, (GRIFFON HOUSE PUBLICATIONS, 1997). IT IS A FICTIONALIZED ACCOUNT OF A NCH PLENARY SESSION. THE DIALOGUE IS MY CREATION; THE CHARACTERS WERE INVENTED TO VOICE OPINIONS AND EXCHANGES NEVER EXPRESSED IN THOSE TERMS IN ANY PLENARY SESSION OF NCH. . . .

" . . . and there are, of course, political implications — " Madam Chairman droned on. "This is a federal agency, after all. . . ."

Curran went on sketching on the pad provided him as part of the working materials for the meeting. His mind was in a meteoric free-fall in which his hand motored his imagination. *John Cleese staring down Barbara Walters. Madonna as a novice in a cloistered order. Alda as Hot Lips' mute gardener. Dan Rather holding up a certificate attesting to his having taken a course in diction. Mayor Giuliani holding a press conference in sign language. . . . Hey, c'mon, what's TV good for except educating us in how to improve our daily casting?*

" . . . a pilot project for television? The going rate is about half a million." Curran looked up, genuinely surprised. It would take an Associate Professor ten years to earn that kind of money!

He returned to his doodlings. For a moment he was tempted to raise his hand and get into the fray, but he thought better of it. Whatever he said would be water seeking its own level. Nothing ever changed, everything remained the same. Just more words to be transcribed at the end of the two-day session.

He sketched a new Mark Russell set, transforming it quickly into the "O" he remembered seeing on the Ashland stage, where he and Dottie had seen Andrew Trainer's unforgettable production of *Waiting for Godot* — concentric double circles, the inner one defining the space for the two major actors, the outer one meant to contain the movements of Pozzo and Lucky. Cables from the back of the theater were stretched over the heads of the audience, right down to the stage — a visible and tangible mathematical analogy for Theater of the Absurd.

Cool summer at Ashland with nothing but theater all day long, walks in between, one small digression out of town, then back quickly to that magic center of their new world together. Imperative, immediate, intravenous happiness.

Loud voices intruded on his reverie. *Who does the casting here? Let me rephrase that. What the hell am I doing at this table, in this room, in the Old Post Office, the new Pavilion?*

". . . and one Abstention."

There was a flurry of movements, a hum of whispers. Curran had drawn himself up in his chair and cast his vote. He had learned early on that there was no point being a martyr to logic and common sense in this particular contest. But some fool had abstained.

"Madam Chairman, I feel I should explain my Abstention."

"Madam Chairman, I feel I should explain my Abstention."

Oh, crazy Kate, what are you up to? Madam Chairman and several of the other members of the group were staring down the long table at Kate Morison. *Will she never learn, poor kid?* Curran returned to his pad and drew a large head with bulging eyes. Lawrence Trebble, the Chairman of Kate's Committee on media grants, was in fact staring at her across the large table, with the carefully spaced microphones now turned off (the meeting apparently had come to an end), as though she had just confessed to murder. Sandy-haired Trebble from Heartland USA-U. A good talker if the audience was on top of the ceiling. One of the constants of the world, who never allows himself to recognize defeat. Once Curran had thought that was good, to be able to disregard people and things, inure oneself against feelings. . . .

Madam Chairman was, in fact, bearing down on Kate. Curran gathered his papers, sketches, notes, the hundreds of pages he had plowed through before coming to the meeting, put his name and address at the top of the pile for them to mail back to him at home. In time, he remembered his sketch pad and retrieved it. He put it inside his briefcase.

Madam Chairman was pissed off. "You should have consulted earlier, with Dr. Trebble. Discussion takes place on the committee level, questions are resolved *there*, and the Chairperson reports the Committee's vote for the record. You *know* our meetings are open to the public! These are *not* matters to be aired in this way!"

Kate seemed genuinely abashed, but she went on stubbornly, nonetheless. "Sorry you feel that way," she replied, her voice less certain. "No one ever told me I couldn't speak in plenary session!"

"Of course one can speak! But there are rules. You were out of order."

"I wanted to make a point. . . ."

"That point was addressed in my memo to the committee, you will recall. I too wanted to bring the amount of funding down. Dr, Trebble reported that the matter had been discussed at length by your committee —"

"But the committee voted *Yes*. I wanted to reject the motion altogether!"

"You just said it yourself. The *committee* voted. That's the democratic process. In any case, I was told that your motion wasn't even seconded in committee."

"All the *more* reason to bring it up!"

"Dr. Morison, a flagged proposal means *let's move carefully on this*. The last thing we need is a public expression of lack of confidence in the process, the proposal, *and* the Chairman!"

"I'm sorry, but I don't agree. If anything, this kind of trimming makes some of us look downright silly! We're talking millions here, and you're insisting on procedures and protocol! What's more important than a candid discussion about funding a project that in my judgment is terribly flawed to begin with!"

Ah, Kate, poor my Kate, you have put the proverbial foot in it this time! You'll have to live out your term under a cloud, and under the heavy downpour of Madam Chairman's displeasure.

He quickly closed his attache case and caught up with Kate at the entrance to the building. She jumped when he slid his arm around her and drew her close. She bumped into him and they both came to an abrupt stop. He maneuvered her to one side so that the people behind them could move toward the door.

"You scared the hell out of me," she said, her hand at her throat.

"I doubt it. More the other way around. You were great back there. But did you realize what you were doing?"

"How do all twits do after a twit holocaust?"

"You survived. Marked for life, but that's O.K." He steered her toward a cab that was just discharging a passenger. He raised his arm and the cabbie waited for them. As they settled back, he gave the driver instructions, then went on quickly, as though to prevent Kate from raising any objections. "Nothing tried, nothing gained. Sometimes, the best is something lost. Like virginity. It can't go on forever without leaving another kind of mark. Right?" She was laughing now. "My hunch is you're ripe for gossip, friendly banter, tactful flirting, gossip, a long break between hassles, more gossip, and some lunch. Not necessarily in that order." She responded to his mood, grateful for his having made a decision.

"An awful morning." She eyed him coyly. "Don't think I didn't see what you were doing, those bloated Dürer atrocities you're always drawing, instead of listening to what's going on."

"I do listen. I don't have to look also, do I?"

"Madam Chairman will never forgive you."

"Maybe I'll take her to lunch some day. You know, gossip, friendly banter — "

Kate interrupted. "What's tactful flirting?"

"Why all of this!" he had replied with a sweeping gesture that took in the space between them.

VIEWS OF THE OLD POST OFFICE PAVILION
(LOOKING DOWN INTO THE LOWER-LEVEL PIT)

VIEWS OF THE OLD POST OFFICE PAVILION
(FRONT OF THE LOWER LEVEL, WHERE RECITALS, READINGS, ETC. ARE GIVEN

VIEWS OF THE OLD POST OFFICE PAVILION
(PLATFORM WHERE RECITALS, ETC. ARE GIVEN)

VIEWS OF THE OLD POST OFFICE PAVILION
(STREET LEVEL LEADING TO STAIRCASE AND THE PIT)

(STORES TO THE RIGHT OF THE CENTRAL STAIRCASE)

VIEWS OF THE OLD POST OFFICE PAVILION
(LOOKING UP FROM THE CENTRAL PIT)

Gaetano Russo's statue of Christopher Columbus shown here was unveiled on October 12, 1892 at the southwest corner of Central Park (Columbus Circle). Professor Herbert B. Adams of Johns Hopkins University called it, in 1892, "the noblest statue of the noble Genoese pilot . . . one of the finest works of modern Italian art." (Photograph c. 1925.)

7. COLUMBUS ON TRIAL
"Columbus: Countdown 1992"

In 1984, two years before I took my place on the National Council on the Humanities, I set up "Columbus: Countdown 1992," a non-profit group to promote new research and encourage original literary and art works, plays, and music commemorating the 500ᵗʰ anniversary of the landing of Columbus in this part of the world.

BRIEF HISTORY OF "COLUMBUS: COUNTDOWN 1992" (EXCERPT)

CC 1992 was launched in the Fall of 1984 by the Hon. Anne Paolucci (a member of the National Council on the Humanities, Commendatore "Order of Merit" of the Italian Republic, and Director of the Doctor of Arts Degree Program in English at St. John's University, where she also served for nine years as Chairperson of the Department). The motto of CC 1992, a non-profit educational foundation, was: "To promote the multi-ethnic legacy of Christopher Columbus, the First Immigrant to the New World."

The launching of CC 1992 coincided with the publication on October 14, 1984 of "Columbus and the Idea of America," a long article (later published separately in two editions as a bilingual 6-page feature and distributed by Griffon House Publications, New York, both here and abroad). The piece was the first important Columbus article of the quincentenary. It appeared in *Il Progresso,* the precursor of *America Oggi.*

Networking with the Council on National Literatures (CNL), which operates in over 40 foreign countries, and with The Bagehot Council and Griffon House Publications, CC 1992 sponsored over the next eight years several important books, plays, video, and art works. Through the outlets of CNL, CC 1992 distributed during this time *Selected Papers on Columbus and His Time (CNL/World Report,* Vol. III), *Modern Views of Columbus and His Time (CNL/World Report,* Vol. V), and a volume in the major CNL series *(Review of National Literatures): Columbus, America, and the World.* Four more volumes in the prestigious *RNL* series will appear netween 1993 and 1995: *Spanish Discoveries of America, English and Portuguese Discoveries of America, French and Dutch Discoveries of America, Native Populations of the Americas.*

Networking with Griffon House Publications, CC 1992 has also published in two separate editions, an original play, *Cipango!* featuring dramatic scenes between Columbus and Queen Isabella and Columbus and Martín Pinzon. The play was staged in showcase productions several times and was also made available in video cassette. This particular project was selected by the federal commission in Washington as an "Official Project of the Christopher Columbus Quincentenary Jubilee Commission."

Artists who have contributed original paintings to the quincentenary celebration include Constance Del Vecchio Maltese, whose 13 "Age of Discovery Navigators" series of portraits won her in 1989 the "Special Recognition in the Arts & Humanities" award of CC 1992 and who has had numerous shows and exhibits, including one on the Intrepid,

---

Rumors were already circulating about a concerted effort to subvert the celebrations of what Peter Sammartino, founder of Fairleigh Dickinson University, called one of the two greatest events in recorded history. This kind of determination and my own resolution buttressed my original intentions but also geared me to the very real possibility of having to waste valuable time to defend Columbus against the scurrilous attacks that might be coming.

What happened was much worse than anyone could have predicted. Factional interests, bent on furthering their own special agendas, were suddenly trashing Columbus and rewriting history to their own specifications. I did not anticipate such hatred and knew that I could not avoid the fray. I've always prided myself on my honesty as a scholar, my fairness as a critic; those who have worked with me can vouch for my insistence on searching out the facts of a situation. I have no ulterior agendas as a critic; except for an instinctive drive to give everyone his due, whether it be an historical figure, or my next-door neighbor. I have never shirked from speaking for those without a voice, who cannot defend themselves, and I have never tolerated the brazen distortion of history.

I knew perfectly well that Columbus and the sovereigns of Spain had done some terrible things, but they had not done them easily or willingly, or were they the first to do so. From the beginning of recorded time, history is replete with the destructive results of conquest. The Spanish did not invent it; nor did they invent slavery. That practice is as old as man himself and is still going on in certain parts of the world, like Africa. The ugly accusations that were soon leveled against Columbus and his time had to be answered, not as an even exchange — I refused to be put on the defensive — but historically, by presenting a full picture. I wasn't out to debate prejudices; I decided to do what I had originally planned: prepare panels, lectures, new art, new drama, new music — what would add to the archives — and review properly the events that were now being condemned out of hand. When asked, or when I lectured on the subject, I put forward what I knew to be true; I explained the historical facts without trying to bleach them squeaky clean.

I did not know at the time I set up "Columbus: Countdown 1992" that President Reagan had in fact formed a federal commission to promote the historical quincentenary of the landing of Columbus in the "new world." Had I known, I probably would have discontinued my efforts. I realized soon enough, however — much to my dismay — that the federal commission was backing down, that it had no intention of taking active part in the celebration. It had decided or had been instructed, instead, to keep a low profile. In the face of that reality, I became more determined than ever to carry out my initial plan. I was not an elected official; I was not prepared to submit to public pressures; I certainly did not share the popular notion of "political correctness," especially in this case.

I decided to "go it alone." It wasn't the first time I'd taken such a stand.

My premise was a simple one: to lay out the facts as we knew them, to avoid controversy if possible, and to steer clear of rewriting history to present-day specifications. George Bush had succeeded Reagan in the White House, but things were not about to change — although the President did acknowledge our existence and praised our work.

COLUMBUS: COUNTDOWN 1992

"TO PROMOTE THE MULTI-ETHNIC LEGACY OF CHRISTOPHER COLUMBUS, THE FIRST IMMIGRANT TO THE NEW WORLD."

My main concern was to build a solid foundation on which to raise a wall that could not be breached. I wasn't prepared to accept what was being dished out. As a scholar and researcher, I had never trimmed facts, no matter how unwelcome they may have been in the context of a particular argument. I wasn't going to start now.

My main theme was irrefutable. The Renaissance marks the great revival of the man-centered civilization of the Greeks, the earliest expression of humanism in all aspects of practical life and the arts. It is a time of great change, the age of Dante, Cimabue, Giotto, Michelangelo, Machiavelli, the Medici, It is also the great age of European territorial and economic expansion that made possible a new outburst of great literature, architecture, painting, sculpture and music. After their long wars with the Moors, the Spanish emerged triumphant and were ready to listen to Columbus and his plans; but eventually their mighty Armada was destroyed by a small but efficient English fleet. The ruthless tactics of Henry VIII to insure England's political and economic independence produced the golden age of Elizabeth, Edmund Spenser, Ben Jonson, William Shakespeare. Portugal had found its new destiny in exploring the Atlantic coast of Africa, setting up trade routes and centers along the way. Its great national hero was Vasco Da Gama, who succeeded in rounding the dangerous southern tip of the African continent and reach India by sailing east from the west. The "discovery" and "conquest" of the "new world" by Europe was inevitable. The European countries were bursting at the seams and looking for new settlements, new colonies, as well as new revenues. Spain was simply the first to take practical steps in that direction, after its victory over the Moors. Columbus was historically the first to hazard the journey that was supposed to discover a short route to India and bring back new wealth for Spain.

Without a country, with minimal support from his sponsors (after a wait of seven years at court) for what most believed to be a reckless journey into oblivion, Columbus deserves credit (for starters) for undertaking that incredible first journey, relying ultimately on his keen "dead reckoning." He was admittedly an expert navigator, with lots of experience sailing the North Atlantic and the Mediterranean, but the conditions he encountered were new and presented many unpredictable dangers. He must be given credit for finding ways to navigate through those dangers. He was by far the most experienced, the most courageous, the most far-seeing navigator of the Renaissance.

The Italians, of course, have adopted him as their own hero. Columbus Day will continue to be an Italian-American national holiday; but the fact is that Columbus left Italy while a teen-ager and, as far as we know, returned to Genoa as an adult, briefly, only once, on business. There is nothing to suggest he spoke or wrote in Italian. He became a Portuguese citizen after marrying a Portuguese woman, hoping perhaps to gain advantage from his father-in-law's connections at court. Rather than be considered a displaced Italian, he should be regarded instead as the greatest navigator of the Renaissance — a much more prestigious title, since the Renaissance was a European phenomenon. And, lest we forget, it was Italy that started the Renaissance and produced its greatest writers, artists, scientists, and navigators. The Italian connection is there, but in those terms. Or, perhaps more to the point: we should think of him as the first to bring colonists to our shores. In the letter he wrote praising our initiative, President Bush acknowledged in his own way the phrase I'd coined to describe Columbus as "first immigrant."

We also know that he wooed the Portuguese first, in his effort to find funds for his voyage. They were, after all, the great navigators of the time, with the personal backing of their king, who had founded a school to train Portuguese seamen. We also know that they rebuffed the foreigner, stole his notes, and tried to murder him in order to get full credit for what they thought they could accomplish. With the detailed information Columbus had compiled, they set out into the Atlantic but soon turned back, too frightened to continue. Used to clinging to the shore, as they traced their trade routes down the western coast of Africa, they were terrified of the wide open ocean that lay before them, which had never been mapped.

It was under the rule of Ferdinand and Isabella that the mad enterprise conceived by a wild foreigner went forward. And once established in this part of the world, those rulers did everything possible to protect their claim. Do we put a nation on trial for defending its own interests, or attack the man who followed the dictates of his time? Can we legitimately cite abstract "rights" and moral absolutes in the light of history? No nation on earth has ever allowed itself to be manipulated by others or destroyed in the name of "justice." St. Augustine's argument about the City of Man is also Machiavelli's argument in defense of *realpolitik*. It is the argument of FDR, Churchill, Abba Eban and those who followed. History is the story of national self-interest. To blame

Spain's actions in the light of our modern moral "enlightenment," to hold Columbus responsible for what had to be done to maintain order in the new Spanish colonies, to express righteous indignation at his having to put the natives to work plantations that were needed to feed them as well as the transplanted Europeans and, later, to sell the same natives as slaves to raise money to continue the enterprise — to take such facts out of historical context is to demean the study of the past and subvert logic itself.

There were other issues that had to be faced.

LEÏF ERICSON SOCIETY

POST OFFICE BOX 301
CHICAGO, ILLINOIS 60690

Leif Ericson Millennium   1003-2003

W. R. ANDERSON   TELEPHONE 312/761-1888
PRESIDENT

22 May 1989

Professor Anne Paolucci
St. John's University - Ch. Eng. Dept.
Grand Central & Utopia Pkwy
Jamaica NY 11439

Dear Professor Paolucci,

Thank you for the glossy "Countdown." Such a pity all the billions being wasted on 1992, with the millions starving. One future year -- or century -- or millennium, it will be obvious that
    "COLUMBUS" WAS NOT CRISTOFORO COLOMBO!!!

In the past couple of years I have sent out at least 250 copies of the enclosure (or prior version with minor differences) and have failed to receive answers to:

    (1) How could "Columbus" sail from Chios to Iceland (perhaps America?) in 1477 and be at his Italian loom -**SIMULTANEOUSLY?**

    (2) After his marriage in Lisbon in 1478, living in Porto Santo with his brother-in-law 1478-83, **HOW COULD HE RECEIVE A COMMISSION IN 1479 TO BUY SUGAR IN PORTO SANTO, OF ALL PLACES?**

Patiently I wait.

       In dismay,

       W. R. Anderson

You are a chemist? I'm a C.P.A. Can't we teach these 'Historians?'"

Among the cries of protest were those attacking the notion of Columbus as the "discoverer," the first to land in this part of the world. Well, who *was* the first? Can we be sure how and where man first appeared on this continent, or on this planet, for that matter? Were the so-called natives Columbus found when he landed the same natives he continued to encounter throughout his explorations, the first and only people who had a claim to the continent? Could any claim be called "legitimate" in the face of the harsh upheavals of history?

FLYER DISTRIBUTED BY THE LEIF ERICSON SOCIETY

VIKING "COLUMBUS," KING OF SPAIN

Viking? He was a descendant — King? He should have been

"His name is one of the best known in history. Yet he is one of history's most controversial and shadowy figures, with mystery surrounding his birth, his character, his career, and his achievement," says Simon Wiesenthal.(1) One fact is obvious: Columbus was NOT Cristoforo Colombo of Genoa ("Genova" in Italian).The first biographer, Peter Martyr, warned history not to confuse Colombo with Cristobal Colon of Spain. (2) As the Universal Jewish Encyclopedia (Vol. 3, page 306) points out, "Local Genoese records referring to the Colombo family are assumed to be identical with the family of the later Spanish admiral." (Emphasis supplied.) That assumption is false.

Morison found about 20 records of Colombo in Italy from 1470-79. He was a weaver, later buyer of wool and sugar, with no sailing experience. (3) A booklet of Colombo family records published by Archivio Di Stato Di Genova in 1978 lists 63 entries, of which only 19 refer to Cristoforo, evidently the same that Morison found. During the same period, "Columbus" was in the crew of pirate Rene d'Anjou (1472-73), on the Greek island of Chios (1473-74), in a sea battle against Genoa (in 1476), sailed as far north as Iceland -- possibly Canada (1477 -- see below), was married in Portugal to Felipa Moniz Perestrello (in 1478), lived with his brother-in-law, governor of the island of Porto Santo in the Madeiras (1478-83). Colombo is believed to have died in 1480.

Who WAS "Columbus?" He was of course the Spaniard Colon. That is invariably shown as the Spanish version of Colombo -- actually he was an entirely different person. Evidence indicates he was a son of Prince Carlos (Charles IV) of Viana and Margarita Colon of a prominent Jewish family in Felanitx, Majorca, born in mid-June, 1460. The village is near Genova, now a district of Palma, the capital ci .(4) Carlos was the elder son of King John II of Aragon, grandson of John I (5. Carlos was the heir to the throne of Aragon but died mysteriously in 1461, so the throne of Aragon went to Carlos's half-brother Ferdinand instead of to Cristobal, the heir.

Records in Norway show many prominent Spaniards to have descended from natives of Gudbrandsdal. Among them was John I of Aragon.(6) And thus his great-great-grandson Cristobal, known to have been tall, with red hair and freckles.

Did Colon and Colombo meet? Several times -- Pohl says they were friends!(7) Italian records (3) show that Colombo made several trips to Portugal to buy wool and to the Madeiras to buy sugar in 1479, when Colon was living with his brother-in-law, governor of the island and the man a buyer would contact for a foreign purchase.

What was Colon's "achievement?" He was "nothing but a good public relations man."(8) His ships Nina and Pinta, and crews of all three ships, had been acquired by Martin Alonzo Pinzon.(9) He had the ship's papers of Alonso Sanchez de Huelva, who had reached the West Indies in 1481, whose first mate had been the same Martin Alonzo Pinzon!(10) He had maps of Viking voyages centuries earlier.(11) His voyage in 1477 is believed to have included a side-trip to Canada. (12) The entire episode deserves an historical niche -- right next to Santa Clau
****

References: (1) Wiesenthal, Sails of Hope, p.93; (2) Ibid p. 113; (3) Morison, Admiral of the Ocean Sea, p. 7 et seq.; (4) Nectario Maria, Cristobal Colon Era Espanol y Judio, p. 3 et seq.; (5) Martorell, CRISTOBAL COLON, La Revelacion del Enima; (6)Hougen,AETTESOGE FOR GUDBRANDSDALEN II, Delaringen og Gudbrandsdal Historielag, p. 100; (7) Pohl, The New Columbus; (8) Tornoe,Columbus in the Arcti p. 78; (9) Morison, p. 136; (10) Nectario, p. 16; (11) Enterline, Viking America and Chapman, The Norse Discovery of America; (12) Prytz, Norseman Magazine, Jan. 1988, p. 9-11;
****

© Copyright 1989, W. R. Anderson, Box 301, Chicago IL 60690

(Excerpt only with full credit)

There has been much speculation about the Jews, the Phoenicians, the Armenians, Leif Ericson, etc. as the first "discoverers," but no historical evidence has ever been found to support those claims.

AMERICA **Oggi** MAGAZINE domenica 24 maggio 1992 **15**

Temi & Dibattiti - Paolo Emilio Taviani e Samuel Eliot Morison lo escludono categoricamente in base a precise ragioni storiche

Colombo ebreo?

DI HENRY PAOLUCCI

Il 1492 è l'anno di Cristoforo Colombo per antonomasia. E' anche l'anno in cui isole e continenti cambiano completamente connotazione, soprattutto nella parte occidentale del nostro globo. E' anche un anno di particolare significato per le tre grandi religioni monoteistiche, - l'ebraica, la musulmana e la cristiana, - che lo hanno segnato in modo speciale nei loro calendari. Per gli ebrei significò infatti la cacciata dalla Spagna, per i musulmani il ritiro quasi completo da tutta l'Europa, per i cristiani l'apertura di nuove frontiere fideistiche.

Colombo non aveva del resto mai fatto mistero dei suoi propositi, di voler creare cioè un impero religioso al di là delle Azzorre. Colombo pensava che la Spagna potesse addirittura riprendere oltremare l'opera di cristianizzazione di Carlo Magno, facendo di tutto il globo un unico tempio per il Cristianesimo.

Al ritorno dal primo glorioso viaggio di là dall'Atlantico, il nostro navigatore fu accolto molto "religiosamente" da re Ferdinando e dalla regina Isabella.

Nella sua biografia di Colombo, Washington Irving ricorre agli occhi di un testimone, Bartolomeo de Las Casas, il primo prete del Nuovo Mondo, per descrivere la scena: "Come Colombo si avvicinò, i reali si alzarono in piedi, com'era d'uso nei ricevimenti di persone d'alto rango; egli si chinò per baciar loro le mani, ma entrambi furono esitanti nel permettere ciò. Lo aiutarono ad alzarsi e a sedersi insieme a loro... Non appena essi ne fecero richiesta, Colombo cominciò a raccontare quanto era capitato durante il viaggio... Quando egli ebbe terminato, i reali s'inginocchiarono ed alzarono le mani al cielo, gli occhi colmi di lacrime di gioia e di gratitudine, e ringraziarono Dio per la sua bontà infinita... La

commozione prese ognuno dei presenti. A quel punto dal coro della cappella reale fu intonato il 'Deum Laudamus'".

Il Genovese aveva anche fatto un voto prima della partenza, un voto collegato con le radici cristiane del suo nome di battesimo che, sia in greco che in latino, significa "il portatore di Cristo". Da sempre il viaggio oltre oceano per Colombo fu un affare di fede. Lui si identificava con San Cristoforo, martire del terzo secolo, forse nativo della Siria.

Il carattere religioso del viaggio della scoperta dell'America è passato purtroppo assai spesso sotto silenzio; alcuni, dicono, perché i conquistatori spagnoli (e poi anche quelli portoghesi, inglesi e francesi) si comportarono con crudeltà nient'affatto cristiana nei confronti delle popolazioni trovate al di là del mare. Qualcuno dice poi che Colombo era religioso per colpa di... Las Casas, che i fini religiosi erano invece solo della regina Isabella e che, in fondo in fondo, il navigatore era ipocrita, cattivo,

assetato di potere e disumano. Stranamente coloro che gli riconoscono una missione religiosa sono quelli che parlano di sue presunte origini ebraiche. Che c'è di vero in questo?

Il problema delle sue origini ebraiche coincise con i festeggiamenti per il quarto centenario della scoperta dell'America. Allo stato delle ricerche attuali, non si possono non riconoscergli però che origini genovesi, e di fede romano-cattolica. Il maggiore degli studiosi colombiani, Paolo Emilio Taviani, lo afferma a più riprese. E nessuno, più di Taviani, ha studiato così tanto estesamente Colombo, i suoi viaggi, le sue origini e tutto quanto, direttamente o indirettamente, è a lui collegato.

Taviani, in particolare, si pone due domande: Colombo era un ebreo che pretendeva di essere cristiano e voleva sfuggire all'Inquisizione spagnola, oppure partì per trovare nuove frontiere agli ebrei e poi, al ritorno, fu costretto a dire che l'aveva fatto per i

cristiani?

La risposta ad entrambi gli interrogativi è già in quanto affermato poco sopra.

Lo stesso Samuel Eliot Morison, nella sua monumentale opera "Admiral of the Ocean Sea" riconosce in pratica le stesse cose: Colombo era genovese e di fede cattolica.

Genova, il Portogallo, la Spagna e le isole scoperte di là dalle Azzorre hanno, ciascuna con un suo ben preciso motivo, ragione di considerare Colombo qualcosa che sia esclusivamente loro. Geograficamente, etnicamente, politicamente il Genovese appartiene certo un po' a tutti. Polemiche a parte, Colombo era genovese e cristiano di religione. Dire il contrario o cercare di sminuirne la figura è semplicemente un attentato premeditato contro la verità e la storia.

Nella foto - "Il sogno di Cristoforo Colombo" di Salvador Dalì (particolare).

Themes & Debates — *Paolo Emilio Taviani and Samuel Eliot Morison*
exclude the idea categorically on precisely reasoned historical grounds

Was Columbus a Jew?

by Henry Paolucci

The year 1492 looms large in the life of Christopher Columbus, of course. It is also the year in which the islands and continents of the world changed their connotations completely, especially in its western half. The year is also of major importance for the three great monotheistic religions — Judaism, Islam, and Christianity — which have marked it as an important date on their calendars. For Jews, it was the year of their expulsion from Spain; for Muslims, the crest of an almost total retreat from Europe; and for Christians, the opening of vast new religious frontiers.

Columbus, moreover, had never made any mystery of his aims — to create a religious empire beyond the Azores. Columbus believed that Spain could easily gain power enough to resume the Christianizing labors of Charlemagne, extending them overseas to unite the entire world in a single universal temple of Christendom.

Upon his return after his first glorious voyage across the Atlantic, our navigator was accorded a very "religious" reception by King Ferdinand and Queen Isabella.

In his biography of Columbus, Washington Irving draws on the eyes of a witness, Bartolomé de Las Casas, first priest to be ordained in the New World, to describe the scene: "As Columbus approached, the sovereigns rose, as if receiving a person of the highest rank. Bending his knee, he offered to kiss their hands; but there was some hesitation on their part to permit this act of homage. Raising him in the most gracious manner, they ordered him to seat himself in their presence . . . . At their request he now gave an account of the most striking events of his voyage . . . . When he had finished, the sovereigns sank on their knees, and raising their clasped hands to heaven, their eyes filled with tears of joy, and gratitude, poured forth thanks and praises to God for so great a providence . . . ; a deep and solemn enthusiasm pervaded that splendid assembly, and prevented all common acclamations of triumph. The anthem *Te Deum Laudamus,* chanted by the choir of the royal chapel . . . rose in sacred harmony."

Columbus the Genoese had in fact made a sacred vow before sailing, a vow that Columbus tied to the meaning of his Christian name, *Christopher,* which is half Greek and half Latin, and means "Christ-Bearer." From the beginning he had made his mission of transoceanic sailing a matter of faith. Columbus identified himself with St. Christopher, a martyr of the third century, probably a native of Syria.

The religious dimension of the Columbus voyages has, unfortunately, been played down — largely because of the charges that the Spanish conquistadors behaved with unchristian cruelty toward the natives of the Americas and were followed in such cruelty by the Portuguese, English, French, and the rest who came later. A case has been made that Columbus was not the religious-minded man Las Casas made him out to be; that his professed religious ends were advanced only to influence a pious queen; that he was a hypocrite, an evil, greedy man, who failed to restrain his men as he should and could have, and became instead an enslaver and exploiter. Ironically, at present, the only Columbus scholars who uniformly ascribe to him a profound religious motive are those who give him a secret Jewish identity. What truth can we find in all of that?

The question of Columbus's possibly Jewish origins hadn't at all been seriously raised until the 400th anniversary of the discovery of America. According to current research on the subject, the best scholarship seems to favor the evidence for a Genoese, Roman Catholic Columbus. The best known Columbus scholar, Paolo Emilio Taviani, has repeatedly affirmed it. And no one more than Taviani has so extensively studied Columbus, his voyages, his origins and all else that is directly or indirectly connected with him.

Taviani breaks down the question into two sub-questions: (1) Was Columbus secretly a Jew pretending to be a Catholic to avoid persecution wherever he chanced to be, whether in Genoa or Portugal, or Spain, or wherever he sailed in the service of "Inquisitional" Spain? And (2) had he perhaps really set out in 1492 to find a New World Zion for his fellow Jews then being forced out of Spain? Taviani's answer to both questions is that already indicated above.

Samuel Eliot Morison also, in his monumental work *Admiral of the Ocean Sea,* comes to the same conclusions — that Columbus was what he said he was: a native of Genoa, and a faithful Catholic.

Genoa, Portugal, Spain, and of course, the islands and continental shores of the world of the West — soon destined to become a "brave new world" for the Europeans — all have legitimate claims on Columbus. Geographically, ethnically, politically, he certainly "belongs" in some measure to all of them. Polemics aside, Columbus was indeed of Genoese origin and of Christian faith. To affirm the contrary or attempt to belittle his person can only be a deliberate assault on truth and history.

Columbus may not have been the "first," but we do know that unlike scattered bands from the north, he didn't cross over for brief hunting expeditions, then go back home. He surely was the "first" to record his adventure and the "first" to establish permanent colonies on these shores. As for the natives: are their claims absolute and indisputable?

Another question often raised: Was it right for Spain to claim parts of the "new world"? Were the countries of Europe entitled to take wherever they could "claim"? Perhaps not, in divine terms; but history is the story of ongoing conquest. And the reality then, as now, is clear: to the victors belong the spoils.

These are difficult statements to accept for those committed to arbitrary and simplistic definitions of "human rights." History cannot be rewritten according to our specifications, current moral and political ideals or prejudices. Columbus had the courage to sail out into an uncharted "unknown ocean sea" and stumbled upon that third of the world the Europeans had not known existed. He charted for the first time the vast ocean which even the Portuguese — the acknowledged master navigators of the time — were afraid to take on. When they tried to do so (after stealing Columbus' notes and charts, and failing in their efforts to kill him), they grew frightened and quickly turned back. But his notes and charts were soon put to good use by others; the French, the Dutch, and, yes, the Portuguese themselves (more confident now) were soon sending ships to claim whatever lands they could, even as Columbus was trying desperately to find the straits that would take him into the Indian Sea.

He provided the impetus for others to follow in his wake. He opened the door for the Cabots, in the north, where England quickly laid claim to those lands. In the south, the Portuguese came away with much greater spoils. France soon entered the frenzied rush to find its own space. Spain, ironically, was eventually left only with the islands and lands in what is now Central America, but they made the most of that relatively small area to establish a strong and permanent sphere of influence in the "new world." Ironically, Italy (or more properly the city-states of what was to become much later the country we know by that name) — without resources to join the race and take some piece of the prize — won a solid claim to history by giving the world its best seamen: Columbus, Vespucci, the Cabots, Verrazzano, men who had been forced to leave their native land to find work elsewhere.

All this and much more was put forward by "Columbus: Countdown 1992." Throughout, our priorities remained fixed: to ride out the yelling and shouting that was clearly undermining the celebration and, while doing some damage control along the way, keeping our sights fixed on promoting new historical, literary and artistic contributions to add to the archives. We reviewed the events of the Columbus story in many different ways, as the positive answer to the attacks that filled the Press and television but also as permanent acquisitions for those interested in studying that period. One of the most important projects undertaken was bringing together in three separate issues of *Review of National Literatures* essays which originally appeared in the massive multi-volume work on early America contributed to by the most eminent scholars of the late nineteenth century and superbly edited by Justin Winsor (first librarian of Harvard University and co-founder of The American Historical Association of America): *Narrative and Critical History of America* .

As 1992 grew near, some leading Italian-American organizations held "Columbus" dinners and gave awards to celebrities (Hollywood stars, business and poiitical leaders, etc.) with Italian names. Our group had no paid members to draw on for fund-raising dinners; only a few dedicated scholars, artists, playwrights, lecturers, hard working individuals who were ready to volunteer their talents to promote the historic figure of the visionary who changed the world. Nor were we interested in spectacular black-tie events and empty rhetoric. Still, we decided from the beginning to hold modest annual dinners honoring those individuals who had contributed to the Columbus story.

At our first annual dinner (Fall. 1985) at the "Club 200" — an elegant room at the end of the lobby of what is known as the "Toy Building" on 23rd Street — we honored Dr. Peter Sammartino, founder of Fairleigh Dickinson University and a long-time supporter of Columbus scholarship, presenting him with a large walnut plaque with the legend in raised bronze letters.

Soon after that, we decided to publicize our multicultural activities by giving two other prizes every year. For the original "Lifetime Achievement" Columbus Award we found a beautiful fifteen-inch high glass "sail" at Tiffany & Co. and had our logo and the legend etched on it, in each case. The plaque became our "International Arts Award." A third award for recognition in the humanities was a gold lapel pin (roughly the size of a dime) crafted by Tiffany, with the logo and the initials of the recipient etched in the center.

TIFFANY "SAIL": THE "COLUMBUS: COUNTDOWN 1992" LIFETIME ANNUAL ACHIEVEMENT AWARD

How the logo came about is an interesting story. I had met in Washington D.C., at the 70th anniversary of the slaughter of the Armenians by the Turks, an Italian artist, "Anselmo," who lived in Paris with his Armenian wife. I had been invited to give the keynote address at the annual event — a reminder of a holocaust as unforgettable as that of the Jews, but, unfortunately, never given the same kind of attention — because of the recent publication of the *Review of National Literatures* volume on Armenian literature, the first such publication in decades.

At the end of my talk, "Anselmo" and his wife came up to me in the grand ballroom of the Washington Hilton and introduced themselves. He asked if I had a few extra minutes to spare; he wanted me to see the exhibit of his paintings of the Armenian massacre, on display across the hall. He led the way into a large room, where twenty or so huge canvases rested against the walls, all depicting the horrors of the atrocities committed against Armenian women, men and children by the Turks, early in the nineteenth century. The collection was a powerful display of intense emotion and tremendous artistic skill. I was impressed by the style — a combination of abstract and real. Afterwards, we talked about the quincentennial and the new organization I had formed. At my request, he sent me, several weeks later, photos of some of his other paintings and sculptures, as well as an idea for a canvas he was planning, featuring Queen Isabella and Columbus, this too projected on a grand scale.

As it turned out, we were unable to afford any of his work; but at a reception at the Rainbow Room, where we met again before he returned to France, he took out a used envelope from inside his jacket and drew on it, in an abstract design, the prows and sails of three ships. He handed me the envelope: "My gift to Columbus Countdown," he said, with a smile. The drawing became our official logo. It was etched on every Tiffany "sail" and on our Tiffany pins. It was also prominently displayed on our stationery, on our programs and promotional flyers — whatever literature was put out.

The 1992 dinner program carried the full list of "Columbus: Countdown 1992" honorees, including that year's recipient, the world-renowned Columbus scholar, Paolo Emilio Taviani (who also happened to be an Italian Senator). Taviani had written a number of excellent books about Columbus and his four journeys, acknowledging his huge debt to and tremendous admiration for his predecessor, the great American Columbus scholar, Samuel Eliot Morison.

Our "International Arts Award" went to people like Helen F. Boehm, President of the most important and internationally prominent company of porcelain collectibles and fine art pieces, who produced a number of exquisite originals for the quincentenary; Maurice Edwards, writer, singer, translator, Executive and Artistic Director of The Brooklyn Philharmonic, and founder of The Classic Theater, for his bold and innovative theater direction and for retrieving from obscurity or introducing for the first time many excellent plays; Nicholas John Stathis, Esq., a nationally prominent patent lawyer and long-time supporter of theater; playwright Mario Fratti, whose award-winning play at Yale became the hit musical *Nine*; Jerre Mangione, perhaps the most prolific writer on the Italian American experience; and others who had manifested in many ways the innovative spirit of Columbus.

Our "Special Recognition in the Arts and Humanities" award went to artists like Constance Del Vecchio Maltese, whose unique "Age of Discovery Navigators" series of thirteen original paintings won a number of other awards besides ours and was on display for two years on the Intrepid, the sea and air museum permanently anchored on the Hudson; Frank D. Grande, who received his D.Phil. degree from Oxford University in the history of science and was Chairman of the Department of History at The City College (CUNY), a long-time supporter of Columbus projects; Helen Greco, the opera singer, one of our most dedicated Columbus promoters, and others like them.

We set up displays at our dinners, to publicize works-in-progress, and especially new paintings. The 1992 display was by far the largest we had had.

SPECIAL DISPLAYS AND EXHIBITS:

• Giovanni Dentoni: *"Columbus Contested"* (Oil on canvas, 22" x 26").

• Comm. Helen F. Boehm: Commemorative Columbus Bowl, Plate, and Bust.

• Bosco Baittinier Ficca: *"Dante's Ulysses, Precursor of Columbus"* (Reproduction of an etching).

• Joseph A. Finelli: Columbus Bust (Bronze).

• Council on National Literatures: *Columbus, America, and the World* (Publ. date, October 12, 1992).

• Marie-Lise Gazarian: *"Encounter/The Miracle of Hispanism"* (20" x 30" Print of original collage [66" x 38"]).

• Fehmi Gerceker (Producer-Director): *"The 1513 Map of Piri Reis: A Historical Puzzle."* (Video documentary, featuring host/commentator Ben Gazzara, sponsored by the Turkish government).
The Piri Reis map, named after a Turkish Admiral, dates back to 1513. Its author completed it after careful study of Columbus's own maps, which have not survived. This important documentary feature, prepared by Quadrant Corporation and directed by Fehmi Gerceker, has already been viewed in Spain, Turkey, Portugal, Brazil, Senegal, and the United States.

• Italian Heritage & Culture Month Fdn.: 1992 Posters & "Events" Booklet.

• Vincente R. Latella: *"First Sighting of San Salvador"* (Oil on Canvas, ca. 68" x 40").

- Constance Del Vecchio Maltese: *"Age of Discovery Navigators"* (Limited Edition Poster, designed by the artist, signed and numbered, of the postcard-size prints of original series of portraits); full size prints of the *"Young Columbus"* and *"Amerigo Vespucci."*

- Anne Paolucci: *Cipango!* (Original Videoplay). Chosen *"Official Project of the Christopher Columbus Quincentenary Jubilee Commission"* (1991). Cipango! *was director for video by Fehmi Gerceker and taped at the St. John's University television studios.*

- "Senatore a Vita" Paolo Emilio Taviani (and Ministero per i Beni Culturali e Ambientali, Italy): *The Voyages of Columbus, The Great Discovery* (2 volumes); *Christopher Columbus, The Grand Design* (1 volume), *Cristoforo Colombo, Genius of the Sea.*

...AND...

- Gabriella Di XX Miglia (Program): Front Cover, "Young Columbus"; Back Cover, "Amerigo Vespucci." Reproductions of original oil paintings.
- Anselmo Francesconi (Program): Insert, "Columbus and the Egg." Reproduction of original oil painting.

Honoring Paolo Emilio Taviani at our eighth and final dinner was a fitting climax to nine years of strenuous activity to promote Columbus, the man who changed history (as well as the maps of the known world). By honoring people who truly embodied the spirit of Columbus, we corrected to some degree the awards given to "celebrities" in the name of Columbus.

Our modest dinners gave us limited publicity, but we didn't expect anything more. Unlike the dinners of the mega-groups and foundations, they were simply footnotes to the major text: our continuing efforts to encourage and produce discussion panels, art exhibits, informal concerts and dramatic readings, lectures and recitals. We did everything possible, within our means, to insure that our offerings were preserved in print or on tapes. I and others in the group took every opportunity to present the facts correctly and rectify the misunderstandings that were confusing the public, made every effort to defuse the hostility toward Columbus. I myself found time to lecture to community and other groups and write a number of articles, including one for the Op Ed page of the *Daily News*.

We met opposition at every turn. Teachers were making headlines denigrating Columbus and Spain in the classrooms and in the Press. No real dialogue was possible. Partisans and factional interests had taken over. Their voices became increasingly shrill. As the weeks and months went by, I found myself not only answering the predictable accusations, but trying to educate the Italian-Americans, who protested vehemently but did not always answer effectively the criticisms leveled against Columbus.

To sum up: although October will always be Italian-American month and Columbus Day will not likely ever be associated with anything but Italian-Americans, neither Italians nor Italian-Americans can lay total claim to the man. He left his native Genoa as a teenager to join an older brother, Diego, who had already settled among the Portuguese. He married a Portuguese woman whose father not only owned a rich library of maps, charts and maritime books, to which Columbus had access, but also had connections at court. To make the best possible use of these advantages, Columbus became a Portuguese citizen. He never seems to have practiced his native Italian (or the language of Genoa); Portuguese was his language. Later, forced to spend seven years at the Spanish Court, waiting for the sovereigns to make good on their promise to fund his journey into the "unknown sea" (funding that turned out to be the equivalent of a mere $10,000), he learned to speak Spanish, as well.

History shows that Columbus was the first to send back the "news" and that Spain was the first nation to see the event as an occasion for colonization and expansion. From there on, the "new world" was on the map — figuratively and literally. The oft-cited case of Vikings having set foot on the continent much earlier than Columbus is part of history as well; but the facts tell us that their trips were seasonal hunting expeditions. They made no effort to colonize but returned back home each time; eventually they stopped coming. Similar claims have been put forth over the centuries, but they remain pure conjecture.

History also tells us that he failed in some of his goals. His ineffective rule of the lands he had claimed and colonized for Spain, his disappointing search for great deposits of gold and pearls, together with rumors created by disgruntled nobles who resented his authority and by the men who fled it by striking out on their own and taking the law into their own hands, all contributed to diminishing his reputation at Court. It is also true that he could not administer settlements which required constant supervision and decisive action at times of crises and still continue exploring the southern waters of the Caribbean and Atlantic. As a result, complaints increased; opposition and mutiny escalated. The former seamen (many of whom had been released from prisons in Palos to provide crew members for the journey) had become outlaws — attacking native villages, stealing and raping native women, setting up their own small fiefdoms, away from all authority. The noblemen who arrived with the second voyage resented his authority and refused to take orders from a commoner or to work side by side with others like him.

It was a battle Columbus could not win.

By the time of his fourth and last voyage into the Caribbean, the administration of the colonies had passed into other hands and many of the promises made to him had been revoked by the Spanish sovereigns. He himself had grown depressed after the many attempts to find a way through the islands to the strait that would take him into the waters that would bring him to the fabled *Cipango* described by Marco Polo. He failed to accomplish the task he had set out to do: to find the short route to the rich spice trade of the East by sailing west. He died a defeated and forgotten man.

Ironically, his calculations proved correct, in a way. Although he never was able to get past the islands of the Caribbean, never thought of exploring what turned out to be an isthmus to the Pacific ocean on the other side, he would, in fact, have reached Japan if this great continent had not been where it is. He would have landed right on target, just as he predicted.

It was for someone else to cross the narrow stretch of land we know as Panama and "discover" the Pacific beyond. And it was for still another to figure out that this part of the word was indeed a continent the Europeans had never dreamed existed.

Sailing with the Portuguese on their mission to check the route taken by Vasco Da Gama around the dangerous southern tip of Africa (now the "Cape of Good Hope") in his historic voyage to India, was another "Italian," a Florentine business man who had left his native city for better prospects: Amerigo Vespucci. It was Vespucci who first realized and recorded the fact that the land mass to the south of the waters Columbus had explored was much too large to be anything the Europeans were familiar with. The captain of the ship on which Vespucci found himself had veered westward – perhaps out of curiosity, perhaps deliberately – and had followed the eastern coast of what is now South America down far enough to discover the truth. Vespucci shared this information in a letter to a fellow-Florentine in Paris, who in turn showed the letter to others. Eventually it came to the attention of a young map-maker and teacher of geography in a small French town, a great admirer of Vespucci, who noted the Florentine's observations on a new map he had created. He named the area "America," after the man who had provided the information (using the feminine form for continents: *e.g.* Europa, Asia). The designation persisted, as new maps appeared. That trip is also historically significant as the fortuitous occasion which allowed the Portuguese to pause long enough to claim the land mass jutting out into the eastern waters, far below the area Columbus had explored for Spain – what was to become known as Brazil.

Vespucci's name ironically pushed that of Columbus into obscurity. This third of the world is named after him, not the bold Genovese – the first European to set foot in the "new world." Even more ironic is the name the former "Indians" have assumed in our time: "Native Americans."

My perseverance in carrying on this crusade to fight the critics who had ganged up on Columbus was no doubt the result of my early training, when – plunged into an alien environment – I had to learn quickly to trust my instincts and fend for myself. In this case, I was drawn to Columbus, not because I was Italian and felt kinship on that score, but because of the incredible twists and turns of his life. He had suffered the plight of the immigrant, his place in the scheme of things questioned at every turn. I recognized in his rejection elements in my own early years. I found especially intriguing the ironies that shaped his life. The man who reached the pinnacle of glory in 1493, when he returned to Spain with new territories for that country and promises of great treasures; the man who stood while the sovereigns of Spain knelt before him (unheard of, in all history); the man who was greeted as a God by the natives of the "new world"; the man who was promised a percentage of all the treasures he found in the lands he claimed for Spain; the man who was put in charge of the new Spanish settlements and promised exclusive and hereditary rule over them — all those wonderful things were wrenched from him in just a few years. When he died in 1506, he had not only been rejected by his royal sponsors but had been virtually forgotten.

He re-emerged slowly over the centuries. The 400th anniversary celebration in 1892 was the most spectacular ever mounted, but — as we know — attempts to honor him in 1992 were severely undermined. Working against the current, "Columbus: Countdown 1992" strove relentlessly to restore his reputation as the most knowledgeable and daring navigator of his time. In an age of incredible expansion, of new ideas and new perspectives in art, music and literature, he led the way. He is one of the great figures of the Renaissance, its gift to the modern world. In this context, Columbus is a sure winner.

It was this story that piqued my interest: the dialectic of history, which is full of reversals. It is a story I dramatized in my play, *Cipango!*, videotaped in 1990 with a grant from St. John's University and recognized the following year as an "Official Project" of the "Christopher Columbus Quincentenary Jubilee Commission" set up by President Reagan. Although, as already mentioned, the Commission kept a low profile throughout the countdown, it did surface every now and then to prove it existed. In any case, the videoplay was produced in several different venues in the tri-state area and listed in a number of catalogs, including Educational Video (Texas). *Cipango! (The Story)* published in 2004 — a mixture of straightforward facts and scenes drawn from the play — was chosen by the Order Sons of Italy as their 2005 Fall book selection. It has gone through three printings since it first appeared.

Cipango! was performed several times on stage in the tri-state area, with different casts and directors. The video is ninety minutes long and has in the lead role my young friend Marco Barricelli, who for many years was in the well-known Shakespeare repertory company of Ashland, Oregon. Called by one drama critic "the best Shakespeare actor in America," Marco was, in my opinion, the perfect choice for the role of Columbus. He accepted our offer and flew to New York from the West coast for the five days needed to tape the video. His performance was superb; his diction — what really singles out a first-rate actor — impeccable. Marco is also a great fan of Pirandello. His grandmother was a friend of Marta Abba (who had married an American after Pirandello's death); his father, Jean-Pierre (who taught French and Italian literature for many years at the University of California/Riverside) had translated, when a young man, *The Mountain Giants*, which Pirandello had written expressly for Marta Abba and to whom he had presented the play, as a gift.

CHRISTOPHER
COLUMBUS

QUINCENTENARY
JUBILEE
COMMISSION

October 16, 1991

Dr. Anne Paolucci
President
Columbus Countdown 1992
166-25 Powells Cove Blvd.
Beechhurst, New York 11357

Ref. No. O-90-062

Dear Dr. Paolucci:

I am pleased to inform you that at its recent meeting, the Columbus Quincentenary Commission granted your "CIPANGO!" an endorsement as an "Official Quincentenary Project." The Commission has recognized the project for its exceptional contribution to the Quincentenary.

Enclosed are two copies of the Agreement between yourself and the Commission including the Regulations for Recognition and Support of Quincentenary Projects, as amended. Please read and sign one copy and return it to the Commission as soon as possible. For your information, I am including a copy of the law which established the Commission.

Please accept my apologies for the extended length of time the Commission has taken in changing your endorsement from "Registered" to "Official." We appreciate your patience and understanding.

We have assigned the reference number listed above to your project. We would appreciate your keeping us informed as your project develops.

On behalf of the members of the Commission and its staff, I am pleased to extend to you our congratulations as well as our best wishes for a successful project.

Cordially,

Frank J. Donatelli
Chairman

Enclosures

1801 F STREET NORTHWEST, WASHINGTON D.C. 20006
202-632-1992

But there were other artistic projects that proved equally satisfying and, in the long run, even more rewarding. The one that truly stands out is the series of thirteen portraits depicting the Columbus story, by artist Constance Del Vecchio Maltese. A successful commercial artist for many years, Connie turned to Columbus in the mid-eighties and in 1988 had completed "The Young Columbus," the first of what was to become our most important contribution to modern paintings connected with the Columbus story, "The Age of Discovery Navigators." Ms. Maltese soon became an expert researcher as well. She sought out designs of the time for her borders and included, around the main figure, highlights of the person's life. She also discovered that living models for the historic figures she was portraying gave the paintings a special quality, an immediacy that most formal portraits lack. Her "models" included judges, plumbers, businessmen, friends and neighbors, her own husband, New York State Senator Serphin Maltese (who posed for both "The Young Columbus" and the last portrait of the series, "Columbus in Chains"). The series was on exhibit for two years on the "Intrepid," the sea and air ship-museum, permanently anchored in the Hudson River.

"The Age of Discovery Navigators" series won many awards, including our "Special Recognition in the Arts and Humanities" gold Tiffany pin for the artist. Connie lectured not only on the Intrepid but also in many colleges, schools, and community centers, bringing to hundreds of people her rendition of the brave men who charted unknown waters and defined new continents.

Other artists included "Sirena," whose "Landfall" graced our dinner programs for the first few years, painter and sculptor Anselmo Francesconi, Marie-Lise Gazarian, and Gabriella Di XX Miglia.

New music for the quincentenary included some haunting melodies by Henry Paolucci, some of which were used for the video of *Cipango!* A number of his songs and lyrics were also featured in recitals held in New York.

The nine years I worked with "Columbus: Countdown 1992" were a struggle all the way, but I could not remain silent in the face of misleading arguments and false accusations. I was troubled by the brazen prejudices put forward as history by so many of our teachers and writers, saddened by so much misinformation being given out to students, by the betrayal of trust on the part of their teachers, whose words were accepted as absolute truth, ostensibly garnered from long study and research. I was constantly reminded that to trim or ignore facts is to destroy the integrity of history and invite the chaos and confusion that heralds a dark age.

In spite of the many difficulties encountered, the effort expended during those frustrating years, in trying to stem the unrelenting tide of criticism was not in vain. Looking back, I can take pleasure and, yes, some pride too, in knowing that we produced important and lasting works in literature and the arts for the Columbus archives.

THE WHITE HOUSE

WASHINGTON

October 11, 1991

I am pleased to send warm greetings to all those
who are gathered in New York City for the "Columbus:
Countdown 1992" Award Dinner. Congratulations to
your honorees: Adriana Scalamandre Bitter, Mario
Fratti, Frank D. Grande, and Joseph Sciame.

As we approach the 500th anniversary of Christopher
Columbus's first encounter with the peoples of the
Americas, we do well to reflect on all that has
transpired as a result of that historic event.
Indeed, it not only helped to usher in a modern age
of exploration and discovery but also launched a
long and fruitful exchange of knowledge, resources,
and traditions between the Old World and the New.

By celebrating the legacy of Columbus through a
variety of cultural and educational projects, Dr.
Anne Paolucci and her colleagues have helped us to
appreciate more fully our heritage as a nation of
immigrants. That heritage is reflected in the
wonderful diversity of American culture, and I
commend the members and friends of the Countdown '92
organization for helping to make the Quincentenary a
truly multi-ethnic celebration.

Barbara joins me in sending best wishes for a
memorable evening.

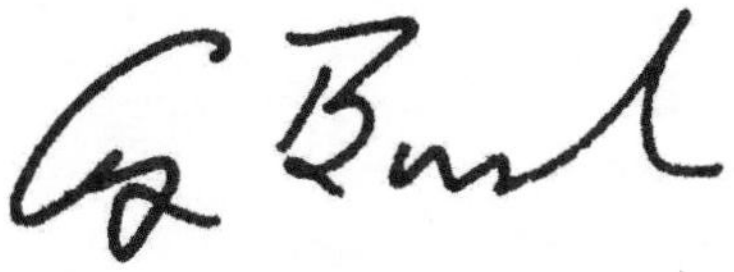

G. Bush

CLAIRE SHULMAN
PRESIDENT

(718) 520-3220
TDD (718) 520-2990

CITY OF NEW YORK
OFFICE OF THE
PRESIDENT OF THE BOROUGH OF QUEENS
120-55 QUEENS BOULEVARD
KEW GARDENS, NEW YORK 11424

October, 1991

Dear Friends,

I would like to take this opportunity to congratulate and extend my best wishes to Dr. Anne Paolucci, the Board of Directors of Columbus: Countdown 1992 and all those who helped make tonight's celebration such a great success.

This year's honorees, like Christophher Columbus himself, have used their own personal talents in a unique way to win acclaim and recognition.

It is fitting, therefore, that we honor them for their achievements on the eve of the quincentennial celebration of the discovery of the New World.

Christopher Columbus linked the Old World with the New World to begin a marvelous story that is still unfolding as a new wave of immigrants arrives at our shores.

The spirit of Columbus, "the first immmigrant to the New World," lives on and thanks to the efforts of Columbus: Countdown 1992 it will never be forgotten.

Sincerely,

CLAIRE SHULMAN
President
Borough of Queens

CS/pc

NINE OF THE THIRTEEN PORTRAITS OF CONSTANCE DEL VECCHIO MALTESE'S
AWARD-WINNING SERIES, "AGE OF DISCOVERY NAVIGATORS"

Amerigo Vespucci
"AGE OF DISCOVERY NAVIGATORS"
by Constance Del Vecchio Maltese

Christopher Columbus
"AGE OF DISCOVERY NAVIGATORS"
by Constance Del Vecchio Maltese

Marco Polo
"AGE OF DISCOVERY NAVIGATORS"
by Constance Del Vecchio/Maltese

Vasco Da Gama
"AGE OF DISCOVERY NAVIGATORS"
by Constance Del Vecchio/Maltese

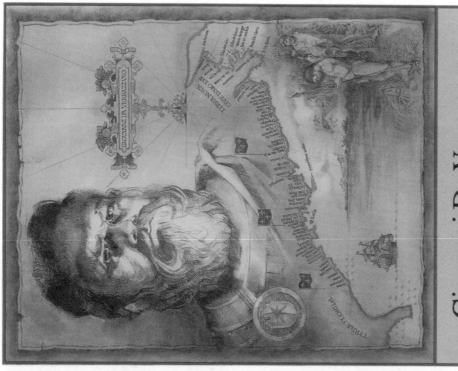

Giovanni Da Verrazzano
"AGE OF DISCOVERY NAVIGATORS"
by Constance Del Vecchio/Maltese

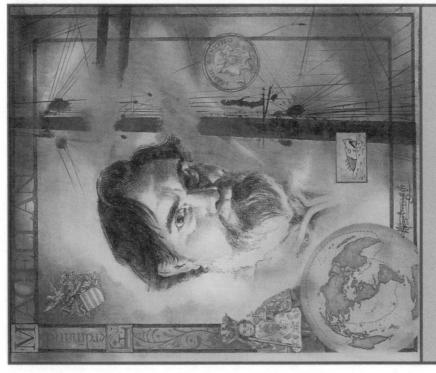

Ferdinand Magellan
"AGE OF DISCOVERY NAVIGATORS"
by Constance Del Vecchio/Maltese

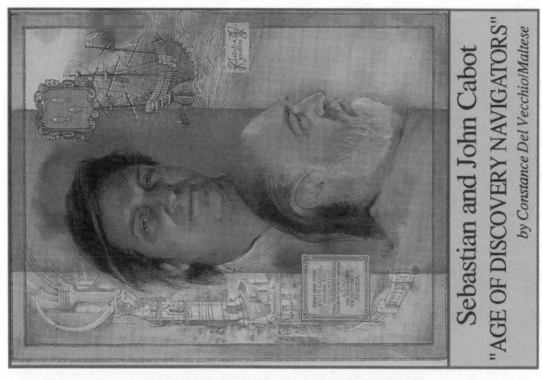

Sebastian and John Cabot
"AGE OF DISCOVERY NAVIGATORS"
by Constance Del Vecchio/Maltese

Vasco Nunez De Balboa
"AGE OF DISCOVERY NAVIGATORS"
by Constance Del Vecchio/Maltese

Painting-collage by Marie-Lise Gazarian

DAILY ◎ NEWS
220 E. 42d St., New York, N.Y. 10017

Monday, December 19, 1994

School where they cross Columbus

By ROB SPEYER
Daily News Staff Writer

Christopher Columbus gets no respect anymore.

At a high school in lower Manhattan, the explorer who became famous for getting lost 502 years ago gets downright dis-respected.

"Columbus was a killer, a murderer and a rapist," said Ebony Smith, an 18-year-old senior at the Satellite Academy, an alternative public school.

"He stole America from the Native Americans who were already here, and he's a mercenary killer," said Xavier Osorio.

"He was a fake, a mad fake," chimes in classmate Aleshia Gibbons. "And Columbus was gay."

Political correctness has long since stripped Columbus of any claim to "discovering" an already well-populated continent. But murderer, rapist, gay? Where do these students get such ideas?

From their teacher, of course. And social studies teacher David Silberg is proud his charges got his message.

"I don't consider Columbus to be a great hero," the 10-year veteran of the city schools told the Daily News. "As a figure of his times, he had all the prejudice and ideas of a typical man of his class and of his day. He was very Eurocentric and strongly Christian."

But gay? On that even Silberg throws up his hands.

"I don't know where they got that from," he said.

For last Columbus Day, Silberg, who insisted he gave "a balanced presentation" of Columbus, asked his 30 stu-

"I don't consider Columbus to be a great hero ... He was very Eurocentric and strongly Christian."

Public school teacher David Silberg

Lesson in history or histrionics?

"Who the hell is teaching them these things? This is blasphemy of an international hero."

William Fugazy President Coalition of Italo-American Associations

DAILY ◎ NEWS
EXCLUSIVE

dents to "share their feelings with the rest of the school" by decorating the building with posters. The signs variously called Columbus "a murderer" and "the beginning of a Holocaust."

"They were hungry for information," he went on. "They basically reacted positively toward looking at Columbus in an alternative light. We got them talking and thinking about the issues a lot."

Last week, two months after Columbus Day, some of the signs remained up at the academy, across Chambers St. from City Hall. And not everyone was reacting positively.

"Who the hell is teaching them these things?" asked William Fugazy, president of the Coalition of Italo-American Associations. "This is blasphemy of an international hero."

Fugazy said he intended to file a complaint with the Board of Education. "Is this part of the New York City public school curriculum?" he asked.

Beckman referred further questions to Satellite Academy's principal.

"We have some beliefs about freedom of speech," said principal Alan Dichter. "We want students to defend their point of view."

OIL PAINTING OF "YOUNG COLUMBUS," BY GABRIELLA DI XX MIGLIA.

OIL PAINTING OF "AMERIGO VESPUCCI," BY GABRIELLA DI XX MIGLIA.

"COLUMBUS AND THE EGG" by ANSELMO FRANCESCONI

Diptych, Oil on Canvas, ca. 13' x 7'

Copyright © 1990, by Anselmo Francesconi. Reproduced by permission of the artist.

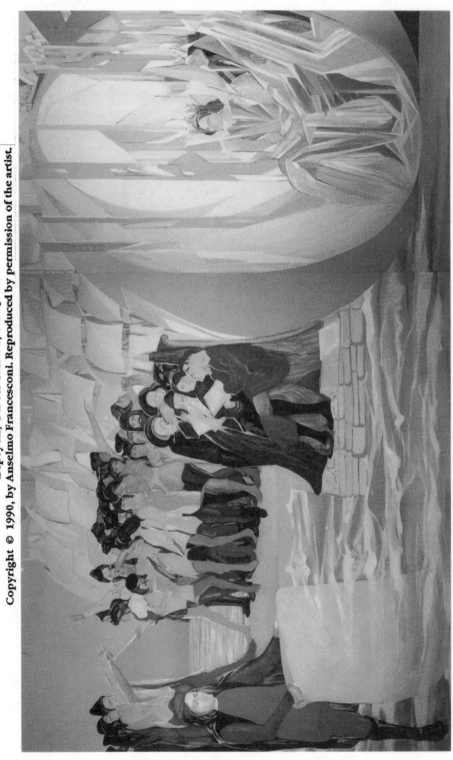

Left panel: Columbus (foreground, left) stands at a distance from the royal advisors (middle right) shown reviewing his plan to reach India by sailing west. Columbus's men (on a third level, left and center), wait in a separate group. Sails crowd the horizon behind them, on the right. Right panel: the monarchs shown alone, in formal attire and crown, encapsulated in an "egg shell." Behind them are the outlines of a modern city still to be defined. The entire concept is at once strikingly realistic and yet symbolic in its isolated and superimposed images. The kaleidoscopic veiled quality of the right panel, conceived in delicate pastels but with sharp angular lines, contrasts dramatically with the more realistic, colorful representation of the panel on the left. A beautifully suggestive painting.

A REDUCED BLACK AND WHITE PHOTO OF THE ENTIRE ANSELMO PAINTING SHOWN ON THE LEFT
(THE COLOR PHOTO WAS CROPPED AT THE FAR RIGHT IN ORDER FOR IT TO FIT THE PAGE.)

WAS "COLUMBUS

by W. R. Anderson

Ridiculous, you say. Every schoolchild knows he was born in Genoa, Italy! Sorry, that was Cristoforo Colombo, who probably could not have navigated a catboat across the bay of Genoa. And Colombo died in 1480, 12 years before the last rediscovery of America!

Cristobal Colon, the real name of "Columbus," was interviewed extensively by Peter Martyr, who wrote the first biography of one of the most famous men in history. Martyr warned history in 1494 not to confuse the two men, in a letter to his friend, Count Giovanni de Borromeo. The letter is translated in Simon Wiesenthal's *Sails of Hope*, page 113. Mr. Wiesenthal wrote to me on June 4, 1984, "I firmly believe it to be an authentic document..."

The Genoan weaver credited with "discovering" America in 1492 actually died in 1480.

Who was "Columbus?" The truth, as I see it, is quite fascinating. He was a son of Prince Carlos (Charles IV) of Viana and Margarita Colon of a prominent Jewish family on the Spanish island of Majorca. He was born in mid-June, 1460. Generally accepted is that in 1472-73, he was in the crew of pirate Rene D'Anjou, on the Mediterranean. In 1473-74 he was on the Greek island of Chios. In 1476 he fought with Casenove-Coullon (possibly a relative) against ships from Genoa. When his ship caught fire, he swam to the tip of southwest Portugal, near the seamanship academy of Prince Henry Sinclair, believed by many to have visited America around 1395.

In 1477 he sailed to England, Ireland and Iceland. Norwegian scholar Kåre Prytz believes on that voyage he examined a book, *Inventio Fortunata*, written by the English monk, Nicholas of Lynn, who had been in the expedition of Paul Knutson. His men left the runestone dated 1362 near Kensington, Minnesota. (The book was owned by Colon's friend, John Jay, who had been on many voyages between Bristol, England, and the North American continent.) Prytz believes that Colon also visited America.

In 1478 Colon was married in Lisbon to Felipa Moniz Perestrello, of a prominent Portugese family. Colon and his wife went to live with her brother Bartholomew, captain of the island of Porto Santo in the Madeiras. From there he made several voyages along the coast of Africa, when he developed his navigational skill. During the same period he broadened his education, as indicated by notations in his extensive library, the first of which was in 1481.

Meanwhile, Colombo was busy at his loom in Italy,

except for trips to Portugal to buy wool and to the Madeiras in 1479 to buy sugar. During those trips he probably met Colon several times—Frederick Pohl (historian and author of *The New Columbus*) believes they were friends.

Colon, having been rejected by the king of Portugal (probably because the king had previously financed a voyage to the Caribbean by Alonso Sanchez de Huelve in 1481) and earlier by Cortereal, guided by Norwegians Pining and Pothorst, realized his only hope was with Ferdinand and Isabel of Spain. But he knew that if Ferdinand learned that Colon was the son of his older half-brother Carlos, and thus the rightful

NORWEGIAN?

heir to the throne he held, Ferdinand would have him promptly exterminated. And so Colon assumed the identity of his deceased friend, Cristoforo Colombo.

The break for me came a dozen years ago. I had occasion to refer to a clipping from Brooklyn's *Nordisk Tidende* (possibly about Cornelius Sand, the Norwegian interpreter in the purchase of Manhattan Island by the Dutch from the Mohawks—but that's another story). On the back of the clipping was an ad by Chedney Press of New York, for their book *Juan Colon alias Cristobal alias Christopher Columbus Was A Spanish Jew*. I immediately ordered a copy. The letter was returned by the post-office, "Addressee out of business."

A few months later I found a card in the Newberry Library—misfiled—indicating they had a copy of the book. From it I obtained the address of the author, Brother Nectario Maria of the Venezuelan Embassy in Madrid. He sent me a copy of his later book with amplified data on Colon. From Spain's major library I learned of a recent book by Martorell, confirming the Nectario findings.

In 19. *Scandinavian Roots* magazine (Lofts-Eik, Norway) had an article about famous descendants of Gudbrandsdal. A name leapt from the page: Juan I of Aragon—an ancestor of Colon! From the editor I learned that the author, Engebret Hougen, was dead, but that his records had been sent to the archives in Maihaugen, Lillehammer, Norway. When we returned to Norway in 1988, of course we had to make a sidetrip to Lillehammer, a beautiful little town a couple hours pleasant train-ride north of Oslo. (Don't go there in 1994 when they hold the Winter Olympics. I have visions of the Fifth Army dropping in to Joe's Diner for lunch.) But in the archives of Maihaugen (Norway's Williamsburg) we spent a futile hour. Then there it was! Juan was indeed of Norse descent!

My story was complete—as far as I want to pursue it. Will I be forgiven if, on October 12, 1992, I chuckle a little? Or laugh out loud?

Jack Norman

The real "Columbus" was Cristobal Colon, of Spanish, Jewish and Norwegian extraction.

Partial Bibliography:

Admiral of the Ocean Sea, Morison (Little Brown, 1942)

Sails of Hope, Wiesenthal (Macmillan, 1973)

Encyclopedia Brittanica, 1973 edition, volume 6 (later editions seem to devote less space to the early years of Colon)

Univ   ' Jewish Encyclopedia, 1969 edition, volume 3. Availabl .n Jewish libraries in principal cities.

Cristobal Colon Y La revelación del enigma, Martorell (Graficas Mundo, Palma de Mallorca, 1986)

The New Columbus, Pohl, (Security-Dupont Press, 1986)

Cristobal Colon Era Espanol, Nectario Mario (Privately printed in Madrid, 1978)

Viking America, Enterline (Doubleday, 1972)

The Norse Discovery of America, Chapman (One Candle Press, 1981)

"Inventio Fortunata" *The Norseman*, (Nordmanns Forbundet, January 1988)

They All Discovered America, Boland (Doubleday, 1961)

La Sala Colombiana Del'archivio de Stato de Genova, Archivio di Stato di Genova, 1978.

GE 2 THE ITALIAN VOICE–October 4, 1990

COLUMBUS '92
AN OCCASION
NOT TO BE LOST

By Anne A. Paolucci

In the months and years ahead, there will be many worthy exhibits, programs and manifestations commemorating the 500th Anniversary of the landing of Columbus in the New World. Many programs have already been implemented, as for example the prestigious Repertorium Columbianum, edited by Professor Fredi Chiappelli and almost ready for publication by the University of California Press; or other programs sponsored by museums and funded by the National Endowment for the Humanities by the state Councils, by the Smithsonian Institution and other groups. Of course, much remains to be done in the years ahead; but there are increasingly disturbing signs that what should be the greatest American celebration of our history may well turn into an ugly confrontation.

Spain and Italy have already set aside large funds for this extraordinary anniversary; Portugal has already appointed a commissioner to monitor the Portuguese contribution to the quincentenary. The United States and Canada have done no less; in 1984-1985, national commissions were set up in both countries, to promote programs and find, is possible, funding for them. Many private groups (as in our area "Columbus: Countdown 1992") have also contributed a fair share to-date of publications, art exhibits, plays, and other cultural programs of many kinds.

Unfortunately, there is mounting anti-Columbus feeling in the United States aimed primarily at emphasizing the violence of the conquest rather than the advantages that the western world has enjoyed as a result of his momentous journey. Moreover, many programs, even international ones, are proving to be nothing more than sheer propaganda.

There is no question that the native population suffered from the discovery. There was bloodshed certainly and many lives were lost. But that is part of our history. There is nothing to be gained by reviewing our history down the ages, to the Second World War and the "wars of conquest" (and not just economic ones) of our own day.

In the days and months ahead, therefore, all public and privately-funded programs must reflect the history and interests of all groups, not just one or another. It is imperative and urgent that we all work together at this point. We are about to enter, in fact, upon a crucial moment in our history, especially with respect to the economic strategies of Europe and North America. We must not lose the occasion.

AMERICA Oggi MAGAZINE

domenica 15 aprile 1990 17

PROGRAMS AND POLEMICS

POLEMICHE & PROGRAMMI

Colombo '92: un'occasione da non perdere

DI ANNE A. PAOLUCCI

Nei prossimi mesi ci saranno molte esposizioni degne di essere visitate, molti programmi e molte manifestazioni per commemorare il quinto centenario della scoperta dell'America da parte di Colombo. Molte di queste iniziative sono già a buon punto come, ad esempio, il **"Repertorium Columbianum"** che, curato dal prof. Fredi Chiappelli, sta per essere pubblicato dalla University of California Press; o come altri programmi di vari musei sponsorizzati dal National Endowment for the Humanities, dagli State Council on the Humanities, dalla Smithsonian Institution e da altri gruppi. Molto, comunque, nei prossimi anni, resta ancora da fare. Ci sono purtroppo molti segnali che indicano già come le prossime celebrazioni colombiane più che risolversi in un fatto storico si risolveranno invece in confronti (e scontri) tra i vari gruppi organizzatori. Spagna e Italia hanno stanziato ingenti fondi per questa eccezionale ricorrenza; il Portogallo, dal canto suo, ha addirittura nominato un commissario speciale per controllare quanto viene fatto per questo quinto centenario. Stati Uniti e Canada non sono state da meno; nel 1984-'85, a livello nazionale in entrambi i Paesi, si è dato vita alla formazione di commissioni che promuovessero le varie celebrazioni e trovassero, qualora fosse possibile, i fondi necessari per farlo. Molte altre organizzazioni a livello privato (come, nella nostra area, il "Columbus Countdown '92") hanno da parte loro contribuito finora con varie pubblicazioni, esposizioni artistiche, rappresentazioni teatrali, e programmi culturali di vario genere.

Purtroppo, in questi ultimi tempi, sta crescendo un po' ovunque in tutti gli States un movimento anti-colombiano teso piuttosto a sottolineare la violenza della sua scoperta che non invece i vantaggi che tutto il mondo occidentale ha goduto dopo il suo memorabile viaggio. Molti programmi poi, anche a livello internazionale, si stanno rivelando pura e semplice propaganda. Non c'è dubbio, storicamente parlando, che le popolazioni indigene "subirono" la scoperta. C'è stato certamente spargimento di sangue e molte vite sono state sacrificate. Ma tutto ciò è storia. Non è qui certo il caso di ripercorrere tutti i secoli della nostra storia, passando per la Seconda guerra mondiale e arrivando alle "guerre di conquista" (non solo di carattere economico) dei nostri giorni.

Nell'immediato futuro è necessario perciò che tutti i programmi, di carattere pubblico o privato che siano, riflettano la storia e le esigenze di tutti, non solo di qualche particolare gruppo. E' necessario, e urgente, che si lavori davvero insieme. Stiamo infatti per vivere un momento assai importante della storia, particolarmente per l'Europa e il Nordamerica. Le festività colombiane sono un'occasione da non perdere.

7-PART PBS SERIES DEBUTS SUNDAY, 3D

COLUMBUS

Hero . . .   or villain?

FRIDAY, OCTOBER 4, 1991 • USA TODAY

COVER STORY

By Metropolitan Museum of Art, New York

MYSTERY MAN: This may, or may not, be Christopher Columbus, painted by Sabastiano Del Piombo in 1519 — 13 years after Columbus' death. No one knows what he really looked like.

His 'seeds of change' bore startling fruit

By Maria Puente
USA TODAY

U.S. events range from silly to serious but explorer didn't see this continent 2A

Christopher Columbus is one of the mystery men of history. Nobody knows where he first landed or where he's buried. Historians can't even decide what he looked like.

Now, as the nation and the world prepare a mega-commemoration of the 500th anniversary of Columbus' arrival in this hemisphere — including Sunday's premiere of a TV documentary on PBS — questions are being raised about the man and the consequence of his achievement.

Was he hero or knave?

Even the most fervent Columbus supporters are learning to pick their words carefully. They don't call it Columbus' "discovery" of the New World. The politically correct term is Columbus' "encounter."

"Everything about Columbus is debatable," says Maria Scarapicchia of the National Italian-American Foundation.

For native Americans, he wasn't the Great Discoverer, he was the Great Invader. For African-Americans, he wasn't the First Immigrant, he was the First Slaveowner. And for environmentalists, he wasn't the Great Explorer, he was the Great Destroyer.

These competing perspectives ensure the quincentennial will be as contentious as it is comprehensive.

Either way, it will be huge.

The quincentennial will be even bigger than the USA's

WGBH, Boston

COLUMBUS? Scholars say there are more than two dozen portraits of Columbus, and no two look alike.

"Not until humans discover life on another planet will there ever be such a diverse coming together of people, plants, animals, microbes and products."

But the counter-Columbus movement, led by native Americans, may end up gaining almost as much attention as the quincentennial itself. On Oct. 12, the day of the Washington kickoff ceremony, native American groups plan a memorial on the Mall to the tribes that died out after 1492.

Some groups — from church leaders to librarians — even question the idea of celebration. They think 1992 ought to be a time of reflection and mourning for the millions of people of the Americas who were killed, enslaved or died of European diseases.

"Our intent is not to rain on anybody's parade, but to get people to think about what really happened and how to make the next 500 years better," says Sandy Toineeta, a Lakota Sioux and spokeswoman for the National Council of Churches.

When replicas of Columbus' caravels, the *Nina*, the *Pinta* and the *Santa Maria*, come sailing into U.S. ports from Spain next year, some native American groups hope to set up blockades — or, as one leader puts it, an "Indian INS."

bicentennial in 1976, costing corporations and local and national governments billions of dollars. Spain is spending more than $4 billion and no one knows what the final cost will be in the United States.

The official U.S. kickoff is Oct. 12, Columbus Day, with a ceremony in Washington, D.C.

There will be hundreds, maybe thousands, of public and private events, from massive to modest, from the crassly commercial to the deeply intellectual. A few highlights:

▶ Oct. 6-8: *Columbus and the Age of Discovery*, a seven-hour documentary airs on PBS.

▶ Oct. 26: The Smithsonian's largest single exhibit ever, "Seeds of Change," will examine how five "seeds" — sugar, corn, potatoes, disease and horses — changed the world after coming together in 1492.

▶ April 1992: The USA's biggest quincentennial event, Amer/Flora '92, opens in Columbus, Ohio. It features the plants exchanged between the Old and New Worlds.

Aside from all that, there will be a smorgasbord of scholarly exhibits, lectures, symposia, debates and books all over the world.

All of this for a guy who probably wasn't the first European on these shores. Remember the Vikings?

"Columbus may not have been the first to make the trip but he was the first to go back and hold a press conference," jokes Marjory Pizzuti, director of a multimillion-dollar celebration planned in Columbus, Ohio. It bills itself as the world's largest city named after you-know-who.

Why the big to-do? Because even the Columbus-bashers agree his linking of the Old and the New World in 1492, celebrated on Oct. 12 in the USA, was probably the most important event ever.

"It was unprecedented in human history," says anthropologist Jack Weatherford of Macalester College in St. Paul, Minn.

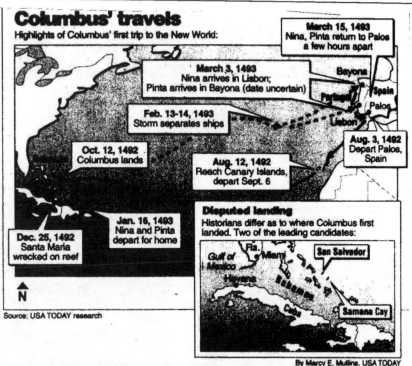

Columbus' travels

Highlights of Columbus' first trip to the New World:

March 15, 1493
Nina, Pinta return to Palos a few hours apart

March 3, 1493
Nina arrives in Lisbon; Pinta arrives in Bayona (date uncertain)

Bayona

Spain

Portugal

Palos

Lisbon

Feb. 13-14, 1493
Storm separates ships

Aug. 3, 1492
Depart Palos, Spain

Oct. 12, 1492
Columbus lands

Aug. 12, 1492
Reach Canary Islands, depart Sept. 6

Dec. 25, 1492
Santa Maria wrecked on reef

Jan. 16, 1493
Nina and Pinta depart for home

Disputed landing

Historians differ as to where Columbus first landed. Two of the leading candidates:

Fla. Miami

Gulf of Mexico

Havana

Cuba

Bahamas

San Salvador

Samana Cay

N

Source: USA TODAY research

By Marcy E. Mullins, USA TODAY

"If we had had this in the beginning — if we hadn't been so lax in our immigration policies — history would have developed differently," says Suzan Harjo, coordinator for the [ ] Alliance of Indian groups planning alternative quincentennial events around the country.

Author Kirkpatrick Sale is the lead debunker of the Columbus mythology, with a best-selling book, *The Conquest of Paradise.* "We have to reassess the Western culture that won, think about the terrible costs of winning and re-examine the values of Indian culture that got lost," Sale says.

His reading of the historical record shows Columbus was cruel and greedy as a person, and incompetent as a seaman and administrator. A rootless man, always searching for something else, Columbus was the epitome of the 15th-century European, Sale says:

"Once they had found paradise, they could not have done anything else but destroy it."

Weatherford, another Columbus revisionist, notes that — aside from past presidents — this country honors only two individuals with national holidays: Columbus and Martin Luther King Jr.

"King stands for the real American values — peace and justice," he says. "Columbus stands for conquest, religious bigotry and greed."

But Columbus defenders say you can't judge him, or those who followed him, by the standards of the 1990s. "All conquest is violent," says Anne Paolucci, president of Columbus Countdown 1992, a New York-based foundation.

And James Axtell, an historian of native American cultures, laments the hijacking of Columbus by "simplistic" political activists.

"There's no balance here," says Axtell, head of the American Historical Society's quincentennial committee.

"There are only caricatures of European society, of Indian societies, of Columbus, and no one's making any effort to be historical."

So it's not going to be a year of unadulterated homage to Columbus. For every admirer who sees him as a symbol of faith, courage and determination, there will be a critic who sees him as a greedy seeker of glory and gold.

But that may be just as well, says Joseph Laufer, a New Jersey college administrator.

Laufer has dedicated the next few years of his life to traveling around the country, dressed up as Columbus, to bring history to life for schoolchildren.

"This will be a tremendous opportunity for all the issues to be aired," Laufer says. "If it were not for the controversy, Columbus would be just another date on the calender."

N E W S M A K E R S

"OP-ED "ARTICLE IN *THE DAILY NEWS*, THURSDAY, DECEMBER 22, 1994.

DAILY ◉ NEWS

NEW YORK'S HOMETOWN NEWSPAPER

Don't dis Chris, the 1st 'immigrant'

By ANNE PAOLUCCI

THE 1992 COLUMBUS quincentenary celebration was marred by empty-headed factional rhetoric, including the suggestion that Christopher Columbus ruined the ecology. Confrontations and debunkings always get a good hearing, and such rantings continue to grab media attention.

Still, it seems strange to read of the bombastic rhetoric of David Silberberg, a so-called teacher bent on rewriting history according to his predilections, undermining in the process both Columbus and the Christian tradition he represented.

The Manhattan high school teacher doesn't consider Columbus a great hero, disparaging him as "very Eurocentric and strongly Christian." His students call Columbus a murderer, rapist and "mad fake" and his great discovery "the beginning of a Holocaust."

Are these opinions a given that all Americans should subscribe to?

Renaissance man

The great historians of Harvard and Johns Hopkins, starting with Justine Winsor, Herbert Baxter Adams and the many qualified age-of-discovery scholars since then (Samuel Eliot Morison, Charles Bump, Fredi Chiappelli, etc.) have made abundantly clear that Columbus not only dared to venture into an unknown vast sea — where even the most famous navigators of the time, the Portuguese, would not go — but in doing so also brought to full flowering the Renaissance spirit of expansion and discovery.

Sooner or later someone would have done what Columbus did. The need for expansion was a historical reality described, for instance, by Thomas More, chancellor to England's King Henry VIII, in his masterpiece, "Utopia" (which was about America).

Successful efforts at territorial expansion have always been accompanied by some measure of violence. Columbus, in fact, was replaced as administrator in Hispaniola, the first New World colony, because he was too mild and compassionate.

Are students given those facts? Are they reminded that we cannot judge past actions in retrospect, on the basis of current values or laws, just as we cannot convict someone of a crime that he or she might commit five or two years from now (as Shakespeare's Brutus convicts Julius Caesar for what he might do and thus justifies killing him "in the shell")?

African tribes are still enslaving other Africans in Africa, as in Columbus' time; certainly the genocide of the Armenians and the massacres in Yugoslavia today are more horrendous than anything which has been attributed to Columbus. The Spanish claim in the Americas is not so different from the claim of the Israelis to their land, which has often necessitated strong measures to restrain and control others who would question that claim. Rewriting history doesn't mean arbitrarily ignoring certain facts.

On the positive side, it must mean (as former Mayor Da-

Christopher Columbus should be judged in the context of his times, not ours

vid Dinkins aptly phrased it in a symposium in July 1992) a shared commitment to the ideal of an America of "Many Peoples, Many Pasts." We are indeed a land of immigrants, starting probably with the northeast Asians who long ago crossed the Bering Strait. And ever since, there has been a sociological "layering" — with diverse peoples following one another, coming full circle, it now seems, with a great second wave of Asian immigrants.

The first immigrant

The contradictory intentions that prodded so many different people to mold our heritage into a new national self-consciousness — a spiraling process of constant redefinition — is what eventually makes us one people and one nation. In this context, Columbus emerges in every sense as the first European "immigrant" to our shores, and one who suffered many of the trials and difficulties of more recent immigrants.

As president of Columbus: Countdown 1992, and having worked for more than six years on special projects commemorating the beginning of our multi-cultural history, I strongly urge that we take a more historical perspective on the matter of Columbus and stop throwing our individual, racial and religious weight around to make gross and untenable points. This teacher should do a bit more reading on the subject and ask his students to do the same. Right now, he flunks the course.

18 domenica 27 maggio 1990   **MAGAZINE/LETTERE**   AMERICA **Oggi**

I lettori ci scrivono

Cristoforo Colombo violento e razzista?

Caro direttore,
la presa di posizione del National Council of Churches contro le celebrazioni colombiane per il quinto centenario della scoperta dell'America è l'ultima, in ordine di tempo, di quelle che accusano di violenza e razzismo Cristoforo Colombo. Da che mondo è mondo, ogni Paese è stato invaso da qualcuno, e ancora oggi, in Africa, la schiavitù è una pratica comune; la sete di conquista poi e la violenza quotidianamente scrivono pagine di cronaca in Medio Oriente e in altre regioni del mondo. E' vero che dopo la scoperta di Colombo la schiavitù è esistita per oltre tre secoli qui in Nordamerica, ma non si può certo ritenere il nostro Colombo responsabile per quanto, fino a Lincoln, è stato fatto. E' un po' come ritenere colpevole di un qualsivoglia atto un individuo, oggi, per qualcosa commesso una decina d'anni fa, per esempio, quando quell'azione non veniva contemplata dalle leggi come peccaminosa e quindi punibile. La parola "scoperta" per giunta non significa certo ladrocinio (qui, contro gli Indiani). "Scoperta" è anche sinonimo di "emigrazione", ricerca cioè di nuove opportunità. Se ciò sia da considerarsi crimine è cosa che fa davvero rabbrividire.

Tutti coloro che sono emigrati qui in America per sfuggire alla povertà, alla discriminazione, ed hanno lottato in questa terra d'adozione per costruirsi una diversa realtà sociale ed educativa dovrebbero prendere posizione contro il National Council of Churches: l'argomentazione di quest'associazione protestante è chiaramente partigiana e antistorica. Indipendentemente dalle molle che hanno spinto Colombo, la sua scoperta ha allargato enormemente i confini del mondo dando a ciascuno di noi una nuova promessa e una nuova speranza.

Anne A. Paolucci
Beechhurst (New York)

CHRISTOPHER COLUMBUS: BRUTAL CONQUEROR AND RACIST?

Editor *AMERICA OGGI*:

The recent statement by the protestant National Council of Churches that there should be no quincentenary celebration of an event that rendered the Indians slaves and was in effect an invasion of their land ("Magazine," Saturday, May 19, 1990, p. 13) is one of many that has been put forward by Indian groups, especially, and their supporters. Countries have been invaded from time immemorial; slaves are still being made in Africa and elsewhere; conquest and violence are still daily events in the Middle East and other areas of the world. Our own history shows that slavery went on for 350 years after Columbus landed; our founding fathers, including ancestors of many members of the National Council of Churches, had slaves. Without condoning the matter one may still insist that where no crime existed no crime can be labeled or punished after the fact. Slavery prospered among us under the triangular trade of the North, which provided cheap labor for the South. We know the devastating results of that choice in the time of Lincoln. History is indeed ironic.

The plight of native Indians is a serious and continuing one; but taking this occasion to accuse Columbus of something that was not considered wrong in the 15th century is like accusing and sentencing a man today for something which was committed ten years ago when there was no edict or law against what he did.

The word "discovery," moreover, does not mean stealing from others. Discovery can mean precisely what one means when one speaks of "immigration," the discovery of new opportunities, etc. If discovering opportunities is a crime then all who leave their native lands to better themselves would qualify as criminals.

Finally, the Arawaks in the Caribbean, and other such tribes, were destroyed not by Columbus but by stronger tribes like the Caribs. The Aztecs, before Cortes put a stop to it, were sacrificing 20,000 captives at a time. With respect to slavery, Columbus was far ahead of his time, as his letters show. To be fair, should we not give the entire case, if he is to be put on trial?

The quincentenary commemorates the landing of the first immigrant to the New World. Those of us who have lived through many trying years of poverty, discrimination, adjustment, the social and educational struggles which every immigrant has had to face, understand the argument put forward by the National Council of Churches; but in all fairness the argument is a partisan, abortive and disruptive one. History has many vectors that converge into a single resultant. Whatever the motives of the countries that sent navigators and explorers into this part of the world, the result has been a world-wide expansion that has given in the past and still provides today new and great promise to all our minorities and to the peoples of the world. And one must be tireless in reaffirming this argument.

Dr. Anne Paolucci, *President "Columbus: Countdown 1992"*

Temi & Dibattiti
Un monumento all'emigrazione
e un ricordo di colui che scoprì il Nuovo Mondo

Ellis Island e Colombo

DI HENRY & ANNE PAOLUCCI

Colombo - è stato suggerito da qualche parte - è americano né più né meno che Ellis Island. Eppure Ellis Island non sta a ricordare il nostro navigatore ma le migliaia di emigrati che per essa sono passati.

È ovvio che l'isola era il primo che gli emigranti cominciassero ad arrivare in massa in questo Paese. I suoi ventisette acri nell'Upper New York Bay, a sud-ovest di Manhattan, sono serviti come forte e come arsenale militare prima di servire, dal 1892 in poi, come centro di accoglienza e di successivo smistamento degli emigranti. Per 59 anni Ellis Island ha svolto questa funzione. Nel 1943, quando milioni di americani vennero mandati via nave o in aereo in Europa a causa della seconda guerra mondiale, le porte di Ellis Island si chiusero. Ci fu l'abbandono alle erbacce, al vento, alla pioggia e alla sabbia; nel 1954 il grande edificio rossastro non era che una rovina patetica.

In che stato Ellis Island si fosse ridotta lo abbiamo sentito per la prima volta da Peter e Sally Sammartino che per primi hanno lanciato l'appello perché fosse restaurata. Ormai il restauro è stato ultimato ed Ellis Island sta per riaprire le porte ai discendenti degli emigranti di un tempo. Ciò accadrà fra giorni, a settembre, e il clima delle celebrazioni si protrarrà direttamente fino alle cerimonie commemorative della scoperta colombiana, in ottobre. Ellis Island sarà un museo, un monumento ai sacrifici e al coraggio di quanti ci hanno preceduto in questa terra.

Tra due anni, in occasione del suo centenario, Ellis Island servirà anche a qualcos'altro, a rendere l'ultimo servizio agli emigranti. Cristoforo Colombo - il primo degli emigranti dall'Europa occidentale - era tornato indietro in Spagna per regolarizzare (usando un linguaggio moderno) "le sue carte". Colombo, proprio come tanti che da Ellis Island furono rispediti indietro, dovette attendere un bel po' di tempo perché esse fossero "regolarizzate". In effetti, morì mentre era ancora in attesa che questo avvenisse. E fino all'ultimo giorno attese la possibilità di un "ritorno" alle isole che aveva scoperto, con innumerevoli vantaggi per tutta l'Europa.

Colombo, in pratica, non morì "a casa", ma lontano da essa. Agognò fino alla fine, senza successo, il grande ritorno. Genova era stata la città che gli diede i natali. Il Portogallo era divenuto "la casa lontano da casa". La Spagna era una "casa di adozione e di convenienza". Il Nuovo Mondo aveva bisogno di colonizzazione e lui chiese invano alla corte di Spagna di essere mandato nelle isole scoperte, insieme alla sua famiglia, come colonizzatore. All'inizio si raggiunse l'accordo, e Colombo poté traversare l'Atlantico per quattro volte. Poi l'accordo venne rinnegato. La corte spagnola decise

che era una missione troppo grande per un solo uomo e per una sola famiglia, anche se grande. Ed avevano ragione. "Colombo, ascoltaci! Centinaia di migliaia, forse di milioni, di spiriti avventurosi debbono fare questo viaggio, prendere possesso dei territori, costruire case. Tu hai mostrato la via. Gli altri dovranno seguirla ed imitarti. E poi, forse fra cinquecento anni, i loro discendenti riconosceranno che ti dovranno molto e che tu sei stato il primo emigrante e finiranno con l'identificarsi con te. Che altro puoi chiedere alla storia?"

Che altro? Riposa, spirito inquieto, riposa. Colombo, la tua casa è qui, in questa terra che ha prodotto i maggiori storici della tua scoperta perché, se l'America non ti riconosce per quello che hai fatto, chi altri mai potrà farlo?

Chi sono i più grandi studiosi dell'opera e della persona di Colombo? Sono certo gli americani! Bisogna infatti risalire a Samuel Eliot Morison. Morison, bisogna ancora ripetere, è stato lui stesso un navigatore ed un ammiraglio nella Navy Usa. Il suo più grande contributo alla storia dei nostri tempi è la sua monumentale (15 volumi) "History of U.S. Naval Operations in World War II". La sua "Oxford History of the American People" è ormai un classico nel suo genere. Ma i suoi volumi su Colombo (comprese le traduzioni di molti documenti) non possono non essere essere considerati ugualmente che "classici".

Il primo volume della sua "European Discovery of America" (1971-1974) sottolinea come modello di Morison sia stata l'opera di Justin Winsor. Egli si rifà particolarmente alla monumentale "Narrative and Critical History of America" (1881-1889), in otto volumi, che ripresentano, in maniera impeccabile e scientifica, monografie e documenti di quanti hanno avuto attraverso gli anni a che fare con la scoperta dell'America. Come lo stesso Morison riconosce, "nessuno in questo secolo, come Winsor, ha cercato di cogliere tutti gli aspetti della scoperta.

Winsor, che ha studiato a Harvard, Parigi e Heidelberg, ha scritto delle opere specialistiche sulle scoperte geografiche e sui navigatori di importanza universale. Ricordiamo, fra le altre, "Christopher Columbus" (1891), "From Cartier to Frontenac: A Study of Geographical History in the Interior of North America in its Historical Relations, 1534-1700" (1894) ed "Exploration of the Mississippi Basin" (1895). Fino al 1889 Winsor, come lo stesso Morison riconosce, ha raccolto e studiato tutti i documenti che era umanamente possibile raccogliere e studiare. Morison fa poi il resto. E chiunque oggi voglia vedere da vicino Colombo e la sua opera non può fare a meno di questi due colossi della storia, che scrupolosamente e scientificamente, hanno "vivisezionato" colui che cinque secoli fa ci precedette qui in America.

Arguments and Debates
*A Monument to Emigration and a Tribute to
the Man Who Discovered the New World*

Columbus and Ellis Island

by Henry and Anne Paolucci

Columbus—it has been suggested—is as American as Ellis Island. Ellis Island was not built to honor Columbus. It was built for humble immigrants.

Of course, the island was there long before the immigrants began to land on it. Its 27-acres afloat in Upper New York Bay southwest of Manhattan had seen many years of service as an arsenal and a fort before their enlistment, in 1892, to function as our country's chief immigration center. The island served in that capacity for 59 years. Then, in 1943, when millions of Americans were being shipped and flown overseas to wage the world's greatest war, its doors of welcome to immigrants were closed. Its abandonment to weeds, wind, rain, and sand in 1954 soon reduced the grand red building of the center to a pathetic ruin

What the abandoned building looked like at its worst some of us have been privileged to hear from the lips of Peter and Sally Sammartino, who first raised the hue and cry for its restoration and preservation. Thanks to many influential people who heeded the cry, restoration has at last become an accomplished fact. In September of this year—in time for our October festivities—the grand old center of immigration will at last open its doors again, this time permanently. And they will open as the entrance to a museum, which is to stand in glory also as a public memorial to our greatest decades of immigration.

But, two years from now, during its centenary, Ellis Island must do a final immigration service. Columbus—the western hemisphere's first European immigrant—had gone back to Spain after his fourth voyage of European discovery in the hemisphere to get his immigration-papers (so to speak) regularized. Like many later immigrants "sent back" from Ellis Island, Columbus waited in vain for his "regularized papers." In fact, he died waiting. He longed until his death to return to the islands and continents which he had first "revealed" to all of Europe.

Columbus, in other words, was not "at home" when he died—far from it. He longed to "go home," but he was prevented from doing so. Genoa had been the home of his birth and youth. Then Portugal had become his "home away from home" for navigational schooling. Next he had made Spain his home of convenience for transoceanic attempts to "reach the fabulous riches of the East by sailing West." And finally, after it was clear that the many islands on which he landed, as well as the continental landmass beyond them, were underdeveloped and in need of development, he pleaded with his royal patrons in Spain to let him and his family become the first resident-developers. And they agreed. That was the deal. But after the fourth voyage, no doubt for valid reasons, those same generous patrons reneged. They had seen that it was too great a project for one man, or one family, however large. And they were right. They might have said, in effect:

"Columbus, listen to us: hundreds of thousands, maybe millions, of adventurous spirits must make such voyages, and take possession, and build. You have shown the way. Others must follow in great waves. And then, perhaps after some 500 years, their descendants will acknowledge that you were indeed the first of their kind, the first immigrant. And they will then celebrate what you did, identifying themselves with it. What more could you ask of history?"

Indeed, if America doesn't fittingly honor Columbus as one of its own, he will not be fittingly honored anywhere else. The record in this respect is more than clear. Who are the greatest Columbus scholars? They are Americans. One must start the list with Samuel Eliot Morison. Morison, it should be stressed, was himself a lifelong sailor and an admiral in the U.S. Navy. His greatest scholarly contribution to the history of our own time is, of course, his monumental (15-vols) *History of U.S. Naval Operations in World War II*. His *Oxford History of the American People* is an established classic of its kind. But his many volumes on Columbus (including good translations of almost all the major documents available) are not less distinctively American classics.

In the first volume of his *European Discovery of America* (1971-1974), Morison explains that his basic scholarly approach to the subject takes the work of Justin Winsor as its model. And he cites particularly Winsor's monumental *Narrative and Critical History of America* (1881-1889), in eight volumes, the first four of which consist of carefully-edited versions of essential documents as well as monographs by the most distinguished scholars who have dealt with the age of American discovery. As Morison put it in 1971: "Nobody in the present century has followed Winsor in attempting to cover the entire field of New World discovery."

Winsor had been educated at Harvard, Paris, and Heidelberg, and was part of the elite group of scholars who labored in his day to lay a solid foundation for serious doctoral studies in America. His specialized books on discoverers and explorers included *Christopher Columbus* (1891), *From Cartier to Frontenac: A Study of Geographical History in the Interior of North America in its Historical Relations 1534-1700* (1894), and *Exploration of the Mississippi Basin* (1895).

Morison reminds us that, in his extensive notes on Columbus, Winsor reviewed all the discovery "hoaxes and 'finds' up to 1889"; and Morison then supplements that with a hundred pages of his own on the subject.

Columbus set the stage for a long age of exploration and development in the Americas. That needs to be remembered when the doors of Ellis Island open again. Columbus must be welcomed home. These continents are his home. He didn't set foot on Ellis Island, of course. But we can make up for that by building a proper memorial to him there:—to begin with, a room with Columbus maps and early books, appropriately named after the leading American Columbus scholars. It could fittingly be called the Winsor/Morison Columbus Study Center of Ellis Island.

This English original of the Italian text is part of an essay by Anne Paolucci, "Columbus: A Paradoxical Legacy Reviewed," in MODERN VIEWS OF COLUMBUS AND HIS TIME (CNL/WORLD REPORT [VI]) published by the Council on National Literatures for its member-libraries in 40 foreign countries and distributed as an independent volume by Griffon House Publications. (To order book: Send $15 prepaid to CNL, P. O. Box 81, Whitestone, N.Y. 11357.)

Columbus and the historic wave of genocide

Opinion 6A

Wednesday, October 11, 1989
Abilene Reporter-News

By JACK WEATHERFORD
Special to the Baltimore Evening Sun

Christopher Columbus' reputation has not survived the scrutiny of history, and today we know that he was no more the discoverer of America than Pocahontas was the discoverer of Great Britain.

Native Americans had built great civilizations with many millions of people long before Columbus wandered lost into the Caribbean.

Columbus' voyage has even less meaning for North Americans than for South Americans because Columbus never set foot on our continent, nor did he open it to European trade.

Scandinavian Vikings already had settlements here in the 11th century, and British fishermen probably fished the shores of Canada for decades before Columbus.

The first European explorer to thoroughly document his visit to North America was the Italian explorer Giovanni Caboto, who sailed for England's King Henry VII and became known to us by his anglicized name, John Cabot.

Caboto arrived in 1497 and claimed North America for the English sovereign while Columbus was still searching for India in the Caribbean.

After three voyages to America and more than a decade of study, Columbus still believed that Cuba was a part of the continent of Asia, South America was only an island and the coast of Central America was close to the Ganges River.

Unable to celebrate Columbus' exploration as a

> Columbus' voyage has even less meaning for North Americans than for South Americans because Columbus never set foot on our continent, nor did he open it to European trade.

great discovery, some apologists now want to commemorate it as the great "cultural encounter."

Under this interpretation, Columbus becomes a sensitive genius thinking beyond his time in the passionate pursuit of knowledge and understanding. The historical record refutes this, too.

Contrary to popular legend, Columbus did not prove that the world was round; educated people had known that for centuries.

The Egyptian-Greek scientist Eratosthenes, working for Alexandria and Aswan, already had measured the circumference and diameter of the world in the 3rd century B.C.

Arab scientists had developed a whole discipline of geography and measurement, and in the 10th century A.D., Al Maqdisi had calculated that the Earth had 360 degrees of longitude and 180 degrees of latitude.

The Monastery of St. Catherine in the Sinai still has an icon — painted 500 years before Columbus — which shows Jesus ruling over a spherical earth.

Nevertheless, Americans have embroidered many such legends around Columbus, and he has become part of a secular mythology for schoolchildren.

Autumn would hardly be complete in any elementary school without construction-paper replicas of the three cute ships that Columbus sailed to America, or without drawings of Queen Isabella pawning her jewels to finance Columbus' trip.

This myth of the pawned jewels obscures the true and more sinister story of how Columbus financed his trip.

The Spanish monarchy invested in his excursion, but only on the condition that Columbus would repay this investment with profit by bringing back gold, spices and other tribute from Asia.

This pressing need to repay his debt underlies the frantic tone of Columbus' diaries as he raced from one Caribbean island to the next, stealing anything of value.

After he failed to contact the emperor of China, the traders of India or the merchants of Japan, Columbus decided to pay for his voyage in the one important commodity he had found in ample supply — human lives.

He seized 1,200 Taino Indians from the island of Hispaniola, crammed as many onto his ships as would fit and sent them to Spain, where they were paraded naked through the streets of Seville and sold as slaves in 1495. Columbus tore children from their parents, husbands from wives.

On board Columbus' slave ships, hundreds died; the sailors tossed the Indian bodies into the Atlantic.

Because Columbus captured more Indian slaves than he could transport to Spain in his small ships, he put them to work in mines and plantations which he, his family and followers created throughout the Caribbean.

His marauding band hunted Indians for sport and profit — beating, Raping, torturing, killing and then using the Indian bodies as food for their hunting dogs.

Within four years of Columbus' arrival on Hispaniola, his men had killed or exported one-third of the original Indian population of 300,000.

Within another 50 years, the Taino people had been made extinct — the first casualties of the holocaust of American Indians.

The plantation owners then turned to the American mainland and to Africa for new slaves to follow the tragic path of the Taino.

This was the great cultural encounter initiated by Christopher Columbus. This is the event we celebrate each year on Columbus Day.

The United States honors only two men with federal holidays bearing their names.

In January we commemorate the birth of Martin Luther King Jr., who struggled to lift the blinders of racial prejudice and to cut the remaining bonds of slavery in America.

This week we honor Christopher Columbus, who opened the Atlantic slave trade and launched one of the greatest waves of genocide known in history.

Weatherford is an anthropologist at Macalester College in St. Paul, Minn. His most recent book is "Indian Givers"

AMERICA **Oggi** **MAGAZINE** 21

domenica 28 giugno 1992

COMMUNITY NEWS   Awards by Anne Paolucci's "Columbus: Countdown 1992

'LEADERSHIP AWARDS' PRESENTED IN NEW YORK

by Antonino Ciappina

The Columbus Club, one of the most prestigious social-cultural headquarters in New York, recently drew many talented personalities chosen by Columbus: Countdown 1992, headed by Anne Paolucci, to receive special **"Leadership Awards"** in this quincentenary year. Parenthetically, while Dr. Paolucci was thinking of honoring colleagues in the Big Apple, someone was thinking of her in Rome: for her play *Cipango!* and for her many Columbus projects and initiatives over the past several years, as well as for her educational and university activities, she was recently singled out for the title of **"Commendatore" Order of Merit** by the Republic of Italy.

Presentations were made by Anne Paolucci to:

Anna Crisci-Santana, founder of SIAMO, an organization devoted to increased awareness of the contribution of Italians in the United States and to promoting role models for the younger generations;

Joseph Amelio Finelli, sculptor, originally from Sannita (Benevento), who has given us two excellent busts—one of Philip Mazzei of Tuscany and the other of Luigi Pirandello of Sicily;

Joseph S. King, playwright and director, who has produced over 200 shows and is responsible for the productions and video direction of *Cipango!*;

Joseph M. Laufer, whose commitment to Italian heritage is unmistakable, a staunch defender of Columbus, especially at a time when he has become the target of other ethnic groups;

Paul Patané, who in the true spirit of Columbus has orchestrated an East-West encounter—a cultural exchange between New York and Tokyo—and who serves as liaison between the New York City Department of Education and the Metropolitan Museum of Art;

Frances M. Rello, USA representative of the magazine *Italy-Italy*, regional head of NIAF (National Italian American Foundation), a member of the "Association of Ligurians in the World" and faithful promoter of the study of Italian in the American high schools;

and, finally, Franco Borrelli of *America-Oggi* and professor of Italian at Montclair State College of New Jersey.

Guest of honor for the evening was painter Antonia Mastrocristino Sirena, who in 1988 was the CC 1992 recipient of the "Special Reccognition in the Arts & Humanities Award."

The group's next scheduled event is on September 30th at the "200 Club," Fifth Avenue and 23rd Street, when CC 1992 will officially celebrate the quincentenary of the discovery of Columbus and will present its prestigious annual awards—the recipients of which, for the moment, must remain "top secret."

In the photo, left to right: Franco Borrelli, Joseph Finelli, Joseph S. King, Anne Paolucci, Antonia Mastrocristino "Sirena" Anna Crisci-Santana, Frances M. Rello, Paul Patané and Joseph M. Laufer. (Photograph by Vito Caruso)

MAGAZINE   MAY 19, 1990

Usa. Da un gruppo di chieste protestanti

Condannata l'impresa di Cristoforo Colombo

WASHINGTON. Un gruppo di chiese protestanti ha sparato a zero contro le celebrazioni per il cinquecentenario della scoperta dell'America: come si può festeggiare un'"invasione" che per gli indiani significò solo "schiavitù e genocidio"?

A condannare senza mezzi termini l'impresa di Cristoforo Colombo è il "National Council of Churches", un'organizzazione a cui fanno capo chiese protestanti ed ortodosse con circa quaranta milioni di fedeli negli Stati Uniti. A convegno a Pittsburgh, il "National Council of Churches" ha approvato giovedì sera una risoluzione anti-colombo presentata dal reverendo George Tinker, della setta "Ecumenica cristiana".

A giudizio di Tinker - che è un indiano della tribù degli Osage - non c'è proprio nulla da celebrare per l'arrivo del navigatore genovese nel nuovo continente: si trattò di un'"invasione" di cui fecero le spese le popolazioni indigene. Dopo un acceso dibattito, la risoluzione del reverendo Tinker è passata a stragrande maggioranza. Contiene anche un appello al governo Usa perché rinunci ai festeggiamenti previsti per il 1992, in occasione del cinquecetenario della scoperta dell'America. "Non possiamo più trascurare i nostri peccati stori-

ci", ha dichiarato il reverendo Tyrone Pitts della chiesa battista progressista.

La risoluzione è una vera e propria requisitoria contro Colombo: "Certi storici hanno chiamato scoperta quella che in realtà è stata un'invasione e un'avventura coloniale, con occupazione, genocidio, sfruttamento economico, un profondo livello di razzismo istituzionale e decadenza morale".

Secondo il "National Council of Churches" anche la chiesa di allora ha le sue colpe: "con poche eccezioni ha accompagnato e legittimato la conquista e lo sfruttamento. Le giustificazioni teologiche per distruggere le religioni locali e imporre forme europee di cristianesimo richiedevano una sottomissione totale dei nuovi convertiti e ciò facilitava la conquista e lo sfruttamento'.

Il reverendo Tinker ha fatto anche dell'ironia sullo scopritore dell'America: "L'unica cosa che Cristoforo Colombo ha davvero scoperto è che si era perduto...". Il viceconsole d'Italia a Pittsburgh Joseph d'Andrea ha detto a giornalisti americani che capisce lo spirito della risoluzione ma non è d'accordo: non bisogna limitarsi agli "aspetti negativi" della scoperta.

Update

Volume 33
Number 7
October 1991

Association for Supervision and Curriculum Development
1250 N. Pitt Street, Alexandria, VA 22314-1403
(703) 549-9110

October 1991   7

Issue

How should schools commemorate the Columbian Quincentennial?

Gilbert Sewall

Although a few educators believe that the Columbian Quincentennial should be an occasion of repentance, a historical morality play in which European explorers enact the role of Darth Vader, teachers can and should approach the event more positively and from more interesting, accurate angles.

The contact between Spain and the Americas in 1492 is the most important historical event of the past 500 years. Much has been made of a European invasion that brought disease and decimation to native tribes in the Americas. The brutality of the conquistadores is well known; the tragic consequences of the Columbian discovery for indigenous cultures are recorded in all major American history textbooks.

But that is only part of the story. The Europeans also brought an expanding sensibility—shaped throughout the Renaissance and Enlightenment—to provide the base of politics, economics, technology, and culture in the Americas today. American agriculture and architecture derive from Europe, as do our systems of health, sanitation, and communication. Roman Catholic and Protestant missionaries made Christianity the dominant faith in the Western Hemisphere. Spanish, Portuguese, English, and French are the languages of the Americas.

In essence, Columbus's arrival on San Salvador was the herald of One World—the global network that, 500 years later, is taken for granted around the earth.

Gilbert Sewall is director of the American Textbook Council, New York, New York.

Suzan Shown Harjo

Schools must tell the truth to kids, not only eliminating lies like the one about Columbus discovering America, but adding our reality and wisdom to the study of history, philosophy, literature, language, medicine, and the arts.

Within a decade from 1492, none of the native people Columbus first encountered were alive, most having been killed off by foreign diseases, churches, states, and Western "civilization." By the fourth anniversary of the Columbus voyage, the native people's numbers in North America had dropped precipitously.

Native people today suffer the residual effects of relocation from our homes, forced changes for the worse in our diets, separation of children from our families for "education," and acts of aggression in reservation border towns and in our sacred places. We have no cause to celebrate this ongoing legacy of destruction.

In order for the next 500 years to be different from the past 500, America must end institutional and societal racism against Indian peoples. This means living up to the U.S. Constitution, which mandates that treaties shall be the supreme law of the land, and taking steps to make up for every broken promise. The United States must rid itself of all dehumanizing, stereotyped images of our people in popular culture, including sports, advertising, and movies. Then, perhaps, we can change a sorrowful and shameful history into a positive future for all.

Suzan Shown Harjo, Cheyenne and Hodulgee Muscogee, is president of the Morning Star Foundation and national coordinator for the 1992 Alliance in Washington, D.C.

Tom Dewing

To make Columbus Day—and especially the Quincentennial—special, schools need to relate the event to students' lives. Instead of *doing* Columbus Day, teachers need to convey to students what the event did and how it continues to do it.

One way to begin is by making connections to students' own life experiences. Many of the students in my district have moved here from somewhere else. These students already know some of the feelings of the explorers who traveled from their safe homes to foreign lands. By discussing with students why they moved and what their feelings were, we would gain a sense of what the men on the Columbus voyage felt and what some of their thoughts might have been. I would continue the involvement by having students role play the voyage or relate it to modern events.

I recommend making connections between other studies and the voyage of Columbus. Use "connections" as a theme and study the effects of the voyage on school subjects or on other historical events. What would have happened to American history if Columbus had not sailed or had landed somewhere else? How would English class be different if Columbus had landed on the mainland? What effect did the trade winds have on exploration that followed?

By making connections between the voyage of 500 years ago and students' lives today, the Columbian Quincentennial will be seen not as a holiday—a day to get away—but as a time to continue to be involved.

Tom Dewing is an elementary teacher from Carol Stream, Illinois, and a member of ASCD's Network and Clearinghouse for the Columbian Quincentennial.

Anne Paolucci

History should not be rewritten to suit changing factional interests or to fit currently fashionable views of morality.

Columbus did indeed land on Caribbean islands and claim them for his Spanish sponsors. Because native inhabitants were on the scene, the landing was not only a "discovery" but an encounter as well, and before long also a conquest. The rise and fall of countries, peoples, and civilizations *is* largely the history of conquests; whether we like to admit it or not, it is so.

Columbus, like the many bold discoverers who followed his lead—Raleigh, Drake, Magellan, Da Gama, and so on—represents the fearless Renaissance spirit of the modern world. It is this spirit that gave us Dante and Michelangelo, that inspired the visions of Sir Thomas More and Shakespeare (whose England had to overcome Spain before it could realize its own aspirations), and that we have seen in the tenacity and daring of the astronauts of our own day.

The coming Quincentennial is a reminder that Columbus started us on a historic journey that has drawn immigrants to a new life. That experience, too, has been filled with struggles. But we must emphasize that out of it, and because of Columbus, our unique multi-ethnic society has flourished and will continue to flourish.

Anne Paolucci is president of Columbus: Countdown 1992, a nonprofit educational foundation, Beechhurst, New York.

| QUINTO CENTENARIO DEL DESCUBRIMIENTO DE AMERICA: ENCUENTRO DE DOS MUNDOS | QUINCENTENNIAL OF THE DISCOVERY OF AMERICA: ENCOUNTER OF TWO WORLDS |

Nos. 43/44 Enero-Febrero, 1993

Nos. 43/44 January-February, 1993

LLEGANDO A PUERTO

SAILING FULL CIRCLE

Este es el último número del *Noticiero del Quinto Centenario*.

This is the last issue of the *Quincentennial Newsletter*.

COLÓN: CONTEO HASTA 1992

COLUMBUS COUNTDOWN 1992

La Octava Cena Anual de Premios del "Columbus: Countdown 1992" tuvo lugar en septiembre de 1992 en el "200 Club" en Nueva York. En la ceremonia, denominada "Una celebración de cinco centurias del espíritu del Renacimiento", el senador Paolo Emilio Taviani, vicepresidente del Senado italiano y erudito colombino, recibió el premio "CC 1992" que se concede a una vida de logros. También se reconoció la obra de Helen Greco, presidenta de la Liga de Beneficencia Italiana; de Serphin R. Maltese, senador en la legislatura de Nueva York y presidente del Grupo de Estudio de la Mayoría del Senado Estatal de Nueva York para la Celebración del Quinto Centenario de Colón, y la doctora Ann Merlino, de la Universidad de la Ciudad de Nueva York. Para más información dirigirse a:

    Columbus Countdown 1992
    166-25 Powells Cove Blvd.
    Beechhurst, New York 11357
    EE.UU.

The Eighth Annual Awards Dinner of "Columbus: Countdown 1992" was held in September, 1992 at the "200 Club" in New York City. At the ceremony entitled " A Quincentenary Celebration of the Renaissance Spirit," the eminent Vice President of the Italian Senate and Columbus scholar Senator Paolo Emilio Taviani received the "CC 1992" award of lifetime achievement. Others whose achievements were recognized include, Cav. Helen Greco, President of the Italian Welfare League, New York State Senator Serphin R. Maltese, Chairman, New York State Senate Majority Task Force for the Christopher Columbus Quincentenary Celebration, and Cav. Dr. Ann Merlino, of the City University of New York. For more information, contact:

    Columbus Countdown 1992
    166-25 Powells Cove Blvd.
    Beechhurst, New York 11357
    U.S.A.

NUEVO LIBRO SOBRE EL QUINTO CENTENARIO

NEW BOOK ADDRESSES QUINCENTENNIAL

Columbus: Countdown 1992, es decir, el Consejo Nacional de Literaturas, publicó recientemente el primero de cinco volúmenes titulado *Colón: América y el Mundo*, el cual incluye versiones ampliadas de trabajos presentados en Conferencias sobre Colón, así como nuevos ensayos críticos y artículos biográficos. Comprende temas tales como: aspectos literarios de la aventura de Colón; un examen de Colón, el hombre, y de la Italia de sus tiempos, y bibliografías anotadas de trabajos importantes sobre Colón, producidos a través de los siglos. Este volumen hace referencia especial al Renacimiento, Era del Descubrimiento, y a su impacto en los siglos subsiguientes. Para mayor información dirigirse a:

    Council of National Literatures
    P.O. Box 81
    Whitestone, New York 11357
    EE.UU.

Columbus: Countdown 1992, in its other persona, the Council of National Literatures, recently released the first of five volumes entitled *Columbus: America, and the World*, which includes expanded versions of papers presented at Columbus Conferences, as well as new critical essays and biographical articles. This publication addresses issues ranging from literary aspects of the Columbus adventure, a review of Columbus the man and Italy at the time of Columbus, to annotated bibliographies of major works on Columbus through the centuries. The volume makes special reference to the Renaissance Age of Discovery and its impact across subsequent centuries. For more information, write:

    Council of National Literatures
    P.O. Box 81
    Whitestone, New York 11357
    U.S.A.

STATE OF DELAWARE
OFFICE OF THE GOVERNOR

MICHAEL N. CASTLE
GOVERNOR

**STATEMENT
IN OBSERVANCE OF
THE 1992 DELAWARE COLUMBUS COMMISSION**

WHEREAS, October 12, 1992 marks the five hundredth anniversary of the voyages of discovery of Christopher Columbus; and

WHEREAS, Columbus' joining of the New World to the Old was the decisive event in the discovery of our planet and began the modern era of human history; and

WHEREAS, the governments and people of Spain and Italy should be recognized and commended for their historic role and contribution to those voyages; and

WHEREAS, all persons in the United States of America should look with pride on the achievements and contributions of their ancestors with respect to those historic voyages; and

WHEREAS, a strengthened awareness of the common history and heritage of the diverse American peoples should be developed with the full cooperation of schools and other cultural institutions.

NOW, THEREFORE, WE, MICHAEL N. CASTLE, GOVERNOR, AND DALE E. WOLF, LIEUTENANT GOVERNOR, of the State of Delaware, do hereby support the celebrations of:

THE 1992 DELAWARE COLUMBUS COMMISSION

in the State of Delaware and urge all Delawareans to support this observance.

Governor

Lieutenant Governor

COLUMBUS 92

mensile di informazioni culturali

Anno 6, numero 2 (43)
Genova, febbraio 1990

direttore responsabile
Mario Bottaro

redazione
Emanuela Demarchi

progetto grafico
Bob Noorda

Direzione e redazione:
via Varese 2, 16122 Genova,
tel. (010) 5388383 - fax (010) 5388386
telex 272300 C92 I

Ufficio di New York:
E.M.C. inc., 251 West 19th St., suite
10, N.Y., N.Y. 10011
tel. (212) 6209081

Editrice proprietaria Publirama s.p.a.

Consiglio di amministrazione:
Cesare Brivio Sforza (presidente),
Giulio Grazioli e Carlo Perrone
(amministratori delegati)

Comitato promotore e di indirizzo
scientifico:
Paolo Emilio Taviani (presidente),
Bartolomeo Attolico, Federico Fellini,
Giovanni Giovannini, Egidio Ortona,
Piero Ottone, Renzo Piano,
Carlo Rognoni, Giorgio Strehler,
Victor Uckmar

Abbonamento annuo (undici numeri):
Italia, lire cinquantamila;
Europa, lire sessantamila;
Continente americano, lire settantamila

Un numero: *lire cinquemila*
Numeri arretrati: *lire cinquemila*

Pubblicità: *Publirama s.p.a. - Milano:*
Galleria Passarella, tel. 02/783841;
Genova: viale Sauli 39, tel. 010/53641

Registrazione del Tribunale di Genova
n. 38/85, 8 ottobre 1985

Spedizione in abbonamento postale
Gruppo III/70

© *All rights reserved*

Stampato da La Stampa S.p.A.
salita Pino Sottano, 3c,
16138 Genova, tel. (010) 850.741

Associata all'USPI - Unione
Stampa Periodica Italiana

SOMMARIO

Hanno collaborato a questo numero: *Giulia Bogliolo Bruna, Giuliano Macciò, B. Passera*
Fotografie: *Silvia Ambrosi, Robert Floyd, Foto Franco, Paolo Welters, Archivio Secolo XIX, Archivio Columbus 92*
Traduzioni: *Marta Matteini (inglese) e Maria Pilar Roca-Alsina Pensato (spagnolo)*

In copertina: Alcuni tipi di imbarcazioni in un'incisione tratta da "Arte de navegar" di Pedro de Medina, 1545

Columbus Countdown 92
I programmi dell'associazione di Anne Paolucci

Fra i diversi comitati di festeggiamento sparsi per tutta l'America, è il *"Columbus Countdown 92"* quello che si segnala maggiormente per attivismo e intraprendenza. Presieduto da Anne Paolucci, docente presso la St. John's University di New York, il *"Columbus Countdown 92"* orchestra le iniziative e le celebrazioni colombiane in tutta la Grande Mela.

Ed è proprio nell'inesauribile attività di Anne Paolucci che sembra trovarsi la fonte di molte fra le iniziative di rilievo che, nel corso del 1989, si sono segnalate all'attenzione colombiana degli Stati Uniti.

La scorsa estate, il dipartimento di Educazione dello stato di New York ha invitato Anne Paolucci a portare il proprio contributo di studiosa al progetto *"Due Case una Tradizione"*, voluto dal governatore dello Stato Mario Cuomo. Il progetto, che si inserisce all'interno dell'*"Italo-American Heritage Curriculum"*, è un corso di studi teso ad approfondire la storia e i contributi degli italo-americani degli Stati Uniti a partire dal primo viaggio di Colombo. Corso di studi interdisciplinare, il progetto *"Due Case una Tradizione"* si propone di ordinare e integrare tutti gli studi sugli italo-americani, con particolare rilievo per l'aspetto legato all'educazione e agli sforzi per mantenere viva la consapevolezza dei propri valori culturali d'origine.

L'obiettivo del governatore Cuomo è quello di promuovere una reciproca comprensione fra gli italo-americani e gli italiani, tenendo presente le opportunità di cooperazione economica e culturale fra lo stato di New York e l'Italia, attraverso scambi commerciali, investimenti e ricerca scientifica. La struttura dell'*"Italo-American Heritage Curriculum"* è articolata in due parti: una basata su materiale di lingua italiana, l'altra su strumenti come video, film e materiale fotografico che verranno utilizzati come mezzi comunicativi da integrare all'insegnamento.

Anne Paolucci è stata invitata dal dipartimento di Educazione, sia per indicare persone e organizzazioni che possono portare il proprio contributo al curriculum, sia per riesaminare il lavoro che già è stato terminato.

L'*"Heritage"* è guidato da un comitato scientifico composto da storici, economisti, linguisti e studiosi della tradizione culturale italo-americana. Il consiglio, riunitosi nel passato dicembre, pubblicherà temi e argomenti da rendere operativi nel corso del 1990.

Ritornando in argomento più strettamente colombiano, il *"Columbus Countdown 92"* ha pubblicato in collaborazione con il Council of National Literatures il volume *"Columbus"*, che raccoglie diversi saggi dedicati alla figura del navigatore.

Fra gli altri, il volume comprende *"Fact, fiction and philology: a re-assestement of the Columbus story"*, di Anne Paolucci, *"Christopher Columbus in historical perspective"* di Frank J. Coppa, *"The earliest literary response of Reinessance Italy to the New World encounter"* di Theodore J. Cachey.

La copertina del libro è un ritratto di Colombo realizzato da Constance Del Vecchio, autrice di un'intera collezione dedicata al Navigatore. La pittrice italo-americana ha ricevuto un riconoscimento speciale durante l'Award Dinner dello scorso settembre, l'annuale riconoscimento che vede il *"Columbus Countdown 92"* premiare coloro che maggiormente si sono distinti nelle attività colombiane.

Oltre a Constance Del Vecchio, l'Award Dinner edizione 1989 ha consegnato il riconoscimento ad Alexander J.J. Roncari, presidente della Commissione per le celebrazioni colombiane canadesi. Nato a Sanremo e naturalizzato cittadino canadese nel 1959, Roncari è oggi direttore della commissione colombiana del suo Paese dal 1984. Laureatosi in Scienze naturali all'Università di Ginevra, Alexander Roncari ha lavorato nel campo della ricerca archeologica, dell'ambiente e della scienza marina. Adesso è membro dell'Associazione dei Fisici canadesi, dell'Associazione americana per l'avanzamento delle Scienze, dell'Istituto chimico canadese. Grazie agli interessi circa l'identità e la continuità culturale degli italiani d'America, Roncari è diventato presidente della Commissione culturale per le arti e le tradizioni d'Italia (Hamilton, Ontario) e membro del consiglio consultivo sul multiculturalismo per media, radio e televisione del Canada.

«Un indomabile spirito e visione della realtà, come quelli colombiani. Una eredità comune intima e personale con la figura di Colombo, essendo l'ultimo discendente vivo del Navegante». Per questi meriti, il *"Columbus Countdown 92"* ha premiato Alexander Roncari durante l'ultimo Award Dinner, affiancandogli, come preziosa first lady, Matilda Raffa Cuomo, moglie del governatore dello Stato di New York, presidente della commissione statale per le celebrazioni colombiane, nonché direttrice del programma *"Due Case Una Tradizione"*.

Lorenzo Fantini

Columbus Countdown 92

Headed by Anne Paolucci, Columbus Countdown 92 is one of the most active committees in America, working for the fifth centenary of the Discovery in the cultural and artistic fields. Among the numerous initiatives of 1989, "Columbus", including several essays about the navigator's life, was published. Moreover, Anne Paolucci took part in the project "Due case una tradizione", an idea of governor Mario Cuomo.

Colombus Countdown 92

Presidido por Anne Paolucci, el "Columbus Countdown 92" es uno de los comités más activos que actúan en América en el ámbito de la cultura y del arte para las conmemoraciones del Quinto Centenario. En 1989, entre las numerosas iniciativas, ha sido publicado en volumen "Columbus" que contiene varios ensayos dedicados a la vida del Navegante. Anne Paolucci ha colaborado también en la realización del proyecto "Due case una tradizione" según una idea de Mario Cuomo, governador del Estado de Nueva York.

Anne Paolucci durante la serata di gala del Dinner Award 1989 (foto Robert Floyd)

DISCOVERY FIVE HUNDRED

1492 ——— NEWSLETTER OF THE ——— 1992
INTERNATIONAL • COLUMBIAN • QUINCENTENARY • ALLIANCE • LTD
——— BOX 1492 • COLUMBUS • NEW JERSEY • 08022 ———

"PUBLIC AWARENESS THROUGH LIVING HISTORY" is the theme of the International Columbian Quincentenary Alliance, Ltd. Through its newsletter, information center, lecture bureau, educational materials, educational travel and public events, the ICQA contributes to the public awareness of the life and times of Christopher Columbus and the 500th anniversary of his Atlantic crossings. Through an informal alliance of the local, national and international groups organized to celebrate the Quincentenary, the ICQA promotes a unified effort in the commemoration of this major historic event.

Volume VII, Number 4   December, 1992

FINAL ISSUE

A COLUMBUS QUINCENTENARY RETROSPECTIVE

REVISIONISTS: A PARTING SHOT

Letters to the Editor, America Oggi
41 Bergenline Ave.
Westwood, NJ 07675

Since 1984, "Columbus: Countdown 1992" has played an active role in providing cultural products -- books, art works, videoplays, music, etc. -- for our great national quincentenary celebration; but it was not until last year that I began to get calls from the media for interviews meant from their point of view to dramatize and exacerbate the ongoing confrontation between "friends" of the native populations and the Western Christian European supporters of Christopher Columbus. Needless to say, it has been difficult to get the precision needed in the press to make our point.

The Minnesota effort to denigrate Columbus and "try" him after the fact for crimes against humanity is a sad joke. I was interviewed by Canadian radio with Kirkpatrick Sale some months ago and told him on that occasion that he was not a worthy scholar, since he accused Columbus of crimes that did not exist in those days (e.g. slavery, which in any case was introduced here after Columbus's voyages), as well as crimes rising out of our modern distorted sense of values (e.g. destruction of the environment, etc.). If all of this were not sad and not destructive of our national celebration, it would be laughable.

The Minnesota descendants of the Vikings, who have paired up with the native populations and their friends for this effort to undermine Columbus, should remember that their ancestors (Eric the Red, etc.) touched the coast of Newfoundland twice (before any other European as far as we know) to build seasonal hunting camps. After two efforts of this kind they returned home and never set foot on this continent again until more recent years. The obvious difference between them and Columbus is that Columbus came to stay; the

mandate was clearly for a long-term wide-reaching enterprise. The entire civilization of Europe was involved in this momentous expansion.

If we're going to accuse, let it be said that the Vikings had no interest in permanent settlements and no plan to start new colonies. They were directed solely by their immediate basic need for food. Columbus opened up this unknown continent to Europe and changed the history of the world.

But, say Sale and his supporters: that was bad. Was it? Are we certain that this vast continent belonged to the so-called Indians? And, if so, to which tribe? As far as we know, the Aztecs destroyed thousands and thousands of other Indians, whom they slaughtered when they conquered those tribes. The Caribs did the same in the area named for them. The so-called native populations of the New World were not "noble savages" after the fashion described by Rousseau!

If anyone was here first it may well have been Adam and Eve!

And why are the native populations so set on accusing Columbus and all of us by extension for their ills? Many of us came to this country with nothing and managed to find ways of rising to some measure of comfort and even success. Why do the Indian populations insist on proclaiming their rights in an absurd and antihistorical way? Are we supposed to give up 500 years of struggle to accommodate them? Is there any other people, nation, or part of the world where such an argument is even remotely considered acceptable? The history of the world is the history of conquest, physical as well as economic and cultural. The Normans conquered the Anglo-Saxons but eventually they fused into one powerful nation, England. And so on.

All of this anti-historical, anti-Western hysteria will dissipate in due course; the native populations will find new ways of making the same point again and again. But this great anniversary year cannot be erased from the historical records. It belongs to Europe and to Columbus and to the World. Most of all, it belongs to the America where the multi-ethnic society he embodies still grows and prospers.

Dr. Anne Paolucci, President
Columbus Countdown 1992

A PERSONAL QUINCENTENARY REMEMBRANCE

Joseph M. Laufer

Anne Paolucci welcomed me into her circle of Columbus enthusiasts and graciously invited me to her annual Columbus Countdown 1992 banquets in New York City. Our friendship continues

and she became very instrumental in the success of a project I planned with Columbia University in 1991. On June 18, 1992, Columbus Countdown 1992 presented me with the Quincentenary Programs Award.

America

COLUMBUS 92

mensile di informazioni culturali

Anno 5, numero 11-12 (41)
Genova, novembre-dicembre 1989

direttore responsabile
Mario Bottaro

America

Il teatro in video
New York. Dalla pièce teatrale "Cipango"! di Anne Paolucci è stato recentemente tratto un videotape della durata di venti minuti che si sta rivelando un buon veicolo di informazione sulla storia di Cristoforo Colombo, rivolto sottutto verso gli studenti. Il video è ...o proiettato in ottobre al teatro Concors, durante l'annuale incontro fra gli insegnanti di madrelingua non americana. Il video di "Cipango!" — prodotto dalla Quadrant productions — vuole essere, più che un documentario, una fonte di ricerche e di spunti di discussione e approfondimento, diretto agli studenti universitari.

"Columbus: Countdown 1992 Award"
New York. Alexander Roncari e Matilda Raffa Cuomo hanno ricevuto il "Columbus Countdown 1992 Award" per il 1989. Svoltasi anche quest'anno al '200 Club di Manhattan, la cerimonia ha voluto premiare alcuni fra gli italo-americani che più si sono segnalati per il proprio lavoro in favore della comunità italiana del Nordamerica. Nato a Sanremo e naturalizzato cittadino canadese nel 1959, Alexander Roncari è oggi direttore della Commissione per i festeggiamenti colombiani nel suo Paese. Roncari è laureato in Scienze naturali e ha svolto anche attività nel campo dell'archeologia e dell'ambiente. Quest'anno Anne Paolucci ha inserito nel programma anche un premio speciale consegnato a Matilda Cuomo per il programma "Due case una tradizione".

Saggi scelti
New York. Preparato dal Cul (Council of National Literatures) in collaborazione con il "Columbus countdown 1992", è stato recentemente pubblicato "Columbus", un volume che comprende diversi saggi scritti a proposito della figura del Navigatore. Fra gli altri, questo volume comprende "Fact, fiction, and phylology: a reassessment of the Columbus story" di Anne Paolucci, "Christopher Columbus in Historical Perspective" di Franck J. Coppa, "The earliest literary response of Reinaissance Italy to the New World Encounter", di Theodore J. Cachey Junior. La copertina del libro è un ritratto di Colombo realizzato da Constance Del Vecchio, autrice di un'intera collezione dedicata al Navigatore.

Theater in video
New York. Anne Paolucci's play, "Cipango!", was recently made into a video of just under an hour, a fine vehicle for disseminating the story of Christopher Columbus, primarily among students. An earlier 20-minute videotape was shown at the Concord (NY) at the annual convention of foreign language teachers. The "Cipango!" videoplay—produced by Quadrant Productions—is not so much a documentary as a source of questions, extended research and disc on meant to prod university students into greater awareness.

"Columbus: Countdown 1992" Award
New York. Alexander Roncari and Matilda Raffa Cuomo were the recipients of the 1989 "Columbus: Countdown 1992" award. The ceremony, once again held at the "200 Club" in Manhattan, also honored other Italian-Americans who have left their mark on the Italian community. Born in Sanremo and a Canadian citizen since 1959, Alexander Roncari is currently the director of the Columbus ccommission of his country. Roncari has a degree in natural sciences and has worked also in archeology and environmental studies. This year, Anne Paolucci also presented a special award to Matilda Cuomo for her work as director of "Due case, una tradizione."

Selected essays.
New York. "Columbus," a volume made up of several articles dealing with the life of the Navigator, was recently issued under the auspices of Council on National Literatures with the cooperation of "Columbus: Countdown 1992." Among the essays are "Fact, Fiction, and Philology: A Reassessment of the Columbus Story" by Anne Paolucci, "Christopher Columbus in Historical Perspective" by Frank J. Coppa, "The Earliest Literary Response of Renaissance Italy to the New World Encounter" by Theodore J. Cachey, Jr. The book cover carries a original portrait of Columbus by Constance Del Vecchio Maltese, who is working on a collection of portraits focused on the Columbus story.

LEADER-OBSERVER

"Serving The Community Since 1909"

Vol. 15   April 12 - 18, 1990   Second Class Postage Paid at Jamaica, N.Y. (USPS 367660)   TWENTY CENTS

Legislators Preview Columbus: Countdown '92

Assemblyman Anthony Seminerio, President of the New York State Italian American Legislators' Association announced that the Association recently hosted "Columbus: Countdown 1992: A Preview", a program on the 500-year anniversary of Christopher Columbus' discovery of the new world.

Through the courtesy of the state Assembly, the program was held in the Assembly Parlor in Albany on March 20. It highlighted the historical background of Columbus' discovery and the various festivities and artistic endeavors that are being planned for the upcoming celebration.

Assisting in the presentation was State Senator Serphin R. Maltese, who is acting as the Legislative Liaison for "Columbus Countdown '92". Dr. Cav. Anne Paolucci, President of "Columbus: Countdown '92" organized and acted as Mistress of Ceremonies for the entire program.

Mrs. Paolucci, a professor at St. John's University, co-authored the book "Columbus: Selected Papers on Columbus and His Time" and has been very active in promoting the 500-year anniversary of the historic discovery of our country. Mrs. Paolucci spoke about the multi-ethnic legacy of Christopher Columbus and premiered an original play she wrote, "Cipango", which depicts the personal tragedy of Columbus as a man of vision and faith.

"Christopher Columbus played an important role in our country's rich heritage. It takes a special courage to challenge the unknown, despite the mockery of others," said Dr. Paolucci.

Dr. Claudia L. Bushman, former executive director of the Delaware Heritage Commission, gave a talk on the commemorative celebrations that took place in New York in 1792 and 1892. Frank C. Cacciutto, chairman of the English Department at East Meadow High School, gave a presentation on Columbus in History, Literature and Art.

The second part of the preview, introduced by art historian Dr. Paul J. Patane, focused on Columbus and the arts. Constance Del Vecchio Maltese, a noted portrait artist who has been commissioned to do twelve portraits of Columbus and his contemporaries, displayed three completed works of Columbus, Queen Isabella and Vasco de Gama. Selected songs from Encounter 500 by Mario Fratti were played by Guiseppe Murolo and sung by soprano Anya Reynatovich.

"Everyone involved in the commemoration of the upcoming 500-year anniversary should be very proud of their efforts and I am most pleased that we in the Italian American Legislators Association were a key part of this early effort to recognize the invaluable contributions of Christopher Columbus and his courageous contemporaries," said Assemblyman Seminerio.

Gli Italiani D'America

il Progresso
sabato 7 novembre 1987

"Tavola Rotonda" alla Fordham, nel Bronx

Cristoforo Colombo marinaio

"Cristoforo Colombo, marinaio" è stato il soggetto di una conferenza che si è svolta recentemente alla Fordham University, Bronx Campus, sotto gli auspici della "Tavola Rotonda Italo Americana".

Nella foto gli oratori; da sinistra: lo scienziato John A. Brown, il dr. Peter Sammartino, fondatore della Fairleigh Dickinson University; la prof.ssa Anne Paolucci, docente d'inglese alla St. John's University; il prof. Michael R. Cioffi, fondatore e presidente della American Italian Cultural & Literary Roundtable.

AMERICA **Oggi** · **SPECIALE**

lunedì 10 ottobre 1988 **13**

COLUMBUS DAY — Realizzazioni e piani futuri

"Countdown":-4

Nata nel 1984, l'associazione diretta da Anne Paolucci ha già al suo attivo una rispettabile serie di successi. Il problema dei fondi. Considerazioni politiche e culturali. Anche l'arte al servizio delle prossime celebrazioni internazionali

Nel 1984, prima che fosse annunciata una qualunque iniziativa a livello federale o statale tesa a celebrare il quinto centenario della scoperta dell'America, un gruppo di scrittori e di docenti universitari suggerì un "countdown" che, fino al 1992, sottolineasse con un crescendo di attività l'avvicinarsi della fatidica data. Tutto iniziò con un articolo di Anne & Henry Paolucci pubblicato nel 1984 (Il Progresso, 14 Ottobre 1984), "Colombo e l'idea dell'America", ripreso e ripubblicato poi per i tipi della Griffon House Publications in edizione bilingue.

Tale articolo costituì così il trampolino di lancio per la promozione e l'organizzazione di tutta una serie di attività culturali: "Columbus Countdown 1992" ebbe così inizio ufficialmente.

Il problema numero uno, allora come adesso, è la reperibilità di fondi e la messa in funzione della macchina delle sponsorizzazioni, una macchina che stenta ancora oggi ad entrare in carburazione. Se si considera poi che per organizzare un qualunque evento che si rispetti occorre una notevole preparazione e un periodo di tempo ragionevole. Si capisce così che lo stesso 1984 non era una data troppo lontana dalla scadenza del 1992; se poi a ciò si aggiunge il fatto che le sponsorizzazioni, a causa di ritardi causati principalmente da considerazioni politiche, hanno tardato (e ancora tardano) a muoversi, il quadro delle difficoltà è più completo.

Malgrado però tutte le difficoltà cui si è appena fatto riferimento, il "Columbus Countdown '92" ha organizzato la prima serata celebrativa nel 1985 con un premio speciale assegnato al dr. Peter Sammartino. Come prologo alla serata fu organizzato un convegno culturale multinazionale i cui interventi vennero pubblicati sul "Review of National Literatures" e distribuiti in oltre quaranta nazioni. Altri convegni, riguardanti soprattutto Colombo e le opere relative alla sua scoperta, furono organizzati a San Francisco, New York City (2) e Dallas. Anche di questi convegni gli atti furono riuniti e pubblicati dal "CNL/World Report", pubblicazione annuale della Griffon House Publications.

Una speciale sezione regionale venne aperta, sotto la direzione del dr. Moses M. Nagy, in Texas, dove sono state organizzati diversi convegni colombiani ed eventi di vario tipo sempre sotto l'egida del "Columbus Countdown '92".

Negli ultimi anni alcuni dei membri del "Columbus Countdown '92" hanno partecipato a notevoli e frequenti iniziative, non solo in campo accademico, tese a sottolineare l'unicità della nostra cultura e la necessità storica di celebrare degnamente il quinto centenario della scoperta colombiana.

Le opere di Colombo sono state ovviamente le prime a suscitare i primi interessi dell'organizzazione. Anche in questo settore, al solito, il problema principale è il reperimento di fondi. Malgrado le difficoltà, è stato possibile mettere in scena, già durante il primo dinner-award del 1985, due arie tratte dall'opera di Cristoforo Colombo, curate da Franchetti e Dario Milhaud.

Il "Cipango" di Anne Paolucci, pubblicato dalla Griffon House nel 1985, è stato più d'una volta rappresentato a New York City e a Washington D.C.; ne esiste anche una versione speciale per le scuole (la Duke University ne ha fatto richiesta) e in North Carolina sarà portato sulle scene da diverse compagnie teatrali.

Il "Columbus Countdown '92" si è anche proposto di diffondere le opere di pittori e scultori. Antonia Mastrocristina Sirena ha recentemente completato una serie di dodici dipinti raffiguranti la vicenda colombiana. "Anselmo" Francesconi, autore dello stesso logo simboleggiante il "Columbus Countdown '92", ha ultimato una statua raffigurante Colombo e un trittico, ispirato da "Cipango", raffigurante simbolicamente un viaggio verso il futuro. Nel campo artistico si sono mossi anche lo scultore Joseph Finelli (autore dei busti di Philip Mazzei e di Luigi Pirandello) e Marie Lise Gazarian.

Per le celebrazioni colombiane si stanno muovendo separatamente anche gruppi di privati ed università come, ad esempio, la St. John's University di Jamaica (Queens). Programmi speciali sono in preparazione presso la Columbia University di Manhattan e la University of California di Los Angeles. Lo scorso mese il "Columbus Countdown '92" ha inaugurato un "International Arts Award" per incoraggiare e diffondere l'arte e la letteratura.

Italian Tribune   COLUMBUS DAY   October 20, 2005 ♦ 25

Anne Paolucci Writes the Story of Christopher Columbus

The story of Christopher Columbus still raises questions and controversies. In *Cipango! (The Story)*, Anne Paolucci reviews the story of the famous navigator in bold strokes, offering the reader the highlights of a life characterized by a brief success and many disappointments in terse and compelling prose.

"It is a life worth exploring as the many books about him attest. New books continue to be written about him. For this author, the attraction of his life lies in its ironic reversals, the incredible ups and downs he experience, from the welcome given him in 1493 by King Ferdinand and Queen Isabella on his return from the first momentous journey – a welcome in which Columbus rode in public side by side with the King 9something unheard of) – to his humiliating return to Spain, in chains, after the third journey. By the time of his death, in 1506, he was forgotten, cast into a double oblivion," Paolucci writes in the Preface.

Each chapter is divided into two parts. In the first, the author gives us a straightforward historical and biographical account of some aspect of the life Columbus, who embodies the spirit of Renaissance discovery. In the second part, she provides us with an original literary narrative drawn, in most cases, from her award-winning play *Cipango!*

The first chapter begins with a quick survey of Columbus's early life, "Looking Back: Genoa?" and ends with "Looking Ahead:

Stranded in Jamaica." Chapter Two details "The Historic First Journey" and "Martin Pinzon," the man who played an important part in the events connected with the first journey. Chapter Three is an account of Columbus's triumphant return to Spain after that first journey in "Return to Spain" and "Fame and Glory" – the second segment is written in the form of a letter describing the excitement generated by that return from the unknown lands discovered and claimed for Spain.

Chapter Four describes the growing tensions and animosity Columbus had to face in "The Second Journey: Accusations and Charges" and "Private Audience with the Queen." Chapter Five includes "The Third Journey: Pearls, Gold and Indians," and "A Letter to the Queen." Chapter Six offers "New Charges: Columbus in Chains" and "Last Encounter with the Queen." Chapter Seven focuses on "The Fourth Journey: Shattered Dreams," and "The Columbus Legacy." This last segment includes a brief summary in the voice of Washington Irving, one of the most prolific writers on Columbus.

The Epilogue raises the question of why Italian Americans honor Columbus instead of Amerigo Vespucci, who did not 'discover' the new world but gave his name to it. The book also carries the reproductions from the interesting 13-part series, *Age of Discovery Navigators* by award-winning

artist Constance Del Vecchio Maltese including "Columbus in Chains" (on the cover), "The Young Columbus" and "Amerigo Vespucci." The first page of *Mundus Novus*, the Latin version of Vespucci's historic account of the landmass south of the equator, appears on the back cover.

This is an unusual and compelling biography for readers of all ages.

About the Author.

Anne Paolucci graduated from Barnard College and Columbia University, where she received the first Woodbridge Honorary Fellowship in the Department of English and Comparative Literature. She was a Fulbright scholar at the University of Rome and later a Fulbright Lecturer in American Drama at the University of Naples.

From 1986 to 1993 Paolucci headed "Columbus: Countdown 1992," a non-profit foundation which promoted new art and scholarship dealing with the life and times of Columbus. In 1991, she received the Gold Medal of the Canadian Quincentenary commission. That same year, her play *Cipango!* was recognized as an official project of the Christopher Columbus Quincentennial Jubilee Commission, set up by President Reagan.

Comitato delle celebrazioni di Cristoforo Colombo per il V
centenario della scoperta dell'America.

· Canadä   Canada's Committee of the Fifth Centennial Celebration
            of Christopher Columbus Discovery of America

            National Chairman

THE QUINCENTENNIAL GOLD MEDAL AWARD

The Christopher Columbus Quincentennial Commission of Canada joins in the spirit of the occasion
of the sixth Annual Awards Dinner "Columbus Countdown 1992" and in paying tribute to Dr. Anne
Paolucci.

She has earned richly deserved recognition for
her distinguished work in Historical Literature and
Theatrical Writing.

Therefore, the Commission Foundation of Canada
do hereby confer this Medal of the Christopher
Columbus 500 Anniversary upon

        Dr. Anne Paolucci

for her scholarly contribution to the Service of
Learning.

        (signature)

        The President

September 21, 1990

32 domenica 31 maggio 1992   **MAGAZINE**   AMERICA **Oggi**

> **Italian-Americans have, for the quincentenary, a greater obligation to fulfill than anyone else**

Columbus, One of Ours

(continued on back page)

By ANNE & HENRY
PAOLUCCI

Every people in the world has at one time or another laid claim to the discovery of America. In the United States we hear mostly of Scandinavian or Irish "precursors" of Columbus, but elsewhere "vigorously defended claims exist for the priority of the Chinese, Japanese, Polynesians, Phoenicians, Romans, Arabs, Turks, Hindoos, Basques, Welsh, . . . French, Polish, Germans, Dutch, and Portuguese. . . . So many are the claims . . . that the question is less 'Who discovered America?' than 'Who didn't?'"

Even when it is agreed that Christopher Columbus was the "effective" discoverer, there are rival claims about his ethnic identity. Was he Spanish or Portuguese, or a Spanish, Portuguese, or Italian Jew whose intention in 1492—so some supporters of the Jewish thesis have claimed—was to find a new-world haven for the Jews being expelled from Spain during that very year? The reason for this great variety of claims is obvious: who could possibly not have wanted to discover this "land of dreams, so various, so beautiful, so new"?

The year 1492, needless to say, is the first and most important of the great centenary dates in the history of the United States. And 1992, the quincentenary year, is a full flowering of celebrations and commemorations. Columbus's voyage had, historically, a long preparation, and there was never any scientific certainty about where it might have ended. When our astronauts traveled close to the moon at Christmas time in 1968, they were able to report back to earth not only all the technical observations that would later be necessary for their actual moon landing, but also confirmation of the make-up of the lunar surface previously observed only through the telescope.

We have Columbus's words on much of what he found on landing; and they are obviously very different from those our Apollo astronauts were moved to use in reporting back to us from the moon. Columbus noted, among other things, that in pressing his explorations he had "taken some Indians by force from the first island" on which he landed, "in order that they might learn our language and communicate what they knew respecting the country, which plan succeeded excellently, and was a great advantage to us, for in a short time, either by gestures and signs or words, we were enabled to understand each other." He mentions that, although initially taken by force, these *interpreters*, as we might say, were later very willing to travel with him voluntarily.

"And yet, though they have been with us a long time," Columbus adds, "the natives continue to entertain the idea that I have descended from heaven; and at our arrival in any new place, they publish this, crying out immediately with a loud voice to the others: 'Come, come and look upon beings of a celestial race'; upon which both women and men, children and adults, young men and

THE STAR-LEDGER, Friday, October 11, 1991

Italian-Americans speak out to restore Columbus' good name

Explorer Christopher Columbus, as seen in three portraits painted after his death. Italian-Americans say his accomplishments can be commemorated without demeaning American Indians or other groups

NEW YORK (AP)—Italian-Americans said yesterday they're sick of "Columbus-bashing" and believe the explorer's accomplishments can be commemorated without hurting American Indians or other groups.

"We see Columbus as the first immigrant who made possible the multi-ethnic society of this country," said Anne Paolucci, director of a doctorate program at St. John's University.

Paolucci was one of seven speakers at a news conference called by the Coalition of Italo-American Organizations.

William Fugazy, coalition president, declared that "a campaign" is under way by the media and some ethnic groups "to cast Columbus as one of the most immoral villains in history." Paolucci also accused the Smithsonian Institution of "studiously avoiding Columbus."

Earlier yesterday, the National Council for the Social Studies said schools should emphasize that Columbus' contribution was that he brought into contact, for good and bad, two rich and thriving civilizations.

It said schoolchildren should be taught that his voyages were the beginning of the near-extinction, through battle and disease, of millions of American Indians.

And it stressed that it was inaccurate to say Columbus, the Vikings or anybody else "discovered" America or the already populated "new world."

Columbus, according to the October issue of American Heritage magazine, actually referred to his destinations as the "other world." Mapmaker Amerigo Vespucci, for whom America is named, coined the phrase "new world."

The Italian-American group asked that Columbus' actions be examined in the context of his own era's standards.

Former Lt. Gov. Alfred DelBello said Columbus got the idea to sail west in his 20s, and lived his dream to age 52. He said that kind of commitment is worthy of celebration.

"Everyone is entitled to interpret history as he or she wishes. . . . God knows, he probably wasn't perfect," said Fugazy, adding that Columbus nonetheless deserves his due because "he did discover this country."

A statement by Tona Gonnella Frichner, attorney for the American Indian Alliance, was read at the news conference.

It said, "The traditional circle of Indian elders declared 1992 the year of the indigenous people and gave us our directive: 'Address the issue of the quincentenary around the world, and in a way that also speaks to the environment.'

"They did not want us to state the obvious: That Columbus' arrival was devastating for indigenous peoples," it said. ". . . . Through this broad notion of respect, harmony and balance, we believe we can make it better for all. So we look to 1992 as a new beginning."

Fugazy said: "It is more important that at this point in time, we look to the future, and that all groups explore their common goals."

American Heritage described Columbus as a great sailor who was high-minded but capable of ruthlessness and cruelty, socially adept, intensely religious, courageous, single-minded and zealous.

He made four trans-Atlantic voyages: In 1492, 1493, 1498 and 1502.

Il Ponte

Italo-Americano

July–August 1992

Italian-Americans speak out to restore Columbus' good name

Italian-Americans said they're sick of - *Columbus-bashing* and believe the explorer's accomplishments can be commemorated without hurting American Indians or other groups.

"We see Columbus as the first immigrant who made possible the multi-ethnic society of this country," said Anne Paolucci, director of a doctorate program at St. John's University. Paolucci was one of seven speakers at a news conference called by the Coalition of Italo-American Organizations.

William Fugazy, coalition president, declared that *a campaign is under way* by the media and some ethnic groups *"to cast Columbus as one of the most immoral villains in history."* Paolucci also accused the Smithsonian Institution of *"studiously avoiding Columbus."*

Recently, the National Council for the Social Studies said schools should emphasize that Columbus' contribution was that he brought into contact, for good and bad, two rich and thriving civilizations.

It said schoolchildren should be taught that his voyages were the beginning of the near-extinction, through battle and disease, of millions of American Indians.

And it stressed that it was inaccurate to say Columbus, the Vikings or anybody else *discovered* America or the already populated *new world.*

The Italian-American group asked that Columbus' actions be examined in the context of his own era's standards.

Former Lt. Gov. Alfred DelBello said Columbus got the idea to sail west in his 20s, and

lived his dream to the age of 52. He said that kind of commitment is worthy of celebration.

"Everyone is entitled to interpret history as he or she wishes.... God knows, he probably wasn't perfect," said Fugazy, adding that Columbus nonetheless deserves his due because *"he did discover this country."*

A statement by Tona Gonnella Frichner, attorney for the American Indian Alliance, was read at the news conference.

It said, "The tradi·· al circle of Indian elders declared 19·· .he year of the indigenous people and ga·· us our directive: 'Address the issue of the quincentenary around the world, and in a way that also speaks to the

environment.' They did not want us to state the obvious: That Columbus' arrival was devastating for indigenous peoples," it said.

"...Through this broad notion of respect, harmony and balance, we believe we can make it better for all. So we look to 1992 as a new beginning."

Fugazy said: *"It is more important that at this point in time, we look to the future, and that all groups explore their common goals."*

American Heritage described Columbus as a great sailor who was high-minded but capable of ruthlessness and cruelty, socially adept, intensely religious, courageous, single-minded and zealous.

He made four trans-Atlantic voyages: In 1492, 1493, 1498 and 1502.

On the first, he went to the Bahamas, Cuba and the island he named Hispaniola, leaving behind 39 settlers. The groundwork laid during his second voyage resulted in three colonies.

One named Santo Domingo after his father, is now capital of the Dominican Republic. On his third journey, Columbus stopped in Venezuela, becoming the first European on record to set foot on a continent of the Western Hemisphere, American Heritage said.

The magazine said during that same trip, Columbus sent to Spain about 500 captured island residents, whom he once had described as a loving people. The 300 who survived the passage were auctioned in Spain, it said. He was arrested on Hispaniola for mismanagement of colonial affairs and was returned, in chains, to Spain in October 1500. He later was vindicated by a court and made his final voyage.

Area Metropolitana

il Progresso
venerdì 30 ottobre 1987

COLUMBUS: COUNTDOWN 1992

Vartan Gregorian e Anne Paolucci al Countdown '92

Quest'anno, durante il terzo "Annual Awards-Dinner" del "Columbus: Countdown 1992", che si terrà questa sera al "200 Club" di Manhattan, saranno premiati alcuni personaggi prominenti che hanno avuto notevole impatto nel mondo della cultura. Il "Columbus: Countdown 1992" è presieduto dalla professoressa Anne Paolucci, docente presso la St. John University.

Il terzo premio annuale sarà assegnato quest'anno a Vartan Gregorian, presidente della "New York Public Library". A consegnare il premio del "Columbus" sarà Denver Frederick, presidente del "Christopher Columbus Quincentenary Foundation". Saranno presenti inoltre il presidente della Pace University, Edward Mortola e padre Joseph Cogo, segretario nazionale dell'Acim. Gregorian è presidente della New York Public Library dal 1981. Sotto la sua direzione la biblioteca pubblica ha ricevuto una spinta organizzativa e culturale non indifferente. "Il dottor Gregorian - ha sottolineato la professoressa Paolucci - viene premiato perché con il suo contributo culturale ha voluto abbracciare un ampio orizzonte etnico".

Denver Frederick, presidente del "C.C.Q.F.", già noto per aver contribuito alle celebrazioni della Statua della Libertà del 1986, è l'"uomo-chiave" delle celebrazioni colombiane per il Quinto Centenario della scoperta dell'America. La dottoressa Anne Paolucci durante la serata parlerà dei programmi futuri del "Columbus: Countdown 1992" e anche degli sviluppi collaborativi tra le sedi "CC 1992" di New York e quella di Dallas.

R.C. Nella foto Anne Paolucci

VARTAN GREGORIAN AND ANNE PAOLUCCI AT COUNTDOWN 1992

During this year's third "Annual Awards-Dinner of "Columbus: Countdown 1992," to be held this evening at the "200 Club" in Manhattan, several important individuals who have had a large impact on the cultural world will be honored. "Columbus Countdown 1992" is headed by Dr. Anne Paolucci, Chairperson of the English Department at St. John's University.

The third annual award will be presented this year to Vartan Gregorian, president of the New York Public Library. The "Columbus" award will be presented by Denver Frederick president of the "Christopher Columbus Quincentenary Foundation." Also present on the dais will be Dr. Edward J. Mortola, Chancellor and former President of Pace University, and Father Joseph Cogo, National Secretary of ACIM. Gregorian has served as President of the New York Public Library since 1981. Under his direction, the public library has enjoyed a noteworthy organizational and cultural thrust. "Dr. Gregorian," emphasized Dr. Paolucci, "is being honored for his ardent support of cultural excellence in the broadest multi-ethnic sense."

Denver Frederick, president of "C.C.Q.F.," already known for his contribution to the Statue of Liberty celebrations of 1986, is a key figure in the Columbus celebrations of the Fifth Centenary of the discovery of America. Dr. Anne Paolucci will review, during the evening, future projects of "Columbus: Countdown 1992" including the joint activities of the main organization in New York and its Dallas affiliate.

In the photograph: Anne Paolucci

Perché tanto odio contro Colombo?

Egregio direttore,

il patetico tentativo messo in atto in Minnesota per denigrare Colombo e processarlo per i suoi inesistenti crimini contro l'umanità è davvero una cosa triste. Alcuni mesi fa, durante un'intervista che la Canadian Radio fece a me e a Kirkpatrick Sale, dissi allo "studioso" che le sue tesi non erano né attendibili né credibili, dal momento che egli accusava il Genovese di delitti che allora neppure si conoscevano (ad esempio la schiavitù, che venne dopo la scoperta dell'America; o quello di carattere "ambientale" concepito dalla sensibilità moderna di questi ultimi tempi). Se tutte queste affermazioni non avessero nuociuto alle celebrazioni del quinto centenario, ci sarebbe stato solo da ridere.

I discendenti dei vichinghi residenti in Minnesota, che si sono alleati con le popolazioni "indie" e con i loro amici per denigrare l'importanza di Colombo e della sua scoperta, dovrebbero ricordarsi del loro antenato Enrico il Rosso che approdò due volte sulle coste del Newfoundland (prima di qualsiasi altro europeo di cui si abbia notizia) per crearvi delle vere e proprie aree da caccia. Dopo questi due tentativi se ne tornò nelle sue terre d'origine ed il discorso finì lì. La differenza con i viaggi colombiani fu che Colombo venne qui per starci: l'impresa di cui era a capo non aveva limiti di tempo, e in quest'opera tutta la civiltà europea era stata coinvolta. Colombo, in parole semplici, scoprì un continente sconosciuto per l'Europa e cambiò il corso della storia.

Kirkpatrick Sale dice che ciò fu un male. Perché? Siamo certi davvero che questo continente appartenesse ai cosiddetti indiani? E, se sì, a quale delle loro tribù? Per quanto se ne sappia, gli Aztechi uccisero migliaia e migliaia di "indiani". I Caraibi fecero opera di sterminio delle popolazioni indigene nell'area che poi da essi prese nome. E gli "natives" non erano affatto quei "nobili selvaggi" che Rousseau vorrebbe far credere.

Perché quindi avercela così tanto contro Colombo? Perché queste popolazioni indigene continuano a proclamare i loro diritti contro la storia e tutti quelli che come noi sono venuti qui dal nulla e hanno poi raggiunto comfort e successo di cui andar fieri? Dovremmo tutti rinunciare a 500 anni di storia per far loro piacere? C'è in tutto il mondo un'altra nazione in cui vengano fatti discorsi così assurdi? La storia del mondo è sempre stata storia di conquista, economica e culturale. Gli stessi normanni, ad esempio, conquistarono gli anglosassoni, si fusero poi con loro e formarono l'attuale Inghilterra.

Non si può correre il rischio di permettere a quest'isteria anti-occidentale di avere il sopravvento e di offuscare le celebrazioni colombiane. Queste appartengono di diritto all'Europa, a Colombo e al mondo intero! E, più che a chiunque altro, esse sono la celebrazione innanzitutto dell'America, dove una società multirazziale continua a crescere, a prosperare e a trovare sempre più nuove vie di collaborazione e di comunicazione!

Anne Paolucci
"Columbus:
Countdown 1992"
Beechhurst (New York)

Preghiamo i lettori di essere più sintetici nelle lettere che ci inviano e, nell'impossibilità di poter usare una macchina da scrivere, di cercare il più possibile di essere chiari nella grafia. Le lettere debbono essere accompagnate da nome, cognome, indirizzo e numero di telefono. La Direzione si riserva il diritto di sintetizzare le lettere quando necessario. Le lettere pubblicate rispecchiano le opinioni dei lettori stessi e non riflettono necessariamente le linee di "America Oggi".

MAGAZINE/LETTERE — AMERICA Oggi

16 domenica 26 febbraio 1995

Chi non vuole il Columbus Day?

Caro direttore,

mai come adesso è necessario fare pressione sui nostri rappresentanti politici e sui responsabili del settore scolastico d'ogni ordine e grado, perché ai nostri figli siano date correttamente tutte le informazioni storiche su Cristoforo Colombo di cui essi, che rappresentano assai semplicemente il nostro stesso futuro, hanno bisogno.

Colombo, si sa, è l'espressione maggiore dell'epoca delle scoperte geografiche in generale e del nostro Rinascimento in particolare. E' stato sotto molti punti di vista, non dimentichiamolo, il primo emigrante su queste terre ove tutti noi oggi viviamo, e il fondatore di quella società multi-etnica di cui si fa un gran parlare. Ogni attentato contro la sua figura e contro l'importanza delle sue realizzazioni umane e scientifiche è un attentato contro ogni nazionalità, ogni cultura, ogni razza. Chi attacca Colombo attacca, in parole povere, gli stessi Stati Uniti.

Da eroe
a delinquente:
perché?

22 domenica 11 ottobre 1992 · MAGAZINE AMERICA Oggi

*Colombo '92 - Alla SUNY di Stony Brook
un simposio sulla figura e l'opera del Genovese*

DI MARIO MIGNONE

Gli storici oggi non si chiedono più chi sia arrivato per primo al di qua dell'Atlantico. Non conta infatti se ad approdare su questo continente siano stati gli africani, i fenici, gli ebrei. Ciò che conta invece è chiedersi: che differenza hanno prodotto? Il viaggio di Colombo fece la differenza, procurando con la sua scoperta degli enormi sconvolgimenti storici, sia nel continente di partenza che in quello d'arrivo. Ciò che oggi conta considerare è cioè l'impatto che il viaggio di cinque secoli fa ebbe sul mondo intero.

Nel numero di ottobre di quest'anno, "Discovery" pubblica un articolo di Jared Diamond, "The Arrow of Desease", sulla facilità della conquista di queste terre ad opera di Colombo e di quanti proseguirono la sua opera. Tra l'altro vi si afferma che l'arma peggiore di Colombo e dei suoi successori era quella rappresentata dai germi di cui s'eran fatti portatori. "Con la conquista delle Americhe iniziata con il viaggio del 1492, numerose come gli indiani massacrati dai conquistadores spagnoli furono le vittime dei microbi esportati dagli stessi spagnoli di qua dell'Atlantico. I microbi sterminarono il 95% della popolazione pre-colombiana". L'articolo termina con questa affermazione: "Non c'è alcun dubbio che Colombo fosse un grande visionario, un marinaio e un leader. Non c'è ugualmente alcun dubbio che lui ei suoi successori si comportarono come assassini... Senza i germi venuti dall'Europa la stessa conquista del cosiddetto Nuovo Mondo sarebbe stata impossibile".

Bisogna ricordare anche la risoluzione approvata dal Governing Board of the National Council of Churches (NCC) nel maggio del 1990: "Non si dovrebbe celebrare questo anniversario, per rispetto dei discendenti di quanti sono stati vittime di genocidio, schiavitù e di irreparabili attentati ecologici".

Un ritratto quindi completamente diverso da quello presentato dalle celebrazioni centenarie del secolo scorso. Fino a non molti anni fa la ricorrenza del 12 ottobre aveva un carattere festivo, un evento che in tutti i libri di storia del mondo segnava l'inizio dell'era moderna, dell'ordine nuovo del mondo economico, culturale e politico. Colombo, sotto questa luce, era l'uomo moderno per eccellenza.

Per secoli, Colombo e la sua impresa hanno simbolizzato il culmine di un periodo unico nella storia dell'umanità, quello del Rinascimento e dell'Umanesimo. Generazioni sono cresciute pensando al carattere di eccellenza di Colombo e della sua epoca. Colombo era considerato il simbolo universale dell'uomo, della sua dignità e della sua indipendenza. Gli europei tutti hanno sempre concordato con ciò, e tutti gli italo-americani hanno sempre coltivato con orgoglio questo retaggio tanto da

ottenerne il riconoscimento ufficiale dal Congresso americano con l'istituzione del Columbus Day.

Tutto ciò oggi è sotto accusa. E ciò è un problema di verità, intellettuale e politica al tempo stesso. Tutto l'Occidente e tutti i suoi valori sono sul banco degli accusati. Nessun ricercatore è mai libero completamente da pregiudizi politici e culturali. Ma lo studioso serio ed onesto sa resistere alle loro lusinghe. La verità non è mai infatti quella di chi grida più forte.

In un'epoca come la nostra in cui s'irridono gli eroi, il pendolo della riconsiderazione dell'opera colombiana ha raggiunto il suo polo negativo. Ci viene presentato non il simbolo dell'era moderna ma un delinquente come ce ne sono stati pochi nella storia, uno che ha distrutto il paradiso in terra, incontaminato fino al giorno del suo arrivo. Un'altra delle accuse più gravi è quella relativa alla schiavitù che fu introdotta qui dai successori di Colombo. Bisogna ammettere che la schiavitù, in quei tempi, era pratica di tutto il mondo conosciuto, un'istituzione universale. Sappiamo anche però di altre civiltà, come quelle degli Incas, degli Aztechi e degli imperatori cinesi, che praticavano si può dire da sempre lo sterminio e la sottomissione delle popolazioni conquistate. L'esperienza coloniale è stata un disastro per le genti indigene. Tuttavia, laddove ci sono state crudeltà ed atrocità, gli storici ne sono venuti a conoscenza tramite la passione per la giustizia che muoveva gli spagnoli del XVI secolo. Molto è stato poi detto sulla cristianizzazione degli indigeni, ma non c'è stata certo apocalisse o risposta monolitica alla spiritualità delle popolazioni indigene.

La storia, del resto, non è interpretata e compresa allo stesso modo da tutti. In questo contesto, per portare un po' di chiarezza nella confusione interpretativa, il simposio "Columbus: Meeting of Cultures", che si terrà il 16 ed il 17 ottobre presso la State University of New York a Stony Brook, offre l'occasione per un dibattito storico sulle realtà del XV-XVI secolo per meglio comprendere Colombo e la sua impresa. Il giudizio etico poi è cosa che non sempre rientra in un discorso storico.

Se vogliamo condannare Colombo ed i suoi successori per aver distrutto la cultura e l'habitat delle popolazioni indigene, bisogna anche sforzarsi di comprendere la mentalità dell'epoca in cui quei fatti si sono verificati. Colombo ed i suoi successori meritano di essere giudicati secondo il metro della loro cultura e delle loro concezioni sociali. In questa misura il simposio della SUNY a Stony Brook servirà a definire in tutti gli aspetti - umani, storici, sociologici, antropologici, medici ed artistici - un equilibrato quadro in cui far rientrare Colombo ed i suoi tempi. Il simposio è aperto al pubblico ed è gratuito. (Per informazioni, 516\632-7444, oppure 516\632-7448).

SUNDAY SUPPLEMENT
OCTOBER 14, 1984

IL PROGRESSO
SECTION B

DUE MONDI

[TWO WORLDS]

COUNTDOWN 1992

COLUMBUS AND THE IDEA OF AMERICA:
COUNTDOWN TO 1992

ANNE PAOLUCCI

HENRY PAOLUCCI

Every people in the world has at one time or another laid claim to the discovery of America. In the United States we hear mostly of Scandinavian or Irish "precursors" of Columbus, but elsewhere, as an eminent scholar has put it, "vigorously defended claims exist for the priority of the Chinese, Japanese, Polynesians, Phoenicians, Romans, Arabs, Turks, Hindoos, Basques, Welsh, . . . French, Polish, Germans, Dutch, and Portuguese . . . . So many are the claims . . . that the question is less 'Who discovered America?' than 'Who didn't?' "

Even when it is agreed that Christopher Columbus was the "effective" discoverer, there are rival claims about his ethnic identity. Was he Spanish or Portuguese, or a Spanish, Portuguese, or Italian Jew whose intention in 1492—so some supporters of the Jewish thesis have claimed—was to find a new-world haven for the Jews being expelled from Spain during that very year?

The reason for this great variety of claims is obvious. Long before America was discovered, peoples had *wanted* such a land, had longed for a distant "brave new world" —as Shakespeare would later refer to it in his *Tempest*—which would lie before them like a "land of dreams, so various, so beautiful, so new," free from the enormous weight of all the heavy ages piled on the old worlds of Europe and Asia. Among the ancient Greeks, scientists and philosophers had speculated about the possibility of there being unknown lands rising in other parts of the earth's vast oceans. And, as any book that deals even superficially with the discovery of America is apt to remind us, it was the Roman playwright Lucius Annaes Seneca—a native of Spain, d. 65 A.D.—who included in his tragedy of *Medea* the prophetic lines: *An age will come, after many years,/When the Ocean will loose the chains of things,/And a huge land lie revealed;/When Tiphys will disclose new worlds,/And Thule no more be ultimate on earth.* Tiphys was the pilot or helmsman of the legendary Argonauts of the ancient Greeks. He was credited with having sailed farthest north in the Atlantic—as far as Thule, which was probably what we know as Iceland. There is a copy of Seneca's tragedies in the Columbian Library at Valladolid, Spain; and in the margin, next to the prophetic lines quoted (378-382), we find the following (written in Latin) in the hand of Columbus's son, Ferdinand: "This prophecy was fulfilled by my father, Christopher Columbus, the admiral, in 1492."

1 *America's Great Centenary Dates*

The year 1492, needless to say, is the first of the great centenary dates in the history of the United States. Just a few years ago, in 1976, we celebrated the 200th anniversary of our Declaration of Independence, and we will be celebrating—in 1987—the 200th birthday of our Federal Constitution. But, if we want a more precise calendar of great dates to commemorate, we need to remind ourselves that, as President Abraham Lincoln observed in his Inaugural Address of 1861, "the Union of the American people is much older than its Constitution. It was formed, in fact, by the Articles of Association in 1774. It was matured and continued by the Declaration of Independence in 1776. It was further matured and the faith of the then thirteen States expressly plighted and engaged that it should be perpetual by the Articles of Confederation in 1778. And, finally, in 1787 one of the declared objects of ordaining and establishing the

EXCERPT FROM A.P. PRESENTATION AT NEW YORK UNIVERSITY CONFERNECE SPONSORED BY THE NEW YORK CITY QUINCENTENNIAL COMMISSION, HEADED BY NYC MAYOR DINKINS (SUNDAY MAGAZINE, *OGGI*. JULY 12, 1992).

"FIVE CENTURIES: MANY PEOPLES, MANY PASTS"

DR. ANNE PAOLUCCI

(Presentation made on July 6, 1992, at a Symposium sponsored by the New York City Columbus Quincentennial Commission and the Humanities Council of NYU)

This quincentenary of the **encounter of two worlds**—one of the great **dramatic reversals of history**—is indeed a most fitting occasion for assessing the **cultural impact** of Columbus's historic voyage on both the original inhabitants of this hemisphere as well as those who came to North America during the next five centuries.

The vectors which put into motion the great age of exploration and discovery were many and often conflicting ones. Spain was desperately seeking an easier route to the wealth of the spice trade of the east. Like the other European nations, it was also very much in need of colonial expansion. Having finally won a long and expensive war against the Moors, Spain was ready to flex its muscles, as England did a short while later with the defeat of the Spanish Armada. In the time of Columbus, Spain was ready to assert its national solidarity through economic expansion, colonies, and homogenous development of its people, not only in Spain itself but also in a global crusade to bring Christianity to the rest of the world. In its effort to define its national identity, Spain expelled those Jews who would not convert to Christianity and the initial effort to find a shorter route to India grew into a global crusade. The past is a complex picture of personal and national intentions against a changing historical scenario, the full implications of which have yet to be fully assessed.

That past also includes the history of the indigenous peoples of the islands and American continents. It took some 400 years to complete a scientific definition of the geography of the Americas from the Baring Sea in the North to Terra del Fuego in the South; and we are still now trying to complete the task of defining with scientific accuracy the ethnic identities and cultural diversities of the major native inhabitants of this part of the world, North, South, and Central.

And even though we know a great deal about Columbus and the nations of Europe that made his voyage possible, our studies go back little more than 150 years, when the original sources in Spain, Portugal, Genoa, and the Spanish colonies in America, etc. were first carefully gathered, collated, studied, and critically published. Harvard University took the lead in the 1880s, followed by the Italian government, with its famous critical collection (*Raccolta*) of those mostly Spanish sources that appeared in the 1890s.

The critical task continues, but the really important work is the one we focus on today: the impact of the Columbus voyage not only on the native populations and their descendants but also on the immigrants who have joined them, wave after wave, first from the great transoceanic maritime powers—the English, French, and Dutch, as well as the pioneering Portuguese and Spanish—but then also from the rest of Europe and Asia, as well as the African continent, from which so many blacks were brought here.

The great vision of Spain and Columbus failed, as we know, as did all the other aspirations to global rule and a united world under one set of laws and one religious belief. The new world opened by Columbus had a very different destiny. It proved in fact to be a haven for immigrants from all parts of Europe and the world, men and women who did not want to be homogenized in their lands of origins much less in a world where universal homogenization—political, religious, and cultural—was the only prescribed way of life. Such are the ironies of history.

Let me summarize, in conclusion, on our own **national American** contribution to the **many pasts** of the Columbus story. The Harvard initiative to bring critical materials together in a large way is reflected in our time in the work of Samuel Eliot Morison, the most famous of our Columbus scholars. In 1971, when he was over 80 and completing his greatest work, *The European Discovery of America*, Morison honored his

NEW YORK CITY COLUMBUS QUINCENTENNIAL COMMISSION

JULY 6

7:00 p.m.

Symposium - Five Centuries: Many Peoples, Many Pasts In cooperation with New York University and the Humanities Council

Moderator: Dr. Leslie Agard-Jones
Director: The Humanities Council, NYU: Leslie Berlowitz
Keynote Speaker: Mayor David Dinkins
Featured Speaker: Dr. Anne Paolucci

MAGAZINE AMERICA Oggi 22 domenica 12 luglio 1992

domenica 12 luglio 1992 23

gli ottant'anni e stava completando la sua opera maggiore, "The European Discovery of America", Morison rese omaggio al suo mentore, il grande bibliotecario di Harvard, Justin Winsor, vissuto il secolo scorso. Morison fece riferimento agli otto volumi della "Narrative and Critical History of America" (1884-1889) come ad un qualcosa di cui non si poteva fare a meno e ai quali Morison voleva solo aggiungere dell'altro, come supplemento. I primi cinque volumi di Winsor contengono infatti l'analisi critico-biografica più accurata di tutta l'età della scoperta del Nuovo Mondo. Nessuno in questo secolo, ha fatto notare Morison, "ha seguito Winsor nel tentativo di coprire tutto il campo" e il risultato, da questo punto di vista, è stato un serio scadimento della ricerca colombiana.

E' nello spirito di Justin Winsor, storico colombiano per eccellenza, che oggi dobbiamo esaminare il passato nel celebrare il quinto centenario della venuta dell'Europa nel Nuovo Mondo. La storia della conquista è parte di questo passato, come lo è pure la storia degli adattamenti avvenuti negli ultimi 500 anni, adattamenti che hanno permesso a moltissimi di vivere insieme in una realtà multiculturale non facile e ancora in ebollizione, lungi ancora oggi dall'essere compresa e studiata fin nel profondo.

Non c'è alcun altro Paese al mondo come il nostro, dove così diverse nazionalità convivono, ciascuna con le sue specifiche caratteristiche e con i suoi particolari valori, ciascuna tendente alla conservazione della propria identità familiare e, al tempo stesso, in collegamento con una non-familiare famiglia più grande. Certamente non c'è nessun'altra città come New York, con l'ondeggiare della sua popolazione, con il suo profilo demografico sempre mutante, capace sempre di fare spazio per i nuovi arrivati che, come gli antichi, vengono qui a cercare nuovi orizzonti.

L'incontro fra le razze più diverse e il processo continuo che New York e gli Usa sperimentano giorno dopo giorno non ha davvero eguali. Colombo non sarebbe mai stato capace però di vedere così lontano. Noi siamo i suoi eredi, i suoi discendenti, malgrado le differenze e le intenzioni di ciascuno di noi e della particolare etnia cui apparteniamo. Considerare solo qualche aspetto di quella scoperta fatta cinque secoli fa è perdere di vista tutto il senso della storia e della realtà che oggi viviamo, che è il ritorno alle nostre radici di nazione costruita sulle ambizioni, sui desideri, sulle speranze e spesso sui contraddittori impulsi di chi ha contribuito a costruirla.

Le contraddizioni della storia, volte assai ironiche, sono anche la base per una continua oscillazione di forze paradossali tendenti alla ricerca dell'identità. Non possiamo, per nessuna ragione, prendere un solo elemento della storia e giudicarlo in assoluto, isolandolo da tutti gli altri. Dagli impulsi molteplici e a volte assai diversi che hanno dato sin qui vita alla nostra storia, dobbiamo riconoscere la formazione di una nuova coscienza nazionale, la ricerca di un'identità che è sempre dolorosa oscillazione tra il desiderio della fuga e quello del ritorno: fuga dai limiti di ciò che eravamo in una potenziale più larga arena e ritorno poi alle nostre radici in un significato più profondo e più comprensivo.

(Dalla relazione presentata lunedì scorso, 6 luglio, al simposio "Five Centuries: Many Peoples, Many Pasts" tenutosi presso la New York University e organizzato dalla New York City Columbus Quincentennial Commission - Anne Paolucci dirige il "Columbus Countdown 1992").

Nella foto - Cristoforo Colombo davanti al Consiglio di Salamanca (Nicolò Barabino, XIX secolo, Palazzo Orsini, Genova). E' il 1486. I sovrani di Spagna hanno riunito la giunta incaricata di esaminare il progetto del navigatore genovese di "buscar el levante por el ponente).

ITALIAN TRANSLATION AS IT APPEARED IN
OGGI (JULY 12, 1882(,

Molti popoli, tanti passati

DI Anne Paolucci

Questo quinto centenario di incontri fra due mondi - una delle più drammatiche contraddizioni della storia - è in fondo la più adatta occasione per "controllare" l'impatto culturale dello storico viaggio di Colombo sia sugli indigeni di questa parte dell'Atlantico sia su coloro che in questi cinque secoli sono venuti a vivere qui in America.

Le vie attraverso cui si è incanalata la grande età dell'esplorazione e della scoperta sono state molteplici e, molto spesso, in conflitto tra di loro. La Spagna era disperatamente alla ricerca di una rotta più facile per il commercio delle spezie con l'Est. Come molte altre nazioni europee, essa era altresì avida di espansione coloniale. Dopo aver vinto finalmente la lunga e costosa guerra contro i Mori, era ormai pronta a "flettere" nuovamente i suoi muscoli, come la stessa Inghilterra fece più tardi nella storia quando sconfisse la grande Armada. Al tempo di Colombo, la Spagna era pronta ad affermare la sua solidità nazionale attraverso l'espansione economica, le colonie e lo sviluppo omogeneo delle sue genti, non solo in territorio iberico ma in una crociata mondiale per portare il Cristianesimo nel resto del mondo conosciuto. Nel suo sforzo di delineare la sua identità nazionale e religiosa, la Spagna espulse quegli ebrei che non volevano convertirsi al Cristianesimo e cominciò a muoversi in direzione di quelle rotte più comode verso le Indie. Il passato, in questo senso, ci appare come un quadro complicato di intenzioni nazionali e personali, sullo sfondo di uno scenario storico che ancora oggi aspetta di essere delineato in tutti i suoi particolari.

In questa visione del passato ci sono, e a diritto, le popolazioni indigene delle isole del continente americano. Ci son voluti circa quattro secoli per esplorare e definire geograficamente questo continente che va dal mare di Bering al Nord alla Tierra de Fuego a Sud; e ancora oggi si fa fatica a definire con scientifica accuratezza le identità etniche e le diversità culturali delle maggiori popolazioni indigene di questa parte del mondo.

Ed anche se conosciamo abbastanza Colombo e le nazioni europee che hanno permesso il suo viaggio, i nostri studi vanno indietro per circa un secolo e mezzo, quando i primi documenti vennero trovati e studiati in Spagna, Portogallo, Genova. e nelle colonie spagnole d'America. Cominciò nel 1880 l'Harvard University, seguita poi dall'Italia, con la sua collezione critica della "Raccolta" contenente per lo più fonti spagnole venute alla luce alla fine del secolo XIX.

Lo sforzo critico continua ancora, ma il lavoro più importante è quello che stiamo facendo proprio nei nostri tempi: l'impatto del viaggio di Colombo non soltanto sugli indigeni e sui loro discendenti ma anche sugli emigranti che li hanno raggiunti al di qua dell'Atlantico, anno dopo anno, ondata dopo ondata, prima dai Paesi potenti sul mare (Inghilterra, Francia, Olanda, Spagna e Portogallo) e poi dal resto dell'Europa, dall'Asia e dall'Africa, da cui sono venute qui le popolazioni negre.

La grande visione della Spagna e di Colombo è fallita, come sappiamo, come tutte le aspirazioni ad un ordine unico mondiale sotto le stesse leggi e le stesse credenze religiose. Il Nuovo Mondo di Colombo ha avuto un destino molto diverso. Si è dimostrato infatti un paradiso per gli emigranti da ogni parte d'Europa e del mondo; per tutti, uomini e donne, che non hanno voluto restare nella loro terra d'origine, per ragioni politiche, religiose e culturali, il Nuovo Mondo di Colombo rappresentava l'unica possibilità di vivere una vita diversa. Questa è l'ironia della storia.

Riassumiamo, per concludere, i nostri contributi nazionali, come americani, ai "molti passati" di Colombo e della sua storia. L'iniziativa della Harvard University di riunire il più possibile il materiale critico trovato si riflette nell'opera di Samuel Eliot Morison, il più famoso studioso di Colombo. Nel 1971, quando aveva già passato

Language Association **Bulletin**

New York State Association of Foreign Language Teachers

| VOL. XLIV | January 1993 | No. 3 |

Book Review

Arnold B. Levine

COLUMBUS, AMERICA AND THE WORLD
Special editors: Anne Paolucci/Henry Paolucci
Published for the Council on National Literatures
N.Y.:Griffon House Publications, 1992, 240 pp.
Price: $23.00

Provocative and contemporary, this literary anthology is truly a *bouquet* of cross-cultural perspectives, scholarly criticism, history and literature. Each of the ten chapters attest to an intense concern with relevant aspects of Christopher Columbus, the man, his times and the 500th Anniversary of the discovery of the Americas. Written by august contributors, each chapter represents a distinct contribution toward the goal of better understanding the impact and many facets of Columbus' voyages. The sheer variety of approaches is so unique as to be stimulating and illuminating to both the novice and the expert. The spectrum of these works include a paper read at a symposium, essays, review articles and transcribed classroom lectures. Much vibrancy is given this collection, avoiding tedium and repetition, which otherwise might flaw a text revolving about a central historic theme. The volume, the first of five projected, is so beautifully diverse that the chapter titles bear mentioning here:

"Introduction: 1992" by Anne Paolucci

"Columbus and the Idea of America" by Anne Paolucci/Henry Paolucci

"Paul Claudel's Christopher Columbus and the Japanese Noh Plays" by John K. Gillespie

"The Myth of Discovery: Edmundo O'Gorman's Perspective" by O. Carlos Stoetzer

"Christopher Columbus and Italy" by Frank J. Coppa

"A Doer, A Dreamer, A Man of Vision" by Marie-Lise Gazarian Gautier

"Dante's Ulysses and Columbus" by Dino Bigongiari

"Bibliographical Spectrum: Christopher Columbus" by Foster Provost

"Review Article: American Foundations of Columbus Scholarship" by Frank D. Grande/Henry Paolucci

"Columbus Bibliography Since 1985" (annotated)

The above collaboration of efforts results in a most comprehensive and engaging text. Unlike many works devoted to a particular historic "hero," and much to

Arnold B. Levine, Ph.D., Department of International Communications and Literature, State University College at Cortland, Cortland, New York.

the credit of the editors, *Columbus, America and the World*, is exceedingly objective. Although much pride and academic affection is presented herein, contemporary attacks upon Columbus, as representative of a system of racial genocide, the commencement of pollution of the American environment, and harbinger of diseases, are dutifully addressed in the book's content. The text further offers details of Columbus' life and explorations, including such issues as: Was he a devout Catholic seeking to spread the cause of Christendom, or was he truly the descendant of Jewish *conversos?* ; Was he a genius/visionary, a man spurred on by intellectual curiosity and scientific hypothesis, or simply a greedy product of an era of exploration?; Was Columbus the first to discover this New World, or were others, such as the Egyptians, St. Brendan, Leif Ericsson, or even Buddhist monks, here previously? Myriad scholarly concerns are proffered from the historic to the absurd. Selections from Columbus' diaries, describing the flora and fauna and the peoples encountered are also delightfully included. There are, in addition, literary comparisons between Columbus and Ulysses, and Columbus' voyages as mirrored in the epic Portuguese poem *Os Lusiadas* by Camoes. The chapter devoted to Columbus as the subject of a drama inspired by the Japanese Noh plays is especially tantalizing from an exotic aspect, while references to the journeys of other New World explorers enhance the flavor of this period of European exploration. There is even a small segment devoted to the artistic topic of Columbus as the subject of historic portraiture.

As with any anthology, there is, regrettably, an unevenness of quality regarding specific chapters. Some entries are exceedingly well documented with copious notes, while others leave the reader less than satisfied with the precision of annotation. Some direct quotations are provided in English translation only, while others, although cited in both the "original" text and translation, offer no accurate notes as to which "original" text or translated edition is cited. Some endnotes are a bit incomplete. The quality of this anthology could have been upgraded by the editor's addition of an index for easy reference, while the absence of even a map(s) is a bit conspicuous. There are also one or two printer's errors, of no consequence, which should be attended to in future editions.

The above criticism is easily forgiven, however, when one considers the overall excellent quality of the scope and content. Indeed, it is a most enjoyable volume for both the novice and the authority. The topic, although historic by nature, is also 100% contemporary. Even the work's small size, coupled with large print, make it easy to carry about, read, and store, as a most welcomed addition to the scholarly library of anyone interested in the myth and the legend of Christopher Columbus.

LETTERS TO THE EDITOR

Dear Italian Voice,

The recent statement by the protestant National Council of Churches that there should be no Columbus Quincentanary celebration of an event that rendered the Indians slaves and was in effect an invasion of their land ("Magazine," Saturday, May 19, 1990, p. 13) is one of many that has been put forward by Indian groups, especially, and their supporters. Countries have been invaded from time immemorial; slaves are still being made in Africa and elsewhere; conquest and violence are still daily events in the Middle East and other areas of the world. Our own history shows that slavery went on for 350 years after Columbus landed; our founding fathers, including ancestors of many members of the National Council of Churches, had slaves.

Without condoning the matter one may still insist that where no crime existed no crime can be labeled or punished after the fact. Slavery prospered among us under the triangular trade of the North, which provided cheap labor for the South. We know the devastating results of that choice in the time of Lincoln. History is indeed ironic.

The plight of native Indians is a serious and continuing one; but taking this occasion to accuse Columbus of something that was not considered wrong in the 15th century is like accusing and sentencing a man today for something which was committed ten years ago when there was no edict law against what he did.

The word "discovery", moreover, does not mean stealing from others. Discovery can mean precisely what one word means when one speaks of "immigration," the discovery of new opportunities, etc. If discovering opportunities is a crime then all who leave their native lands to better themselves would qualify as criminals.

Finally, the Arawaks in the Caribbean, and other such native tribes, were destroyed not by Columbus but by stronger tribes like the Caribs. The Aztecs, before Cortes put a stop to it, were sacrificing 20,000 captives at a time. With respect to slavery, Columbus was far ahead of his time, as his letters show. To be fair, should we not give the entire case, if he is to be put on trial?

The quincentenary commemorates the landing of the first immigrant to the New World. Those of us who have lived through many trying years of poverty, discrimination, adjustment, the social and educational struggles which every immigrant has had to face, understand the argument put forward by the National Council of Churches; but in all fairness the argument is a partisan, abortive and disruptive one. History has many vectors that coverage into single resultant. Whatever the motives of the countries that sent navigators and explorers into this part of the world, the result has been a world-wide expansion that has given in the past and still provides today new and great promise to all our minorities and to people of the world. And one must be tireless in reaffirming this argument.

Dr. Anne Paolucci
President
"Columbus: Countdown 1992"

Point of View

Where is Christopher Columbus?

By Donna Marie Iadipalo

This guest editorial will end October, Italian Heritage Month.

If your children or grandchildren attend school in most states, they probably will never hear this traditional rhyme about Columbus or learn anything positive about this historic Italian at all.

COLUMBUS AS VILLAIN

A case in point is the school district of Ann Arbor, Michigan where a current evolving "controversy" is keeping any facts about Co-lumbus' accomplishments out of the local schools-replacing them with a negative portrait of this 15th century Italian explorer.

As a result, few children in Michigan will learn what a skilled and intrepid navigator Columbus was or that he was once so admired that there was a movement to canonize him.

"The only specific material we use about Columbus is a picture book in the fifth grade that is rather anti-Columbus," says Linda Prieskorn, the Ann Arbor Public Schools (AAPS) curriculum coordinator.

The textbook she is referring to is Encounter writ-ten by Jane Yolen and illustrated by David Shannon. It portrays an imagined encounter between Columbus and the Tainos, a native tribe, told from the perspective of a fictional Taino boy, who says, "I watched how the sky strangers touched our golden nose rings and our golden armbands but not the flesh of our faces or arms. I watched their chief smile. It was the serpent's smile - no lips and all teeth." The "chief" is Columbus whom the picture accom-panying the text depicts with a green complexion and prominent teeth and drooling as he examines the gold.

Although the author claims to have used his-torical records and "the storyteller's imagination" to write the text, she does not cite any solid facts. Instead, she implies that Columbus and his men committed geno-cide. "Though there were originally some 300,000 native islanders, by 1548- a little more than fifty years later-less than 500 remained. Today, there are no full-blooded Tainos."

Columbus made only four voyages to the New World in a ten-year pe-riod. He brought with him fewer than 100 men, It is physically impos-sible, therefore, for a handful of Europeans to wipe out more than a quarter of a million Tainos, but Yolen does not point this out to her young readers.

Columbus As Hero

Such current interpretations are at odds with the fact that for most of our story, historians have recorded Colum-bus as a hero. >From 1776 until about 1992, American school children studied him as an important figure in American history, who represented the American ideals of cour-age and leadership.

Columbus Day is one of America's old-est patriotic holidays, first celebrated in 1792. A century later in 1892, the Pledge of Allegiance was written to commemorate the 400th anniversary of Columbus' ar-rival the New World.

Columbus was a deeply religious man 10 took his baptismal name, Christ-barer, literally. He believed part of his mission in the New World was to bring Christianity to the native tribes he found. His deep religious convictions, in fact, led a group of Christian intellectuals to launch a movement to canonize him in the mid-1800s. This movement was even-tually supported by the Pope.

According to historian David Fabre, author of "Columbus: the Im-possible Hero," [The canonization move-ment's] discourse worked out a symbolic, providential interpretation of 'Christophorus' as an inspired navigator 'who carried Christ' to the New World. At the last minute, this movement failed, as has every attempt to canonize Columbus since then."

1992 AND ALL THAT

Ironically, Columbus's reputation began to suffer as the 500th anni-versary of his first voyage approached in 1992. At that time, special interest groups representing Native Americans and Hispanics began at-tacking Columbus as the explorer who "opened the floodgates" to Europe's exploitation of the New World and its peoples.

In their books and articles, such writers as Glen Mor-ris and Kirkpatrick Sale charge Columbus and his crew with genocide, slavery, rape and plunder. However, they are hardly objective historians.

Morris, who is chairman of the political science de-partment at the University of Colorado, is also a leader of the American Indian Move-ment, a political activist group while Kirkpatrick Sale is a radical envi-ronmentalist not an historian. Sale's book, The Conquest of Paradise, pub-lished in 1990, is clearly anti-European and pro-Indian in its indict-ment of Columbus and the European civilization he represents.

His arguments, however, are undermined by the fact that Sale is a leading exponent of the Luddites, a move-ment that warns of the dan-gers of progress and technol-ogy. If ever a man was responsible for progress, that man is Christopher Columbus.

"What we are seeing is an attempt to modify the his-tory of Colum-bus to fit the political agendas of special interest groups," says Theodore Grippe, a lawyer and founder of the American Italian Defense Associa-tion (AIDA), a national defamation group that fights Italian American stereotyping. "Some of that has to do with a strong anti-Catholic... and anti-Southern Mediterranean bias in the media," he says.

The results of such anti-European sentiments are beginning to appear on the campuses of America's top universities, "Columbus = genocide," "Murderers don't deserve holidays" and "Columbus = murderer" are some of the graffiti found on the buildings of the University of Michigan's Ann Arbor campus last year.

Similar sentiments were painted on the buildings of New York State's Cornell University. The local and nation-al news media gave little cov-erage to this vandalism

Re-Discovering Columbus

As a result of this historical revisionism, some teach-ers are reluctant to offer any positive information about Columbus to their students because they fear a backlash from those who do not want the study of Columbus to be part of a public school's curriculum. But failure to teach about Columbus and his ex-plorations objectively and ratio-nally could result in a generation of children who despise him and the European civilization he rep-resents.

This Columbus 'blackout' is not necessary, accord-ing to John Sala, who has taught English at schools in Michigan's top-rated Birmingham Pubic School district for 40 years. Sala believes that the study of Columbus has enormous untapped potential from elemen-tary school through college.

"(When teaching about Colum-bus) my intention is to have stu-dents learn how to avoid a rush to judgment, to learn how to fully explore an issue with an open mind and to have them appreciate the complexity of seemingly simple issues," says Sala.

Fact vs. Fiction.

The controversy over Colum-bus may take years to set-tle, but the fact remains that he was the greatest explorer in history: a fear-less sailor, a great mapmaker, a nautical genius, and a deeply reli-gious man. Thanks to Columbus and the millions of immigrants who followed him, the New World gave birth to the United States of America and its noble experiment in democracy.

What happened to the honors given by the American Govern-ment over the centuries such as?

COLUMBUS IMMORTALIZED:

A portrait of Columbus by Constantino Brumidi, graces the US Capitol and for two centuries, the US considered Columbus a hero.

HONORING COLUMBUS:

For more than 90 years, Wash-ington, DC has laid a wreath at the Columbus statue near Union Sta-tion on Columbus Day. For the past

COLUMBUS 92

Mensile, Anno 6, Numero 4 (45) - Genova, aprile 1990 - Lire 5.000
Spedizione in abbonamento postale Gruppo III/70 - Imprimé a Taxe réduite - Taxe perçue - Tassa Riscossa - Genova (Italie)

America

Una conferenza per il 1992
Albany. L'Italian-American Legislators Association ha presentato lo scorso 20 marzo ad Albany una speciale conferenza di preparazione ai festeggiamenti colombiani del 1992. Il presidente l'assemblyman Anthony Seminerio, dopo l'apertura ufficiale dei lavori da parte del senatore statale Serphin Maltese, ha presentato ai membri dell'associazione la professoressa Anne Paolucci, direttrice del "Columbus Countdown '92"

la quale ha fatto il punto sull'attività dell'organizzazione da lei presieduta e, soprattutto, su quanto resta invece ancora da fare. All'incontro nella capitale dello stato di New York hanno partecipato Claudia Bushman del Delaware Heritage Commission, Frank Cacciutto e la pittrice Costance del Vecchio Maltese. La cantante Anya Reynarovich, accompagnata al piano da Giuseppe Murolo, ha interpretato brani dall'"Encounter 500", il musical allestito dal commediografo Mario Fratti. E' stata pure presentata la versione filmata del "Cipango" di Anne Paolucci, in cui viene ripercorsa la vicenda della scoperta del Nuovo Mondo.

Thursday, April 12, 1990   THE LEADER OBSERVER

Legislators Preview Columbus: Countdown '92

Assemblyman Anthony Seminerio, President of the New York State Italian American Legislators' Association announced that the Association recently hosted "Columbus: Countdown 1992: A Preview", a program on the 500-year anniversary of Christopher Columbus' discovery of the new world.

Through the courtesy of the state Assembly, the program was held in the Assembly Parlor in Albany on March 20. It highlighted the historical background of Columbus' discovery and the various festivities and artistic endeavors that are being planned for the upcoming celebration.

Assisting in the presentation was State Senator Serphin R. Maltese, who is acting as the Legislative Liaison for "Columbus Countdown '92". Dr. Cav. Anne Paolucci, President of "Columbus: Countdown '92" organized and acted as Mistress of Ceremonies for the entire program.

Mrs. Paolucci, a professor at St. John's University, co-authored the book "Columbus: Selected Papers on Columbus and His Time" and has been very active in promoting the 500-year anniversary of the historic discovery of our country. Mrs. Paolucci spoke about the multi-ethnic legacy of Christopher Columbus and premiered an original play she wrote, "Cipango", which depicts the personal tragedy of Columbus as a man of vision and faith.

"Christopher Columbus played an important role in our country's rich heritage. It takes a special courage to challenge the unknown, despite the mockery of others," said Dr. Paolucci.

Dr. Claudia L. Bushman, former executive director of the Delaware Heritage Commission, gave a talk on the commemorative celebrations that took place in New York in 1792 and 1892. Frank C. Cacciutto, chairman of the English Department at East Meadow

High School, gave a presentation on Columbus in History, Literature and Art.

The second part of the preview, introduced by art historian Dr. Paul J. Patane, focused on Columbus and the arts. Constance Del Vecchio Malteses, a noted portrait artist who has been commissioned to do twelve portraits of Columbus and his contemporaries, displayed three completed works of Columbus, Queens Isabella and Vasco de Gama. Selected songs from Encounter 500 by Mario Fratti were played by Guiseppe Murolo and sung by soprano Anya Reynatovich.

"Everyone involved in the commemoration of the upcoming 500-year anniversary should be very proud of their efforts and I am most pleased that we in the Italian American Legislators Association were a key part of this early effort to recognize the invaluable contributions of Christopher Columbus and his courageous contemporaries," said Assemblyman Seminerio.

AMERICAN SOCIETY OF THE ITALIAN LEGIONS OF MERIT
INVITES YOU TO A SPECIAL "COLUMBUS PREVIEW"

CONSTANCE DEL VECCHIO MALTESE
Portrait Artist
Winner, 1989 "CC 1992 Special Recognition in the Arts & Humanities Award"

THE ARTIST AS RESEARCHER: COLUMBUS PORTRAITS

FRANKLIN C. CACCIUTTO
Chairman, English Department, East Meadow High School

THE IMAGE OF COLUMBUS IN CHAINS

DR. CAV. ANNE PAOLUCCI
President, Columbus: Countdown 1992
Member, National Council on the Humanities

COLUMBUS IN A MULTI-ETHNIC SPECTRUM: PROS AND CONS

COLUMBUS: COUNTDOWN 1992   FRIDAY, JUNE 22, 1990
8 East 69th Street
New York, New York 10021

National Journal

Cultural Collision

Native Americans and Hispanics lobbied hard to get this year's commemorations of Columbus's 1492 achievement to portray it as an encounter between two old worlds, not the discovery of a new one.

BY ROCHELLE L. STANFIELD

The Native American lobby may have found a secret ally in a long-time nemesis. It hopes to share the spotlight in this year's commemoration of the 500th anniversary of Christopher Columbus's historic voyage.

Representatives of Indian tribes have argued aggressively—and with some success—that observations of Columbus's 1492 landing serve as a forum for a reappraisal of the history of Native American cultures and of the status of Indians in contemporary society. The ultimate goal is to parlay the quincentennial hoopla—which will reach a peak on Oct. 12—into pro-Indian social legislation and land policies.

The Native Americans confront a monumental task. Generations of American schoolchildren have been taught that Columbus's arrival opened their country to the advances of European culture and technology. The Indians hope to turn that story on its head; they argue that their ancestors had already established sophisticated civilizations and that Columbus's so-called gifts were devastating: the eventual death of 90 per cent of the indigenous population—as a result of what many Indians regard as genocide—and the institution of slavery.

On the ceremonial front, at least, the Indians have scored a substantial victory. In large measure, 1992 has officially been transformed from the celebration of Europe's discovery of a new world to a commemoration of an encounter between two old worlds.

Some traditionalists call that rewriting history. But Rep. Ben Nighthorse Campbell, D-Colo., a Cheyenne who is the only American Indian in Congress, responds: "Hell, we didn't have a chance to help write it in the first place. We're just trying to set the record straight."

Expanding the record hasn't been easy. Before they could even begin their campaign, Indian leaders had to revise their approach to politics, persuasion and the press. When Congress, in 1984, began to discuss plans for a quincentennial jubilee celebration, the Native American community reacted in traditional fashion:

Many Indians ignored it, some protested loudly and largely ineffectually, but most greeted the plans with silent resentment.

"In Indian country, when we don't like something, we stay at home," said Suzan Shown Harjo, a Cheyenne and Hodulgee Muscogee, who is national coordinator of the Washington-based 1992 Alliance, a clearinghouse founded in mid-1990 for Native American responses to the quincentenary. "It took a long while for many of us to really see the pressing need for our involvement in 1992."

Actually, it took about five years. By 1989, however, Indians had begun contacting the planners of quincentennial events to seek recognition of the Native American perspective. State, local and church officials were also asked to lend their support for a more balanced presentation of early American history. And Indians began to plan a variety of alternative events of their own.

Perhaps most important, Native Americans began to cultivate the press. "We learned to play the media game," said Sandra Toineeta, a Lakota, who is the American Indian consultant to the New York City-based National Council of Churches and coordinator of the council's 1992-related activities. "It is a media event, so the media had to pick up on it."

CONVERGENCE OF FORCES

It can't be said that the Indians mounted a well-oiled lobbying operation to influence the Columbus commemoration. In fact, they still disagree among themselves over how to proceed this year. Harjo's Alliance, for example is by no means a typical umbrella coalition of like-minded interest groups. The major Native American organizations, such as the National Congress of American Indians in Washington, the Association of American Indian Affairs in New York City and the Boulder (Colo.)-based Native American Rights Foundation, go their separate ways, albeit they all hammer away at basically the same themes.

"I wish I could point to someone who orchestrated this, but there's nobody who can really take credit for it," said La Donna Harris, executive director of Americans for Indian Opportunity in Washington. "There has been no major institutional change [in the country], but rather a new sense of awareness that's come mostly because people like ourselves [in the Native American leadership] have said: 'Wait a minute. This really isn't a celebration. You don't have the full story.' "

A combination of outside factors helped the Indians get their message across. Timing was crucial. The nation's changing ethnic makeup, fed by new patterns of immigration, moved issues such as multicultural education to the front burner in the 1980s. Also, the 1960s generation, weaned on a diet of inclusiveness, had come of age and assumed positions of authority in schools, churches and some political offices. Many of them were receptive to the ideas the Indians were pushing.

"Independent ideas coming from many different groups sort of coalesced," said Alicia M. Gonzalez, director of the Smithsonian Institution's office of quincentenary programs.

Other interests clamoring for a place on the quincentennial stage bolstered the Indians' efforts. A major assist, for example, came from Hispanics, a population bloc with its own Columbus-related political agenda and its own claims to indigenous ancestry.

Ironically, Native Americans may have received their biggest boost unintentionally from the Christopher Columbus Quincentenary Jubilee Commission, the official body established by Congress in 1984 to plan a traditional Italian-centered—Columbus Day-parade-writ-large—celebration. Lack of funds, mismanagement and scandal sidetracked the commission, delaying and perhaps precluding lavish preparations for festivities.

The recession has also kept some corporate backers from their checkbooks, as has their fear of investing in projects that could turn out to be controversial because of the stir raised by the Indians.

A lack of consensus among historians has contributed to the debate over how the quincentenary should be commemorated, whether as a glorification of European explorers or a repudiation of rapacious slave traders. In the main, the federal agencies that have the money to mount major exhibitions and produce television documentaries—the Smithsonian Institution and the Library of Congress, for example—are playing it down the middle by adopting the encounter-of-two-cultures theme.

Predictions vary greatly as to how the year's celebratory events will unfold. In some cases, Native American mourning services will be held simultaneously, or there may be heckling by Indians, like that at some Columbus Day parades last October. Among the major events will be Columbus (Ohio)'s ambitious April-October Ameriflora festival, a horticultural and theatrical exposition budgeted at $53 million. Most such observations are expected, at least minimally, to acknowledge Native Americans in a positive way.

The main hope within Native American circles is that it not be all over when it's over. "A lot of people in the Indian community worry that this is going to be a five-minute shot in the arm for Indian problems and everybody is going to forget it after 1992," Campbell said. "Everybody will go back to business as usual, and the Indian people will still be suffering the way they did before."

POLITICAL AGENDAS

However the 1992 events turn out, Indians, Hispanics and other groups have already assured that the quincentenary will differ greatly from what Congress had in mind when it created the Columbus jubilee commission eight years ago.

Like the annual Columbus Day parades in big cities such as Boston, Chicago and New York, the quincentenary jubilee was initially envisioned by many as an excuse for a yearlong celebration of Italian heritage. Nearly half of the public members named to the 30-member federal commission were prominent Italian-Americans.

"I don't think anybody viewed this as anything more than another significant chronological anniversary to 'do' in the same way all the other commemoratives had been done," said Robert B. Blancato, now the director of institute and public policy for the National Italian-American Foundation in Washington, who at the time worked for then-Rep. Mario Biaggi, D-N.Y., one of the act's sponsors.

"As far as an Indian person being a full member of the [national quincentenary] commission, I don't think that occurred to them collectively at the very beginning," said Bill Ray, a Klamath Indian who is a member of the Oregon Commission on Indian Services. Thanks to pressure from Native American, Hispanic and church groups, Ray was named to the commission last month. He had served as an honorary member and chairman of its Native American Advisory Committee since 1989.

The political turn of events has even surprised the academic world, where vociferous argument has been going on for decades, if not centuries, about what kind of a person Columbus was, where his ship actually made landfall, the

Suzan Shown Harjo of the Native Americans' 1992 Alliance
Indian involvement in Columbus fetes is a "pressing need."

exchange of foods and diseases that resulted from the encounter, the full extent of the indigenous civilizations and the reasons for their demise.

"We thought there would be much more [in the way of] vigorous intellectual debates [as 1992 approached]. Those haven't taken place," said Franklin W. Knight, a professor of Latin American and Caribbean history at the Johns Hopkins University in Baltimore and an adviser to various projects to observe the quincentenary. "What we have are a lot of polemical debates."

A hard core of Italian-Americans is determined to proceed along traditional lines. Columbus: Countdown 1992, a private, nonprofit organization based in New York City, for example, has commissioned portraits of 15th-century navigators, published books about Columbus and the Italian Renaissance and produced a video of a puppet play about Columbus.

"I say it's the discovery of America by

celebrating the quincentenary and instead to engage in activities of reflection and repentance.

"It was a highly controversial resolution at the beginning, but they hung in with it and took the punches with it," said Council of Churches' consultant Toineeta. "And now many of the denominations have adopted resolutions with similar flavor."

The council's resolution lists African-Americans among the victims of the 1492 encounter but does not emphasize their plight. In fact, surprisingly little attention has been focused on the whole aspect of slavery. A probable reason is the absence of black voices in the general clamor over the quincentenary.

In 1984 and 1985, black organizations reacted to the initial quincentennial plans in a manner similar to that of Native Americans, John Hebert, the Library of Congress's quincentenary coordinator, recalled. "They asked, 'Why should we celebrate?' " Hebert said. Unlike the Indians, however, who have taken a "very forceful and vocal and demonstrative position, I have not seen a similar sharpening of focus from African-American society," he said. "There hasn't been the same follow-up that says 'What we will do instead is this.' "

SHAPING THE STORY

Although Native American activists say that the film documentaries and museum exhibits developed for the quincentennial are not sufficiently pro-Indian, most such efforts have taken pains to acknowledge the cultures Columbus encountered in 1492. There have also been fewer re-creations of the event than many observers had expected.

"We thought we would be overwhelmed by movies and television programs about Columbus, and that certainly has not yet happened," Johns Hopkins's Knight said. "I heard talk about three movies, but I don't know of any of them in advanced production." The recession, the disarray of the quincentenary commission and fear of arousing controversy are generally given as reasons why such projects have had difficulty attracting financial support.

Knight was an adviser to the only television series that has aired so far, the seven-part *Columbus and the Age of Discovery*, produced by WGBH in Boston and shown on PBS last October. The documentary used the disputed word *discovery* "because this is what it was," Knight said. "Everybody discovered something about themselves, about others and about the wider world."

Some television critics complained that the series, which took pains to include

European, Native American, African, Asian and Middle Eastern perspectives, was boring.

But advocates on all sides agreed it presented a balanced picture. During the course of filming from 1986-88, Knight said, Indians interviewed in several countries expressed increasing political interest in how the Columbus story was being presented. The National Endowment for the Humanities (NEH) contributed

Rep. Ben Nighthorse Campbell, D-Colo.
"Just trying to set the record straight."

$650,000 toward the production's $6.5 million budget.

But the NEH rejected a request for financial aid by an independent filmmaker, Yanna Kroyt Brandt, for his proposed four-part series called *1492—A Clash of Visions*. NEH deputy chairwoman Celeste Colgan said it was turned down because its script characterized the Aztecs as "very benign" in contrast with "the rapaciousness and greed of the Spanish conquistadors." She added that "the word genocide was applied to Columbus in a way that our national council members felt was really troubling."

Complaints about NEH financing decisions have also come from those who wish to honor Columbus's role in history. "It's so sad to see the energy expended on confrontation when here we are working on a shoestring," the pro-Italian Paolucci of St. Johns University said. "We have no grant money, no nothing. How we manage, I don't know."

Colgan said the NEH's goal in awarding grants was to avoid presentations that are "directed at persuading an audience to a particular political, philosophical, religious or ideological point of view or advocate a particular program of social action."

Two museum exhibitions mounted in Washington—the National Gallery of Art's recently completed *Circa 1492: Art in the Age of Exploration* and the Smithsonian's *Seeds of Change*—epitomize the emphasis on objectivity and balance (Harjo called them "safe and boring"). *Seeds of Change* is only one of more than 100 quincentenary events the Smithsonian plans, but it is the centerpiece of the institution's commemorative calendar.

"Very sensitive issues were being dealt with," the Smithsonian's Gonzalez acknowledged. "So [the institution] tried to discuss it in as objective a way as possible." One way that was done was by emphasizing disease as the major killer of the indigenous population rather than violent acts by European discoverers and colonizers. "If you want to get away from genocide, it's easier to talk about disease," said James Axtell, a humanities professor at the College of William and Mary in Williamsburg, Va., and chairman of the American Historical Association's Columbus Quincentenary Committee.

But Gonzalez doesn't interpret the encounter or the institution's depiction of it as totally neutral. "You can't deny that there was a deliberate intent [to destroy or at least weaken the native cultures]," she said. "Every group approached us," she said. "Many groups came ready to battle. In the end, we worked with many of them."

Hebert of the Library of Congress criticized the Smithsonian show for not hitting hard enough at the problem of slavery in a segment that focused on the development of the sugar trade. "That was hardly really a response, to damn one product rather than the process," he said. Hebert said the library is planning an exhibit, *1492, An Ongoing Voyage*, that will present manuscripts and other archival items in which slavery will be given greater stress.

Some scholars, such as Axtell, worry that the politics of the quincentenary could prove counterproductive to the aims of the Indians and others. "I see dangers in the abrupt kind of moralizing that's going on, using little pieces of information from the past for political or moral purposes," he said. "It treats the Indians like nothing but victims, passive helpless victims who just got run roughshod over. And they weren't that; they were much stronger."

To many Native Americans, the real reason for dwelling on this issue is not the past but the future. "There's certainly the historical perspective," Ray said. "But the real important thing for tribes today is what do we do now. We have crucial issues that the tribes have to face. What can be done to help them solve those problems?" ∎

COLUMBUS: COUNTDOWN 1992

CIPANGO!

1990: Special Performance sponsored by the Wintherthur Museum (Wilmington, Delaware) as part of their 1990 Columbus Program: Saturday, October 13.

1989/90: Original Puppet Version prepared by P.I.P. (Puppetry in Practice)—Tova Ackerman, Jorge Fantini and others. Ready for showing in the Fall.

1990: Puppet Version in Portuguese to be shown in Brazil: late 1990 and on.

1989-90: Professional 55-minute Videotape prepared with a grant from the Television Center of St. John's University and featuring AFTRA/EQUITY actors—including Marco Barricelli, Sandra Dickinson, Michael Dorkin, Maurice Edwards, and Jeff Robins. Directed for TV by Fehmi Gerceker. Stage Director, Joseph L. King. Original Music by Henry Paolucci (arranged by Robin Escovado). Ready for distribution after February.

1989: Showing of 20-minute video segment at NYSAFLT annual convention (Concord Hotel) as part of special program, "Columbus: An American Celebration"—featuring actors and director of first showcase production (Vera Lockwood, Dino Narizzano, Kircker James, Robert Dahdah, etc.): Sat. October 14.

1989: Presentation by Jorge Fantini of Columbus puppet and plans for the 1990 puppet version for the schools at NYSAFLT: Sat. October 14.

1988: Professional Reading at Lincoln Center, sponsored by American-Italian Cultural Round-table, featuring Joseph Capone, Dan Grimaldi, Vincent Gugliotti, D. J. Mendel, Eileen Roehm, Ellis Santone, and Rose Vizziello: October 1st.

1988: Reading on WFUV-FM: October 20.

1988: Play "package" with live actors and panelists made available for schools and community centers ($500 to $1,000 plus expenses).

1987: Showing of 20-minute video segment at St. John's University: October.

1987: 15-minute program featuring excerpts and interview with author on RAI-USA: October.

1987: Second (short TV) Edition published by Griffon House Publication, NY.

1986: First Edition published by Griffon House Publications. NY.

1987: Second Showcase Production at Little Theater of the Singers' Forum, featuring Sunny Taylor, Gino Fedele, etc.: Oct.-Nov.

1986: First Showcase Production at Hunter College, CUNY, featuring Vera Lockwood, Dino Narizzano, Kricker James, Robert Dahdah, etc.: October.

1986: Dramatic Reading of excerpts, featuring Marie Henderson etc., at Washington Hilton, as part of NIAF annual weekend: September.

1986: Showing of 20-minute video segment at Washington Hilton as part of NIAF "Columbus" Program. September.

1986: Showing of 20-minute video segment of First Production at CC 1992 Annual Awards Dinner: October.

CHRISTOPHER COLUMBUS

QUINCENTENARY JUBILEE

Lecture
and
Video Presentation
of a puppet adaptation of

CIPANGO!

by **Dr. Anne Paolucci**

*President of Columbus Countdown 1992
Award-Winning Playwright and Poet
Chairperson of the English Department
of St. John's University*

CIPANGO! is a play about Christopher Columbus, Queen Isabella, Martin Pinzon and Washington Irving. It is the only dramatic work that has received the title "Official Project of the Christopher Columbus Quincentenary Jubilee Commission" from the federal commission in Washington, DC.

**1pm Sunday, October 18, 1992
THE FERGUSON LIBRARY AUDITORIUM**
One Public Library Plaza Stamford, CT 964-1000

Cosponsored by the Stamford's 500th Anniversary of Christopher Columbus Committee

CIPANGO!
By Dr. Anne Paolucci

An official project of the Christopher Columbus Quincentenary Jubilee Commission

**Sunday, May 31st
4 p.m.
Empire State Plaza
Concourse Meeting Room VI**

COLUMBUS JUBILEE WEEKEND
Sponsored by the New York Conference of
Italian American State Legislators

Nicholas A. Spano
President

Anthony J. Genovesi
Chairman

NEW YORK STATE
ITALIAN-AMERICAN LEGISLATORS' ASSOCIATION
PRESENTS

"COLUMBUS: COUNTDOWN 1992: A PREVIEW"

Tuesday, March 20, 1990
9:30AM - 12:30 PM

Assembly Parlor (Room 306)
The Capitol, Albany, N.Y.

Welcome and Opening Remarks
The Hon. Anthony Seminerio
President, NYS Italian-American Legislators' Association
The Hon. Serphin R. Maltese
New York State Senate

PART I: HISTORICAL BACKGROUNDS

DR. CAV. ANNE PAOLUCCI
President, "Columbus: Countdown 1992"
The Multi-Ethnic Legacy of Christopher Columbus, the First
Immigrant to the New World

DR. CLAUDIA L. BUSHMAN
Former Executive Director, Delaware Heritage Commission
Columbus Commemorations in New York in 1792 and 1892

FRANK C. CACCIUTTO
Chairperson, English Department, East Meadow High School, NY
Columbus in History, Literature and Art

PART II: COLUMBUS IN THE ARTS

Introduced by Dr. Paul J. Patané, *Educator, Art Historian*

CONSTANCE DEL VECCHIO MALTESE
Portrait Artist, Winner of the CC 1992
"Special Recognition in the Arts & Humanities Award" (1989)
The Columbus Story from the Artist's Point of View

SELECTED SONGS
ENCOUNTER 500 by MARIO FRATTI
Music by Giuseppe Murolo
Based on a Story by Lou Marola and Nick Montaldo
Giuseppe Murolo (piano), Anya Reynarovich (soprano)

Premiere Video Screening of Original Play about Columbus,
Queen Isabella, Martin Pinzon, and Washington Irving

CIPANGO!

by ANNE PAOLUCCI

Original Music *Director* *Stage Director*
HENRY PAOLUCCI FEHMI GERCEKER JOSEPH KING
Produced at the Television Center of St. John's University

————

Closing Remarks

————

Luncheon and Reception immediately following the Program
(By invitation only)

CIPANGO! FEATURED BY THE "COLUMBUS 500 SAIL ON COMMITTEE OF DELAWARE" (SUMMER, 1990)

Columbus 500

Published by the Columbus 500 Sail On Committee of Delaware
Vol.I.No.1   *for the 500th Anniversary of Christopher Columbus's voyages and the opening of the New World*   *Summer 1990*

CHRISTOPHORVS COLOMBVS   REYNA YSABEL

Columbus 500 October Conference Will Feature Play, "Cipango"

Saturday, October 13, will see the Delaware opening of the play, "Cipango"--an original play by Anne Paolucci featuring dramatic encounters between Christopher Columbus, Queen Isabella, and Martin Alonso Pinzon (captain of the Pinta) with Washington Irving as a commentator. The play focuses on the personal tragedy of Columbus as a man of vision and faith, fated to seek his fortune away from his native land. The dramatic encounters are set at a time when Europe was as agitated by its new awareness of impending global changes as it is today. Columbus and his royal Spanish patron, as depicted here, belong as much to our dawning "EUROPE 1992" as to the Europe of five hundred years ago.

"Cipango," or Japan, is so named because Columbus was looking for a new route to China, India and to Japan, and planned to make Japan his first stop.

Washington Irving was the first American biographer of Columbus and was a devoted fan of the man whom he considered to be one of the most outstanding in all the Renaissance period. The appearance of Washington Irving is a genial touch reminding us of the multi-ethnic legacy of Columbus and the American focus of the play. This one-hour play will be directed by Paula Lehrer of Dover.

Author Anne Paolucci's first play, "The Short Seasons," premiered in Naples, Italy, and later at the Cubiculo in New York. Her one-act play, "Minions of the Race" (about More, Cromwell, and Wolsey) won a national award when it first appeared and was staged several times in New York. Her recent "the Actor in Search of his Mask," featuring Machiavelli writing his dramatic masterpeice "Mandragola" appeared last year on Italian television. Chairperson of theEnglish Department and Director of Arts

Degree Program in English at St. John's University, Dr. Paolucci has written extensively on Edward Albee, Shakespeare, Pirandello, Theater of the Absurd, and dramatic theory. Her recent short stories, "Sepia Tones," were review in <u>The New York Times</u>.

"Cipango" will be available for a fee for community performances after January, 1991. Any group interested in the play should contact Ms. Lehrer in Dover at 736-4303 or in New Castle at 368-6881.

The rest of the half-day conference will include a 15-minute musical presentation by the Holly Consort group of Dover playing16th century music, updates on the activities and programs planned for Delaware in 1992, announcements of the annual *Columbus 500* awards, and will end with lunch.

Anyone interested in registering for the October 13 half-day conference shouldcomplete the form on page 7.

CIPANGO!

*A 50-minute video play about the ironies of the Columbus sto
by* ANNE PAOLUCCI; *original music and lyrics by* HENRY PAOLU
featuring MARCO BARRICELLI *as Christopher Columbus*

---

produced by

"Columbus: Countdown 1992"

and

Awarded recognition in 1991 as
*"Official Project of the Christopher Columbus
Quincentenary Jubilee Commission"*
set up by President Ronald Reagan

CHRISTOPHER
COLUMBUS
500
QUINCENTENARY
JUBILEE

SPECIAL LIMITED EDITION PRICE: $25.00

CIPANGO!

BY BOB BYRD

ADAPTED FOR PUPPET THEATER FROM
ANNE PAOLUCCI'S *CIPANGO!*

"Puppetry in Practice" (P.I.P.), headed by Dr.
Tova Ackerman, has made available a puppet
adaptation of Anne Paolucci's dramatic play
about Columbus, Queen Isabella, and Martín
Pinzon (*and*, with Washington Irving as
Commentator). This entertaining puppet play
brings the voyage of Columbus into classrooms (with audience participation).

Prepared in collaboration with "Columbus:
Countdown 1992," the project originated in
cooperation with Sia Santa, a puppet theater
in Campinas Brazil headed by Jorge Fantini,
who designed the original puppets with Alberto Camerera and Jesus Seda. The script
was adapted from Anne Paolucci's stage play
by Bob Byrd. The performance team includes
three actors from "Teacher Actor Teams," (a
collaborative project between P.I.P and the
Actor's Work Program). These are: Victoria
Demtchenko, T. Michael Dalton, and Bob
Byrd. Another P.I.P. member, George
Voyzey, can provide sign interpretation
(optional).

FOR SCHOOLS, COMMUNITY GROUPS, FUNDRAISERS!

CIPANGO!

A PUPPET PLAY

BY BOB BYRD

**ADAPTED FROM
ANNE PAOLUCCI'S *CIPANGO!****

(*An Official Project of the
ristopher Columbus Quincentenary Jubilee Commissi

*A COLLABORATIVE MULTI-FACETED
PROGRAM PREPARED BY*

**"PUPPETRY IN PRACTICE"
"TEACHER ACTOR TEAMS"**
(Actor's Work Program)
"SIA SANTA"
and

COLUMBUS: COUNTDOWN 1992

Italian Tribune   COLUMBUS DAY   October 20, 2005 ♦ 25

Anne Paolucci Writes the
Story of Christopher Columbus

The story of Christopher Columbus still raises questions and controversies. In *Cipango! (The Story)*, Anne Paolucci reviews the story of the famous navigator in bold strokes, offering the reader the highlights of a life characterized by a brief success and many disappointments in terse and compelling prose.

"It is a life worth exploring as the many books about him attest. New books continue to be written about him. For this author, the attraction of his life lies in its ironic reversals, the incredible ups and downs he experience, from the welcome given him in 1493 by King Ferdinand and Queen Isabella on his return from the first momentous journey – a welcome in which Columbus rode in public side by side with the King 9something unheard of) – to his humiliating return to Spain, in chains, after the third journey. By the time of his death, in 1506, he was forgotten, cast into a double oblivion," Paolucci writes in the Preface.

Each chapter is divided into two parts. In the first, the author gives us a straightforward historical and biographical account of some aspect of the life Columbus, who embodies the spirit of Renaissance discovery. In the second part, she provides us with an original literary narrative drawn, in most cases, from her award-winning play *Cipango!*

The first chapter begins with a quick survey of Columbus's early life, "Looking Back: Genoa?" and ends with "Looking Ahead:

Stranded in Jamaica." Chapter Two details "The Historic First Journey" and "Martin Pinzon," the man who played an important part in the events connected with the first journey. Chapter Three is an account of Columbus's triumphant return to Spain after that first journey, in "Return to Spain" and "Fame and Glory" – the second segment is written in the form of a letter describing the excitement generated by that return from the unknown lands discovered and claimed for Spain.

Chapter Four describes the growing tensions and animosity Columbus had to face in "The Second Journey: Accusations and Charges" and "Private Audience with the Queen." Chapter Five includes "The Third Journey: Pearls, Gold and Indians," and "A Letter to the Queen." Chapter Six offers "New Charges: Columbus in Chains" and "Last Encounter with the Queen." Chapter Seven focuses on "The Fourth Journey: Shattered Dreams," and "The Columbus Legacy." This last segment includes a brief summary in the voice of Washington Irving, one of the most prolific writers on Columbus.

The Epilogue raises the question of why Italian Americans honor Columbus instead of Amerigo Vespucci, who did not 'discover' the new world but gave his name to it. The book also carries the reproductions from the interesting 13-part series, *Age of Discovery Navigators* by award-winning

artist Constance Del Vecchio Maltese including "Columbus in Chains" (on the cover), "The Young Columbus" and "Amerigo Vespucci." The first page of *Mundus Novus*, the Latin version of Vespucci's historic account of the landmass south of the equator, appears on the back cover.

This is an unusual and compelling biography for readers of all ages.

About the Author.

Anne Paolucci graduated from Barnard College and Columbia University, where she received the first Woodbridge Honorary Fellowship in the Department of English and Comparative Literature. She was a Fulbright scholar at the University of Rome and later a Fulbright Lecturer in American Drama at the University of Naples.

From 1986 to 1993 Paolucci headed "Columbus: Countdown 1992," a non-profit foundation which promoted new art and scholarship dealing with the life and times of Columbus. In 1991, she received the Gold Medal of the Canadian Quincentenary commission. That same year, her play *Cipango!* was recognized as an official project of the Christopher Columbus Quincentennial Jubilee Commission, set up by President Reagan.

COLUMBUS: COUNTDOWN 1992

by ANNE PAOLUCCI

(Copyright © 1994 by Anne Paolucci

You ask what I felt?
My tracks are epic (I'm told),
But, really, I stumbled into fame.
Shores are simply a need,
A lure, a claim.

You ask what I want?
Oceans closing behind me,
Wind singing before me
Filling canvas with promise.
On land I grow dizzy, impatient, tired.
My shadow on the ground tells me
I have yet to keep my sea bargain . . . .

You ask what I dream?
A map that proves me right,
The heavens chartered,
Another ocean sea to the moon,
New storms to be outraced,
I long for grace of waters
Softly folded over sleep.

Who else dares (you ask?)
Ah, many sought new lands
Sifted through so many sands
Back to the sea! Even Ulysses
Sailed the length of Venus
To measure his will against the sky,
Every star fixed to his purpose,
Lighting his orbit.

Touching land is daily bread.
What matters is definition
Of the event—
Giving birth is only the first
Dim sighting of earth.

Land scattered before me
I battered my way through a wall
Of islands strung out
To wear me down —
Indians were there to greet me
(As Indians are there in India),
Unknowing, unaware;
I blessed their untroubled nakedness,
Our hopes and all to come —
Surely that's worth something?

Well, we know the rest.
So: Let me ask you this:
Is reaching Ithaca really best?

*[*The original version of this poem first appeared in 1986 and was included in* GORBACHEV IN CONCERT (AND OTHER POEMS) *by Anne Paolucci, published by Griffon House Publications, New York, 1991. The present version has been slightly revised.]*

REVIEW OF NATIONAL LITERATURES

ANNE PAOLUCCI / HENRY PAOLUCCI
SPECIAL EDITORS

COLUMBUS, AMERICA, AND THE WORLD

Includes: *D. Bigongiari*, "Dante's Ulysses and Columbus"; *F J. Coppa*, "Christopher Columbus and Italy"; *M.-L. Gazarian*, "A Doer, A Dreamer, A Man of Vision"; *J.Gillespie*, "Paul Claudel's *Christopher Columbus* and Japanese Noh Plays"; *F. D. Grande* and *H. Paolucci*, "Review Article: American Foundations of Columbus Scholarship" and "Columbus Bibliography Since 1985"; *A. Paolucci*, "Introduction, 1992"; *A. Paolucci* and *H. Paolucci*, "Columbus and the Idea of America"; *F. Provost*, "Bibliographical Spectrum"; *O. C. Stoetzer*, "The Myth of Discovery: Edmundo O'Gorman's Perspective."

An "Age of Discovery" Publication of
COUNCIL ON NATIONAL LITERATURES

"Columbus: Countdown 1992":
The Curtain Falls
on a Decade
of Cultural Activities

The "200 Club" in Manhattan, at Fifth Avenue, was once again the setting last September 30th for the last "Awards Dinner" of "Columbus: Countdown 1992," headed by Dr. Anne Paolucci. That organization, which with this event has brought to a close a decade of various activities (conferences, books, video, etc., focused throughout on the Columbian theme), will be transformed in the near future into the "American Foundation of Italian Arts and Letters" and will continue to champion, with the same devotion and fervor of the past, the cultural and artistic excellence of our Italian legacy.

The Hon. Paolo Emilio Taviani (who at the last minute had to forego the trip across the Atlantic), the greatest living exponent of the life and accomplishments of the Genoese, was awarded the special prize for his achievements in the field of Columbus scholarship. Others honored included Helen F. Boehm (International Arts Award), and Helen Greco (Special Recognition in the Arts & Humanities Awards). Special Quincentenary Awards were presented to former Congressman Mario Biaggi, Dr. Ann Merlino, The Hon. Pam Grella, and NYS Senator Serphin R. Maltese.

EXHIBITS, PLAYS, READINGS, LECTURES, WORKSHOPS, PANEL DISCUSSIONS, SEMINARS, PUPPET-MAKING, AND PUPPET THEATER, VIDEO PLAYS AND VIDEO "SPOTS," EXCERPTS FROM OPERAS AND MUSICALS, ART SHOWS, BOOK FAIRS

LECTURES AND WORKSHOPS (15 minutes to one hour):

* Columbus and His Time
* Major Navigators of the 15th and 16th Century
* The Spanish Sovereigns, the Conquest of the Moors, etc.
* Washington Irving—the First Biographer of Columbus in English
* Columbus as a "Tragic" Hero
* The Maps of Columbus's Time
* Portuguese and African Navigation of the 15th Century
* Marco Polo and his Journals about China
* The Writing of Columbus
* The Young Columbus
* The Four Journeys of Columbus and the Islands Named by Columbus
* The Foods of the New World
* Literary Works about Columbus
* Plays about Columbus (Lope de Vega, Claudel, Ghelderode, Anne Paolucci, Frank Cacciuto, etc.)
* Operas about Columbus (Claudel/Darius Milhaud, Franchetti, Carlo Gomes [Brazilian/Italian, 1892], etc.)
* Monuments to Columbus in America
* Columbus Celebrations in New York State and Elsewhere
* Genoa in the Time of Columbus

ART SHOWS/LECTURES (one hour, with or without slides and prints):

* Contemporary Art on Columbus: Portraits, landscapes, statues, etc. depicting the Columbus story
* The Image of Columbus in Chains (with slides)
* The Agony of Columbus (with slides)
* Existing Portraits of Columbus and Other Navigators and Personalities of the Time

THEATER (one hour):

* CIPANGO! by Anne Paolucci. An original play about Columbus, Queen Isabella, Martin Pinzon, with commentary by Washington Irving. (Live performances on royalty basis through author's representative or agent.)
* Dramatic Readings from CIPANGO!
* Video Play of CIPANGO! A stunning 55-minute video of Anne Paolucci's CIPANGO! with Marco Barricelli (Columbus), Sandra Dickinson (Isabella), Michael Dorkin (Pinzon), Maurice Edwards (Washington Irving), Jeff Robins (Scout), and with original music by Henry Paolucci, arranged by Robin Escovado. Stage Director: Joseph King; Director: Fehmi Gerceker. (Arrangements through author's representative or agent.)
* Puppet Play Based on CIPANGO! (IN SEARCH OF THE TREASURE) Available in English, Portuguese, Spanish.
* Puppet-Making Demonstration Based on CIPANGO!
* ENCOUNTER 500 by Mario Fratti. An original musical based on a story by Lou Marola and Nick Montaldo. Music by Giuseppe Murolo. (Live performances on royalty basis through author's representative or agent.)
* Excerpts from ENCOUNTER 500 (with music)
* Songfest from ENCOUNTER 500

COLUMBUS: COUNTDOWN 1992

The projects of the organization headed by Anne Paolucci

Of all the various groups in America planning celebrations, it is "Columbus' Countdown 1992" that has emerged as the most enterprising and the most active. Headed by Anne Paolucci, Professor at St. John's University, New York, "Columbus: Countdown 1992" orchestrates the initiatives and Columbus celebratory projects throughout the Big Apple.

It is precisely in Anne Paolucci's inexhaustible activity that we find inspiration for most of the important initiatives which in 1989 attracted Columbus-focused interest in the United States.

Last summer, the New York State Department of Education invited Anne Paolucci to contribute her scholarly abilities to "Due Case una Tradizione," a project launched by Governor Mario Cuomo. The project, part of the "Italo-American Heritage Curriculum," consists of a course of study aimed at extending popular knowledge of the history and contributions of Italian Americans in the United States, beginning with the first voyage of Columbus. Working toward an interdisciplinary program of studies, "Due Case, una Tradizione" proposes to reorder and integrate all Italian-American studies, with particular emphasis on furthering education and the efforts to keep alive the cultural values and legacy of our people.

Governor Cuomo's objective is to promote mutual understanding between Italo-Americans and Italians, keeping in sight the advantages that can result through economic and cultural cooperation between New York State and Italy, by means of commercial exchanges, investments and scientific research.

The "Italo-American Heritage Curriculum" is conceived in two parts: one based on materials in Italian, the other on such learning devices as video, film and photography, all of which will be used as means of communication to be integrated into the actual teaching experience.

Anne Paolucci was invited by the Department of Education to suggest names of individuals and groups that might contribute to the curriculum and to reassess what has been done so far.

The "Heritage" project is directed by a scientific committee of historians, economists, linguists and scholars of Italian-American culture. The group, which met in December, will publish themes and ideas to be implemented and put into position during 1990.

On Columbus, more particularly, "Columbus: Countdown 1992" published, in cooperation with the Council on National Literatures, a volume called "Columbus" in which a number of recent essays dealing with Columbus were brought together.

The volume includes "Fact, Fiction, and Philology: a Re-Assessment of the Columbus Story" by Anne Paolucci, "Christopher Columbus in Historical Perspective" by Frank J. Coppa, "The Earliest Literary Response of Renaissance Italy to the New World Encounter" by Theodore J. Cachey.

The cover of the book carries an original portrait of Columbus by artist Constance Del Vecchio Maltese, who is working on an entire gallery of portraits having to do with the Columbus story. The Italian-American painter was honored at last year's awards-dinner in September, when "Columbus: Countdown 1992" singles out for recognition those who have distinguished themselves in Columbus projects.

In addition to Constance Del Vecchio Maltese, the 1989 Awards-Dinner honored Alexander J. J. Roncari, president of the Columbus commission of Canada. Born in Sanremo and a naturalized Canadian citizen since 1959, Roncari has served as director of his country's Columbus commission since 1984. A graduate in natural sciences from the University of Geneva, Alexander Roncari has worked in archeology and in marine science. He is currently a member of the Association of Canadian Physicists, the American Association for the Advancement of Science, the Canadian Institute of Chemistry. Thanks to the continued interest in backgrounds and cultural continuity among the Italians in America, Roncari was made president of the cultural commission on Italian art and tradition (Hamilton, Ontario) and serves as a member of the advisory board on multiculturalism in the media, Canadian radio and television.

"An indomitable spirit and a vision of the world, like those of Columbus. A common heritage, both personal and intimate, shared with Columbus himself, of whom he is the last descendant." For these singular qualities, "Columbus: Countdown 1992" honored Alexander J. J. Roncari at its recent awards dinner, together with the accomplished First Lady, Matilda Raffa Cuomo, wife of the governor of New York State, who serves as President of the State Columbus Commission and is also Director of "Due Case, una Tradizione."

LORENZO FANTINI

DESCRIPTION OF AWARDS

"COLUMBUS: COUNTDOWN 1992"

Imported Italian Glass "Sail" with Legend and CC 1992
Logo Engraved by Tiffany & Co.

To an outstanding representative of the
Quincentenary Community

*****

"INTERNATIONAL ARTS"

Bronze Plaque with CC 1992 Logo and Legend, including
the Name of Honoree and the CC 1992 Motto.

To an artist, composer, musician, playwright, producer,
actor, writer, singer, dancer who has realized one or
more outstanding works in some area of the arts.

*****

"SPECIAL RECOGNITION IN THE ARTS AND HUMANITIES"

Gold Logo Pin Crafted by Tiffany & Co.

To gifted artists and energetic promoters
of the Humanities.

ROSTER OF "COLUMBUS" COUNTDOWN 1992" HONOREES

1985: DR. PETER SAMMARTINO
(Founder and Chancellor Emeritus,
Fairleigh Dickinson University)

1986: AMBASSADOR JOHN A. VOLPE
(Former Ambassador to Italy)

1987: DR. VARTAN GREGORIAN
(Former President and CEO, NYPL;
President, Brown University)

1988: DR. FREDI CHIAPPELLI
(Director, Medieval and Renaissance
Institute UCLA; Renaissance and
Columbus Scholar)

1989: DR. ALEXANDER J. J. RONCARI
(President, Christopher Columbus
Quincentenary Commission of Canada)

1989: MATILDA R. CUOMO
(SPECIAL AWARD)
(Chairperson, New York State Christopher
Columbus Quincentenary Commission)

1990: DR. VASCO GRAÇA MOURA
(Commissioner-General for the
Commemoration of the
Portuguese Discoveries)

1991: ADRIANA SCALAMANDRÉ BITTER
(President, Scalamandré Silks)

1992: THE HON. PAOLO EMILIO TAVIANI
("Senatore a vita" and Columbus Scholar)

Fall 2005 Selection

THE SONS OF ITALY BOOK CLUB

CIPANGO! (THE STORY)
By Anne Paolucci

Marco Polo's description of *Cipango*, (Renaissance Italian for "Japan"), inspired Columbus to cross an ocean to find it, as we learn in this short but powerful biography of the greatest navigator of the Renaissance by noted Columbus scholar Anne Paolucci. She starts with Columbus' early life in Genoa where he began sailing at age 15 and ends with his tragic fourth and last voyage when a storm sank almost his entire fleet of 32 ships. The facts are enhanced by excerpts from Paolucci's award-winning play, also named *Cipango!* A "must-read"

FOUR NEW *RNL* VOLUMES FEATURING

THE AGE OF DISCOVERY

EXCERPTS FROM *NARRATIVE AND CRITICAL HISTORY OF AMERICA*, BY JUSTIN WINSOR, WITH INTRODUCTIONS

✳ SPANISH DISCOVERIES OF AMERICA ✳
✳ ENGLISH DISCOVERIES OF AMERICA ✳
✳ PORTUGUESE, FRENCH, AND DUTCH
DISCOVERIES OF AMERICA ✳
✳ NATIVE POPULATIONS OF THE AMERICAS ✳

8. CHAIRWOMAN OF THE BOARD
BOARD OF TRUSTEES, CITY UNIVERSITY OF NEW YORK (CUNY)

In June 1996, I retired from St. John's in order to give more time to my writing; but before my plans could take shape, Fate stepped in again, this time with a call from Albany. New York State Governor George Pataki had chosen me to serve on the Board of Trustees of The City University of New York (CUNY), the largest urban complex of its kind anywhere, with 19 colleges and, at that time, a student population of 220,000. I saw the offer as a perfect transition from active teaching and administration to another kind of educational challenge. I would still have plenty of free time for my own work: the Board met only a few times in the year. During the summer, I filled out forms and went through a number of interviews, both in New York and Albany. By the Fall, FBI clearance had been obtained. I attended my first Board meeting in September.

There were several old-timers on the Board. Herman Badillo had been a member for about 14 years; Edith Everett, for about as long. James Murphy, a Democratic appointee like Everett and several others, was Chairman. Raising educational standards ostensibly was the Board's primary concern, but its members — I soon discovered — had different "readings" on what "standards" meant. Our common interests as Board members were often affected, also, by liberal and conservative agendas.

I also learned that Dr. Ann Reynolds, the Chancellor then in place, was being criticized by many, including New York City Mayor Rudolph Giuliani and Governor Pataki, for being ineffectual in getting CUNY's problems resolved. Many of the newer colleges, as well as The City College (once "New York's Harvard"), were showing poor graduation figures and below standard performance. Programs like nursing and teacher-education had come in for serious attacks in many of the colleges. In my first six months on the Board, I came to realize that major organic changes would have to be made, from bottom to top, if any substantive improvement was to take place.

My first hard decision as a member of the Committee on Academic Policy, Program, and Research (CAPPR), to which I'd been assigned, was forced on me at the October 27 meeting of the Board. Earlier that month, I'd been asked by the Chancellor to stop by to discuss a "performance test" she and her staff had worked out to improve existing conditions, a test she'd christened the "Academic Certification Exam" (ACE) and which she intended to offer for Board approval at the next meeting. I don't believe I was singled out for my credentials as an educator but because Dr. Reynolds wanted to be sure she had the votes needed for ACE to be approved. I was still an "unknown quantity," potentially disruptive. Other new members, I'm sure, had been approached also, in the same way and for the same reason.

We all were aware of the dismal statistics on remediation and low performance levels across the CUNY system. The Chancellor also had received and surely had read the copy I'd sent her of my letter to Governor Pataki, on my appointment to the Board, in which I stated my strong views about the need for drastic changes in remediation, University-wide restructuring, and general financial retrenching. I'd promised to do all I could to insure "access to excellence" within the bounds of "fiscal responsibility" — a phrase I would repeat many times in the months ahead. I looked forward to working closely with my fellow Trustees and the Chancellor on matters crucial to the University but was soon disillusioned. The Board was split along liberal-minded Trustees, repeating empty platitudes, and the more aggressive among us, who wanted to see substantive and basic changes. The Chancellor, whom the old timers had rarely challenged, had an agenda of her own. She wasn't about to listen to a brash newcomer.

Of course by this time the problem of remediation had surfaced as a major nation-wide educational issue, and the Press — thriving on controversy — had found the perfect "continuing story." The first rumbles announcing a major storm were heard as early as 1991, when CUNY (and other universities) were facing a financial crunch. Remediation had been targeted as the greatest financial drain on universities across the country. CUNY, with its notoriously poor performance levels, was singled out in a *New York Times* article by Samuel Weiss ("Panel Asks Stiffer Preparation for CUNY Students," March 10, 1991), where the author pointed up the dilemma faced by CUNY in having to accept students with the required high school diploma but poorly prepared notwithstanding and unable to keep up with college-level work. The article read in part:

A faculty panel has recommended that students entering the City University of New York complete a set of college preparatory courses as tough as those New York State requires for its best high-school graduates.

University officials say they want to put pressure on the city's public school system to prepare students better for college work. In approving their broad plan, the trustees did not specify the high-school course requirements to be met by freshmen but gave the chancellor until January 1992 to draw up a list.

In anticipation of this, Dr. Reynolds several months ago charged the University Faculty Senate with preparing a preliminary set of "expectations" to be met by university freshmen. A copy of the proposals of the Senate's Advisory Committee on the College Preparatory Curriculum was obtained by the *New York Times*.

The committee calls for students entering the university to have taken four years of college-preparatory English, four years of social studies, three years of mathematics, two years of laboratory sciences, two years of a foreign language and one of visual and performing arts.

New York State high school students now earning a Regents' endorsed diploma must complete four years of college-preparatory English, four years of social studies, three years of foreign language, two years of sciences, two years of mathematics, and one year of art and music.

According to the New York Board of Education, only about 20 percent of its high-school graduates now earn such a diploma.

By 1996, when I joined the CUNY Board of Trustees, press coverage of remediation had escalated to a daily "breaking story." The controversy had polarized and become more than an educational issue. In a short time, it had turned into a political crisis as well.

In "Remedial. Paying Twice for the Job the Public Schools Didn't Do" (July 23, 1996), *The Houston Chronicle* reported that "the growth in the cost of remedial education at state colleges and universities is alarming. State spending for remedial instruction in mathematics, reading and writing has increased from $38.6 million in 1988-89 to $153.4 million for 1996-97."

A *Newsday* editorial, "America's New Information Age Economy Has Closed the Door to High-Paying Jobs for the Ill-Educated" (September 5, 1996), noted that "[President] Clinton's approval to spend $2.75 billion on a nationwide effort to see that every child learns to read by third grade is a worthy endeavor. But it's also an indictment of the public schools. That 40 per cent of 8-year olds cannot read as well as they should is a travesty. If a million volunteers are recruited to tutor students in reading their efforts must be focused where they're needed most — in the troubled inner cities."

The refrain was picked up by Clifford Adelman, in "Point of View" (*The Chronicle of Higher Education*, October 4, 1996):

> From the City University of New York to the California State University System, authorities have begun reducing the number of remedial courses available to postsecondary students. Some legislatures have made it clear that they do not want to pay colleges to teach what public high schools already receive tax dollars to teach: other legislatures want community colleges to handle all remediation, to eliminate duplication of such programs at four-year institutions. . . . The first lesson that one learns from . . . transcripts is that the bulk of remediation is a traditional role of community colleges. . . . The second lesson is that the extent of a student's need for remediation is inversely related to his or her eventual completion of a degree. Of the students in the study who had earned more than a semester of college courses by 1993, 55 per cent of those who took no remediation courses and 47 per cent of those who took only one remedial course had earned a bachelor's. . . . If a student requires remediation only in writing or needs to repeat an intermediate algebra course, four-year colleges can handle the problem quickly. They are not very efficient with more daunting cases, and we defraud students if we pretend otherwise.

CUNY soon became the major target. The circumstances that had forged the controversial policies it had inherited were reviewed in "Making the Grade: Reforming America's Schools" ("Briefly: Notes." "Open Admissions in New York," *The Ford Foundation Report*, Summer/Fall 1996, p. 32):

In 1970 a new policy called "open admissions" was introduced at the City University of New York (CUNY). The policy, which guaranteed a place in the CUNY system to any graduate of a New York City high school, was controversial from the start. The most frequent criticism was that open admissions would drastically lower the university's high academic standards, erode the quality of education provided, and diminish the value of a CUNY degree. In *Changing the Odds: Open Admissions and the Life Chances of the Disadvantaged* (Yale University Press, 1996), a study funded by the Foundation, David E. Lavin and David Hyllegard counter criticisms which have persisted for a quarter of a century, and conclude that open admissions at CUNY produced thousands of graduates — many of them minorities — who otherwise might never have earned a college degree.

Although there was much to be said in favor of "Open Admissions," the immediate problem, for most critics, had to do directly with remediation programs already in place and administered after students had already been admitted. No one was seriously considering ending "Open Admissions."

The controversy soon moved into high gear.

Richard Riley, U.S. Secretary of Education, commented in "Colleges Should Change Course" (September 20-22, 1996, p. 6): "The remedial condition (at colleges) has gotten out of line and become almost unacceptable."

In "Remedial Courses Are Widespread at American Colleges, Report Says" ("Go to Today's Headlines" ["Academe Today," *The Chronicle of Higher Education*, October 24, 1996]), Lisa Guernsey zooms in on the major arguments: "Critics of such courses say that colleges should not be in the business of helping unprepared students or of making up for the deficiencies of the public schools. But others say that colleges are not doing enough to provide such courses for their students."

CUNY had no ready answers. Some critics (myself included) were quick to point out that the low levels of performance and graduation rates were due, to a significant extent, to the dramatic demographic changes that had taken place in recent years and which were difficult for the schools and colleges to absorb. The tremendous ethnic diversity that had come to characterize the Big Apple could not have been predicted at the time that the "Academy," the original City College, had opened its doors, a hundred and fifty years earlier; nor could it have been anticipated as late as 1970, when "Open Admissions" went into effect. The large influx of new students, many of them recent immigrants who could not speak English at all, as well as culturally-deprived students — Blacks especially — had created a massive problem that had yet to be properly assessed.

In 1970, when the so-called "Open Admissions" policy went into effect, there were only a few minorities at City College — the flagship of a still rather small system — primarily Jews and Italians. With the many new nationalities that since that time had found their way, legally or illegally, into the large cities, especially New York, a unique and interesting social mosaic had emerged, but one that brought with it major problems throughout the educational spectrum.

At the time I joined the Board of Trustees, these factors had already had a huge impact within CUNY. Remediation programs that had been set up to help students to overcome their various deficiencies were only marginally or sporadically effective. A problem was that there was no common system for measuring remedial success: students passed out of remediation in some of the schools simply by completing the remedial sequence. Reading and writing skills were at a low, especially in the community colleges where "Open Admissions" insured access to just about everybody. (The senior colleges had a choice of sorts). Courses and programs designed to bring students to a basic level of proficiency were no longer adequate to achieve the desired results.

Many, including the Mayor and the Governor, felt that the Chancellor was to blame for allowing the problem to escalate. The report she had asked for was anything but reassuring. Other measures had to be put forward, and quickly.

I myself had come to recognize some of the more troublesome aspects of the controversy. For one thing, students taking remediation often did so at the same time they attended regular courses — counter-productive, to say the least. How could a student with writing and reading deficiencies, who could hardly speak English and couldn't put an English sentence together, take notes, participate in class discussion, ask questions, absorb what the professor was saying or write reports and take tests? I had come to be convinced, even before coming on the Board, that a first basic step was to train properly teachers in place (not ask for more) and to streamline existing programs according to current needs — not the least of which was recognizing the new ethnic spread, the many new nationalities that had settled in New York since "Open Admissions" was introduced. I felt strongly that the demographic changes that had taken place in New York City since the 70s had to be recognized as an important element in any discussion about remediation reform. It was a factor that could not be ignored in proposing solutions.

I understood Chancellor Reynolds' need for a quick remedy. Her relationship with the Governor and the Mayor had seriously deteriorated. She had to come up with something to regain their confidence and to silence other critics.

The answer she proposed was ACE.

At our meeting, I was handed a sample copy of the test. I scanned it quickly — an essay of several single-space pages, bluntly political, a call for drastic social action. More to the point, it was not easy reading. I was informed that students would be allowed to take the test home, answer the questions at leisure, and return the test by a certain date. I commented on the obscure, heavy prose, suggested that it was not the sort of essay that encouraged clear writing. I also objected to having students take the test home; even more strongly to their being allowed to repeat it — if they failed — not once, but several times, with one-to-one tutorials and other help in-between, until they got through. Guidelines for grading were vague or ambiguous.

I questioned its value as a testing tool for measuring comprehension, writing, and reading skills, even on an advanced level, and found it unacceptable as a diagnostic test on any level. It might work, I explained, as a competitive exam for more sophisticated, better-prepared students applying for grants or fellowships — not exactly what we were looking for. I failed to see how it could possibly improve or adequately measure performance levels for students who still desperately needed very basic skills. I also wondered about the cost of such a project. Individual tutorials for indefinite periods of time, aimed at passing a test; faculty hours for grading such tests several times over; open-ended remedial help along the way until the student "Passed" — all this called for a generous budget. Had the Chancellor money in the till for all that, if it were approved? The funding agencies were anything but sanguine about shelling out more money for such a doubtful experiment, when they were trying desperately to cut down remediation expenses, which had skyrocketed. They were looking for basic, effective changes. I didn't believe they would be convinced that ACE was the answer.

I listened to long explanations and watched the Chancellor go through dozens of blown up colorful charts resting on an easel. I focused on the numbers and percentages shown in the pies drawn on those charts, restrained from comments as she went over those numbers and pointed to those pies, doing her best to convince me. The Trustee-Chairman of CAPPR, also present, stepped in with arguments of his own, in an effort to support the Chancellor.

I told them bluntly that I could not vote in favor of such a test.

My answer clearly drew the lines. I was now part of the "opposition."

It was no surprise (in spite of my objections and those of other Board members) to hear Dr. Reynolds introduce and defend ACE at the October 28th meeting of the Board. She had made no discernible effort to address the comments she had received from some of us. Anticipating such a move, I had prepared a memo of my own and had distributed it prior to the meeting. I reviewed my arguments against the test, stressing that it was badly thought out, a disaster as a testing instrument, and inadequately applied even as a limited experiment. Moreover, by allowing students any number of "retakes," providing them with special tutoring in-between, and encouraging them to appeal a "Fail" grade at the end of a prolonged process, ACE was producing artificial statistics showing positive results in the face of transparent failure.

In spite of tremendous pressure on the part of the Chancellor, the Board voted down her proposal and ACE became a dead issue. The battle for control, however, continued to rage. By now, the Chancellor had come under serious scrutiny. With so much criticism battering CUNY, both the Mayor and Governor were impatient for results. Dr. Reynolds was not producing them.

Looking back, I suppose what happened next was predictable, under the circumstances. Chancellors (as well as college presidents and most deputies) were appointed by the Board, at the recommendation of search committees set up for the purpose. They could also be censured or fired by the Board. But Board members were appointed by the Mayor and the Governor — which meant that the recent Republican victory would be felt on the CUNY Board. Several vacancies had to be filled and, as everyone knows, to the victors belong the spoils. The structure of the Board was about to change; and with that, the Chancellor's chances to weather the storm of criticism leveled against her would diminish considerably. The Board would be in a position to act decisively — censuring or even firing her.

As expected, Board vacancies were quickly filled by the Mayor and the Governor. It was also assumed, correctly, that Jim Murphy, the Chairman in place and a Democratic hold-over, would soon be replaced and a new Chairman appointed by the recently-elected Republican Governor.

In February, 1997, I received a call from Albany: the Governor had appointed me Chairwoman of the CUNY Board of Trustees (the first woman and the first Italian-American to hold that position), replacing Jim Murphy (who continued his term as a Trustee). I was stunned, elated, and depressed, in that order. I had plenty of constructive ideas: in fact, I'd already started to map out an outline that took in the immediate and other problems that plagued the University; but I had no illusions about what lay ahead. I knew I had a fight on my hands. Those first six months had been difficult; the months ahead would be even more trying — how much more trying, I didn't come close to predicting.

NEWSDAY, SUNDAY, FEBRUARY 23, 1997

Pataki Names New Chief to CUNY Board

THE ASSOCIATED PRESS

Gov. George Pataki yesterday rearranged the leadership of the City University of New York, ending the 17-year reign of its board of trustees chairman and replacing its vice chairwoman.

Anne Attura Paolucci, an English professor at St. John's University, was named the new chairwoman of CUNY's board of trustees. She replaces James Murphy, who assumed the post in 1980.

CUNY graduate Herman Badillo, a former congressman and the city's first Latino deputy mayor, was appointed vice chairman. Badillo is also Mayor Rudolph Giuliani's special adviser on education and is a senior partner in Fischbein, Badillo, Wagner and Harding.

Badillo replaces Edith B. Everett.

Both Everett and Murphy will remain on the board of trustees. The chairman and the vice chairman positions are unsalaried.

Giuliani praised the appointments yesterday and said Pataki had consulted him about them.

"We were very pleased. We think this means a lot of the problems that haven't been addressed will be," the mayor said. He praised Badillo for his "tremendous knowledge of education."

The CUNY system includes seven community colleges, nine four-year colleges, a technical college, a graduate school, a law school, a medical school and an affiliated school of medicine.

Liz Willen contributed to this story.

IT'S A CHALLENGE, says Anne Paolucci of her now role as chairwoman of the CUNY board of trustees. She comes to the job with impressive credentials as a scholar.

IVY MASES DAILY NEWS

METRO *SUNDAY, FEBRUARY 23, 1997*

Pataki Appoints a Professor As CUNY Board Chairman

By KAREN W. ARENSON

Gov. George E. Pataki moved to put more of his stamp on the City University of New York yesterday, naming Anne A. Paolucci, an English professor at St. John's University, as chairman of the board and Herman Badillo, a lawyer and adviser to Mayor Rudolph W. Giuliani, as vice chairman.

"The two appointments are people who, in the Governor's view, are tough-minded thinkers who will re-examine some of the assumptions underlying CUNY and bring in fresh thinking," said Bradford J. Race Jr., secretary to Governor Pataki.

Since last summer, the Governor has named five new trustees, including Dr. Paolucci, and there had been some speculation about when he would name his own chairman and vice chairman.

In a statement yesterday, Governor Pataki thanked James P. Murphy, the current chairman, and Edith B. Everett, its vice chairman, for their leadership and commitment and said both had agreed to remain on the board.

It is too early to say how the two new top officials might shift CUNY's direction at a time when its budget continues to be squeezed and many of its campuses have been torn apart by budget battles. But Dr. Paolucci has already called for more interaction between the trustees and the faculty and the presidents of CUNY's 21 campuses.

"We have to have a healthy dialogue and hear what the faculty, the presidents and even the students are thinking," she said.

Commenting on the budget pressures facing CUNY, Dr. Paolucci said it is important to maintain "the access to excellence that CUNY provides, but to be aware of the fiscal necessities facing us. The question is how to provide cost efficiencies without doing damage to the programs in place."

Mr. Badillo was out of New York, and attempts to reach him through his office were unsuccessful.

Some faculty members expressed pleasure that the Governor had chosen an educator and scholar as chairman. "She will be a person who will understand the university from the standpoint of the faculty," said Robert S. Dombroski, Distinguished Professor of Italian at CUNY. He called her a very capable academic, organizer and administrator.

On the CUNY board, Dr. Paolucci has already become an active member. At a meeting earlier this month, she insisted that the university not proceed with its plan to give students mid-college assessment tests on a pilot basis this spring until the trustees received adequate information.

At the same board meeting, she called for the trustees to act more independently from CUNY's administration, including its Chancellor, W. Ann Reynolds. Dr. Paolucci suggested that the trustees meet at least twice a year with college presidents with no CUNY administrators present. And she proposed that the trustees prepare their own budget documents separate from the Chancellor's, and that they have their own legal committee and legal counsel.

Although Dr. Paolucci did not attend CUNY — she graduated from Barnard College and Columbia University — she did teach at City College for 10 years before leaving for St. John's. From 1986 through 1994, she was a member of the National Council on the Humanities.

At St. John's, she headed the English department for 10 years and has directed its Doctor of Arts degree program. She is expected to leave St. John's at the end of the school year.

Although more an educator than a politician, she has had long ties to conservative politicians in New York. State Senator Serphin R. Maltese of Queens said he has known her since 1963, when he was chairman of the Conservative Party in New York. Her husband, Henry Paolucci, ran as a Conservative candidate for the United States Senate.

Mr. Badillo was first appointed to the CUNY board by Gov. Mario M. Cuomo in 1990 and has been a vocal advocate of more stringent academic standards. A City College graduate and longtime Democrat, he was a Congressman, Bronx Borough President and Deputy Mayor.

He ran unsuccessfully for city comptroller on the Republican ticket with Mayor Giuliani in 1993 and has been an adviser to the Mayor on education since then.

One of the first items of business was to come up with a proper exam that would do what ACE should have done. I instructed CAPPR and the University staff working in that same area to join forces to produce an effective mid-career proficiency and performance test. This was done. The first pilot was administered early in 1998. A second test was scheduled for early 1999, when the results would be reviewed and the test adjusted, if necessary, before mandating it for all CUNY units.

Working to insure the "seamless transition" into college was, in my opinion, a crucial first step. To facilitate the long-overdue dialogue with the Schools' Chancellor, I set up, in the Spring, an "ad hoc" committee, headed by Trustee Nilda Ruiz, to study the matter. That committee met several times during the months that followed, dutifully reporting to the Board. At the same time, I set up a second "ad hoc" committee on remediation, chaired by Mr. Badillo. This committee, working with the University's Office of Institutional Research, documented the extent of remediation, the average length of stay in remediation and the overall cost. In spite of the urgent business on hand, however, the committee met only two or three times and did not suggest any action based on those findings. (The data was used much later, by the Schmidt Commission, as a starting point for change.)

During budget preparations, I also recommended to the administration that they include allocations for more "College Now" programs for other units in the system. "College Now" — a collaborative "partnership" effort with selected high schools in the community — had first been introduced at Kingsborough Community College (Brooklyn) to prepare juniors and seniors for what I called the "seamless transition" from high school into college. That program had proved extremely successful and was recognized nationally as a model of its kind. Already tried and tested, it could prove equally successful at other community colleges in the system. And a positive outcome could nudge Albany into finding funds to support the program on a wider scale. It might also induce the New York City Schools' Chancellor to work closely with CUNY, possibly including some elements of "College Now" into his own agenda for the City's high schools.

The mixed reaction to my suggestions was the first indication that other priorities were in place, that certain Trustees had other plans and were not averse to undermining mine. It was like working with an opposition government in exile — only in this case, whatever was happening was kept under wraps, for as long as possible. I had enough to worry about, but the Machiavellian in me advised caution.

From the start, it was tough going. Turning the big ship around could not be done quickly, but the major difficulty was having to work with a less-than cooperative Chancellor, and, as I soon discovered, a certain number of less-than-supportive Trustees who, in some cases, were openly hostile.

In spite of less-than-perfect conditions and with my usual perverse determination, I sought answers to problems I'd inherited as Chairwoman of the Board. Finding practical solutions for remediation was high on my list, but there were also mundane, routine matters that needed attention. I tackled these too, but even on this level I met with resistance every inch of the way.

The Press, meanwhile, was all too happy to get stories from disgruntled Trustees and administration personnel who felt threatened in their support of the Chancellor or in other ways, stories in which I was described as inarticulate, incompetent and generally inadequate as Chairwoman of the Board. It was reported that I dragged my feet and was indecisive. The *New York Times* carried an article in which an unknown source described how I mumbled at Board meetings — a piece that brought irate letters to the Governor's desk from places as far away as California. It was a concerted move to frustrate me to the point where I might resign. My plans for change seemed to pose a threat to the *status quo*, especially to the Chancellor and her supporters. Others, including several Trustees, had agendas very different from mine, and openly or privately did what they could to undermine my authority.

In spite of this atmosphere of suspicion and open hostility, I was able to implement some important administrative and academic changes and make a few "housekeeping" improvements as well, along the way — although these too came in for criticism by the "opposition," ready to challenge anything I proposed. Still, I managed the following.

☐ Board meetings were increased from six to ten a year. I also called for special meetings at least twice during my tenure.

☐ The venue for Board and committee meetings, Public Hearings, and other official gatherings, was moved from the small third-floor conference room next to the Chairperson's office to the large Kibbee Lounge on the first floor, a more fitting place for public meetings. The conference room was a tight squeeze for the ten people seated around a table that practically filled the small room, for the additional twelve seated against the walls, and for the three to five who stood throughout, just inside the closed door. The Kibbee Lounge had a huge table, the entire length of the room, that could comfortably seat thirty or more college presidents, Trustees, and delegated staff. Several permanent rows of seats, on one side of the room, were for the public.

(I often wondered whether the third-floor conference room had been deliberately chosen by the Chancellor, somewhere down the line, as an effective way to limit the number of persons who could participate in the business on hand and discourage both long discussion and public attendance.)

☐ Board space was enlarged and re-apportioned to provide much needed additional work areas for the Secretary of the Board and her staff, cubicles for Trustees to work in, a lounge, and a library. (Provision for the latter dated back to Board Minutes of 1988 but had been consistently ignored.)

☐ An "ad hoc" committee was formed to suggest ways of reducing operating costs (personnel/services/materials, etc.).

☐ An "ad hoc" committee was formed to study security conditions across the campuses.

☐ The Board considered and approved a resolution (March 24, 1997) to enable the Chairwoman to hire a full-time secretary for herself and the Board, a part-time consultant on academic affairs to serve as a liaison between the Chairwoman and representatives of the various constituencies, and a part-time researcher to help collect data and prepare memos on matters of concern to the Board generally and to the Board committees in particular. An outside Legal Counsel also was hired to represent the Board.

☐ After a long hiatus, the Board re-established contact with Albany on a regular basis. The first visit was in March, 1998. At that time Board members met with legislators, Senate and Legislative committee members, and other groups. The new initiative proved a success and was repeated the next year.

☐ "Open Forums" were set up for the first time in Board history. Their purpose was to encourage informal discussion and dialogue among the various constituencies on matters of mutual concern. They were to meet four times a year, just before regularly-scheduled committee meetings.

☐ "Ad hoc" committees were set up to monitor remediation initiatives and to encourage networking with the New York City Schools' Chancellor.

☐ At least two meetings were held with the New York City Schools' Chancellor, together with the Interim Chancellor of CUNY (once he had been chosen and assumed office).

☐ The Long-Range Planning Committee was revived, after years of inactivity, to study the Comprehensive Action Plan (CAP) I'd submitted to the Interim Chancellor in the Fall of 1997.

☐ Guidelines for presidential and other high-administrative searches, which had grown lax over the years, were streamlined; relevant by-laws reviewed and reworded to make the mechanism run more smoothly; and, most important, the Board reclaimed its role in the handling of such searches, effectively reminding the Chancellor that they were the Board's responsibility.

New guidelines for presidential searches became an immediate priority when, soon after I became Chairwoman, the Board was forced to abort two such searches they felt had been compromised. One was for a new president at New York City Technical College; the other, for a new president at Queensborough Community College. At NYCTC, the Acting President persisted in her efforts to be considered a candidate for the opening, when by-laws clearly stated that no one in her position could be considered for the permanent post. When asked for her opinion, the Chancellor agreed that the Board should stand firm. It was one of the few times we would agree about anything.

Events took a somewhat rocky course when, on April 2, 1997, outgoing President Schmeller of Queensborough Community College, rescinded his decision of May 20, 1996 to retire after thirty years of service and asked for a few more weeks on the job. The Chancellor (who officially had no vote in the deliberations), came down strongly against honoring the request for reasons hard to accept. One of the Trustees, a member of the search committee, opposed President Schmeller's request with even greater force.

It was not an unusual request. Faculty members all along had been allowed to change the date of retirement already noted on the books (within the parameters defined in the by-laws, and in some cases after having collected TAVIA money); why shouldn't the same courtesy be extended to a loyal and dedicated president? Two days later, in a rather confused "brief" by CUNY's legal counsel, where the words "resign" and "retire" were used arbitrarily and interchangeably, I was informed that President Schmeller could not rescind his earlier decision.

I reviewed the By-Laws carefully with regard to procedures to be followed by search committees and was convinced they needed tightening. Moreover, mounting evidence showed that the Chancellor might well have exceeded her authority in taking an active role in search proceedings (perhaps to insure that her candidates were in place before the Fall semester began).

On March 5th I reached eight Trustees by phone to find out what they thought about all this. Their responses convinced me that the Board should meet in special session to discuss what had happened and clear the air. I tried to reach the Chancellor as well, but I was told she was out of town. The next day, she was back and informed me she would attend the special Board meeting. (As I recall, she didn't show up.)

After noisy and tumultuous deliberations, the Board concluded that it could not tolerate flagrant disregard of by-laws, procedures, and precedents and voted to abort both ongoing searches. New committees were set up (not without loud protests from certain Trustees), new timetables, and a new competition. Fresh candidates were interviewed. By Fall, there was a new President at NYCTC and, while the search continued for a new President at Queensborough, President Schmeller was allowed to remain at his post, as he had requested.

I had grown used to criticism, but I was surprised to find myself a personal target in this case. One rumor that had been put out was that I had a special interest in Schmeller and was, in fact, having an affair with him!

These two appointments were a landmark event for the Board. They reasserted its legitimate control of the search process and gave a strong signal as to what might be expected in the future.

The new set of guidelines for presidential and other high-level search committees came at an especially crucial time, for not long after the events just described, the Board was faced with the difficult task of replacing the Chancellor. One important point the Board insisted on, in its new instructions to search committees, was that "no member of the Administration take part in the committee's deliberations unless specifically invited to join the meetings." To improve procedures in our high-level "searches" I also empowered the

Board to hire outside firms to help find the best candidates available and to provide search committees with background information about potential candidates. The earlier practice of using a staff member to "investigate" candidates and report back to the Chancellor was illegal and therefore discontinued. In addition, I set up:

☐ an "Investment" sub-committee within the Board's Fiscal Committee to review CUNY portfolios and to scrutinize periodically the firms that dealt with CUNY accounts. The sub-committee was drawn from the regular one and reported to its chairman, who was an ex officio member of the sub-committee.

☐ a committee to report on economic development possibilities that could encourage networking with private and public corporations.

☐ special committee meetings to insure Board input in budget preparations. These resulted in operational budget changes in what was submitted to Albany.

One of the charges leveled against me during this time was that I had in many ways usurped the Chancellor's job. The reply should have been obvious: in the absence of an effective Chancellor and during the time it took to find an Interim Chancellor, after Dr. Reynolds resigned in September of 1997, the Board had inherited a number of urgent administrative tasks. I didn't feel I had to apologize for having assumed some of the pressing obligations the Chancellor had not met or for the Board's having taken on a more active role in the intense drama that was unfolding. We had no choice.

The most memorable moments in that drama were three: the public outcry over Hostos Community College's administering of illegal tests in Spring, 1997; the resignation of the Chancellor early in the Fall; and the resistance to the Comprehensive Action Plan (CAP) which I had written up and handed over to the Interim Chancellor, who was prepared to take it on but did not foresee the dogged opposition that surfaced by staff and certain Trustees.

The "Hostos crisis" made headlines for weeks and intensified earlier criticisms that the Board meant to get rid of remediation and close down "Open Admissions." The situation threatened to become explosive when it was discovered that a mandatory writing test (CWAT) had not been properly administered for some time at Hostos Community College, one of the 2-year colleges in the system and the one that catered primarily to Latino students. The test being given at Hostos, which every student had to pass either before entering college or following remedial efforts, was not the test called for, in English, but an "equivalent" test in Spanish.

When the President of Hostos, Isuara Santiago, was asked to explain why the test, meant to pinpoint weaknesses and help students overcome them as soon as possible, had not been given as mandated by the By-Laws, she replied that the "equivalent" in Spanish served just as well. The Board at once informed the Chancellor and President Santiago that the test in Spanish was illegal and that a proper test in English should be administered, as required.

The Board had stumbled into a mine field but could not retreat. It had to insist (on one hand) that proper action be taken by the colleges affected (other units had been found delinquent in this), that they comply with the existing mandate, and (on the other hand), it had to do everything possible to minimize the crisis that such action would bring about.

The Chancellor and President Santiago appeared before the Board to explain why they had allowed this to happen, but all they did was rationalize and fall back on rules they had arbitrarily introduced, hoping the Board would relent. We had no choice: compliance was mandated. The Chancellor thought otherwise and stubbornly refused to follow our directives.

The circumstances called for Board action. It could not be avoided. On May 24, the Trustees passed a resolution that, in order to graduate, all students must have passed CWAT as officially described. Although it had been made clear that the exam was not an "exit" test but a diagnostic test (preferably to be taken on entry), the immediate implications of the resolution were obvious. On those campuses affected, it would mean forcing unpleasant actions at a critical time. The Press dramatized the plight of students who would not graduate because of an "exit test."

Avoiding the difficulties, The Chancellor had became unavailable until, finally, an urgent conference call from the Manhattan office of Michael Hess, the New York City Corporation lawyer, on June 5, forced her to the phone. There were five others present, besides myself, listening to the conversation between her and the Corporation's legal counsel. When Mr. Hess reminded Dr. Reynolds that she was avoiding *compliance*, that she must at once implement the instructions issued by the Board, she replied bluntly that she had no intention of doing so. She insisted that waivers should be allowed students who had not passed the test or had not taken it, resting her argument on flimsy and arbitrary grounds. The conversation went nowhere, but she must have realized even before that conference call was made, that her days at CUNY were numbered.

The battle that ensued was exploited by Press and TV. Demonstrations in front of Board headquarters were reported and filmed. The whole City was in an uproar. Representatives of minorities had a field day: their rhetoric made headlines. No one cared to hear the reasoning behind the Board's decision. The sequence of events that had forced our resolution was never mentioned — especially the fact that the Chancellor had conveniently refused to do what her job demanded: implement what was officially mandated. Perhaps she saw herself (in her public image) as the protector of the minorities at CUNY, or, more probable (and more shrewd), decided to stall for as long as she could, while sorting out her personal options for the future.

When files related to the Hostos test disappeared from President Santiago's office (they were never recovered, as far as I know), I set up an "ad hoc" committee to investigate their disappearance, to recover the missing files, and to look into charges of incompetence that had been leveled against President Santiago. Mr. Badillo asked to be put in charge of that committee and to let him handle community relations with regard to President Santiago's inevitable resignation. He had already lined up community and political groups, he said, who would in due course put pressure on Santiago and "ease her out." He also reminded me, as he had reminded the Press and TV whenever he got the chance, that he was the person who had made Hostos possible, having played a major role in giving the Latinos a college that would serve their special needs. Since he and I had been the major targets in the preceding weeks — I, as the unbending, unfeeling Chairwoman of the Board; Badillo, as a traitor to the Latino cause — I felt I should give him a chance to redeem himself. I put aside any doubts I might have had and agreed to let him handle the situation.

I was eager to settle the Hostos business and get on with other pressing matters, especially finding an Interim President to take over when Santiago stepped down; but whenever I asked Mr. Badillo for an update, he would simply say "things are coming along," he "was working on it." In November, after almost six months of waiting for results, I decided it was time to take action.

The morning of the scheduled monthly Board meeting, I instructed the University legal counsel to contact President Santiago's lawyers and come to a final agreement that would allow her to step down. Objections were raised by Santiago's lawyers. The entire morning and part of the early afternoon were spent dismissing those objections. Finally, I asked to be put through to President Santiago herself and told her I expected her resignation on my desk by 3:45 PM, before I went into the Board meeting at 4 PM. I explained that if that didn't happen, the Board would be asked to take action. She knew that from the beginning of the troubles in May, many people, inside and outside the University, wanted her fired and that the Board would have no qualms about getting rid of her, if such a motion was made.

By 3:45 that afternoon, the signed resignation was on my desk.

My decision to bring matters to a head caught Mr. Badillo by surprise. He was indignant that I had moved so precipitously, without consulting him. It was then that I realized he probably had reasons of his own for delaying. I strongly suspected that he had done little if anything to help bring closure to the Hostos situation when later that evening — after the Board had accepted President Santiago's resignation — he told the Press that not only had I been "dragging my feet" all along but that I had given President Santiago a "golden parachute" to ease her fall from grace!

I had never been a party to the negotiations. It was not my business, and I didn't get involved. To this day, I have no idea what the terms of her resignation were, besides the pension she was legitimately entitled to receive after eleven years of service. President Santiago's lawyers and University officials had worked out the terms of her separation; I never asked for or was given the details. Mr. Badillo's comments to the Press were a clear signal that I could not count on his cooperation. Looking back, I suspect he was already setting the stage for the mayoralty bid he launched soon after and possibly, also, hoping to take over the Chairmanship of the Board, howsoever briefly, if I could be forced out. Whatever the reasons for his outrageous public statements, I knew I was fighting a lonely battle in a no-win war.

There was no time to brood. I set up a search committee that worked diligently but quickly to find an Interim President for Hostos. We soon had an excellent candidate, whom the Board approved without any difficulty.

DAILY NEWS

JULY 31, 1997, p. 97

CUNY chief hits Hostos

Sez many students barely do college-level work

By RUSS BUETTNER

Daily News Staff Writer

Students at Hostos Community College are being held to such low standards that many are barely doing college-level work, a memo by City University Chancellor Ann Reynolds shows.

The internal report, obtained by the Daily News, says students at the Bronx campus have been allowed to take too many classes in Spanish — despite the college's stated goal as a bi-lingual institution.

Hostos does "not appear to facilitate students' progress toward the stated goal of mastering English" on a college level, the report states.

It also found that students' grades fall dramatically when they transfer to a four-year college — and they are in danger of losing state financial aid because they're being given too many class hours to learn math.

The report says that under the 10-year reign of President Isaura Santiago Santiago, Hostos has been "destabilized" by high administrative turnover — 13 deans replaced and six chief financial officers. It also says an audit of "certain fiscal issues" at Hostos is under way.

The July 23 memo will be provided to City University of New York trustees tomorrow. It was requested by the trustees after a scandal erupted in May

over Hostos' English language writing-test requirement.

Anne Paolucci, CUNY chairwoman, said she had not seen the memo, but that its findings "will be addressed efficiently."

The report concluded that many Hostos students were allowed to graduate without passing an English language writing test — in violation of CUNY policy.

As for math, students have been given three hours' worth of credits for math classes but actually five hours of instruction, giving them a leg up on students taking similar courses at other campuses. That's in violation of state education regulations, the report points out, and is jeopardizing financial aid.

Awilda Orta, Hostos' dean of planning, said the math course issue will be resolved by October.

The report also shows that grades at Hostos don't mean the same as those at other CUNY community colleges: Average grade-point averages fall nearly a full point, from 2.99 to 2.06, after Hostos students transferred to a CUNY four-year school. For students from other CUNY community colleges, the fall was only a half point, from 2.76 to 2.26.

Professors said that's because Hostos students are coddled in remedial courses and take too many courses in

Spanish. "Santiago is in the remedial business," said one professor. "What she's done is pervert bi-lingual education."

Some students at the campus yesterday agreed.

"We already know Spanish. We need to learn in English. That's important," said Ana Infante, 22, a Dominican Republic native and two-year Hostos student.

But Yamile Mendez, president of student government at Hostos, defended Santiago.

"Our degrees are being devalued and graduates are not getting jobs because of the [trustees' and the chancellor's] political attacks," Mendez said.

With Rafael A. Olmeda

The New York Times THE NEW YORK TIMES METRO SATURDAY, DECEMBER 27, 1997

Deal Is Sought To Persuade

Hostos Leader To Step Aside

By KAREN W. ARENSON

The City University of New York is negotiating to have Isaura Santiago Santiago, the president of Hostos Community College, step aside voluntarily following criticism that the bilingual college in the South Bronx has lax academic standards.

University officials negotiating with Dr. Santiago's lawyer have drawn up a tentative severance agreement calling for her to step aside as active president on Jan. 1, but allowing her to retain her title and salary through August 1999.

The chairwoman of the university's trustees, Anne A. Paolucci, said yesterday that no agreement has been reached yet, but she said that efforts to remove Dr. Santiago were under way.

"We are hoping she will step down voluntarily," she said, adding that the negotiations are "not mature" yet. She said that she has not yet seen any document.

Another top CUNY official, speaking on condition of anonymity, said the document was a draft intended to serve as a vehicle for discussion.

The tentative agreement on university stationery has been circulated among some of the university's trustees and also among some CUNY and Hostos officials. A copy was provided to The New York Times by a person critical of the proposal.

Dissatisfaction with Dr. Santiago has risen steadily since May, when the university's trustees learned that students at Hostos were not being required to pass an English-language writing test that the trustees believed was necessary for graduation from all CUNY colleges. More than three-quarters of the students at Hostos speak English as a second language.

Efforts were made to reach Dr. Santiago by asking the security desk at Hostos to forward a message to her, but no responses had been received by yesterday evening.

City University presidents serve at the pleasure of the CUNY trustees and are not under contract. But people close to the trus-

tees said that by reaching a swift settlement with Dr. Santiago, the board hoped to avoid a messy battle and to start work on correcting the college's problems. Dr. Santiago has been president of Hostos since 1987.

The draft agreement, which is being negotiated with Gladys Carrion, Dr. Santiago's lawyer, calls for Dr. Santiago to continue to receive her annual salary of $127,575 through August 1999 while she takes sick leave, study leave and annual leave.

Under the deal being negotiated, she would also receive her housing allowance of $1,420 a month through 1998. When she officially steps down as president, the draft says, she will become a professor at the City University Graduate School for at least two years at $99,277 a year.

In May, after Hostos was criticized for its graduation requirements, the CUNY trustees voted just before commencement to require all students to pass the writing test to receive their diplomas. The trustees scheduled special last-minute tests to give the students another chance. Only 13 of the 104 students who took that emergency test passed.

The trustees later learned that students at other colleges were also being allowed to graduate without passing the examination. But the board believed that the standards at Hostos were so weak that it set up a committee to examine the college's performance. The committee is headed by the trustees' vice chairman, Herman Badillo, a frequent critic of CUNY standards. It is scheduled to meet on Monday to discuss the proposed severance agreement and other issues.

The trustees also brought in outside auditors to look into the college's finances.

University officials said yesterday that settlement terms will have to be discussed by the trustees.

"The university has entered into no agreement whatsoever," said Rita Rodin, a spokeswoman for the university. "There are no signatures."

Dismissing a sitting college president is always ticklish. But some of the CUNY staff and officials who have seen the draft that circulated

this week said it was more generous than other agreements that City University had reached with presidents whom it wanted to resign. They said that the housing allowance and the length of the paid leave were unusual.

The draft, which specifies that the terms are to remain confidential, says that while Dr. Santiago holds the president's title, but is not active as president, she will not be allowed to use any college credit cards, vehicles or drivers or to transact business on behalf of the college.

Another issue that Mr. Badillo's committee will consider Monday, some CUNY officials said, involves a break-in this month at an office at Hostos that contained questions for the university's writing test. In a letter to trustees this week, the officials said, Interim Chancellor Christoph M. Kimmich expressed concern that Hostos officials did not report the incident.

DAILY⊚NEWS (Metro) January 5, 1998

Pol blasts CUNY for 'lynching'

BRONX — Bronx Assemblyman and Democratic Party chief Roberto Ramirez has gone to bat for departing Hostos Community College President Isaura Santiago Santiago, charging unfairness over a dispute involving her financial settlement package.

In a letter last Wednesday to Anne Paolucci, chairwoman of the City University of New York's board of trustees, Ramirez charged the board turned what normally would be an "internal confidential administrative practice . . . into a public lynching."

The discovery of an unreported break-in at a college office where English writing tests were stored led CUNY officials to suspend talks on a possible severance deal for the outgoing president of the bi-lingual Bronx school.

Isaura Santiago Santiago of Hostos College.

---

el diario/La Prensa
Fri. Dec. 11, 1998

CUNY Students Will Have to Take English Exam
By María Vega
Translated by
Office of University Relations of The City University of New York

Forty-five ex-students of Hostos Community College will have to come back to take classes and English exams in order for them to get approval for their graduation, if a court ruling issued this week is sustained.

The forty-five were part of a group of students who graduated last year without taking an English exam imposed as a requisite days before the graduation.

The controversy for the exams gave bad reputation to the college, because more people saw Hostos as a school where it was possible to graduate without knowing English.

Due to the scandal, the then Hostos President Isaura Santiago Santiago lost her job, as did her entire cabinet.

Affected students had taken an English exam exclusively designed for Hostos Community College.

However, the Board of Trustees of The City University of New York decided that that exam was not acceptable.

On May, 1997, five days before graduation, the Trustees, lead by Anne Paolucci and Herman Badillo, dictated that students who had not passed the exam used by some of the rest of the system colleges, were not allowed to graduate.

Dozens of students who had not taken or passed the exam required by the Trustees could not get their diplomas.

Those students sued claiming that the Trustees' decision was arbitrary and capricious. A Supreme Court judge agreed and ordered the issuing of diplomas to the students. However, the Trustees appealed immediately. The outcome of that appeal is the decision made public this week.

Four judges who signed the decision said that the Trustees had not acted arbitrarily or capriciously. The exam required by the Trustees, according to the judges, had been a requisite at Hostos Community College since 1979.

The judges said also that the college does not have the authority to alter the general requirements of the University System, and therefore, it had no authority to substitute its own exam for another English exam.

The decision mandates that the college has to offer free tutoring to affected students in order to prepare them for the exam. Hostos Community College spokesperson Ramon Rodriguez said yesterday that the administration will do so.

Meanwhile, Julio Alcantara, Hostos student leader, said that the judges had taken a "discriminatory" decision.

"Those students had gone through a series of calamities," Alcantara said. "Today, they have no recourse." He also pointed out that the English exams controversy is a first step toward eliminating bilingual education and close doors to Hispanics.

He said that the students will take their case to the court of appeals, the State's highest court.

Other problems still loomed large.

All through the summer, the Chancellor had been on the firing line. Her non-compliance in the Hostos crisis, however, was not our only concern. On June 26, 1997, I'd sent her a memo — the fourth — requesting explanations in matters that had come to our attention, especially what had to be construed as unofficial absences on June 6, 10, and 16 and unreported income from outside sources. The memo read in part:

As you know, the Board of Trustees set forth explicit procedures with regard to approval of extended absences from the workplace in its *Minutes* of September 24, 1990 (6B., p. 222), and the *Terms and Conditions of Employment for Staff in the Executive Compensation Plan* (p. 12) clearly states that reporting is mandated for any professional absence of over 2 consecutive days in any one month of the year. It is also clear that the "Employer" to whom the Chancellor must report absences of more than 2 consecutive days in any one month is the Chair and Vice-Chair of the Board of Trustees. Honoraria, stipends, and reimbursements of over $1,000 during any one year, from any one source, agency, and/or sponsor organization other than CUNY must also be reported.

I urge you, once again, to comply with this official request and to provide me with the following by July 1.

☐ Signed Time Sheets for March, April, May, and June.

☐ Signed list of absences (over two consecutive days) for each of those months, together with places visited, length of each trip, sponsor organization(s), and reason(s) for absences during each of those months.

☐ Signed account of honoraria, stipend, and/or any other moneys received for absences during each of those months from agencies, sponsor organizations, etc. other than CUNY.

☐ Signed account of projected absences of over 2 days for July and August, together with reason for absences, length of absences, sponsor organization, expected honoraria, etc.

I must also remind you that time sheets and the information listed above with regard to completed trips and absences must be submitted to me, as a routine matter, at the end of every month.

I had no illusions that she would cooperate. But serious allegations had been received by my office and called for answers.

In a meeting I had requested, with Mr. Badillo also present, the Chancellor insisted that she had done nothing wrong, that when she first took office she had received assurances from someone in Albany, a "verbal agreement" that excused her from reporting such information as I had requested. We reminded her that no one was empowered to do that; the By-Laws were unambiguous. Any income over $1,000 had to be reported, as well as extended absences from the workplace. She persisted in claiming special privilege, and the meeting ended in a standoff.

She must have known that since questions had been raised they could not be ignored. Rumors persisted that for years she had been getting large fees for serving on several corporate boards. After our meeting, she was once again hard to reach. It occurred to several of the Trustees and to others as well that she had firmed up plans of her own and had no intention of answering our questions. She seemed to be stalling for time, while stories and rumors continued to circulate.

Once again the Board was in the spotlight: this time the controversy raged between those who supported the Chancellor of seven years, in spite of the cloud that now threatened her job, and others who saw her as a willful, self-serving administrator who had been allowed to have her way for too long. In its deceptively non-committal style, the *Times* ran a story on its front page (together with a large posed photograph), reviewing her seven years in office. Other newspapers denounced her. CUNY staff for the most part remained impassive and uncommunicative.

Again, the lines were drawn. A new battle was under way.

In a last ditch effort to assert herself, the Chancellor had made some calls of her own, right after the June 5 conference call, when she had refused to act on legal counsel's order to instruct community college presidents to administer a proper CWAT, as the Board had ruled, in accordance to the By-Laws. She had contacted several Board members to find out where they stood. In a memo addressed to me later that same day, she reported that "the majority of Board members . . . did not concur with [the Chairwoman's] belief that [the Chancellor] had been remiss in addressing the recent writing testing problems at Hostos Community College." She had conveniently forgotten or was brazenly ignoring the fact that nine days earlier the Board had voted overwhelmingly (one negative vote only) in favor of compliance. The Board had clarified its position in that resolution and reaffirmed a policy that was in place and had to be respected. Under the circumstances, we would have no choice but to charge her with non-compliance. Her actions were now a legal matter; there was no turning back. Eventually she would either have to implement the Board's directive and provide the information we had requested or come under censure and, very likely, be asked to leave.

She could not be reached when the Board tried to do so, prior to its scheduled meeting in September. Instead, on the 15th of that month, she sent in her resignation — a blunt three-line memo informing the Board of her decision. All pretenses had been dropped. She was moving out quickly. It was an open secret that she had a new job waiting at the University of Alabama.

The New York Times

June 25, 1997　　　B3

CUNY Board's Leader Says Chancellor

Is Under Review and Suggests She Resign

By KAREN W. ARENSON

Escalating their attacks on the performance of W. Ann Reynolds, the Chancellor of the City University of New York, the new chairwoman and vice chairman of the university's board said yesterday that they would assess her performance in coming months to see whether she should continue in her job.

But the chairwoman, Anne A. Paolucci, also suggested that Dr. Reynolds could ease the process by simply resigning.

Dr. Paolucci and the vice chairman, Herman Badillo, criticized Dr. Reynolds for failing to monitor the performance of students at CUNY's 21 branch campuses sufficiently, for tolerating grade inflation, for failing to inform them about important problems on campuses, and for creating an environment of intimidation that made college presidents unwilling to give information to trustees.

Board members recently stepped up their public criticism of Dr. Reynolds following their decision to require that students at CUNY's six community colleges, including Hostos in the Bronx, pass a university writing test to earn their degrees. When they made their decision, board members say, they thought they were simply reinforcing existing policy, since Dr. Reynolds had assured them that all the colleges already required the test.

They also say that the community college presidents, who were at the board's meeting, failed to tell them that most of their colleges did not require the test.

The board was recently reshaped by Gov. George E. Pataki and Mayor Rudolph W. Giuliani, and while some trustees still strongly support Dr. Reynolds, who was named to the post seven years ago, the new board majority has been increasingly critical. The complaints about Dr. Reynolds, made during a meeting yesterday with editors and reporters at The New York Times, were their strongest yet.

Also attending the meeting was Ronald J. Marino, the chairman of the board's fiscal affairs committee, and a lawyer, Michael D. Hess, of

---

New trustees have intensified criticism of the head of community colleges.

Chadbourne & Parke, whom the board recently hired as its own counsel. Dr. Reynolds did not attend.

Contacted after the meeting, Dr. Reynolds declined to be interviewed but issued a statement reiterating her desire to work with the trustees: "Whenever new trustees are appointed to a higher education governing board, the chief executive officer is obliged to adjust to new expectations. I welcome the opportunity to work with all trustees to assist in the formulation and implementation of new policies to further advance CUNY's mission and well-being."

Despite their criticisms, the trustees yesterday said again that they had no formal plan to dismiss her. But Dr. Paolucci suggested strongly that the Chancellor should resign, citing a recent article in The Chronicle of Higher Education, which she said made the case that when presidents or chancellors do not agree with or implement the policies of their boards, they should leave.

Chancellor Reynolds, however, has given no sign she will do so. Asked whether they had the nine votes on the 16-member board necessary for dismissal, Dr. Paolucci quickly responded, "Oh yes, we have the votes." Mr. Badillo hedged a bit, and said it might be close. Mr. Marino said it is "up in the air."

Dr. Paolucci then added: "There isn't a block of votes. There are new people on the board who vote with us some of the time, but are not always in accord with us."

"I can't say the new trustees will vote as a block," she said, alluding to Alfred Curtis and Kenneth Cook, the newest Pataki and Giuliani appointees, who joined the board last week.

Dismissing the Chancellor, Dr. Paolucci said, is a process that "has to be explored and discussed very carefully. We have to go along with what we have until it can be discussed in clear terms."

Complicating the issue, Mr. Marino added, is that the Chancellor "is not an incompetent person."

"If she was," he said, "it would be easy. This is a very competent, very skillful, very intelligent person. The issue is more one of, can a chief executive work with a new group of trustees who view their fiduciary responsibility very differently from the former board, which appears to have taken a more passive role."

"There might be philosophical differences between our views and the views of the last board," Mr. Marino continued. "So it is only fair to give the chief executive time to deal with these differences, and to provide us with adequate time to evaluate her."

He and his colleagues said that they would be watching the Chancellor's actions on such issues as remedial classes, grade inflation and the budget, as well as English as a second language.

At the board meeting on Monday, the trustees asked the Chancellor to report to them by Aug. 1 on whether the community colleges have been requiring the university writing test for graduation, and if not, what re-

quirements they have imposed.

They also told Dr. Reynolds to direct the colleges to require the exam for all graduates. And finally, they asked for her recommendations on how they should reprimand the community college presidents for not being more forthcoming.

And Mr. Badillo said the Chancellor had let the colleges inflate grades. He said that at Brooklyn College, one of CUNY's strongest four-year colleges, nearly half of the college's 1,450 graduates in 1996 graduated with honors of cum laude, magna cum laude and summa cum laude. He also said that at Hostos Community College, the bilingual college he helped to found, half of the students were getting A's and B's.

A 22   L   *THE NEW YORK TIMES* /**LETTERS** THURSDAY, JULY 10, 1997

CUNY Can Do Without a Chancellor's Office

The New York Times

To the Editor:

"Intramural Warfare at CUNY" (editorial, July 7) deplores the conflict between Chancellor W. Ann Reynolds and Anne A. Paolucci and Herman Badillo, the chairwoman and vice chairman of the City University of New York's board of trustees. You say the conflict is creating a crisis that may "cripple a valuable institution." This overestimates what goes on at the Chancellor's central administrative offices and underestimates what goes on at the university's 21 campuses.

The central administration run by Chancellor Reynolds has few functions that are not already taken care of at the individual community and senior colleges, which have their own budget offices, deans, provosts and presidents. Many campuses were established long before being merged into City University in the 1960's. These campuses functioned brilliantly in their heyday without the oversight of any chancellor.

The central administration, which handled only admissions and testing standards at first, took over the budgeting process in the 1980's. Hold-

ing this new power, the Chancellor has over the past decade begun a vast series of "initiatives" to take over academic areas that at private institutions are the traditional purview of the deans and faculty.

This has resulted in duplication not merely of administrative functions, but also of academic operations like the centers for remedial classes the Chancellor has created that wastefully compete with the remedial education already going on at the various campuses.

When Dr. Paolucci suggests it would be easy to find an interim chancellor to replace Dr. Reynolds, she has not gone far enough. CUNY's colleges would function more effectively if the enormously expensive central administration were simply eliminated. The money saved — perhaps 30 percent of CUNY's budget — could be put into the classroom where it belongs.   DAVID HENRY RICHTER

Flushing, Queens, July 7, 1997
The writer is director of graduate studies for the English department at Queens College.

The Board quickly moved to find an Interim Chancellor.

In this action, as in previous ones, I was forced to take the initiative. All kinds of rumors reached me about the Mayor's preferences and the Governor's, but I was not prepared to act on rumors. Two months after Dr. Reynold's resignation, and after a thorough investigation of the candidates, the Board voted in, as Interim Chancellor, Dr. Christoph Kimmich, who had served many years as Provost of Brooklyn College. It turned out to be an excellent choice.

Soft-spoken, dedicated to CUNY, Dr. Kimmich quietly assumed his new duties and helped stabilize both the University's academic and financial situation. I valued his experience and his lucid mind. We worked extremely well together.

THE WEEKLY NEWSPAPER OF NEW YORK STATE GOVERNMENT

The Legislative Gazette

ALBANY, NY

JANUARY 5, 1998

THE LEGISLATIVE GAZETTE

New chancellor

Dr. Anne A. Paolucci, chairwoman of the City University of New York Board of Trustees, welcomes new Interim Chancellor Christoph M. Kimmich. Kimmich, who earned his Ph.D. from Oxford University and has served as Brooklyn College provost and vice president for academic affairs since 1989, will serve while a search continues for a permanent chancellor.

Dr. Kimmich continued as Interim Chancellor — together with Patricia Hassett (Vice-President for Finance and Budget at Brooklyn College), whom the Board had chosen as Interim Deputy Chancellor — for almost two years. Eventually Dr. Matthew Goldstein, former President of Baruch College, who had left to become President of Adelphi, returned to CUNY as its new Chancellor. Dr. Kimmich returned to Brooklyn College, as its new President.

While still Chairwoman, I watched Dr. Kimmich deal efficiently with several serious problems that had been waiting for Administration action. One was to find ways to restore the reputation of the beleaguered nursing and education programs. Many of these had come under harsh criticism from Albany. The poor preparation in CUNY's teacher-programs was especially targeted, since those programs furnished 80% of the New York City's public school teachers.

He also took on the Comprehensive Action Plan I had submitted to staff members, after Dr. Reynold's resignation. Dr. Kimmich, according to protocol, asked for input from his committees, who produced several versions of the original. I didn't want to rush things. CAP was a long-range blueprint designed to tighten the lines of communications on every level and to put new strategies in place in a systematic way, especially new remediation initiatives. On the other hand, it was a cohesive and integral plan that could be launched without too much fuss.

Specifically: CAP mapped out the sequence that would insure proficiency in basic skills, cooperation among the constituencies, periodic assessments of new and existing programs, and carefully-monitored new remediation strategies from bottom up. It began by describing the need to network closely with the New York City Public Schools; for CUNY's Chancellor and the Chancellor of Schools to devise better ways to prepare high-school juniors and seniors for entering college. It then went into projected remediation measures that would improve proficiency in basic skills quickly and effectively once students were admitted — especially more intensive "Summer Immersion" courses and additional "College Now" partnership programs. The increase in the number of "Summer Immersion" courses offered in the summer of 1997 had resulted in a stunning increase in admissions that Fall. "College Now" — already recognized as a national model — would produce equally positive results if made available on other campuses. These were good starters. The plan also projected the gradual elimination of remedial courses in the four-year colleges.

What CAP described was a re-ordering and overall tightening of what was already in place and working, and the introduction of new initiatives where needed.

To expedite matters, I had distributed copies of CAP to top-level administrative staff even before Dr. Kimmich was brought in. I watched as they scanned the pages. A stunned silence followed. After the initial shock wore off, they began asking questions, but it soon became obvious that they were not ready to discuss the plan in any way.

A copy of CAP had also been sent to the Governor. I described its contents as a "blueprint for moving ahead toward reconstituting standards in both the senior and community colleges" and repeated its major premise: that "new entry and exit requirements beginning February 1, 1999" would insure that students by then "will have overcome basic deficiencies before being accepted for regular course work." The plan would require a certain redistribution of tasks and faculty, as well as some additional funds. It would also require close cooperation with the New York City Schools' Chancellor. It was a clear signal to CUNY constituencies and to the community at large that things were moving in the right direction.

At the beginning of April, I had informed the Governor's office, as a courtesy and to keep the lines of communication open, that I soon intended to ask the Board to consider and approve CAP. An aide to the Governor contacted me to say they were pleased with the document and promised to get back to me. As things worked out, I never heard from him again: he had left his job abruptly on April 6. No one else tried to contact me.

In the months that followed, the Administration submitted three revisions of CAP for general approval. The Interim Chancellor and I also took time to meet personally twice with Mr. Thompson, New York City Deputy Schools' Chancellor, setting a precedent for regular meetings in the future. In answer to our several concerns and in the light of our efforts to get things rolling, Mr. Thompson assured us that they would soon do away with "social promotion," perhaps the most serious criticism leveled against the schools. They were also thinking of extending the school year. And, yes, they were ready to collaborate with us in every way to improve the preparation of juniors and seniors aiming for college. Another piece of good news was that Albany would soon mandate regents exams in the schools. The time was ripe for launching the multi-level restructuring outlined in CAP.

The document had been given also to the Long-Range Planning Committee, recently reactivated and headed by Mr. Badillo, with express instructions for feedback, as their top priority item on the agenda. In the Spring of 1998, I discovered to my dismay that the Committee had not been meeting as expected and there had been no feedback. Instead, sometime in May, Mr. Badillo handed me a short statement that fixed a timetable by which the four-year colleges were to dismantle all remediation programs.

I tried to explain that, taken out of the larger context of CAP such a move might gain publicity and even praise but that remediation on that level should not be the immediate priority: it was less problematic than in the two-year colleges, where the matter was urgent and should be addressed first, before going on to the next level. I tried to explain that the sequence established in the CAP document was essential for overall success. I also cautioned him that the statement, as he had worded it, was ambiguous and misleading in a number of places and would certainly be questioned if he presented it to the Board in the form he had handed me. His reply was a terse "You can't change a single word!"

THE WEEKLY NEWSPAPER OF NEW YORK STATE GOVERNMENT

The Legislative Gazette
ALBANY, NY

—— MARCH 30, 1998 ——

CUNY trustees to examine chancellor's action plan

Tired of the attacks on the City University of New York (CUNY)? Interim Chancellor Christoph M. Kimmich might have an answer.

The plan calls for a cooperative exchange of resources between CUNY and New York City public schools, a summer school for students who need remedial assistance prior to enrollment, requires a Scholastic Aptitude Test or Test of English as a Foreign Language score with application, offers refresher courses for adult students, limits remedial course repeats for the associate degree, limits the time a student can complete pre-college preparatory course-work, a competency exam after the remedial

sequence, and a strengthening of the advisement program.

If CAP is approved by the Board of Trustees, it would start in February of 1999, and be subject to an initial review 18 months later.

Kimmich submitted a draft of his Comprehensive Action Plan (CAP), which is designed to raise standards, to the CUNY Board to Trustees. Anne A. Paolucci, chair of the board, said the plan would be discussed at today's board meeting.

Actually, he was kicking down an open door (no pun intended); the senior colleges had had minimal remediation for years. (An interesting point: when I questioned one president who kept insisting that they had "zero" remediation at his college, he finally had to admit that they did in fact have remediation but called it a variety of other names.) It was easy enough to discontinue (or reroute) remediation in the senior colleges. But what about the community colleges? I was opposed to jumping to what appeared to be an easy solution on the senior college level; Mr. Badillo's resolution was no answer to the long-term disorder that was affecting the weaker parts of the system.

I didn't linger on why he wanted to push that resolution through; my immediate concern was his peremptory demand that the resolution be put on the agenda for the next Board meeting. He seemed sure of getting the votes he needed, mine included: indeed, how could I reasonably *not* vote for something that was part of the blueprint I had worked out? I was caught between the rock and the hard place.

The resolution was premature and poorly written; but at the May 26,

1998 Board meeting, Mr. Badillo moved that the Trustees accept it. There was, as expected, much confusion as to what exactly was being approved, much discussion of the wording of the short paragraph we were being asked to accept — but, in the end, after a number of changes, the motion passed.

The opponents of change, students (minorities especially) who were convinced the Trustees were trying to make things hard for them, politicians who saw this as an opportunity for soap-box tirades against me and certain other Trustees, made the most of the drama. Newspapers carried stories and pictures, television stations carried live and taped commentaries and action shots describing or showing police holding back demonstrators; police vacating the public section of the Board room, on my orders, so we could get on with our business and not be constantly interrupted by yelling and shouting; police forcing people out, police hauling demonstrators into vans.

Outside Board headquarters, faculty members, some wearing their academic caps and gowns for greater effect, mingled with students and other supporters to shout the all-too familiar refrain about the Board having put an end to remediation and "Open Admissions." The chaos on 80th Street was recorded and taped for posterity that evening, on all the major channels.

No one bothered to note that the resolution, out of the larger context of CAP, did not hail the harsh revolution the Press and the campus activists made it out to be, that it was nothing more than a rhetorical gesture addressing what was essentially a minor issue within the larger picture: once entry-level problems were resolved, it would be easy enough to eliminate altogether remediation at the four-year colleges, without resorting to hard measures. Still, the resolution succeeded in diverting attention from the urgent need to improve the situation at the community colleges.

Like the emperor's new clothes, Mr. Badillo's motion was praised by many, anxious for change, as a major event; no one (besides me) recognized it as the illusion it truly was. No one (except me) mourned the fact that CAP had been effectively torpedoed.

DAILY ◉ NEWS

450 W. 33rd St., New York, N.Y. 10001

CUNY reform
springs a leak 3/98

CITY UNIVERSITY'S REFORM package du jour is called the Comprehensive Action Plan. But, as the plan withers under the bickering of a fractious board of trustees, it is painfully evident that when it comes to action and CUNY, the twain shall never meet.

This time, the blame falls squarely on board Chairwoman Ann Paolucci. In the 14 months since she was appointed by Gov. Pataki, Paolucci has gone from hope to disappointment. Unable to unite the board around a clear plan or even articulate what she herself is committed to, Paolucci is squandering the momentum for reform that she inherited. It is a situation that cries out for action — either by Paolucci or a successor.

To her credit, Paolucci did manage to force out Chancellor Ann Reynolds, the unrepentant standard-bearer of no standards. But that was nearly a year ago. Today, most of CUNY's 17 undergraduate campuses remain what they were under Reynolds: second-chance high schools with no clear demand to change. The clock is ticking. But, sadly, Paolucci, an esteemed academician, does not seem to know what time it is. Pataki must set her straight: The time is now.

Now for the trustees to agree to set strict admissions standards, phase out remediation and sever the automatic admissions link between two-year and four-year colleges. Now for raising graduation rates. Now to end grade inflation. Now for Paolucci to give the college presidents benchmarks and order (not ask) them to come up to snuff — or send them packing.

Now, now, now.

The CUNY board's membership will not change for a year, when the terms of the two staunchest opponents of change, Edith Everett and James Murphy, expire. And the search for a permanent chancellor promises to drag on for at least that long.

Pataki must not allow Paolucci to dither away that year in endless meetings, studies and focus groups. Says the chairwoman: "I purposely am not rushing. This is too serious to rush." She has it backward. The situation is too serious not to rush.

Taxpayers spend about $21,000 a year per CUNY student, more than the tuition of many private colleges. Yet most students enter unprepared — 70% of incoming freshmen wind up in remediation — and count on being coddled with remedial courses and wildly inflated grades. And in the end, only 9% of senior college students graduate in four years, and only 1.3% of community college students graduate in two years.

Those who doubt the urgency of the crisis should consider this: Four of the state's five worst-rated teacher-training programs are at CUNY, yet CUNY grads account for 80% of the city's new teachers. No wonder the schools are such a shambles.

It is Paolucci's job to put an end to this travesty. And Pataki's to make sure she does. Now.

DAILY ◎ NEWS

DAILY NEWS   •   Tuesday, April 21, 1998

VOICE OF THE PEOPLE

CUNY under attack

Brooklyn: Of course "CUNY reform springs a leak" (editorial, April 13); it is being stabbed in the heart by our governor and mayor! Board of Trustees Chairwoman Anne Paolucci is caught between the full-court press of politicians (and editors) who know nothing about education, and the faculty, students and some administrators who know what is needed.   *Nancy Romer*
Professor, Brooklyn College

The illusory nature of Mr. Badillo's resolution was predictably ignored by the media and the soap-box minority spokespeople and politicians who saw a chance to gain public attention with their unfounded, strident charges that we were undermining "Open Admissions." The chaos that marked the May 26 meeting soon after were followed by court actions and law suits.

By this time, it was clear that the Mayor had an agenda of his own. He had threatened publicly to close down remediation and had put forward a plan to underwrite charter schools. The Governor, on the other hand, was keeping a wary distance and was not easily accessible.

My main task had turned out to be a necessary but disagreeable one. Before anything positive could be accomplished, I had had to "clean house." I'd done that pretty effectively and was ready to focus on constructive measures, according to the large plan I had envisioned and the Interim Chancellor was ready to implement. But, by Fall 1998, I knew that the integral structure of CAP had been undermined and that any changes would likely be approached piecemeal, not as part of an organic multi-level blueprint. Any hopes I might have had about CAP were now wishful thinking. I realized, too, that the climate had shifted. A new Chancellor would be taking over, a new phase was beginning. It was up to him to accept, change, or ignore the actions already taken and to make new decisions. I could only hope that some of the Board's initiatives would not be scrapped.

Bottom line: I had served my purpose, performed long overdue surgery, brewed some new ideas. I'd handled any number of crises. I'd worked out a long-term comprehensive plan that could be implemented economically and easily, if adopted. I'd given my no-pay job my best shot, but I could not ignore the inexorable dialectic of history even in this narrow application. My job was done. It was not the job I'd hoped for as an experienced administrator and educator, but I could not be effective for much longer, working with people who sought "band-aid" solutions to serious problems and basked in the limelight insured by their public show of indignation.

In April 1999 I sent in my resignation.

Chairwoman of CUNY Resigns, Leaving Yet Another Vacancy

The New York Times   *THURSDAY, MAY 27, 1999*

By KAREN W. ARENSON

In another blow to the troubled leadership of the City University of New York, Anne A. Paolucci, the university's chairwoman, announced yesterday that she was resigning from CUNY's board on June 1.

Dr. Paolucci's resignation is likely to further unsettle the nation's largest urban university, which already has several vacancies in top positions and has been run by an interim chancellor for 18 months. Her abrupt departure with less than a week's notice comes as the university faces two potentially critical reviews, one by the State Board of Regents and another by Mayor Rudolph W. Giuliani's advisory commission on the university.

Dr. Anne A. Paolucci

"This is not a relaxed month, and the question of leadership on the board now is critical," Christoph M. Kimmich, CUNY's interim chancellor said yesterday.

The trustees are about to consider CUNY's long-range master plan, which must be submitted to the Regents by July 1. Mr. Kimmich said they probably will have to respond to the Mayor's task force report, expected next month. "These are things that require seasoned leadership," he said.

Virtually since Dr. Paolucci was appointed chairwoman 27 months ago by Gov. George E. Pataki, the university has been under attack by Mayor Giuliani and others who say it does not have sufficiently high standards. The Mayor has charged that CUNY's graduation rates are too low, that it accepts too many weak students and that it does a poor job providing remedial education. At times, some of the trustees, including Dr. Paolucci, have joined the criticism.

Dr. Paolucci said in a statement "that we are entering a new phase in the restructuring of CUNY and that a new chair should be in place for that purpose."

Dr. Paolucci's resignation creates yet another opening in CUNY's vacancy-ridden top management. The university, with 17 undergraduate colleges and nearly 200,000 students, has been without a permanent chancellor since September 1997, when W. Ann Reynolds resigned after battles with Dr. Paolucci and other trustees.

The Mayor and Governor effectively vetoed the three candidates for chancellor that Dr. Paolucci and the board's search committee, which she led, had nominated last summer, leaving the search in limbo.

In addition to an interim chancellor, the university also has an interim deputy chancellor and two interim vice chancellors, and the presidencies of five of its colleges are either vacant or about to be.

"I'm trying to avoid using the word chaos, but it certainly hangs out there in front of you," said Edward C. Sullivan, chairman of the State Assembly's Committee on Higher Education, commenting on the Paolucci resignation.

The Governor is responsible for choosing the university's chairman. He can either select a new chairman from the existing board or name a new trustee, who would require approval from the State Senate.

Although aides to Mr. Pataki have privately raised questions about Dr. Paolucci's leadership for more than a year, her announcement appears to have come as a surprise. She submitted her resignation to the Governor on Monday and informed CUNY's interim chancellor yesterday morning.

The Governor praised Dr. Paolucci for her service but had no comment on a successor, his office said yesterday.

"We'll take all the time necessary to find a qualified candidate, but only the time necessary," said William Van Slyke, a spokesman for Governor Pataki.

Because of the Governor's continued criticism of her, there has been continued speculation about possible replacements. Two names that have emerged recently are Lewis E. Lehrman, a former candidate for New York governor in 1982 and a former executive of the Rite Aid drug store chain, and Robert Price, of Price Communications Corporation, who served as a deputy mayor under

The Governor and Mayor have been critical of CUNY.

John V. Lindsay and as a CUNY trustee in 1996 and 1997. He resigned to devote more time to his business.

Until a new chairman is appointed, Herman Badillo, the vice chairman of the board and a close adviser to Mayor Giulianni, will preside over meetings.

Dr. Paolucci was a professor of English at St. John's University and director of its Doctor of Arts Degree program in English when Conservative Party officials promoted her as a candidate for chairwoman.

Although her post was not an administrative one, she said she sometimes spent as much as 60 hours a week on university work. She led the board to set tougher admissions and graduation standards and installed new tests to measure student progress. But she still found herself at odds with both Mayor Giuliani and Governor Pataki on issues such as remedial education and whether the university was moving fast enough to raise its standards.

Dr. Paolucci did not respond to requests for an interview yesterday, but said in her statement that she wanted to return to her scholarly work and that the timing seemed appropriate.

"This was not an easy decision, but after giving it much thought I felt it was right and proper to do so at this time," she said in the statement.

Some CUNY officials said that Dr. Paolucci's enthusiasm for the job seemed to have waned since the death of her husband in January. They also speculated that she wanted to leave before facing what is expected to be a critical report from the Mayor's task force, lead by Benno C. Schmidt Jr., the former president of Yale University. Yesterday, Mr. Schmidt called Dr. Paolucci "a person of strong academic values who deserves a lot of credit for seeing that CUNY needs to change itself in some fundamental ways."

CUNY chairwoman quits, ending rough 2-year ride

Thursday, May 27, 1999 • DAILY NEWS

DAILY NEWS NEW YORK'S HOMETOWN NEWSPAPER

The chairwoman of the City University trustees resigned yesterday after a bumpy tenure that witnessed landmark votes to toughen standards and accusations of political meddling by Albany and City Hall.

Anne Paolucci, who was a little-known English professor at St. John's University when Gov. Pataki picked her to run the 200,000-student system, issued a statement saying she will step down Tuesday to return to writing and publishing. She referred to her 27-month term as a "difficult period of transition" for CUNY.

After a lengthy political battle, CUNY trustees voted in January to ax remedial courses at four-year colleges starting in January 2000. Paolucci said the system was moving into a "new phase in the restructuring" and that "a new chair should be in place for that purpose."

In a written statement, Pataki called Paolucci an "untiring advocate for public education." He did not mention a successor.

Michael R. Blood

After about fourteen years as a Trustee, Mr. Badillo (who had suddenly decided to turn Republican), was made Chairman of the Board, following my departure — a brief tenure, for he had other plans. His real goal was to become Mayor of New York City. No one was surprised when he made public his intentions and stepped down from his recent appointment as Chairman of the Cuny Board to give full time to his campaign.

He lost the election (as he had lost earlier ones) but never returned to CUNY. Benno Schmidt, called in as a consultant while I was still in office, became Chairman of the Board after Mr. Badillo left.

I have not followed closely the Board's more recent deliberations and actions, but I sincerely hope that the changes being made do more than offer temporary relief to symptoms of the serious ills that have plagued CUNY in recent years, and which — in many areas — still pose a threat to the future of the University.

🗁 *FROM THE FILES* 🗁

ISSUED AFTER CHAIRWOMAN'S RESIGNATION IN APRIL 1999

CUNY Board of Trustees Accomplishments Over Past Year
Under the Leadership of Dr. Anne A. Paolucci

1. Documented extent of remediation at CUNY's two- and four-year campuses; acted to remove remediation from baccalaureate campuses so that students can start on a higher plane and end on a higher plane.

2. Initiated programs to insure that students entering CUNY are better prepared so they don't need remediation:
   - Early administration of FSATs (Freshman Skills Assessment Tests) to high school juniors is now underway so they can address deficiencies at high school level.
   - College Now expanded to all community colleges and 6,500 high school seniors.
   - CUNY professors and NYC high school teachers collaborating to implement more effective writing instruction at both levels and across curriculums.
   - CPI requirements are being steadily hiked so more students will have taken the coursework they need.
   - Summer immersion programs were revamped last summer, drawing more students, testing new remediation methods and achieving improved results.

3. Initiated a proficiency exam to insure that students who graduate with an associate's degree or move into the junior year have mastered essential writing and thinking skills.

4. Installed a new administration at Hostos Community College to restore confidence in that degree and insure that graduates are able to function and communicate in English.

5. Instructed campuses to review their grading policies to assure that grade inflation was not occurring and that policies were being uniformly applied.

(CONTINUED)

6. Instructed presidents to revamp their teacher education programs and requirements to meet higher state standards; put low-performing programs on notice they could be closed if improvements are not immediate.

In addition to raising standards, the Board has:

1. Re-established the Trustees' authority in policy matters, made the business of CUNY more open through more meetings and open forums.

2. Brought the budget process into the open for greater fairness and increased input by Trustees; introduced the concept of performance funding in the budget allocation process and are working to develop greater accountability measurements.

3. Begun a review of school missions and programs to focus resources into areas of excellence, merge overly duplicative programs and close those with poor performance.

4. Begun to review city and state training needs to insure University programs meet them.

NEWS STORIES ABOUT GOVERNOR PATAKI'S APPOINTMENT OF A.P. AS CHAIRWOMAN OF THE CUNY BOARD OF TRUSTEES

Raising the grade at CUNY

DAILY NEWS

450 W. 33d St., New York, N.Y. 10001

MORTIMER B. ZUCKERMAN, *Chairman & Co-Publisher*
FRED DRASNER, *Chief Executive Officer & Co-Publisher*
PETE HAMILL, *Editor In Chief*
DEBBY KRENEK, *Executive Editor*   ARTHUR BROWNE, *Managing Editor*
MICHAEL GOODWIN, *Editorial Page Editor*

Fall, 1997

A GLIMMER OF LIGHT is breaking through the gloom shrouding the City University of New York. And holding the lantern is the new board Chairwoman, Anne Paolucci.

In a vote that shows little confidence in CUNY Chancellor Ann Reynolds, Paolucci and a group of new trustees agreed to spend $1 million to hire their own researchers and auditors. The mission: Shed light on CUNY finances, study the performance and graduation rates of each of the university's 20 campuses and determine why so much time and money are spent on remedial courses. The results should make fascinating reading.

That the trustees had to make an end run around the chancellor is indisputable. Reynolds has presided over a disaster — one that is getting worse. Only she doesn't seem to notice.

Twenty-six per cent of incoming freshmen cannot pass 11th-grade reading or 10th-grade math tests, worse than the 20% in 1993. Even with doses of remediation nearly double the national average, only 15% of community college students finish their two-year programs in less than four years. Turn that number around and it is staggering: 85% do not graduate in four years!

The results aren't much better at the system's four-year senior colleges: A mere 31% earn a sheepskin within six years, compared with 56% in the state university system.

Last year, Reynolds inched toward reform. To enter a four-year college, students now must have taken college-prep courses in high school. Those who need more than a year of remedial work can attend only community colleges.

Sounds good. But 77% of students entering CUNY's two-year

colleges last fall required English as a Second Language courses or remedial work just to meet high school-level standards. Still Reynolds refuses to consider entrance exams.

And officials have no alternative plan. They seem content to dip endlessly into public pockets to fund remediation programs. Reynolds says the cost is $20 million, but given the vast numbers of students involved, the true cost may be much higher.

One part of Gov. Pataki's plan is a $400-a-year tuition hike. That's not likely to pass the Legislature, and it gives the status-quo gang a weapon to use against the push for standards. Indeed, the battle over tuition is a distraction that will divert attention from what really ails CUNY: the impact of paying college-level prices for a second-chance high school.

Reynolds has been put on notice. If she is serious about wanting to turn CUNY around, she had better get on board Paolucci's train. It's pulling away from the station, with or without her.

Staten Island Advance

FEBRUARY 23, 1997

Pataki changes CUNY leadership

ASSOCIATED PRESS

Gov. George Pataki yesterday rearranged the leadership of the City University of New York, ending the 17-year reign of its board of trustees chair and replacing its vice chair.

Anne Attura Paolucci, an English professor at St. John's University, was named the new chair of CUNY's board of trustees. She replaces James Murphy, who assumed the post in 1980.

CUNY graduate Herman Badillo, a former Congressman and the city's first Latino deputy mayor, was appointed vice chairman. He replaces Edith B. Everett.

Both Everett and Murphy will remain on the board of trustees. The chair and the vice chair positions are unsalaried.

The CUNY system includes seven community colleges, nine four-year colleges [including the College of Staten Island], a technical college, a graduate school, a law school, a medical school and an affiliated school of medicine.

Scholar for all seasons

New CUNY honcho's no lightweight

By RUSS BUETTNER
Daily News Staff Writer

The new head trustee of the city university system is sitting in her dining room issuing a lesson about the need for an institution to live within its means. Emphasizing her point, Anne Paolucci slices gently authoritative karate chops to the dinner table.

But a moment later, she is cupping her hands and tilting her head in a gentler discussion about the poetry and plays she has written.

"I wish I would have had more time for creative writing," she lamented.

It might be the only regret Paolucci will allow. A poor Italian immigrant child who struggled with English, she went on to a rich literary and academic career as a writer and English professor.

She was a Fulbright Scholar, a Reagan appointee to the National Council on the Humanities and founder of the doctoral program at St. John's University in Queens, where she has taught for three decades.

At 69, she sees leadership of the nation's largest urban university system as just another challenge.

"I'm not lying down to die," she said. "I hope to die on my feet."

Gov. Pataki last week named Paolucci chairwoman of the 17-member City University of New York board of trustees, the oversight body for the 21-campus system. Pataki and Mayor Giuliani appointed Paolucci and eight others to the CUNY board last summer, a move that signaled a political shift for a board that had for years been filled by Democratic appointees.

Rumors started immediately that Pataki's board would end Chancellor Ann Reynolds' reign and amend the controversial open admission policy, but Paolucci insists she's been given only one marching order — to use her good judgment.

The governor saw in Paolucci's 50-page résumé signs of a forceful and independent intellect that could breathe new life into a static board, said Bradford Race, Pataki's chief of staff.

"You don't need to spend a lot of time looking at her c.v. [curriculum vitae] to know that she has had a remarkable academic career," Race said. "The governor was awed by it."

Paolucci came to the Bronx from Rome at age 8. Her father died months later from the delayed effects of mustard gas exposure in World War I, leaving her mother with three children in the depths of the Depression.

Paolucci remembers most from those years "the difficulties. Because we had very, very little. I remember my mother shopping with one dollar for a whole week."

Young Anne spoke only Italian. At Public School 32, she earned high marks in math, but flunked English and history. Then the language clicked.

"Suddenly, I had it, and I was getting A's in every subject," she said. "But to this day, I don't remember . . . that very important change."

She then skipped three grades. And language became an obsession; her enunciation, though warm, can snap a room to phonic attention.

"I brought myself to a kind of perfection on my own," she said.

As a graduate student at Columbia College, she met her future husband, Henry Paolucci, who shares her boundless intellectual energy.

A prolific author of history and political books, he was the state Conservative Party's first U.S. Senate candidate, running against Robert Kennedy in 1964.

After their marriage, Anne Paolucci

DAILY NEWS SATURDAY, MARCH 1, 1997

taught at City College for nine years before starting at St. John's — where her husband taught history and politics — in 1969.

The Paolucci home — two apartments combined in a high-rise facing the East River from Whitestone — is simply decorated. On the walls are Paolucci's own paintings (a hobby for which she no longer finds time), paintings by friends and a collection of Peruvian masks that was a gift.

But down the long hall off the living room, the essence of the home reveals itself.

A door to the right leads to his office; a door to the left to hers. Books and files pack every horizontal surface in both rooms. This is the center of the Paolucci brain trust.

There are kept the collected works of Anne Paolucci: a book of poetry — "Queensboro Bridge" — that was nominated for a Pulitzer Prize in 1995; books of criticism, including "From Tonic to Tension, The Plays of Edward Albee"; and short-story collections, including "Sepia Tones: Seven Short Stories."

She also publishes the Review of National Literatures, a journal she founded to explore literary and cultural traditions of other countries.

"She is one of those perfect intellectuals," said Talat Sait Halman, a retired New York University professor and contributor to the issue on Turkey. "She is balanced and has imagination. She has a vivid style. Yet she has depth of knowledge and great personality."

Paolucci plans to retire from St. John's in May, creating many voids, said her supervisor, the Rev. David O'Connell.

"To say that Anne Paolucci is among the most energetic, passionate members of our faculty would not do her justice," he said.

Her encyclopedia of accomplishment was aided by a blinding focus. The Paoluccis have no children. They don't take vacations. Asked about her best friends, Paolucci gave an answer that would sadden some.

"I don't have personal friends, as such," she said, without remorse. "I don't socialize, per se. I have colleagues."

Her husband remains active in the Conservative Party. Though she's not an active player, it was the state chairman, Michael Long, who recommended her to Pataki.

"She's a very strong-willed person, but yet not uncompromising," said Long. "I think she'll go a long way in carrying out the governor's agenda."

Paolucci said she's still learning about the issues before the board. She says she doesn't necessarily oppose open admissions, but wants to maintain standards and will explore better ways to do remedial instruction.

She plans to protect programs that directly affect students, though she insists she will not yelp the sky is falling every time the budget is cut.

"We have to work within the budget; that's the reality," she said. "I think that can be done looking for cost efficiencies in certain areas."

Sunday, February 23, 1997 • **DAILY NEWS**

By George, CUNY given a shakeup

By DAVE SALTONSTALL
Daily News Staff Writer

Gov. Pataki yesterday shook up the embattled City University of New York board of trustees, naming a new chairwoman and vice chairman from within the board's ranks and promising a new "vision" for the 215,000-student system.

Anne Paolucci, a St. John's University English professor since 1969 and CUNY board member since July, is now chairwoman.

Herman Badillo, a CUNY graduate, board member and former New York congressman, was named vice chairman.

Paolucci, a Queens resident who has written four books of poetry, replaces James Murphy, who has led the board for 16 years, a period during which the 20-campus system has been criticized for lowered standards and deep cuts in educational offerings.

Badillo, a former adviser to Mayor Giuliani who now lobbies the administration on behalf of numerous clients, will replace vice chairwoman Edith Everett. Both Murphy and Everett will remain board members.

Recent studies show only about one-third to one-half of all CUNY students actually receive degrees under the system's open admissions policy. Last year, more than 80% of incoming students required some kind of remedial course work.

In an interview yesterday, Paolucci said she saw no reason to replace CUNY's top leaders, including Chancellor Ann Reynolds. "It would be presumptuous of me to even suggest that at this point," Paolucci said. "We need to cooperate."

She also offered strong support for the open admissions policy, adding that "whatever adjustments might need to be made — and I don't know what they may be at this point — the board is ready." On remedial education, she said, "There isn't a single college or university that doesn't have some kind of remedial education. We have to help the students who, for whatever reason, are not able to keep up."

March, 1997
Volume XXVII
Number 2

UNIVERSITY FACULTY SENATE NEWSLETTER

Scholar Named Board Chair

Dr. Anne Paolucci, a Professor of English at St. John's University, has been named by Governor George E. Pataki as Chair of the CUNY Board of Trustees.

Dr. Paolucci, a distinguished scholar and writer, is published widely. Among her scholarly books are Hegel on Tragedy, From Tension to Tonic: The Plays of Edward Albee, and Pirandello's Theater: The Recovery of the Modern Stage for Dramatic Art. She has also published several volumes of poems and short stories. Her published plays include Minions of the Race and Cipango! She holds a Ph.D. in English and Comparative Literature from Columbia University, an M.A. in Italian Literature from Columbia, and a B.A. from Barnard College.

Among her many honors, Dr. Paolucci has been a Fulbright Lecturer in American Drama at the University of Naples, a Visiting Fellow at the Humanities Research Centre at the Australian National University, and a Distinguished Visiting Professor at Queens College. She was also awarded an Honorary Degree in Humane Letters from Lehman College in 1995.

In addition, Dr. Paolucci has also served on the National Council of the Humanities, helped to found
(continued on page 6)

Scholar Named Board Chair

(continued from page 1)

the Council of National Literatures, and is on the board of directors of the American Society of the Italian Legions of Merit. She is a member of the American Comparative Literature Association, the Shakespeare Association of America, MLA, PEN, the Pirandello Society, and the Dante Society of America.

In Who's Who Dr. Paolucci is quoted as saying, 'There is enough room in the day for doing a number of things - and for creating "space" every so often to do one's own special work (writing fiction or poetry or plays, in my case.) Organization is all-important; but perhaps the basic premise in intellectual things is organic growth, letting "in" those things that are meaningful because they already suggest an intrinsic pattern.'

At St. John's, Dr. Paolucci chaired the English Department for ten years and currently directs its Doctor of Arts Program in English. Before joining the St. John's faculty, she taught at City College for ten years. Dr. Paolucci intends to retire from St. John's this year.

Under the leadership of Chair Paolucci, the Board will probably take a more activist role in CUNY affairs. At the February Board meeting, Trustee Paolucci proposed several changes in procedures to facilitate the deliberations and resolutions both in Board committees and meetings. These proposals included meetings between the Trustees and the University Faculty Senate, the Professional Staff Congress, and the Presidents at least twice a year.

CUNY Matters

A Newsletter for The City University of New York • Winter 1997

Governor Taps Paolucci, Badillo to Head CUNY Board

The following press release was issued by Gov. Pataki's office on Feb. 22:

Governor George E. Pataki today designated Dr. Anne Attura Paolucci as Chair of The City University's Board of Trustees. Dr. Paolucci will replace James P. Murphy, who has served as Chairman since 1980. Gov. Pataki also designated Herman Badillo to be Vice Chairman of the Board, replacing Edith B. Everett.

"I am grateful to Mr. Murphy and Ms. Everett for their steadfast commitment and leadership during their tenure as Chair and Vice Chair," Gov. Pataki said. "I am pleased they will remain as Board members and look forward to working with them to provide the highest quality education to each and every student in the CUNY system."

Chairman Murphy said, "It has been a great honor to have served as Chair since 1980. My principal focus as Chair has been and will continue to be to preserve and strengthen the mission of the University in providing access to affordable quality higher education for thousands of New Yorkers."

Gov. Pataki said, "Dr. Paolucci's and Mr. Badillo's exceptional credentials will ensure that CUNY students continue to receive the highest quality education possible as we move into the 21st century. I am confident they will bring commitment, leadership, and vision to their new roles as Chair and Vice Chair of the CUNY Board."

Mayor Rudolph Giuliani said, "Herman Badillo has a proven record on education. He has committed his career and his livelihood to the betterment of New York City schools. I am sure that Herman, a product of CUNY himself, will continue to be a role model for the thousands of students who have entrusted The City University with their hopes and dreams for a quality education."

Chancellor W. Ann Reynolds said, "We look forward to working with Chair Paolucci and Vice Chair Badillo. We share a deep commitment to the vitally important educational mission of the University."

Dr. Anne Attura Paolucci

Paolucci has been a full-time English Professor at St. John's University since 1969 and the Director of the Doctor of Arts program in English since 1982. "I look forward to working with the Governor, Mayor, City Council, State Legislature, Chancellor Reynolds, and members of the CUNY Board to continue the University's tradition of providing access to a first-rate education for all students of New York City," Paolucci said. "The

Board of Trustees will work to deliver our services as effectively and efficiently as possible, within the bounds of fiscal responsibility."

Paolucci was Chair of the English Department at St. John's from 1982 to 1991, taught as "Distinguished" Adjunct Professor at Queens College in the Fall of 1982, and was an Instructor and Assistant Professor of English at City College from 1959 to 1969.

Paolucci has received numerous honors, including: appointment by President Regan as a member of the National Council on the Humanities (1986-94); Honorary Degree in Humane Letters, Lehman College, 1995; nomination for the Pulitzer Prize for *Queensboro Bridge (and other poems)*, 1995; the First National Elena Cornaro Award of the Order of the Sons of Italy, 1993; and the City-Wide Italian Heritage Award, 1982.

A Fulbright Lecturer, Paolucci, a resident of Queens, has a B.A. in English Literature and Creative Writing from Barnard College and an M.A. in Italian Literature and a Ph.D. in English and Comparative Literature from Columbia University.

Badillo said, "As a graduate of City College, I found that my degree was the avenue of opportunity for me. I am pleased to serve on the Board in any capacity Gov. Pataki wants me to. I want to make sure the high standards that enabled CUNY to open doors for me will enable those of generations after me to benefit as well."

Badillo is currently practicing law at Fischbein, Badillo, Wagner, Harding in New York City. He currently serves as a member

Herman Badillo, Esq.

Photos: André Beckles

Her view from the bridge is full of hope and promise

Anne Paolucci's slender volume of poetry, "Queensboro Bridge," speaks to the hopeful glitter of New York.

The book, which was nominated for a Pulitzer Prize in 1995, opens with a quote from F. Scott Fitzgerald's "The Great Gatsby": "The city seen from the Queensboro Bridge is always the city seen for the first time, in its first wild promise of all the mystery and beauty of the world."

In the title poem, Paolucci explores Fitzgerald's wonder at the city's possibilities. She adds a theme of doubt or insecurity, only to emerge with Fitzgerald's optimism again.

*My favorite too, of all crossings
Into the City. Fitzgerald was right.*

*Canyons, gorges, suddenly rising
Before you, are part of a mystery
Never unraveled, a wild promise.
I understand the words,
But when I try to see what he saw.
In his leap across the span
Of his own startled vision
I'm not sure I can.
And yet, as I turn off,
The bridge behind me,
Driving faster than he ever could
Or did, down the avenue,
I know I'm in Gatsby country.*

NEW YORK POST

America's oldest continuously published daily newspaper

WEDNESDAY, MARCH 26, 1997

Time to rebuild CUNY

Gov. Pataki's and Mayor Giuliani's newly appointed trustees of the City University of New York (CUNY) — led by Chairwoman Anne Paolucci and Vice Chairman Herman Badillo — are wasting no time in tackling one of the system's long-standing problems: The remedial-education morass that still soaks up much of CUNY's resources.

Remedial education was an inevitable consequence of the CUNY's 1970 open-admissions policy, which guaranteed a classroom desk to virtually every holder of a city high school diploma — whether or not they could do college-level work.

Seventy-five percent of students now admitted to CUNY's two-year, or community, colleges need remedial education courses in math, reading, writing, or all three.

As a result, many students spend semesters, if not years, on the remedial track — so-called "college students" taking elementary- and high-school level courses. Naturally, they require a long time to earn their degrees: A CUNY study of students who enrolled in community colleges in 1990 revealed that 66 percent failed to obtain a degree in six years.

To be sure, CUNY Chancellor Anne Reynolds has already made considerable gains in raising academic standards at CUNY.

Since her arrival in 1990, Reynolds has improved matters considerably by helping institute the College Preparatory Initiative (CPI), an academic program for college-bound students in the city's high schools.

CUNY's four-year colleges now require that all remedial work be completed in the freshman year, with any additional make-up work to be done at community colleges. Since 1995, there has also been an experimental language-immersion program for students with limited English.

But Paolucci, Badillo & Co. want the changes to proceed further and faster. Badillo says he wants to consider re-establishing an entrance examination for CUNY, and suggests that remedial education could be pursued in a special high school rather than at a community college.

That the commonsensical idea of requiring students to pass a test showing they can do the work strikes many as unfair reveals how thoroughly the ideal of academic excellence has been subverted during the open-admissions era.

The new trustees have also approved funds to hire their own staff and lawyers to study all aspects of the university; they are wary of not getting sufficient cooperation from CUNY's entrenched bureaucrats.

Gov. Pataki wants to help the process of reform along by limiting state scholarship aid to four semesters, remedial courses included. That surely would limit the number of professional students marking time at CUNY.

After a generation of open admissions — and an inevitable descent into mediocrity — CUNY is now moving forward on several fronts.

For an institution that once had a real claim to academic greatness, change can't come a day too early.

28

DAILY NEWS

450 W. 33d St., New York, N.Y. 10001

MORTIMER B. ZUCKERMAN, *Chairman & Co-Publisher*
FRED DRASNER, *Chief Executive Officer & Co-Publisher*
PETE HAMILL, *Editor In Chief*
DEBBY KRENEK, *Executive Editor*   ARTHUR BROWNE, *Managing Editor*
MICHAEL GOODWIN, *Editorial Page Editor*

Summer 1997

Restoring trust by degrees

GOV. **PATAKI DAWDLED FOR MONTHS,** but he finally has put his stamp on the City University Board of Trustees. By naming Anne Paolucci as the new board chairwoman, the governor signals he is ready to join with Mayor Giuliani in the herculean task of pulling CUNY out of its decline.

Paolucci, an English professor at St. John's, has been on the board only since the summer, when Pataki and the state Senate installed a host of new members. In interviews, she has been noncommittal about any sweeping plan, saying she needs time to learn more about the 200,000 students and 20 campuses.

But Paolucci already has shown that her tenure will be different from that of James Murphy, who was chairman for 17 years. It was a reign that should have ended long ago.

Paolucci has asked that trustees be more independent of the administration of Chancellor Ann Reynolds. In terms of budgets and communications with individual college heads, Paolucci wants the trustees to have data not filtered by Reynolds.

That's a good start, for Reynolds has taken it upon herself to undermine the efforts to cut costs and raise standards pushed by Giuliani and Pataki. Reynolds, for instance, has rallied students against city and state budgets and once called all criticism of open admissions "partly sexist, partly racist." And she has resisted the workfare program, sounding as though students on welfare are entitled to handouts without reciprocity.

Changing that attitude will be Paolucci's first order of business. As for structural problems, she must must not delay in asking her new vice chairman, Herman Badillo, for help.

Badillo is a CUNY alumnus and long-time board member whose criticism centers on falling standards and their source: open admissions. He has warned that carte blanche access to a college education would devalue it. The facts prove him right.

Once one of America's premier urban universities, CUNY has seen its reputation sink with its standards. Too many campuses and classes now play the role of a do-over high school. The proud university that produced Colin Powell and a host of Nobel Prize winners now has a graduation rate of only 16% in its two-year colleges — and that's after four years.

As she learns the ropes, Paolucci will be disappointed by CUNY. But she now has the power to make a difference.

MORE ON THE HOSTOS CRISIS

December 1998

America's oldest continuously published daily newspaper

The War on CUNY Excellence

Supporters of high standards at City University this week won an important battle in the Appellate Division of state Supreme Court — but the enemies of excellence immediately opened fire on another jurisprudential front.

First, the good news.

A four-judge appeals panel unanimously upheld CUNY's power to deny diplomas to prospective graduates who cannot meet basic literacy standards.

This would seem to be a no-brainer — awarding a sheepskin to someone who can't read it is beyond bizarre — but a trial judge had found otherwise.

At issue was a decision by Hostos Community College to exempt itself from a CUNY-wide policy requiring prospective grads to pass a test that measures basic reading and writing skills.

Hostos' motives were clear enough: If it hadn't waived the test, it could have held its 1997 graduation in the back seat of a taxicab, so few kids could actually read English.

But even CUNY Chancellor W. Ann Reynolds — no strong supporter of stringent academic standards — couldn't stomach what Hostos was up to. She, in effect, canceled graduation and ordered most of the college's almost-graduates back to the classroom.

The inevitable lawsuit followed in short order — with the appellate court Tuesday permanently affirming CUNY's power to set system-wide graduation standards.

Whether this victory will have lasting significance remains to be seen, however.

That's because yet another effort to enforce perpetual mediocrity on CUNY was undertaken this week: A coalition of "civil-liberties" groups went to court effectively to derail the university's efforts to raise admissions standards to reasonable levels.

What civil rights has to do with the imposition of reasonable admission requirements at CUNY is beyond us. Still, this is New York — so we're not surprised the suit has been brought.

It seeks to give final review of CUNY admissions standards to the state Board of Regents — a panel in total thrall to the same gang of unionists, racialist zealots, ivory-tower academics and hack Democratic politicians that brought the once-world-class university to its present low state.

There are some legal subtleties in this suit that make for something less than the slam-dunk situation the Hostos case represented.

A failure to raise standards at CUNY would be good for the professors' union — but a disaster for kids who'll need a respectable degree to earn a living in New York City.

That, basically, is what's at issue.

The New York Times

THE NEW YORK TIMES **METRO** TUESDAY, JULY 15, 1997

A Judge Tells CUNY to Give Diplomas to Hostos Students

Chester Higgins Jr./The New York Times

Two Hostos students, Yamile Mendez, left, and Miguel Castillo, were pleased by a judge's decision that diplomas should not be withheld.

By KAREN W. ARENSON

Hostos Community College students won a temporary victory yesterday in their effort to get their college diplomas without passing a university writing examination.

A New York Supreme Court Justice in the Bronx, Kenneth L. Thompson Jr., ruled yesterday that the City University of New York could not withhold diplomas from any students who had met all other graduation requirements.

More than 100 students were scheduled to graduate from Hostos in June without having passed the writing test that CUNY's trustees set as a condition of graduation in late May.

Lawyers for the university said they were appealing Judge Thompson's ruling and that they expected to get a stay against the order.

Ronald McGuire, a lawyer representing the students, called the decision a "tremendous victory" for them and said that it "showed that they are blameless and are entitled to a degree."

"People have to take a look at the administration of Chancellor Ann Reynolds and the board, headed by Anne Paolucci, and ask whether they are trying to raise standards or cut costs," he said. "It turns out the board was misguided and wrong on the facts."

Judge Thompson, too, was critical of the CUNY trustees yesterday. In his decision, he said that hasty efforts to impose criteria for evaluating students retroactively were "arbitrary and capricious, and in the present case must be held to be undertaken in bad faith."

The decision to impose the test as a graduation requirement five days before graduation "was not based on informed, lucid and cogent deliberative processes," Judge Thompson said. "The obvious unfairness in changing the degree requirements immediately before graduation is manifest."

The trustees have said that they passed a resolution calling for the essay test as a graduation requirement at all community colleges after being told that, while the test was required for graduation in the university system, Hostos had substituted its own procedures.

Even after learning later that the test was not being required at five of CUNY's six community colleges, the trustees reaffirmed the requirement. Of 104 Hostos students who took the last-minute exam, only 13 passed it.

In granting the injunction, Judge Thompson said the students must put up $20,000 to cover CUNY's costs if it is ruled later that they were not entitled to an injunction. The students said they did not know how they would raise the money. Their lawyer, Mr. McGuire, is handling their case without pay.

Last month, the same judge gave the students a temporary restraining order that would allow them to graduate, but the city got an automatic stay.

Although the students were allowed to participate in the Hostos graduation ceremony, they will not receive diplomas when they are mailed out in August unless they win their lawsuit or pass the writing test.

The New York Times

THE NEW YORK TIMES **METRO** THURSDAY, DECEMBER 10, 1998

CITY   B 25

CUNY Wins Ruling in a Dispute Over Graduation Requirements

By KAREN W. ARENSON

In a victory for the trustees of the City University of New York, a state appellate division panel has upheld the university's right to withhold diplomas from students at a bilingual community college in the South Bronx who did not pass an English writing examination.

The four-judge panel ruled unanimously, overturning a lower court. "It would contravene public policy to force an institution of higher learning to award degrees where the students had not demonstrated the requisite degree of academic achievement," the panel said in a strongly worded decision issued late Tuesday.

Just days before graduation in May 1997, in the face of questioning by Mayor Rudolph W. Giuliani and others about the rigor of CUNY standards, the board's new majority made the university exam a condition of graduation at Hostos and CUNY's five other community colleges. More than 500 prospective community college graduates, including more than 100 at Hostos, were denied diplomas.

The students sued, and Judge Kenneth J. Thompson Jr. of State Supreme Court initially ruled in their favor last year. Judge Thompson ruled that imposing new graduation requirements on students just five days before graduation was "arbitrary and capricious," as well as unfair.

Ronald B. McGuire, the lawyer who represented the Hostos students in the case, said that he would try to appeal to the Court of Appeals, the state's highest court. He said most of the 100 Hostos students denied their diplomas still had not graduated.

CUNY officials reacted happily to the ruling. The chairwoman of the trustees, Anne A. Paolucci, said, "The true beneficiaries of the decision are the students of Hostos, who must be assured that the completion of their academic requirements will have credibility in the workplace and at other institutions of higher education."

The question of whether Hostos Community College students were being allowed to graduate without having met appropriate standards started the trustees of the City University of New York on their campaign to revise CUNY's standards, just 19 months ago.

A bilingual college in the South Bronx, Hostos attracts many Hispanic students for whom English is a second language. Although some Hostos students were strong — its nursing graduates, for example, score exceptionally well on the professional nursing examination — others struggled to master English.

At an emotional board meeting in May 1997, just days before graduation, the trustees made the university exam a condition of graduation. The board faulted the Hostos president for failing to require students to pass the CUNY exam and using another test instead. The president, Isaura Santiago Santiago subsequently resigned.

Herman Badillo, the vice chairman of the CUNY trustees and the sponsor of the policy on the graduation rule, called Tuesday's court decision an important one. "It is a very basic recognition of the principle — over and above the disputes — that the value of a diploma has to be preserved, and that the trustees have to have the authority, not the president of a college," he said.

The board had also faulted CUNY's chancellor, W. Anne Reynolds, for the problem at Hostos, saying it was a sign of lax management. She testified during the Hostos trial that the CUNY writing test had been a requirement for all students even before the board's action in May, although Hostos and other colleges had substituted other requirements for their students. Dr. Reynolds resigned as chancellor last year.

Concluding that the writing test had been a requirement since 1979, the appellate division judges ruled that the board's action was not "arbitrary or capricious." Furthermore, they said, officials at Hostos and the other colleges had no authority to substitute their own rules for those laid down by the university.

"The City University Board of Trustees possesses the sole and exclusive statutory authority to impose graduation and course requirements for all CUNY colleges," the judges wrote. The individual colleges, they said, "lack the authority to modify, unilaterally, course prerequisites."

The decision also specified that Hostos "is to continue to provide tuition-free remedial assistance" to prepare students for the writing test.

The college offered free workshops to the students affected by the board decision last year, and is willing to provide additional help, said Dolores M. Fernandez, the interim president of Hostos.

Hostos now makes it clear to students that the writing exam is a requirement, Ms. Fernandez said. "Whatever it is, if CUNY requires it, Hostos students will meet that requirement," she said.

DAILY NEWS

22

Facts don't matter much in CUNY's quest for Hostos prez' head

Monday, December 29, 1997 • DAILY NEWS

ISAURA Santiago Santiago, in her last days as president of Hostos Community College, sat at her desk yesterday almost in shock.

It was the Sunday between Christmas and New Year's, a time when most educators are enjoying quiet days with their families. But here was Santiago, still hard at work doing what all good teachers do: Separating fact from myth.

For 11 years she has presided over a college whose student body has the lowest income and highest proportion of immigrants with limited English skills in the country. And for most of those years, Santiago has been accorded nothing but praise for her single-minded dedication to serving the educational needs of her students.

Just five years ago, she received one of the top evaluations of any City University of New York college president from the board of trustees.

But since early this year, when Hostos became embroiled in controversy over the failure of many students to pass an English writing test, Santiago has become the prime target of a witch hunt masquerading as a search for "higher standards" at CUNY.

Like most witch hunts, this one has been big on steamy headlines and bereft of many

JUAN GONZALEZ

facts.

Take the latest "incident" — a burglary that occurred a few weekends ago in a professor's office at Hostos. Press reports the past few days have

claimed that Santiago failed to report the incident to interim CUNY Chancellor Christoph Kimmich, and that, when asked about the break-in, she told a different story than Hostos' security director did.

Further, the reports say, the break-in may have involved someone obtaining copies of the CUNY Writing Assessment Test, known as the CUNY WAT. Santiago's failure to report it has now scuttled private negotiations for a severance package top CUNY officials have offered her to resign.

I spent yesterday afternoon interviewing several Hostos officials with direct knowledge of the break-in, including Clyde Isley, the Bronx school's director of security. Isley is a retired 20-year veteran detective of the New York Police Department and the former police chief of Mount Vernon.

According to all those officials, the college administered this semester's CUNY WAT test in early December. None of those tests nor any questions for any future test was stored in the burglarized office, so there was no possibility of the test "being compromised."

"Nothing was taken from the office," Isley said, adding that because university regulations require only burglaries exceeding $5,000 be reported to the CUNY central office, he saw no need to do so.

But facts no longer matter. Anything to make Santiago and Hostos look bad is fair game. Take the press leaks several weeks ago about alleged misuse of college funds by Santiago and others.

"I've been deluged by auditors since August who have been poring over all our records," said Eugenio Barrios, a Hostos dean. "They haven't

found anything of substance wrong. Why don't they issue a final report?"

Santiago refused yesterday, under advice from her lawyer Gladys Carrion, to talk about the attacks. She decided weeks ago that staying at Hostos was impossible. Not only have the public attacks become more intense lately, but major illnesses in her family have sapped much of her energy.

"I just want to save the mission of Hostos as a bi-lingual school for the most needy," she said yesterday.

For a decade, in a school where 80% of the students are women, most of them with children, and where 40% are on welfare, Santiago has functioned not just as an administrator but as an inspiration and role model.

She has supervised $120 million in new construction, including a first-class cultural center and Allied Health program that has turned Hostos into a small oasis in an area long starved by downtown interests.

Those who say Hostos failed under her tenure have never visited the college, nor have they talked to its students, nor do they know what a wasteland the South Bronx was when Santiago arrived.

CUNY Vice Chairman Herman Badillo, who has spearheaded the attack on Santiago, claims his only aim is to improve standards.

Last spring, Badillo was named head of a committee to study the Hostos situation. In all these months, that committee has met once. It never responded to written requests from faculty leaders and administrators to meet. It certainly never thought to meet with students.

The New York Times

Civil Liberties Groups Sue City University Over Remedial Program

THE NEW YORK TIMES **METRO** WEDNESDAY, DECEMBER 9, 1998

By KAREN W. ARENSON

In another legal challenge to the City University of New York's new policy on remedial education, six civil liberties groups have accused CUNY's trustees of violating state law because they did not submit the policy to the State Board of Regents for approval.

The lawsuit, filed late Monday in State Supreme Court in New York, was brought on behalf of a CUNY professor, Sandi E. Cooper, the former chairwoman of the CUNY Faculty Senate, and three New York City high school students who say they want to attend the university's senior colleges but expect they will need remedial help.

"The whole process by which the CUNY trustees arrived at their resolution to eliminate remediation at the senior colleges was fundamentally flawed," said Jonathan D. Bassett, of Van Lierop, Burns & Bassett, a lawyer who joined the coalition of civil liberties groups in bringing the lawsuit. "The failure of the CUNY trustees to submit their plan to the State Board of Regents is further evidence of that."

The policy, adopted in May, calls for students to pass tests in reading, writing and mathematics before they are allowed to enroll in the university's bachelor's degree programs. Students unable to pass the tests by registration day would be referred to CUNY's community colleges. The policy is scheduled to be phased in beginning next September.

The groups that brought the lawsuit are the Puerto Rican Legal Defense and Education Fund, the NAACP Legal Defense and Educational Fund, the New York Civil Liberties Union, the Center for Constitutional Rights, the American Jewish Congress and the Asian American Legal Defense and Educational Fund. Ronald B. McGuire, a lawyer, also joined in the suit.

DAILY ⊙ NEWS

450 W. 33d St., New York, N.Y. 10001

Wednesday, October 1, 1997 • **DAILY NEWS**

CUNY bigs: The write test was all wrong

By RUSS BUETTNER

Daily News Staff Writer

City University trustees have voted to eventually replace a writing test that just four months ago they thought was important enough to make a graduation requirement for community college students.

The original vote to require the test — on May 27, just a week before graduation — sent hundreds of students' commencement plans into turmoil.

In response, emergency testing sessions were given this summer. And students at Hostos Community College sued the trustees, challenging their right to pass the 11th-hour requirement. The suit is still pending.

Critics of the original vote said the decision Monday night showed the trustees realized they made an error.

"They made a mistake, and some of us have been working all summer to unravel it," said Sandi Cooper, the faculty representative to the Board of Trustees.

"They should never have voted for it in the first place," said trustee Edith Everett, who was not present for the May vote. "My impression is that they know it was the wrong thing to do."

Students at Hostos, the City University of New York's only bi-lingual college, did particularly poorly on the test. During testing this summer, 95% of the students failed, even after weeks of extensive class and tutoring time.

Trustee Herman Badillo, who had criticized the Hostos administration for low graduation rates and for scheduling too many classes in Spanish, said the test results provided further evidence that Hostos President Isaura Santiago Santiago is doing a poor job.

Last week, Hostos students called for Santiago to resign, saying Hostos might be closed in a political struggle if she stays.

About 75 Hostos students, fearing the criticism of Santiago was part of a plan to close the Bronx campus, protested yesterday outside CUNY headquarters on E. 80th St., chanting, "Hey, hey, ho, ho, Badillo has to go."

Badillo, who proposed the May resolution requiring the test, arrived late to the meeting yesterday and left soon afterward without comment.

CUNY faculty members have objected to using the CUNY Writing Assessment Test to both determine a student's need for remediation and to measure the ability to write on a college level after remediation. Yesterday's resolution acknowledged that and set a review process in motion to find new tests.

Anne Paolucci, chairwoman of the Board of Trustees, dismissed critics who said the resolution represented an acknowledgment of error on the test requirement. "It's perfectly in accord with what we were thinking of back then," she said. "There's nothing changed."

Metro Report

October, 1997

The New York Times

Bilingualism At Hostos Is Receiving A Hard Look

By KAREN W. ARENSON

Thirty years ago, when Herman Badillo, as Bronx Borough President, first dreamed of opening a college in the economically depressed South Bronx, he wanted a college in which Spanish-speaking students could receive degrees as quickly as possible, learning English while taking other courses taught in Spanish.

Thus was born Eugenio María de Hostos Community College of the City University of New York, a rare experiment in bilingual higher education in America.

Today the success of that experiment is in question. City University's trustees, Mr. Badillo among them, accused Hostos last month of giving diplomas to students who do not know English, and voted that all university students must pass an English writing test to receive a degree.

"If you can't express yourself in English, you shouldn't graduate," said Mr. Badillo, who proposed the writing test requirement as vice chairman of the university's board of trustees and is Hostos's leading critic. "Bilingual means two languages, English and Spanish. You have to be fluent in English to have a career. No one would ever have approved Hostos if they thought it meant monolingual."

While bilingual education is widely used in elementary and secondary schools, few colleges have picked it up. In Florida, Texas and California, for example, all of which have large immigrant populations, college courses taught in English are the rule.

"We want students who are proficient in English," said David Spence, executive vice chancellor for the state university system of Florida, who said college bilingual education was not a big issue in his state.

English remains a stumbling block for many students.

And at Boricua College in upper Manhattan, which describes itself as the only four-year, bilingual liberal arts college in the United States, all classes are in English, although faculty members and administrators are required to be bilingual so they can help students with language problems.

"We don't believe we should give students the option of taking a degree in the United States of Spanish courses, because we don't believe it would be helpful to them," Roland Marrero, a student services official at the college, said.

At Hostos, which straddles the Grand Concourse in the Bronx just a mile from Yankee Stadium, and where more than three-quarters of the nearly 5,000 students are Hispanic, college officials defend their approach and say they are achieving their mission.

"The bilingual model has been effective in providing access to large numbers of students," the president of Hostos, Isaura Santiago Santiago, said in a recent interview in her office. "They've left here skilled. Our career programs are nationally recognized in a variety of fields. And we've been particularly effective in giving access to minorities."

"We should build on what people know, and teach them English," she added.

About 22 percent of the college's classes, mostly introductory subjects, are taught in Spanish, and many students spend term after term taking English-as-a-second-language courses. Some of the college's departments, like its highly respected health science programs, require that their students be proficient in English to enter.

Despite Hostos's success in areas like nursing and dental hygiene, where virtually all of its graduates pass state and national certification exams, English — and passing the City University writing exam — remains a stumbling block for many students. Although students at other City University colleges have similar difficulties, none of the other colleges have seen such large portions of its students repeatedly fail the university writing test. When the university offered the test to prospective Hostos graduates earlier this month, only 13 of the 125 who took it passed it.

Hostos is a tough place to run any education experiment. Not only do many students enter speaking little English, but many are poor and poorly educated.

On the writing placement examination given to all City University entering freshmen, fewer than 15 percent of Hostos's students passed last fall, a rate lower than at any other university college.

Teaching English to adults is not easy. Young children pick up new languages fairly naturally. Adults rarely, if ever, gain the proficiency that children do. Language experts have also found that adults who are more literate in their native language do better learning a second language than less educated adults.

"That's what makes this so complex," said Henry M. Levin, a Stanford University professor and expert in remedial education who is a visiting scholar at the Russell Sage Foundation in New York. "It's the dirty little secret; it's more a literacy problem."

Many immigrants who enter City University with limited English do quite well, passing the university writing test, excelling in their studies, sometimes graduating at the top of their classes and going on to elite graduate schools.

(EXCERPT)

NATIONAL CROSSTALK

A Publication of the Higher Education Policy Institute

Vol. 5 · No. 3 · Fall 1997

Ms. Machiavelli

City University of New York's controversial chairwoman

Machiavelli: Well, be sure you remember. What these people lack is proper direction from the top, proper government, real political leadership, laws that will...

Actor: Wait, wait, wait! What's all this political stuff! Let's keep politics out of it!

Machiavelli: "But you can't! That's my whole point. Like I said, it's a kind of siege! We're in a political universe from beginning to end!"

—From "The Actor in Search of His Mask," a play by Anne Paolucci, chairwoman of City University of New York's Board of Trustees.

By Joe Mathews

NEW YORK

ANNE PAOLUCCI fills her plays with bold, historical characters: Thomas More and Cardinal Wolsey, Confucius and Sophocles. She quotes *Dante* to reporters. And when not writing drama, she translates Machiavelli. Paolucci has the Prince's affection for

> *In nine short months, Paolucci has made herself de facto chancellor of CUNY's 18 colleges and 200,000 students.*

politics, particularly the broad strokes.

In February, this state's Republican governor, George E. Pataki, appointed Paolucci to the chair of the City University of New York Board of Trustees. Immediately, this 71-year-old retired English professor from St. John's laid personal siege to the country's largest urban university, criticizing it from all angles and working full-time to bring the central administration under her control. In nine short months, she has made herself *de facto* chancellor of CUNY's 18 colleges

The New York Times

VOL. CXLVII .... No. 51,083   Copyright © 1998 The New York Times   NEW YORK, SUNDAY, MARCH 1, 1998

CUNY Proposes Stricter Rules On Students in Remedial Classes

Plan Would Require Intensive Summer Courses

By KAREN W. ARENSON

Stung by criticism that it is wasting resources and lowering its standards in teaching students basic skills that they should have learned in high school, the City University of New York is proposing a sweeping overhaul of the way it handles students who are not ready for college-level work.

Under the plan, entering students who did poorly on placement tests would have to attend intensive remedial summer classes before being allowed to enter one of the university's 17 undergraduate colleges. Some remedial instruction would also be moved out of the college curriculum into special institutes run by the colleges.

All students, including those at the community colleges, would be required to complete their remedial work in one year. Those who could not would be allowed to take additional instruction through adult education or special immersion programs, but could not continue as enrolled students at the community colleges. Students who failed a remedial course twice would also be directed to intensive workshops or adult education classes.

The proposal, drawn up by CUNY's interim Chancellor, Christoph M. Kimmich, with the backing of the chairwoman of the university's board of trustees, Anne A. Pao-

lucci, would represent one of the most aggressive efforts by any public university in the nation to deal with the chronic problem of underprepared students. Nearly all colleges and universities offer students remedial classes to make up for deficiencies. Last fall at CUNY, 22 percent of entering freshmen failed all three of CUNY's placement tests in reading, writing and mathematics, and more than 70 percent failed at least one, placing them in remedial classes. , The plan is being circulated among trustees and other university officials this weekend and needs the board's approval. The plan calls for implementation by February 1999.

Top CUNY officials expect some version of this comprehensive plan to win board approval. "Whatever differences there may be on the details, I believe the board will get behind this," Dr. Paolucci said. "The timing is right. There is such pressure on the schools now. We can't do much unless the schools do something, too."

She said that the committee on long-range planning, which she heads, will take up the plan on Thursday, and that she hoped to be able to present it to the board at its meeting March 23. "It is a flexible document and we will continue to refine it up to the 23d," she said.

University officials said the comprehensive plan had been developed to deal with the continued criticism by Mayor Rudolph W. Giuliani and CUNY trustees that the colleges' preoccupation with remedial classes was dragging down the university's standards.

The Mayor has said that unprepared students should not be admitted to the university and that the remedial education function should be conducted by private companies or by private universities.

Randy M. Mastro, New York City's Deputy Mayor for Operations, said yesterday that he had received a copy of the plan but was withholding substantive comment until he had had time to study it in detail.

Dr. Kimmich wanted the university to consider a broad program rather than deal with smaller piecemeal solutions that have begun to surface in recent months.

Changes contained in the proposal, which is called the Comprehensive Action Plan, include the following:

¶All recent high school graduates applying to CUNY would be required to submit their scores on the S.A.T., which is traditionally used by selective colleges and universities but rarely for community colleges. Louise Mirrer, CUNY's vice chancellor for academic affairs, said that besides providing more information about incoming students, requiring S.A.T. scores would force applicants to think more seriously about college and the preparation they need.

¶Adults who have been out of high school and simply need to brush up on skills they once knew but may have forgotten would have the option of taking "refresher" courses, rather than regular remedial classes.

¶Students in remedial courses would be required to pass university approved competency exams before being allowed to move on to college work. Currently each college determines when students are ready.

¶CUNY will cooperate further with the New York City public schools to insure that students are better prepared for college work. The university hopes to expand Co

lege Now, a program offered by Kingsborough Community College. In the program high school students take CUNY's placement exams in 11th and 12th grades, and if they do poorly, they can enroll in special classes on nights and weekends to better prepare themselves.

These proposals come nearly 30 years after CUNY adopted a far-reaching open-admissions policy to allow a broader range of students into its four-year colleges. Beginning with New York City's budget crisis in the mid-1970's, that program has been gradually cut back, but CUNY's six community colleges still take anyone with a high school diploma or its equivalent.

These new proposals, however, are sure to draw fire from those concerned that disadvantaged students most in need of remedial help, particularly minorities and immigrants, would face an entirely new series of obstacles to earning their degrees.

Stefan Baumrin, a professor of phi-

A public university's response to the issue of underprepared students.

---

losophy at Lehman College and the Graduate Center, said the plan "looks like a rushed response by a board roiled up by mayoral and press criticism."

"The panic to stop the threat of a halt to all remediation, and the call for an end to open admissions, yields, I think, in this case a half-baked solution. The right solution in my mind is to rebuild the university, and simply require better performance by its students."

But even among those with reservations about the plan, there seems to be a widespread sense that some change is necessary.

Mizanoor Biswas, the student representative on the board of trustees, said he is "not in favor of unlimited remediation" and that he has been impressed with the immersion programs CUNY has now.

But, he added, he wants to be sure that whatever plan is adopted has the approval of the college senates, which includes students, faculty and administrators.

Edith Everett, another trustee, said she was willing to accept limits on remedial work as long as there were opportunities for students to get up to par. "It's not as if we are saying we don't want you," she said. "It has to be emphasized that we are not walking away from this."

Dr. Mirrer said yesterday that the summer immersion programs should give such students a better chance of succeeding when they get to college. She said CUNY has run such programs since 1985 as part of its SEEK and College Discovery programs, which accept students who are disadvantaged.

Last summer, nearly 12,000 students were in the summer programs, which run four days a week for six weeks. A recent review of the results, she said, showed that the students performed better than similar students who were not in the immersion programs.

"It works better because it's intensive, students are focused and they are highly motivated to succeed," Dr. Mirrer said.

By moving some remedial study to immersion programs that are separate from regular course work, CUNY may improve its performance statistics in two ways. Graduation rates may rise if students learn better. And the clock that measures the time students take to graduate will not start ticking until the students finish the immersion program and enroll as regular students.

Mayor Giuliani has repeatedly attacked the fact that only 1 percent of students at the community colleges graduate after two years, a process slowed by their remedial work.

CUNY officials said they hope to keep the charge for the summer immersion program modest, perhaps at about $100. Such programs do not qualify for some of the major government financial aid under programs like T.A.P. and Pell, but CUNY officials are lobbying for some kind of support in Albany.

Gov. Pataki's Rogue Reformer

NEW YORK POST, MONDAY, FEBRUARY 16, 1998

POSTOPINION

NEW YORK POST

23

BOB McMANUS

WHEN George Pataki one year ago placed Ann A. Paolucci in command of the City University's fortunes, he thought he was getting a tough, traditionalist educator wholly committed to the resuscitation of a dying municipal institution. It now appears that what he *actually* got was double-crossed.

He has time to do something about it, but not a lot.

Wednesday afternoon, CUNY's Trustees Committee on Remediation will serve a preliminary eviction notice on the panderers and pettifoggers who now run the university.

Or it won't.

It is Paolucci, and Paolucci alone, who will decide which. But there is real cause to doubt the willingness of the former St. John's University professor, who now chairs CUNY's board of trustees, to do the right thing.

Wednesday's agenda consists almost solely of resolutions aimed at converting CUNY's 30-year open-admissions policy into an effective dead letter.

They're not draconian, and by no means do they represent the final word, but they're meant to set a timer ticking on the institution's bizarre operating philosophy — which, in a nutshell, is that in a truly progressive society, illiteracy must be no barrier to matriculation at a public university.

Trustees on the proper side of the issue will be Herman Badillo — Mayor Giuliani's man on the CUNY board, its vice-chairman, and a street-fighter for educational excellence — and Alfred Curtis, a mayoral appointee who shares Badillo's sensibilities.

On the other will be Edith Everett and Susan Mouner, Cuomo-administration board holdovers and committed advocates of unrestricted CUNY admissions.

Squarely in the middle will be Kenneth Cook, a Pataki appointee who, barring the unexpected, will have the deciding vote Wednesday — and who, for the moment anyway, can be expected to cast it in whichever direction Paolucci sees fit.

And what direction will this be? Hints abound, including these:

■ Paolucci didn't have to assign hard-line business-as-usual advocates like Everett or Mouner to this strategically critical committee — but she did it anyway;

■ Lately, she's been relying heavily for advice on another Cuomo-era hanger-on, James P. Murphy — her immediate predecessor as board chairman and a poster boy for preservation of the CUNY status quo, and;

■ She makes scant effort to hide her disdain both for Giuliani's high-decibel criticism of CUNY and for his unambiguous prescription for reform.

The university's problems need no elaboration: Its 35-percent-plus remediation enrollment in the four-year institutions, and its 1 percent on-time graduation rate at the community-college level, speak eloquently enough.

Pataki, in the past, has been no wallflower regarding these shortcomings. He campaigned on the need for radical CUNY reform — and Paolucci was to have been his agent for change.

At the outset, she was — targeting CUNY's fossilized bureaucracy and deftly engineering the departure of its principal champion, then-university Chancellor W. Ann Reynolds.

When it came to finding a successor to Reynolds, however, Paolucci suddenly went all wobbly: She began increasingly to defer to Murphy's views — so much so that it's unlikely that a permanent chancellor can be selected without bone-jarring conflict.

But that's for the future. Right now, the action's with the remediation committee — and this presents Pataki with a clear and present dilemma.

He must contend with Giuliani, who — with an eminently legitimate interest in the outcome — has gone to war over remediation and open admissions. The mayor sees the issue as critical to the city's future, and he says he'll withdraw municipal financial support from the community colleges if it isn't resolved in his favor. Does anybody want to bet that Giuliani doesn't mean it?

And Pataki must come to terms with the Conservative Party, upon which he depends both politically and for the advancement of his gubernatorial agenda — but which counts among its leading lights Paolucci's three principal patrons. These are her husband, party stalwart and one-time gubernatorial candidate Henry Paolucci; former party chairman Serphin Maltese of Queens, now a powerful state senator; and the conservatives' current leader, Brooklyn's Mike Long.

Earlier editions of Pataki would have had no problem here: He'd quietly have dragged Paolucci on board. Period.

But the governor is in re-election hyperdrive at the moment; this means no waves are to be made 'til well after November — and a messy CUNY fight would, to put it mildly, make waves.

A battle wouldn't *necessarily* hurt Pataki, of course: If Giuliani has proved nothing else, it's that challenging the conventional wisdom often can pay huge political dividends.

On the merits, moreover, November may be too late for CUNY; a critical moment of sorts may well have passed by then. Outside the Murphy-Everett orbit, there exists in the city a broad-based, but probably ephemeral, consensus supporting fundamental reform — at least in principle.

Certainly one need not cleave fully to Giuliani's scorched-earth CUNY agenda to concede that his essential diagnosis is correct. Indeed, the most compelling response to the mayor to date has been the astonishing assertion, no doubt true, that the community colleges must admit illiterate students in large numbers because the institutions themselves are financially dependent on the sale of remedial services.

Still, it's not always necessary to go to war to preserve the status quo. Artful foot-dragging often is enough — and it sure helps when the reformers' tactical commander decamps to the other side.

So the critical question becomes this: Does Pataki have the will to retrieve the portfolio he handed Ann Paolucci 12 months ago? By the time CUNY's Committee on Remediation finishes its work two days hence, the answer should be in sight.

> *It's not always necessary to fight hard to preserve the status quo. Often artful foot-dragging is enough — and it sure helps when the reformers' tactical chief decamps to the other side.*

NEW YORK POST, THURSDAY, AUGUST 13,

10

HIGHER EDUCATION AT CUNY

The New York Times

THE NEW YORK TIMES **METRO** *THURSDAY, APRIL 23, 1998*

C I T Y   B6

CUNY May Let Politicians Plan Remediation

By KAREN W. ARENSON

Despite what appeared to be a growing consensus among many of the trustees of the City University of New York on a plan to limit remedial education, some trustees predicted yesterday that no plan would be adopted at a monthly board meeting on Monday because a solution acceptable to both the Mayor and the Governor had not yet been reached.

At a meeting of the board's long-range planning committee yesterday, attended by 9 of the board's 17 trustees, a consensus seemed to emerge around a plan drawn up this week by CUNY's chairwoman, Anne A. Paolucci. That proposal would limit remediation to one semester at the senior colleges and one year at the community colleges.

Such limits are more moderate than those in a previous version the board was considering, which would have eliminated remedial courses at the senior colleges. The imposition of any time limits, however, would still make CUNY unusual, since most public universities take in many students who need catch-up work in one or more subjects before they are ready to tackle college-level courses.

Despite this, many of the trustees and college presidents at the long-range planning meeting yesterday said the new plan was an acceptable compromise, and that with minor changes, they could live with it. Edith Everett, a trustee, complemented Dr. Paolucci on assembling a consensus after weeks of deadlock.

But some trustees said the plan falls far short of the more radical change that Mayor Rudolph W. Giuliani has been demanding, and, as a result, would not have the nine votes needed for passage. They said that Dr. Paolucci herself, who was appointed chairwoman by Gov. George E. Pataki, would most likely follow Mr. Pataki's lead once he and Mr. Giuliani had agreed on a plan.

The Mayor appoints 5 trustees and the Governor 10, and the students and faculty each have one representative on the board, although the faculty trustee does not vote.

The Mayor has said repeatedly that CUNY's standards are too low, and that all remedial instruction should be conducted by a private company or by another university, not by CUNY. He has also urged that students be barred from the university until they have completed all remedial work. The proposals being discussed by CUNY's trustees so far would allow students to take remedial courses at the colleges under CUNY's direction.

One person close to the Mayor's negotiations over CUNY, who spoke on the condition that he not be identified, said that the Mayor and the Governor were discussing a plan that would impose a stricter limit on remediation at the senior colleges, following the Baruch College model, which calls for ending all remedial courses but providing extra tutorial help to students who need it.

He said that what would happen at the community colleges was less clear, but that a decision on that front might be postponed while the Mayor and Governor keep searching for a mutually acceptable plan.

The Governor's office said yesterday evening that no one was available to comment because of work on the budget.

But Dr. Paolucci said in a telephone interview that the remedial plan was still a work in progress, and that what is put before the board on Monday may look different from this week's plan. She also said that a vote might need to be put off to allow the public to comment on a new version.

"It is really not clear yet," she said.

Some CUNY Officials Are Cautious About Mayor's Proposal, but Others See Disaster

The New York Times
THE UNIVERSITY

FRIDAY, JANUARY 30, 1998

By KAREN W. ARENSON

Mayor Rudolph W. Giuliani's sharp attack on the City University of New York — and his proposal to remove all remedial work from the community colleges, a cornerstone of the university's open access policy — took officials there by surprise yesterday.

Despite the radical nature of the Mayor's remarks, some top university officials sounded both a diplomatic and conciliatory response to the proposal. But some on the board of trustees were indignant, suggesting that the Mayor did not understand the role of community colleges in educating the most disadvantaged or the difficulty of that task.

In a brief statement issued late in the afternoon, Christoph M. Kimmich, the interim Chancellor, said the university was "eager to work with Mayor Giuliani to strengthen the educational preparation of incoming freshmen before they are admitted to CUNY community colleges." He stressed, however, that CUNY remained committed to open enrollment.

The chairwoman of the board, Anne A. Paolucci, was also measured in her response, saying she was "willing to consider all options" but that she hoped the Mayor would give the board a chance to pursue its own changes. "The Mayor has a right to bring up these things," she said. "We're in the midst of a very serious overhauling of all programs, and I do believe we have to give these efforts a chance."

Other trustees, however, were sharply critical of the Mayor.

Edith Everett, a longtime trustee, called Mr. Giuliani's proposals "politics, not education."

And Sandi E. Cooper, the chairwoman of the university Faculty Senate and the faculty representative on the board of trustees, said the Mayor's proposals were "a recipe for closing down the colleges, and a move a lot of small private colleges with empty seats have been salivating over for a long time."

Educators say a plan could jeopardize open enrollment.

"The irony is that the university has been the pioneer in this area," she said, "and many people nationally come to us to learn how to do this."

It is not clear how CUNY would be affected if the Mayor succeeded in removing all remedial classes from the university in a proposal that parallels those laid out by Heather MacDonald in an article in the winter issue of the Manhattan Institute's City Journal.

As Mr. Giuliani noted, among CUNY's entering classes, about four-out of five students fail at least one of the three placement exams in reading, writing and mathematics, and some fail two or three.

Newsday

MONDAY, JANUARY 11, 1999

CUNY Trustees Plan New Vote

Revisit issue of remedial classes

By Mohamad Bazzi
STAFF WRITER

Seeking to bypass a court challenge from faculty and students, the City University of New York board of trustees plans to retake a vote ending remedial classes at its senior colleges.

The board will vote Jan. 25 on a proposal nearly identical to one it approved last year at a gathering that critics say violated the state open meetings law. The trustees voted 9-6 to phase out remedial classes at all 11 CUNY senior colleges, starting in September. But a judge barred the university from implementing the plan until a lawsuit challenging the vote winds its way through the court system.

This month's vote will be taken in strict adherence to the open meetings law, said CUNY Vice Chancellor Jay Hershenson. The trustees plan to move the meeting from their headquarters on East 80th Street in Manhattan, which seats about 100 people, to a theater that seats about 750 people at LaGuardia Community College in Long Island City.

A state judge had ruled that the trustees limited public access to the meeting by holding it "in a room which they knew to be too small."

"The board is not conceeding that it violated the open meetings law, but the leadership is eager to get the remediation policy back on track," Hershenson said.

The move to end remedial classes drew criticism from faculty members and some trustees, saying most universities provide some form of remedial education in writing, reading and math. But the changes have been championed by Mayor Rudolph Giuliani and Gov. George Pataki, who appoint most members of the CUNY board. Proponents say students who need remedial courses should be barred from entering CUNY's senior colleges and sent to take them at community colleges instead.

One trustee who opposes ending remediation said the board shouldn't vote on the issue until it hears from a task force created by Giuliani last year to study changes at CUNY. That panel held public hearings last week, but it hasn't issued any recommendations.

"Let's see what they have to say," said Edith Everett, a CUNY trustee from Manhattan. "It's such a foolish thing to say that we're not willing to accept students who would be accepted at all kinds of other schools like Fordham, Columbia and NYU [New York University]."

Under the new plan, which is expected to pass, remedial classes would be eliminated over three years, starting next January at Baruch, Brooklyn, Queens and Hunter Colleges.

A university study projected last year that 46 percent, or more than 12,000, of the incoming bachelor's degree students would not be able to pass at least one of CUNY's three placement exams, effectively barring them from entering a senior college. Students who fail one of the exams now may take remedial classes and test again.

Meanwhile, one of the faculty members who sued the trustees said he was glad that they plan to move the next meeting to a larger space.

"Our lawsuit has forced them to obey the law," said William Crain, a psychology professor at City College. The suit accused CUNY trustees of violating the state open meetings law when they approved the remediation changes on May 26. Before the vote, Chairwoman Anne Paolucci ejected all spectators, except reporters, from the meeting room because of disruptions. Twenty-six people were arrested after refusing to leave.

In August, State Supreme Court Justice Elliot Wilk ruled that the trustees violated the law not only by holding the meeting in a room that was too small, but also by reserving seats for their staff and the press and by ejecting the entire audience, "including those watching and listening peacefully."

An appeals court heard arguments in the case last month but has not yet ruled on the issue.

Newsday

NEWSDAY, MONDAY, APRIL 27, 1998   A5

CUNY Plan Gets Remedial Attention

By Mohamad Bazzi

STAFF WRITER

In hopes of gaining support for a compromise, the chairwoman of the City University Board of Trustees has delayed a vote on a controversial plan to limit remedial education.

Anne Paolucci decided to send a revised plan for review by a board committee May 6 instead of bringing it before the monthly trustee meeting this afternoon. The new plan, drawn up by Paolucci last week, backs away from completely eliminating remedial classes at CUNY's 10 senior colleges. Instead, it calls for a one-semester limit on remediation at these colleges, which currently allow students to take up to one year of remedial classes for credit.

"The major issue under discussion has been the role of senior colleges in providing remediation," CUNY Vice Chancellor Jay Hershenson said yesterday. "No vote will be taken on the plan because Chairwoman Paolucci felt there was need to have further discussion."

The revised plan allows individual college presidents to request a longer or shorter limit on remediation. Such requests would have to be approved by the CUNY chancellor.

Like the earlier plan, proposed last month, Paolucci's compromise also calls for stricter admissions requirements and a one-year limit on remedial classes at community colleges.

The initial plan came under intense criticism from students, faculty members and politicians, who argued that it threatens the university's historic mission of allowing poor and working-class students to attend college. More than 200 people spoke against the proposal at a hearing last week, including students who testified that remedial classes paved the way for their success.

But some faculty members are opposed to any plan placing a time limit on remediation, arguing that most public universities nationwide allow students to take remedial classes until they're ready for college-level work.

"This will make CUNY into a national exception when it comes to remedial education," said Barbara Bowen, an associate English professor at Queens College.

University sources said the delay indicates that Mayor Rudolph Giuliani and Gov. George Pataki, who control most of the votes on the board, have yet to agree on the plan's scope.

Any plan requires nine votes to pass. Proponents of the initial plan needed support from Giuliani's five appointees on the 17-member board. The mayor had said that proposal did not go far enough in raising standards at CUNY. The panel also includes 10 gubernatorial appointees, a voting student member and non-voting faculty member.

Last month's proposal was drafted after Giuliani called for privatizing remedial programs and ending open admissions, which allows any city student to enroll at a CUNY community college with a high school diploma or its equivalent. The mayor could not be reached to comment on the revised proposal.

Staten Island Advance

TUESDAY, APRIL 28, 1998

CUNY board again delays vote on remedial education

y KERRY MURTHA
VANCE STAFF WRITER

For the second consecutive onth, the board of trustees of the ty University of New York UNY) decided to delay a vote on e controversial plan to revamp ·medial education at the univer- ty's colleges.

The decision was announced at e trustees' full board meeting ·sterday by chairwoman Dr. nne Paolucci, who said a meet- g of the board's long range com- ittee is scheduled for May 6 at 3 m. to continue consideration of e Comprehensive Action Plan 'AP).

She said yesterday that she)ped a resolution would be ·ached at that time which could : presented to the full board.

Susan Moore Mouner, a Staten land trustee and member of the ng range committee, has indi- ited that she for one would like ore information before moving rward.

Meanwhile hundreds of students id faculty gathered outside UNY's Manhattan headquarters ·sterday to lambaste the trus- ·es' plan as well as the recent reats by the mayor and gover- r to cut CUNY funding.

Gov. George E. Pataki vetoed $36 million yesterday that the state Legislature had added to its draft budget for the state and city universities. Those cuts included approximately $5 million that would have been used to hire new faculty at CUNY.

Mayor Rudolph W. Giuliani an- nounced that he would cut $110 million in city money from CUNY's community colleges and its senior colleges that offer asso- ciate degree programs if more stringent attendance policies were not implemented.

The College of Staten Island (CSI), one of the university's 10 senior colleges, grants approxi- mately 400 associate degrees to its 1,800 or so graduates each year.

Critics have accused trustees, who are appointed by the mayor and governor, of caving to such political whims at the expense of CUNY students.

"This is our university not the university of the trustees in there making the decisions," said Wil- liam Wharton, CSI's student gov- ernment president, who was among the many protesters out- side CUNY's headquarters.

The current remedial overhaul plan — which was drawn up in re- sponse to the mayor's call to end

remediation at CUNY's colleges — essentially sets out to limit the amount of time students have to complete their remedial course work and calls for intense sum- mer programs and other alterna- tives to handle remediation.

A plan to ban remedial classes at the university's senior colleges is also being considered.

Trustees' more recent proposals call for limiting remediation to one semester at the senior col- leges and one year at the universi- ty's six community colleges.

Staten Island mayoral appoin- tee Alfred B. Curtis Jr., called the more moderate plan "discussa- ble," yesterday and said it war- rants a "long lengthy discussion."

The overwhelming majority of CSI freshmen take at least one re- medial class in English, reading and math.

"It's important for students to take a stand against the downsiz- ing of CUNY," said Jessica Siegel, a CSI professor of journalism who joined yesterday's protesters. "CUNY offers students who haven't taken advantage of the ed- ucational system for whatever reason — whether they be 18, 30 or 40 years old — a chance to do so. And for them to close that down is outrageous."

No Vote Is Expected Today on Remedial Programs at Meeting of CUNY Board

By KAREN W. ARENSON

Despite lobbying by Mayor Rudolph W. Giuliani's office, trustees of the City University of New York said they were not likely to vote on any change in remedial programs at their meeting this afternoon, because no plan seems to have enough support for passage.

"I don't think there will be a vote," Anne A. Paolucci, the board's chairwoman, said yesterday. "We don't seem to be ready for it." Nine votes are needed to approve any plan on the 17-member board, with 5 trustees appointed by the Mayor, 10 by the governor, a student representative and one nonvoting faculty member.

Mr. Giuliani has been pressing for a resolution offered by Herman Badillo, the vice chairman of the board, and John J. Callandra, a trustee, that would require students to pass placement tests in reading, writing and math before being allowed to enroll in a CUNY bachelor's degree program at its 11 four-year colleges.

Those who did not pass could take intensive remedial immersion programs or enter a community college and would still have to pass the placement exams to transfer to a bachelor's degree program.

The plan, said to have been hammered out by Gov. George E. Pataki's office and the Mayor's office, would be phased in over a three-year period starting in September 1999. High school graduates from other countries who need some work in meeting of the trustees' long-range planning committee but does not appear to have enough votes to pass.

The balance of votes could change slightly by the June meeting if the State Senate approves a trustee to replace an appointee of former Gov. Mario M. Cuomo, Susan M. Mouner, whose term expired last year.

The New York Metropolitan Region of the American Jewish Congress urged CUNY's board to reject the Badillo/Callandra proposal, saying the problems "cannot be addressed with simple one-dimensional solutions such as ending remediation or making entry standards suddenly so high that huge numbers of New York's ethnic, racial and religious communities are barred from pursuing higher education."

But the Committee for the CUNY Future, associated with the American Council of Trustees and Alumni, a conservative education policy organization, said CUNY was overestimating how many students would be barred from bachelor's programs by the Badillo/Callandra plan. "Giving the colleges an incentive to develop successful programs will provide true benefits to students," it said. English but could show they need no remedial work in reading, writing or mathematics would be exempted.

A proposal by John Morning, another trustee, calls for the colleges to develop their own plans to limit remedial work. It had more support than the Badillo/Callandra plan at a

NEW YORK POST

TUESDAY, AUGUST 11, 1998

Judge blocks CUNY effort to cut remedial ed

By DAREH GREGORIAN

A judge yesterday put a temporary stop to City University's plans to end remedial classes, ruling the university board violated open-meeting laws before passing the controversial resolution.

The faculty members who filed the suit showed "the CUNY trustees violated the Open Meetings Law, and that there is a strong likelihood that the May 26, 1998, resolution will be voided," Manhattan Supreme Court Justice Elliott Wilk wrote in granting a temporary injunction halting the university's plan.

Anthony Coles, a senior adviser to Mayor Giuliani, blasted the decision as "ludicrous" and said the judge "considers his own personal political viewpoints to be more important than the law."

"There is very little question that this decision will be promptly reversed on appeal," he said.

The CUNY resolution, which was heavily backed by Giuliani and Gov. Pataki, would phase out remedial classes at all four-year city colleges by 2002. It was passed during a raucous open meeting in May.

The vote was taken after CUNY Chairwoman Anne Paolucci ordered all members of the public out of the small, packed meeting room because of a few hecklers in the crowd.

Six people who refused to leave were arrested, including two who did nothing wrong — Assemblyman Edward Sullivan and Sister Elizabeth Kelliher, a Franciscan nun — Wilk said.

The judge said it was "unreasonable" for Paolucci to clear the room instead of having just the hecklers tossed out. And after the room was cleared, the judge said, the board refused to let in other people who had been waiting outside for hours.

"The actions of a disruptive few did not justify depriving the public of its right to observe the vote," Wilk wrote. He added the board members knew there was tremendous interest in the vote, and that they should have held the meeting in a larger location.

Wilk's decision means City University can't even start planning new remedial-class-free budgets for the various colleges, pending a trial or appeal.

That could be a major blow to CUNY, because some colleges were slated to end their remedial programs in September of next year, and 1999 school budgets are supposed to be presented to the City Council within the next two months.

A CUNY spokeswoman said the university is reviewing the decision. The ruling does not affect CUNY's plans to develop summer and high-school remediation programs.

Judge: Not So Fast

Enjoins CUNY from eliminating remedial classes

NEWSDAY, TUESDAY, AUGUST 11, 1998

Newsday

By Pete Bowles
STAFF WRITER

A State Supreme Court judge yesterday enjoined the City University of New York from eliminating remedial education at its 11 senior colleges, ruling that the CUNY Board of Trustees had violated the state's Open Meetings Laws when it ended the courses.

The 20-page decision was hailed by advocates of remedial education, including students and faculty members who had brought a lawsuit charging that the board had illegally voted to curtail remedial-education programs.

In his ruling, Justice Elliot Wilk said there is a "strong likelihood" CUNY's May 26 resolution eliminating the courses would be rejected at trial.

"This is a huge victory for the forces of democracy in this city," said William Crain, a psychology professor at City College and one of the plaintiffs in the lawsuit. "Hopefully, it will force the CUNY board to reconsider their closed-meetings policies, as well as the destructive decision to eliminate remedial education for thousands of students who need it."

Rita Rodin, a CUNY spokeswoman, said, "We are reviewing the decision and consulting with the state attorney general to decide on an appropriate course of action."

The plan to eliminate remedial education was drafted a few weeks after Mayor Rudolph Giuliani called for privatizing remedial programs and ending open admission, which allows any New York City student with a high school diploma or its equivalent to enroll at a CUNY community college.

Many who opposed that plan said it threatened the university's historic mission of allowing poor and working-class students to attend college. Giuliani and those favoring the change said it would raise standards.

Giuliani was on vacation and not available for comment. Anthony Coles, a Giuliani adviser, called the ruling "ludicrous," and added: "There is very little question that this decision will be promptly reversed on appeal and will not stand in the way of CUNY's efforts to raise standards. The opinion clearly is written by a judge who considers his own personal viewpoints to be more important than the law."

The ban, which was to be initiated at four colleges next year and then phased in to include other senior colleges over the next two years, was passed at a raucous meeting during which 20 demonstrators and six members of the audience were arrested. Among those arrested, noted the judge, were Assemb. Edward Sullivan (D-Manhattan), chairman of the Assembly Higher Education Committee, and a Franciscan nun who were not being disruptive.

Wilk said the board violated the Open Meetings Law by limiting public access to the meeting by holding it "in a room which they knew to be too small," by reserving seats for their staff and the press and by ejecting the entire audience, "including those watching and listening peacefully."

"This behavior was unreasonable, designed to deny public access to the meeting and inconsistent with the fundamental principles of the Open Meetings Law that 'the public business be performed in an open and public manner,'" Wilk said.

In his ruling, Wilk also referred to Board Chairwoman Anne Paolucci's comments in the New York Times the day before the meeting that no vote on the remedial resolution was expected. "Her statement had the effect, if not the intent, of dissuading interested members of the public from attending the meeting," the judge said.

The New
New York Beacon | **June 4 - June 10, 1998**

Trustees Approve End To Remediation At CUNY

The Board of Trustees of The City University of New York adopted a resolution on May 26 to phase out all remedial education in the baccalaureate degree programs at CUNY's eleven senior colleges, starting in the fall of 1999, and continuing through September 2001, Chairman Anne A. Paolucci announced.

The four colleges to be affected in the first phase will be Baruch, Brooklyn, Queens, and Hunter Colleges. Lehman College, John Jay College of Criminal Justice, The College of Staten Island, New York City Technical College and City College will be part of phase two in September 2000. York College and Medgar Evers College will be included in September 2001.

Students will be required to pass all three Freshman Skills Assessment Tests, (reading comprehension, essay writing and mathematics) as well as other admissions criteria in order to enroll as a freshman or to transfer into those college's baccalaureate programs.

The resolution adds that "students seeking remediation shall be able to obtain such remediation services at a CUNY community college, at a senior college only during its summer sessions, or elsewhere as it may be made available."

The resolution does not apply to ESL (English as a Second Language) students who received a secondary education abroad and who otherwise are not in need of remediation.

Detailed plans to implement the resolution at the respective colleges are requested by Interim Chancellor Christoph M. Kimmich and the senior college presidents by September 1998.

Board Chairwoman Paolucci emphasized that "the University will focus on strengthening collaborations with the public schools and developing innovative alternative to current remedial instruction."

Among the strategies being reviewed for broader and more effective applications are:

. The College Now program, designed to help students make a smooth transition from high school to college.

. The pre-freshman summer skills programs, evening and weekend classes.

. Basic skills immersion programs and language immersion programs during the academic year.

. Tutoring and mentoring services and programs.

. Collaborative strategies planned with the high schools also include closer cooperation on the Colege Preparatory Initiative. In addition, CUNY Assessment Tests will be administered in due course to high school juniors in order to target weaknesses and help overcome them before students graduate.

The New York Times

THE NEW YORK TIMES **METRO** FRIDAY, AUGUST 14, 1998 **B5**

CUNY Review By Regents Is Questioned By Governor

By KAREN W. ARENSON

Gov. George E. Pataki questioned yesterday whether the State Board of Regents had the authority to approve or reject a plan by the City University of New York to bar remedial students from CUNY's senior colleges.

CUNY is resisting the Regents' efforts to conduct a review of the policy, which the university wants to introduce at four colleges in September 1999, and seven other colleges after that.

"We've got some lawyers looking at it, and their preliminary analysis is that it's not clear at all that the board has this power," Bradford J. Race, Mr. Pataki's chief of staff, said yesterday.

The Governor's office, together with Mayor Rudolph W. Giuliani, strongly supported efforts by CUNY trustees this spring to make significant changes in how CUNY handles remedial education, saying that such changes were necessary to raise the university's standards and to force students to take their education more seriously.

Mr. Race said he called Carl Hayden, Chancellor of the State Board of Regents, yesterday morning after reading about CUNY's battle over the Regents' authority in The New York Times. He said he suggested that the Chancellor meet with the Governor's staff and CUNY "to talk about the differences in our conclusions and to reach common ground."

Mr. Hayden said: "We're very confident we have the authority, and we also have the responsibility. That's the long and the short of it."

Although Mr. Hayden said he had also received calls yesterday from members of the City Council who opposed the CUNY resolution, he added: "We have no political agendas. We are not carrying anyone's water. We're simply doing our job."

CUNY's chairwoman, Anne A. Paolucci, and its interim Chancellor, Christoph M. Kimmich, challenged the Regents' authority to review the new policy in a letter this week.

The Regents are required by law to approve the master plans of all higher education institutions in the state. But CUNY officials noted that the Regents streamlined that process in 1995, and that the remedial changes do not come under the list of items that warrant review under those revisions. They also say that they made comparable changes in the remedial programs and admissions standards in 1995 and were not required to submit those for a lengthy review.

But State Education Department officials said yesterday that the streamlining they did was aimed at reducing the need for a lengthy review of minor amendments to a university's master plan, not significant changes like admissions standards at a public university or its mission.

Reviewing CUNY's Admissions Policy

FRIDAY, AUGUST 14, 1998· A20

The New York Times

The proposal by trustees of the City University of New York to bar admission to CUNY's senior colleges for students who have not passed skills tests in reading, writing and mathematics is too far-reaching not to be reviewed independently by state education authorities. The plan, to be phased in over three years, could affect nearly half the students entering the 11 four-year colleges. Such sweeping change demands a full public review, as provided for under state law.

Yet the CUNY board is resisting pressure by the state Board of Regents, which oversees the university's master plan, to comply with a formal review process. The trustees argue that changing admissions standards does not require amending the university's master plan, and therefore does not require the Regents' approval. But the proposed change is not a minor adjustment to the entrance requirements. It represents a fundamental shift in the mission of CUNY's senior colleges, which up to now have provided substantial remediation to students who failed the skills tests. By pushing nearly all remedial instruction to the two-year community colleges, the proposal will change the very structure of the CUNY system.

The State Education Department and the Regents are right to call for a state-level review. A key issue is whether the plan will maintain sufficient access to education while it raises standards. That question must be answered before the change is allowed to go forward. The Regents are prepared to expedite the review so that the new policy, if approved, can be put in place at four colleges next year. The CUNY trustees, avowedly confident about the rightness of their plan, should have no hesitation defending its merits to the Regents and the public.

Fall, 1998

Gov to Regents: Let CUNY steer own course

By GREGG BIRNBAUM
Post Correspondent

ALBANY — Gov. Pataki told state education officials to butt out of CUNY's sweeping plan to eliminate remedial classes, fearing the stricter new admissions standards could be delayed or watered down.

Pataki launched his broadside at the state Education Department and the state Board of Regents for claiming they have the power to approve or veto any upgrade in admissions policies at CUNY.

The Post has learned the Education Department is hiring private consultants to undertake a detailed analysis of CUNY's controversial admissions proposal to help the Board of Regents make its decision.

"I think the CUNY board should be allowed to run the City University system, and I was just unaware that the Regents thought they had this power," Pataki said. "I was surprised to see the Regents take this position."

Pataki's chief of staff, Brad Race, said he called Regents Chancellor Carl Hayden to find out why that group is sticking its nose into CUNY's business.

"I told the chancellor I thought it would be a good idea if we had a little more dialogue on these things before I read about it in the paper," Race said.

"And I said I am not sure we agree you have a legal responsibility or authority over the CUNY admissions plan, he added.

CUNY plans to put the tougher requirements into place at four schools — Hunter, Queens, Baruch and Brooklyn colleges — in September 1999 and phase them in at the seven other colleges in 2000 and 2001.

But some officials fear a review and vote by the Board of Regents could stall the start of the plan for a year or even longer, and CUNY is in a jam now because it can't tell potential students what the admissions policy will be.

Under the proposed new rules, incoming students would have to pass CUNY freshman placement exams in reading, writing and math before enrolling. Remedial courses at the colleges during the school year would be canceled.

State education officials said they are required under state law to OK or nix the admissions plan or request changes.

"We aren't seeking to intrude in anyone's business. We are just doing our job," Hayden said, adding that Pataki's staff had previously been informed of the Board of Regent's role in signing off on the plan.

"They [CUNY] have the burden of satisfying us on the merits that the [admissions] plan won't compromise access."

Hayden said the Regents review would not jeopardize CUNY's timetable.

Newsday   NEWSDAY, WEDNESDAY, SEPTEMBER 23, 1998

CUNY Remedial Phase-Out Challenged

By Dan Janison
STAFF WRITER

The City University of New York's new policy of ending remedial education at senior colleges starting next year appears likely to be delayed — even if CUNY ultimately defeats a court challenge to its plan.

In a ruling released yesterday, a state Appellate Division panel in effect ordered CUNY not to move forward with the change for at least two months while the court challenge, from professors and students, goes through the system.

CUNY spokesman John Hamill said the institution is abiding by the latest court ruling pending a final outcome.

That means November would be the earliest CUNY administrators could even draw up exact plans to phase out the remedial-education programs at 11 senior colleges, officials said. "November makes things tight at best for putting the change into effect as scheduled in September, 1999," said one CUNY source who declined to be identified. The process of admitting students for that class and budgeting funds for the university's various divisions begins a year in advance.

Opponents of the plan said the ruling means the phase-out now couldn't begin until 2000 at the earliest.

On May 26, CUNY's board of trustees approved a resolution calling for the phase-out. Plan proponents said basic courses in English and other subjects belong in high schools and junior colleges where they'd be shifted.

Opponents of the phase-out say the classes help students who did not have adequate high school preparation. Additionally, the plan would disproportionately affect minorities, they say.

On Aug. 10, State Supreme Court Justice Elliot Wilk barred CUNY from moving ahead, saying there was a "strong likelihood" that a lawsuit, still to be tried in court, would succeed in blocking the plan.

Wilk said the trustees violated the state's Open Meetings Law when it voted to end the courses.

By a 5-0 ruling, a Manhattan Appellate Division panel has now upheld Wilk's order until the matter can be argued further in November.

"This is another major victory for us," said CUNY professor William Crain, one of the plaintiffs.

The New York Times
Fall, 1998

By KAREN W. ARENSON

In another legal challenge to the City University of New York's new policy on remedial education, six civil liberties groups have accused CUNY's trustees of violating state law because they did not submit the policy to the State Board of Regents for approval.

The lawsuit, filed late Monday in State Supreme Court in New York, was brought on behalf of a CUNY professor, Sandi E. Cooper, the former chairwoman of the CUNY Faculty Senate, and three New York City high school students who say they want to attend the university's senior colleges but expect they will need remedial help.

"The whole process by which the CUNY trustees arrived at their resolution to eliminate remediation at the senior colleges was fundamentally flawed," said Jonathan D. Bassett, of Van Lierop, Burns & Bassett, a lawyer who joined the coalition of civil liberties groups in bringing the lawsuit. "The failure of the CUNY trustees to submit their plan to the State Board of Regents is further evidence of that."

The policy, adopted in May, calls for students to pass tests in reading, writing and mathematics before they are allowed to enroll in the university's bachelor's degree programs. Students unable to pass the tests by registration day would be referred to CUNY's community colleges. The policy is scheduled to be phased in beginning next September.

The groups that brought the lawsuit are the Puerto Rican Legal Defense and Education Fund, the NAACP Legal Defense and Educational Fund, the New York Civil Liberties Union, the Center for Constitutional Rights, the American Jewish Congress and the Asian American Legal Defense and Educational Fund. Ronald B. McGuire, a lawyer, also joined in the suit.

Jay Hershenson, vice chancellor for university relations, said that the university's officials could not comment on the suit since the matter is in litigation. But CUNY officials have said they do not believe they are required to seek the approval of the Regents for their policy. When the Regents asked the university to submit the plan for review last summer, its officials rejected the request, saying that they disagreed with the Regents' contention that such a review was mandated by state law.

That disagreement between CUNY and the Regents is on hold because the university is barred from working on the remedial policy by a court injunction in an earlier lawsuit. That suit, brought by a City College professor and student, said that the public was excluded from the CUNY board meeting on May 26 at which the remedial policy was adopted, in violation of the state's open meetings law. An Appellate Division hearing on the injunction, which was issued by Justice Elliot J. Wilk of the State Supreme Court in August, is scheduled for Friday.

The suit filed Monday calls the remedial policy "an unprecedented resolution that, if implemented, would drastically alter the admissions policies of CUNY" and cut the number of baccalaureate students in half.

The student plaintiffs in the new lawsuit are all juniors in New York high schools. Caresse P-Orridge is described in the court papers as a student at the Urban Academy High School with an average of about 80, but who expects that she will need remedial courses in math since she does not perform well on standardized math tests.

Wilfred Gomes, also an Urban Academy student, has a 90 average, but since he came to the United States from India a year ago, his vocabulary is limited and he believes he will need remedial education in writing, the papers say.

The third student in the case, Sung Pyo Ma, is a student at William Cullen Bryant High School, and also expects that he will need remedial courses in writing.

Lawyers for the civil liberties coalition said that although this week's lawsuit focused on a procedural issue, it did not preclude a later suit on the merits of the policy itself.

DAILY NEWS

RUSS BUETTNER
y News Staff Writer

Sunday, November 23, 1997

Seeking new head of class for makeover of university

A NEW ACTING chancellor is about to launch a Rambo-style attack on the City University system, and one of the first targets will likely be CUNY's troubled flagship: City College.

The once-proud Harvard on the Hudson has produced eight Nobel Prize winners and titans of literature, politics and business.

But it now stands for everything that CUNY's tough new trustees despise.

Graduation rates are low. Remediation rates are high. And its teacher-education program does such a lousy job that its students can't pass a certification test.

"The failure of [City College's] teacher-education program is typical of what I consider to be the fall from grace of the bellwether college of City University," said Herman Badillo, vice chairman of the CUNY trustees and a City College alumnus.

The trustees plan to change that. Tomorrow, they are likely to select an acting chancellor willing to shake the very foundations of the system — a "kamikaze pilot," as one activist trustee put it.

They'll empower their choice to turn CUNY's 21 campuses into a performance-based system — one in which bottom-line results, such as graduation rates, matter more than mushy interpretations of academic freedom.

In other words, trustees said, the CUNY of tomorrow will not look like the City Col-

The new model, driven by hard-nosed conservative pragmatics, is more like Baruch College, the restructured business school on Manhattan's East Side, whose president, Matthew Goldstein, is considered a contender to be CUNY's next permanent chancellor.

The trustees applaud and regularly quote a vision Goldstein described for CUNY in a recent speech: "Gritty, urban academic rigor: tough to get in, tough to stay in, with few amenities along the way."

BAD AND WORSE

CCNY is not the worst of CUNY's 11 senior colleges. Medgar Evers, Lehman and York Colleges show greater reasons for concern. And the new trustees have expressed even stronger doubts about CUNY's six community colleges — especially Hostos, the system's bi-lingual campus.

But as CUNY's first campus, City College has always been its centerpiece.

City graduates includes Dr. Jonas Salk, writers Paddy Chayefsky and Bernard Malamud and Gen. Colin Powell.

City students of old were mostly the white sons of hard-working immigrants. Many went on to boast that a free education at City gave them their crucial start.

Critics say the City College of today is better exemplified by the dubious scholarship of Leonard Jeffries, chairman of the black studies program, than the accomplishments of leaders such as Powell.

The decline, they said, can be traced back to 1970 — the year the system adopted open admissions.

The policy was a direct outgrowth of the tenor of the times — the late 1960s, when the Harlem campus was awash in civil rights and anti-war protests. Activists set their sights on increasing access for blacks and Hispanics to a free college education.

Critics said that was the start of an era in which students set the rules.

"One of the things that changed was that the students said, 'You shouldn't make us do anything we don't want to do,'" said Bernard Sohmer, a City College math professor for more than 40 years. "There were massive changes."

The core curriculum — a stringent set of minimum requirements for all students — was loosened. New programs, many in ethnic studies, were created in a flurry of racial politics. That also led to the creation of new CUNY colleges — Medgar Evers in Brooklyn and Hostos in the Bronx.

Leonard Kriegel, who retired from City in 1991 after 30 years as an English professor, said liberal arts programs stopped pushing students and started coddling them.

"The study of literature isn't supposed to make you proud of your heritage — it is supposed to bring you into the world," he said.

But open admissions was, in reality, a misnomer — and has been scaled back significantly in recent years. Requirements for entering freshman have in-

creased several times since 1970 — and the campus founded as the Free University in 1847 hasn't been tuition-free for 20 years.

LOW GRAD RATE

Only 17% of City College students graduate within five years. Fewer than half finish within eight years.

Last month, the new trustees showed they were serious about timely graduation as a measure of each college's success: The number of faculty positions each college receives next year will be tied to its graduation rate.

"It begins to introduce performance-based budgeting, and performance-based standards, and I think that's important," said trustee Ronald

Marino, whose committee crafted the plan.

Many argue that the City College students of today face obstacles that their predecessors didn't. CUNY students today are poorer, older and the products of deteriorated high schools.

But others counter that the problem lies with the open-admissions policy.

"They are admitting — and I don't even call this open admissions anymore — people who are not ready for college work American-style," said Andrew Hacker, a just-retired Queens College professor and author. "Those who defend open admissions, they've just run out of ammunition."

DAILY ◉ NEWS

NEW YORK'S HOMETOWN NEWSPAPER

PHOTOS BY BILL TURNBULL DAILY NEWS

MAKING STRIDES: City College President Yolanda Moses says the college's teaching program has some work to do. "I take responsibility for that," she says.

When they do finally graduate, there is troubling evidence that City failed to adequately prepare its students for the job market.

City College's teacher-education program, for instance — among the largest in the state — is also seen as one of the worst.

Only 40% of the 1,113 City students who took the state's teacher certification exam in 1995-96 passed — compared with an 82% passing rate statewide. Only two colleges in the state — one being Medgar Evers — had a lower pass rate.

"There is an absence of standards at City College, and the saddest example of that is the teachers program," Badillo said.

The state Board of Regents is crafting a proposal that would kill teacher-education programs whose graduates can't pass the test — including those at City and Medgar Evers.

"Our teaching program has some work to do," said City College President Yolanda Moses. "I take responsibility for that."

Several trustees have privately said that what angers them most are complaints they hear from New York businesses about the quality of CUNY graduates.

"You just can't imagine the frustration of employers in the City of New York when you can't hire people who can do the job," said H. Dale Hemmerdinger, president of Atco Properties and Management.

MATTER OF DEGREES

City College embodies another by-product of the 1960s and '70s that the trustees want to end: academic sprawl.

1998

Friday, December 11, 1998

DAILY ◼ NEWS

450 W. 33rd St.. New York. N.Y. 10001

CUNY reform inches along

MANY PEOPLE MAY BE AMAZED to learn that it took a state appeals court to enforce the City University's right to require that students at Hostos Community College prove they can read and write English before they are granted a degree. Those people do not know CUNY.

At Hostos, where more than half the students last year received A's and B's but nearly 30% failed a high-school level writing test, the appellate decision was a major victory for reform. It upheld a requirement — actually deemed radical by some — that students pass a basic English test to graduate.

The unanimous ruling is reason to celebrate. But that the issue got to court at all — thanks to a lawsuit by students — is cause for alarm. It's a warning sign that powerful forces remain aligned against even minimal academic standards at CUNY and that they will continue to make mischief until a strong chancellor takes charge of the sprawling 20-campus system.

Almost a year and a half has passed since Chancellor Ann Reynolds, the unrepentant standard-bearer of no standards, was given her walking papers and CUNY board chairwoman Anne Paolucci promised a "wide search" for a replacement.

This page greeted that development with much optimism. It was premature. Extremely premature. By late October last year, when CUNY was still without a chancellor, we warned that "too much is at stake to move at such a snail's pace."

Paolucci and the board of trustees whipped the snail for a month more before finally picking an interim chancellor, Christoph Kimmich, the provost of Brooklyn College. Kimmich is respected and capable. But the job is temporary and his authority vague. The board still has not found a permanent chancellor.

Until that happens, the voices of reform at CUNY will be drowned out by the din of the status quo.

To her credit, Paolucci dumped Hostos' rebel president, Isaura Santiago Santiago, who ignored the English test requirement and used her own weak substitute. And she won a crucial vote from the trustees to end remediation at the senior colleges — a stunning move toward transforming CUNY from a second-chance high school into a true citadel of learning. But that effort, sadly, is now stalled in the courts. Meanwhile, CUNY drifts.

Crisis management reigns. There is no rational allocation of resources, and none of the colleges has a clear mission. No one is held accountable, from presidents to the lowliest student.

So, by all means, raise a toast to the judges who upheld graduation standards at Hostos. But remember that their decision is as a Band-Aid on a cancer: no substitute for a cure.

NEWS STORIES ABOUT OPERATIONAL CHANGES INITIATED BY THE CHAIRWOMAN

The New York Times

THE UNIVERSITY

THE NEW YORK TIMES **METRO** *TUESDAY MARCH 25, 1997*   L   **B 3**

CUNY Trustees Vote to Hire Own Staff

Some Complain That the Administration Is Stinting on Information

By KAREN W. ARENSON

In a move that reflects the split between the trustees of the City University of New York and the university's administration, the trustees yesterday approved a budget of up to $1 million to finance their own research, auditing, management consultants and legal counsel.

Although it is not uncommon for trustees to have their own staff and consultants, the decision is apparently based on the belief by some trustees that they have not been getting adequate information from administrators. While few of these complaints have been made publicly, some trustees — mostly those appointed last summer by Gov. George E. Pataki and Mayor Rudolph W. Giuliani — have complained for several months that the administration has not been responsive enough to their questions. But at the meeting, much of the debate centered on whether the staff would be duplicative and on the lack of a budget.

Edith Everett, the former vice chairman of the board, and a long-time trustee, called the proposal "ill-considered and ill-advised" and said that it would create a shadow bureaucracy at a time of budget stringency.

But Anne A. Paolucci, the new chairwoman of the board, said such help was critical. "The need is very urgent if we want to get going," she said. After promises that any money spent would be tracked closely, with regular reports given to the board, the move was approved by vote of 11 to 1, with 2 abstentions.

The board also established three committees. One would study the performance and graduation rates of each of CUNY's 21 campuses and one would study whether CUNY is spending too much on remedial programs for students who need help with math, writing and English. Dr. Paolucci said last week that CUNY's costs for remedial courses are high compared with other colleges. A third committee would study the process of finding new college presidents.

The meeting was the first run by Dr. Paolucci as the university's new chairwoman. She was appointed last month by Governor Pataki. He and Mayor Giuliani had established a majority on the board last summer.

A new board of trustees is adopting new priorities.

The new board members have questioned everything from whether the administration has too many employees, too many offices and too much power to whether the university has too many campuses. They have also raised questions about the quality of teaching.

It was only with the naming of Dr. Paolucci as chairwoman that the new board's priorities have begun to take shape. From the beginning, there has been an uneasy relationship between the new trustees and Chancellor W. Ann Reynolds, who was hired in 1990. Some new trustees, including Dr. Paolucci, have complained that she and her administration have not been giving them enough information. "I think it is just a question of her adjusting to the new board," Dr. Paolucci said in an interview last week. "We have to give her time. But she has to come around; she has to adjust."

Chancellor Reynolds, who sat quietly through most of yesterday's meeting, said she had no problem with the board's desire for outside help.

As they look to reshape the university, the trustees face campuses that have been squeezed sharply in recent years by successive cuts in state support. At a recent meeting between trustees and college presidents, several presidents said their budgets have already been cut to the bone. Others said that they have hired so many part-time faculty members to replace full-time teachers who have left that they have been concerned about retaining their schools' accreditation. Loss of accreditation could make it more difficult for students in some fields to obtain licenses or certifications. "Fifty-seven percent of our instruction is delivered by adjuncts," or part-time teachers, said Charles C. Kidd Sr., president of York College. "We can not stand an accreditation visit."

Frances Horowitz, president of the CUNY Graduate Center, said that when she arrived at CUNY from the University of Kansas five years ago, "My initial impression of CUNY was how threadbare it was." Since then, she said, it has sustained many cuts, "that are incompatible with the kind of education we are trying to offer."

Marlene Springer, president of the College of Staten Island, said that she, too, had been astonished at CUNY's poverty when she arrived in 1994. "I had departments that had not hired in more than 20 years," she told trustees. "We need new blood."

Newsday

NEWSDAY, TUESDAY, MARCH 25, 1997

CITY
CUNY Expenses Probed

By Graham Rayman
STAFF WRITER

In an unprecedented move, the City University Board of Trustees approved last night up to $1 million to create its own staff to examine CUNY expenditures and possibly pay for an outside auditor.

In the past the board relied on the staff of CUNY Chancellor Ann Reynolds to provide it with background information on university expenditures. But now board members will have — for the first time — what amounts to their own investigative staff.

What duties the staff will assume was largely left to future debate but a brief description of the resolution indicated that the money will be used to "provide the board with staff to perform their fiduciary duty efficiently and expeditiously."

Board member Ronald Marino said last night the money would be used to hire up to five staffers, including two researchers, two clerical staffers and a part time legal adviser.

In addition the funds may be used to hire an independent auditor to review unspecified expenditures.

The vote was seen last night as another example of a change in direction by a more skeptical board than has existed in the past.

In recent months a number of new trustees were appointed including a new chair, Anne Paolucci, who supported last night's resolution.

Defending the resolution vice-chair Herman Badillo said, "the board needs resources and a small amount of money to provide the resources."

Badillo added that he had attempted to convince an accounting firm to provide free auditing,, but had not found any takers.

"Part of what this would be is an independent audit and there are issues that need to be specifically looked into," said trustee Jerome Berg. Longtime CUNY board member Edith Everett who cast the lone no vote said "the impression given by this resolution is one of a takeover or junta rather than an orderly transition of new trustees and leadership for CUNY."

Trustee James Murphy, a former chair, also objected to the resolution but ultimately voted in favor once he was assured that specific expenditures would be brought back to the board for approval.

"The main issue is the tremendous growth of CUNY," Murphy said. "We need to get the deck chair rearranging out of the way quickly and get back to work."

CUNY big in office flap

DAILY NEWS, July 14, 1997, p. 17

By RUSS BUETTNER
Daily News Staff Writer

The new chairwoman of the City University trustees has ordered 15 people to vacate their offices so CUNY's part-time trustees can have full-time digs.

Anne Paolucci, appointed by Gov. Pataki in February, gave the CUNY legal staff 30 days to move off the third floor of the system's upper East Side headquarters.

Paolucci said the trustees' two staffers and stacks of files

are crammed into small offices

She added that the trustees need offices to conduct personal business on board meeting days.

But Edith Everett, a long time trustee now in the minority among 12 new appointees said trustees don't need a suite of offices to sit vacant just so they'll have occasional access to a telephone.

She said the Paolucci order showed a "lack of respect" for the legal staff.

"I think she's mixed up about who runs the university on a daily basis," Everett said. "This really is like a junta."

Everett has been critical of Paolucci and vice chairman Herman Badillo since March, when the trustees voted to spend $1 million to hire their own staff so they could circumvent the flow of information through Chancellor Ann Reynolds' office.

Everett has accused Paolucci of ignoring opposing opinions on the board and of issuing broad criticisms to gain political momentum so they can oust Reynolds and

downsize the 21-campus system.

CUNY's legal staff — 11 attorneys and four staffers — is to be moved to smaller quarters on another floor. The trustees' staff already occupied most of the third floor.

Paolucci issued the order in a July 1 memo, citing the trustees' need for permanent offices for a secretary, a part-time consultant and a part-time researcher.

"In addition, there is no office space for trustees to use when they are in the building," said Paolucci in the memo.

"Our trustees are very busy individuals and need offices where they have privacy to conduct their business when they are here volunteering their time to the university."

By contrast, the 16 trustees of the State University system have access to a single office with a desk and a phone when they travel to Albany for board meetings, said SUNY spokesman Ken Goldfarb.

In an interview, Paolucci said the CUNY trustees need more space than their SUNY counterparts because of the "special projects we are doing."

"We need the space," she said. "I don't have to justify anything."

Paolucci said the trustees once occupied the entire third floor: "We're trying to recapture what we had."

But Everett disputed that.

"Not in my lifetime," she said. "It has never in the last 20 years been anything but legal offices."

CITY COLLEGE IN CRISIS

CCNY'S FALL FROM GRACE

DAILY ◎ NEWS

June 14, 1997

CUNY head is knocked

By RUSS BUETTNER

Daily News Staff Writer

In her strongest attack yet, the head of the City University board of trustees yesterday accused Chancellor Ann Reynolds of "grave dereliction of duty" and said she won't tolerate it much longer.

Stepping up pressure on the beleaguered Reynolds, CUNY Chairwoman Anne Paolucci repeated her criticism that the chancellor has not provided accurate information to the trustees so they can make informed decisions.

In particular, she blamed Reynolds for the ongoing fiasco over an English language writing test required of all CUNY students.

The CUNY board, in a hasty vote days before graduation, decided no CUNY student could graduate unless they were able to pass a standardized writing test. The trustees voted believing Hostos Community College in the Bronx was the only CUNY campus that didn't require students to pass the test. In fact, they later learned, three others also exempted students.

Paolucci said Reynolds' explanation — that her administration didn't know until later that the other campuses weren't using the CUNY test — was unacceptable.

"If they didn't know, that was a tremendous and grave dereliction of duty," Paolucci said. "We have a chancellor who has been remiss in her duties. It's as simple as that."

She rebuked a resolution, passed Thursday by faculty leaders, slapping the trustees for their vote.

"We were doing our job," she said. "The chancellor was not doing her job.

"This is not going to last much longer — it can't," she added.

Reynolds is out of the country on a personal trip, and her spokeswoman declined comment. But in a June 10 memo responding to Paolucci's criticism of the Hostos mess, Reynolds sounded a conciliatory note.

"It has always been my goal to raise academic standards at the City University," Reynolds wrote. "But I also believe that much more can and should be done, and the willingness of this board to courageously raise standards is most welcomed."

Paolucci said the trustees will not respond to the resolution by the Council of Faculty Governance Leaders expressing regret "about the public savaging of Hostos" and will not revoke the writing test requirement.

"It's a clear signal of what we intend to do, and what [Reynolds] should have done a long time ago," Paolucci said.

And she criticized a new plan by Reynolds to spend $100,000 on an emergency language immersion program for students at the bi-lingual campus as "a lot of nonsense."

"To save her skin, she's putting something out that was put together overnight without board approval," Paolucci said.

DAILY ◉ NEWS

Fall, 1997

Clock is ticking on CUNY reform

THE ANNALS OF HISTORY are littered with generals who pulled defeat from the jaws of victory while resting on the laurels of a single triumph. That could well become the fate of Chairwoman Anne Paolucci if she continues to dawdle over reform of the troubled City University system.

In forcing the resignation of Chancellor Ann Reynolds, the bearer of the standard of no standards, Paolucci scored a coup in the war to save CUNY. But that was more than two months ago. Now, Paolucci's inability — or refusal — to take the next step is jeopardizing the momentum for substantive changes.

A respected academician and poet, Paolucci nonetheless has failed to rally other trustees around even an interim chancellor, leaving them deadlocked and bickering over three finalists — with the very real possibility of having to begin a new search.

While it would be a mistake for her simply to opt for a benchwarmer, as some frustrated trustees are beginning to urge, Paolucci must find a way to bring the majority of the board behind a single, qualified candidate. And if she can't — or won't — Gov. Pataki, who appointed her, and Mayor Giuliani, who has five seats on the board, must cooperate to force the issue.

Too much is at stake to move at a such a snail's pace. Put another way, if this is the pace at which Paolucci pursues a tempo-

rary chancellor, what is the hope that a permanent replacement will be hired anytime soon? And what happens to the long list of policy changes that must be put in place to save CUNY?

Without a chancellor, for example, the trustees are blocked from ousting Isaura Santiago Santiago, the rebel president of Hostos Community College who supported granting degrees to graduates who couldn't pass a high school English test.

In other ways, too, CUNY looks pretty much the same as when Pataki appointed Paolucci last summer. Despite some modest advances and promises of more, remediation remains the cornerstone of the university's education. Professors still hide their failures by inflating students' grades. And administrators continue to put a happy face on disaster in a way that makes Nero look like a man of action.

Graduates' pathetic pass rate on teacher certification exams — 62% compared with SUNY's 95% — is a prime case in point.

The state Board of Regents has told the university that for its colleges not to be banned from training teachers, 55% of the program's grads must pass the exam by next year, 75% in 2000 and 85% in 2001. None of the colleges comes even close to 85% now — and Medgar Evers and City scrape the bottom at 40%.

If Paolucci grasps the urgency, she's not letting on. Minutes of the academic policy committee's Oct. 6 meeting reflect only that she "displayed her pleasure in seeing everyone working together." That sounds more like a feel-good report card from a benign grade-school teacher than a serious prescription for change.

If Paolucci aims to meet the challenge before her, she must pick up the pace. Or risk turning victory into defeat.

Newsday

July 18. 1997　A7

Reynolds Quits

Embattled CUNY chief to head Alabama university

By Robert Polner
STAFF WRITER

After months of attacks by top trustees, City University of New York Chancellor W. Ann Reynolds is leaving.

Reynolds said yesterday she intends to walk away Sept. 15 from the $166,000-a-year job to accept an offer to become president of the University of Alabama at Birmingham.

"It has been a magnificent experience to serve this superb university," Reynolds said in a parting memo to the trustees.

Her decision marked the culmination of relentless challenges to her leadership by CUNY Chairwoman Anne Paolucci and Vice Chairman Herman Badillo, who once referred to Reynolds as a "potted palm."

Faculty union representatives were also upset with what they termed her exclusionary style, with professors working without a contract for more than two years.

Paolucci and Badillo — appointees of Republicans Gov. George Pataki and Mayor Rudolph Giuliani, respectively — have raised questions in recent months over Reynolds' commitment to high academic standards, controlled spending and improved teaching.

"I don't think the CUNY system is in very good shape right now," Giuliani said yesterday after voicing surprise at Reynolds' decision. "Fortunately or unfortunately, the person in charge has to take responsibility for that."

But Reynolds' defenders said that in her nearly seven years on the job she created a key college-preparatory program for public school students, brought in $72 million more in science and math grants, and organized support for imperiled state and federal tuition assistance.

"She has met several important objectives for the university — enriching college education, improving the quality of the students coming to us and defending the university from tuition hikes," said Edith Everett, a trustee appointed by former Gov. Mario Cuomo.

Everett called Reynolds' departure unfortunate and blamed it on a power grab by Paolucci and Badillo, who represent the trustee board's new conservative majority.

"Their hostility had nothing to do with Reynolds

W. Ann Reynolds

being up to the job or not up to the job," Everett said. "From the very beginning they wanted their own people who they can manage and control, and Ann Reynolds is not someone you can manage and control. Frankly, they are power hungry."

Badillo insisted the resignation augured well for CUNY's students, saying a search for a replacement would be organized soon. In his eyes, CUNY is at a key juncture, in need of big changes. "There's been grade inflation," he said. "Practically everyone gets A's and B's. My view is we need to have standards."

At Paolucci's urging, the trustees recently set up a $1-million audit committee to evaluate the sprawling, 21-campus university system, a move widely seen as encroaching on the chancellor's turf.

Speculation about a successor focused yesterday on the president of CUNY's Baruch College, Matthew Goldstein. Other names have included Frank Macchiarola, a former city schools chancellor, and Peter Salins, of the Institute for Policy Research.

Now, Time to Find A CUNY Chancellor

By Graham Rayman
STAFF WRITER

With the resignation last week of City University of New York Chancellor Ann Reynolds, the spotlight turns to her loudest critics, Trustees Anne Paolucci and Herman Badillo.

In a short letter to trustees, Reynolds announced she was stepping down from the post she had held for seven years to take the helm at the University of Alabama at Birmingham, an institution of 16,000 students.

The responsibilities of choosing an interim chancellor and eventually a new one, and of curing what ails CUNY, now fall on Badillo and Paolucci, who mounted a campaign over the past several months against Reynolds, blaming her for everything from low academic standards to a lack of strong leadership.

Paolucci is a retired English professor from St. John's University who became chairwoman of the board in February. Badillo, the vice chairman of the

Ann Reynolds

board, is a member of Mayor Rudolph Giuliani's kitchen cabinet. They are among a 16-member board, three-fourths of which was appointed in the last year by Gov. George Pataki and Giuliani.

In telephone interviews on Friday, Badillo and Paolucci talked about what they see as the chief issues facing CUNY while declining to specify how they would be addressed.

The issues included the English as a second language writing test, the huge remedial education program, grade inflation and low standards across the board.

"We have laid the issues out," Badillo said. "We need to establish a clearer program for remediation, for entrance into the university. We need to look at why graduates of the school of education fail the teachers' exam, and we need to look at the question of grade inflation, where more than 50 percent of our students get A's and B's."

Badillo added that he wants to see CUNY's 19 college presidents speak up more at board meetings. Badillo recently scolded the presidents for remaining silent at a board meeting on the controversy at Hostos Community College over the ESL writing assessment tests, which a significant number of students failed.

Asked if CUNY's students need to be concerned about more budget cutbacks, Paolucci said, "We have no intention of cutting programs. The cost efficiencies we're looking for are there. We don't need to get more and more money. You just redistribute what's already there."

Paolucci said the board is also looking at hiring an outside auditing firm to look into the financial side of the university.

"The crucial issue is remediation," she said. "We need to see if we are doing the best for these programs and get a monitoring mechanism . . . These kinds of programs are draining the budgets of many states."

Both trustees said an interim chancellor will be chosen within the next few weeks, and then a search committee will be formed to assemble a list of candidates for the permanent position.

The New York Times

WEDNESDAY, MARCH 24, 1999

The Metro Section

Leadership Void Hobbles CUNY

as It Faces Severe Problems

Lack of Permanent Chancellor Feeds Sense of Crisis

By KAREN W. ARENSON

Two years ago, Gov. George E. Pataki gave the trustees of the chronically troubled City University of New York a new chairwoman with a mandate to steer the university in a new direction. Less than five months later, the trustees got the chance to shape their own management team when they forced the resignation of Chancellor W. Ann Reynolds.

But in the 20 months since, the opening the trustees created at the top of the university has turned into a yawning gulf.

Not only has the board failed to find a permanent chancellor. Other top executives at the university have been leaving one by one. Five of CUNY's top jobs are now filled by temporary appointees: there is an acting chancellor, an acting deputy chancellor, two acting vice chancellors, and an acting dean for student services.

The presidencies of 5 of its 17 undergraduate campuses are open or about to open, and at least 2 more presidents have been seeking other jobs.

While CUNY continues to function despite all these openings, there is a pervasive sense of crisis and lost opportunity as the university awaits a report from a task force appointed last year by Mayor Rudolph W. Giuliani. The panel, led by the former Yale president Benno C. Schmidt Jr., was asked to investigate CUNY and draw up a plan for the future; the report is expected next month.

There are few hard numbers by which to gauge the cost of the leadership vacuum.

But officials and faculty members say it has had tangible effects.

¶Long-range planning has virtually stopped.

¶Major administrative functions, like preparing budgets, are now being performed by the board itself.

¶Morale has suffered. "The level of morale is in the basement," said Sandi E. Cooper, a history professor at CUNY's College of Staten Island who is a former chairwoman of the faculty senate, "because of the insecurity of not knowing whether you are going to be rewarded or blown up at, respected or not believed."

¶Recruiting of faculty members and high-level administrators has been handicapped.

"The number of people applying for the college presidencies is much lower than it used to be," said Edith B. Everett, a trustee. "Without a permanent chancellor, they have no idea of the kind of leadership they will be operating under, the direction of the university, what its philosophy is and the support they will receive. Right now, there is a perception of chaos."

The trustees had hoped to have a new chancellor in place months ago, and their search committee had selected three finalists last summer. But the process broke down when the Governor and Mayor failed to approve any of them; they did not even summon them for interviews.

To some, the stalled search was a sign that the university and its trustees, who are responsible for appointing the chancellor, did not control their own destiny.

While the acting chancellor, Christoph M.

Kimmich, has earned great respect inside CUNY and outside — Governor Pataki's office last week said he had done an "excellent job" — there is a widespread awareness that he and many of his staff are caretakers. "It's not that we don't like Christoph Kimmich; he's done an unbelievably great job under the circumstances," said William P. Kelly, provost at CUNY's graduate center. "But how can you plan when you don't know who is going to be in charge in a year or two?"

And Herman Badillo, the vice chairman of CUNY's board, says the interim appointments also color the way the university is perceived on the outside. "You have to have a new chancellor for the Governor and the Mayor to have confidence in CUNY," he said. "An interim chancellor doesn't do it, because he doesn't have the authority to move."

Even Dr. Kimmich says the university is "not best served by a state of uncertainty."

"There is a sense of being a bit on hold," he said.

A permanent chancellor could be expected to grapple more forcefully with the critical problems facing CUNY: its tattered reputation, its shrinking financial resources, the demands for changing the way it operates.

Without such a leader, the trustees and the Mayor and the Governor have involved themselves in policy matters on an unusually detailed level.

"The gap in leadership has empowered the worst aspects of the trustees, who are trying to micromanage the university," said Bernard Sohmer, the faculty representative on the CUNY board. "Most of the presidents are terrified about what might come next."

In addition to the lack of permanent leaders, CUNY faces challenges on many fronts.

It has come under fire from the Governor and Mayor, among others, over academic standards they say are far too lax.

Enrollment has fallen, at a time when other New York colleges are seeing their applications soar. This semester's total of 193,505 students is off about 2 percent from last year, and down 9 percent from the 1994 peak of 212,634, raising questions about underused capacity on some campuses.

The university is in severe financial straits. Its budget has risen little since the early 1990's after inflation is taken into account. State and city support have fallen sharply, leaving CUNY more squeezed than many public universities. Both the Governor and Mayor are refusing to pay for faculty salary increases approved in the union contract for next year.

The trustees themselves are sharply divided over CUNY's direction and priorities, and have lacked both strong leadership and the confidence of elected leaders in Albany and New York City.

Instead of a Buffer, 'A Conduit for Politics'

The largest urban university in the United States, CUNY was once a beacon in public higher education, and in some ways it still burns brightly. But in other ways it is under siege.

"I wouldn't want to characterize what happened before as higher-education nirvana," said Patrick M. Callan, president of the National Center for Public Policy and Higher Education, in San Jose, Calif. "But CUNY is now caught in the middle of a partisan, ideological circus."

It is not unusual that the trustees are political appointees. At CUNY, the Governor appoints 10 of the 17 trustees and the Mayor 5. (There is also one faculty trustee and one student trustee.)

What is unusual is the Mayor's and Governor's close involvement in shaping CUNY's policies — and in choosing a new chancellor.

"Usually, boards are meant to be a buffer from the politics," said Joseph Burke of the Rockefeller Institute of Government in Albany. "Here, it is more like they are a conduit for the politics."

For his part, the Governor is happy with the trustees' progress, his chief of staff, Bradford J. Race, said. In particular, Mr. Race commended the passage of a hotly debated measure in January that will bar students from bachelor's degree programs if they need remedial work in reading, writing or mathematics, although they can still enroll in the community colleges.

He added that the Governor's office was also now pleased with CUNY's chairwoman, Anne A. Paolucci, whom Mr. Pataki had attacked after he grew dissatisfied with the slow pace of change.

But as the trustees themselves note, much of the board's progress has come in close, hotly contested votes. Although the votes of the Mayor's appointees have generally been consistent with his vision, Governor Pataki's appointees have splintered.

Dr. Paolucci denies that anyone outside the board is affecting policy. But others on the board say that the Mayor has been a primary force in drawing up policies like the one on remedial education.

The Mayor's press office did not respond to several telephone calls seeking comment about CUNY.

Trying to Provide A Sense of Direction

Dr. Kimmich, the mild-mannered historian who was appointed interim chancellor in November 1997 and had expected to return to his job as Brooklyn College's provost long ago, has tried to provide a calming influence and a sense of direction amid the disarray.

In the fall, for example, he worked with the trustees to draw up a five-year budget proposal for Albany, rather than the usual one-year request. This month, he led college presidents and other top administrators on an off-campus retreat to discuss long-term planning.

"Regardless of my tenure, we need to set targets and engage people in forward planning process and make sure things do get done," Dr. Kimmich said. "It may not be the norm for someone who is in a temporary position, but I don't think we can wait."

The trustees set up a committee to find a new chancellor in late 1997. With the help of a search firm, the committee conducted interviews and by last summer had produced a short list of finalists: David Adamany, the former president of Wayne State University; Richard H. Ekman, the secretary of the Andrew W. Mellon Foundation, and Warren H. Fox, the executive director of the California Postsecondary Education Commission.

What was most notable about the list, however, was that it did not include the man described as the Mayor's and Governor's candidate, SUNY's provost, Peter D. Salins. Although CUNY's search committee interviewed Mr. Salins, trustees on the committee said last summer that his presentation went poorly. Mr. Salins has declined to discuss the CUNY search.

Neither CUNY's bylaws nor state or city laws call for the Governor or Mayor to approve the appointment of a chancellor. CUNY's trustees hold that power. Although the chairwoman called the forwarding of the three candidates' names to the Mayor and the Governor last summer a courtesy, other trustees say it is one more sign of the Governor's and Mayor's influence over CUNY affairs.

One of the three candidates, Dr. Adamany, has since withdrawn, and the search committee has not met since.

Dr. Paolucci, who heads the search committee, would not comment on the events so far. She said the search firm was supposed to be finding more names, but was not finding many.

"We have good candidates," she said, "but we want to build up the list. It is a very important job."

Other members of the panel say they have heard nothing about the resumption of the search, but they and others wonder if they can even find a plausible candidate who will want the job. Some college presidents who were approached said the position involved too many political land mines.

"How do you get the kind of leadership you want when the position begins to look like a municipal appointee?" Mr. Callan asked, referring to the Mayor's role in prescribing policy. "The person has got to be accountable, but not in the same way as a municipal employee."

Moving Ahead In Spite of Turmoil

Beneath the turmoil at the top, the university has continued to function, often in impressive ways: the Carnegie Foundation for the Advancement of Teaching named a Queens College professor the state's 1998 Teacher of the Year, the third CUNY faculty member in four years to be so honored. John Jay College of Criminal Justice was rated the leading graduate program in criminal justice last year, ahead of Harvard, by U.S. News & World Report.

CUNY is also working to improve student preparation so more students can pass its placement tests when they arrive. It has expanded its College Now program to 50 high schools, so 10th, 11th and 12th graders can take CUNY's placement examinations and receive remedial help before they graduate. The university is also expanding its intensive "immersion" programs for students who fail the tests.

Officials say they are encouraged that new applications are running 2 percent ahead of last year and that applicants to the senior colleges, which are raising their entrance requirements, are better prepared than those of a couple of years ago.

The mood on campuses is varied. While some students and faculty applaud the attempts to remake the university and see the turmoil as the cost of making sweeping changes, others say they are worn down by the constant attacks on the university, using words like "battle fatigue" and "numbness" to describe how they feel.

Some who follow CUNY politics predict that no serious chancellor candidate will be put forward until summer, when Mr. Pataki has the opportunity to make new appointments to the board, solidifying control.

But Mr. Race said that the Governor's office had no such plan, and added that he believed CUNY's board was pressing ahead with its search.

Although he expressed admiration for Mr. Salins, he said the Governor had no particular candidate. "I know Peter well, and he's doing a great job at SUNY," Mr. Race said, "but I would have an interest in anybody with his qualities who expressed an interest in the job."

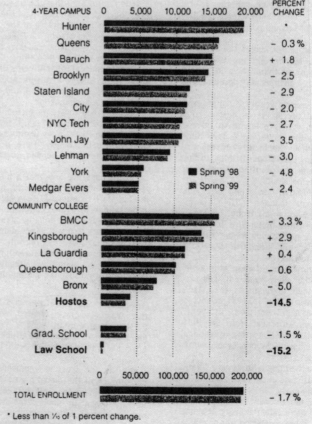

KEEPING TRACK

Missing Class at CUNY

Enrollment at the City University of New York declined 2 percent this year and has fallen 9 percent since 1994. Below, spring enrollment at the 19 campuses; the largest declines are given in **bold**.

4-YEAR CAMPUS	PERCENT CHANGE
Hunter	*
Queens	– 0.3 %
Baruch	+ 1.8
Brooklyn	– 2.5
Staten Island	– 2.9
City	– 2.0
NYC Tech	– 2.7
John Jay	– 3.5
Lehman	– 3.0
York	– 4.8
Medgar Evers	– 2.4

■ Spring '98
▨ Spring '99

COMMUNITY COLLEGE	
BMCC	– 3.3 %
Kingsborough	+ 2.9
La Guardia	+ 0.4
Queensborough	– 0.6
Bronx	– 5.0
Hostos	**–14.5**

Grad. School	– 1.5 %
Law School	**–15.2**

TOTAL ENROLLMENT	– 1.7 %

* Less than 1/10 of 1 percent change.

Source C.U.N.Y.

MORE ABOUT A.P. RESIGNATION

The Metro Section

𝕿𝖍𝖊 𝕹𝖊𝖜 𝖄𝖔𝖗𝖐 𝕿𝖎𝖒𝖊𝖘   MONDAY, MARCH 30, 199

Aides Say Pataki Is Unhappy With CUNY Leader He Chose

By RICHARD PÉREZ-PEÑA

ALBANY, March 29 — Thirteen tumultuous months after Gov. George E. Pataki picked a little-known English professor with powerful political connections as chairwoman of the City University of New York's board of trustees, he has already soured on her, aides to the Governor say.

The Governor appointed Anne A. Paolucci, who headed the English Department at St. John's University, believing he had found a tough conservative to shake up an institution whose academic standards he considered lax. It helped that she had longstanding ties to two important Pataki allies, the state Conservative Party chairman, Michael R. Long, and State Senator Serphin R. Maltese of Queens, a Conservative-turned-Republican. Her husband, Henry Paolucci, once ran as the Conservative candidate for United States Senate.

But the Pataki administration has grown frustrated with Dr. Paolucci, believing that she is not conservative enough and that her political skills are weak, said Pataki aides who insisted on anonymity. At times, the Governor has agreed with his fellow Republican, Mayor Rudolph W. Giuliani, that she has not been moving aggressively enough to raise academic standards and to cut back on remedial instruction for students who are not prepared for college work.

Mr. Pataki is not looking to replace her as chairwoman, but it may come to that, the officials said.

The administration's concerns have intensified during the continuing dispute over remediation, which has pitted those who would do away with all remedial classes against those who want to keep the courses as a central part of the curriculum. As Dr. Paolucci has tried to build a consensus behind a plan to do away with all or nearly all remedial classes at the university, Pataki aides say, she has often failed to tell the Governor's office what she was up to. They say she has surprised them with some of her positions, and with the apparent shifts in her stand, leading to questions about her commitment to change.

In an interview, Dr. Paolucci said it came as a surprise to her that the Governor or his aides had reservations about her, adding, "I'm in frequent communication with the Governor's advisers." She said she was doing as well as could be expected at the difficult task of trying to find a compromise on remediation that would gain the support of a majority of the trustees.

Mr. Giuliani contends that CUNY should end its policy of admitting anyone with a high school diploma — a policy now nearly three decades old — and should refuse to accept students who do not pass the entrance exams. He would have the university get out of the remediation business entirely and turn it over to private concerns. The Mayor's office did not return calls about Dr. Paolucci, but he and his aides have made their frustrations with her clear.

The CUNY board is essentially divided into three factions. One takes the Mayor's position. Another faction, which includes Dr. Paolucci, is searching for something slightly less radical, and the third insists, as many students and professors do, that broad-based remediation at the colleges should continue.

Given Mr. Giuliani's apparent unwillingness to compromise, and the chronic tensions between him and Mr. Pataki, university officials say that if Dr. Paolucci cannot gain the Governor's faith and strenuous backing, she may be unable to get a majority behind any plan.

Mr. Pataki favors a sharp reduction in remediation programs — though not an end to open admissions — but he also recognizes the sensitivity of the issue. Though it is the Governor who has the greatest influence over the board — he appoints 10 of the 17 trustees — he has been content to say little publicly about it, letting the Mayor and the trustees draw the fire. Indeed, the Governor's office declined to discuss Dr. Paolucci for the record.

But some state and CUNY officials say that if she cannot resolve the board's current stalemate over remediation, Mr. Pataki could be drawn more directly and more publicly into the affair.

Frustration at how a trustee has handled the issue of remedial courses for students.

Last month, John J. Calandra, a trustee appointed by Mr. Pataki, proposed ending remediation at all the system's four-year colleges by September 1999. The idea had the support of Herman Badillo, a trustee named by Gov. Mario M. Cuomo who is a close adviser to the Mayor.

But Dr. Paolucci balked, saying the plan moved too fast, surprising the Pataki administration. That came after she had named two Cuomo-appointed trustees, James P. Murphy and Edith B. Everett, who opposed any fundamental change in the university's role, to important positions.

"It looked like she was getting co-opted," said a Pataki aide.

Dr. Paolucci said she did not warn the Governor's office of her position on Mr. Calandra's proposal, because, "personally, I don't think it's proper to bother people about half-baked notions."

But less than two weeks later, Dr. Paolucci proposed a remediation plan that was, in its own way, nearly as aggressive as Mr. Calandra's. It would require students who do poorly on placement tests to attend intensive summer classes before entering four-year colleges, and would move much of the remedial education out of the colleges and into separate institutes. And all senior and junior college students would have to complete remedial education and pass the placement exams in one year.

Then, days later, she put forward a broader version of that plan, one that would eliminate all remedial classes from the four-year college curriculum, requiring students who needed them to take them in the summers or at night. But she has had to postpone a vote on that plan, admitting that it did not have the votes to pass.

To be sure, she has taken on a tall order. Seriously reducing remedial efforts would mean a profound shift in the university system's role, and she has been determined to wrap that goal into a comprehensive plan that would still accommodate students who need extra help, while addressing the role of the New York City schools. "It has been called the most aggressive plan in the nation, short of creating chaos, which we mustn't do," she said. "It's obvious that for some people this is much too radical, already."

Dr. Paolucci contends that since being appointed chairwoman, she has dealt successfully with a series of crises, a view supported by some university administrators. During her tenure, the board has forced out W. Ann Reynolds as university chancellor, found an interim chancellor, Christoph M. Kimmich, and begun the process of finding a long-term replacement. The board also weathered the storm over Hostos Community College's allowing foreign-born students to graduate without passing an English writing test, forcing a change in the school's policy and forcing out its president.

But from the beginning, many university officials have thought her an odd choice, in light of her relative lack of administrative experience. And her critics within the university and in the Governor's office say she has handled the job clumsily, from being unaware of the rules for running a board meeting to being unsure who her allies were.

A university trustee who said he was a frustrated ally of Dr. Paolucci pointed to last Monday's board meeting, when the trustees took up a motion to let individual campuses end remediation as they saw fit, before a systemwide policy was decided on. Dr. Paolucci supported the motion and brought it to a vote, where it fell one vote short.

"You don't go to a board meeting and ask for a vote unless you know in advance you're going to win," the trustee said. "It's just not smart politics."

Newsday

NEWSDAY, THURSDAY, MAY 27, 1999

A8

CUNY Vacancy

Board chairwoman resigns abruptly

By Dan Morrison
STAFF WRITER

The conservative chairwoman of the City University's board of trustees resigned abruptly yesterday, leaving vacant the top two spots in the nation's largest urban university system.

Anne Paolucci, 72, a scholar and published poet, said she was stepping down effective Tuesday.

Herman Badillo, a Republican mayoral hopeful and the board's vice chairman, will become acting chairman until Gov. George E. Pataki appoints a successor.

In a letter to the board, Paolucci said she wished to return to "writing and publishing tasks" and felt that the university needed a new person at its head as efforts to restructure the system reach a new phase.

Badillo to Run For Mayor, Page A41

One year ago yesterday, Paolucci persuaded the board to eliminate remedial classes at CUNY's 11 four-year campuses, by far the board's most contentious issue.

The resignation came as a surprise. "She just announced it today," said CUNY spokesman John Hamill. "She said she had been thinking long and hard and that she had agonized over the decision."

Paolucci could not be reached for comment.

The City University, which enrolls 355,000 degree- and non-degree students, has not had a permanent chancellor since November, 1997, when Anne Reynolds resigned under fire from Paolucci. Since then, Christoph Kimmich has been acting chancellor.

Badillo, an ally of Mayor Rudolph Giuliani who had pushed for the job of chairman before Paolucci was appointed in February, 1997, said he did not know when the governor would appoint a permanent successor.

"He could well appoint someone as chairperson other than me," Badillo said in an interview.

In a short statement, Pataki praised Paolucci for "always demanding the best for and the best from her students." He made no other comment.

Giuliani lauded Paolucci for her "dedication and aggressive advocacy for higher standards."

While many were taken aback by the abrupt announcement, some CUNY officials said Paolucci had not been the same since her husband, Henry, died on Jan. 1.

Paolucci, a retired professor at St. John's University, joined the board with no political experience. She and her husband were close to Michael Long, president of the state's Conservative party, and Henry Paolucci once ran for U.S. Senate on the Conservative line.

As chairwoman, she inherited a 17-member board torn by a dwindling number of Democratic appointees and appointees of the governor and the mayor, who are frequently at odds.

Newsday File Photo / Michael E. Ach

Anne Paolucci announced she is leaving her CUNY post.

Before a vote to eliminate remediation last year, she ordered the room cleared of unruly spectators, leading to the arrest of 26 people, including a state assemblyman. When protestors shouted, "You have no right," Paolucci responded, "I have every right."

She also found the university under pressure from the mayor last year when Giuliani appointed a commission chaired by former Yale president Benno Schmidt to audit the CUNY administration.

A report by the commission "should be released in about two weeks," said Badillo, who is a member of the commission. "It points out that we have to do much more to bring the university up to high standards."

Albany bureau chief Liam Pleven contributed to this story.

NEW YORK POST

America's oldest continuously published daily newspaper

18　　　　NEW YORK POST, THURSDAY, MAY 27, 1999

CUNY chief quits under fire

By DAVID SEIFMAN
City Hall Bureau Chief

The City University of New York's chairwoman quit yesterday — after a barrage of criticism for not moving quickly enough to enact reforms.

Anne Paolucci, a former English professor, said she planned to leave June 1 to resume "writing and publishing tasks" and so a new chairman could be in place as the university enters "a new phase in its restructuring."

Gov. Pataki immediately accepted her resignation, while praising Paolucci as an "untiring advocate for public education" in her 27 months at CUNY's helm.

She wasn't scheduled to step down until 2003.

The Post reported last November that Paolucci was on her way out amid criticism that she hasn't been able to unite the 17-member board as it grapples with such critical issues as higher standards and the search for a new chancellor.

The terms of two other CUNY trustees appointed by former Gov. Mario Cuomo — James Murphy and Edith Everett — end on June 30.

That gives Pataki an opportunity to reshape the CUNY board at a time when he and Mayor Giuliani are trying to push through several controversial changes, including an end to remedial education in the senior colleges.

Among the candidates for Paolucci's job is Herman Badillo, vice-chairman of the CUNY board.

But Badillo told The Post, "I haven't heard a word from the governor's office."

Sources said that other names being mentioned as board members are businessman Lew Lehrman, the Republican candidate for governor in 1982, and Bob Price, a former deputy mayor in the Linsday administration.

The City University is comprised of 11 senior colleges, six community colleges, a graduate school, a law school and a medical school.

AMERICA OGGI   LA GRANDE CITTÀ　　　　Friday, May 28, 1999　**13**

Anne Paolucci resigns as chairwoman of the university
TOO MANY BLOWS, I'M LEAVING
The Professor had been under constant attack by Giuliani and Pataki

CUNY

By John Cappelli

"This past year we took many blows," said Professor Anne Paolucci, Chairwoman of the Board of Trustee of CUNY, "but the climate is different now and having done a great deal during my tenure, it's time to step down. After all, I can't be expected to stay on forever."

The "different climate" Prof. Paolucci refers to must be construed as the ongoing positive restructuring phase at CUNY, brought about largely through her efforts, but in this climate we have also had, out of a clear blue sky, the rough lightning jolt of her resignation effective July 1st.

It has been accepted with equally rough suddenness by Governor Pataki, who appointed her to the Board in 1996 and made her Chairwoman in February 1997.

How did Paolucci officially explain the reasons for her decision to step down? "For some time I've been neglecting my writing and publishing, and I am convinced moreover that we are entering a new phase of restructuring at CUNY, a task which a new Board Chairperson should assume."

Generous euphemisms aside, it is well known that from the moment of her selection as Board Chair, the Professor has been subjected to unremitting open attacks by Giuliani, more subtle ones by Pataki, so that for over a year now the repeated efforts to bring before the Board names for a new Chancellor (after the equally rough resignation of Dr. W. Ann Reynolds) have been met with an implacable "veto" by both Giuliani and Pataki.

If you listen to "the other side," Anne Paolucci has brought about some reforms, but too slowly. We'll come back to that.

In accepting her resignation, Pataki said, among other things: ". . . your efforts have helped to make CUNY more efficient, more accountable and better prepared to equip students with the knowledge and tools they will need to meet the challenges of the new millenium."

A half-hearted bureaucratic thank-you considering what, according to many, the Chairwoman deserved, who in her letter of resignation, made a point of thanking the Governor for his support but made no similar reference to Mayor Giuliani.

When we pointed out to Professor Paolucci that her hasty exit comes on the eve of a review of CUNY's "Master Plan" by the Board of Regents of New York on the 1st of July, she replied that many long hours of hard work have gone into the preparation of it, that she will have contributed, in fact, a great deal to it, in and out of office.

The fact remains that the review of University operations by the special task force appointed by Mayor Giuliani, also due to come out in a few days, will be "negative," to put it mildly, and the entire complex will be back to interim in all its major areas.

Currently interim, in fact, is the Chancellor, the Vice-Chancellor, the Chairman of the Board, the Vice-Chairman of the Board. Anne Paolucci will be replaced in interim by Giuliani's man on the Board, Herman Badillo, who because of his position vis-a-vis Pataki is not likely to succeed her.

To prove how unfairly critics have insisted, openly and behind the scenes on "how little was done" for the 17 colleges and 200,000 students of CUNY during her tenure, Professor Paolucci's Public Relations office sent the press a FAX listing her "30 major initiatives" from May 1996 to May 1999. Among them, "remediation" (for students who need help with basic skills) at the junior not the senior colleges, a move backed by both Giuliani and Pataki and accomplished by Anne Paolucci, to give CUNY "stature" once again, but for many critics an elitist solution that ignores the burden placed on minority students.

HER SCHOLARLY CURRICULUM

Born in Rome, "Fulbright Scholar" from 1951 to 1952, Anne Paolucci was a professor of English at St. John's University and at CUNY, has a Ph.D. in English and Comparative Literature from Columbia University, a Master's degree in Italian Literature also from Columbia, and a B.A. [from Barnard College]. "Fulbright Lecturer" in American Drama at the University of Naples, 1965-67, a scholar in Chinese culture, poet and playwright, president of the Council on National Literatures, married to Professor Henry Paolucci, renowned professor, scholar, and political figure, who died in January 1999. Appointed to the Board of Trustees of CUNY in July 1996, she became Chairwoman in February 1997.

In the photo, Professor Anne Paolucci.

Today's News

The Chronicle of Higher Education

Thursday, May 27, 1999

CUNY Chairwoman Resigns; Action Is Likely to Strengthen Pataki's Hold on Board

By PATRICK HEALY

Anne A. Paolucci, a prime mover behind the controversial remedial-education reforms at the City University of New York, resigned Wednesday as chairwoman of its Board of Trustees -- an action that may strengthen Gov. George E. Pataki's influence over the future leadership of the system of 350,000 students.

Ms. Paolucci, a poet and playwright and a retired professor of English at St. John's University, said Wednesday that she wanted to return to her scholarly research after three tumultuous years heading the public-university system, one of the nation's largest. She has pushed policies -- often approved on sharply divided votes -- to create assessment tests, raise graduation standards, and end most remedial education offered by the system's 11 senior colleges.

That last measure, which is now being phased in, has been the subject of lawsuits by professors and civil-rights leaders, who contend that limiting remediation will close off college options to disproportionately high numbers of minority students.

Ms. Paolucci described her work as a "critical first phase of restructuring."

"That first phase is over," she said in a statement. "What lies ahead is a period of implementation, negotiation, adjustment, reaffirmation in new terms."

Governor Pataki, a Republican who appointed Ms. Paolucci as chairwoman, thanked her Wednesday for her service. He did not immediately name a successor.

Anne A. Paolucci
RESOLUTION of APPRECIATION

WHEREAS, The Honorable Anne A. Paolucci has served as a member of the Board of Trustees of The City University of New York from July, 1996 to May, 1999; and as Chairwoman of the Board from February, 1997 to May, 1999; and

WHEREAS, She has been an untiring advocate for public higher education, always demanding the best for students; and

WHEREAS, During her tenure as Chairwoman she oversaw the phasing-out of remediation at the senior colleges, the expansion of collaborations with the City's public schools to improve the academic preparation of students prior to college entry, and the establishment of a University proficiency examination to assess student progress; and

WHEREAS, Dr. Paolucci encouraged the revamping of teacher education programs to include new admission standards and incentives to recruit high quality teacher candidates; and

WHEREAS, She has worked tirelessly with deep dedication to the mission of The City University of New York with an unwavering commitment to providing an education of high quality to the people of New York; now therefore be it

RESOLVED, That the Board of Trustees of The City University of New York extends most sincere thanks and deepest appreciation to the Honorable Anne A. Paolucci for her outstanding service to the Board and the University community, and wishes her continuing success in her public and private endeavors.

CUNY BOARD OF TRUSTEES MEETING
JUNE 28, 1999

PART THREE

CONCLUSION:
FINDING MY NEW STRIDE

CONCLUSION: FINDING MY NEW STRIDE

I was seventy-three, when I resigned as Chairwoman of the CUNY Board of Trustees, but I wasn't ready to call it quits. In the midst of the pressing demands of a no-pay but challenging job, I had continued to find time for my writing, as well as my tasks as President of Council on National Literatures and for other personal demands. Free of all official obligations, I could now give my full attention to a long-range plan which no human being could subvert.

Henry, my beloved partner of five decades died on January 1, 1999 of complications from prostate cancer. He had published a great deal during his life but had left behind a great deal more. I now assigned myself my own non-paying job. I would put my long experience as an editor and writer to work at preserving as much as possible of Henry's scholarship and research on a variety of literary, political, and historical subjects; as well as his incisive analyses of American foreign policy in his monthly political newsletter, *State of the Nation*, published without interruption from 1969 to 1980.

To insure the success of my plan, I made an offer to Griffon House Publications — a small mail-order academic press that Henry had helped launch in the late 60s with his monthly newsletter. With the approval of CNL's Board of Directors, an agreement was reached whereby CNL would pay for handling and mailing expenses of certain books issued by GHP, to be sent, free of charge, to a selected list of about 600 libraries here and abroad. It was also agreed that a certain number of those books would be Henry's or by authors important in his life and my life. The cost of publishing the books would be covered by GHP, with the help of grants and donations elicited by CNL.

I then drew up a preliminary list of libraries that would receive the CNL "bonus gift books." It included The National Library of Scotland, The British Museum Library, the libraries of the Sorbonne, libraries in Canada, Japan, England, Australia, Italy, etc., as well as scores of libraries in the United States — many of which had been dues-paying member-libraries of CNL for over three decades.

With the mechanism in place, I was ready to provide the publisher with my first offering: a collection in one volume of some of Henry's major articles and monographs (some in print, but scattered and hard to find; some unpublished) under the title *Selected Writings on Literature and the Arts, Science and Astronomy, Law, Government, and Political Philosophy*. This first volume in my plan to preserve Henry's rich legacy appeared in 1999, several months after his death. The following eight books followed (most of them authored solely by him).

James Thomson's The City of Dreadful Night (2000);

Hegel on the Arts (reprint of Henry's translation of selected passages from Hegel's entire *opus* (2001);

The Achievement of Galileo (reprint, 2002);

Zionism, the Superpowers, and the P.L.O. (reprint, 2002);

Public Image, Private Interest: Kissinger's Foreign Policy Strategies in Vietnam (drawn mostly from articles written for *State of the Nation* [new edition, 2002]);

Presidential Power and Crisis Government in the Age of Terrorism, with Richard C. Clark (reprint, 2003);

Lectures on Roman History (new, 2004);

A Brief History of Political Thought and Statecraft (reprint, 2004).

Two books carry both our names. *Hegelian Literary Perspectives* (2002) is a collection of essays — some Henry's, some mine, some a collaborative effort — on a variety of literary subjects from an Hegelian point of view. The essays on Shakespeare are especially important. Shakespeareans have consistently ignored Hegel, or — worse — have criticized him without having actually read him. Hegel, whose philosophy of fine art had become part of my intellectual life soon after I met Henry (who was already a thoroughgoing Hegelian), brought fresh insights to the works of authors both my husband and I knew and loved. We first offered the collection to two publishers, both of whom were ready to accept a new study on Hegel — something we were not interested in doing. We felt that our essays, written over a number of years, were the perfect way to introduce Hegelian thought to literary critics and scholars, much like the great Italian Hegelian critic, Francesco De Sanctis, brought Hegelian thinking to bear on his many essays on major Italian authors and works, producing also a superb history of Italian literature from the same perspective. There is no such collection in English, that systematically applies Hegel's theory of the arts to major works and authors. When Hegel is mentioned at all, it is very often to cite A. C. Bradley and, more often than not, to perpetuate the few errors that crept into the great British Shakespearean's otherwise excellent analysis of "Hegel's Theory of Tragedy" (*Oxford Lectures on Poetry*).

A second book that carries both our names is *Hegel on Tragedy*. First published by Doubleday as an Anchor Book, it was later picked up as a Torchbook by Harper & Row, and, still later, was made available in hard cover (and is still being published) by Greenwood Press. It was reissued in a new paperback edition by GHP in 2001. This is a one-of-a-kind book, not apt to be repeated. Only someone who knows every aspect of Hegel's work could have put it together, someone who could find and order relevant passages from the entire Hegelian *opus* into a seamless whole. Henry could do that. The excellent choice of excerpts is his, as is most of the editing. I was there to help the master. I drafted the Introduction, but he perfected it. I helped with the detailed Index (which has proved invaluable over the years, even to me). We consulted constantly about every aspect of the work, but the final decisions were his. We both considered this book one of the most important scholarly tools for serious scholars willing to read Hegel in English. It gives anyone interested in drama (and tragedy in particular) access to Hegel's provocative analyses of ancient and modern tragedy, his keen evaluation of playwrights from the time of the Greeks down to the moderns. At the same time, it gives the reader some idea of the wealth and breadth of Hegel's command of the subject. No one has come close to his systematic analysis of dramatic theory or to his detailed applications of it. To lure the reader into the subject, we paid for and included, as an "Appendix" to the volume, Bradley's essay on Hegel.

I also reissued three books of my own, which I know Henry would have wished me to do.

The first was *From Tension to Tonic: the Plays of Edward Albee* – as mentioned earlier, the 100th volume in the Crosscurrents/Modern Critique series edited by Harry T. Moore for Southern Illinois University Press. It was reissued by GHP in 2000.

The second was *Pirandello's Theater: the Recovery of the Modern Stage for Dramatic Art* – this too written at Professor Moore's suggestion and for which he again wrote a Preface. First published by Southern Illinois University Press, it was reissued by GHP in 2002.

The third was *The Women in Dante's* Divine Comedy *and Spenser's* Faerie Queene (2006), my dissertation at Columbia, which won the first Woodbridge Honorary Fellowship in the Department of English and Comparative Literature. I had no intention of ever publishing it but relented at the personal urging of Dr. Frank D. Grande, President of GHP.

Four more additions of mine to this ongoing project are *Cipango! (The Story)* (2004), a biographical/historical account of the ironic reversals in the life of Christopher Columbus – each chapter a blend of facts and dramatic scenes drawn from my videoplay *Cipango!*; two mystery novels – *In Wolf's Clothing* and *Slow Dance to Samarra* – and *Selected Poems of Giacomo Leopardi,* one of my most difficult undertakings as a translator.

This last work started out as a collaborative project with Thomas Bergin, Sterling Professor at Yale. The occasion of our meeting (the first and only one) was a spectacular, week-long international congress and exhibition of manuscripts commemorating the 600th anniversary of the death of Petrarch. I'd been invited to present a paper at a panel Tom was chairing. He was then at the peak of his career, by far the most prominent academic attending the conference, known throughout the world for his translations of Boccaccio, Dante, as well as Petrarch and several French Poets of the Renaissance. After the Washington meeting, we corresponded and often chatted on the phone. One day, our phone conversation turned to the familiar subject of translation, the miseries and frustration a translator suffers, his constant urge to revisit a text, to do more with it. I told my friend about the many times I worked on the poems of Italy's second greatest poet, after Dante, and how I was always dissatisfied with the result and inevitably pushed the work-in-progress back into the recesses of a desk drawer or a filing cabinet, where it would remain for another several months. When I was through, he told me a similar story. We both had published some translations of Leopardi here and there, over the years; but, in talking, we realized that we shared the same secret hope of some day producing a volume of his poems in English. Impulsively, I asked: "Why don't we work together at it?"

Tom liked the idea. From January to October of 1986, we exchanged translations, consulted, suggested changes. During that year, Tom's health had began to deteriorate (he had been fighting lung cancer for some time), and I didn't want him to expend any further energy on the project. I assured him we had enough material for a book. The last translation he sent me was of "La ginestra" ("The Broom"), one of the most pessimistic and difficult of Leopardi's poems. I now had the responsibility of sorting out what we had done.

After Tom's death in 1987 (at the age of 88), I made some half-hearted attempts at finding a publisher, but I soon realized it was too early to offer the project for publication. It required a great deal of work. Not knowing exactly how to proceed at that point, I put aside the many pages that had accumulated and didn't pick them up again until fifteen years later, in 2002. As I started to go through those pages again, as I read and re-read Tom's translations and mine, I was struck, as never before, by the immense task that lay ahead. Instinctively, I knew that the job would demand more than I had anticipated. There was a moment of utter dejection, when I almost abandoned the project.

When the book was finally published, I explained in my Introduction some of the difficulties that had loomed large:

> When I pulled out the manuscript, early in 2002, I excused my delay with the reminder that time always sharpens the focus and refines the critical judgment. The break, in fact, made me appreciate Tom's efforts at searching for the right "voice" and meaning. I found, also, that at this distance I was able to see the whole with greater clarity and therefore could make consistent decisions as to the final disposition of language and of its parts — the final assignment entrusted to me. Still, there were many things that needed to be reviewed and revised if the translations were to be both readable and accurate. So I pushed everything else aside and gave myself to the task.
>
> I found that in quite a few instances both Tom and I had been misled by [Leopardi's] incredibly flexible but too often ambiguous syntax; that Italian word endings often had to be re-examined carefully as a clue to adjective-noun relationships and therefore to meaning; that the terse construction characteristic of Leopardi was easily lost in trying to maintain the original meter in English, and that perhaps it would be best to retain Leopardi's tight, often abrupt transitions after all. In short, I found myself returning to the Italian text and working directly from it once again, then comparing my current versions with both my earlier ones and Tom's.

This took time, and the result was not reassuring. My earlier versions read well; but perhaps because I'd written a great deal of poetry, my voice dominated. Tom, on his part, had expressly said, early in the project, that his priority was to maintain Leopardi's meter and produce something of an archaic flavor, as well. The result — in his case — was connectives, phrases and constructions not in the Italian, word relationships not present in the original, shifts in emphasis, and a style altogether different from Leopardi's direct, almost colloquial tone. Neither version succeeded in rendering an English equivalent that approximated Leopardi's crisp, terse, and ultimately simple language. As I scrutinized Tom's work and my earlier versions, I also realized that our separate translations were too far removed (for different reasons) to be integrated successfully into one fluid text. With growing apprehension, I soon had to admit that the only solution, the only way to realize what Tom and I had envisioned, was to scrap everything and start all over again, from scratch.

Was I prepared to do that? I had no illusions about what was in store for me. It would be an awesome undertaking. Would I be able to tune out all other voices and concentrate on Leopardi's? I almost gave up, as I surveyed the situation — also because, to carry on alone, to live under the pall of Leopardi's pessimism until the job was done, was not a pleasant prospect: it meant a sustained mental and emotional drain. On the other hand, two people had spent precious months on the project; I could not accept the notion that all the hours, days, and months spent on it were going to be lost. When I finally decided to bring the work to completion, I applied totally new guidelines. I explained my decision in the Introduction to the volume.

> My main consideration was to maintain, as closely as possible, Leopardi's language, and avoid all extraneous words. No effort was made to retain rhyming lines or, as in the case of poems like "Primo amore" ("First Love"), the difficult *terza rima*; [but I tried] wherever possible, to keep adjectives as adjectives, nouns as nouns, participial and other phrases as they appear in the Italian; to retain correspondences, repetitions, and inversions, in order to maintain the precision of meaning and give words and phrases the weight they carried in the original.

My last big decision came when the work was finished: should Tom's name appear on the cover? I brooded hard and long about this. We both had spent months on the project, but Tom had left everything up to me. When I finally came around to it again, I'd been forced to conclude, after reviewing what we had done, that our first efforts missed the target. It was not an easy decision to start all over again, alone. This other decision was even harder. In the end, I left Tom's name on the cover of the book — even though none of his hard work is in evidence. I've had to explain my decision more than once since the book appeared, but I felt that Tom's effort should be acknowledged in some way. It was a gesture of friendship and respect.

I've done other translations but never felt about them as I do about my Leopardi poems. Pirandello's "History of the Italian Theater" appears as the Introduction to Eric Bentley's *The Genius of the Italian Theater*; a long segment from Pierre Duhem's massive *Le Système du Monde* is included in an anthology Henry prepared, *The Achievement of Galileo*); Machiavelli's comic masterpiece, *Mandragola,* published in the late 50s, has gone through at least 39 printings and several publishers — its success as an academic and theater text undoubtedly due, in large part, to the Introduction Henry wrote, where that

bitter exercise in diplomacy, applied to satisfying personal and self-serving ends, is explained in terms of Machiavelli's realistic political conclusion: that only one end justifies the means, and that end can only be the safety and preservation of the state. Yet, in spite of its continued success, I never looked at that translation (or any of the others) after it was published. *Mandragola* continues to be an academic "best seller," but I still feel that somehow it isn't quite "finished," that if I had it in my hands again, I would want to continue working on it. My reaction to the Leopardi translations was altogether different, even as I re-read them for publication. When I read them in print, I discovered I was still pleased with the results. I hear Leopardi's voice, I find his abrupt transitions in English match the quick changes in mood of the Italian text. I am satisfied that the terse tight English verse echoes his. I felt a certain justification when the work was singled out for recognition and awarded a cash prize by the Italian Ministry of Foreign Affairs.

Recently, I took on and brought to completion something especially dear to Henry and me, something we had started many years ago but somehow never got around to finishing while Henry was alive. This was the Bigongiari notes we took, while graduate students at Columbia, of his two-semester course on Dante. I'd learned shorthand expressly for the purpose (and completely forgot it afterwards). Henry used his own version of abbreviated words and phrases. In the evening, after class, we would return to our apartment, a few blocks from the University and, after a quick supper, we'd tackle the two sets of notes until two or three in the morning — I, reading my shorthand notes out loud, as I transcribed them on the typewriter; Henry consulting his own notes, then dictating what we felt was the first draft of a readable text. Years later, we tried to edit those notes, but each time we found the task daunting. Too much would have to be cut out, too many changes and adjustments would have to be made. Much of the excitement of the Socratic exchanges in the classroom and Bigongiari's habit of interrupting with timely comments or anecdotes would have to be trimmed or deleted altogether to turn even the running text we'd put together into a readable book. It seemed an awesome responsibility. We simply kept postponing it. After Henry's death, I picked up the project again. I felt I owed it to Bigongiari (who shaped so much of our thinking), as well as to Henry and myself, to get it done.

The first book (representing the first half of the course) finally appeared in 2005 with the title *Backgrounds of the* Divine Comedy. The second, *Readings in the* Divine Comedy, came out in 2006. An earlier book, *Essays on Dante and Medieval Culture,* edited by Henry at the request of Giuseppe Prezzolini, Bigongiari's friend and colleague (who, as I explained earlier had left a successful world-wide journalistic career to teach at Columbia), contains the few pieces Bigongiari actually wrote at the request of colleagues and publishers. First printed by Leo S. Olschki, the Florentine publisher, the book was reissued by GHP, as part of the "bonus gift books" library project in 2000.

These three books are among the most important contributions to Dante studies in the last century.

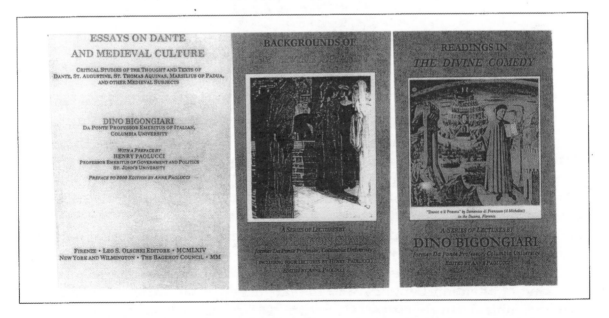

CNL has also made available for the "bonus gift books" library project the work of interesting old and new writers and talented artists.

The "CNL/Anne and Henry Paolucci International Conference Center" in Queens, New York, which I founded soon after my husband's death, hosted in 2001 an exhibit by artist Vincenzo R. Latella — 35 oil paintings, each depicting a scene from Dante's *Inferno* and a portrait of the poet himself. The CNL Board decided, after the exhibit closed, that the collection was worth preserving in some way. The result was a lovely volume — *Dante's Gallery of Rogues*. Each individual print fills the right-hand page; the *terzina* (in Italian and English) describing the event depicted is on the left, near the bottom of the page. At the request of the publisher, I wrote a rather substantial general introduction to the *Inferno*, "The Strident Voices of Hell."

In 2004, GHP added to their list of new books a collection of poems and short stories that had won annual prizes set up by CNL in 1995 in *Potpourri Magazine* (*Potpourri Magazine: Council on National Literatures Annual Awards in Poetry and Fiction [1995-2003]*).

Another book published under the CNL/GHP agreement carries the title *Beyond the* Commedia (2004). It contains three unusual offerings that should be of interest to Dante scholars, each published at some earlier date but hard to come by in recent years. The first section reproduces a work attributed to Dante, *A Question of the Water and of the Land*. It reminds some scholars of the kind of attention Dante gave to the languages of the various parts of the Italian peninsula, in *De Vulgari Eloquentia*. Others refuse to accept the work as Dante's. The question of authorship seemed important enough to preserve for future scholars the contents of the brief treatise, which appeared in an English translation by Charles Hamilton Bromby, in London in 1897, and which I came upon in the Columbia discards (a book now virtually impossible to find).

The second section consists of three papers originally presented at the Modern Language Association's annual convention in New York in 1976, as the annual program of The Dante Society of America for the Bicentennial year: "Dante's Influence on American Writers (1776-1976)." The Consul General of Italy in New York, Alessandro Cortese DeBosis, and Congressmen Lester Wolff and Mario Biaggi welcomed the group; presentors were J. Chesley Mathews, James J. Wilhelm, and Glauco Cambon. The event drew over two hundred (we had to move quickly to a large hall in order to accommodate the crowd that had assembled) — an all-time record for any MLA "Affiliated Association," I learned later. (I'd also suggested a second Bicentennial project: a collection of essays by eminent American Dantists, starting with the Harvard scholars who first introduced Dante studies in America, early in the 19th century, right down to the present, including a piece by Dino Bigongiari — a project accepted by the Board and entrusted to the Society's President, A. Bartlett Giammati, who later became head of Yale University. It was published in the late eighties.)

The third section of *Beyond the* Commedia contains a long article, first written by Henry and me for the *India* volume of *Review of National Literatures*, "Dante and the 'Quest for Eloquence' in India's Vernacular Literature" (1979). (It was singled out in a number of journals and newspapers, here and abroad, and was the lead review in the *India Times* Literary page.)

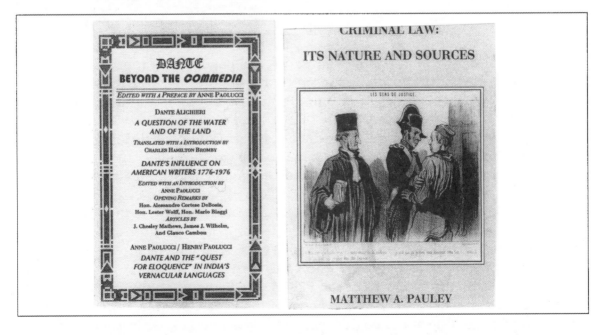

Another work we thought deserved to be published was *Criminal Law: Its Nature and Sources*, with a Preface by New York State Supreme Court Justice, Joseph G. Golia — an authoritative, witty, and readable introduction to the subject by Matthew Pauley, brilliant young scholar from Harvard.

One of the most unusual, certainly the most handsome book published by GHP to-date is Constance Del Vecchio Maltese's *An Artist's Journey of Discovery*. I would like to expand here on what I said earlier about this memorable product of the Columbus Quincentenary.

COVER OF CONSTANCE DEL VECCHIO'S *AN ARTIST'S JOURNEY OF DISCOVERY*, WITH THE PHOTOGRAPH OF THE ARTIST AND, IN THE SHADOWED BACKGROUND, THE "YOUNG COLUMBUS."

The large-format volume contains full-page color reproductions of thirteen original portraits of Renaissance navigators, as well as some later masters of the sea, who played an important role in the continuing history of "discovery." The series begins with the "Young Columbus" (1988) and ends with "Admiral of the Ocean Sea," which depicts Columbus in chains (1992). Others in the series are Vasco Da Gama, Amerigo Vespucci, Juan Ponce De Leon, John and Sebastian Cabot, Ferdinand Magellan, Giovanni Da Verrazzano, Hernando Cortez, Vasco Nunez De Balboa, Henry Hudson, and Queen Isabella, the Spanish sovereign who played such a crucial part in the history of Columbus's four journeys and continued to support him until her death in 1504. Although of an earlier time, Marco Polo is also part of the series as the man who for centuries triggered the imagination of so many — including Columbus — with his accounts of the island of *Cipango* (Japan) and the fabled treasures of the Far East. The series (as mentioned earlier) won several awards, including CNL's "Special Recognition in the Arts and Humanities" award and was featured for two years on the museum-ship "Intrepid" in New York.

What is unusual about these portraits is that the artist used living models for the facial features and other basic details, then gave her subject what she conceived as his/her characteristic expression. The result is a stunning departure from the kind of formal portraits we are accustomed to see in corporate offices, university Board rooms, and other similar places. Maltese's series has a vital immediacy; her figures seem to be thinking and breathing, communicating with us rather than staring out at us. They are depicted in costumes of the time — testimony to the meticulous research by the artist to insure scrupulous accuracy in details.

A second feature that gives these portraits historical as well as artistic value, reminding us of the artist's careful research, is the "legend" surrounding her subjects. These "highlights" are often inside a design that serves as an inner frame. At the bottom of the portrait of Marco Polo, a parade of horsemen stretches across the canvas; on the sides, we see cameos of Kubla Kubla and others whom Marco Polo encountered on his historic journey. In the portrait of Verrazzano, the artist has turned the edge of the subject's cape into the eastern coast of North America, the names of places the explorer claimed for France (under whose banner he sailed). These are executed in small print that gives the impression of a fringed edge to the cloth. In the foreground is a drawing of the ship on which Verrazzano sailed and the inlet or harbor where he weighed anchor. On the bottom right are two figures of Native Americans. In the portrait of the "Young Columbus," the inner frame was taken from an authentic design of the time; on the bottom is a drawing of the Santa Maria; opposite it is the crest Columbus adopted after receiving many honors at the Spanish Court on his return to Spain from the first journey. Just above that, is the profile of a Native American; facing it, on the other side, is Queen Isabella, also in profile.

These details of the subject's life are never executed in the same way. Each canvas is a new surprise. A special feature of the book is a photograph — facing the full-page reproduction of the portrait — of the model who posed for it, as well as a brief anecdotal account of how that person came to be chosen. The book also contains photographs of events connected with the series, as well as other interesting data and illustrations.

How the project came about is worth telling.

One evening, in the Fall of 1984 (I was just about to launch "Columbus: Countdown 1992"), as Constance and I waited for the men to retrieve our coats after a fund-raising dinner out on Long Island, she said casually: "You know, I'd like to try something new. . . ." Constance was a successful commercial artist but — as she went on to explain — she was ready for a fresh challenge. "What about my doing something for the Quincentenary?" she asked. The answer was easy enough: "What about a painting connected with the Columbus story?" Neither one of us was thinking of portraits — although she had done a few in the past, including a fine drawing of Ronald Reagan — but portraits it turned out to be.

In the months that followed, she and Henry had long conversations about Columbus. Henry provided historical and other materials and lent her a number of books from our library that he thought she would find useful. One day in October 1988, Constance called. She wanted to stop over and show us something. The "something" was the finished portrait of "Young Columbus." We were the first to see it, she explained, and she wanted to know what we thought. "You should be home packing," I scolded. Serphin had just won his first victory as a New York State Senator (a job he still holds), and he and Constance were flying down to Washington later in the afternoon to attend victory celebrations. "Plenty of time for that," she said, shrugging off my words as she tore the brown wrapping from the framed portrait.

Neither of us could ever have anticipated the result of that first effort. She had obviously learned a great deal about the time and about Columbus himself; she didn't need anyone's help any more. But what really struck us was the force emanating from the painting and her innovative approach to portraiture. She had obviously gone much further in her research, as well. Clearly, she had found a new style. My first reaction was: What else is left for her to do? She quickly disabused us. She was planning other portraits. Before she left that afternoon, we had worked out the title for the series: The "Age of Discovery Navigators." What materialized were the thirteen portraits listed earlier — a collection worthy of any major museum. I was pleased when GHP accepted her book as one of its "bonus gift books" titles.

My most recent additions to the project are three "samplers" of essays drawn from the various *RNL* volumes published since 1970. The first contains a selection of essays Henry and I wrote, separately and together. The second contains essays on the emergent and neglected literatures and carries an Introduction by Gerald Gillespie, former (now "Honorary") President of the International Comparative Literature Association and Professor Emeritus at Stanford University. The third contains selections on the European literatures.

Publication of *RNL* was discontinued in 2001. That same year marked the opening of the CNL/Anne and Henry Paolucci International Conference Center in Queens, New York, where, for the last seven years CNL has invited the general public to enjoy lectures, art exhibits, dramatic readings, musical recitals, book signings, and book fairs, free of charge. Soon after the Center opened, a former D.A. student of mine, Dr. Clara Sarrocco, agreed to become my Assistant and help with the ongoing task of inviting speakers and arranging monthly programs. At the same time, she took on the editing of *Book Digest*, CNL's one-page review of important new titles, sent out with the "bonus gift books" to libraries. In 2006, the Board elected her Director of the Center and Executive Director of CNL — jobs she had taken on, even before the titles made them official: running a vital cultural center, supervising the activities of a restructured CNL, allowing me more time for other projects. Without her help, things would not have worked out or run as smoothly as they did.

Between 1999 and the end of 2007, with the support of friends and colleagues, the backing of the CNL Board, the cooperation of GHP's energetic President Dr. Frank D. Grande and its long-time and most helpful Director Jack Ryan, I have edited and/or written over thirty books for distribution to libraries here and abroad, as part of the CNL/GHP "bonus gift books" project. I am pleased to say that the libraries receiving the books have expressed genuine interest in them and are grateful to us for adding to their collections.

In 2004, another possibility for preserving Henry's legacy opened up unexpectedly, and I quickly set about exploring it.

At the prodding of friends who were living in Wilmington, Delaware, my husband and I bought a second apartment there in 1996. I had just retired from St. John's and had been named to serve on the Board of Trustees of CUNY (the call came to me while we were actually visiting our friends in Wilmington). Henry had been diagnosed with prostate cancer some time earlier, but a program in which he had agreed to participate at Columbia Presbyterian Medical Center had kept him in remission for several years. The hopes that had been raised during those years were dashed when the cancer flared up again, soon after we bought the second apartment. We had quickly found a place where he could have dialysis treatments (his kidneys had begun to fail), but when in August of 1998 he developed a high fever and had to be rushed to Wilmington Hospital and then to Christiana Care Hospital, I knew that drastic changes were coming. At Christiana Care (rated third in the country for patient care) the doctors could not diagnose the new symptoms Henry had developed. They tried a number of medications, but after two weeks without any change in his condition (except that the fever had been brought under control or had gone down for whatever reason), I hired a private ambulance and took him directly to Booth Memorial Hospital in Queens, not far from where we lived in Beechhurst. He came home after two weeks, was back in the hospital in

September, and again, for the last time, at the beginning of December. I still scold myself for not having kept him home or at least placed him in a hospice for that last month of his life, instead of leaving him to the mercy of doctors who knew he was dying and yet subjected him to useless tests and surgeries. On the very day he died, when he was already in a coma, a team came into his room and tried to convince me that he should have a feeding tube inserted!

Neither of us had really had time to adjust to Wilmington. As his illness progressed, Henry was not too happy with the prospect of driving down to Wilmington every so often. After his death, I was tempted to sell the new apartment but resisted making hasty decisions. Instead, I continued to drive down on a regular basis. I also began searching out universities where I might set up a memorial fund in his name but the results were not encouraging. As Fate would have it, in the Fall of 2001 I accepted a friend's invitation to attend a lecture at the Intercollegiate Studies Institute (ISI), on Centerville Road, a few minutes away from my apartment.

Not many people have heard of ISI, even in Wilmington, although it has close to 60,000 members (at least half are students and professors on campuses throughout the country). Their headquarters or "campus" boasts many acres of land and a lovely mansion. I enjoyed the event, but when I left I was no more aware of the group's main activities than I had been when I arrived. After a few more visits, I began to learn things that alerted me to the possibility that ISI might be the perfect place to set up a fund and promote certain activities in Henry's name.

I learned, for starters, that ISI's main efforts were directed toward monitoring academic programs, especially the teaching of American history in our colleges and universities, where their campus-based members were trying to counter the prevailing liberal views, which undermine in different ways the work of our Founding Fathers, as well as the men themselves. I discovered that in many schools and colleges, the name of George Washington, for example, has disappeared from the textbooks and history classes. At the request of students and professors, ISI was providing lecturers, discussion panels and special seminars at college and university centers to encourage the kind of debate not found in the classrooms. The Wilmington lectures, I soon discovered, were a kind of "bonus"; their main work was monitoring the teaching of history and other subjects on liberal-dominated campuses across the country. They found speakers who could challenge and respond to arguments that put down our historical traditions; writers and educators who could effectively answer the current practice of rewriting history according to current fads and prejudices — in short, it had taken on the awesome challenge of stemming the erosion of educational values on our campuses and tried whenever and wherever possible to counter the current prejudices that often pass for history in our classrooms. In 2006, they launched a dramatic new initiative: formal debates on the campuses themselves, with the approval (or at the invitation) of campus officials.

My interest in the group was prodded one evening as I chatted with two of ISI's young executives at a reception that followed a lecture I had gone to hear. I discovered to my great astonishment that their first president had been William F. Buckley, Jr., who knew Henry well and had asked him to write for *National Review* a number of times. It was Bill (as I mentioned earlier) who had nominated Henry for the United States Senate, at the Conservative Party Convention in 1964, when Clare Boothe Luce had to step down. I also learned that among the early and continuing supporters of ISI, until their deaths, were Henry Salvatori, a West coast businessman who shared Henry's views and visited us when in New York, and Henry Regnery, the publisher, for whom Henry had prepared and edited two important books: *The Political Writings of St. Augustine* and the *Enchiridion.* (Later, when I was given more literature about ISI, I found the two books listed in a small catalog of recommended titles ISI distributes to students and offers at below-cost prices.) In talking with the two young men at the reception that evening, I also learned that we had friends in common, including a colleague of Henry's at St. John's, a history professor who admired Henry and still remembers him vividly.

To me, an intellectual conservative and an educator who has witnessed the slow deterioration of the public schools and colleges across the nation; who experienced first-hand the almost insurmountable difficulties connected with any attempt to correct deficiencies and improve the quality of education in a systematic and integral way; who has watched the erosion of traditional values as teachers and professors rewrite history according to current fads, ISI was a breath of fresh air. I was delighted to have found a group that is both well-organized and well-funded, with qualified people who can carry out its goals.

By 2003, I had made up my mind. ISI was the kind of place and had the kind of people running it that Henry would have appreciated. I nudged my new friends and told them what I had in mind. Early in 2004, I entered into an agreement with ISI to establish an annual book prize of $5,000 in Henry's name or, more accurately, "The Henry Paolucci/Walter Bagehot Book Award," since Henry was a great admirer of the British economist and man of letters and resembled him in many ways. He had, in fact, named the organization he founded in the late 60s after the author of *Lombard Street*, calling it "The Walter Bagehot Research Council on National Sovereignty," a sign of his admiration and respect for the British writer.

The first book award went to Professor Derek Beales of Cambridge University for his *Prosperity and Plunder: European Monasteries in the Age of Revolution (1650-1815)* — not a "popular" subject, but one that is of immense archival value and that only a few scholars remain with enough solid preparation to tackle it. Professor Beales flew in from Cambridge, England for the November 11, 2004 event, and gave an excellent lecture.

More recently, I signed a second agreement with ISI which redirects the activities of Council on National Literatures to include four lectures a year on ISI-member campuses throughout the country, an annual conference, and an annual prize to an ISI faculty-member who has introduced into his or her syllabi authors or works from literatures not in the mainstream.

STORY IN THE ISI MAGAZINE, *THE CANON*, ABOUT THE FIRST "HENRY PAOLUCCI/WALTER BAGEHOT BOOK AWARD" TO PROFESSOR DEREK BEALES OF CAMBRIDGE UNIVERSITY, ENGLAND, ON NOVEMBER 11, 2004

LEGACY GIFT MEMORIALIZES EMINENT CONSERVATIVE HENRY PAOLUCCI AND ENDOWS NEW ISI BOOK AWARD

Henry Paolucci lived an extraordinary life. As an aviator in World War II, he flew numerous combat missions over Africa and Italy. After the war, he taught courses at Columbia and St. John's College on subjects ranging from Greek and Roman history to Dante and modern science. He wrote, translated, and edited hundreds of scholarly

Dr. Anne Paolucci, center, joined ISI's Jeff Nelson, family friend Frank Grande, award-winner Derek Beales, ISI's Jeff Cain, and New York State Senator Serphin Maltese on the night of the book award presentation honoring her late husband.

papers and books, most notably *War, Peace and the Presidency* and the *Political Writings of St. Augustine.* A frequent contributor to the editorial pages of the *New York Times* and *National Review*, Professor

Paolucci actively participated in politics, running against Robert F. Kennedy for the U.S. Senate in 1964 on the New York Conservative Party ticket. Until his death in 1999, Professor Paolucci remained a vigorous force in New York politics and a prominent conservative intellectual.

Last year, Anne Paolucci, Henry's widow—herself an internationally acclaimed scholar, teacher, playwright, author, translator, and poet—decided to honor her husband's achievement through a memorial gift. For decades, she had labored with him on numerous academic, political, and cultural projects. Establishing an endowment at a major university seemed like the logical way to preserve their legacy, but she worried that the intent of her gift would eventually be lost among a large university's other priorities and ever-changing political commitments.

Because of this, Anne Paolucci turned to the Intercollegiate Studies Institute, whose first president—William F. Buckley, Jr.—had been a close friend of her husband's. ISI also had a well-known reputation for defending liberty, honoring donor intent, and exposing universities when they played fast and loose with donor funds. Moreover, because Henry Paolucci was a prominent man of letters, ISI's publishing enterprise, ISI Books, was a fitting place to preserve his memory.

ISI Books was launched in 1994 with the hope of leavening the publishing industry with books that were conservative and humanist in orientation. ISI Books has since published dozens of such volumes, offering quality titles that might endure, or at least argue afresh some enduring truths: the kind of books that stand out from the constant flood of meaningless words the public is subjected to each day. With a deep interest in perennial ideas, ISI Books demonstrates respect not merely for words, but for the truth embodied "from the beginning" in The Word—a commitment that ISI Books shares with Anne Paolucci and with the great tradition represented by the name of her husband.

These reasons led Anne Paolucci to select ISI and ISI Books to administer her legacy gift. Working with Dr. Jeff Cain, ISI's director of Institutional Advance-

ANNE PAOLUCCI'S LEGACY
GIFT BOTH ADVANCES THE ISI
MISSION AND HONORS HER
HUSBAND: AN EMINENT AMERICAN
CONSERVATIVE THINKER,
POLITICIAN, AND TEACHER.

Derek Beales, author of Prosperity and Plunder: European Catholic Monasteries in the Age of Revolution, 1650-1815, *won the 2004 Walter Bagehot/Henry Paolucci Book Award.*

ment, and Jeffrey O. Nelson, vice president of ISI Books, Dr. Paolucci helped craft her gift in a way that enables ISI to recognize and reward a scholar or public intellectual who has exemplified in their work the ISI idea of educating for liberty through an annual cash prize of $5,000. The name of the award, the Walter Bagehot/Henry Paolucci Book Award, also honors the great British political economist and man of letters Walter Bagehot, whom Henry Paolucci long admired and studied.

On November 11, 2004, the very first Walter Bagehot/Henry Paolucci Book Award was presented to Derek Beales, author of *Prosperity and Plunder: European Catholic Monasteries in the Age of Revolution,*

1650-1815, at a full ceremony at ISI's national head-quarters in Wilmington, Delaware.

As Jeff Nelson noted in his presentation of the award that evening, the core mission of ISI is to articulate for new generations the importance of the foundations and principles of Western civilization and of the American experience within it. The late Russell Kirk, himself a great admirer of both Walter Bagehot and Henry Paolucci, recalled in his last work: "We Americans live in an era when the general outlines and institutions of our inherited culture still are recognizable; yet it does not follow that our children or our grand-children will retain a great part of that old culture."

In an effort to promote this culture throughout the generations, Anne Paolucci's legacy gift advances the ISI mission while also honoring her husband.

Other initiatives with ISI are being planned. Of special importance to me personally is to consolidate and expand the work of CNL. ISI seems the perfect place for this to be done. Until recently, most of their efforts to restore educational values have been history-oriented; by offering CNL lectures, conferences, and other multicomparative programs to their 30,000 or so faculty and students (roughly half their total membership), they will be in the forefront of literary studies, adding to their agenda a literary dimension that will prove just as interesting and academically significant. Toward that end, and to allow for other collaborative projects that will insure the educational legacy of logical thinking, historical accuracy, and intellectual integrity to which both Henry and I dedicated our lives and to which ISI is firmly committed, I have set up the Anne and Henry Paolucci Fund.

Anticipating this new joint enterprise, I have prepared three volumes of "samplers" (mentioned earlier) — essays drawn from the *Review of National Literatures* series — for distribution to libraries in the GHP/CNL "bonus gift book" project but also to be made available to ISI academic members interested in promoting multicomparative literary studies on their campuses. The first two are already in print (a selection of essays written by me and/or Henry, and selected essays on the emergent and neglected literatures, with an Introduction by Professor Gerald Gillespie). A third volume focuses on the European literatures. The "samplers" — an ideal introduction to *RNL* — will be ready for distribution to those attending the first CNL/ISI conference tentatively scheduled for the Spring of 2008.

Over the last 37 years, CNL has provided valuable materials to help facilitate the systematic restructuring of comparative literary studies to include the many national literatures not in the traditional canon. Its companion series, *CNL/World Report,* has proved an important forum for exchange of ideas and for debate about the future of the profession. The need for both continues as we move toward effective guidelines for multicomparative literary studies. ISI, with its large faculty membership, can prove most effective in any effort to introduce into academic studies areas now at the periphery of the literary canon or altogether ignored by it.

My collaboration with ISI has become my major "project," after the GHP/CNL "bonus gift book" initiative. Both will keep me busy; but other interests have not been abandoned. Looking back, the year 2001 seems to have been a turning point of sorts. That was the year that the CNL Board held a dinner at "Players" to commemorate the 25th anniversary of the founding of CNL – and, as the committee insisted, to celebrate my 75th birthday as well. I was presented with a gold pin, about one and a half inches square, with the CNL logo reproduced on the surface in slightly raised letters. I was also given a large handsome book, in which dozens of testimonial letters were collected, each carefully inserted in a plastic sheath.

SOME OF THE LETTERS RECEIVED ON THE OCCASION OF THE 25TH ANNIVERSARY OF CNL AND A.P.'S 75TH BIRTHDAY.

ANNE PAOLUCCI

One of the terrors facing a creative writer early on in his career is the awareness that sooner or later critics and scholars are going to start interpreting and dissecting his work, beginning the long and wearying misunderstanding and misinterpretation that will plague any writer who is brave or foolhardy enough to go on writing in the face of it.

It is a lucky writer, indeed, who finds an Anne Paolucci at him early on, writing with intelligence, insight and perception. Her book, *__FROM TENSION TO TONIC__,* made this writer a happy man, and while Dr. Paolucci's accomplishments are many and varied, and her championing of Pirandello essential to our understanding of 20th century drama, her lucid and encouraging essays on my first handful of plays still burns bright for me.

Now ....if she would only write volume two!

Established in 1987, The Shakespeare Guild
is a global not-for-profit corporation that celebrates,
and endeavors to cultivate larger and more appreciative audiences
for, the dramatist who has been applauded in every society
as history's most reliable guide to the mileposts of life.

2141 Wyoming Avenue NW, Suite 41
Washington, DC 20008-3916
Phone (202) 483-8646   Fax (202) 483-7824
E-Mail shakesguild@msn.com

Presenter of THE GOLDEN QUILL
The Sir John Gielgud Award for Excellence in the Dramatic Arts

FOUNDER AND PRESIDENT
John F. Andrews

BOARD OF DIRECTORS
Kenneth L. Adelman
J. Leeds Barroll III
Letitia Chambers
Esther Coopersmith
June Oppen Degnan
Janet A. Denton
Susan Eisenhower
Barbara Hammerman
R. Robert Linowes
Mark Olshaker
Walda W. Roseman
John Safer

ADVISORY COUNCIL
F. Murray Abraham
Brian Bedford
Ralph Berry
Livingston Biddle
David Birney
Winton M. Blount
John Russell Brown
Nedda Casei
Tony Church
Robert Aubry Davis
Barry Day
Jan Du Plain
Irwin Glusker
Janet A. Griffin
Marifrancis Hardison
Kitty Carlisle Hart
Jeffrey Horowitz
Michael Kahn
Michael Learned
Ken Ludwig
Maynard Mack
Robert MacNeil
Sherry L. Mueller
Adrian Noble
Peggy O'Brien
Andrew Oehmann
Stuart Omans
William W. Patton
Roger Pringle
Tony Randall
Lynn Redgrave
Michael A. Rosenberg
Sir Donald Sinden
Susan Stamberg
Jean Stapleton
Patrick Stewart
Homer Swander

GIELGUD AWARDEES
Sir Ian McKellen, 1996
Sir Derek Jacobi, 1997
Zoe Caldwell, 1998
Dame Judi Dench, 1999
Kenneth Branagh, 2000

July 29, 2001

Dear Anne,

May I add my congratulations to those you'll be receiving from all your dozens of other well-wishers on this special occasion.

Through all the contributions you've made, both personally and professionally, to all the individuals, institutions, and organizations you've touched, you've taught us all that there are no limits to what a dedicated creative spirit can do to bring light, joy, and love to a world in which these qualities become increasingly precious with each passing year.

With immense gratitude,

John

DEPARTMENT OF ENGLISH,
DEPARTMENT OF COMPARATIVE LITERATURE,
COMMITTEE ON THEATER AND PERFORMANCE STUDIES,
and COMMITTEE ON GENERAL STUDIES IN THE HUMANITIES
1050 East 59th Street
Chicago, Illinois 60637
bevi@midway.uchicago.edu tel. 773/288-7905 fax. 702-2495
Tue, Jul 17, 2001

Azar Attura
P O Box 4115
Arlington, VA 22204

Dear Azar Attura,

I'm happy to have your letter on the 25th anniversary of the Council
on National Literatures and about your plans for a celebration of the
75th birthday of Anne Paolucci, whose work I much admire. I fear that
the date is such that I cannot attend; I have to be teaching in
Chicago on the 24th of October. But my best wishes and thoughts will
be with you. I do hope that you will convey to Anne my warmest
greetings and congratulations. Hers has indeed been a remarkable
career. Just to cite one instance, it's very significant that the
CNL, to which she has given so much of herself, will be sponsoring
activities and publications of the Pirandello Society. My warmest
greetings also to Mr John Martello, Executive Director of the
Players. In addition to that, it's remarkable to recall how Anne has
chaired the Department of English at St John's University, where she
served as first University Research Professor. She has of course been
a distinguished professor at Queens College, as well as series editor
of the *Review of National Literatures* and editor of the *Pirandello
Society of America's* annual publication. She amazes us all with how
much she gets done.

I do wish I could join you to enjoy all that promises to happen on
the 24th.

Sincerely,

David Bevington
Phyllis Fay Horton Distinguished Service Professor in the Humanities

Oct 22 01 02 0752

THE CONSUL GENERAL OF ITALY
IN NEW YORK

October 10, 2001

Ms. Azar Attura
Member, CNL Board of Directors
Council on National Literatures
68-02 Metropolitan Avenue
Middle Village, New York 11379

Dear Ms. Attura:

Thank you for your kind invitation to attend the reception/dinner to celebrate and honor Comm. Dr. Anne Paolucci's 25th year as President of CNL as well as her 75th birthday on Wednesday, October 24, 2001.

In as much as I would have be delighted to attend, regrettably, due to a series of previously accepted engagements in New York I will be unable to attend.

However, I would like to extend my most sincere and heartfelt congratulations to Commendatore Paolucci. She wholeheartedly deserves much credit, praise and recognition for the excellence of her work especially for the commitment with which she dedicates herself to all that is Italian. Her remarkable career as a scholar, writer, playwright and poet is truly inspiring. She is a beacon among academics as well as among the young men and women who benefit from her experience as an accomplished educator. An extraordinary woman who is an extraordinary role model for young Italian Americans.

It is fitting that you celebrate and honor her during Italian Heritage and Culture Month for she is a true Renaissance woman.

Sincerely yours,

Giorgio Radicati

690 PARK AVENUE · NEW YORK, N.Y. 10021 · TEL. (212) 737-9100 · 737-9112 · FAX (212) 439-8677

October 10, 2001

I would like to extend my most sincere and heartfelt congratulations to Commendatore Paolucci. She wholeheartedly deserves much credit, praise and recognition for the excellence of her work especially for the commitment with which she dedicates herself to all that is Italian. Her remarkable career as a scholar, writer, playwright and poet is truly inspiring. She is a beacon among academics as well as among the young men and women who benefit from her experience as an accomplished educator. An extraordinary woman who is an extraordinary role model for young Italian Americans.

It is fitting that you celebrate and honor her during Italian Heritage and Culture Month for she is a true Renaissance woman.

Sincerely yours,

Giorgio Radicati

Giorgio Radicati

Before leaving the Pirandello Society of America, in 2002, I prepared and edited for the Society (and for distribution through GHP) the last four volumes of the annual journal, *PSA* (1999-2002). I had decided to resign from the group, not because my interest in Pirandello had diminished but because I wanted to set up new initiatives that would draw especially younger scholars to the contemporary theater by way of the playwright who had revolutionized it. The Society continues to draw scholars to its MLA meetings and provides an outlet for ongoing research, with *PSA*; but what I now have in mind is something broader. Ideally, I'd like to see in our colleges and universities more theater-oriented programs featuring Pirandello and the many contemporary playwrights who gained so much from him. I hope to work with ISI in establishing annual prizes to encourage such activity.

That same year, I received a grant from Queens Public TV to produce a video of my award-winning short play, *Minions of the Race*. The play premiered in November of that year and continues to be shown periodically on QPTV stations. *Cipango! (The Story)* — a combination of fictionalized and factual history about the ironies of the Columbus story— has gone through three printings since it was first published in 2004. (In 2005 it was singled out as "must reading" by the Book Club of OSIA).

A few surprises were in store as well. In 2003, I was chosen by the Queens Women in Business as one of the "Top Ten Queens Women in Business." I have never asked why I was singled out for this particular award; the closest I've come to an explanation is that for a number of years I headed two independent non-profit educational organizations. Enough to qualify, I guess — though hardly "big business"!

ANNE PAOLUCCI, PH.D
CHOSEN AS A
TOP 10 WOMAN IN BUSINESS

BEECHHURST RESIDENT AND WRITER ANNE PAOLUCCI, Ph.D. was born in Rome, attended public schools in New York City and went to Barnard College. She went on to earn her doctorate degree from Columbia University in English and Comparative Literature. For many years she taught at City College and later at St. John's University. There, Dr. Paolucci launched the publication *Review of National Literatures* and served as both the Chairperson of the English Department and Director of the Doctor of Arts degree program in English.

In 1986, Dr. Paolucci was appointed by President Reagan to the National Council on the Humanities and remained in that position until 1994. Governor Pataki chose her to serve on the Board of Trustees of City University in 1996, and from 1997 to 1999, she served as chairwoman of the Board.

Dr. Paolucci has written four books of poetry, two books of short stories, a novella and several plays. She has also written a classic work on Edward Albee, and scores of books and articles on dramatic theory, Shakespeare, Greek tragedy and the Theatre of the Absurd.

The Courier
THE AWARD WINNING COMMUNITY NEWSPAPER

COURIER
The Largest Weekly Serving Our International Borough   "WE'RE ALL ABOUT YOU"

Visit Our Website At:
www.queenscourier.com

Be There!
FIRST ANNUAL TOP 10
Queens Women in Business
AWARDS EVENT*

MARCH 27, 2003
AT TERRACE ON THE PARK FROM 6:00PM

TICKETS NOW ON SALE FOR EVENT.

TICKETS: $75 EACH   TABLE OF 10: $700
MAKE CHECK PAYABLE TO: QUEENS BUSINESS TODAY 38-15 BELL BLVD., BAYSIDE, NY 11361
FOR MORE INFORMATION CALL: (718) 224-5863

And The Winners Are......

JACKIE ARRINGTON — CITIBANK

DR. GISELE WOLF-KLEIN—PARKER JEWISH INSTITUTE

JO-ANN JONES — FLUSHING TOWN HALL

CARYN SCHWAB — MT. SINAI QUEENS

CONSUELO QUINTERO — NATIVES

☐ DR. ANNE PAOLUCCI — PROFESSOR/AUTHOR

LENA BRISKIN — ALICIA'S JEWELERS

LOIS CHRISTIE — CHRISTIE & CO. SALON • SPA

MAUREEN BUGLINO — NEW YORK HOSPITAL QUEENS

LIZ SULIK — EXECUTIVE DIRECTOR,
CHAMBER OF COMMERCE, THE ROCKAWAYS

PIONEER AWARD
GERT MCDONALD

ROOKIE OF THE YEAR
DEPUTY INSPECTOR SUSAN MORELY

THE CLAIRE SHULMAN COMMUNITY SERVICE AWARD
ASSEMBLYWOMAN NETTIE MAYERSOHN

A.P. ACCEPTING THE "TOP TEN BUSINESS WOMEN IN QUEENS" AWARD.
STANDING, LEFT OF PODIUM: VICTORIA SCHNEPS (CEO, SCHNEPS COMMUNICATIONS);
SEATED, AT RIGHT OF PODIUM: HELEN MARSHALL (BOROUGH PRESIDENT OF QUEENS).

Albee's work continues to hold a special attraction for me. In 2004, at the request of a West coast agent who liked my writing and had a client who specialized in biographies, I suggested a book on Albee. I had no intention of competing with Mel Gassow's definitive work on the playwright's life, so I sent her an outline for something I tentatively called *Backstage with Edward Albee.* My idea was to interview directors and actors like Rosemarie Harris and others who had worked with Albee (as well as Albee himself) and come up with some interesting insights into how they approached the plays and dealt with difficulties of interpretation (avoiding what had already been said). I still believe the idea has merit; but I wasn't prepared to stop my other work to tackle this new project, unless there was real interest in it and possibly a contract. Unfortunately, the agent backed off when she learned that my book was not a "biography" and that, in fact, one already existed.

Busy with other compelling deadlines, I pushed the idea aside — until new circumstances made me reconsider. I pulled out the few pieces I'd written on Albee since my 1972 volume on his major plays and decided that a new critical study might be worth the undertaking. There were many things I still wanted to say about his work. *The Man Who Had Three Arms*, especially, should be better known; it closed only a few days after it first appeared (possibly because the critics panned it, thinking it was aimed at them). Albee himself had asked me on a number of occasions to write a second book, focusing on the later plays, so I contacted him to let him know that I was considering doing so but that, if I did take on the project, I would have to ask for his cooperation, especially for copies of recent scripts or published texts

His reply was the nudge I needed.

EDWARD ALBEE
THE OFFICE
14 HARRISON STREET
NEW YORK, N. Y. 10013

February 23, 2007

Anne Paolucci
166-25 Powells Cove Blvd.
Beechhurst NY 11357

Dear Anne Paolucci:

Thank you for your letter, your new book, and the essay.

For years now when people have asked me what the best critical work on my plays is, I always tell them: "As far as it goes, Anne Paolucci's *From Tension to Tonic* is without question the most intelligent and comprehensive analysis of my work."

Over the years I've been hoping that you could be persuaded to bring your magic to the plays following those that you include in your book. Then we would have an intelligent, comprehensive book of essays on my work. And that would make me very happy.

I hope you could be persuaded to take this task on, for we need such a book--I need such a book--and I could think of no one other than you who could do it so well.

So don't stint, don't be content doing minor additions to your existing book on me. I do not want a new biography. I just want a continuation of your intelligent examination of my work. Let me know if you're willing to do the thorough job I know you're capable of. Given that, of course I and my office would work with you in detail.

Best wishes,

[signature]

Edward Albee

The book on Albee won't slow me down with other projects I have in mind, two or three of which have already been mapped out. I'm used to handling several things at once; my work patterns haven't changed much since retiring. Still, setting my own priorities and schedules, not having to deal with obligations dictated by others, is at best a mixed blessing. I've been my own boss for over a decade, but during that time I've taken on more projects than I ever did when earning a living. Of course, I've had more "free" time to do so; but left to my own devices I discovered that I kept increasing my "work load." More recently, I find myself sitting at the computer or sorting out materials from morning right through the afternoon, with a quick lunch around three or four o'clock. The one positive aspect in this new regimen is that all casual distractions have fallen by the wayside, although I interrupt myself at some point in the afternoon to venture out, usually for light marketing and other necessary errands. I then stop off at Caffè Italia (or a similar place, when in Wilmington) for a cappuccino and (in Queens) a friendly chat with Maria or Nino, owners of the Caffè. As far as a social life: I can take it or leave it. Usually, I leave it; although I enjoy lunches and dinners with my associates, colleagues, and old friends, as well as former students, where the conversation is anything but casual. I avoid cocktail parties and formal dinners.

Albee's book definitely is high priority on my list, but it won't take up all of my time. I will also be working on two separate volumes of essays I wrote for journals and other academic publications on Dante and Pirandello, as well preparing a new edition of a 1949 translation of Dante's *De Monarchia* by Herbert W. Schneider (Professor of Philosophy at Columbia in the 1940s, 1950s), with an Introduction by Dino Bigongiari. This little treasure, published in 1949 by Oskar Piest (The Liberal Arts Press), was falling apart when I came across it in my files, but that's not why it deserves to be reissued. Anything that carries Dino Bigongiari's name is, in every sense, a "collector's item." I have also started to work on an account of Henry's 1964 campaign for the U.S. Senate and his role as Vice-Chairman of the New York State Conservative Party, from 1964 to the time of his death, on January 1. 1999. In this last, I'll miss the advice and practical help of Dr. Frank D. Grande, for over three decades President of Griffon House Publications. It was Frank who urged me to put such a book together and who drove faithfully into Queens, once a week, for several months, to put into some kind of order the materials I'd pulled out from the files. His untimely death on Thanksgiving Day of 2006 was a tremendous loss to his colleagues, family and friends; for me, it was a professional as well as a deeply personal loss. He had been dedicated to Henry and had already helped me with the publication of my husband's class notes on Roman history, a course which Henry taught at The City College of New York for several years and which Frank had audited more than once.

Luckily, I've had the time and means to allow my intellectual curiosity free rein along the various paths described. Perhaps even more important, I've been blessed with the energy to consolidate and make permanent acquisition of what I and my husband have managed to achieve over the years. Money, obviously, has never been an important factor in my adult life. As a teenager and in my early years at Columbia, I was forced into whatever job I could find, in order to pay for my education and contribute to the family's day-to-day needs. Later, I discovered that teaching was a "natural" habitat for me and provided a decent livelihood. My deep-rooted frugal habits helped to make my life and Henry's comfortable on teachers' salaries. I knew how to buy (always good things on sale) and was never tempted to follow fashion trends dictated by others. And since time is money, I learned how to organize mine to insure getting the most out of it. I was a fair cook but didn't waste time in the kitchen. I had no wish to experiment with new recipes. I dubbed myself a "fast-order cook" and still pride myself in how quickly I can put a decent meal together. When Mom was with us (and for as long as she could handle it), I let her do the cooking. She was excellent at it and had the time to indulge her passion for well-prepared food. She took over completely, when family came to dinner. Her "cappelletti" ("little hats") were everyone's all-time favorite. She made her own dough for them, kneading with strong strokes of the roller until it was almost transparent, literally falling off the edges of the large board and table on which she worked. The result was wafer thin, without a single break. We "little helpers" (whoever was standing around watching) were then put to work cutting what seemed hundreds of small rounds with the rim of a special vermouth glass she kept for that sole purpose. She would then place, on one side of each round, a small teaspoon of the filling she had prepared: a mixture of "white" meats — ground boiled veal, chicken, and pork — a package of Philadelphia cream cheese, some powdered nutmeg and (but I'm not sure about this) a beaten egg. Each round was then carefully sealed, the ends brought together to form what appeared to be a tiny hat. These were then dropped into a mega-pot of her rich broth. The result was a dish for the gods. We all preferred it to pasta or any roast, no matter how excellently prepared. My fare is healthy enough but dull by comparison.

Although I never sought out "big money," I learned to respect what it could buy in my case: an experienced staff. I have even entertained (briefly) the notion that were I to win the lottery, my life would not change radically; I would simply hire people who could help me put out more books.

But that will never happen, since I don't play the lottery.

🗁 *FROM THE FILES* 🗁

MISCELLANEOUS DOCUMENTS, NEWS STORIES, AND PHOTOGRAPHS

ADDITIONAL TESTIMONIALS ON THE OCCASION OF THE
25TH ANNIVERSARY OF CNL AND A.P.'S 75TH BIRTHDAY (2001)

(718) 286-3000
TELECOPIER (718) 286-2885
TDD (718) 286-2656

CITY OF NEW YORK
OFFICE OF THE
PRESIDENT OF THE BOROUGH OF QUEENS
120-55 QUEENS BOULEVARD
KEW GARDENS, NEW YORK 11424

October 24, 2001

Dear Friends:

I join you tonight in celebrating the achievements of one of our City's outstanding individuals, Anne Paolucci.

It was a quarter century ago that she founded the acclaimed Council on National Literatures and opened the hearts and minds of people around the world. Here in Queens, she has contributed greatly to our institutions of higher education, including St. John's University and Queens College.

Anne's pioneering efforts in so many fields have earned her an enviable reputation without parallel. Her latest venture, sponsorship of the Pirandello Society of America, is just the latest event in her remarkable life. With the creative support of Mr. John Martello, this latest chapter in the Council's history is certain to be a huge success.

On behalf of all our residents, I congratulate Anne on reaching this latest milestone in her life and wish her Godspeed in all her future endeavors.

Sincerely,

CLAIRE SHULMAN
President
Borough of Queens

23 September 2001
For transmission through the good offices of Azar Attura

To: Anne Paolucci Anne and Henry Paolucci International Conference Center
68-02 Metropolitan Avenue
Middle Village
New York, NY 11379

Dear Anne,

It is a pleasure to join the throng of your well-wishers on the occasion of your 75th birthday by means of this letter. Your many accomplishments and gifts have provided innumerable reasons to mark October 24 as a special day of tribute to you. While I shall be omitting quite a lot which others can justifiably think should earn first mention, I trust my personal select list of highlights will resonate with fellow academics looking back over the success story of the Council on National Literatures and your distinguished record of public service.

I recall the heady days when, with the support of eminent scholars like Frank Warnke, Victor Lange, Henri Peyre, and more, you launched the Review of National Literatures and, next, what evolved into the CNL/World Report. Because of the sustaining energies you invested, today students of comparative literature and culture can draw with enormous profit upon dozens of rich volumes completed in the RNL and CNL/World Report series. I felt it an honor to participate in the CNL/World Report volume entitled Multicomparative Theory, Definitions, Realities (1996), a major gathering of theoretical insights into the dynamic evolution of our field -- a pioneering saga in which you have been a leader.

Over the years I have enjoyed reading your poems, stories, and plays. I found admirable the way that you combined so many aspects of an active literary and civic life. Not just a scholar, not just an editor, not just a creative writer, not just a cultural commentator -- no, you were the genuine article, and I needed to refurbish a better, honored term from the Enlightenment to describe you. You are a woman-of-letters.

More recently I have been (re)reading some of Henry's wonderful writings on literary topics, cultural history, and political theory. I was touched by your concern to bring back into the public sphere the important intellectual contribution of a husband whom you both loved and respected. Surely I am speaking for a huge part of the New York citizenry, too, when I explain why so many scholars cherish you as a colleague because, in a time of terrible adversity, while caring for Henry, and instead of enjoying a well-merited furlough as an emerita, you were willing to assume the onerous duties of chairing the Board of Trustees of the City University of New York.

A remarkable episode in the life of CUNY ensued because you stood as a bulwark against further degradation of academic standards. One has to reach for operatic metaphors to describe how you skewered the raging dragon, the collective malaise. I have filed some amazing clippings from the bootless vilification campaign waged against you in my special drawer labeled "troglodytic". You were an inspiration to concerned fellow professors across the nation who knew the time had arrived to resist the antinomian attack on culture and who wanted to see CUNY regain the prominence it had once enjoyed. I took a message of hope from your courageous stand; you and Henry exemplified the best of New York as a citadel of the arts and education, a place where civic virtues and cultural vision could and should be allied.

Thank you, Anne, for the spiritual companionship you have so generously demonstrated and continue to demonstrate to so many of us.

With warmest wishes for the future,

Gerald Gillespie
Emeritus Professor, German Studies and Comparative Literature, Stanford University; Honorary President, International Comparative Literature Association

Gerald E. P. Gillespie
Stanford University
Stanford, CA 94305-2030 U.S.A.

Supreme Court
of the
State of New York

851 GRAND CONCOURSE
BRONX, N.Y 10451

CHAMBERS OF
DOMINIC R. MASSARO
JUSTICE

July 10, 2001

Dear Ms. Attura:

Thank you for the opportunity to comment on my

friend Anne Paolucci.

In a word: "Extraordinary"!

Sincerely,

Ms. Azar Attura
P. O. Box 4115
Arlington, Virginia 22204

Congratulions, A nne, on this historic moment!

And a special thank you for all the support I have
had from you since we met some fifty years ago!

ERIC BENTLEY   in the year 2001

love
Lill

4th of July, 2001

For Anne Paolucci:

I have known Anne Paolucci since 1963 and have many fond memories of these years. One of the most charming comes not from an incident I witnessed, but from an interview with her that I read not long ago. Reflecting on her life with Henry, Anne told the interviewer they had met at Columbia University, in a graduate seminar on Dante, conducted by the great Professor Dino Bigongiari. She described how involved they became in analyzing *La Commedia*, and then added: "The term came to an end, but there were so many questions we still had to ask that Henry and I decided to get married and explore them together." That they certainly did. Never have I known a couple who, over the years, developed such a perfect αγαπε. It was a joy to watch these two strong people interact with each other. In their love for the truth and for each other they certainly lived what Dante described in the *Paradiso:*

> . . . *gia mai non si sazia*
> *nostro intelletto, se 'l ver non lo illustra,*
> *di fuor dal qual nessun vero si spazia.*

> *Posasi in esso, come fera la lustra,*
> *tosto che giunto l'ha; e gigner puollo:*
> *se non, ciascun disio sarebbe frustra.*

Frank D. Grande

> . . . there can be no satisfying
> of our intellect if the Truth doesn't enlighten it,
> outside of which no truth can place itself.

> In truth it finds rest, like the beast in its lair,
> once it has attained it; and it can attain it:
> else every desire would prove itself to have been vain.

Potpourri Publications Company
A not for profit literary corporation
P. O. Box 8278   Prairie Village, Kansas 66208
(913) 642-1503   Fax -3128
editor@potpourri.org

Missouri Office: 1215 W. 65 St.
Kansas City, MO 64113

We at Potpourri Publications have had a delightful—albeit a long distance—relationship with Dr. Anne Attura Paolucci since 1993.

Potpourri's association with Anne Paolucci began when Herman M. Swafford, our founding publisher, "discovered" her poetry. He was impressed by what he read and wrote to her:
"Some of your poetry reflects the East Indian culture as it commingles with the West, and the result becomes most interesting. It is the comparing, the bringing forth, the unisons, the differences, the subtleties, the nuances, the weaving of the cultures that make the poetry unique. And, of course, your own special way as a poet."

Later in a Contemporary Profile, "Le poesie di Anne Paolucci" in *Potpourri, A Magazine of the The Literary Arts*, he wrote:
"I know the Anne Paolucci who writes poetry…and so, Anne Paolucci, like all who travel the East, you will journey the Pacific trough to Australia and New Zealand, and you will take us with you in your poetry."

Since that time Potpourri Publications has not only published her poetry in our magazine but also served as publisher for her fourth collection of poetry, *Queensboro Bridge* (1995), which was nominated for a Pulitzer Prize, and her first novella, *Terminal Degrees* (1997).

We also know and appreciate Anne as an energetic, innovative advocate for the Literary Arts. In 1995, she established for *Potpourri* a Council on National Literatures Award to be given annually for a poem or short story (alternating years) which best "expresses in a positive way our multicultural diversity or reflects on our national heritage in historical terms." Through her generosity, many authors, new and established, have been inspired to pursue excellence in their creative writings.

So thank you, Anne Paolucci, from all of us at Potpourri Publications for your support and friendship and for the countless writers whose lives you have touched in your remarkable career. Happy Birthday to you and congratulations on your twenty-five years of leadership of the Council on National Literatures.

Sincerely,

Polly W. Swafford

Polly W. Swafford
Publisher/Senior Editor

Happy Birthday, Anne!

Best Wishes from Dr. Jeanne J. Smoot
Secretary-General International Comparative Literature Association

Anne, like so many of your admirers and friends, I honestly can't remember when I first met you. I think it was when we both served together on the National Humanities Council, but certainly we had talked together before then, and I knew you by name and reputation.

I have not been privileged to know you in all the facets of your life, nor do I think I possess the knowledge to follow you into all the many intellectual pursuits you have undertaken, but in those moments when we have interacted and your good mind has stirred mine, we have always enjoyed cordiality. Certainly, I respect you for your tough mindedness, and I have also always admired your work ethic. You worked hard as a young woman to get an education, and you continue to work hard and to share your wealth—both intellectual and otherwise--with others.

Your work on Pirandello is inspirational to those of us who wish to understand the Italian playwright, and your presentations at the American Comparative Literature Association and other such national and international venues have always been outstanding.

But what I remember and will always treasure most about you is your love of your departed husband, Henry, and your delight in learning. I also shall cherish the conversations we had when we shared dinner or another meal at a professional meeting. Those times with you were fun and intellectually quickening.

You are a fine woman, Anne Paolucci, and I am proud of you, your work, and your loving manner and approach to life.

Happy Birthday, dear lady, and may the Council on National Literatures continue to flourish.

The Best to you always,

Jeanne

PRESENTATION BY A.P. OF CONSTANCE DEL VECCHIO MALTESE'S OIL PAINTING
OF HENRY PAOLUCCI. CONSERVATIVE PARTY ANNUAL DINNER, THE NEW YORK HILTON.
L/R: JIM GAY, A.P., MICHAEL LONG, CHAIRMAN OF THE NYS CONSERVATIVE PARTY.

INTERCOLLEGIATE STUDIES INSTITUTE
THE HENRY PAOLUCCI/WALTER BAGEHOT BOOK AWARD

It is only fitting that the award commemorating the life and work of Henry Paolucci should also carry the name of Walter Bagehot – bringing into sharp focus a true partnership of mind and soul.

In the late sixties, Professor Paolucci established The Walter Bagehot Research Council on National Sovereignty (a not-for-profit educational foundation), named after the great British political economist and man of letters, Walter Bagehot, who founded and edited for many years *The Economist*, one of the most important journals of the time, and who also wrote many literary essays.

For many years, Professor Paolucci helped organize Bagehot Council lectures and panels at the annual American Political Science Association annual meetings, encouraging younger scholars to participate and find their place in the academic community. In 1969, The Bagehot Council became the publisher for *State of the Nation* – a political newsletter dedicated primarily to current issues dealing with American domestic and foreign policy. Paolucci continued to publish *SN* through 1980, serving as its chief editor and major contributor. The monthly series deals with some of the most dramatic events and major "players" of a difficult period in American history, viewed from a keen long-range historical perspective. At this distance in time, those assessments, unlike most of the journalistic reporting of the time, take on a clarity that seems prophetic. The entire series is well worth preserving; portions, in fact, have already appeared in recent publications of GHP.

His books, like the early classic, *War, Peace and the Presidency* (1969), and his last, *Iran, Israel and the United States* (1995), are indicators of his extraordinary grasp of political matters and display the range and accuracy of his political insights. Since his death, in 1999, a number of Professor Paolucci's out-of-print books, as well as works not published during his lifetime, have been edited by his wife Anne Paolucci and published by Griffon House Publications. Through an agreement between GHP and Council on National Literatures (founded in 1975 and still headed by Anne Paolucci) these reprints and new additions to Professor Paolucci's long list of books and articles are being made available, free of charge, to major libraries here and abroad.

Henry Paolucci was without a doubt the best disciple of Walter Bagehot. Like Bagehot, he had a wide mastery of political thought and knew how to bring the past into present political realities. But his intellectual interests included much else. He was an avid reader of Aristotle, Plato, Hegel, Einstein, Newton, Adolf Harnack, Dante, T.S. Eliot, Francesco De Sanctis, St. Augustine, Machiavelli, Benedetto Croce and Giovanni Gentile, as well as Bagehot himself, and pursued subjects as diverse as astronomy, mathematics, literary theory, political philosophy, Greek and Roman history, Christian dogma, church history, the history of the Jews, American history and foreign policy.

In recent years he had found a new scholarly focus: the age of European discovery and early American exploration, especially the massive work of Justin Winsor — first librarian of Harvard, founder of the American Library Association, and co-founder of the American Historical Association — an interest reflected in several volumes of *Review of National Literatures*, which he edited with his wife Anne.

His impeccable scholarship in all these subjects and his dedication to learning will long be remembered by those who were privileged to hear him in the classroom and in public forums; but they are clearly in evidence, as well, in his books, articles, and speeches, some of which have been gathered in a collection published in 2000: *Selected Writings on Literature and the Arts; Science and Astronomy; Law, Government, and Political Philosophy* — a sampling which also reflects his literary flair.

In 1964, he was asked by William F. Buckley to accept the NYS Conservative Party nomination for the U.S. Senate, as the high-profile third candidate, running against Kenneth Keating and Robert F. Kennedy. His stimulating speeches, debates, and interviews drew considerable interest and brought the newly-formed Party into prominence as a result of his vigorous campaign, during which he was featured by *The New York Times* as "The Scholarly Candidate." In 1995, the Party honored him with its prestigious Kieran O'Doherty Award.

At the time of his death, on January 1, 1999, Henry Paolucci had been retired for eight years from St. John's University as Professor Emeritus of Government and Politics and still served as Vice-Chairman of the Conservative Party of NYS.

After a BS degree from The City College of New York (1942), Paolucci joined the US Air Force as a navigator. He flew many missions over Africa and Italy. Toward the end of the war, he was placed in charge of 10,000 German prisoners and in that capacity remained in Italy for over a year. When he returned to New York, he resumed his education and received the MA and Ph.D. from Columbia University. In 1948 he was chosen Eleanora Duse Traveling Fellow in Columbia University and spent a year studying in Florence, Italy. In 1951, he returned to Italy as a Fulbright Scholar at the University of Rome.

His wide range of intellectual interests was reflected in the variety of subjects he taught, including Greek and Roman history at Iona College, Brooklyn College, and The City College; a graduate course in Dante and Medieval Culture at Columbia University (at the invitation of the President of Columbia at the time, Nicholas Murray Butler); and, from 1968 to 1991, undergraduate and graduate courses in U.S. foreign policy, political theory, St. Augustine, Aristotle, Machiavelli, Hegel, astronomy and modern science at St. John's University, New York, where he helped design an interdepartmental and interdisciplinary Doctor of Arts Degree Program in History, Sociology, and Government and Politics.

On his own initiative, he became proficient in Greek, Arab, and Jewish texts. He translated several important works, including Cesare Beccaria's *On Crimes and Punishments*; Machiavelli's bitter play, *Mandragola* (first published in 1957, with a fine introduction placing this late work in Machiavelli's political spectrum), still in print; and sections of Hegel's *Philosophy of Fine Art* in *Hegel on the Arts*. Among his other works are *The Achievement of Galileo* (with his original translations of a number of important pieces for inclusion in the work); Maitland's *Justice and Police*; *The Political Writings of St. Augustine*; and a unique anthology on dramatic theory drawn from Hegel's entire opus into a single volume, *Hegel on Tragedy*. (first published as an Anchor Book by Doubleday Co, then as a Torch Book by Harper and Row, later in a hard-bound edition by Greenwood Press [still in print], and recently in a new paperback edition by GHP). His keen analyses of political affairs and US foreign policy are still available in the classic *War, Peace and the Presidency* (1968), *A Brief History of Political Thought and Statecraft* (1979), *Kissinger's War* (1980), *Zionism, the Superpowers, and the P.L.O.* (1964) and *Iran, Israel, and the United States* (1995).

Like Walter Bagehot himself, Henry Paolucci was also a literary man. After Dante, and perhaps in a more personal way, James Thomson, author of *The City of Dreadful Night*, was his favorite poet. He was also familiar with the works of Giacomo Leopardi, the major European writers of the Romantic age, Greek and Latin philosophers and the writings of the Church Fathers — as well as the work of Harnack, Caspar, and other great scholars of Church history. At the time of his death he was still active as Chief Researcher and Feature Writer for the two international annual publications of Council on National Literatures, *Review of National Literatures* and *CNL/World Report*.

A frequent contributor to the Op Ed pages of the *New York Times* and magazines like *National Review* and *Il Borghese* (Rome), Professor Paolucci was also a lover of Brahms, Schubert,

Mozart, Chopin, and Beethoven, as well as Scott Joplin and others of that period. He also found occasion, over the years, to develop his own musical skills, especially as a composer. A number of his haunting melodies were used in Anne Paolucci's videoplay *Cipango!*

INTERCOLLEGIATE STUDIES INSTITUTE, INC.
F.M. KIRBY CAMPUS, 3901 CENTERVILLE ROAD • POST OFFICE BOX 4431 • WILMINGTON, DE 19807-0431
(302) 652-4600 • FAX: (302) 652-1760 • E-MAIL: isi@isi.org
www.isi.org

For Immediate Release
October 21, 2004
www.isi.org

Contact: Sarah Longwell
(800) 526-7022 x168
media@isi.org

ISI Announces This Year's Henry Paolucci/ Walter Bagehot Book Award Winner

Author to receive $5,000 award and lecture at ISI's headquarters

Wilmington, DE—The Intercollegiate Studies Institute (ISI), a national academic organization headquartered in Wilmington, DE, is pleased to announce this year's recipient of the Henry Paolucci/Walter Bagehot Book Award: Derek Beales, author of *Prosperity and Plunder: European Catholic Monasteries in the Age of Revolution, 1650-1815.*

Derek Beales will give a public lecture and slide presentation entitled, "A Lost Society: Monasteries in post-Reformation Europe" at ISI's F.M. Kirby campus on November 11th at 5:30 p.m. The award presentation and reception will follow.

Derek Beales is Professor Emeritus of Modern History, University of Cambridge, and a Fellow of Sidney Sussex College and the British Academy. His publications include *England and Italy, 1859-60* (1961), *From Castlereagh to Gladstone, 1815-1885* (1969), *The Risorgimento and the Unification of Italy* (1971), and *Joseph II: In the Shadow of Maria Theresa, 1741-1780* (1987).

This prestigious award was first launched two years ago by the Walter Bagehot Research Council, an organization founded by Professor Paolucci in the late sixties. Beginning in 2004, the annual award will be presented by ISI to a deserving scholar whose intellectual achievement—as made manifest in the form of a book published in the previous year—embodies the spirit, range, and scholarly rigor of the award's namesakes. Walter Bagehot, a man of letters, was the founder and long-time editor of the *Economist*. Henry Paolucci, a Fulbright scholar and prolific author, taught at several institutions, including Columbia University.

Founded in 1953, ISI works to "educate for liberty"—to identify the best and the brightest college students and to nurture in these future leaders the American ideal of ordered liberty. For more information on ISI, the award, or this event, please visit www.isi.org or contact Sarah Longwell at (800) 526-7022.

-30-

**HENRY'S OBITUARY IN THE JOURNAL OF THE AMERICAN POLITICAL SCIENCE ASSOCIATION (APSA).
A SHORTER VERSION APPEARED IN THE *NEW YORK TIMES*.**

Political Science & Politics

Volume XXXII   Number 2   June 1999

Henry Paolucci

Henry Paolucci, professor emeritus of government and politics at St. John's University and vice chairman of the Conservative Party of New York State, died Friday. January 1, 1999, at New York Hospital Queens Medical Center from complications caused by prostate cancer. He was 77.

After graduating from the City College of New York with a B.S., he joined the Air Force as a navigator and flew numerous missions over Africa and Italy. Later, he resumed his education, earning an M.A. and Ph.D. from Columbia University.

Professor Paolucci's wide range of intellectual interests was reflected in the variety of subjects he taught, including ancient Greek and Roman history at Iona College, Brooklyn College, and City College; a graduate course on Dante and medieval culture at Columbia University; and, since 1968, courses on U.S. foreign policy and political theory, Aristotle and Hegel, and others in the department of government and politics at St. John's University. He is especially known for his studies of the political thought of Aristotle, St. Augustine, Machiavelli, and Hegel.

A frequent contributor to the Op Ed page of *The New York Times* and magazines like *National Review* and *Il Borghese* (Rome), Dr. Paolucci wrote a number of articles for the Columbus quincentenary and helped to prepare three volumes drawn from the massive work of Justin Winsor, the great historian of early America. He translated Cesare Beccaria's *On Crimes and Punishments* and Machiavelli's *Mandragola* (in its 32nd printing) and edited Maitland's *Justice and Police,* as well as a notable collection of *The Political Writings of St. Augustine.* His books on political affairs and foreign policy analysis include *War, Peace and the Presidency* (1968), *A Brief History of Political Thought and Statecraft* (1979), *Kissinger's War* (1980), *Zionism, the Superpowers, and the PLO* (1964), and *Iran, Israel, and the United States* (1991). In 1948 Professor Paolucci was chosen Eleanora Duse Traveling Fellow in Columbia University and spent a year studying in Florence, Italy. In 1951 he revisited Italy as a Fulbright Scholar at the University of Rome.

In 1964 he was asked by William F. Buckley Jr. to accept the New York State Conservative Party nomination for the U.S. Senate and he ran against Kenneth Keating and Robert F. Kennedy. His stimulating campaign drew considerable interest and he was written up in *The New York Times* as the "Scholarly Candidate." In 1995 the party honored him with its prestigious Kieran O'Doherty Award.

Founder and president of the Walter Bagehot Research Council on National Sovereignty (a nonprofit educational foundation), Paolucci was for many years chief editor of its newsletter, *State of the Nation,* and organizer of its annual discussion panels at meetings of the American Political Science Association. He also contributed to the international publication *Review of National Literatures* as research coordinator and feature writer. He leaves his wife, Anne Paolucci.

Anne Paolucci
Chair, Board of Trustees, CUNY

GRIFFON HOUSE PUBLICATIONS

FRANK D. GRANDE, D.PHIL(OXON), *President*   JOHN J. RYAN, *Director*

Contact: Jack H. Ryan
P. O. Box 30727
Wilmington DE 19806
Tel./FAX (302) 656-5651
e-mail. griffonhse@aol.com

January 14, 2005

FOR IMMEDIATE RELEASE

COMM. ANNE PAOLUCCI RECEIVES À TRANSLATION INCENTIVE AWARD FROM THE ITALIAN MINISTRY OF FOREIGN AFFAIRS FOR *SELECTED POEMS* OF *GIACOMO LEOPARDI*

The Italian Ministry of Foreign Affairs has chosen *Selected Poems of Giacomo Leopardi*, by Comm. Anne Paolucci, for its 2004 translation initiative prize. The prize is given to promote the translation of Italian literary and scientific works abroad and carries a cash award, in this case, of E.4,000. The presentation ceremony will take place in New York City.

The 153-page book, published by Griffon House Publications, carries both the original and the translated texts, as well as prose excerpts drawn from Leopardi's notebooks, journals, and letters that provide welcome insights into the poet's psychological and literary motivation. Also included in the slim volume are a "Brief Chronology" and an important and very readable "Introduction" by the translator, in which the work of the great Italian poet is put into historical and literary perspective and his pessimism assessed in the light of statements by eminent writers like Giovanni Gentile (the leading Italian Hegelian philosopher of the twentieth century) and Francesco De Sanctis (who still ranks as one of the most important literary critics of Italy).

"We at Griffon House Publications are delighted with the prestigious recognition accorded Commendatore Paolucci by the Italian Ministry of Foreign Affairs. She took on a very difficult task and brought it to an excellent conclusion," commented Dr. Frank D. Grande, President of Griffon House Publications, on hearing news of the award. "We are proud also for having been the ones to recognize the value of the project and publish the book."

Reviewing the volume in *Oggi* ("Libri," February 15, 2004), Franco Borrelli wrote: "A clear and seemingly simple language, Leopardi's, accurate and accessible, in the choice of words and sounds; extremely difficult, however, to translate into another idiom (above all into English). . . . How, then, to translate him?" After quoting Comm. Paolucci's description of some of Leopardi's "seemingly simple" style, Borrelli concludes:

> . . . reading these translations . . . one truly has the impression that Leopardi "sings" very well also in Shakespeare's language . . . [we have here] a Leopardi more than ever alive, reading whom, moving from one language to the other, one has the strong and very real impression of reading also the everyday contemporary soul, with its fears, its hopes, and its awe in the face of the great mystery of being. [*Translated from the Italian*]

The project, begun in 1986 with Thomas G. Bergin, then Sterling Professor Emeritus at Yale, was set aside when Professor Bergin died in 1987. The difficulties encountered fifteen years later, when it was taken up again, and the decisions that had to be made along the way, are recorded in the "Introduction," where Comm. Paolucci explains how she took as her working premise Leopardi's observation that all great poetry had simplicity and clarity, and went on to seek those images, resonances, and correspondences in English that would at least suggest what the poet — in spite of (or perhaps because of) his unique linguistic agility — accomplished so well, with such seeming ease, in his own poetry.

Internationally known for her work on Shakespeare, Edward Albee, Theater of the Absurd, Machiavelli, Pirandello, and Columbus, and especially for her Hegelian approach to literary subjects, particularly ancient and modern drama, Comm. Paolucci is also a prize-winning poet and playwright. Born in Rome, she returned to her native city as a Fulbright Scholar from Columbia University at the University of Rome and later taught for two years as Fulbright Lecturer in American Drama at the University of Naples. She toured Yugoslavia twice as guest of the Ministry of Culture and, at the invitation of the Humanities Research Center of the Australian National University, spent several months there as their special guest. A graduate of Barnard College and Columbia University, Comm. Paolucci is the recipient of an honorary degree from Lehman College of City University and of the Elena Cornaro Award of the New York State Grand Lodge of Order Sons of Italy, as well as the only woman singled out for that group's national Elena Cornaro Award. For her initiatives to promote Columbus studies, she received Canada's gold medal for the quincentennial. In 1986, President Reagan appointed her to the National Council on the Humanities, where she served until 1993. In 1996, New York State Governor George Pataki named her to the Board of Trustees of City University and the following year chose her to head that Board. The New York State Legislature has also honored her on a number of occasions.

Comm. Paolucci is currently editing the lectures of the late Dino Bigongiari, the eminent Dante and medieval scholar, who taught at Columbia for over five decades.

— 30 —

A Special Woman
A Special Poem

Anne Paolucci, chosen as one of *Queens Business Today's* top 10 Women in Business, is an award-winning poet and playwright, as well as a writer of fiction. She is a graduate of Barnard College and Columbia University and also studied at the University of Rome as a Fulbright scholar. She has written extensively on Theater of the Absurd (especially Edward Albee), as well as Shakespeare and ancient tragedy. Currently Director of the

Anne Paolucci

Doctor of Arts Degree Program in English at St. John's University, Dr. Paolucci was Fulbright Lecturer in American Drama for two years in Italy. She is a Whitestone resident and the author of this lovely poem taken from the book of poetry "Queensboro Bridge (and Other Poems)":

WINDOW BOX

My day-to-moon calendar
Turns yellow as I wait for
Basil leaves to shed unsuspecting
Fragrance from my window box.
Are they happy in their green?
Do they dream of salads?
One moment, please.
I want to hear
What this piece of lettuce
Has to say.

COUNCIL ON NATIONAL LITERATURES
CELEBRATING OUR 25ᵀᴴ ANNIVERSARY

May 3, 2001

DESCRIPTION OF RESTRUCTURED CNL: *AIMS AND ACTIVITIES*

BACKGROUND

CNL was founded in 1976 as the parent "umbrella" for two annual series, *Review of National Literatures* (1970-2000) and *CNL/World Report* ((1985-2000). The volumes were distributed to member-libraries throughout the world. This concentrated activity provided a much needed academic forum for multicomparative literary studies: overviews of literatures not in the traditional mainstream (*RNL*) and a continuing dialogue among comparatists and other literary scholars on the future of the profession (*CNL/WR*). The series, meetings, and other activities of CNL have been called by experts in the field of comparative literary studies "A pioneer effort." *RNL* volumes have received excellent reviews throughout the world.

Over the years, CNL has held joint meetings at a number of universities, including the School of International Affairs at Columbia University, major universities in Australia, Canada, etc., and, until recently, as an "Allied Organization," at the annual meetings of the Modern Language Association of America.

NEW AGENDA: 2000 ⇨

In 2000, CNL decided to discontinue its two academic series (the last *RNL* volume on Italian literature since 1950 has just been distributed to member libraries here and abroad) and to redirect its activities to provide public- and community-oriented programs as well as scholarly conferences, lectures, dramatic readings, exhibits, and special events in the arts, literature, and science. An annual volume is planned, to record the activities of each year.

SUMMARY:

Briefly, since early 2000 CNL ⇨
- has launched the CNL ANNE AND HENRY PAOLUCCI INTERNATIONAL CONFERENCE CENTER (Middle Village, New York) as the site for future activities;
- has held an international conference on multinational studies (March 25, 2000) which included panels and lectures followed by an awards dinner, at which time prizes were awarded to both university and high school teachers who had effectively promoted, in their writings and in the classroom, the expansion of curricula to include authors and literatures not in the traditional mainstream;
- has sponsored a book-signing reception for artist Constance Del Vecchio Maltese's *An Artist's Journey of Discovery*, which features the thirteen paintings of her award-winning series, "Age of Discovery Navigators" (1988-1992);
- has published and distributed to libraries throughout the world *An Artist's Journey of Discovery*, in which artist Maltese traces the evolution of the "Navigators" series;
- has sponsored an exhibit of 34 paintings by Vincenzo R. Latella, depicting the 34 cantos of Dante's *Inferno*;
- has published and distributed to libraries throughout the world *Dante's Gallery of Rogues*, containing reproductions of artist Latella's Dante series, and an Introductory Essay ("The Strident Voices of Hell") by Anne Paolucci;
- has taken on the activities of The Pirandello Society of America, including publication of its annual volume *PSA*;
- has negotiated with publishing outlets to distribute as bonus/gift items to over 700 libraries, here and abroad, important new books and reprints;
- has expanded its Board of Directors.

A forum for scholars and teachers concerned with the comparative study of the established, emergent, and neglected national literatures that make up the written and oral artistic legacy of the diverse contemporary peoples of the world.
• PUBLISHER OF *REVIEW OF NATIONAL LITERATURES* AND *CNL/WORLD REPORT* •

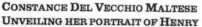

CONSTANCE DEL VECCHIO MALTESE
UNVEILING HER PORTRAIT OF HENRY

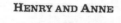

HENRY AND ANNE

HENRY VISITING WITH
CHARLES BURTON
MARSHALL, FORMER
CHIEF AIDE TO
DEAN ACHESON
(WASHINGTON, D.C.
EARLY 80s).

HENRY RECEIVING THE KIERAN
O'DOHERTY AWARD (MID 80s)

WITH MINISTER GIORGIO RADICATI, CONSUIL GENERAL OF ITALY IN NEW YORK

WITH CLAIRE SHULMAN FORMER PRESIDENT OF THE BOROUGH OF QUEENS

WITH ACTOR KEVIN KLINE

WITH COLIN POWELL, FORMER SECRETARY OF STATE, AT THE 150ᵀᴴ ANNIVERSARY DINNER OF THE FOUNDING OF THE CITY COLLEGE (1997)

WITH U.S. SENATOR PHIL GRAMM

BOOK SIGNING (FEATURING U.S. PUBLICATION OF *SEPIA TONES*)

ANTICIPATING THE 10ᵀᴴ ANNIVERSARY OF CNL

COUNCIL ON NATIONAL LITERATURES
10TH ANNIVERSARY RECEPTION-DINNER

Friday, December 28, 1984
National Geographic Society Headquarters
1600 M Street　　　　　Washington DC 20036
Reception: 7 PM; Dinner: 8 PM

A W A R D S

RENE WELLEK
Presentor, Frank J. Warnke

AMBASSADOR ROBERT W. SEARBY
Presentor, Henry Paolucci

VARTAN GREGORIAN
Presentor, Vahe Oshagan

VICTOR LANGE
Presentor, Marilyn Gaddis Rose

Black Tie Optional
$150 per person　　　　　Table of ten: $1,500.

JULY, 1976

JULY, 2006

A.P. BIRTHDAY DINNER HOSTED BY SENATOR SERPHIN R. MALTESE AND WIFE, ARTIST CONSTANCE DEL VECCHIO MALTESE. SEATED (LEFT): FORMER CONGRESSMAN MARIO BIAGGI AND A.P. STANDING, L/R: MIMI VALENTI, DEVELOPMENTAL OFFICER, CHRIST THE KING REGIONAL H.S.; DR. CLARA SARROCCO, EXECUTIVE DIRECTOR CNL; BARNEY COHEN AND WIFE DOLORES SCORCA COHEN; NIECE JOAN ATTURA LOVLER; NIECE CLARE ATTURA KRETZMAN. STANDING, FAR RIGHT: THE MALTESES.